LET
the
GAME
BEGIN

KIRA SHELL

sourcebooks
casablanca

CENTRO
PER IL LIBRO
E LA LETTURA

This work has been translated with the contribution of the Center for Books and
Reading of the Italian Ministry of Culture.

Originally published as *Kiss Me Like You Love Me Vol. 1: Let the Game Begin* © 2019
Mondadori Libri S.p.A.
Published by Mondadori Libri for the imprint Sperling & Kupfer. Translated from Italian
by Nicole M. Taylor.

Published by Sourcebooks Casablanca, an imprint of Sourcebooks
1935 Brookdale RD, Naperville, IL 60563-2773
(630) 961-3900
sourcebooks.com

Originally published as *Kiss Me Like You Love Me Vol. 1: Let the Game Begin* in 2019
in Italy by Sperling & Kupfer, an imprint of Mondadori Libri S.p.A. This edition issued
based on the Pickwick BIG paperback edition published in 2021 in Italy by Sperling &
Kupfer, an imprint of Mondadori Libri S.p.A.

Cataloging-in-Publication Data is on file with the Library of Congress.

The authorized representative in the EEA is Dorling Kindersley Verlag GmbH. Arnulfstr.
124, 80636 Munich, Germany

Manufactured in the UK by Clays and distributed by
Dorling Kindersley Limited, London
001-351752-Aug/25
10 9 8 7 6 5 4 3 2 1

For all my readers

CONTENT WARNING

This is a dark romance series. It includes some sensitive themes as well as explicit content. It contains scenes of nonconsensual and dubiously consensual sexual activity as well as depictions of violence and child sexual abuse. It is recommended for a mature and aware audience.

People often ask me if I love
And I tell them that I do, in my own fashion
Because love is not a single concept
It comes in many forms
And the most powerful of them
Is silent.

PROLOGUE

········

November was particularly cold that year. Usually I hated the cold, but that night I had discovered its utility. The icy air froze my thoughts.

"Kiddo, look at me." A uniformed stranger captured my face in his hands, trying to see if I was aware of my surroundings. I was sitting on the porch steps, naked, save for a blanket someone had put around my shoulders. I was shaking and sweaty. I couldn't speak, though I understood everything that was said between him and his colleagues.

The man, tall and bearded, was misty-eyed as he continued to stroke my cheeks. I usually loathed any type of human contact, but I allowed him to touch me because I wasn't feeling myself.

"He's in shock, but he's okay," he declared.

The officers continued to speak to me, but I just stared into the red and blue of the lightbars. They flashed, blinding me, and I squinted at their intensity. I was the one who had called the police, even though I was just a child. They thought it was a prank until they saw with their own eyes the horrible situation I had wound up in.

"What'd they do?" The police officer took my chin gently and tried to force me to look at him, but my face just kept turning back in the same direction. I stared at the patrol cars, not saying a single word. There were three of them. Next to one of them, two other officers gathered around a small, slight body crowned with black hair.

It was a little girl. The same one who had been with me just before. She was drinking water; her bare feet were filthy with dirt and a blanket covered her still-immature frame.

"We called your parents. They'll be here any minute," the officer informed me, but no emotion disturbed my impassive face. I could no longer feel my heart beating—maybe I didn't even have one anymore. My body was empty, without a soul.

The man tried to get my attention, but I was far away. Had they really called my parents? I didn't feel anything about them, either. I didn't want to run into my mom's arms or explain things to my dad.

They were the ones who had never noticed.

My mother thought I needed a psychologist. I'd often listened in on her telephone conversations with a man who wasn't Dad. I had listened to one just that afternoon, crouching on the stairs that led to the floor above.

I recalled every detail.

Mama walked nervously back and forth in her high heels. She had always been a refined woman, high-class even at home. Her platinum blond hair was gathered severely into a neat bun; pearl earrings decorated her perfectly symmetrical earlobes. Her skin was translucent. Her blue eyes, ringed by long lashes, looked at everything, but in actuality, they saw nothing. She had all the clues right in front of her. I did everything I could to show her, but she just thought I was disturbed, troubled, deviant.

"How can I know if a child needs a child psychologist? You're a psychiatrist, right? What do you suggest we do?" she asked the person on the other end of the phone. The same person she turned to every time there was an issue regarding me or my strange behavior, especially when my teachers complained about my conduct. I had no learning difficulties; my teachers considered me very intelligent and intuitive, but they claimed that something was wrong with my personality development.

"Why does your son behave so differently from his brother, who comes from the same nuclear family?" my teacher just kept asking.

"He's not like other children," Mama answered tersely.

"There's something wrong with him," the teacher said, icily.

The worst part was the answer to all of their questions was right in front of their noses.

"I don't know what to do," Mama said suddenly, pulling me away from the memory of what had happened at school. Then she burst into tears. She cried frequently during that time. Then she rubbed her belly with one hand. She was pregnant with my sister, Chloe, and I knew that all this stress wasn't good for her. I felt guilty about all the trouble I was causing. I sighed as I wrapped my arm around my knees and balanced my chin on top of them. My family wasn't happy anymore because of me.

My father, the CEO of a large company, always came home late at night and was angry all the time. I knew that he had made us one of the richest families in New York, but he was most often a cold man, especially when it came to me. His eyes, as clear as ice, flayed my skin every time he stared contemptuously at me. He hated me. He hated me because Mama almost lost Chloe. He was the one who told me to stop making problems or he'd really hurt me. He insulted me however he could—said I was evil, crazy, a little pervert. He said I'd ruined his life, that he hated the color of my eyes, and he didn't want me around. He said that I was dangerous, and sooner or later, my mother would realize it too...

I turned to look back at the police cars in fascination.

The police had unwittingly created another problem for me: Mama and Dad were definitely going to yell at me for making public a scandal that I had kept secret for too long.

A secret that was killing me slowly. It was all my fault.

"Two young kids. They were locked in a basement. Naked and terrified," the officer said to someone else while I floated among my thoughts, staring out into the space in front of me.

"No signs of bruising." The officer continued to examine me, but I didn't listen to him. My legs and fingers were numb from the cold, but not a word escaped my sealed lips. I didn't have the strength to speak. Partly from shame, partly from disbelief that it was all over or, perhaps, just beginning.

I wanted to forget all the ugly things and take refuge in my Neverland.

I wanted to journey to distant lands and rescue myself.

That day, though, escape was impossible because I had to live and face reality.

I couldn't flee to some alternate dimension. No Neverland.

I found myself at a crossroads: I could live or I could die.

I chose to live, but from that day on, I was never the same.

1

SELENE

They say in life we have to make the right choices, but we don't always have the ability to recognize them. Who establishes right and wrong? Does the right thing really make us happy?

I was lying comfortably on my bed and surfing on my laptop. I was supposed to leave for New York that morning, though I wasn't enthusiastic about it. I lived with my mother in an apartment in Indian Village, a residential neighborhood of Detroit. At least that's where I *had* lived until my mother had the bright idea to turn my life upside down overnight.

I hooked one ankle around the other and kept on scrolling through the gossip blogs about one of the most famous surgeons in New York, Matt Anderson, and especially about his partner, Mia Lindhom, the high-profile director of an important fashion house.

I carefully examined the photos of her taken at various moments in her day. She was all sophisticated beauty: tall, with a refined, slender frame. Her hair was the color of gold, her eyes a luminous gentian blue.

"He chose well," I commented to no one as I chewed on my index fingernail.

Yes, Matt Anderson (also known as my father) had, after a series of affairs, finally decided to leave my mother for a younger, more beautiful and more famous woman.

I wondered if she had children too, but there was no information on the subject.

"Selene! Don't pretend you can't hear me!" My mother came into the room, huffy after shouting my name for several minutes. Still, I didn't pull my gaze away from the pictures of Matt and Mia looking happy and carefree together.

"Since when does he like blonds?" I asked, scowling seriously as she walked around my room, gathering up the clothes scattered here and there. I wasn't a neat freak like her.

"Since he met Mia, probably? Anyway, I have your suitcase packed downstairs," she reminded me, though it was hardly necessary. I knew full well that my flight was scheduled for ten o'clock. I had already bathed and dressed, albeit reluctantly. I didn't want to repair any relationship with Matt, much less become part of his life after he had been so completely uninterested in mine for so long. So, I kept opening random web pages, just to keep my mind occupied even as I could feel the anguish rising inside me.

Parents rarely understand how much their actions affect their children's emotional state. My adolescence was marred by fighting and my father's constant affairs. Indelible memories that I tried to fight against every day in vain. Going to live with him was a terrible punishment for me that was probably going to bring all sorts of unhealed wounds to the surface.

"Selene…" Mom sighed, sitting down on the bed beside me. She closed my laptop gently and smiled at me, finally getting my attention. "I just want you to try," she said in an indulgent murmur.

Sure, she wanted me to *try* to accept a man who had long since ceased to be my father.

Four years had now passed since he left us to live with his current partner. Four years in which he had tried to call and talk to me but got no response. Four years in which, every time he tried to see me, I locked myself in my room and waited for him to leave. I sighed at those nagging memories and tilted my chin down to hide my pain from the only person I truly loved.

"I can't do it…" Memories of her weeping and raving over the lack of respect shown by the man she'd married were embedded too deeply in my mind.

Matt had started off by sleeping with a nurse ten years his junior. One lover became two, three, four…until I lost count. Or rather, until Mia came along and took him away from us for good.

"Sure you can do it. You're a bright girl…" She stroked the back of my hand and gazed lovingly at me. She believed in me, and I never wanted to let her down. Never.

"I don't want anything to do with Matt," I muttered like a wayward child. I needed to act like a woman, put on the mask of acceptance and display a certain maturity, but it was nearly impossible to act rationally when anger had taken me over inside.

"Selene, I know it's not going to be easy. I don't expect the two of you to get along right away, but I at least want you to give it a chance… You've refused to speak to him for too long." She looked at me with the pained expression that inevitably corralled my pride. She was fully aware that her big blue eyes—identical to my own— had the power to make me surrender. Still, I tried to make my case.

"Mom, that man doesn't deserve my respect. *You* know…" I answered, scowling, and it was the truth. After everything she and I had gone through *by ourselves*, my mother knew very well how much it cost me to go along with her request that I live with a "father" who was nothing of the sort.

"I get it, sweetheart. But I've forgiven him for what he did. You should, too."

I stared silently into her eyes. My mother had the enormous fortitude required to forgive that man's wrongdoings, but I wasn't like her. I didn't have her strength.

....

The trip to the airport went by too quickly.

My mom waited with me until I had to go through security and spent the time reassuring me, even if her words were heavy and difficult to accept for a twenty-one-year-old. I once read somewhere that someone of my age was on the threshold of adulthood, but at the same time, lacked definitive maturity. That was probably why I vacillated between childish behavior and moments of utmost thoughtfulness.

The plane ride took about two hours. It felt like the longest flight of my life, even though I had outfitted myself with a couple of books that partially relieved some of my perpetual anxiety.

On our descent, from my window seat I observed the giant skyscrapers rising in the distance and all the cars speeding by on the streets of the great city. It was clear to me in that moment exactly why they called it the city that never sleeps.

When I arrived in New York, the cool air and chaotic atmosphere hit me immediately, catapulting me into an entirely new reality. I sighed and let my mother know that I had arrived. She'd asked me to call her the moment the plane landed, and knowing all too well how excessively anxious she got, I tried to reassure her. Then, I tried to spot Matt in the crowded arrivals area of the airport. How could I find one person in such a giant space? Maybe I should have held up a sign? "Wanted: Matt Anderson, asshole father." Or: "Selene seeks asshole father, Matt Anderson, and his new family." Either way, I would have kept the "asshole."

I remembered what model car Matt had—a black Range Rover.

He would bring it to come get me, but how many of them might drive by? I looked around me; there were so many people concentrated in one space it made my head spin.

However, I must have had a lucky star on my side, because during all the chaos of people and cars, I spotted a shiny black Range Rover pulled up a few feet away. I wasn't completely sure it was the vehicle I was looking for, but I had a feeling. I hadn't seen my father yet, but inside I could sense his presence.

I stuck my cell phone into the pocket of my jeans and grabbed my suitcase, dragging it along toward the luxurious vehicle. As I approached, I squinted, trying to pick out any details of the interior—a figure that I could associate with him for certain. Every step I slowly took toward that car became more and more uncertain, as if I were walking to the gallows.

Then, suddenly, the door opened and dispelled all my doubts. My father appeared, a man of sophisticated charm, decidedly in shape, dressed in an impeccable suit undoubtedly from some famous brand. He looked like he'd made a deal with the devil. Despite his age, he was still handsome and alluring in a way few other men were. And that was his biggest problem. He had always been a magnet for women and incapable of controlling his urges. It was no coincidence that fidelity was a moral commitment he struggled to keep.

I looked at him, but his warm hazel eyes were hidden behind his sunglasses, which gave me a moment to regain my composure. I didn't want him to see the effect he still had on me.

"Hi, Selene." He gave me an almost embarrassed smile and immediately reached to take my suitcase, giving every appearance of a kind and considerate person. His voice... I had forgotten the sound of it.

"Hi, Matt." I didn't call him "Dad" anymore; he knew how it was between us.

"How are you? How was your trip? I'm happy you agreed to come and stay with us—"

I interrupted him immediately to avoid listening to all those worthless pleasantries. He was good with words, with speeches and little soundbites, but I was certainly not the kind of daughter to be so easily duped.

"I only did it for my mother. Can we go?" I opened the car door and slid into the passenger seat. Neither of us said a word for the entire journey. It was a truly embarrassing situation, but it couldn't have gone any other way. That man had left us to make a new life, and even during my parents' marriage, he had never acted like a husband or, more importantly, like a father. I could still remember every birthday he missed, all the performances he promised to come to but never showed up at, and the calls he didn't answer because he was too busy getting some younger coworker in bed. It happened again and again. His distraction, his absence, I remembered all of it…especially my mother's tears.

I sighed and stared out the window, trying to think about something else, like the fact that I would be starting my sophomore year of college at Pace, where I would need to study rigorously while trying to fit in and make friends. A difficult task for an introvert like me.

"I'm glad I finally get to introduce you to Mia," Matt said awkwardly, breaking the heavy silence that hung over the two of us. It wasn't exactly the first thing I was expecting to hear.

"Since when are you into blonds?" I ask tartly. I had only seen pictures of her, but I already knew, deep down inside, that it would be impossible for me to get along with Mia.

Matt gave me a brief, blank look before turning his attention back to driving. "You could make friends with her kids…" He deflected my pointed question quickly and cleared his throat, tightening both hands on the steering wheel.

"Children? For real?" I gave a mocking shake of my head. "And to think I'm an only child because you didn't *want* any other kids. So, do you share a house with your partner's progeny now? What a twist of fate…" I commented, both sarcastic and indignant.

Yeah, I believed in fate—an impersonal force that governed human affairs in some unknowable way. I was convinced that everyone had a destiny, for better or for worse.

"Selene, I understand your perspective, but I want you to try to—"

"Don't start with that bullshit! The only reason we are doing this is because Mom convinced me to make an attempt, but I already know that nothing is going to change between you and me!" I answered adamantly, pulling my cell phone out of my jeans pocket.

I didn't want to talk to him.

I knew it wasn't exactly the mature thing to do, but I also knew that this was a consequence of his behavior and he would have to deal with it. Immediately, I noticed a text notification flashing insistently on my screen.

It was from Jared, my boyfriend: Did you get there yet, baby? I'm waiting for your call.

I answered immediately, not caring if I seemed rude. I'm with Matt now. I'll call you later. XOXO.

"Are you listening to me?" Matt burst out suddenly. He had said something before that I didn't catch, so I decided to be honest.

"No…I was responding to a text." I smiled at him with the same indifference he had shown me for years. I wondered how he was feeling at that moment. Had he been hoping for a hug from me, the kind he hadn't gotten in a while? The situation wasn't easy for me because, although I always put on a good face, I had missed having a father figure.

During those first few years, it hadn't been easy to accept that I was the daughter of a powerful man who thought only about himself and his career. A man who regularly sought pleasure from other women because he wasn't satisfied with the pure love that his wife gave him. A man who was only ever able to carve out a tiny space in his life for me, for being a father.

Then, I got used to it.

When Matt pulled the car in front of an enormous iron gate, I knew we had reached our destination. He took a remote control out of his pocket and pressed it, the gate opening automatically. He turned down a stone driveway and parked between a white Audi and a black Maserati. I resisted the urge to make an inappropriate comment and instead just opened the door and got out of the car to grab my suitcase from the trunk.

I turned my gaze to the palatial manor before me and was astounded: it was a luxurious three-story house with a manicured garden, an illuminated swimming pool, and windows everywhere to provide a view of the splendor inside. It was a high-profile property located in wealthy Westchester County, but all that opulence only served to remind me of Matt's empty and superficial personality. He flaunted his prosperity and cash, not understanding that no house or car could ever make up for a lack of paternal love.

"Here we are." He cleared his throat awkwardly, breaking the silence with a banal observation.

"Yeah, thanks... I kinda figured," I answered sarcastically with an insolent smirk. I pulled the suitcase along with me and dodged his hand when he kept trying to take it. My heart was unsettled. I felt like *Alice in Wonderland*, except that nothing about this situation was wonderful. I had only just gotten there, and I already wanted to run away.

Shortly thereafter, a woman with gold-colored hair, cornflower blue eyes, and a skimpy blush pink dress appeared before my eyes, draped in what I hoped was a *faux* fur. It was like a jump scare in a horror movie.

"I've been waiting for you! Finally, you're here!" she declared euphorically, clapping her hands like a delighted child. Then she turned her joyful smile on me while I scrutinized her carefully.

I'd definitely had a different impression of her based on the Mia Lindhom that I had seen in the newspapers. I had imagined her as a conceited and haughty sort of person, but instead she had revealed herself to be friendly and eager to get to know me.

"You're so beautiful, Selene! Wow, I'm just thrilled, I—I'm Mia." She smiled again, adjusting her dress. She seemed genuinely abashed and apprehensive, possibly about the impression she was making on me.

"Yes, thank you, and I hope my stay here is a short one," I told her automatically, watching her smile slowly fade as she began to compulsively touch her bright hair. I, on the other hand, stood motionless in front of the entrance to the sumptuous manor, with its sophisticated, modern design, feeling wholly inadequate—a tiny fish struggling to survive out of the water.

"Are the kids here?" my father interrupted, uneasy with my excessive candor.

"Oh! Yes. They're inside. Let's go in." Mia tried to take my suitcase out of my hand, but I moved to avoid her.

"I'll carry it, thanks." I pasted on a polite smile and continued dragging my luggage along as I followed the lady and my father into the house. The interior of the enormous home was exactly how I'd imagined it from the outside. A marble staircase that led to the upper floor was all high-quality craftsmanship, which gave it a unique and compelling look. Heavily laden crystal chandeliers decorated the ceiling and threw off opulent, multifaceted light in gold and silver. It illuminated the entire room, dazzling the eye. Every detail of the place was a fashion statement: elegant and refined. Even the walls were made of fine marble veined with gold.

"Kids, come here!" Mia shouted, and I continued to admire the vivid colors that surrounded me while I waited to meet her children.

"What do you want, Mom?" a petite blond girl muttered acidly, all while she continued to chew gum and tap rapidly on her phone's screen. *She can't be older than sixteen*, I thought, based on her not-yet-mature body and her delicate, childlike face.

"Sweetheart, I'd like you to meet Selene," Mia said excitedly. Her enthusiasm embarrassed me more than it should have.

The girl looked up from her phone and cocked an inquisitive eyebrow. Her gray eyes were overly made-up. She wore a cropped, figure-hugging sweater, and skinny jeans covered her slim legs.

"Chloe," she answered with an arrogant air.

I just stared at her. It wasn't at all polite and perhaps a little defensive as well, but I was very nervous and the agitation had put me in a bad mood.

"What did you want, Mom?" asked a male voice.

A moment later, a boy came down from the upper floor and broke some of the overbearing tension in the air. His eyes immediately found mine, and I saw that they were a warm, earthy brown. Neat chestnut hair framed his fresh face while his athletic physique was highlighted by a pair of dark pants and a lightweight shirt.

He approached me slowly, examining me meticulously. "Logan. Pleasure to meet you. You must be Matt's daughter." He held his hand out to me while his sister continued to regard me skeptically.

"Yeah, I'm Selene." I shook his hand in return and smiled.

"Pretty name," he said. He lifted one corner of his mouth in a sensual fashion. It was an expression that I was sure had captivated many a girl before.

"Thanks," I answered, obviously embarrassed, as I stared into his gorgeous eyes.

He was a very good-looking guy. I had to admit it.

"Wonderful, darlings. Now, I think Selene needs to see her room. Which of you would like to volunteer to show her?" Mia interjected coquettishly, and I suppressed a huff of irritation.

14

She had a particularly strident voice, which I would—with great reluctance—have to get used to.

"I'll do it. Come with me, Selene." Logan immediately demonstrated his readiness with a jerk of his chin, though, for a second, I just stood there, lost in my own thoughts. It all felt so surreal. Me, Matt's new family, Matt himself, and our already shattered relationship... What the hell was I doing there?

"Are we going?" Logan called, grabbing my attention. And I just nodded rather than spilling all my inner torments to a complete stranger. I made a grab for my suitcase, but he very politely beat me to it, so I followed him up the stairs, watching his broad shoulders and trying to tamp down the misery of the moment.

"So, Selene... You like it here?" He glanced at my body, and I tensed up automatically, as though he were judging me. Or, more likely, judging my decidedly relaxed and casual look.

"Are you asking if I like luxury, expensive cars, swimming pools, and all this crap?" I couldn't help but be honest with him. But Logan only gave me an amused smile, not at all offended by my words. He was the kind of boy who exuded his own unique charm, with an elegant bearing and a pure, radiant smile.

"Yeah... all this crap. Do you like it?"

All at once, he threw open the door of a room at the end of the long, bright hallway and put my suitcase down on the floor. There were at least twenty bedrooms in the house and who knew how many bathrooms. I was sure it could have housed several families.

"Not really. I'm here as a favor for my mother because she made such a big deal about trying to get me and Matt to reconcile, though I think that's unlikely to happen," I said and took a look at what would be my new room. I approved of the bright colors and the restrained furnishings—luxurious but not ostentatious.

In the center of the room there stood a four-poster bed with a tufted headboard, embellished with a cascade of pillows in all shapes and sizes. A mirror with gold-leaf accents adorned a vanity covered with perfumes, makeup products, and creams of all varieties. One entire wall was dedicated to bookshelves, each shelf strung with bright, decorative lights that gave it a particularly chic vibe.

"Just give it some time, Selene. Everything will fall into place," Logan said and I turned to look at him. In his eyes, I saw a clear understanding, even though we didn't really know each other at all.

"You've got one of the best rooms," he declared before clearing his throat and glancing away. "For two reasons," he added, giving me a sly look.

"Which are?" I noticed the desk, then the white velvet seat where I would probably put my clothes or my bags. The room was truly every girl's dream.

"Reason one," he raised an index finger as he moved toward the French doors that opened onto a huge balcony. "You have a view of the pool." He opened the doors, and I approached him slowly, taking in the incredible exterior panorama. The rectangular swimming pool was located to the left of the house, near a Mediterranean garden with an ample variety of colorful plants, each one unique.

"And the second reason?" I cocked an eyebrow while I tried to hide a shy smile.

"Your room is right across from mine." He gave me a mischievous wink and grinned.

Though I did not feel threatened by him for whatever reason, I still wanted to set him straight. "Don't get any funny ideas. I'm not that kind of girl," I answered tersely, even as I put on a cheerful expression to make myself appear less harsh.

"Mmh...then this room could be a problem for you." He smiled sarcastically with a strange gleam in his eyes.

"Why?" I asked curiously.

"Because the room next door is Neil's," he answered, amused, but I still didn't get his meaning.

"Who's Neil?"

"My older brother," he said immediately, and it was only then that I remembered Matt telling me about *three* children.

"And why should that worry me?" I continued questioning him, undaunted, while he shook his head, mocking me.

"Get some earplugs," Logan answered cryptically. Then, he simply winked and walked away.

....

I tried to make myself feel comfortable for a change by giving myself time to take a hot shower and put on clean clothes. Though, inside, I could feel the usual annoying sensation of rising anguish that I knew wasn't leaving me anytime soon.

About an hour later, I joined Matt and Mia promptly for lunch. Everyone had already taken their seats, and I quickly sat down next to Chloe, who just continued to text without paying anyone else the slightest bit of attention.

"So, Selene, I know you're starting at Pace tomorrow. You've already completed your freshman year, right?" Mia immediately tried to make conversation but to no avail, naturally, as I wasn't in the mood to chitchat with my father's girlfriend.

"Yeah," I answered indifferently, immediately cutting off the exchange. Logan was sitting in front of me, constantly looking at me with a smile I couldn't decipher. Maybe he liked my excessive candor?

"Where's Neil?" my father asked, pulling our gazes to him.

"He's probably out with his friends," Logan muttered with a shrug. Anna, the housekeeper—whom I had the pleasure of meeting when I got lost in the immensity of these new spaces while trying to make it to the living room—was roaming around the table making sure that everything was just as the master of the house had requested.

"Or screwing somebody," Chloe added with a cheeky smile on her face.

"Chloe!" her mother scolded while my father shook his head uncomfortably. I turned my attention from Anna back to Matt and sank into the whirl of my thoughts, reflecting on the absurdity of the situation. Him sitting at the head of the table with his family and me, a total stranger, showing up just to please her mother and trying to salvage a relationship that she already knew was unsalvageable.

Nevertheless, lunch continued with Mia repeatedly trying to make small talk with me while Matt seemed particularly tense.

"I'm going to hang out with Carter," Chloe said suddenly, leaping to her feet.

"You haven't finished your lunch yet." Matt's authoritative voice surprised me; he had never taken that tone with me.

"I know, Matt, but he's already there. We're going to the mall and then the movies. I promised him." Chloe argued her point sweetly, as though he really was her father, and she owed him that kind of respect.

Air.

All at once, I needed air because that anguished feeling was turning into an invisible rope, tight around my neck.

"That asshole again?!" Logan grumbled. Clearly this Carter wasn't the kind of guy he wanted his sister seeing.

"Logan, mind your own business," Chloe shot back, not at all intimidated by her brother's butting in.

"Kids!" Mia scolded them.

"Okay, but when he dumps you like all the other ones, don't come crying to me!" Logan insisted, pounding his fist on the table.

"Kids!" Mia admonished them again, but no one seemed to hear her.

"He's not going to dump me... Carter cares about me!"

"Do what you want." Logan gave up, though irritation was still evident on his face. His sister was a teenager, and holding back a girl at that age wasn't easy at all. They were governed exclusively by hormones and social instincts.

Chloe hurried off, leaving the rest of us to lapse into an awkward silence. Lunch continued, albeit with discomfort that was hard to ignore.

"Is there a good bookstore nearby?" My voice cut through the tense atmosphere, drawing the eye of everyone else to me. I'd only been there for a few hours, and I already felt like I needed to be alone. I felt inappropriate; the ink splotch on a white sheet of paper, the scribble on a spotless wall, and I needed to do something comforting.

"Well, there's one downtown, or you could go into the city. The Strand is great but…why?" Matt answered before looking at me like I'd just sprouted a horn out of the middle of my forehead.

"I can take you if you want," Logan added, smiling, probably taking it for granted that I would accept his invitation. It was nice of him to offer, but I needed to perform my familiar ritual alone: on every trip I took, I had to buy one new book that would accompany me throughout my journey. It was a little secret of my own, a kind of good-luck charm.

"No, I can take the train, and I have Maps on my phone. I'm good." I got up from the table and took my phone out of my pocket to illustrate my point. They looked at each other strangely, but I didn't care. I said goodbye to them and headed for the door, planning to walk to the train station a couple of miles away.

I didn't have a great sense of direction; I tended to get lost easily, even in places I knew very well. New York was large and fast paced, so it would be a struggle not to get lost, but I wasn't afraid. After all, there were people I could ask for directions and a map on my phone.

In short, I had everything under control. The train ride took less than an hour and spit me out in real NYC, where I gawked like a tourist on vacation. I felt instant euphoria over the idea that I was going to attend college so close to the city. I walked around in raptures for about half an hour. From time to time, I stopped to examine the store windows, the imposing skyscrapers, and some buskers. When hunger started knocking on my stomach, I bought a hot dog at a cart.

I felt light, buoyed, and intrigued by this new reality. The weather was crisp, and strolling the streets of Manhattan turned out to be much more pleasant than I'd thought it would be. I lost track of time and only stopped when I spotted a store window with a display of books of all varieties. I drew closer to it with a dreamy look on my face and had pressed both hands to the glass before I realized that this was the exact bookstore that Matt had mentioned.

I immediately went in through the automatic doors and found myself in a magical environment. There were three floors exclusively full of books, a true reader's paradise. The scent I was breathing in—of wood, of dreams, of imagined lives—transported me into another world. I could have spent the whole day there, forgetting everything else.

I set off, trying to keep my out-of-control enthusiasm in check and asked a sales assistant where I would find classic fiction and literature. The modern classics were my favorites, and I felt the need to start this new life with one of them. The girl directed me to the third floor, and I admired the immense size of the place as I climbed the stairs.

"Excuse me..." I passed a couple absorbed in leafing through books right in the middle of the great classics section. I smiled. It seemed I wasn't the only person who loved them. I stroked the rows of books with my fingers, soaking in the smell of the pages as I closed my eyes. A sleepy calm came over me as it always did whenever I sought refuge in this kind of environment. The thud of something falling to the floor, however, had me on alert again.

A book lay open not far away from where I was standing. I glanced around to see who had dropped it, but the couple was gone so I assumed I must have knocked it over. I bent down to pick up the volume and saw the title: *Peter and Wendy*. Something about those words caught my attention and convinced me to buy it. This would be the book that marked the start of my new journey.

I paid for the book and slipped it into my bag, politely telling the cashier goodbye. By the time I got off the train back in Bedford, it was dusk, and I had a two-and-a-half-mile walk before I got back to Matt's home. I sighed and opened my Maps app again, typing in the address of the house. I started off and tried not to notice all the dark, deserted streets that crossed my path as I headed for my destination.

My phone indicated that the battery was running low, and I swore softly, hoping it wouldn't die before I could navigate back.

"No, shit, no... Hold on." I turned down the brightness and prayed that luck would be on my side, at least for another two miles or so.

I kept going, following the directions down the street until the display went black. My phone was officially dead.

"Great. Fantastic," I grumbled, rubbing my face. I shook my phone as if to jostle it back to life, but unfortunately, it needed a charger and my pleas and curses were of no use. I didn't even have Matt's number memorized.

"Shit. Shit. Shit," I burst out. I wanted to kick something. I threw my phone into my bag and just kept walking, following my instincts. I hunched my shoulders as the sun started to set and the streetlights lit up. It was the time of day when the brightness of the colors began to fade and disappear into the textured shadows of the dark. I had no idea whether my father would have been worried if I didn't make it home for dinner. Maybe he would have just given me up for missing or—worst-case scenario—dead.

"How many times do I have to tell you about the importance of car maintenance! You're such a dumbass!"

I stopped on the edge of the sidewalk under a streetlight and saw an old black Cadillac parked in the street with a tire that was either punctured or entirely flat—I couldn't tell which. A guy, whose shadow looked deformed from so far away, was shouting angrily, waving his arms in the air. I frowned and stared curiously at him.

"Calm down, Luke. We'll figure it out," answered another guy, this one tall and slim with black hair. I couldn't make out his features, but I could see a piercing glinting from his lower lip.

"Doubt it. How are we supposed to get home if you don't even have a spare tire?" A girl with bizarre blue hair put her hands on her narrow hips, which were clad in a pair of black shorts with fishnets in the same color underneath. She gave her friend a snort and then crossed her arms over her chest, pushing up her small breasts. I didn't know what these people's deal was, but whoever they were, they didn't inspire a lot of trust.

I sighed and tried to walk past the group without being noticed. I kept my head lowered and my posture rigid as I passed them. I'd almost made it, but then I heard their voices falter and the silence build around me, and I knew I'd been clocked. I sped up but someone behind me yelled, "Hey, baby doll. You in a hurry?"

I didn't know which of the boys had spoken, but I froze. The deep timbre of the voice was confident and menacing, and everything inside of me vibrated with fear. I didn't know whether I should try to run or turn and face the situation. In any event, I didn't get the chance to think it over before the voice called out to me again.

I turned and looked at the boy, whom I could now see more clearly. He had dark eyes, a small nose, and a thin mouth. His features were almost delicate, but the look he was giving me was disturbing to say the least.

"We're out here flat on our asses, and you're trying to holler?"

the other guy, the blond one, huffed noisily, running a hand through his short hair.

I startled at his words and cleared my throat awkwardly. I needed to get out of this situation—make up something, anything.

"I am in need of some information," I hazarded, smiling tightly. The dark-haired man cocked an eyebrow, and the blue-haired girl moved next to him, looking me up and down as though I were a prostitute. She was wearing too much makeup, and her hazel eyes were rimmed with extra-long fake eyelashes; she looked like a dollar-store version of Harley Quinn from *Suicide Squad*.

"And what would you be willing to give me in exchange?" The boy approached me slowly, analyzing my body with deliberation while I backed away in alarm.

Who are these people?

"Xavier!" The blond boy called him back, irritated. Maybe he was the sane one of the two? Nevertheless, the boy named Xavier didn't give up and just kept staring at me like an animal in rut.

"Shut up, idiot. Have you seen her?"

"Yeah, I saw her, but here comes another problem." The blond pointed at the car just as another guy emerged from it, followed by curvy blond Barbie. The guy slammed the car door hard, making everyone turn in his direction. He leaned arrogantly against the hood and stared the other two down grimly.

For a moment, I forgot about the situation I was in and just lost myself admiring the virility of his muscular body.

He was tall, so tall.

A leather jacket tugged on his folded arms, his biceps bulging with a strength that was entirely masculine. His jeans, though not especially tight, wrapped around a pair of firm, athletic legs with the muscled calves of an athlete. A white sweater, not at all showy, clung perfectly to the lines of his clearly defined chest.

More than his magnificent body, however, it was his face that stunned me—finely drawn features in striking contrast to his explosive physicality. There was a hint of well-groomed stubble on his jaw. His nose was straight, the tip upturned ever so slightly. His plump, perfectly shaped lips looked like they were drawn on him, and his eyes were an eerie golden color, like honey in the sunlight. Then there was his hair, a thick mass of unruly brown curls.

He looked around at his friends and smiled, amused by the strange circumstances we had all found ourselves in.

"So…do you plan to keep acting like idiots for a while longer or are you going to engage your brains and figure out a solution?" His voice was a raspy baritone, and the vibe he gave off was that of a superior to his cohorts.

"You're so hot when you do that…" The blond girl rested a hand on the guy's chest and then rubbed all over that Adonis body, planting a kiss on his jaw as she did. He, however, remained unmoved. He stood imposing as a god, focused on the two other guys who still hadn't responded.

"This girl here wants some information…" Xavier pointed, shifting Tall, Dark, and Handsome's attention to me. I blushed unexpectedly when I felt his gleaming, golden gaze on me. I looked at him and he looked back at me for seconds that felt like an eternity. His eyes were truly something special. Never in my life had I seen anything like them.

"What information do you need?" he asked me, and it felt like his voice lit up still-unexplored corners of my body. He was intense, certain. More than anything else, he inspired awe with his towering frame, even though he wasn't specifically attempting to intimidate me.

"I think I'm lost. My phone is totally dead, and I need to get home," I explained with a miserable sigh. I would never have approached these people to ask for help before, but now that I was here, I had to seize the opportunity.

"We have our own damn problems. We don't need hers," the blond guy grumbled in exasperation.

"Baby doll is lost, dickhead, be nice," Xavier said, giving him a lewd wink. "Do you at least remember where home is, princess?" he added, extending an arm out toward me while I backed away apprehensively. The two girls burst into laughter, delighted by my reaction. Xavier pivoted to grab his crotch instead in an obvious obscene gesture. He was aroused. I knew I couldn't appear to be submissive or frightened. I prepared myself to fight back if he tried anything.

"Okay, that's enough." The Adonis, whose name I still didn't know, pushed up off the car and that movement was enough to make his friends go pale. He was a giant for real, at least six three, and his broad shoulders suggested a physical power that would have cowed anyone.

"Where do you live?" He turned to me again and I gulped. I couldn't say exactly by how much he towered over me, but I had to tilt my head back to look him in the eyes. When I did, I was able to see the tiny amber stripes in his otherwise light, sandy irises. I just kept staring vacantly at him.

I had lost the power of speech. I felt so disoriented and confused. His eyes scanned me while mine darted to the blond who wouldn't stop glaring at me as though I were some irritating insect that needed squashing. Was she jealous? I just wanted some basic information, not to steal her boyfriend.

"I live nearby," I replied. And then I managed to recall my new address. The guy wrinkled his forehead into a frown while the blond beside him looked like she was having a lightbulb moment. I waited a few seconds, staring at the boy's full lips, which had flattened into a serious, considering expression. He must have noticed where I was looking because he gave me a soft, satisfied smile that made me blush.

"I'll go with you, then," he suggested, and for a second, I thought I'd misheard him.

"What? You're going to ditch us and leave?" Xavier said, as shocked as I was.

I stopped and considered. I didn't ask him to go with me, I just wanted him to—

"Are you serious?" The blond gave him an indignant look, clearly feeling possessive. Then she stamped her heel on the ground and my eyes slipped down the leather skirt that wrapped around her long, firm thighs. Her blond hair fell almost to her butt, and her curves were generous and flourishing. She was objectively beautiful, but I doubted that she had much going for her beyond the physical.

"Yes, Jennifer. Get back on your own." Then, after those harsh words, he touched her cheek and talked to her like he was about to strip her naked right there in front of me. He stared at her breasts, propped up on display, and his face showed barely suppressed desire. She bit her lip.

"We'll go to mine tonight," he whispered in such an erotic tone that it sent shivers down my spine. He touched her hip, and it felt as though his fingers were touching my body instead. It was a ridiculous feeling. He let her go and started walking down the sidewalk without paying any further attention to his friends. I, on the other hand, stood frozen, debating which option was better.

"You coming?" He turned to me, and I startled. He wanted me to go with him, but the guy was a total stranger to me. I didn't even know his name, why should I go anywhere with him?

"I don't know you," I admitted, sounding like a little girl who had been warned not to talk to strangers. The boy cocked his head and examined my outfit, from the dark jeans to the light jacket open over my sweater with Tinkerbell printed on it. I had a special fondness for it because it had been a Christmas present from my grandmother

Marie, who was no longer with us. Even though I was in college, I'd always choose to wear something that connected me with her.

"Listen, Tinkerbell, I'm not a very patient person. So, pick: either you stay here with Xavier and Luke—and, trust me, you don't want to get to know them better—or follow me and get home. I live in that area too..." he answered, irritated.

I flushed and stiffened my spine, trying to look somewhat fierce. "Why should I go with you? You could be some kind of crazy person, a psychopath, a serial killer..." I hardened myself, crossing my arms over my chest. I could hear his friends behind me grumbling about their car, but I didn't turn to look at them. The boy stared at me and a thin layer of shadow fell over his perfect face. I tried to find a single aesthetic flaw in it, but I couldn't. Not even when an inexplicable darkness appeared in his golden eyes.

"Or maybe I'm someone who can show you the way..." He gave me a sly wink and kept walking, but once again, I stood still and pondered his response.

Sure, a guy like that could "show me the way." That boy looked like the devil incarnate with a mysterious, forbidden appeal, but he didn't actually seem like a crazy person or a serial killer. Though appearances could be deceiving. In any case, I needed to be wary of him.

"You wanna get a fucking move on? It's not like I'm doing you a favor here or anything, little girl!" He turned violently around, and I jumped. Nice manners. Why did he have to be so surly and ill-tempered? We didn't even know each other. I didn't have much of a choice, though. Staying with his friends was completely out of the question and going on by myself would have gotten me completely lost.

"I'm only coming with you because you live around there as well. Assuming that's even true..." I pointed out, earning myself an unfriendly look. "And you should try to be less arrogant," I added. I was aggravating him, and he let me know it with a menacing stare. Then he turned once more and started walking casually away again.

I took the opportunity to study his form undisturbed. Everything about him suggested a particularly masculine strength, especially his firm glutes, which I observed admiringly. His bearing was proud and determined. He looked like a damned soul strolling happily through a hell of his own, detached from everything around him.

"In any case, if you tried to do something to me against my will, I know how to defend myself. I'm dangerous to men who don't show respect," I declared. I was lying, I didn't even know how to kick someone away, but I had to pretend and at least try to generate some apprehension in the beguiling man beside me.

He looked over at me, cocking an eyebrow.

"Anything I've ever done to a woman has not been against her will, believe me." He gave me a lingering look, and for a moment, I suspected he was ogling my breasts, but I wasn't sure so I couldn't call him out. I decided to ignore his comment. Men, after all, were always prone to boasting about their lovemaking prowess, so he was probably spinning bullshit, too.

"What's your name?" he asked me abruptly, pulling my mind back to our halting conversation. He grabbed a pack of cigarettes from his back pocket and took one out. He offered it to me politely, and I declined, shaking my head.

"I don't smoke, thanks." I trailed alongside him, trying to keep up with the pace of his strides. Compared to his imposing size, I felt even smaller than usual.

"But my name is Selene," I added, trying not to stare too much, though it was difficult not to be drawn to him. No one else had ever had that kind of effect on me. I was so intimidated; I couldn't even ask for his name in return.

"Where are you from?" he asked. He lit the cigarette, his toned biceps contracting. He rounded his full lips to expel a grayish cloud.

I coughed and stepped back a bit to avoid the wave of smoke coming for me; I hated the smell.

"Detroit. I'm here with my father…on vacation, you could say." I made a skeptical face. I wasn't sure if one could really call this time in my life a "vacation," but I didn't want to tell a total stranger my actual reasons for coming to New York.

I glanced at him and focused on his sharp, straightforward profile. Forehead, nose, and lips all seemed to have been artfully crafted.

Several moments passed in silence, during which I didn't dare open my mouth, not even to ask what his name was. He finished his cigarette and put it out. Even though he had just finished smoking, he had a nice smell, like clean amber.

"You realize it was irresponsible to wander alone around the streets of a city you aren't familiar with yet, right, Tinkerbell?" I went rigid and instinctively did up the buttons of my coat to cover my sweater.

"Stop calling me Tinkerbell," I snapped in irritation, ignoring his scolding. The boy grinned without looking at me. I noticed again how attractive he was, despite his impudence.

"I'll call you whatever I want." He paused for effect. "Tinkerbell," he said again with amusement in his voice. I heaved a sigh and glared at him.

"And what am I supposed to call you, then?" I groused, finally getting up the nerve to ask him for his name. The boy looked at me with his beautiful honey-colored eyes and my own eyes caught on his lips, which moved finally to say his name.

"Neil," he said. Then we walked in silence for a long time, stopping only when we reached the enormous gate that I'd passed through with Matt hours before. I looked at the gold plaque engraved with the words "Anderson–Lindhom Residence" and then back to Neil. I was about to thank him when he reached into the pocket of his dark jeans and produced a set of keys with a remote fob.

"We've reached our destination, Tinkerbell." He opened the gate and gestured with fake gallantry for me to go through it. I stared at him in disbelief while a smirk spread across his face. I realized then that he had always known who I was and that he'd just enjoyed screwing with me.

That Adonis with his indisputable allure and enigmatic smile was the same Neil whom Logan had told me about, Mia's oldest. Before me stood...Neil Miller.

....

Mia and Matt were pleased when they saw us walk in the front door together. My father clapped Neil on the shoulder as if he were some hero who had rescued the princess from her remote tower. I, on the other hand, just tried to avoid Neil's constant mocking glances at my beloved Tinkerbell sweater.

When Matt asked me if I'd gotten lost, I reassured him that I hadn't, even though that wasn't entirely true. I didn't stay and chat for too long, though, because I really needed to lock myself in my room, take a hot bath, and go to sleep. So, I took my leave quickly, paying no further attention to Neil, who had decided to go back out instead. Probably with those friends of his whose names I had already forgotten.

Hours later, deep in the night, I found myself lying awake in bed, my brain continuing to play back images of everything that had happened in the day. I rolled over on my side and tried again to fall asleep. I tossed and turned endlessly, closed and opened my eyes, sighed, huffed. In short, I did everything except allow myself to fall into a restful sleep.

"Goddammit!" I swore, lifting my torso up off the bed. I peered around anxiously before I hopped out of bed and decided to head down to the kitchen for a drink of water. Maybe the walk would calm me down and allow me to fall into a deep sleep.

I checked my phone and saw that it was already three in the morning. I crept slowly down the stairs, careful not to wake anyone. Silence and darkness reigned in the house, and it was blissfully relaxing.

Having made it to the kitchen—albeit with some wandering—I opened the fridge, grabbed a bottle of water and took a long drink.

"Ah, finally," I sighed in satisfaction. I felt the cool water run down my dry throat and straight into my hungry stomach, reminding me I hadn't had any dinner.

Just then, I heard the front door open and some odd sounds echoing around in the sitting room. All my senses went on high alert and my legs began to tremble.

"Shh...try to control yourself, you little slut" came the whisper of Neil's deep, raspy voice. I could have picked it out from a thousand whispers. Hold on a minute... *What* did he just say?

"It gets me so hot when you talk to me like that... I want you now," the girl he had just described in such a vulgar way murmured breathlessly. I heard the door close with a thud and then the smacking of kisses, passionate and greedy.

My eyes grew wide when I realized what was happening just a few feet away from me. My breathing sped up, and I bit my lip anxiously. I had no idea what to do; I began to panic as I heard stifled gasps and moans from the next room. I remembered what Neil had said—*We'll go to mine tonight.*—and everything became much clearer. The girl was Jennifer, the blond from earlier.

"Then I'll fuck you right here. Right now," he agreed with conviction, and even though I wasn't actually looking at them, I felt like I was in the middle of porn shoot.

"Yes..." she breathed while I was busy dying of embarrassment. Immediately, I tried to tiptoe out of the kitchen. The soft moonlight filtering through the numerous windows gave me a faint view of the house; enough to get back to my room. Until I accidentally ran into a chair, and it made a sound loud enough the catch the pair's attention.

"Oh, boy," I muttered, fully aware of the mess I had just made. I felt my heart beating so loudly that I was afraid they could hear it, too.

"What was that?" the girl asked, worried.

"What are you talking about?" he answered, too worked up to take notice of anything besides the lust building in his body.

"Someone's here, Neil," she whispered, and from the way her voice shook, I presumed that she was worried and frightened, maybe even more than I was.

"Wait…" he answered firmly. A few hurried footsteps followed; he was surely headed for the light switch. I pressed my lips together tightly and mentally counted the seconds that separated me from the moment when I would be caught red-handed, embarrassed, and afraid.

All at once, the light came on and Neil and Jennifer jolted when they noticed my presence.

"What the hell are you doing here?" Neil roared.

2

·····

SELENE

I swallowed uncomfortably as Neil continued to stare me down. His eyes skimmed lightly over my features. His lips were reddened, probably from the mauling they'd been subjected to just a few seconds before, and his imposing body loomed over me.

"Well?" he prodded me, and for the first time in my life, I felt incapable of speech or response. So, I stood there silently, looking closely at his pecs under his light turtleneck and thinking about how well defined they were.

"I came down for a drink of water." It was all I could manage to say. Then I cleared my throat and tried to get some control over myself. I had been in New York for how long? Not even a day? And already I was racking up the faux pas.

Neil, meanwhile, furrowed his brow and scrutinized me from head to toe. I was wearing a basic set of baggy pajamas with tigers on them, not remotely seductive. Jennifer, whose presence I had briefly forgotten, folded her arms over her chest, visibly annoyed that I had interrupted them.

"Could this be the famous Selene? The girl you told me about today?" she asked. I couldn't fail to notice the derisive way she said it.

"Yeah, that's her," Neil confirmed, and I just kept trying not to look at his broad chest because it would have undercut my appearance of indifference.

"What were you doing here in the dark, Selene? Did you perhaps want to join us?" Neil asked before leering suggestively at my childish pajamas. Jennifer burst out laughing, like she'd just been waiting for a chance to make fun of me. But I wasn't about to let that slide. I straightened up, fixing her with a sharp glare. She cut off mid-laugh. Then, I turned to Neil.

"Oh, of course." I grinned smugly, displaying a distinct boldness. "But if your penis is anything like your brain, I think it'd be too small to satisfy two women at the same time," I replied. Neil raised his eyebrows in surprise at my insult, and I watched his smile fade with satisfaction. Jennifer, meanwhile, didn't have the guts to utter a single syllable.

I knew all too well how keenly men felt it when their male pride was struck, but my moment of victory didn't last long. Neil shook his head and gave me the smile of a man with so much expert experience that he was completely unaffected by the absurdity I'd just spouted.

"Watch what you say, Tinkerbell." He got so close to me that I could feel his breath touching my face and strangely, I shivered. "I can show you how wrong you are right now, if you're brave enough." His eyes locked on mine, waiting for an answer. The flicker of guile in his stare made me stiffen. I just kept staring at his eyes, glittering like two stars behind which a dangerous fiend hid, and I knew with absolute certainty that I had never seen such a singular color before.

"Hard pass." I pulled myself together. "I'll spare you the embarrassment," I snapped with false bravado. We were standing so close to each other that we could feel the battle playing out between our bodies.

"You're just a baby," he whispered into my ear, breathing in my scent. "And, by the way, you should change up your look if you ever want to get a man hard." He examined my perplexed face and smiled in victory.

Then he snatched Jennifer's hand and dragged her up the stairs behind him. I was overwhelmed with frustrated embarrassment.

I thought that was the end of it, but I was completely wrong. That shameless, rude, and horribly sexy boy made sure I had a sleepless night. I heard every one of Jennifer's moans. The pair could count on Mia and Matt being unable to hear them as they slept on the other side of the sprawling palace.

But I could hear everything. Absolutely everything. And it was truly a nightmare.

At five in the morning, after tossing and turning in my bed all night with a pillow over my head, I fell asleep for such a brief period of time that I didn't even get to enjoy it. At seven, I rushed downstairs, grumpy and looking like a sleep-deprived panda. My head was pounding, and the thought of starting my first day at a new university like this only made it worse. Fortunately, my father had already taken care of the registration and various enrollment documents.

When I walked into the kitchen, Matt looked up from his newspaper and watched my exhausted form lumber toward the table.

"Good morning, Selene." He smiled and gave me a suspicious look. I wasn't looking so hot. I was well aware.

"Good morning," I grumbled tonelessly.

Next to him, Logan smiled kindly, his neat hair and still-drowsy eyes making him look both silly and sexy at the same time. Chloe, on the other hand, always looked like she was drifting through life in her own private bubble, oblivious to the world around her.

35

"Did you sleep well?" asked Logan, whom I had decided was the superior stepbrother.

"Not remotely." There was no point in denying it, and my tone even drew Chloe's curious eyes to me.

"Neil, right?" He chuckled, obviously amused.

"I'm think I'm actually going to need earplugs," I sighed in frustration, leaning back against my chair. Meanwhile, Matt just watched us in confusion.

To make the situation even worse, Mia jumped in, yelling, "Good morning!" in her coquettish voice. Her voice was so high-pitched, it made me jump. I rubbed my temples and silently cursed the day my mother had the bright idea to move me into this horror house.

Then I thanked Anna, the housekeeper, when she handed me a steaming cup of warm milk, and I forced myself to give her a polite smile. After all, she seemed like the only normal person in the place.

"Today is going to be a fantastic day, isn't it?" chirped Mia, who, despite the earliness of the hour, was happy and radiant. Furthermore, she was perfectly made up; her bright hair was pulled back into a ponytail, and she had on a black pantsuit that displayed a bit too much of her large yet firm breasts.

I quit examining her and instead mentally organized my tasks for the next few hours. I was concentrating entirely on myself when someone loudly yawned. My attention was immediately drawn to the giant striding through the kitchen doorway whom my body had bizarrely learned to recognize. Every one of my senses went on alert when he appeared.

Neil was bare-chested, only wearing a pair of gray sweatpants. It was a sight that would send any woman's hormones into overdrive, and I was no exception. I noticed a peculiar tribal tattoo adorning his right bicep and shoulder and another strange tattoo that looked like interwoven lines on his left side. His brown hair was mussed, and his lips were notably rosy and swollen. It pained me to admit it, but his physical beauty was almost indescribable; he was strapping and masculine.

He noticed my presence and smiled slyly at me, turning to the pantry to get a chocolate pistachio protein bar, the kind that are a staple in every athlete's diet. Each muscle in his back tensed, drawing my eyes to the perfection of his toned physique.

He turned back toward me and opened the bar. He bit into it slowly while leaning lazily on the counter behind him. I followed his every movement helplessly. He oozed sex from every inch of his body. Every breath, every hungry stare, every movement of his lips. He was a wild creature, carnal and greedy.

"Good morning," he said in a deliberately lewd murmur while staring at me. The irony of his greeting did not escape me. He knew that I hadn't gotten a wink of sleep because of him, and he was proud of it.

"Neil, could you put on a shirt?" Chloe muttered huffily. I didn't know whether she was protective of her brother or just annoyed by him. He didn't answer her and kept staring at me. Involuntarily, my eyes sank down his lean torso to the elastic waistband of his pants, hanging so low that it revealed the V leading to his pelvic area. Though he wasn't aroused, the bulge in his underwear was still perfectly visible. Yep...extremely visible.

I'd probably been wrong about his size last night, but at the same time, I was glad I got to make fun of him. Neil noticed my inappropriate glances and continued to stare me down, this time smugly.

"Shut up, Chloe. The ladies dig it."

I went back to frantically sipping my milk, fully aware that I'd been caught staring. There was no point in denying it.

"Are you ready for classes to start?" Mia asked suddenly, coming to my rescue.

"Yeah, Mom. Carter's here; he's going to take me." Chloe looked elated when she left, but I caught her brothers' frowns upon hearing that unwelcome name.

"I have to get to the hospital. I have a full schedule today," my father, the famous surgeon, cut in. He rose from the chair with his customary elegance, told everyone goodbye, and then turned to me. "Selene, would you like to…um…spend some time together later?" he mumbled, obviously afraid I would refuse him.

"No. I have things to do, Matt," I answered shortly. I saw no surprise on his face, only grief. It wasn't true, of course. I'd been there for such a short amount of time that it was impossible for me to have any solid plans yet. I only gave him that answer because it's what he always told me when I used to beg him to spend time with me.

Matt left without saying anything else, followed by Logan, who ran upstairs to get ready. Once Mia and Anna had also disappeared, Neil and I were left all by ourselves. I watched him warily.

I knew I should have restrained myself, but that perfectly proportioned body was made to be appreciated. So, I stared at him like he was a statue on exhibit in a museum and I was a visitor intent on memorizing every seductive angle of him. I consoled myself with the knowledge that he hadn't torn his eyes away from me either. We were assessing one another.

"Why are you staring at me?" I murmured, feeling like the walls of the room were inexplicably closing in on us.

"Isn't that what you've been doing to me this whole time, Tinkerbell?" That nickname again. That deep, rough voice combined with his cocky self-assurance scattered all my intentions of standing up to him.

All at once, he advanced on me, and I scrambled to my feet and backed up. I was visibly embarrassed, but I didn't want to give him any power over me. "Don't answer a question with another question. We were staring at each other," I told him as I felt the circular counter behind me hit my butt, bringing me to a halt.

What were his intentions here?

I didn't know, but I had a gut feeling that this boy was dangerous, and every time I looked at him, I felt shaken.

That was the truth.

Neil advanced again, and in a slick move, put his palms on the counter on either side of my body. He loomed over me—too tall, too powerful, too intimidating.

"What are you doing?" I babbled in a voice so feeble that I barely recognized it as my own. I had always been immune to guys like him. I'd never focused much on men in general, not even Jared. I'd always had other more important things on my mind.

"I know what you want…" His honey-colored eyes slid along my entire frame, lingering on my breasts. Utterly shameless. "And I don't mind you also knowing what I want…" he whispered, soft but certain.

"You're a pervert." I tried not to look overcome by the strong scent of bath gel that his body emitted, or by his lips, which, from this close distance, seemed even more plush than last night.

"Oh, you have no idea, Babygirl…"

I drowned in his eyes for a moment. He was drugging me with his venomous stare. A stare that penetrated me, stripping me of all my defenses and…

Ridiculous. It was just a visual spectacle, like a rainbow or the picturesque colors of a sunrise.

"Stay away from me!" I summoned all my strength to put some distance between us. "I'm your stepfather's daughter… You shouldn't talk to me that way."

"Chill out, we're just playing," he said, blatantly staring at the curves of my body, covered as they were by a long-sleeved shirt and a pair of jeans. He wanted me to understand that he wanted me and how determined he was to get whatever he wanted, but I wasn't going to give in so easily. We didn't even know each other and for him to presume that I was like last night's blond was an affront.

"How are we playing? What does this game consist of? Let's hear it." I folded my arms over my chest, challenging him fearlessly. I was young and maybe a bit naive, but I had enough fight in me to fend off such an obvious bad boy like him.

"If I told you, what fun would that be?" he answered. Then he gave me one last hungry look before turning and leaving with a sardonic laugh that promised nothing but trouble...

....

That morning, I decided to put Neil and his muscles out of my mind and got a ride to the university with Logan, who was just as pleasant and friendly as I'd expected. He was also attending Pace. We chatted on the way about his brand-new Audi R8 and the lovely relationship he had with his siblings. But despite all his attempts to draw me into engaging conversation, I was still anxious about the new program I was about to start at school. New city, new home, new family, new college... All of it scared me. I wasn't used to change, and the fast pace of it all made me nervous.

Logan, with his placid, understanding manner tried to put me at ease, and he partially succeeded. I also discovered that while we were both undeclared majors, we did have several classes in common. I would be spending a lot of time with him, which reassured me, oddly enough.

He also introduced me to his group of friends, and I got to know Alyssa, an energetic girl who was full of life, and Cory, a dark-haired boy with a lean frame and a perpetual smile on his lips. He had the strange habit of calling every living being of the feminine persuasion "doll." Then there was Jake, a super-tattooed blond guy with a rebellious charm, and Adam, with dense curls and olive skin. And finally, Julie was the brainiac of the group. I shook hands with each of them, and when it was Cory's turn, I said, "Pleased to meet you. I'm Selene. Don't call me 'doll' and keep it in your pants, thanks." Which for some reason made him laugh.

"She's a tough nut to crack," Logan said, chuckling.

"I've noticed," Cory answered sardonically.

As we passed through the main atrium of the school, I tried to get to know each of them and commit their names to memory. All of the girls were nice and friendly, and I found that I particularly clicked with Alyssa. I also appreciated their infinite patience in showing me around campus. The university was huge. I went to the theater, the library, and the main annexes, trying to memorize the corridors and lecture halls I'd have to find to attend my classes. Acclimating wouldn't be easy, but I was now surrounded by people who were ready and available to help me if I needed it.

A few hours later, while I was walking with Alyssa and the others across the wide university lawn, our conversation was suddenly interrupted by the roar of a powerful vehicle. It drew everyone's attention, mine included.

A gorgeous black Maserati pulled up in front of campus, and a guy with a black leather jacket and a cigarette dangling from his lips emerged. He stared straight ahead intently, and perhaps because of this removed and mysterious attitude, he gave the impression of a violent, even obscene beauty.

It was Neil. It couldn't have been anyone else.

The luminous highlights in his tousled hair gleamed in the sun, and his full lips were stretched into an insolent smile.

"Your brother is such a snack," Alyssa remarked to Logan before lapsing into all sorts of praise for Neil. Her opinion was shared by most of the girls present; I was the only one who seemed upset or surprised about finding him here at the school.

"What the hell is he doing here?" I practically yelled. I couldn't stand having to put up with him, even in a controlled environment like the campus. I'd never been a weak person before, but I inexplicably knew that this boy had the power to annihilate me.

"Neil's in his senior year. He'll be graduating soon," Logan explained, surprised by my reaction.

I didn't give a crap whether he was in his senior year. I didn't want him anywhere near me. Period.

We all continued to stare at him. Though only I did it angrily. In truth, the anger was more for me than for him, because I was afraid of the effect that Neil had on me.

"I'm begging you: don't let me run into him too often," I grumbled, praying an unseen God would heed my plea.

"Well, you do live in the same house as him, so school is probably the least of your worries there." Logan chuckled. I had hoped to at least avoid his insidious presence and walk carefree through the halls of my university.

I was still mourning when, a moment later, Jennifer appeared wearing a black miniskirt and slim knee-high boots. Her hair was a golden cascade over her bombshell curves. She wrapped her arms around Neil's neck and kissed him passionately, paying no attention to the students around her.

"My goodness…in a public place and everything," Julie remarked, sounding prim and proper.

"You are talking about Neil Miller here. You know the reputation he's got…" Adam pointed out.

So, he was known to be a lothario? Shocker.

"Jennifer's body is insane…" Cory interjected, staring speculatively at her backside.

I couldn't say exactly why, but the situation became too much for me to handle. I said my goodbyes to everyone and headed for the building's entrance, ready to start classes. I didn't want to hear anything more about that swaggering jerk. Our relationship had started off on the wrong foot, and I already knew it was going to continue in the same fashion. I was better off just walking away. Or running.

My classes flew by. In my literature course, I met the odd Professor Smith, who had a soft spot for Shakespeare. In just the first half hour, he quoted him approximately one billion times. Then I met the art history instructor, Amanda Cooper, who was less fanatical but equally dedicated. She was lively and appealing. So much so that Logan, Adam, Jake, and Cory's observations on the class were limited to comments about the tight skirt she was wearing and debates about her possible age.

"That's what I'm saying. She's got to be about forty," Adam insisted once again as we walked away from campus. I couldn't wait to get home; there was a jackhammer pounding in my head, and all I wanted was a good night's sleep.

"And I'm saying no way," Jake said.

"Guys, either way she's a MILF. Everyone knows that's the best kind," Cory declared.

I smiled at their debate. It was true, young men often seemed especially attracted to older women.

"You want to knock it off?" Julie grumbled in annoyance, but no one paid her any attention.

"As I was saying: she's a dime piece," Adam went on. Their collective hormones were running wild after getting a glimpse of their professor's shapely bottom.

"You aren't wrong," Logan added, and I gave him a disbelieving look.

"So, you got the famous perv gene like all the other men, huh?" I cocked a sarcastic eyebrow at him and stifled a grin of amusement.

"Well, I make the typical male observations," he explained with a shrug of his shoulders.

I shook my head, and at the same time, two large hands landed on my hips, startling me.

"What the…" I spun around and, to my amazement, encountered a pair of emerald-green eyes.

"Jared!" I shouted in delight, throwing my arms around his neck.

"Hey, baby," the man I still thought of as my boyfriend whispered in my ear. I couldn't believe my eyes. Had he really come all the way out here just to see me?

"What are you doing here?" I surveyed him, from his elegant overcoat to the dark pants that hugged his athletic legs. He looked particularly handsome and sexy. He pushed a strand of hair behind my ear and smiled.

"I wanted to surprise you, and I was worried I wouldn't be able to find you on a strange campus," he admitted, but I was distracted by all the curious stares burning a hole in us. I turned to find Logan and the others, all very interested in the situation.

"Um…this is Jared. He's my…" I cleared my throat awkwardly because I was always deeply uncomfortable sharing personal information, to say nothing of hashing out complicated personal situations. He wrapped an arm around my shoulders, and I forced myself to relax.

"Her boyfriend." Jared came to my rescue, flashing a beaming smile.

Logan was the first to hold out his hand, and then everyone else followed his lead. But my boyfriend wasn't there to visit campus or to meet my new friends, he was there to spend time with me, so he offered to take me home. We got an Uber, and when we arrived at the house, we lingered together outside for a few minutes.

Jared explained to me that he'd come to New York for something related to his father's company and that he was supposed to go back to Detroit the same day. He was such a busy go-getter; his life was full of commitments. His days were taken up with either work or studying, because he was determined to forge a solid future for himself. He was a keeper, and I admired his maturity so much. Jared never made mistakes; he always knew the right thing to do. It made him a great touchstone for me.

We'd just met not so many months before during a time in my life when I felt alone and was really in need of someone who could understand me—someone with whom I could share my daily struggles. We were just friends at first, then he confessed his feelings for me, and we'd been going out at that point for three months. We had agreed to a sort of pause on the formal relationship while I was in New York. Jared insisted we were serious and would quickly pick up where we left off when I got back to Michigan, but I wasn't sure how we would be impacted by the time apart. It would certainly test how connected we really were.

"I want to go home," I murmured miserably after explaining to him about Mia and her children while deliberately trying not to dwell on Neil too much. Jared would not have liked a guy like that.

"I know, baby, but you need to spend some time with your father. You know, patch things up between the two of you." He touched my cheek, and I delighted in his sweetness, a part of him that had stood out to me from the moment I met him.

"There's nothing to patch," I complained. "When can you come back to see me again?" I locked my eyes on his, hoping to get one answer in particular.

"Soon, baby. I have to get my studies sorted out, and my dad is on my ass about work..." He glanced around, sighing in frustration. I knew his father was an arrogant, despotic man. I'd only met him on one occasion, but that was enough for me to see how terribly he treated his son. And to know that I could never respect a man like that.

"I understand," I answered sadly. It wasn't what I wanted to hear, but I decided not to make a big deal out of it. I realized that his eyes were glued to my lips, and I understood immediately what he wanted. I gave him a mischievous smile before deciding I needed to thank him for his delightful surprise.

And then I kissed him.

I kissed him like a schoolgirl kisses the boy she's crushing on. I kissed him like a teenager kisses the cutest boy in the group during a high school game of truth or dare. I kissed him like the boy someone writes about in their secret diaries and then chuckles over as the pages weather and adulthood sets in.

I felt his hand pressing on the back of my neck to deepen the kiss. Then, slowly, he leaned me against the wall next to the gate, joining our feverish bodies together. I heard him emit a small, sensual moan from the back of his throat as I continued to taste his clean flavor.

As always, though, something wasn't quite right. I didn't want to admit it, but that thrill that I had heard so much about and never experienced firsthand just...wasn't there with Jared. The blazing passion, the irrepressible desire, the heart pounding in my chest— all of it was missing.

The feeling of *love* was missing.

He gave me affection and protectiveness, but I never got those famous butterflies in my stomach from him. In fact, I had stopped even believing they were real. When he kissed me or touched me, I knew for certain that I wasn't in love with him.

I put my hands on his abdomen to try to slow down his demanding, impatient movements, but he didn't relent in the slightest. With his free hand, he grabbed my butt cheek, and my heart leaped into my throat. My moment of apparent happiness gave way to tension that began to pulse in my veins, making me stiffen. My body just seemed to react differently to touches that other women would probably enjoy quite a bit. His kiss began to feel smothering, and it made me anxious.

The roar of an engine interrupted us, and we abruptly broke apart, looking for all the world like a happy couple caught in the act.

I pulled my mouth away from Jared's and turned to the noise, where I found Neil...my nightmare. He rolled down the window of his car and looked speculatively at both Jared and me, pushing his sunglasses up on his forehead. He blew out a cloud of smoke; he was holding the lit cigarette with the same hand that rested on the steering wheel. Stupidly, I wondered what he thought of me in that moment, and then I tried to figure out why I cared. I wasn't doing anything wrong, yet I felt soiled in his eyes.

"Selene, a little discretion, please. Daddy might see you," he scolded me with an insolent smile that I longed to slap right off his face.

I couldn't stand it—no one had ever sparked such instant dislike in me before. He looked me up and down like I was nothing before fixating on my lips, which I touched with an index finger. They felt wet and swollen. I experienced a pointed sense of discomfort, even though I knew I had no reason to.

"Thanks for the concern, but I know what I'm doing," I answered cheekily. (I did not know what I was doing.)

Neil just shook his head and revved the engine, making a deafening racket. He opened the automatic gates to the house but tossed me one last smirk before driving through.

"And he is?" Jared asked, frowning with confusion and obvious concern as he watched the expensive car roll through the palatial entrance. What could I have said? Nothing that would have reassured him.

"Neil," I answered in a gloomy whisper, because, alas, I was going to have to spend a lot of time with him, and I knew it was going to cause problems. That was for certain.

"You mean Logan's brother, Neil?" he clarified.

"The same."

"And he lives with you?" I could see his justified jealousy. Neil evoked competitiveness in men and desire in women. On me, however, he had another effect: I found him frightening and compelling at the same time.

"Yeah, Jared," I said dejectedly.

Yeah, Neil and I lived together and the incredible electricity that flowed between our bodies would need to remain a secret I kept buried deep inside of me and something I fought against at all costs.

48

3

SELENE

I often found myself alone among people, locked in a world of my own. A world where I felt safe and could truly be myself. A world where I didn't have to prove anything to anyone. I firmly believed that solitude was the key to discovering and understanding ourselves.

"The man who is unable to people his solitude is equally unable to be alone in a bustling crowd." I read aloud this passage from a poem by Charles Baudelaire, one of those books I always kept on me in those days so I could escape into a reality other than my own. I loved to read; I would have devoured books all day long if I had the time.

"What?" Logan raised an eyebrow and gave me a confused look.

"Uh…nothing. I was just reading out loud." I showed him the book that had completely captured my attention.

"Selene, you haven't been listening to anything we've said, have you?" Alyssa asked.

"Nope," I shrugged and continued reading, laying the book open in my lap. We were all off campus, taking a break from classes, and in my case, the world entirely.

"Are you going to Bryan Nelson's party this weekend?" Adam asked me.

"Nah, Adam, I'm not feeling it," I said without looking up at him.

I really didn't feel like spending my free time surrounded by sweaty bodies, deafening music, and a veritable river of alcohol.

"It'll be fun. Bryan always throws bomb-ass parties," Corey wheedled. I looked at him, squinting slightly against the sun and shook my head. He snorted and I smiled.

"You have to come!" Julie batted her eyelashes sweetly and pleaded with her most angelic face, but I just rolled my eyes and ignored her.

"Yeah, sis, you're coming with us whether you like it or not," Logan chuckled.

"I'll come, but only if you stop calling me that," I retorted.

"Okay, it's a deal, sis," he answered, and I gave him an admonishing glare. "Starting now," I specified. Logan only smiled and didn't say anything else.

I'd been living in New York for a week at that point, so Logan was getting familiar with me. With Neil, however, it was a very different story: we had yet to have a normal conversation. Instead, he only directed suggestive jokes and sly smiles at me while he wandered half-naked around the house. I'd started sleeping with earplugs in because of the sheer number of girls he brought home. Jennifer, apparently, didn't have that locked down. But I was trying not to think about Neil; I needed to mind my own business instead.

After some more small talk with the group, Logan and I got into his car and headed for the house. "So, Jared goes to school in Detroit, right?" he asked during the ride.

"That's right," I answered, staring out the window at the buildings passing rapidly by.

"And how long have you guys been together?" he continued.

"Okay, Dad, what's with the third degree?" I teased, even though I didn't mind answering his questions.

"Just curious." He shrugged, keeping both hands firmly on the wheel.

"About three months," I told him. Strangely, I didn't feel any discomfort talking about myself or my life in Detroit when it was with Logan. "And how about you? Do you have a girlfriend?" I added, hoping I didn't sound too nosy.

"You mean like a steady girlfriend or..." Logan gave me a suggestive look and I grinned.

"No, I don't think you're like your brother," I said immediately.

"What's that supposed to mean? I have an active sex life, too," he teased, and I gave him a light nudge.

"Come on, dummy." I shook my head and thought about how lovely and natural it was, laughing and joking with Logan as though we'd known each other for years.

"I am happily single, for the moment. I've only had one significant relationship, and that was a while ago." He grew serious again. "Her name was Amber. I met her during basketball practice; she played on the women's team," he explained, his voice getting melancholy.

"And how did it end with you two?" I asked before I'd really thought about what I was saying.

"She cheated on me with some guy at a party," he answered casually, shrugging one shoulder as if it didn't really matter. I bit my lip and tried to cheer him up anyway.

"Then she didn't deserve you. You're a great guy, Logan. You'll find someone better," I told him with conviction.

"I've always thought the same thing," he said, with admirable self-confidence. Logan was a together guy and aware of his value. Whatever misery his ex had caused him, he seemed to have overcome it and come out stronger than before.

"Do you still play basketball?" I asked, mostly to change the subject. With his height, he probably could have been a pro player.

"I quit. I decided to focus completely on school." He smiled and kept driving, occasionally reaching to touch his hair. Some of his mannerisms were identical to Neil's, and it niggled at me. But I tried not pay attention to the feeling.

We kept talking, but I carefully avoided any further questions about Amber. Instead, we talked about his basketball career, how his passion for the sport was born, and how many years he'd played. I discovered that Logan had other hobbies besides sports: he also played the guitar and collected antique coins. He promised he would show me his collection someday.

When we got home, I went right to the kitchen and got a bottle of water from the fridge. I was just about to drink it when someone snatched it roughly away from me. I scowled, my arm still poised in mid-air and looked up to see Neil in his sweatpants, soaked in sweat, hanging on to the neck of what had been, up until a few seconds before, *my* water bottle.

I watched the muscles in his arm contract, tank top clinging to his gleaming, muscular chest. Black sweatpants hugged his long, toned legs, and his hair was even more disheveled than usual. It looked good on him, too.

I was starting to think that Neil was the one guy in the world who always looked good, even immediately after a workout.

"Hey!" I cried as he continued to drink from the bottle while staring at me from under his long eyelashes.

"I was thirsty," he answered. He shrugged and wiped the back of his hand over his lush mouth. I couldn't help but stare in fascination.

"That was *my* bottle," I snapped back irritably, despite the way his eyes cut into me like daggers.

"Sure, but I wanted... *yours*," he whispered playfully.

Our bodies were very close to each other. I could feel my breath speed up and my heart beating faster. I couldn't figure it out… *Why does he have this effect on me? Why does his mere presence send me reeling?*

"Why weren't you on campus today?" I tried changing the subject to recover a bit of my equilibrium. I put some more distance between us and pushed a strand of hair behind my ear.

"I didn't want to be there." His tone abruptly changed. He no longer seemed mischievous or amused but altogether absent, even annoyed. I took a step back from this coldness and looked at him uneasily.

"Why?" I realized that this was perhaps the first truly normal conversation the two of us had ever had. Neil was really quite reserved, and I began to suspect that a lot of his arrogance was a mask he used to hide from the world.

"I don't think that's any of your business," he answered stiffly. He heaved a sigh and then scrubbed a hand over his face and through his hair, as if to shake off some disturbing feeling that was eating away at him.

Since I had no idea how to reply to that statement, and he didn't seem like he had anything to add, I started to leave. Then, he spoke again and stopped me in my tracks.

"Martin Luther King Jr. argued that darkness could not drive out darkness; only light could do it and that hate could not drive out hate, only love could do it. Hate multiplies hate and creates a destructive downward spiral."

I turned and found him staring into space, his golden eyes lost in dark thoughts. He looked down at himself as though venomous spiders were crawling across his skin. I stood there, just staring at him, trying desperately to understand what he was trying to communicate, but Logan's voice cut in, shattering the moment.

"Hey, you two, what's going on?" Logan walked into the kitchen, eyeing his brother and me, both of us frozen like statues.

"Nothing," I answered quickly. Neil, by contrast, remained motionless with his jaw clenched in a grim expression. Slowly, his eyes moved over to Logan who, unlike me, seemed to understand where his brother's thoughts were.

After a long, tense moment, Logan cleared his throat and distracted us with conversation about that weekend's party, which I had forgotten about entirely. He told me that he was driving, but only if I got my butt in gear by nine. I threw one last unsettled look at Neil, and after reluctantly confirming that I would go to the party, I said my goodbyes to the brothers and fled to my room.

I spent the entire time studying and brooding over Neil's strangeness. I probably shouldn't have even been worrying about it. My stay in New York was temporary, and I would soon be saying goodbye to everyone here and going back to my mother in Detroit. Neil was only ever going to be a slim chapter in my life, and I didn't need to care about his stupid mood swings.

4

NEIL

I had no idea what time it was.

I sat on the edge of the bed staring into space, thinking about how life had drained all the essential energy from me. I was trying to survive, to hold on to this world, but I would have to give up soon.

I blinked repeatedly as the sun's rays filtered through the window, lighting up the dark interior of my room. My desire to rise and face another day was nil. It was happening to me more and more often in recent days.

Why me?

It was the same question I asked myself every morning.

I rubbed my temples, throbbing because I'd had too much to drink the previous evening. Then, I glanced down at the bed, where the crumpled blankets beside me still held the imprint of the girl I'd spent the night with. I didn't even remember her name. Luckily for me, she was already gone.

Lots of guys bragged about racking up women like they were collectible figurines, but I felt nothing but disgust toward myself. I just couldn't find any other way to release the frustration inside me. That wasn't an excuse, I knew, but it was what my life had taught me to do.

I got out of bed and grabbed the condom wrapper off the floor and threw it away. I walked into the bathroom, still nude, and halted at my reflection in the mirror. The memories rose up again and lit the fuse of my rage, which I knew would blaze inside of me until nothing was left but a pile of ashes and pain.

Why me?

I touched my lip with my index finger and licked the bitter taste from it. Then, I stared at my neck, wearing evidence of greedy kisses; my chest, crisscrossed with scratches. It wasn't hard to guess how I'd gotten them.

Sex was essential for me. I didn't just derive pleasure from it; I had an extreme, even sick need for it. Yet I still hated the filthy feeling I got afterward. I hated feeling the residual traces of strange hands or lips on me. Most of all, I hated my body and my face that made me so desirable in the eyes of women.

Was it because of the way I looked? Was that why I had been picked?

I didn't know, but I was determined to exploit those characteristics to the fullest. I would use them like a weapon against anyone who ever tried to hurt me. Never again would someone be allowed to destroy me.

I brushed my teeth, scrubbing them so hard that my gums bled. Then I got immediately into the shower and used an entire bottle of body wash to scour the memories from my skin. The boiling hot water alternately burned and the soothed the pain. The pain reminded me that I was alive.

I got out of the shower and wrapped a towel around my waist. Then, unexpectedly, a new and different train of thought interrupted my usual internal torments.

I thought about her.

About Selene.

I remembered the good smell given off by her silken hair. It smelled like purity—the scent of a woman and a girl at the same time. Maybe it was just a figment of my imagination, but I couldn't remember ever having smelled anything like it before.

No woman had ever drawn me in like her. I wanted to unearth her, provoke her, talk with her...and take her to bed. Selene had become another trophy for me to covet, but oddly, I didn't just want to fuck her. I wanted to kiss her and lick slowly all over that slender, delicate body. I wanted to touch her hair and suckle her breasts, push her thighs open... I wanted to give her pleasure instead of just receiving it.

Instead of just demanding it.

These ridiculous thoughts made me smile. I quickly got myself together, and decided I would confine myself to just toying with her. She would be just one of many for me, even if she was Matt's daughter. I could just have some fun without worrying about feelings I didn't believe in. Feelings I couldn't believe.

I had known a different kind of love, one that I would never want to push onto another human being. Still, I never knew how to control the impulses, and I felt the lure of the forbidden like a moth feels the flame.

I shut down all that rumination and went back into my room. Voices from outside in the garden caught my attention. Chloe and Logan were down there talking and joking with each other. I watched them from my balcony and felt a warming sensation in my chest.

My siblings were my reason for living.

I decided I would join them, so I put on a clean pair of boxers and some dark pants. On my way to the garden, I passed the kitchen and spotted my mother reading a fashion magazine. I hesitated for a few moments in the doorway. I didn't want to talk to her, but I knew I couldn't avoid it forever. I sighed as I walked into the kitchen, praying to whoever might be up there that she wouldn't immediately start busting my balls with the usual questions.

"Good morning, darling." She smiled at me, and I smiled in return, noting her severe pale pink suit and the way her blond hair was scraped back in an elegant hairstyle.

"Good morning," I answered cooly. I poured myself some coffee, hoping both that it would ease my hangover headache and that my mother wouldn't realize I'd been drunk the night before.

"Sleep well?" she asked, and I immediately noticed a suspicious tone in her voice that put me on alert.

"More or less," I answered. I sipped my coffee with an indifference that was both affected and calculated. But I knew full well that war was going to break out at any moment.

"So, I saw something strange this morning…"

And here it is, shots fired. This enemy had a machine gun.

"Strange like?" I pretended not to know what she was talking about, but I was only wearing pants so my mother's sharp eyes had no trouble spotting the incriminating marks on my chest.

"Like a girl coming out of your room, Neil!" she scolded me, and her voice bounced around between my temples until I had to squeeze my eyes shut.

"How many times do I have to tell you…" she went on but was interrupted when Matt appeared in the kitchen, unwittingly coming to my rescue.

"God, my back is killing me, but I have to go to work to today," he complained, and my mother turned to console him for a few moments. I took advantage of her distraction to sneak away and avoid what would undoubtedly be a tedious dressing-down. She had long suspected what I got up to in my room, but I hadn't given her confirmation before. Living in a big house like ours gave me some freedom to fully dedicate myself to my sex life but didn't provide all the privacy I would have liked.

Sure, I could smuggle the girls out through the service stairs or the back gates, but that wasn't enough to hide the assiduous way I plowed through my quarry. I was like the worst kind of beast: always starving, always unsatisfied. It was a psychologically ruinous sort of existence that would eventually lead me to destroy myself as both a person and a man.

Brushing off these grim thoughts, I went out to meet my siblings where they were sitting at a table under our gazebo. The rays of the sun were warm and gentle on my bare shoulders as I walked.

"Oh, to what do we owe this honor?" my sister teased with a smirk.

"Love you, too," I answered. I gave her a wink and then looked around for Selene. I couldn't say exactly why, but I'd been hoping to run into her this morning. Or maybe just see her around the house, poured into those jeans of hers and filling up the space with her sass.

"It's almost lunch time. You were up late, huh?" said Logan, giving me a suggestive look. My brother knew how I lived, and I'd never tried to deny any of it with him.

"Well, you're the fucking romantic. I make my own fun," I said shortly, because I was too focused on trying to determine the whereabouts of the lovely tigress who had invaded our house days ago now. I didn't want to ask Logan about her and make him suspicious, but I couldn't keep quiet any longer.

"Selene come out?" I scratched one eyebrow with my thumb and feigned a lack of interest, like I was just passingly curious about where she was. But my brother wasn't stupid.

"No, she's up on the third floor at the indoor pool," he answered.

The fact that we had two swimming pools, one outside and one inside, had never seemed so practical as it did to me that day. Was Selene all alone there?

The idea thrilled me and sent a strange rush of adrenaline down my spine. It was completely inappropriate, but my deviant mind wanted to see her. Against all my good sense, I quickly excused myself, pretending that I'd forgotten my pack of Winstons in my room.

I avoided the kitchen and headed straight for the house's elevator on the first floor, because I was in an atypical hurry to find Selene, even if I didn't fully understand why. When the automatic doors opened on the third floor, I crept down the hallway that led to our pool. I mentally counted down the seconds that divided me from her and then…then I saw her.

I froze, just watching her for what felt like endless minutes. She was stretched out on a chaise lounge wearing just a black bikini that fit her like a dream. Her pale skin glowed, and her damp hair looked like polished amber. Her rounded lips were parted slightly, and occasionally, she would lick them, which generated increasingly indecent thoughts in my twisted mind. I refused to even blink, perhaps out of fear that she might vanish at any moment like a dream or an illusion.

I approached her like the most lethal sort of predator and threw myself down on the empty chaise next to her.

"Morning, Tinkerbell," I said politely, nudging her side. Selene jumped and pulled out her earbuds.

"You scared me!" she cried irritably and turned my way. The ocean in her eyes dazzled me, and she seemed somehow even more beautiful than she had been the night before.

"Are you afraid of me?" I asked, picking the container of body lotion she'd left on the table next to her and raising it to my nose. "Mmm…coconut," I murmured, taking in the pleasing fragrance. She snatched the lotion away from me with an agitated look. Apparently, Tigress didn't like people touching her things. So, I decided to get in her space, push her boundaries a bit just to test her.

"I'm not afraid of you," she declared and then lay back down, pretending to ignore me, but I could feel her agitation. I could sniff out her desire the way any animal sniffs out its dinner.

"You should be," I answered. I lay down, propping myself up on my elbow and leaning my chin on the palm of my hand. I could feel her stare burning into me.

"Fear can be an ally, if you know how to handle it," she answered firmly and gave me a cunning look. Nothing turned me on more than a woman with a killer body and a beguiling mind.

"And do you, Selene? Know how to handle it?" I sat back, resting my elbows on my bent knees. I looked her up and down, from her glistening lips to her long, slim legs—the ones I yearned to feel clasped around my hips. She was so small; it would have been effortless to overpower her and the idea...it excited me.

And she seemed to understand exactly what I was thinking because she went red.

"Stop looking at me that way!" she snapped at me. I almost came when I heard the low, apprehensive sound of her voice. It was breathy, like she'd been running fruitlessly for hours in a maze. She sat up and hunched her thin shoulders as if trying to protect herself. From me? Hadn't she just implied she knew how to handle her fears?

"You have to... You have to stay away from me, Neil." She got up in a rush and leaped into the pool to escape me. Where did she think she was going? This was my territory. She was in the wolf's den now, and the wolf certainly wasn't going to spare her.

With a shameless grin, I got up off the chaise and undressed. I pulled off my pants and was left in just my black Calvin Klein boxers. I considered taking those off as well and joining her naked, but I didn't want to push it too far. At that point, she still only *suspected* that I was a pervert.

I followed her, slowly immersing myself in the warm, crystal clear water. The two blue gems that were her eyes followed my every feline movement. I gave her a smile that communicated every one of my bad intentions and swam elegantly toward her.

I stopped a short distance from where she was now pressed against the wall of the pool, and I took a moment to admire her. If I'd gotten any closer to her, I wouldn't have been able to restrain myself.

"Face your fears, Selene." I stared—first at her eyes and then at her lips. Finally, when she didn't retreat, I closed the distance between us once more. I touched her hip, and she jolted. I smiled at her reaction, but I didn't stop. My hand just glanced over her bikini bottoms, and I tried to stroke her between her thighs, but Selene clamped them together tightly to keep me from going any further.

"You shouldn't…" Her voice shook, tears of resignation clung to her eyelashes. I could have stopped then and apologized for my behavior, but I wanted her. Craved her. Demanded her. I was a profoundly selfish person; I always had been and now I needed to have her.

"Push me away," I challenged, and she lifted her tiny hands to put them against my chest. She applied light pressure, and I saw the way her pupils dilated at even that small contact. "That's it?" I said mockingly. But the Tigress had begun to tremble, possibly from excitement, fear of giving into me, or simply the awareness of her own desire blooming to life inside her. I gave her a satisfied smile, because I knew that she had lost her capacity to reason. I was well aware that she had a boyfriend in Detroit, but I didn't care. I wanted her and that was enough for me.

That was how I survived, after all. I attacked a woman's mind; I ferreted out the things she craved, then I sated myself with her body. In that way, I was able to cling to the slim thread keeping me tied to this life.

I pressed closer and tilted my head slightly until our lips touched. Hers fell open, demonstrating her willingness to taste me. I brushed her lower lip with mine; hers was smooth and soft. Selene narrowed her eyes as though locked in an internal battle between right and wrong. My vote was for wrong, as always, but I knew she didn't entirely agree with me. I grasped her hips and toyed with the ties on her swimsuit, ignoring her discomfort. I demanded more; my body was trembling with the need for greater contact, so I pressed my hips into her and closed my eyes, savoring the connection between us.

I pressed my nose to the place beneath her ear and I imagined I could feel the beating of her heart and smell her arousal mixed with the scent of chlorine. Her hands rested on my shoulders and her breasts were plastered against my front. Her stiffened nipples poked into my chest, and I had to stifle the urge to lean down and take them between my teeth. We stared into each other's eyes.

This was my favorite part: the moment before a kiss. When hearts are frenzied, minds are turned off, everything is waiting with bated breath. I brushed her soft cheek with the tip of my nose before reaching her mouth, the gates of paradise.

Would she let a poor devil like me in?

I licked the curve of her mouth and tried to kiss her. Initially, I found a barrier of clenched teeth and struggled to get a response. But I courted one slyly, moving my tongue slowly until the moment when she was inevitably forced to give in to damnation. After a few seconds, her lips parted like the petals of a flower, finally giving me access.

She kissed me back, and from the uncertain way she followed my movements, I could tell just how inexperienced she was. How far had she gone with other men?

I was used to women who were fully capable of exciting, seducing, and satisfying a man. Women who were confident in themselves, charmers who were good in bed. They were well-practiced at kissing, fucking, and fulfilling even the most depraved male fantasies.

I liked this contrast between us.

I adored the shy, dainty way this girl moved her tongue, the prim way she tried to hold back her moans, and the subtle way she tried to push our bodies apart at the most sinful, yet natural, point of union that there could be between us. Between a man and woman. I felt no awkwardness or bashfulness about letting her feel how aroused I was and how my body reacted to the feeling of her mouth. I pushed my erection between her thighs and heard her gasping and trying to move away from me, to no avail. I held her still, squeezing her hips and continued to kiss her the way I wanted to fuck her.

I wanted to do it right there, in the middle of the pool, in broad daylight, and that was absolutely no good. I had to stop, or it was going to be another one of my typical fuckups. I backed away and allowed her to gulp down some air before resting my forehead against hers.

"Now, you can say you've faced your fears," I whispered.

Selene's breathing was labored, and she seemed dazed, possibly incredulous. She stared at me, absolutely mortified by her reaction to my attack. She touched her lips with her index finger and gulped, as if trying to understand what had just happened to her. It was at that moment that I realized the kind of truly selfish bastard I was, taking this piece of her.

I wished she would hurl insults or slap me. I wished she'd do anything, so long as she didn't blame herself for following her instincts over her reason.

"Now I can say that I've basically cheated on Jared," she said in a deeply harsh tone, but her eyes were glittering with a new light. Selene was finally conscious of the attraction that linked us, and this knowledge sent her spinning.

She jumped out of the pool and ran her hands through her hair in confusion. "I'm still in a relationship! I still have a...a...some-one!" she screamed furiously. An instant later, she was in tears. Then she snatched up a towel to shield herself from my eyes, which ran longingly over her curves.

Those were the effects I had on people: confusion, dismay, guilt, lust, rage, and disappointment. I had brought nothing but evil to the people around me, and Selene would be just another one of my victims.

"So, we'll make sure he doesn't find out," I answered cynically, but that only made the situation worse. Selene knew perfectly well that I didn't care about whatever relationship she had, just that I had her, if only for a few minutes. She looked at me in disgust before fleeing.

I could understand her reaction. I kissed women to torment them—a kiss from me was simply a prelude to more carnal sins. It created desire; it was ardor and vice.

I got out of the pool and dried myself off hastily with one of the many towels we had around before peeling off my wet boxers and getting dressed. I took the stairs back to my bedroom to grab a sweatshirt and the pack of cigarettes I'd use to explain my absence to Logan. When I returned downstairs and found out that my mother had instructed Anna to set up the table under the gazebo in the garden. We were taking advantage of the sunny autumn day and having lunch outside.

I joined my family in the garden, feeling blissful as the crisp breeze fluttered my damp hair. I took the only available seat, right next to Selene.

Fate was not on her side.

I looked at her and paused to analyze every bit of her. She had pulled her hair back into a loose ponytail and was wearing her usual jeans, along with a light T-shirt that clung to her small breasts.

Suddenly, despite my empty stomach, I could only feel hunger for her. I sighed and tried to get myself under control. If I got a hard-on, it would be difficult to conceal, as I wasn't wearing boxers anymore. Selene, for her part, tried in vain to ignore me. She drummed her fingers nervously on her thighs, and instinctively, I grabbed her hand under the table and squeezed it.

"What do you want?" she whispered furiously, trying to pull away from my grasp.

"Don't be mad," I answered tonelessly.

It wasn't like she'd committed murder. She'd just gotten a little more proof that no one could win against powerful physical attraction.

"Easy for you to say." She freed herself from my grip and pointedly turned her attention to my mother and siblings for the rest of lunch.

I should have regretted what we'd just done, but I didn't. For me, it had become a game. A game of strategy that I had to win at all costs. It was a bet I was making, between me and life itself.

Selene didn't yet know just how profoundly I deviated from the norm, and she never would have understood.

Suddenly, Chloe's voice saying that idiot Carter's name, shook me out of my twisted thoughts.

"Have I mentioned that I hate that guy?" Logan hissed through gritted teeth, and I found myself in perfect agreement with him. Carter Nelson, Bryan's younger brother, was neither a trustworthy nor respectful boy, contrary to what Chloe believed. I knew him, and he didn't have a good reputation. He treated women like playthings, and I didn't understand how Chloe could talk about him like he was Prince Charming straight out of some fucking fairy tale.

"Our little sister is too blinded by the illusion of love to see what an asshole he is," I blurted out, never considering her feelings. I was used to saying whatever I thought and wasn't about to start holding back then.

"What? Do you think he's like you?" she challenged me. Yes, I did think that. Carter *was* like me. Although I didn't have room to judge his attitude toward women in general, I did have a right to protect my little sister from guys like him. Guys like me.

"We're your brothers; we just want you to be careful," Logan cut in, but Chloe had inherited all the same bullheaded obstinacy that I had. It was no coincidence that we argued constantly.

"You're a deluded kid who understands fuck all about real life," I added testily. Losing control like that was easily one of my worst flaws. I reacted instinctively, often insensitively. I realized much too late how my words might have landed for a young girl still not fully capable of identifying the dangers around her.

Chloe threw her cutlery furiously onto her plate. "Because *you* understand anything about life? Do some self-reflection. You don't even know what it means to love another person. Do you think it's right? Sleeping with all these women and lying to them like you did with Scarlett?"

My reaction was instantaneous: I was suffocating. Scarlett was a difficult chapter in my history. I hated talking about her; I hated remembering her, and I hated even hearing her name. I stood up so furiously that my chair tumbled to the floor. My mother shot me a pleading look, begging me not to make one of my typical scenes. The ones to which my family had now become so accustomed.

My family, yes. But not Selene.

I met her crystalline stare and saw fear and confusion there, the same feelings I inspired in anyone who met my grimy little world. Anyone in my vicinity had to deal with it: what I was, what had happened to me, and what it had made me into.

For a fleeting moment, I regretted kissing her. I shouldn't have drawn her into my problems, no matter how much I liked the sweet taste of her on my tongue. And so began the eternal struggle within me that would only ever tear me up even more.

I was anxious. I felt like breaking something, the way I always did when my higher intellect went out the window and gave way to the other side of me—the hair-trigger, intractable side. I stepped back from the table and did what I did best: I hid away from the world.

I talked instead to the monsters that lived inside my head. Sometimes, I thought they were the only ones who could understand me. I relived the past in search of the Boy I had been, and when I found him, I fought him. I loathed him, I tried to block him out, but I always emerged defeated.

The Boy remained. He lived inside me. He was in the innermost chamber of my soul, and he was never, ever going to leave.

5

SELENE

I stared at my reflection in the mirror as I gathered my hair into a messy bun. I'd done nothing but think back on that kiss from the previous day. Neil's lips against mine; our bodies fused together in that pool. I'd never encountered feelings like that before...so all-encompassing.

While I hadn't technically cheated on Jared, I had betrayed myself, the Selene who never would have even thought about another boy like that, who would never have let Jared down or given into that kind of base temptation. The awareness of what I had done took hold of me, painful and oppressive.

What is happening to me?

I'd known that Neil had an uncontrollable power over me, but I still couldn't understand my total inability to resist him.

Sighing, I tugged on a pair of light-washed jeans and a gray sweatshirt. I grabbed my messenger bag and immediately felt my phone vibrating. I glanced at the screen: it was Jared. My heart leaped into my throat, and I nearly stopped breathing. What was I supposed to say to him?

I tried to tamp down my panic and took a deep breath.

"Hey?" I answered after a few rings.

"Baby, how are you?"

Awful, but I couldn't tell him that. Hearing his voice only intensified my guilt.

"Well, I'm about to go to campus with Logan. What are you doing?" I asked him while I balanced on one leg to put on my shoes.

"I just finished my first class today, so I thought I'd take the opportunity to catch up with you. I've missed you," he told me lovingly, and I decided that I needed to clarify things for myself. That kind of behavior wasn't like me; I couldn't live peacefully with this. I felt soiled, contaminated by some awful thing.

"I'm glad to hear from you, but I have to get going because I'm already late," I said all in one breath, deciding to cut off the conversation before I started crying. I couldn't freak Jared out; I needed to talk to him about this in person.

"Okay, baby. I'll call you later. I love you!" I could picture his smile and sweet expression when he said those three little words, which are so difficult for me to repeat. I had never told him I loved him. I was firmly convinced that love was unique feeling, something precious that I could only give to the right person. Someone who would then have the power to crush my heart in their hands.

"Later." I hung up and searched the house for Logan. I looked briefly into the kitchen and spotted Mia having breakfast with Chloe and my father.

"Good morning, Selene," Mia said, raising a hand in greeting.

"Morning, everyone," I replied with a forced smile as I adjusted the strap of my bag on my shoulder.

"Won't you have breakfast with us?" my father offered, but I didn't feel up to it. My stomach was closed tight, still tortured by what had happened the day before.

"I'm running late, and I need to find Logan so I can get to class,"

I answered stiffly, hoping against hope that I wouldn't run into the wrong brother while I was waiting.

There had been no sign of Neil that morning, but we were still living under the same roof and the chances of encountering him were high. Considering how weak and irrational I got whenever he spoke to me or even just looked at me with those golden eyes, I had decided it was in my best interest to steer clear of him.

Fortunately, Logan already appeared ready to go. Not even bothering to say goodbye, I grabbed his wrist and dragged him out the door in hopes of avoiding any more inappropriate encounters.

"Get up on the wrong side of the bed today?" Logan asked me once we were safely in the car and he could really see my thoughtful scowl.

"It's the only side I ever seem to get up on," I admitted

"You know, Selene, I think you'd really benefit from looking at things from a new perspective," he said, stepping on the accelerator to pass the car ahead of us.

"What do you mean?" I turned to him, but he was staring ahead at the road looking focused and reflective.

"Well, this is your chance... Your chance to change things, make them go the way you want. Don't look at your life as being dark; think of it as a blank canvas waiting to be filled with color," he said, quietly and seriously.

"Where did you read that?" I grinned, silently thanking him for chasing away my terrible mood.

"Eh, somewhere, but that doesn't make it less true," he answered in an amused tone.

We lapsed into silence for the rest of the trip. I was so lost in my thoughts that I didn't even notice when he parked right next to an unmistakable black Maserati. But as soon as I saw it, I was shaken.

Neil was there. *Calm down*, I told myself. I would just have to avoid him. And that was all there was to it. Bolstered by this decision and feeling just a hint of fear, I strode through the long corridors of the university.

....

Six exhausting hours later, and I hadn't seen hide nor hair of Neil. I was comforted enough by this that I could even relax as I drove home with Logan.

We had the house to ourselves, since Mia was working, Chloe was studying at a friend's house, and my father would be at the hospital until late.

"Weird that Neil isn't home," Logan muttered. Though I was deeply relieved by his brother's absence, Logan seemed unsettled and concerned about it. Why was he so worried? His brother was plenty old enough to take care of himself, right?

"He's probably having fun with his…friends," I suggested. I would have just said "girls," but I didn't want to offend him.

Logan was getting increasingly agitated.

"Come on, let's go to the living room," I said. We sat down on the couch, but Logan kept moving around like he was sitting on needles; a sure sign of how unsettled he was. I tried to start a conversation with him about our classes, the professors, even the thongs that Professor Cooper very clearly wore, but nothing could distract him from his draining thoughts.

"Can you stop talking for one second, Selene! I'm really worried here!" he snapped at me in a way he'd never done before and got up to pace the room. I immediately clammed up, embarrassed by my lack of tact, but then he sat back down next to me and took my hand, apologizing for the way he'd spoken to me. He'd had no reason to do that, he said.

Maybe I didn't understand his worry because I didn't really know his brother. Was Neil prone to getting into trouble? Or, even worse, did he have some sort of addiction issues? I didn't have the nerve to ask him those questions, so I limited myself to simply offering him comfort.

I really understood then how much Logan cared about his brother and the unbreakable bond that united them. I almost envied him—I hadn't been lucky enough to have brothers or sisters.

"You'll see, he's going to come walking through that door any moment in his 'no fucks given' attitude," I tried to put a positive spin on things to defuse some of the tension in the air.

Suddenly, the lock on the front door clicked open.

"Neil! Thank goodness!" Logan exclaimed. He sighed in relief before pouncing on his brother. "Where have you been?"

Logan's fear became more comprehensible when I noticed the purpling bruise on the upper part of Neil's cheekbone. It seemed obvious that he'd been punched in the face.

"What happened to your eye?" Logan asked, alarmed. I got up from the couch and approached the two of them.

"Nothing." Neil tossed his car keys onto a stand in the entryway and shrugged off his leather jacket with utter indifference.

"Tell me what the hell happened!" Logan yelled, making me flinch, but his brother didn't seem at all fazed by this display of anger. Neil just looked at him with a serious, almost irritated frown.

"Some asshole pissed me off…that's it," he said shortly.

"That's it?" Logan put his hands on his hips and moved to block Neil's way so he couldn't leave and evade his questions.

"Yes. He provoked me so I left him in the dirt to rot, which is exactly where a piece of shit like him belongs."

Oh. Cool. And he was proud of this? To think, for a moment there I'd been glad he hadn't broken any bones.

"W… What?" Logan managed. "Fuck's sake, Neil! Are you trying to catch another charge or what?" He pointed a finger at his brother, who just stared back at him emotionless. It was inhuman coldness. He looked like a young man who had been disappointed and defeated by life to the point where he was incapable of feeling sorrow. Or, maybe, he felt so much of it that he had to put up a wall of steel to protect himself from everyone else.

Neil remained a mystery to me. I knew next to nothing about him or his past. I'd seen only what he'd shown me, the most superficial part of him, brash and a bit perverse. Now, as he stood in front of his brother, his dark clothing seeming somehow like an extension of the shadow that encompassed him, and he provided no further clues about the enigma that he was.

"He'll be fine," Neil said in a cynical, impassive tone. Then, he brushed past both of us and walked upstairs, leaving us behind in a whirlwind of questions and doubts.

"He'll never change," Logan announced, looking battle weary. He shook his head and sighed, staring at an indeterminate point on the floor. I didn't know what to tell him, so I just rested a hand on his shoulder.

"I thought he was making an effort, but I was wrong," he continued before vanishing wearily up the stairs himself.

I holed up in my own room at that point and just studied until eight o'clock. I should have been getting ready to go out, but doubts preyed on my mind. I wondered why Neil behaved the way he did, what he was rebelling against and why he seemed so angry at the whole world. I would never get the answers to those questions unless I got to know him better, which I was too afraid to do because the attraction that pulled me toward him was too perilous. It was palpable between us…that kiss had only confirmed what I already knew.

Even worse, when he had showed up this afternoon looking all handsome and shadowy—even with that purple bruise marking his manly face—my heart had leaped in my chest. It was almost painful. It was insane the way my body reacted to his nearness, and it wasn't just because I wanted to be touched again by those lips. I wanted so much more than that, and admitting it even to myself made me squeeze my eyes shut and curse my own weakness.

When I realized I was about to be late to Bryan Nelson's party because I'd been so lost in my thoughts, I quickly got myself ready for the evening, opting for a black blouse and simple skinny jeans under my long coat.

Logan and I drove to a house almost as sprawling as Matt and Mia's. I had resisted the urge to ask him any more questions on the trip there. Neither of us said anything about what had happened with Neil that afternoon. But I couldn't help but break the uncomfortable silence.

"So, who is this Bryan guy anyway?" I asked Logan as we got out of the car.

Logan chuckled and more of the tension dissipated. "Oh, you'll see. Wait until he meets you." With no further explanation, he gestured for me to follow him to find his friends, who were waiting for us in the yard.

"There you are! Finally! We've been waiting for you," exclaimed Alyssa when she met us in front of the house. She was wearing an incredible white floral dress, and I didn't miss the long, slow look that Logan gave her legs. I got the vibe that the two of them liked each other but hadn't quite gotten up the courage to confess their mutual interest.

"C'mon, c'mon, let's get in there before the good booze runs out," Cory urged us. I grabbed Julie, who was standing around looking bewildered, and we all walked inside.

When we walked into the party, I was immediately hit with the combined smells of booze and smoke, which made me cough. I glanced around and saw some guys on the sofa drinking intently while other people were dancing, already half-drunk or stoned.

"Everything okay?" Logan noticed my bewilderment, and I gave him a reassuring smile. This wasn't exactly my scene, but I was going to make an exception, just for one night. We walked over to the table where alcohol of all varieties was available, and a tall, muscular man with deep blue eyes approached us.

"Hey, Miller." He turned to Logan and shook his hand. I remained on the sidelines, observing them.

"Hey Bryan," Logan answered. From the way Bryan immediately started leering at me, I knew he was a jackass to be avoided. I sized him up warily. He was wearing a basketball jersey with the logo of a team I didn't know and tight jeans that showed off his thick legs, undoubtedly the result of the same obsessive workout routine that had shaped his body into a mountain of muscles and hormones.

"Wow, and who is this angel?" He looked me straight in the eyes and gave me a seductive smile, as though that was going to have me falling at his feet.

"May I present Selene Anderson. She's the daughter of my mom's boyfriend, Matt," Logan said, apparently not registering that his friend was obviously undressing me with his eyes while I tried to avoid his persistent gaze.

"Mmm…enchanted. I'm Bryan Nelson, master of the house." He gave me a sly look and winked before grabbing my hand to kiss it gallantly. "If you like, I can give you a full tour later, angel. What do you think about that?" he asked, clearly assuming I was just another chick in his hen house. I was never moved by guys like that. I could always tell what was on their minds right away, and I usually managed to avoid them.

"Sorry, not interested," I answered flatly and walked away from the creep. I grabbed a drink to ease some of the tension I could feel seeping into my body. I emptied the cup in one gulp, put it back on the table, and then I started wandering around the house in search of an exit. I needed some fresh air. But the partiers kept jostling me around, and I frequently tripped over my own feet because my heels were too high.

"I'm willing to show you an escape route, if you'll indulge me in one quick dance?"

It seemed that I could hear Neil's voice—that low, deep baritone, the one that raised goosebumps on my arms. I turned around to look for him but saw no one except for anonymous bodies and fluttering hair.

Am I hallucinating?

I shook my head and started walking again, disoriented by the overly loud music, but then someone grabbed my wrist. Before I could react, I met Neil's golden eyes, bright as any beacon. The feeling of arousal was so strong in my chest that it sent a jolt through me, though I couldn't explain why I was so incredibly attracted to a guy I'd known for such a short amount of time.

His body dominated even that large space. Though we were surrounded by other people, my eyes were glued to him because Neil had this shine to him, making everything else pale in comparison.

"Oh hey, it's you," I teased him but I didn't object when he wrapped his arm around my waist and pulled our bodies together. He gave off a heady smell of amber and tobacco, a combination that seemed to burn up my brain and paralyze my reason.

"If I were you, I wouldn't wander alone around a party like this, it could be dangerous." He flashed a small smile that I could reasonably classify as sincere, and I was shocked that he'd care. Neil wasn't the kind of guy who paid attention to that kind of thing.

He took a step toward me and I realized how close we'd gotten. I feared I might drown in his eyes, and I felt shivers pass from my skin all the way to my heart.

"Doesn't that seem like a bit of an exaggeration? What other things do you consider' 'dangerous,' Mr. MLK?" I bit my lip to keep from laughing aloud, and he must have noticed because he arched an eyebrow at me.

"Love," he said so decisively that it extinguished my smile. How was love dangerous?

"You're afraid of love?" I asked incredulously, and it occurred to me that we had somehow become enclosed in this little bubble where the attraction crackled between us and neither of us seemed to care who else was around.

"No, I'm afraid of the dependence that love creates." His stare fell to my lips, and I flushed. The way he stared intimidated me, but at the same time, I felt the urge to know him fully.

"And how do you protect yourself from that kind of dependence?" I asked him.

Instead of answering me promptly, however, Neil abruptly spun me around, forcing my back against his chest. My breath caught, and I could feel the pounding of my heart. These were completely new sensations for me, and they terrified me.

My body felt like it had been designed to mold to his. My brain was wiped clean of my previous life, wiped clean of Jared and the guilty feelings that struggled to rise back out of the depths of my consciousness. I tilted my face back slightly to meet his burning gaze.

"Simple. I don't love," he answered firmly.

Immediately thereafter, his lips settled on my neck, branding it with a delicate kiss. His hands wandered from my sides to my thighs. My head was spinning, and I felt breathless.

"You should learn to protect yourself, too, Tigress," he murmured into my ear. I closed my eyes; my legs felt weak, and I feared I would collapse at any moment. I was about to put my full weight against Neil, but suddenly, there was nothing but empty space behind me and a cold feeling along my spine. I turned and saw that he had vanished, like a magic trick.

I touched the curve of my neck as though emerging from a dream before I shook off the feeling and started searching for him.

It was stupid of me to run after him. I basically still had a boyfriend, after all; I shouldn't have been trying to get closer to any other guys. But my instinct fought my intellect on all fronts.

I searched for him like a madwoman, shoving aside anyone who got in my way. I stopped abruptly, though, when I spotted his messy hair and saw his hands clasped around another girl's body. I recognized her immediately: it was Jennifer. The two of them were dancing close together. She whispered something into his ear, and he smiled, slowly feeling his way down her back, then to her hips, then her ass.

I stood motionless, staring at them. I should have expected it, but I was still shocked by the anguish that uncurled inside of me. It was completely irrational, especially considering that I barely knew Neil.

When he caught my gaze, Neil stopped smiling, but he didn't stop touching her or push her away. But why would he have done that?

A while later, I found my friends and went up to the bar. While the others were busy ordering cocktails, I glanced around, bored as ever. I was looking for something more interesting than throwing back shots. Then, when I least expected it, among the crowd of people cheering for the band, I spotted a familiar mop of unruly chestnut hair. Neil's powerful, robust body was wrapped around Jennifer's much smaller form. She danced sensually with him, grinding her backside into his crotch.

Every cell in my body was drawn to him; it was a force as incontrovertible as it was dark. It was frightening, the way I could always sense his presence. When my eyes eventually found his lips, they were pressed against Jennifer's exposed neck. I met his ravenous gaze, and I felt it like a punch to the stomach. I jumped like I'd just been caught shoplifting by a police officer. But I didn't stop staring and he didn't stop dancing his attentions upon the blond girl's body.

He kissed her, touched her delicately, squeezed her tightly, and I could see the hidden malice in every gesture. It was right there behind his eyes. He danced with her, but he looked at me, which only intensified the odd feeling in the pit of my stomach. Again, it occurred to me how unreasonable and out of control my reactions to him were.

Jennifer tilted her head to seek Neil's lips. And he did not deny her—far from it. He kissed her fervidly, giving me a sneak preview of what was going to happen shortly thereafter, possibly in an empty bedroom. And all at once, I realized exactly who he was like: my father.

It was as though I was transported back in time, remembering an incident when I had caught Matt in the act. The image was still perfectly clear in my mind, despite the passing of the years since then. I had only been fifteen, and my father hadn't been expecting me back home so soon. I'd spent the afternoon out with my high school bestie, Sadie, but a sudden storm had forced us to come back early. When I went upstairs to his office to ask him if we could watch a movie together, I was halted by the sounds of female moans. I wasn't so naive that I didn't understand what was happening behind that door, but I had sincerely hoped that it was my mother with him and not some stranger.

My breathing was labored as I approached the half-open door and peered inside only to see my father with his coworker, Leslie Hellen. I knew her pretty well; she had even gone out to lunch with us a few Sundays before. I was disgusted, particularly by the obscene way she begged for him to go harder and how Matt obliged her, grasping her hips aggressively.

The force of the unexpected memory had me staggering backward until I ran into one of the drink tables. I leaned a hand on it to avoid falling over.

"Selene, are you okay?" Julie touched my shoulder, giving me a particularly worried look.

"Let's get a drink, Julie," I suggested stupidly and proceeded to drink way more than a lightweight like myself should have been allowed. I couldn't tell her how I felt at that moment, how all I wanted was an escape from reality. I brooded about the move, my alarming kiss with Neil, about Jared and all the sudden changes I had undergone. I considered how toxic this current situation had become and how I suddenly had the desire to take the completely wrong path at every turn. It was as though my body was now running my life, and my brain no longer got any input.

I got wasted like an idiot, even though I knew perfectly well that I was only hurting myself. I'd lost track of the number of drinks I'd downed, but I did notice that I was struggling to pronounce familiar words. In fact, I could barely recall my own name.

"Wesh... We should...stop," I said to Julie, who wasn't in much better shape. She mumbled something unintelligible while I laughed like a lunatic.

"Mav... Maffey... Maybe you're right..."

I slumped against the bar and blinked several times. My vision was no clearer than my mind.

"Girls..." someone said. It was probably Logan's voice. I turned to check. Yeah, it was him. But wait a minute...just how many Logans were there?

"Hello to every Logan present!" I waved a hand in greeting to all the Logans, even if the reproachful looks on their faces didn't bode particularly well.

"Are you drunk, Selene?" I heard his words as a distant echo. I felt completely unmoored from reality, so I just nodded and wrapped my arm around his shoulders. I couldn't stand it, and if I tried to walk, I would trip over my own feet.

Less than an hour later, I found myself back at home with Logan, who had also dropped off Alyssa and Julie along the way.

"D'ya know why the ladybugs are red, Logan?" I rhapsodized

on the front stoop before stopping to closely examine the exterior wall.

"No, Selene," he sighed, opening the front door.

"Because, in ancient times, red was the color of good fortune," I continued, holding forth like I was some great expert on the subject.

Logan, by contrast, was tired of my ramblings. "That doesn't explain why they're red," he grumbled, propping me up wearily.

We got into the house, and he dragged me toward the stairs. Fortunately, everyone else was already in bed, and Logan navigated us skillfully through the darkened house to make sure that no one would hear us.

"Explains why they're good luck, though," I argued after a few moments. He was no match for my incredible deductive reasoning.

"Yeah, yeah, okay. I think you've talked enough, and it's time for us both to go to sleep," he huffed and guided me slowly up the stairs. Every now and then my legs would give out and I'd hit my knees like a sack of potatoes, but Logan was always there to get me back on my feet.

He brought me into my room and helped me stretch out on the bed, pulling off my shoes. I muttered a subdued "thank you" and followed his shape with my eyes as he disappeared out the door of my room. I could feel my head throbbing and my stomach getting tight. I'd already thrown up on the ride home, but the nauseous feeling still lingered.

I tried to close my eyes. Sleep might have made me feel better, but the sounds coming from the next room were keeping me awake. I knew it was Neil getting his rocks off with some girl, and I decided that I wasn't going to let him get to me tonight.

I stumbled out of bed and toward the door. I tossed furtive glances up and down the empty hallway before making my way to his room, one hand on the wall next to me for stability. The walls kept rotating and the floor looked like an ocean of marble, rocked by invisible waves. I blinked and refocused on my goal.

I pounded insistently on his door until Neil appeared, in the flesh, wearing just a pair of track pants with his torso bared. I examined the well-defined lines of his solid musculature, including those sculpted pecs that I would have happily stroked before forcing myself to look back up and meet those eyes, gleaming like gold. He had a confused expression on his face, but I was determined not to let his perfect body distract me this time.

I cleared my throat and started in on him. "What are you doing? You want to knock it off with all this noise? And don't tell me you have someone over tonight, because I need to sleep!" I shoved him aside and forced my way into his room. I looked at the king-sized bed and was surprised to find no one in it. There was just a punching bag, swinging from a hook mounted on the ceiling and the scent of amber and tobacco in the air.

"Are you crazy? What do you want? I'm not fucking anyone; I was just training." He brushed past me irritably, and I looked first at the contours of his sweaty back then at the powerful muscles in his arms before I finally noticed the white wrappings around his hands and wrists.

I kept silent, aware that I had screwed up, while Neil bent down to grab a bottle of whiskey. I tilted my head and stared intently at him. His eyes were glassy, and his cheeks were flushed. Suddenly, there was a flare of understanding on both of our faces.

"Are you drunk?" we asked each other in unison. I was suddenly very aware of the danger in this moment because, with neither of us sober, there was no one to keep the situation under control.

"I-I-I'd better get back to my room." I went to leave but stopped in the doorway and turned back. "I apologize. That I thought you were… I mean, that I came over here because…" I didn't know what to say, I had screwed up, and it would have been better to just apologize and then walk away. But my body remained motionless. Waiting. For what, even I didn't know.

Neil set the now-empty bottle on the floor and walked over to me. He was covered in sweat; it turned his skin into polished amber stretched over the clean lines of his body. For a second, my eyes caught on the Māori-style tattoo on his right bicep, and I wanted to ask him why he'd chosen that particular design.

I quickly snapped out of my silly thoughts, however, when I felt his big, warm hand touching my cheek. I wanted to squirm away from the gesture. I wanted to feel disgust. I wanted it to be an unwanted advance. Instead, it just reignited those sensations in me that I had now learned to recognize as lust, fear, and confusion.

"You're very beautiful. Do you know that?" He seemed to be murmuring it more to himself than to me. I stared at his lips and wondered what it would feel like to taste them again. I hadn't forgotten how soft they were and how skillfully they moved against mine. Those lips could scramble a woman's brain.

"So are you," I answered.

It suddenly seemed to me that the two of us standing there together, saying what we were thinking, just might be the most right thing in the world. Why did I have to be so attracted to someone so far removed from who I was? In that moment, I didn't even care. Neil and I were just two young people trying to figure ourselves out against every rule and all good advice.

"Why'd you get drunk?" He brushed my lower lip with his thumb, and I opened my mouth breathlessly, feeling the rough texture of his fingertip.

"Why did you?" I asked him back and he smiled at me…almost sweetly.

"You know what Bukowski said about that?" he asked abruptly, still touching me. I shook my head, and he went on: "If something bad happens, you drink in an attempt to forget; if something good happens, you drink in order to celebrate; and if nothing happens, you drink to make something happen." He wrapped his arms around my waist and pulled our bodies tightly together.

Feeling awkward, I looked down at his bare chest, which did absolutely nothing to banish the odd feeling of arousal inside me. His knuckles brushed my cheek, so I slowly raised my eyes until they locked on his. All I saw there was desire. I wondered what he was reading in my gaze, but then his lips touched mine for the second time and the real world fell away.

I couldn't reason; my brain shut down completely. All I knew was the heat of his body against me, my skin presented for his kisses, our hearts pounding together, our tongues chasing one another feverishly.

Neil tasted like alcohol, tobacco, sin, and mistakes. But also like dreams, certainty, experience, knowledge. I was drowning in his eyes. We freed ourselves from our clothing. A mix of pain and pleasure coursed through my body, carrying me away to some other plane. I felt my eyes stinging and moisture on my cheekbones... *Am I crying?* I didn't realize it in the moment, but my nails were digging up his back while my body was racked with tremors and sensations I'd never experienced before. I felt at one with him and complete. Bound to this troubled boy about whom I still knew so very little.

We were gazing deep into one another, our bodies hot and intertwined, our minds clouded and dim. We were all irrationality and instinct.

Lust and error.

Reality and dream.

6

SELENE

Weird.

That's how I felt.

I was warm, lying in a soft bed, wrapped up in fluffy blankets.

I was awake, but I couldn't seem to open my eyes.

I had no idea what time it was, though I knew I had definitely missed some of my classes for the day.

Slowly, I raised my eyelids and stretched my sluggish muscles, feeling an odd soreness in them. I glanced around and immediately spotted a dark wall in front of me, decorated with a poster of a... basketball team? When did my room get such...masculine furnishings? Everything ranged in color from cobalt blue to black.

Perhaps I was still sleepy? Or was this some bizarre hallucination?

I sat up, my head spinning, and discovered that I was completely naked. I sat there staring down at my breasts for an unknown amount of time, trying to reconstruct what had happened the night before. I racked my brain for some reasonable explanation, an excuse that could justify my lack of clothing, but nothing came to me.

I was starting to feel confused and lost when I felt a body moving next to me. I felt like dying when I turned immediately and saw the powerful shoulders of some guy with his face buried in the pillow. My hands started trembling, and my stomach felt like it was being crushed in a vise. I leaped out of the bed and pulled the warm blankets along with me, revealing the naked form of the boy who continued to sleep unconcerned.

I could see solid legs, buttocks like carved marble, and an expanse of relaxed muscles, all completely exposed. Under normal circumstances, I might have been able to appreciate an Adonis like that, but not when I was inexplicably naked in his room.

"Oh my God!" I shrieked uncomfortably, clutching a long white sheet to my chest. I swallowed down a retch triggered by the disgust I was feeling toward myself. This was an actual tragedy; I had done irreparable damage this time!

Who was this guy? Had I just gone to bed with some stranger I met at the party?

"Mmh…" the boy muttered, burying his head deeper in the pillow. He didn't seem aware of anything.

I looked around, and from the corner of my eye, I saw a photo on a shelf. It was of Logan and Neil as children at the beach. I reached out to the boy in bed. I touched his disheveled hair and stared at his bent arm, which was marked with a tattoo. Māori style…the same one…

The room began to spin around me as reality sank in.

"N-Neil," I stammered, in shock. Then, the boy, no longer a mystery, lifted his face up and greeted me in a tired fashion, not even bothering to look at me.

"Hey, whatsyourname…last night was great but you can go now." He clearly hadn't yet realized the gravity of the situation but… Wait, was this the way he typically dismissed his conquests the morning after?

"Bukowski got it right..." I pulled the sheet more tightly around me and watched the muscles in his neck tense at the sound of my voice. He propped himself up on his elbows and turned his head toward me. He couldn't hide the shock that showed in his still-sleepy golden eyes. Probably the same as mine.

"Selene?" he asked, sounding troubled, and I saw a flicker of surprise cross his face as he kept his gaze fixed on me. His lips were swollen, and his hair was a riot. Was I the one who had done that to him? And what about me? What sort of state was I in?

I began to pace the room like a maniac. I didn't want to accept what had happened. I felt so profoundly soiled and wrong. I wished for nothing so much as the magical power to go back in time so that I could turn this reality into just a bad dream.

"What are you doing in my room?!" He tried to get up, but I immediately raised a hand to halt him. Was he insane? The last thing I wanted right then was to see more of his nude body.

"Do not sit up!" I demanded sternly. Neil registered first the sheet wrapped around my body, then that he himself was completely naked.

Sigh.

"Calm down, Selene." He balanced on his elbows, motionless. He was beautiful, brazen, and terribly attractive as he stared at me like a guilty little imp, but that didn't change the reality of the situation: I should never have made a mistake of this magnitude.

"Calm down? Calm down?" I shouted furiously. I knew, though, that the fault was mine, not his. If I was going to be angry with anyone, it should have been myself.

"Hand me a pair of clean boxers. I can't just stay like this all day." He sighed and adjusted a chestnut-brown lock that had fallen over his left eye. Every movement he made was alluring. I shook my head; now was not the time to be bewitched by his erotic energy. Not after I had already fallen victim to it.

"Are you seriously more worried about your boxers than about what happened between us?" I was stunned by his equanimity.

"Do you want me to deal with this while I'm naked and not allowed to stand up? Check the dresser."

He had a point. I immediately went hunting for a pair of boxers. Once I'd found them, I threw them to him and turned around so he could get dressed. In the meantime, I stared first at the blank wall and then at the desk, where there was a laptop, some books, and two photos of him with Logan. Neil couldn't have been more than eight or nine in either of them. I noticed that there was no sign of any mementos from his adulthood.

"You can turn around now," he ordered after a few moments, and I obeyed. I found myself presented with a spectacular tableau: Neil was seated on the bed, his muscular body saved from nakedness only by a pair of boxers. He had the weary but satiated expression of someone who'd had a really good time the night before.

"This is a real shitshow," he remarked, chewing nervously on his lip as he took in our clothes, scattered all over the floor.

"What were we thinking? Neil, I was wasted." I started pacing again in total panic. "I'll never be able to forgive myself." I accidentally stepped on something, and I froze when I looked down and realized with was a torn condom wrapper. Neil followed my stare and was silent for a few moments. The overwhelming evidence of what we'd done the night before just kept piling up.

"Selene, it was an accident. We weren't thinking clearly." He was trying to comfort me, but a bitter laugh escaped my lips instead. Sure, it was an accident. One that could have been easily avoided if I had been just slightly less stupid or slightly more mature in my decision-making.

"That's easy for you to say, Neil. How many people do you sleep with in a week? How many of their names do you even remember? But it's not like that for me; it's never been like that." The guilty

89

feeling washed over me, and I felt deeply disconcerted. I could no longer recognize myself. The old me would never have just slept with some guy like that, not even while drunk.

I felt like crying, but I didn't want to appear weak in front of Neil. On top of that, my head was spinning, and I felt a distinct burning sensation between my legs with every step I took. The bottom of my abdomen ached, as did my hips. Muscles I hadn't even known I had before were sore.

The worst part, however, was seeing the evidence of my virginity on the mattress. My innocence, which I had guarded so carefully only to throw it away without a second thought. That was a real blow to my heart, one that took my breath away and made me feel sick. I stood there motionless with a blank look on my face, and even Neil didn't have the guts to say anything to me.

"I'm so disappointed in myself. This wasn't how I wanted it to happen." I continued looking at the red stain and Neil frowned, not realizing what I was talking about. Once again, he followed the direction of my stare, and from the surprised look on his face, I guessed that he hadn't noticed, and I hadn't told him. Of course, I'd never talked about it with anyone before, why would I have started with him? I felt his fiery honey gaze turn to me, but I was too ashamed to meet his eyes. I bowed my head so I wouldn't have to see pity on his face.

"I would never have figured that you were…" He left this horrified sentence hanging in mid-air and got out of the bed, rubbing a hand over his face in disbelief.

"Yeah…"

There was no need to say anything else. He was the first man I had ever been with. I died a little inside at the idea of him laughing at me, bragging to his friends about deflowering Selene, the sad virgin who had come all the way from Detroit to fix her relationship with her daddy.

"I'm not going to say anything. It'll be our secret. You have my word." He moved in front of me, and he smelled so good it was almost stunning. I lifted my face and was further amazed by his extremely sincere expression. Still, the thing that worried me the most wasn't my secret that was no longer a secret, but...

"Jared." I swayed dizzily and Neil stabilized me. I rested my forehead on the warmth of his chest and closed my eyes. He put his hands on my hips and then, in a completely unexpected move, he pulled me close into a comforting embrace. Somehow, it only made the whole thing worse. I was a collection of indecipherable feelings, all screaming and demanding to be free, but I just wanted to erase every one of them. To forget all of this and start thinking of Neil as something wrong and deleterious in every way.

Neil took my shoulders and shook me.

"Look at me," he demanded, and I raised my chin, distraught. "I am so sorry. Genuinely. I didn't want you to lose your virginity that way either but there's nothing we can do about it now. If one of us had been sober, we could have dealt with the situation, but..." He searched my face for any reaction, but I turned away again so I wouldn't see his pity. It would have been easy for him to tell me to leave then. I would have been just one more of many: forgotten.

But instead he was... He was being... I pushed him away and grasped the sheet, turning my back to him.

"I have to shower," I said simply. "I'll wash your sheet and give it back to you when it's clean." I continued, sounding like an automaton, "I hope you can get rid of that stain."

I opened the door, and after making sure no one was around, I went out into the hallway. I quickly darted into my room and locked the door behind me. Then I slumped down on the floor and started sobbing, hugging my knees to my chest.

I had made an unfixable mistake. I would have to accept it, but I couldn't forgive myself. I spent God knows how long curled up on the floor there wallowing in a river of despair, but that wasn't the right attitude. I had to come back from this somehow.

I swiped my wet cheeks with the backs of my hands and got to my feet. I was exhausted, like I'd just run for miles. My heart was pounding, and my head was throbbing. A part of me was still hoping that this was all just a dream or, rather, a nightmare. But I knew that wasn't the case.

I trudged to the bathroom and allowed the sheet to slip down. I felt weak, my legs ached. There was a different smell on my skin—a smell that didn't belong to me. I observed myself carefully in the mirror. People said that, after your first time, something changes, and you became a woman. But all I saw was the same girl I'd always been, only with more guilt.

I scrutinized every inch of my reflection's skin and frowned when I saw purple bruising on my right breast and at the base of my neck, right beside my collarbone. Neil had also been drunk last night. From the marks on my body, it seemed he hadn't curbed his impulses very much, but I didn't actually remember anything.

I touched myself slowly, following the trail of marks and stopping at my pubic mound. My heart battered my chest as, instinctively, I dipped the pads of my fingers inside. I pulled them away covered in little smears of purple-red.

I released a tiny hiss of pain as I contracted my pelvic muscles. I was probably going to feel where he'd been inside me for days to come. I climbed into the shower and thoroughly scrubbed my hair and body. I hoped in vain that the spray of hot water could also wash away some of my guilty feelings.

After, I dressed quickly, putting on a clean pair of underwear, a pair of jeans, and a dark T-shirt. I dried my hair and put it up in a long braid before using concealer on the marks around my neck. I didn't want to arouse suspicions or court any tough questions.

I stuffed the dirty sheet in the washing machine, and then I remembered that I'd left the clothes I was wearing last night in his room. There was no way I was going to go see him again. I had made quite enough trouble for myself already.

I had just returned to my room when someone knocked on my door. I hoped it wasn't Mia or Matt; there was no way I'd be able to hold a conversation with them in my current condition. I gathered my strength and opened the door.

In front of me, I found Neil wearing sweats. His hair was damp, and he gave off a strong smell of body wash, as always. I suspected he must just go through bottles of body wash, because I had noticed that he took several showers per day.

"Your clothes," he said, like he'd heard my thoughts.

"Yeah, thanks." I grabbed them while trying to avoid his gaze, which made me feel naked, psychologically as well as physically. He had stripped me down and touched my soul—nothing was more intimate than that.

"Selene..." he said in a horrified whisper, and it was clear he wanted to talk, but I wasn't in the mood. I felt like a withered flower, and his amber scent was only making me more uncomfortable. It was the same smell that had been on my skin before I'd washed it away. The same smell that still lingered on me.

"It's fine, Neil. I'll be down for breakfast soon." I was so embarrassed, but I managed a tense smile. Fortunately, Neil saw my unease and didn't push. He left promptly, giving me plenty of time to prepare myself for the day ahead.

Down in the kitchen, I ate breakfast silently. My father kept giving me suspicious looks, but he didn't ask me any questions.

I was grateful.

"How are you feeling?" Logan grumbled, interrupting my silence as he crunched on his cereal.

"Huh?" I pretended not to understand.

"After last night," he whispered and for a terrible moment, I imagined Logan spying intently on us during the incriminating act. I swallowed hard and looked at him, alarmed.

"What are you talking about?" I played dumb, trying not to be overheard by my father or Mia as she walked into the kitchen.

"You getting blitzed," he chuckled, and I could breathe normally again. *Stupid!*

"Oh, yeah… Let's just say I'm much better now." I got a grip on myself and breathed a sigh of relief. I was pretty sure I'd gone completely white in that first moment of uncertainty.

Of course. Logan was the one who had gotten me back to my room and put me to bed. It was completely natural that he'd ask how I was doing. He couldn't have been talking about anything else. I smiled at him, and at the same time, my heart did a bizarre somersault because I saw Neil come into the kitchen with a pensive look on his face.

He poured himself a cup of coffee, looking perfectly cold and indifferent, despite what had happened. With me. In his bed.

"How long have you been awake?" his mother asked him as she leafed through a fashion magazine propped up on the table.

"I went out to smoke a while ago." Neil didn't meet my eyes, not even accidentally. It seemed like he wanted to avoid me, and he was succeeding wonderfully.

And wasn't that what I wanted, too?

So why, then, did his apparent indifference needle me?

I snorted at myself. I was contradiction embodied. Even I couldn't stand myself ever since I'd moved to New York.

"Hey, Jennifer stopped by," Logan told his brother, and my eyes immediately shot to Neil's face, which reacted not at all to that name.

"What did she want?" He pulled his iPhone out of the pocket of his track pants and swiped a thumb across the display. I couldn't figure out why I was scrutinizing his every movement so carefully.

What was I trying to understand? If he really liked Jennifer or not? He was probably going to text or call her right then, and what was I going to do about it? Stop him? Neil wasn't my boyfriend; I had someone waiting for me back in Detroit.

Well, probably not after he found out what I'd done.

I had to laugh bitterly at myself. I pitied this new person I had become in just the space of a couple weeks.

"Dunno. I told her you were still sleeping. She wanted to go up to your room." Logan made a displeased face. Evidently, he didn't like the blond with her tight miniskirts, either.

"I get it; I'll deal with her." He stuck his phone back in his pocket with a shrug. How was he going to "deal" with her? I shook my head, unable to understand why I felt so possessive over a guy to whom I meant nothing. After all, the only thing between us was one night of sex, and he'd had plenty of those.

I decided I needed to put some distance between myself and Neil and all the feelings he stirred up in me, so I got up and went into the living room. Before I could get there, though, a hand grabbed me firmly by the wrist and pulled me into an isolated corner. I could smell his amber scent, and I shivered.

"What are you doing?" I whispered furiously.

"Shh. I just needed to make one more thing clear." His breath was warm against my face, and I had to close my eyes to keep from thinking about that last time I'd felt that sensation, when we were…

"Let's hear it." I cleared my throat, trying to hide the effect he had on me, though it was a difficult task.

"I don't want you to be weird around me. We're going to have to share this house for a while. What happened was a mistake. I understand that you feel bad about it and—"

I shook my head abruptly, halting the flow of his words. "I don't think you're capable of understanding how I feel." It was easy for him to give himself to a series of strangers. Sex was a hobby for him. A game. It wasn't for me. I had always believed that sex and love should be connected, and I'd never questioned those beliefs.

"I didn't realize you were a virgin." It was as though he didn't know what else to say. Like he was trying to excuse himself or apologize, maybe. Either way, he wasn't succeeding.

"This isn't easy for me; I need time to process everything that happened," I said, looking down at the place where his hand was closed around my wrist. It felt like my skin was burning. My emotions felt unstoppable. I tried to fight them back, but they crushed me beneath them as easily as a stone would crush a tiny, helpless butterfly.

It occurred to me that I needed to talk to Jared soon.

"It won't happen again. It was just a terrible mistake," he said and then his gaze fell to my lips, and I knew with certainty that no one could believe those words.

Least of all us.

7

SELENE

It was especially sunny when I finally decided to take a walk in the park with Matt. In reality, I'd only agreed to go out with him to avoid Neil—the tsunami that had upended my life.

So, I walked alongside my father in silence until he sat on a bench and motioned for me to join him. I took a seat next to him and put my hands on my knees, rubbing my palms over the surface of my jeans.

"You know, Selene," he began, watching as a group of children pushed each other on the swings, "I feel regret every day that I wasn't a better father to you." I regretted it too, but I didn't say that to him. Instead, I chose to keep quiet and hear what he had to say. "I know what you and your mother went through, but I think I deserve..." he trailed off, hesitant.

"Another chance?" I finished for him with a bitter smile. If he thought I was dumb enough to give him one, he was sorely mistaken. "I still remember when I walked in on you and your coworker. Do you realize that?" I added in disgust. Matt adopted an embarrassed look. His embarrassment, though, was nothing compared to the disillusionment I had felt.

"I am so sorry…" he murmured, not looking at me.

"Should have thought about that before you did it." Ours was not an evenly matched fight. Matt was in the wrong, and he knew very well that it was contemptible for a father to put himself in a position where he was caught with another woman by his own daughter. He fell silent, and my anger, repressed for so long, swelled and then exploded.

"You have no idea how many times I watched Mom cry when she smelled someone else's perfume on your shirts or when you gave her some flimsy excuse for why you were going to be late." My voice shook, and I couldn't hide how upset I was. It was still so painful for me to talk about this, and as far as I was concerned, his actions were unforgivable.

"Selene, I…"

"You have no idea how many times we waited for you pointlessly. To eat dinners, to celebrate birthday parties, to watch school plays." Matt hung his head, and I turned my face away so I wouldn't have to see his contrite expression. Ironically, the new angle gave me a perfect view of two parents holding their daughter's hand.

"I used to love you so much," I murmured, staring at the happy little family just a stone's throw from us.

"I'm sorry," he whispered, more to himself than to me. I got to my feet and looked back down at him.

"We'd better head back now," I said with finality. Matt got up as well and followed me.

Back at the house, my father went upstairs to find Mia while I remained downstairs alone. I sat down in the living room, worn out and bummed out by my conversation with Matt and watched as Logan emerged to grab the keys to the Audi.

"Where are you going?" I said curiously. He was all dressed up, like he was going out on a date, but I didn't ask directly if he was because I didn't want to seem nosy.

"I'm going to watch the game at Adam's place with the guys," he answered immediately, but I didn't believe him. He wasn't dressed for a night with the boys. Still, I just smiled at him and shrugged. Logan's love life was none of my business, though I would have been pleased if he had finally decided to date Alyssa.

"Okay, have fun," I told him. He gave me a wave and hurried out the door. A moment later, Chloe appeared. She was wearing a magnificent red dress, and her blond hair tumbled softly around her shoulders. All dressed up like that, she was a carbon copy of her mother. She walked to the door without acknowledging me, and I didn't say anything to her either.

Alone once again, I turned on the TV and started surfing with the remote control.

"Selene!" I was startled when Mia's playful voice echoed through the room.

"Your father and I are leaving for a conference. Anna will also be going shortly." She pulled on a long, elegant coat and gave me a smile that I did not reciprocate.

"That's fine."

"Are you sure you'll be okay on your own? You can call me if you need anything," my father added, sounding worried as he entered the living room. His show of concern annoyed me.

"Yup." I didn't even look at him and focused on the television until I heard the door shut and silence fell. Finally, I was free from their presence.

I got up then and went into the kitchen to get a bowl of the popcorn Anna had made. She really had a gift—she was a magician in the kitchen and even her simplest dishes made my mouth water.

"Miss, I'm heading out now. My children are waiting for me," said Anna, appearing behind me and taking me by surprise. I smiled at her, still holding the bowl in my hands and watched her pick up her purse.

"How many children do you have?" I asked, hoping she wouldn't think I was prying.

"Two, dear. Two boys." She told me about her children as I walked her to the door. Ethan, her oldest, was eighteen and dreamed of becoming a great baseball player. The younger boy, Jace, was fifteen and played the piano. I didn't ask any questions about the father of her children, but I got the impression that he hadn't stepped up for them. Anna had worked for Mia for so many years precisely because of the generous salary that Mia offered, which gave her enough to support herself and her kids without anyone else's help. She had been looking after Neil, Logan, and Chloe since they were little. She told me that Neil had been a very smart but mistrustful boy; curious but introverted. I looked at her as she spoke, and it occurred to me that she could help me. She had known Neil for a long time; perhaps she could shed some light on the shadows surrounding him and his mood swings. But Anna was in a hurry, and it wasn't really the time to pepper her with questions. I said a polite goodbye to her and watched her leave.

I returned to the living room and sat back down on the sofa. I intended to take advantage of the solitude to eat some popcorn and watch a movie. I just needed a break from everything that was happening, especially with Neil. I was still deciding on what to watch when I heard footsteps on the staircase. Seconds later, his imposing frame appeared in the living room. I hadn't realized Neil was even home. I'd thought he was out with Jennifer or his other friends.

"What are you doing here?" I asked before choking on a piece of popcorn and coughing.

"I'll remind you that this is my home." He smiled and looked at me in such a seductive way that it gave me goosebumps.

"I thought you'd gone out as well." I cleared my throat and went back to pressing remote buttons randomly. My brain was already all static and the closer he got the more precarious I felt.

"No. Jennifer left half an hour ago, and I need to relax." His hair was damp, and he smelled like body wash, a sure indication that he'd just taken yet another shower. I could deduce that he and Jennifer hadn't met up to talk.

Heedless of my discomfort, Neil sat down near me and stretched out his legs, crossing one casually over the other. I went rigid and instinctively moved slightly to increase the distance between us.

"Leave it here," he said when I landed on a channel with a boxing match on. Was he a fan of the sport? Suddenly, I had a vague memory of a punching bag swinging in his room. Too bad for him: I had no interest in watching dudes punch each other.

"I'm anti-violence. I don't like to watch certain programming," I argued, and he just smiled, his eyes locked on the screen. I rolled my eyes and continued chowing down on the popcorn as I gave him a furious look. Although I was visibly irritated by his intrusion and his presumption, I couldn't help but be dazzled by the line of his profile and those full lips that generated all sorts of fantasies in the female brain.

I sighed and reluctantly bid goodbye to my peaceful evening. I focused on my popcorn. Suddenly, Neil's hand invaded my field of vision and thrust into the bowl.

"Hey!" I exclaimed in annoyance, the way I might react to a naughty child as he grabbed a handful.

"Yes?" he asked, chowing down with his typical indifferent air.

"This is my popcorn. There's more in the kitchen if you want some." I held the bowl out of his reach, though I was sure he would have just taken it if he really wanted it. After all, he always found a way to get the things he wanted.

"Don't be greedy, Selene. Be generous, like you were last night." He gave me a sly look, and his luminous eyes seemed even brighter than normal.

"Knock it off," I demanded and stared at the TV screen, trying not to look at him.

"The details..." he murmured thoughtfully, as if his mind were wandering off somewhere else.

"What?" I asked, turning to him in confusion.

"The truth is hidden in the details." The low timbre of his voice drove the air from my lungs.

"What are you talking about?" I whispered. Though we weren't sitting that close together, it felt like the space between our bodies was shrinking.

"True intelligence means knowing exactly how to read them, Selene, and when you do, nothing makes sense anymore." He pulled the popcorn bowl from my hands and set it on the glass table in front of us before drawing closer and touching my cheek. His cold fingers glided across my skin, and I didn't pull away from them.

I did, however, close my eyes, because surrendering to him hurt like a dagger to the heart.

"Except everything makes sense, and we can't upend our whole situation," I answered hesitantly. I wish I had the strength to reject him outright, but no matter how hard I tried to resist him, I was overwhelmed by the emotions he generated within me.

"My bed smelled like coconut this morning," he whispered beguilingly. I could feel his breath on my lips. It smelled of tobacco and popcorn. I had to admit it: he knew what he was doing, and he had a talent for manipulating a woman's mind. But that didn't excuse my own weakness.

I opened my eyes and put my hand over his as I chewed on my lower lip.

"Stop," I begged him, trying not to give in to this temporary madness that had already cost me so much just the night before. I was just one of many for Neil, and he likely didn't have any of the same feelings I had. More importantly, he completely ignored my pleas, too focused on bending me to his will.

"I want to kiss you..." He traced the contour of my lower lip with his thumb, hypnotizing himself with his own movement. I saw the flicker of desire in his eyes and flushed.

"No," I said with a decisiveness that I didn't feel. I kept trying to put up a wall that might protect me in some way, but our commingled breaths battered it down.

"I wasn't asking for your permission." In a wild, impulsive motion, he pressed our mouths together. I went rigid, putting my hands on his chest with the intention of pushing him away. But my desire was obvious to a man like Neil. The sort of man who could make me feel completely naked without ever undressing me and who could read my every thought.

My lips moved slowly against his in a silent, teasing dance. I couldn't catch my breath; my heart was pounding—I felt so alive. When our tongues intertwined, the kiss became something divine: powerful and magical.

He climbed on top of me and pushed me into the sofa, positioning himself between my legs. All the while, his hot and hungry mouth continued to tease me. I could feel his body's reaction to mine. I sucked in a breath when I felt his erection rub between my thighs, giving me unimaginable pleasure. Secretly, I felt nothing but satisfaction about how excited I had gotten him.

I gave a moan of pleasure, and he smiled, pleased with himself. I dug my hand into his hair and kissed him passionately, blushing as a tiny gasp escaped his plush lips. I was fully aware that I was making another mistake, but I had already made a decision in my own mind: I was never going to get back together with Jared. By that point, I had realized that our relationship had always lacked one crucial element: love.

I hooked my legs around Neil's hips, and we groaned together.

Neil began to rock his pelvis slowly against me and my breathing got heavy. Even when I was completely at the mercy of these physical sensations, I still couldn't help but marvel at how comfortable I felt with him.

So comfortable that I dug my nails into his powerful back and clung violently to him. All my muscles tensed and my knees trembled, but the pleasure merged with the guilty feeling. Though I intended to more firmly break things off with Jared, I was currently going further with someone else than I'd ever considered going with him, so I dug deep and tried to find the strength to put on the brakes.

"Please, stop," I begged, panting as I broke our kiss. Neil's face hovered a few inches from mine, looking both aroused and upset. For a moment, he looked at me like a child who had just been told he couldn't have an ice cream cone. Then, he adopted the expression of a seducer so skillful that he could make heaven's most devout angel commit the worst of sins. He licked his pink, swollen lips slowly, savoring the taste of me there.

"Why do you keep trying to reject me?" He stood up, and finally I could think clearly again. I felt hot and disoriented, but above all else, I felt…unsatisfied. I wanted him inside me again, and this time, I wanted to remember every single second of my transgression. When the full realization of that thought dawned on me, I turned red, ashamed of myself.

"Because of Jared!" I cried, my voice heavy with frustration. Neil shook his head, scrubbing a hand over his face.

"Fuck!" He turned his back on me, furious. Was he mad because I'd rejected him or because I'd brought up Jared?

"I'm different from the kind of girls you're used to…" I began, though my recent behavior suggested that wasn't at all true. Was that the kind of person I had become? I used to have principles. Now, though, I didn't even recognize myself.

"Don't you dare. Don't you dare judge me. You don't know shit about me!" Neil burst out menacingly, turning back around and advancing on me. I retreated. His stare had become dangerous. His anger seemed to come from somewhere far away, some other world. I caught a glimpse of something that dwelled in the depths of his soul: a monster that needed to remain undisturbed.

I kept silent; talking would only have made the situation worse. Instead, I looked at him. At all of him: the rumpled hair, the straight nose, plump lips, the sharp jawline, and then there were his eyes. Sometimes the gold of honey; other times as dark as coal. This was all their fault. What kind of spell had they cast on me?

"Neil!" Someone called out in the entryway. A moment later Jennifer, with her slender legs, curvy body, and flowing blond hair entered the living room, swaying her hips. What was she doing here? Was she always underfoot?

"Babe, I forgot my phone in your room," she said, not sparing me a single glance. Then she threw her slim arms around a motionless Neil's neck with the devil's own shamelessness.

"How did you get in here?" he asked her, not moving away.

"The back door wasn't locked. Sorry for sneaking in, but since I left my phone here, I couldn't exactly call you," she said coyly. "Will you take me upstairs to get it?" she continued in a suggestive whisper. She moved her body sensually against him, purring and rubbing on him like a kitten desperate for affection.

The Cheshire grin on Neil's face told me that he was prepared to give her his full attention. They would undoubtedly be having all the phenomenal sex that I, in my stubbornness, had just talked myself out of moments ago.

"Let's go…" he told her, taking her upstairs with him. They hadn't even gotten to the first landing before my cell phone rang, Jared's name appearing on the display. I felt a stab of anguish. I should have answered him, but instead I just stared blankly into space.

I felt like a ship adrift on the ocean and I could see the storm on the horizon, but I couldn't seem to change course. What would become of me? Would I survive?

Or would I sink below the waves forever?

8

NEIL

I miscalculated.

I had miscalculated everything because of a girl with ocean eyes and an angel's face who had invaded my house, my libido, and my brain.

I had to get her out of my head.

Selene had no idea who I really was and the kind of burdens I bore. She was innocent, and I should have been thinking of her as a little sister, but instead I could only picture her underneath me, screaming my name.

I didn't deserve her. I was a deviant, a demon of perversion squatted in the innermost part of my soul. It sat upon a throne in my heart and was suffocating me, killing me slowly. That was why I couldn't help but destroy everything I touched.

I leaned against the door and crossed my arms as I observed Jennifer, her tight miniskirt riding up her hips and her flowing blond hair—the part of her that excited me most—hanging down. I knew her lost phone was just a ruse to eke out a little more time with me, but I decided to play along because I still—as always—wanted to fuck.

"Come and get what you want," I ordered, gesturing for her to approach. It was satisfying in an unhealthy way: using her, humiliating her, treating her like an object upon which I could vent my darkest instincts and not just in the bedroom.

In exchange, I gave her my body because I had nothing else to offer. My soul had been torn from me long ago. I was a fallen angel surrounded by the paper swallows from a Carrieri book. I was trying to shake off the dust, to open my broken wings and tend to the wounds inside me. I was trying to endure, to subdue the fires of hell, but all I could manage was hobbling around on the rubble.

It felt bad, behaving that way. I was disgusted with myself, but at the same time, I had no other means of communicating with other people, and I still hoped that someday, someone might understand me. So far, no one had.

Jennifer didn't, either. Instead, she gave me a seductive smile and obeyed me promptly. I immediately grabbed her by the arm, shoving her against the door face-first. Gentleness wasn't my strong suit, but she enjoyed that about me. She loved it when I acted like an animal. And hadn't I been spat out by society? Crushed like a worm? So why should I treat people with a respect they'd never shown me?

I shook my head and put a stop to my thinking, determined to get some relief from my constant torments in sex. I could sense her arousal, and it gratified me.

Jennifer wanted me.

I pressed a kiss against her neck and shoved her skirt up over her hips. I wasn't one for a lot of sweet nothings or foreplay—oral sex was a concession that I made only rarely—but a few kisses and touches were usually enough to get my prey wet for me anyway.

I touched her all over, from her firm breasts to her slim thighs and her high ass. I did worship women, in my own way.

I slid my hand between her partially opened legs and pulled her thong to one side before pressing two fingers inside her.

She was already warm and yielding, ready to take my cock, which women typically described as "impressive." Jennifer panted, turning to lick my neck. It was the erogenous zone that immediately triggered my animal instincts.

I partially closed my eyes. I could feel my body tensing as my muscles contracted. I needed to come hard and find oblivion in an overpowering orgasm that I hoped wouldn't take too long to arrive, as had been happening more and more to me lately.

I tugged down my pants and retrieved a condom from my pocket. I rolled it on as I bent her over in front of me, pushing myself between her ass cheeks. Her tight ass was a nice distraction as I gripped her hair in my fist and started thrusting, sucking and biting her bent neck. With one hand, I teased her pussy, which was drenched for me.

As I did this, the sound of Jennifer's body slamming into the door echoed around the room. I rested my forehead on the back of her neck, but I didn't stop thrusting. I sank into her again and again, without regard for her, without sensitivity, without respect. My hips moved desperately, pounding her with strong, decisive blows.

Jennifer jerked and moaned. A couple of times she asked me to slow down but I paid her no mind. Every time she pleaded with me, I slapped her ass and pushed myself deeper.

I tried to concentrate on her and our entanglement, but I couldn't seem to fully abandon myself to pleasure. I'd never been a two-pump chump, and sex always lasted a little longer than I'd like, but this time I was getting an unfamiliar feeling of confusion.

My thrusts were too controlled. Mechanical. Something wasn't right.

I stopped and pulled out of Jennifer, staring at the globes of her ass, which were red from the unrestrained slaps I'd given her. I was about to drive back into her again when I felt a sudden anger rising up within me.

I didn't know what was happening to me.

I blinked repeatedly and didn't move. Jennifer got down on her knees in front of me and peeled off the condom. Then she looked me right in the eye as she took me in her mouth.

My blondie knew me so well. She knew that when I was feeling unsettled, I needed to receive pleasure rather than give it. In that moment, though, it was more than just a typical male desire.

I closed my eyes and Selene appeared in my mind's eye. I couldn't remember exactly what had happened between us the night before, but I imagined how it would have felt, penetrating her soft body, losing myself in those ocean eyes as I watched them flood with desire. I imagined hearing her shy yet sensual gasps, feeling her little pink nails sink into my back flesh with each thrust while her flexed thighs strangled my hips. And more: her cheeks painted a delicate pink with every filthy word I said, the way she bit her plump lower lip, the silky hair that slid through my fingers, and the smell of coconut that intoxicated me.

I opened my eyes and stared at Jen's blond head between my thighs. I wondered if Selene had ever fooled around like this, if she was even capable of using her tongue in such a sinful way. I wondered what her inexperienced mouth would feel like around me. I felt a tremor in the bottom of my abdomen.

All at once, my arousal evaporated. I yanked away from Jennifer and pulled up my boxers and pants.

Game over.

"Get out." I walked over to my desk and picked up a pack of Winstons. I needed a smoke and to clear my head.

"What's your deal? Have you lost your mind?" she demanded, still on her knees with her makeup smeared, her lips shiny with saliva. She looked disappointed and furious at the same time. One of her cheeks was red where I had slammed her face against the door. The sight of her repulsed me and made me feel like an uncontrollable animal. I was disgusted with myself and this madness of mine. I didn't understand how women could tolerate it.

"I'm not feeling it tonight," I told her while lighting a cigarette. My hands were shaking, especially my right. I should have stayed in alone and gotten myself under control the way I usually did.

"You're a fucking asshole," Jennifer screeched, coaxing a malicious smile from me. She had no idea how right she was.

"I never claimed I wasn't." I took a drag and stared at the glowing cherry on the end of the cigarette as it slowly burned. Sometimes I felt like that bright ember, other times like a pathetic pile of ash.

Jennifer left, slamming the door behind her. She knew she wouldn't get any more of my attention tonight. Silence fell inside my room and I tried to get my thoughts in order. I had to admit that I was surprised—that had never happened to me before. I'd never thought about one woman while I was with another like that.

I didn't even remember exactly what had happened with Selene, and that tormented me. I knew that I was her first and that I'd taken her virginity, but all the details were fuzzy. I felt an irrepressible urge to relive that singular moment between us—sober this time—and commit it to memory. I wanted to brand her slender body as my own.

Out of love? No. Out of pure selfishness.

....

The next morning, I got up with the sun. Ever since I was small, I had believed that by doing this I would be able to anticipate my own fate for the day and change it. Obviously, it was just a delusion of mine, but I still did it when I needed to keep a wretched feeling at bay. Like my anger, which had gotten increasingly unmanageable since I'd quit therapy.

I took a shower—the first of many—and went down to the kitchen for a coffee. Then, I went out into the garden and lit up a cigarette.

"Good morning, Neil," said Anna, appearing before me with her hands folded in front of her, already looking tired. It couldn't have been easy, taking care of a huge house like ours without any help. Yet Anna was always good natured. Maybe that was why I actually got along with her.

"Good morning, Miss Anna." I stubbed out the cigarette butt in the ashtray and got up out of the deckchair. Anna tilted her head to look me in the face and smiled at me.

"I made breakfast for you," she informed me sweetly with that maternal air that she had always reserved for me, ever since I was a child.

"It's freezing out here," she chided me, as I was wearing just a pullover and a pair of jeans. It was cold outside, but I didn't care.

"I'm not hungry. You don't have to worry about me." I rested my hand on her shoulder and we walked into the kitchen together, where we found my mother and Matt deep in conversation.

I muttered a cursory "good morning" and went up to my room to grab my car keys before I needed to head to campus. I was thinking about becoming an architect, despite firmly believing that graduating with a degree was an impossibility for someone like me. I had given up on life. Hope was the small, bright lamp in the recesses of the soul, but mine worked only intermittently. When it flickered off, I became more unstable and the nightmares of the past came back to me. Though, if anyone ever asked, I would deny those nightmares even existed.

I walked back to my room, lost in these dark reflections, when my attention immediately snagged on Selene's half-open door. I drew closer and saw her sitting on the end of her bed, trying to put her shoes on one-handed while holding a cell phone in the other.

"I can never forgive him, Mom," she said decisively. A lock of auburn hair fell across her face and she immediately tucked it behind her ear. "Yes, I know that. I *am* trying to build a relationship with Matt."

What a little liar.

She wasn't trying to clear up anything with her father; she simply ignored him whenever she found herself sharing space with him. I knew that the state of affairs was hurting Matt quite a bit.

Selene got up from the bed and bent over to pick up her bag off the floor, giving me the opportunity to study her ass. The tight jeans she wore showed it off to divine effect. It was small but high and firm—the perfect size for my hands and for all those fantasies about her that I wanted to make reality.

I'd been with many women in my life, but in that moment, I must have looked like a teenage boy, drooling over an ass like I'd never seen one before. *You are an idiot,* I thought to myself, leaning against the doorframe. Slowly, I nudged the door open with my foot.

Selene got off the phone, turned around, and jumped.

"How long have you been there?" she demanded, annoyed, as she eyed me up and down. The way she flushed told me that Babygirl liked what she saw—more than just a little bit, too.

"Long enough to know that you're lying to Mommy," I teased, winking at her.

"Were you eavesdropping?" She looked at me like I was a serial killer. It was honestly adorable.

"Actually, I was checking out that cute little ass of yours, Tinkerbell," I admitted easily. Her ocean eyes grew wide, and she blushed again. She still hadn't gotten used to my plain speaking. She stood there, defiant, with her arms folded.

"You have a few screws loose," she said rudely. Then, she approached me and tried to pass, but I stuck out my arm to block her way.

"Where do you think you're going, Tigress?" I teased her in a low tone. Selene drew herself up stiffly, and my eyes fell to her breasts, small and perky, left partially exposed by her simple camisole. I wanted to rip it off her and suck on her skin until I left bruises. Yes, I very much wanted to do that. Again.

"What the hell is your problem?" She stared me down. She was pretending to be mad at me, but I knew full well that my attentions did not displease her.

They never displeased any woman.

"I have this one in particular…" I grabbed her wrist and pushed her back against the doorframe. "Between my legs." I spread myself over her like a blanket and heard her small, surprised gasp when I pressed my pelvis against her.

I adored her innocence. She was just a girl, ignorant of the world's dangers.

"Is there no one else available to resolve your…problem?" she asked challengingly, but she didn't move away. We remained pressed against each other, our skin separated only by a few layers of clothing.

"I know of several available people, but the usual gets so boring. More difficult challenges, however, get me going." I stressed the last few words, and just to really clarify the concept, I pushed my hips forward to make her feel every bit of my desire for her. From her burning face, I deduced that I had done this quite thoroughly.

"Stop it; someone could see us." She shoved me roughly away, and I burst into laughter at her delayed reaction. The contact between us had made her feel all the same things I did; I was sure of it.

I backed away and Selene ran off, taking all her embarrassment and her innocence with her. I hoped she'd never stop being herself—genuine in everything she did. It was what set her apart from all the rest.

Once the Tigress had vanished down the stairs, I checked my watch and saw what time it was. I hurried to my room and grabbed my car keys before heading back downstairs. Before I got to the front door, I spotted Selene asking Anna about Logan. She probably needed a ride to school, but my brother had gone out the previous night and hadn't yet returned. So luck was on my side today.

"Great, so I'm getting there on foot. I'll have to catch the bus," she groused before telling Anna goodbye. Then she turned, spotted me, and tried to pretend she hadn't, but her shimmery eyes were drawn like a magnet to my smug smile.

"What are you grinning about?" she snapped at me, and I found it absolutely hilarious.

"Want a lift?" I offered kindly. Selene shot me a suspicious look. Maybe she had realized that unmotivated kindness wasn't something I possessed?

"Thanks, but no." Her rejection was firm and came with a rude scowl. Surrender, however, wasn't in my wheelhouse either.

"I won't bite, Tinkerbell. Come on," I murmured slyly and headed out the door toward my car. Selene didn't answer me, but I heard her footsteps following along behind me. The sky had turned leaden, and it looked like rain.

I sat down behind the wheel and watched her settle herself in the passenger seat without saying a word. The interior of the car was instantly invaded by the smell of coconut. I tried to focus on driving, but my eyes kept getting pulled her way. I glanced furtively at her for the umpteenth time and caught her producing a sleepy little yawn.

"Didn't get enough sleep?" I drummed my fingers on the steering wheel as we paused at a traffic light.

"Actually, I stayed in the living room, so no, I didn't get very good sleep," she grumbled irritably, watching the world outside through the window.

"Why?" I asked. I already knew why, but I liked messing with her.

"Because Jennifer was in your room, and I didn't want to listen to her yowling," she explained, just a hint of annoyance in her voice. It was then that I burst out laughing for real. Babygirl really was adorable.

"What's so funny?" She cocked an eyebrow and gave me a side-eye.

"Nothing, I just think you're genuinely funny."

The green light appeared. I accelerated, returning my focus to the road.

"And I think you're genuinely an asshole. It doesn't matter a bit to you that our rooms are close together and that I can hear everything, does it?"

She was right—being generally inconsiderate was another of my many flaws. If I needed to fuck, I fucked. If I wanted to get loud, I got loud. Simple. I didn't care about anyone's complaints, least of all hers.

"Sex is relaxing; you should give it a try. Maybe when you're sober," I taunted her. It was a shame I couldn't turn my head to watch her blush.

"I focus on other activities to relax, like reading or walking in the park. You could consider something like that, you know?" she responded, and I was reminded once again of just how different she was from the other girls I dated.

"You're such a child," I said, just to needle her.

"Excuse me?" She sounded surprised and perturbed.

"You're still a girl," I repeated, parking the car in front of campus. We had reached our destination.

"Just because I hadn't had sex with anyone before..." She stopped herself and stared through the windshield at the students walking into the university. She struck me as pensive.

"Don't get me wrong, I'm honored to have been your first," I admitted in a subdued tone. Selene had ducked her head and was wringing her hands, avoiding my stare. I got the feeling she was still guilty over having given herself to someone who was essentially a complete stranger. I was used to sleeping with girls whose names I wouldn't remember or even care about forgetting. My body had no value in that way, but hers still did.

"I wasn't trying to be insulting." I cleared my throat, trying to smooth over some of the awkwardness that I had created.

"It doesn't matter," she whispered, but I knew full well that it did matter to her.

"You and Jennifer… Are you…?" she asked abruptly, probably trying to change the subject.

"Together?" I finished for her. "Nah," I grinned, shaking my head. "I'm not the relationship type."

"Yeah, I figured. After all, sex is like a sport for you, isn't it?" she taunted me. I could see from the look on her face that she disapproved, but that was nothing new.

"I get the feeling that there's a lot of suffering in your past…" she stated with a certainty that struck me dumb. I scratched my eyebrow with my thumb and sighed. I never talked to anyone about my past. It was a part of me that I couldn't let anyone but myself see. I couldn't show her the monster that I really was.

"And I get the feeling that you still haven't forgiven yourself for what happened between the two of us," I answered, shifting the focus of the conversation back on to her.

While we were talking, a few girls waved hello to me as they passed my car, and I acknowledged them with a lift of my chin but never took my attention from Selene.

Babygirl licked her lower lip and then bit it, shaking her head. "You didn't need to say that." She tried to get out of the car, but I immediately grabbed her by the wrist.

"Wait," I whispered, my eyes drilling into hers. "I think we should have a redo," I told her. I knew that she'd think I was insane, but I didn't give a shit. I needed her. If I just fucked her one more time, maybe I could stop imagining how her face would look as she climaxed beneath me.

"What?" she asked incredulously. She clearly wasn't expecting me to make that kind of proposition to her.

"I want you, Selene. I may seem like a lunatic to you, but that's the way I am. I always say what I'm thinking, especially to women. I'll say it again: I want you," I told her, never taking my eyes off hers. In that moment, she looked smaller, more afraid and more confused than ever, and I got the feeling that we occupied two different universes, light-years apart. Still, I didn't retract my suggestion.

"God, Neil," she sighed, running a hand through her hair. She sat back against the seat, and I released her wrist so I wouldn't hurt her.

"I have to sort things out with Jared. And besides, I'm Matt's daughter... I'm... I..." she stammered, confused and torn between her guilt and her desire. I imagined her walking a slender tightrope, balanced precariously between the world of perdition—my world—and her world, an illusion of perfection.

"You lost your virginity to me, and you don't even remember it. I just wanted to give you the opportunity to make up for it, because I get that your first time was a big deal for you," I said softly, trying to sound convincing. Still, she resisted me, shaking her head.

"Are you trying to do me a favor?" She laughed hysterically, like the entire situation was totally surreal to her.

"No, I'd just like to give you another shot," I admitted, staring into her eyes. I wanted to stop thinking about her in such a sick way—I'd even conjured her up when I was with Jennifer, for Christ's sake. I was certain that us having sex again would put an end to my torment and her feelings of guilt. We could sleep together one more time, and it would fix everything. Both of us could go on with our lives without ever again thinking about what had happened between us.

"You're insane! Truly nuts! I'm going to class." Selene started to open the door, but I reached out and pulled it shut. We weren't finished yet. I and I alone was the one who decided when my games began and when they ended.

"We've kissed already, and you've slept with me. What's the point of fighting something that you want just as much as I do?" My face was very close to her. The smell of coconut was drugging; it shocked me. I wanted to kiss her in a way I'd never wanted to kiss anyone before. Typically, I kissed women to disarm them so I could fuck them, not because I actually wanted to kiss for its own sake.

"I'm not promising you a love story out of a movie or a book. I'm just offering you the opportunity to use me to jog your memory."

Selene stared at me like I'd lost my mind.

"*Use* you?" she echoed, horrified. "I don't use people, Neil." She didn't understand me. No one could, least of all her. I sighed in exasperation, but I didn't lose my patience, which was unusual for me.

"At least think about it." I pulled back and dug in my jeans for my pack of Winstons.

"About getting fucked by you?" She grinned sarcastically before muttering incomprehensibly under her breath.

"We can make love, if you want…" I suggested. Selene burst out laughing—it seemed that she couldn't believe her ears.

"How do you make love to someone without loving them?" she asked reflectively. Her attitude was making my head hurt. I was tired of constantly coming up with new forms of persuasion.

"You're sharp," I told her. I brought a cigarette to my lips and lit it, buying myself some time.

"You're screwing with me, aren't you?" she asked indignantly. She pinched the bridge of her nose with two fingers like I was causing a nervous breakdown.

"Perceptive, too." I exhaled my smoke into her face and she squinted, coughing.

"I'm out of here. I don't waste my time with assholes," she spat out irritably. She climbed out of the car furiously and gave the door an aggressive slam for good measure.

"Have a great day, Tinkerbell," I said, waving at her from the half-open window. She didn't respond, except to lift her middle finger at me. I watched her firm, beautiful ass walk away and found myself thinking that she really was a fairy creature.

Just adorable.

But Babygirl had already lost me too much time.

I ran a hand through my hair as I walked across campus toward the art building, trying not to notice the furtive glances some of the other students gave me. Some of them were attracted to me; others were afraid of me and just wanted to stay out of my way. All of them knew my reputation.

"Look who finally showed up." Jennifer appeared alongside me with a frosty look and an irritated tone.

"Hey, Blondie." I stopped to loom over her, touching her cheek and giving her one of my winning smiles. Though I felt no regret about how I'd treated her in my room and would never apologize to her, I still needed to at least pretend to be sorry, if only to maintain the harmony of our friend group. I hated fighting with Jennifer or Alexia in particular because, like all women, they tended to hold grudges and dragged out disagreements forever.

"Oh, now you wanna acknowledge me," she answered stiffly. I wasn't sure if she was actually still angry, but what I did know was that Jennifer loved to be on the receiving end of my attention. They were suffocating—her jealousy and her habitual pushiness. She wanted to know who I was seeing, who I was talking to, who I was going out with. This behavior of hers often reminded me of Scarlett, and I wondered if I was the common denominator, driving women to new levels of crazy.

Scarlett…

Every time I thought about her, anguish bled into me like a poison.

"Are you bringing your stepsister to school now, too? How cute." Jennifer's mocking voice shook me from my reverie. My first class started in less than ten minutes.

"Get off my back," I snapped, annoyed. "I do what I want with whoever I want."

I walked away from her, feeling in my pockets for my package of Winstons. I could never tell Jennifer about what happened with Selene, otherwise Babygirl would become a target like every other person I slept with. I'd already said too much when I told her Selene was Matt's daughter.

"You never turn me down," Jennifer said as she followed along behind me, intending to continue the argument. She was right. I never turned her down, and I certainly never turned down her top-notch oral skills. Blondie really knew how to work her tongue.

"There's a first time for everything." I lit up a cigarette and continued walking briskly, listening to her hastening footfalls behind me. I smiled in satisfaction at the thought of her having to chase me. It always pleased me to know that I was pushing her buttons.

"Bullshit, you—"

I didn't let her get any further. I turned abruptly and grabbed her by one of the French braids along the side of her head. Then I used it to tug her face up until it was barely an inch from mine, staring into her eyes. Jennifer held her breath and swallowed hard, alarmed by my vehemence.

"Don't make me angry, Jen," I hissed furiously.

I could feel the stares of the students all around us but no one seemed surprised by the pathetic scene, nor did anyone attempt to intervene.

Jennifer grimaced in pain but said nothing, aware that she was on thin ice.

"Just shut the fuck up, and quit busting my balls." I released her, letting her stagger back and then walked away.

There were limits with me that couldn't be pushed. It was dangerous, because beyond those limits lay the territory of the beast.

9

SELENE

Neil was completely insane.

Did he seriously think that making the same mistake all over again was the answer? No way.

And yet, there was a part of me that wanted to take him up on it, and I felt tortured by my need to do right by Jared. I rolled over in bed and shut the book I was reading. I tried every way I could think of to distract myself, but nothing could get it out of my head: the wicked temptation to give in to him again.

When it came to Neil, it seemed that my rational mind always lost out to my need to know more about him, to understand his troubled soul. I could tell that his careless front was just one of the many masks he wore, and I couldn't say why, but I wanted to peel away each one and learn all the facets of him.

I picked up my phone and tried texting Jared again. I'd asked him to come visit me in New York so we could talk, but his commitments prevented him from traveling.

"Dammit!" I said aloud when he answered with yet another

message saying that he couldn't come to New York that weekend either.

I was so tired of living with the burden of what I had done. Telling him the truth and setting him free for good was the right thing to do, but I couldn't bring myself do it over a text message or even a phone call.

I headed downstairs for dinner and took my seat at the table with Matt, Mia, and Logan. Chloe was out with Carter again, and Neil was in the wind. I had promised myself that I was going to get something in my stomach—I was eating very little, and it was making me feel increasingly fuzzy and anxious.

On top of everything else, I didn't have any friends I could trust with my troubles, and I felt so awfully alone. I'd thought about confiding in my mom, but the idea of her getting angry at me was horrifying. She wasn't the right person to ask for advice about this. I would just have to face it on my own. Like always.

I toyed with the food on my plate and smiled at Anna when she asked me if everything tasted all right. In reality, I only reluctantly ate the delicacies she had prepared. I was too torn up inside, worried, and depressed.

"Hey.... everything okay?" Logan asked, scooting closer to me. I just nodded, hoping I looked convincing.

"So, kids…" Matt patted his lips with his napkin and looked at me and Logan. "How's school going? Tell me all about it." He rested his chin on his fist and awaited our responses.

"Well, I'm ready now for a test at the end of the month," Logan began, giving me some time to come up with something cogent to say.

"Glad to hear it, you never let us down, Logan," my father commented with pride.

"Good job, Pup," Mia praised him, one hand pressed to her chest.

"Mom," he chided her sternly and reddened in embarrassment.

124

I barely restrained my laughter.

"And what about you, Selene? What's going on with you?" Matt prompted me.

"I'm adjusting," I answered shortly, nibbling on a piece of bread just to keep myself busy.

Matt didn't push and dropped his eyes to his plate, clearly disappointed by my attitude. Mia patted his shoulder in reassurance, but I didn't feel any pity for him.

After that, dinner proceeded in monastic silence. Occasionally, I would respond to Jared's text messages, but Neil was the one who was really on my mind. I jumped at every noise from outside and expected to hear the roar of his engine at any moment. How was I supposed to ignore that sinful smile and matching body when he walked in the door? Would I even be capable of it?

Though I was feeling tense, I remained politely seated at the table until everyone had finished their dinner. For a second, I thought I was going to get away clean, but then I heard the click of a lock and the front door opened.

I stiffened immediately and poured some more water into my glass just to hide my obvious nerves.

"Neil, darling, is that you? Come in here with us for a minute. There's still some dessert left." Mia gestured toward the kitchen, but her son didn't bother to dignify her with a response. He took the stairs briskly and retreated into his room.

Logan threw a worried glance at his mother, and a strange sort of understanding passed between them. A moment later, Mia nodded almost imperceptibly at Logan, who immediately stood up and cleared his throat.

"Uh, please excuse me, I'm going upstairs for a minute," he announced before backing away from the table and heading quickly to the stairs. What was going on? I tried to project an air of indifference, but it was obvious to me that something wasn't right.

Unable to tolerate the fraught atmosphere at the table anymore, I made my excuses and left to go to my own room. I wanted to take a hot bath and watch a movie in bed.

I was almost there, too, when I was stopped in the hallway by the sounds of shouting coming from Neil's room.

"It's none of your business!" Neil's deep baritone voice bellowed.

"I'm just trying to help you; don't you get that?" Logan responded, alarmed.

I chewed nervously on the inside of my cheek. I wanted to hear what they were arguing about, but it seemed like a sibling issue, and I had no right to eavesdrop on them. It would have been disrespectful.

So, despite my curiosity, I walked to my room, determined not to insert myself. Then, suddenly, I heard a loud thud and instinctively ran for Logan to make sure that he was okay and hadn't run afoul of Neil's wrath.

I threw open the door of the next room, looking first at Neil, standing in front of his brother, and then at the room surrounding them, which appeared to have been devastated by a tornado. A lamp had been shattered against the wall, tiny shards lay on the floor among a few loose books.

"It's fine, Selene. Get out of here," Logan said placatingly. I should have listened to him but my legs wouldn't obey me.

"You leave too, and get off my dick!" Neil thundered at his brother. His golden eyes were dull and blank. The black of his pupils sucked up all the gleaming honey that I'd admired so much. Neil was dripping sweat, his fisted hands were trembling and his breathing was irregular.

"Selene, please go away," Logan pleaded, shooting me a worried look. It was wrong of me to butt in, but...

"I-I thought something had happened to you. I heard a loud noise and..." My voice trailed off.

"Nothing happened. It's best if you just go back to your room," Logan pressed, and I decided to listen to him. I nodded and apologized, and I was about to walk out the door when Neil let out a wicked laugh that nailed me to the spot, sending shivers down my spine.

I spun around, terrified.

"Yeah, Selene, go back to your room. But come back to mine when you want a ride later. Maybe when you're drunk." He gave me an evil wink, and I blushed with shame. Was he crazy? Did he want Logan to figure out what had happened? I paled, unable to speak.

"What the fuck are you talking about, Neil?" Logan cut in obliviously. "Selene, don't listen to him, he's not himself right now," Logan added, scrambling to excuse him.

I tried to walk away, I really did. I was on edge and afraid as Neil approached me. Immediately, I could smell his distinctive scent and I stared at him. Dressed all in black with a cruel expression on his face and both fists clenched, he looked like the devil incarnate. The fresh purple love bite on his neck and his disheveled hair told me he'd just been with someone, which caused a stab of pain in my chest.

"Tigress..." he whispered, his eyes fixed on my mouth. I swallowed and waited for him like a sacrificial victim offering herself up to the executioner.

"Do you want to know what happened with Jennifer the other day?" he asked, and I could feel his breath on my face.

I tried to stay cool, but my legs had started to tremble. Slowly, I turned my gaze to Logan, who was staring fixedly at his brother. I slowly exhaled, aware that any misstep here could endanger me.

"I thought about you while she was trying to blow me." He walked past me and stopped right behind me. Logan's eyes narrowed warily while I remained completely motionless.

Neil stood behind me for a few seconds, smelling my hair and gently touching my arm, which grew tense under his provocative touch.

"Do you know what hell really is?" He moved a strand of hair away from the side of my face and blew softly into my ear. I shivered, trying to keep my wits about me, trying to keep breathing.

"Hmm?" he murmured, slowly pressing his pelvis against my butt. I tried to pull myself free, but Neil put a hand on my stomach to keep me plastered against him.

"I don't think I do," I managed nervously. I felt trapped against the solid marble of his body, which could have crushed me at any time.

"Hell is a world away. Away from hope, love, trust, and reason. It's an empty space where all you do is fight to survive among people just as evil as you are." All at once, he grabbed me by the hair and forcefully pulled my head back. I let out a cry of surprise, and Logan took a step toward us but froze when Neil gave him a warning look.

I squeezed my eyes shut from the pain in my scalp. I wasn't processing anything. Why was he acting like this? It occurred to me that I didn't actually know him at all. When I twisted my head slightly to meet his eyes, I found them distant, completely disconnected from reality.

"If my brother wasn't here…" he whispered in my ear, "I would've already pounded you into that bed," he finished, pressing a brief kiss to my neck. A second later, he let me go roughly, and the only reason I didn't fall over was because Logan caught me before I could.

"Out," Neil ordered in a tone that brooked no argument and gestured at the door. Logan and I obeyed him.

I turned one last time before I left the room and saw Neil sitting on the floor in a shadowy corner. He hugged his knees to his chest and wore a lost look on his face. Slowly, he began to rock back and forth, hitting his head against the wall, his hands crawling up to his temples. It was disconcerting to see him like that, suddenly so fragile and vulnerable.

There was no trace left of the confident, menacing young man of just a few moments before.

He looked instead like a lonely and remote child, cast out and suffering.

Logan shut the door, preventing me from continuing to look at him, and I shook myself.

"We should go to bed." He gave a frustrated sigh. He seemed used to living with that kind of incident.

I, on the other hand, was shaken, unable to even move.

"But…" I didn't want to go and leave Neil all alone like that. We needed to call someone, maybe a doctor or even an ambulance. He might do something drastic. I was terrified, but Logan seemed significantly calmer than I was. He gave me a searching look as he rested his hands on my shoulders, which still wouldn't stop shaking.

"He'll get better. Today was just a bad day."

His calm tone of voice reassured me even though it was clear that he was also hurting a lot for his brother.

What had happened to him?

One thing was clear to me: hell existed, because I had seen it Neil's golden eyes.

10

·····························

SELENE

That night was one of the worst.

    I was restless, just tossing and turning in my bed. Every tiny noise agitated me further, and the sound of rain pattering on the window panes only made me more miserable.

I jumped at the thunder, lightning intermittently illuminating the walls around me. I pulled the blankets up to my nose, willing myself to calm down.

Sigh. I couldn't stop thinking about Neil and what had happened in his room just a few hours earlier. What was supposed to be a simple "bonding trip" to see my father was now turning into something else entirely. All of my plans had been upended. Neil had torn through the flowery meadow of my life like a hurricane.

I no longer knew who I was or what choices were the right ones or even what was going to become of me if I continued to live in this world of chaos. The adrenaline I now regularly felt coursing through me was not normal. I'd always lived a steady life, characterized by methodical actions and carefully considered choices. But now I was a ship at the mercy of the waves, not knowing where they might take me.

I had no idea what awaited me from one day to the next. But strangely, the not knowing made me feel alive.

Still restless, I stretched my arm out for the switch on the lamp and turned it on. I sat up in bed and looked around the room thoughtfully. If the thunder outside didn't stop, I wouldn't get a wink of sleep.

I was considering trying to go back to sleep when two raps at the door startled me. I threw aside the blankets and got out of the bed, creeping over to the door in my bare feet. I opened it slowly only to find Neil's honey-colored eyes fixed on me. It was then that it occurred to me that I was only wearing a pair of sleep shorts and a white T-shirt without a bra, so I blushed.

Neil stood with one hand resting on the doorframe, just a short distance from me.

"Can I come in?" he asked in a low tone, and his voice seemed somehow even deeper and more masculine to me. I had a moment of concern. After what happened earlier, I wasn't sure that I could trust him. He seemed calm at the moment, but I had clearly seen his rough, mercurial side.

"You don't need to be afraid of me; I just want to talk to you," he said softly, like he could read my mind.

After a couple more seconds' hesitation, I moved aside to let him in. He towered over me with his six-foot-plus frame, and I shut the door behind him.

He wanted to talk?

Well, I was listening.

"Talk to me," I prompted him, and he turned to face me. The dim lamp light only lit up half his face, but it was enough for me to linger on his unique, finely drawn features.

"No bra?" he started thoughtfully, staring at my chest. His eyes

131

were bright and intense now but no longer threatening. I tracked the direction of his stare and then folded my arms over my chest to shield myself from him.

"Do you think it's polite to point that out to me?" My voice trembled and I blushed. Before him, no one else had seen me naked.

"No, I'm sorry. I wasn't trying to embarrass you." He rubbed his neck and sighed, sitting down on the edge of the bed. He clasped his hands and balanced his elbows on his knees. He was buying himself some time before beginning his speech while I stayed right where I was.

I figured it was better to keep a good amount of distance between the two of us.

"At times..." he began, "I have these periods when it is very difficult to control myself..." Talking to me about this was clearly an enormous effort for him. His eyes were fixed on the floor, his muscles all tense and contracted. "I'm not trying to make excuses for myself, but I want you to know that I would never hurt you." He paused. "Not voluntarily," he added, sounding mortified. He looked so different from the boy I'd encountered just hours earlier. He was contemplative and present in the moment.

"I don't know who you are, Neil," I whispered, drawing his beautiful eyes to me.

"My name is Neil Miller. I was born on May third in New York. I have a brother and a—" he answered sardonically, but I shook my head and he stopped.

"I mean I don't know who you *really* are. You don't allow yourself to be known." I stood apart from him with my arms folded, but when his gaze dropped first to my bare legs and then to my bare feet, I trembled.

"I don't want you to know anything about me. I'd rather leave you the freedom to imagine me however you'd like." He got up from the bed and moved toward me.

No, no, no.

He was definitely crossing the boundary that I had internally imposed upon him to maintain my clear head. I backed up until I hit the wall, and he stopped and looked sorrowful.

"You don't want me to get near you." It wasn't a question; he saw how frightened I was. I gulped and shrugged.

"I'd rather you didn't," I admitted, and he winced like I'd slapped him. He stepped back and sat down on the bed again. I didn't understand how he could go from being so surly and vulgar to docile and compliant.

The variability alarmed me.

"Sometimes, difference is not accepted because it is not understood. That's the way of the world." He raised his eyes to me and his gaze had changed yet again. I could see the indomitable fire in his eyes, and once again, I caught of the glimpse of his anger, that part of himself that he was always trying to keep at bay.

I didn't want him to misinterpret me and think I was rejecting him for the same reason everyone else did. People usually didn't even try to explore the mysterious world inside him. But I had never been a surface-level kind of girl.

I took a few steps toward him. Unsure, weak, and slow, but still moving toward him. He kept still, watching me warily. I stopped a few inches from his body, my stomach level with his face. I could smell amber and tobacco. Instinctively, I reached out to stroke his hair, and he let me do it. It was soft to the touch. Clean, fragrant, and messy, just like always.

"Sometimes, we need a little help to understand difference. Some special people are a bit more complex than us mere mortals," I told him, and then I smiled and Neil looked at me with such blazing heat. He reached out for my right knee, still staring at me. He was tacitly asking for permission to touch me, and I didn't have the strength in that moment to push him away, so I nodded.

My consent obtained, he put both of his hands, warm and strong, on my knees. He moved them slowly up my thighs until they reached the hem of my shorts. I shivered at his seductive touch, freezing and yet fiery at the same time. He rubbed the fabric and then started upward again, this time all the way to the elastic band.

I could feel my heart pounding in my throat and shivers running down my spine, but I allowed myself to be explored. And when he hooked two fingers around my waistband, I let him. He slid the shorts down my legs and I stepped out of them. I was left in only my panties and T-shirt.

We stared into each other's eyes, fully aware of what was about to happen. Even I, who just moments ago had been so afraid of his presence, wanted nothing more than for his fingers to keep tracing new routes across the map of my body.

"Softly…" was all I said. He hadn't done anything to prompt me to whisper that small request, but he knew that he needed to be gentle, and he smiled at me. Then he delicately raised the hem of my T-shirt and pressed a kiss to my lower abdomen. I startled when I felt the stubble on his jaw, and Neil shot me an amused glance.

With another smile, he continued kissing my stomach, raising the fabric with one hand. He kissed my hips and my belly before I lifted my arms up to help him get my shirt off completely. The garment had landed somewhere on the floor, and I saw how his eyes were trained on my bare breasts.

I turned red, and he shook his head at my embarrassment. He rested his hands on my hips and traced the shape of them, like an artist might do with a sculpture. He was contemplating me, adoring me, even with all my flaws. He encircled my breasts with his large hands, then he coaxed out my nipples and took one between his lips. Softly, out of deference for my earlier request. I felt his damp tongue moving in circles, and I squeezed my eyes shut. Rising and falling to the silent music of our desire, I slipped a hand into his hair and pulled him tight against my chest.

I had never experienced anything like it before, but I immediately understood why women loved this kind of thing. A strange warm feeling spread from where his lips touched me to down between my thighs. I still had time to stop it—to stop him—but I wanted him.

Sure, it was a contradiction, fearing and wanting a person at the same time, but I couldn't seem to help myself.

All at once, Neil quit teasing my breasts and stood up. I found myself leaning on his still fully clothed body and shivered from the cold. He stared deeply into my eyes, maybe wondering if he should stop or keep going. There were so many things I wanted to tell him, but my feelings were so intense they prevented me from speaking.

He brushed his knuckles across my cheek and studied the features of my face: my forehead, my eyes, my nose, my lips. I was afraid he wouldn't like what he saw, and that insecurity had me lowering my chin to escape his stare. Neil however, dispelled my fears, taking my hands and putting them on the hem of his tank top. He wanted me to undress him, that was obvious, and I felt a thrill of embarrassment over my inexperience.

Were there certain rules one was meant to follow when undressing a man? I didn't know, and I couldn't think clearly with all the tension in the air.

"I'm nervous," I whispered, and he gave me knowing, indulgent look. He moved without haste, in a reassuring sort of way, because I was so terribly awkward and taut as a violin string.

"Keep going." He put his hands over mine and guided them slowly upward before letting me continue on my own. I pulled his shirt up to his shoulders, but he was so tall that he had to help me out for the last bit. I took it off him and tossed it carelessly somewhere on the floor.

Then, I examined the half-moon shape of his pectoral muscles, the delineating lines of his abs, and the V of his pelvic area, still mostly covered by his pants. Once again, my eyes snagged on the tattoo around his left hip, the lines of it intersecting to form some sort of symbol, but I was too flustered to examine it in detail.

I had no idea what I was supposed to do.

Should I touch him? Kiss him? Seduce him in some way?

I started to panic. I stepped back and all my inexperience reared its head just to remind me how completely inappropriate and unprepared I was for an expert like him.

He was going to laugh when he realized what a little nothing I was, how incapable I was of pleasing him the way other girls did.

"Sorry... I... I..." I babbled. I wanted to run—run anywhere—just to get away from that powerful, imposing body. "I don't know what to do... I don't know where to start..." I blathered on, shaking. I even forgot about my near-nudity. My legs were beginning to feel unsteady, and I nearly fell, but Neil caught me with one arm. My breasts pressed against his bare chest, and I sucked in a breath. For the first time, I was skin to skin with him, and it felt incredible.

"Everything's going to be okay. Calm down. Keep going," he repeated in a low voice, and I nodded along. He pressed closer to me and kissed my neck while my frozen hands remained motionless on his hard abdomen. I closed my eyes and tried to focus on nothing but the slow, expert way his lips moved over my skin. I was sure that he could feel the beat of my heart, now noticeably erratic.

He kissed me just underneath my ear, and I couldn't help but smile because his stubble created just the right amount of friction there—pleasant and arousing at the same time. He kept peppering my jaw and cheeks with kisses before moving on to my lips. He paused and I opened my eyes to find him staring right at me.

Was he still looking for confirmation from me? It was clear by this point that I didn't want him to stop.

"Keep going," I whispered and our gazes intertwined like a golden rope between us.

Then, Neil brushed my lips with a series of small, fleeting kisses that only deepened my desire for more contact with him. Unconsciously, my hands drifted down, and I traced the ridges of his sculpted abdomen. I'd never touched anyone that way before.

A moment later, his mouth crashed down onto mine. I shut my eyes and welcomed his hot tongue as it began to gently swirl in time with mine. I touched his hips then moved up to his back. I drew my fingers down the line of his spine all the way to his firm ass. I realized that, under his tutelage, I was developing some ease and a sense of spontaneity.

He continued kissing me, and as he did so, gently pushed me down until I was lying on the bed. I felt my naked shoulders hit the coolness of the sheets.

"Everything all right?" he asked, holding himself over me on his elbows. I nodded and spread my legs so he could position himself between them. I could tell that he was trying not to crush me with his weight, and I felt something hard pressing against my groin. I went red, and in that moment, it really occurred to me how men and women were perfectly matched in this way.

"What are you thinking?" he whispered, giving my neck a soft kiss. He was trying to give me time to get used to what was happening, and I appreciated it.

"It's silly," I answered as Neil's mouth roamed freely over my body. He stopped kissing me and looked down at me curiously.

"I want to hear it anyway," he insisted and I sighed.

"A man and a woman..." I cleared my throat awkwardly. "Our bodies fit together so perfectly. I hadn't really noticed before. It's... ordinary but also kind of magical," I said softly, hoping he wasn't about to laugh in my face.

But his face remained serious as he leaned in close to my ear, his chest pressing against mine. "I haven't even begun to show you how perfectly a man and woman can fit together," he said in an obscene whisper as he kissed my cheek. I stared dazedly at him, my thighs trembling as though he had a direct line of communication to them.

Neil began kissing my neck again, moving his hips slowly against me. At first, I didn't understand what he was trying to do but when I felt his erection bumping into my still-panty-covered clit, I figured it out. Then, I got so aroused that I didn't need to understand anything anymore.

I held still, though, and let him take the lead.

"Relax..." He'd noticed how tense I'd gone and slowed down his ministrations. I closed my eyes and focused on the feelings his body produced in me. Before I could stop myself, I had reached out and grasped the waistband of his pants and started writhing underneath him. As I did so, Neil continued to kiss me everywhere. Anywhere his hands touched, his lips followed. All at once, he descended to play with my breasts. He sucked softly on them and my back bowed.

Then, he moved down further and dragged his lips across my stomach. He licked my abdomen and toyed with my belly button. He circled it with his tongue and then looked up at me, his fingertips brushing the edge of my panties.

I stared at him in confusion before I understood what he intended to do. "No! Not that!" I threw out an arm to stop him. I slammed my legs together and went rigid again. Letting him do *that* for me would have been mortifying. I was not yet an uninhibited person and still retained my sense of modesty.

"No? You sure? Women usually like it quite a bit." I would have preferred it if he hadn't reminded me of just how many other women he'd pleasured right at that moment. I frowned and looked up at the ceiling, realizing that I was putting some unfair expectations on him. Neil was no Prince Charming. He had been clear about that:

this wouldn't a love story out of a novel or a movie. So why did I have that strange, uncomfortable feeling in the pit of my stomach?

I needed to protect my heart. I was so much more sensitive than him. If I wasn't careful, I was going to get burned.

"You're thinking too much." He crawled back over me and stroked my hair. I was still considering the possible fallout of my feelings.

"I know...." I sighed, attempting to look anywhere but at his eyes. The alarm bells had started going off in my head by this point, but I didn't want to heed them.

"Let's take it one step at a time, okay? I want you to be comfortable," he whispered, trying to draw my focus back to him.

"I…"

He kissed me, interrupting all of my thoughts. His tongue found mine, and I allowed myself to be carried away by the kiss because Neil demanded every bit of my attention. He was gentle but firm. He knew what he was doing; his greater experience was very obvious, and I felt somewhat lacking when I realized I wasn't participating at all. I was practically motionless beneath him, frigid and apathetic.

So I mustered my courage and kissed him back more intensely, moving against his body. I heard him emit a pleased sigh, which flattered my feminine pride. Then, Neil reached down to fondle my breast before going even further, all the way down until he reached my pubic mound. He slipped a hand into my already-damp panties and began touching me. I turned a violent red at the realization that I was already wet for him, but I shoved aside the embarrassment and just kept kissing him as his fingers worked between my legs.

I panted, trying to take in more air while Neil teased me all over. He was so assured and capable of pleasuring multiple points on my body all at once with the same intensity. I, on the other hand, could not keep up. I was afraid I was going to have a heart attack before we even got to the main event.

"Softly…" I whispered again when I felt his fingers grow more fervent against me. He wasn't hurting me, but my brain had fully short-circuited, and I was afraid of feeling pain even as my body was adapting to these mysterious new feelings.

"I'm not going to hurt you. I promise," he whispered against my lips and one of his fingers slipped inside me, followed swiftly by a second. My body received his touch as though it had been designed just for me. It didn't hurt. It made me feel hot, liquid, overstimulated. Neil moved his fingers in a rhythm that seemed precisely calculated to deliver just the right amount of pleasure.

I kissed him with everything I had, biting his lip. The next moment, Neil stopped to take off his pants. I was too embarrassed to risk looking down, but Neil didn't give me time to overthink it: he stretched out on top of me again and his arousal pressed between my thighs. It was hard and formidable. Extremely formidable, even covered by the thin fabric of his boxers.

"You ever touch yourself here?" he continued to rub himself against that small single point at the top of my sex, so central to a woman's physical pleasure, and my body's reaction was instantaneous: descent into a state of pure lust.

"No," I admitted timidly, and he began kissing me again. My inexperience didn't seem to discourage him; if anything, it was the opposite: a new light gleamed in his brilliant eyes.

"Selene…" He stopped suddenly and pressed his forehead to mine. Both of us were panting, ready to possess and be possessed. Only our last small layers of fabric kept us apart. "You have to tell me now if you want to stop. After this… it's not going to be possible anymore." We stared at each other, and I felt a flicker of uncertainty, immediately swept away by our labored breaths that chased one another and our heartbeats that sounded in unison.

"I don't want you to stop," I told him.

Neil dropped a chaste kiss on my lips and then sat up on his knees, exposing his incredible body to me. It was too perfect, too virile. I knew that he was only going to be mine for this one night, because I could see for myself just how unattainable he really was.

He touched my thighs and grasped my panties. He pulled them down and off, kissing my ankle and still looking directly at me. I searched his eyes for the certainty I needed to keep following his lead, and Neil knew it. I blushed as his golden stare caressed my entire body, lingering on my sex, which was now completely exposed. I wanted to shut my legs but I couldn't move. Neil smiled reassuringly at me and then took off his boxers. Instinctively, I looked up at his face because I didn't have the courage to look anywhere else. I was pretty sure I was blushing again.

"Are you embarrassed to look at me?" He was stretched out on top of me and feeling him, completely naked and warm and in contact with every part of me was more lovely than I could have imagined. His erection pressed stiffly against my lower abdomen. I realized definitively that I'd been incorrect about his size in our earlier interaction. But it had only ever been random nonsense anyway, my stupid desire to get a dig in on him.

"Yes," I admitted, still trying to control my curiosity and not glance down. Just feeling him against me was enough to know that I was done for—I was going to be sore tomorrow.

"You can't have passion without nudity," he informed me. He shifted slightly, lining himself up with my entrance, the place where my body would welcome his. I parted my lips and exhaled rapidly. I grabbed his biceps and he gave me a reassuring look, warm and intense. In his eyes, I saw the sun, the moon, the stardust sprinkled across the night sky.

All at once, I was ready. I wanted it.

It was then that his member began to glide slowly over my sex, presaging the pleasure it would give me once it got inside. The feeling was new and overpowering; so beautiful that it hurt.

"Ready?" he whispered in my ear. I flattened my hands against his powerful back, gripped his pelvis between my knees and looked at him.

"Yes." I touched my nose to his and Neil kissed me. At the same moment, I felt his penis pushing against my opening. He applied a little more pressure when my muscles resisted and then, with a single thrust, he slowly entered me.

I let out a hiss of pain, exhaling it against his lips as I felt him fully, in all his glory.

"Relax." He thrust again and my body molded itself to him, inch by inch, accommodating him. It felt cumbersome inside me, and I gave a pained moan at the acute discomfort of it. I bit my lower lip and he halted, concerned.

"Are you okay?" he asked softly. My knees were shaking and my heart had begun to pound. I was cold and sweating and yet, I still felt good. It was an odd sensation—painful and pleasant at the same time. My body seemed too small to fit around his. Thinking about this, I instinctively looked down at the place where we were joined. Neil was only halfway inside me. His penis was big, enormous. My anxiety swelled. I couldn't do this. It was too much. I... I...needed to get away.

"Your body can take me. Don't be afraid." He kissed the corner of my mouth and stroked my cheek with his thumb. It was incredible the way he seemed to read my mind. Had he been in this situation before? Perhaps some of his exes had been virgins like me? The thought sobered me. I wanted exclusivity. I wanted to be the only *something* for him, but with Neil, that was probably an impossibility.

"Quit thinking," he said before pushing deeper into me. I let out a moan of pain and pleasure, but then I immediately felt ashamed and shut my mouth.

He grinned at my involuntary reaction, stopped again, and we stared at each other for an indefinite period of time. Neil was thoughtful, while I was like a child, incapable of doing anything for herself.

"I should put on a condom, but I don't want to get up, walk naked down the hallway, go into my room, and grab one…" Neil had thought of a crucial detail that I myself had completely missed, and I cursed my stupidity. Protection was essential, how could I have forgotten? I'd been too horny to really comprehend what was happening.

"So?" I prompted him.

"Are you on the pill or anything? If you were, we wouldn't need one," he suggested and my eyes went wide. Sex between us could be even more intimate—maybe *too* intimate. I nodded and he shot me a sexy smile.

We communicated silently, then, our breath intermingling as we absorbed the feeling of our bodies adjusting to one another. Neil licked my bottom lip; he liked tasting me, and I liked it too. He stuck his tongue into my mouth, and automatically I raised my shoulders up slightly to suck on it.

Something flashed in his gleaming eyes, and he began penetrating me slowly again, stealing my breath. He sank into me and withdrew at a moderate, carefully calculated pace. I could see from the rigidity of his back muscles just how hard he was working to control himself and avoid hurting me.

He pulled out a little bit at a time before thrusting back in firmly, banking his strength. He closed his eyes and rested his forehead against mine. His elbows rested on either side of my face, his forearms supporting his weight and leaving his chest free to press down on me.

He continued to move carefully, moderately, but something in his face told me that this was costing him.

Maybe I was supposed to do something, too? Participate,

generate the right sort of chemistry and ease the way? The pain had evaporated by then and had been replaced by pleasure. I was yielding to him, accepting him without any barriers—physical or psychological—and I wanted him to be able to let go as well. So I began touching him back, mimicking his languid, measured motions. He breathing turned into a pant and I was delighted to realize that he was enjoying my taking initiative.

"Selene…" he gasped. We were both sweating and breathless yet neither of us had reached our climax.

"What is it?" I pushed damp strands of hair away from his forehead and stared at him. He was somehow even more beautiful with his face tightened in expectation.

"If you keep moving like that, I'll probably lose control. I'm trying to be gentle and…"

I touched his lip with my thumb and he licked it, bold and lustful.

"Be yourself," I told him. Neil gave me an amused grin and nipped at my finger.

"I like fucking, Selene. Kisses, soft touches, good manners—that's not me. Just enjoy this moment; I promised you I'd go easy."

So he was just faking this?

He moved to kiss me again, but I turned my face away to stop him. Once again, I found myself feeling small and too hopelessly naive to even understand his feelings. But I knew then, deep in my heart, that I needed to resist that impulse, to stop allowing myself to be the victim. So I looked him in the eye again and caught him giving me an evaluating look.

"So do it, then. Come on. Show me who you are, Neil," I challenged him, and his forehead creased up. My request surprised him, but I would rather he showed me his true face than the mask he felt the need to wear instead.

"You don't know what you're saying." He shook his head as he spoke, sounding derisive.

No, I didn't know, but I could find out.

"Come on!" I slapped his arm, and he lifted his torso slightly, arching his back. The movement shifted his penis inside me and drove it deeper, sending a pang of pleasure-pain through me until my teeth clenched.

"Just use me, Selene. I'm yours tonight. I want you to have the memory of this, the first time you always wanted." He leaned in for another intense kiss, picking up right where we'd left off before my request. And so I decided to stop insisting and stop worrying. I was going to think only about myself for once.

I would need to take responsibility for actions eventually, yes, but not in that moment. I could also stop worrying about the fake Prince Charming mask that Neil had put on. I was going to be selfish, even though I knew that I'd be sorry soon enough. I pulled him closer to me and let myself go.

We kissed each other and touched each other and joined with each other. Neil began to move more vigorously inside me. He thrust into me forcefully and then slowly withdrew, making me so aware of how fully he dominated me, even though I could tell he was still only using a fraction of the force he could have.

I bit his throat, and to my surprise, he let out a sigh of pure delight. Neil was quiet during sex, and hearing him moan was like spotting a shooting star in a sky full of clouds, both astonishing and extraordinary.

His panting breaths, which accelerated from time to time, also thrilled me. I was similarly enraptured by his body tensing beneath my fingertips. I had to frequently ask him to pause and let me breathe. He was too powerful, and my much smaller frame was frequently overcome by the mountain of muscles and testosterone that he was.

"You're so tight," he commented after what felt like an infinite amount of time. His baritone and the obscene tone of his voice made me blush.

"And you're too big," I sputtered, and he gave me a sly look.

"You should be happy about that." He gave me a chaste kiss on the lips and started moving again. Firm but measured. The bones in my hips and the muscles in my legs and my sex burned, but still Neil maintained his gentle yet passionate pace.

"I think I'm going to…" I wasn't exactly sure how to recognize an oncoming orgasm, but I believed that the magic was about to happen for me. His thrust his hips more fervently as my body tensed, craving more and more and more. I curled my toes into the mattress and tossed my head back into the pillow. I dug my nails into the smooth skin of Neil's back, and he moved his head to mouth my breast, which only intensified the already overwhelming sensations. I felt his tongue tease my flesh, his teeth sinking in, his lips enveloping me.

I writhed beneath him, the headboard hitting the wall in time with his thrusts, but neither of us could care that someone might hear us. I was on the brink, walking the edge of a precipice. My head spun and my heart was thumping like crazy. Was this how he'd made the others feel?

I tightened my knees around Neil's hips, and he must have liked that because he started moving more emphatically and clenched his glutes. I ran my hands all over him, delighting in that Adonis body that was so strong from every angle.

I focused on his reactions. He was silent, but he couldn't hide the change in his breathing. He was approaching his own limit.

"Come now," he ordered in a whisper. It was ridiculous, how my muscles actually reacted to that masculine, decisive tone. And it was then that I discovered the closest we humans get to the divine: the ecstasy of orgasm.

Neil covered my mouth with his to muffle my screams, and I scratched down his back. Desire painted all over his perfect face was the last lovely vision I got before my eyelids closed. Pleasure had suffused every part of me. I lacked the strength to properly recip-rocate his kisses—I didn't have enough breath in my lungs and my heart was pounding in my temples.

My body was sweaty—boiling—racked by uncontrollable shiv-ers and muscle contractions. When they had, finally, began to sub-side little by little, I was swamped by a wrung-out, sleepy feeling that brought me back to reality.

When I opened my eyes I saw Neil hovering over me, not moving, wearing a smug smile filled with masculine pride. We stared at each other, and I could see my reflection in his brilliant eyes. He was also sweaty and out of breath, but unlike me, he was still in full command of himself. I, meanwhile, barely knew where I was.

He didn't give me any time to familiarize myself with the after-glow, but instead he began to move again so forcefully that I was afraid I was going to have a second climax, just like the first. It would have been embarrassing, coming twice. I was so wet, though, that I felt nothing but pleasure when he slid easily inside me. I allowed him to do as he pleased, because I wanted him to feel good too. I wanted him to have what he had just given me.

Ten more minutes of interminable pounding went by. Neil seemed genuinely inexhaustible, but I was so tired. Satisfied, but tired. Did all men have this kind of stamina?

"Neil..." I pleaded, and after a few more minutes of firm and uninhibited thrusts, I felt him stiffen against me. He raised up his torso and looked at the place where our bodies were joined. He began to move faster, more lustfully and just as shameless as he'd been all along. His back tensed, his muscles flexing, and when he looked at me, his jaw went tight. He pulled out of me immediately and grasped his erection, shiny with my fluids.

It was the first time I'd gotten a really good look at him. He was long, thick, and covered in veins. It was frighteningly swollen. The sight aroused me and all the embarrassment I'd felt before fell away.

He quickly slid his hand from the base to the tip and aimed it right between my legs, where I was still wet and aching. His biceps strained and his abdomen spasmed, briefly but intensely. In one long, soundless exhalation, he released his seed onto my pubic area and the sheets below me. Small, pearlescent drops began sliding down his shaft like threads of silver.

Neil provoked the most indecent thoughts—the kind I hadn't even imagined I could have. I wanted to worship him, like he was some brazen god who had manifested right in front of me.

At that point, I realized I'd been staring at him way too hard during that lewd performance, and I directed my eyes back up to his face, blushing.

Neil, however, was still kneeling and hadn't noticed anything. He seemed confused, almost lost. He took his hands off himself and tried to catch his breath. The veins standing out in sharp relief on his neck and arms betrayed the lusty adrenaline rush still making its way through his body. He blinked a few times and stared at me like he didn't know who I was before lying down next to me on his back, staring up at the ceiling.

I admired him. I admired him from top to bottom. The musculature covered in a thin coating of sweat that only made his tanned skin gleam, his powerful chest rising and falling with his breath, his damp, disheveled hair. His lips, still swollen from our kisses. He was so beautiful, and for a moment, I wondered if I had dreamed all of this. How could someone like him, someone who was on another plane of existence entirely, want an ordinary girl like me?

I wanted to ask him that and so many other things besides, but his silence had become deafening. I had no idea what to do. My embarrassment came rushing back like a weight on my chest, and I forced myself to wait for some sort of sign from him.

When none arrived, I shifted and felt my muscles coming back to life. There was a pang in my groin and my nipples tingled. I tilted my chin down and saw that they were red and protruding. Neil had been holding himself back from start to finish, and despite all that, I could still feel his lips on my skin and the reminders of his body inside mine. What would it be like if he had shown me how he really treats women? His true self? That part of himself that so often tried to surface but which he had gotten so good at pushing back down?

I turned to him, and unexpectedly found him staring at me. Soft light from the bedside lamp illuminated just enough of him to outline his facial features.

"You okay?" His low, raspy voice gave me goosebumps. It was hot as hell, like the way an enigmatic, trickster devil might sound.

"Yes, thank you," I answered cooly, as though I were talking to a stranger rather than a guy I had just slept with, but that was how I always behaved when I felt uncomfortable. Did other people feel the same way after sharing this kind of moment with another person?

"You'll have to change your sheets," he informed me seriously. With no sign of any embarrassment, he gestured to his cum. I looked down at my pubic area, dappled with thick drops of it. I slowly ran a finger over the substance and then rubbed it between my thumb and index finger to examine its consistency.

All of this was novel to me.

Neil sat up partially and ran a hand through his hair while I lay motionless, filthy with him. I found myself staring at the Māori-style tattoo that extended from his bicep to his shoulder. The black ink was intense, free from smudges, and all of the lines were precise and perfectly spaced, like the artist had used a ruler to draw them. I knew that tattoos like that sometimes symbolized a warrior identity or a fighting spirit, but I didn't know why he'd chosen that one in particular. I squinted, trying to find the pattern that hid among the intersecting lines.

"It's a toki," he murmured, looking at his arm. "I chose it because it symbolizes strength, authority, courage, and determination," he explained, like he'd read my mind. I scanned the rest of Neil's body to see if he had any other tattoos, and he stuck out his left hip, showing me his penis again in the process.

I cleared my throat and focused on the smaller tattoo that I had barely noticed before.

"This one's a pikorua," he explained. I craned my neck to see better and allowed myself to trace the lines of it with my index finger. Neil startled at this light contact. My fingers were cold, and his skin was boiling, so I offered him an apologetic look.

"A pikorua..." I repeated thoughtfully. I could feel him breathing from such a short distance away. We were lying next to each other like we'd known each other our whole lives. It was a strange intimacy, nearly as intense as the act we'd just shared.

"That's right. It represents the strength of interpersonal bonds, the spiritual joining of people or communities for all time. I got it for my siblings."

I smiled at him and continued my journey across his body. I got to my knees beside him, heedless of the way I'd exposed my breasts for his viewing pleasure, and I used my fingers to draw a line from his hips to his abdomen and then on to his pectoral muscles. I could feel his eyes on me, scrutinizing every motion. Maybe he didn't entirely trust me, or maybe he was just surprised by my curious exploration. His breathing, however, remained perfectly controlled. I was almost miffed that I hadn't generated any excitement.

Then, I noticed the circular scars, like small burns on his left forearm. But before I could even touch them, Neil grabbed my wrist. I sucked in a breath at the strength of his grasp.

"Those are none of your concern," he scolded me, serious and succinct. I looked him in the eyes and he released me, standing up immediately from the bed.

I would have loved to know more. But despite the fact that we'd gone to bed together, there still wasn't enough trust between us for me to ask about him or his past.

Neil turned away from me and started getting dressed in just his boxers and pants.

"You should open the window; it smells like sex in here," he warned before bending down to grab the black tank top that he was apparently deciding not to wear.

"What?" I felt confused and a little dizzy. Where was he going?

"You don't want them to figure it out, do you?" he said derisively, a smug look on his face. "When people fuck, the irrefutable evidence—besides the sheets—is the smell in the air. But you wouldn't know that. How is there still so much stuff you don't know?" He glanced first at my face, and then at my naked body, which probably smelled like him.

I wasn't sure exactly what he was talking about, but he was absolutely right about one thing: I didn't know enough. Still, his superior tone made me feel worthless and small. So, out of reflex, I just nodded at him and instinctively tried to cover my breasts with one arm and my sex with the other hand.

But my sense of modesty, however unconscious and automatic, was useless now. I'd already let Neil take everything he could possibly want.

He bit his lip to keep from laughing at me before giving me a pitying smile. "Good night," he said, walking toward my door.

That was all? He was just going to leave like we'd just finished up a chat over coffee? I crawled to the edge of the bed and called out to him, which made him turn back toward me.

"Where... Where are you going?" What a stupid question! I bit my tongue, but I was too late.

It was obvious: he was running away. From me.

We weren't a couple struggling with the admissions he'd made;

we were two people who'd had some fun for an hour or so and would now go back to being total strangers.

"I'm going back to my room," he said positively. He rested his hand on the doorknob and looked back at me. He paused to consider something for a few moments and then sighed, perhaps irritated or possibly a little guilty.

"I told you, Selene. No fairy tales or love stories." He pushed open the door and then, with one last, brief glance, he left and closed the door behind him. I felt a sudden emptiness in my chest and a strange sinking feeling in my stomach.

There was no reason I should have felt so bad. I knew, deep down, that all Neil wanted was to give me a first time that I could actually remember. Intellectually, I had accepted this arrangement between the two of us. Emotionally, however, it was much harder to face. We were nothing. Or maybe we were something that was impossible to identify.

I ran a hand over my face and felt my lips. They were puffy and sore from the kisses we shared. The taste of him had mingled with mine so completely that I still felt him on my tongue. I would need to take a shower and brush my teeth to truly rid myself of him.

But nothing was going to help me forget.

11

SELENE

If being able to remember my first time was truly the solution to my feelings of guilt, then why hadn't I eaten or slept in days?

I avoided Neil in the days after our…well…whatever it was that we did. And I pretended that everything was fine.

At the moment, I was hanging out in one of the many green areas on campus with Logan and his friends, trying to act like a regular student, a model girlfriend, and a young woman who was perfectly measured in all her decisions.

Except that I was none of those things.

I felt like I was going insane all the time, and I just kept making massively irrational choices. Like giving in to Neil's suggestion, which had only created even more problems.

I was afraid of how I was going to react when I saw him with other girls. We'd shared something significant, and knowing that his many lovers also got the same thing from him was difficult to accept. Neil had been mine completely, if only for a little while, and I still somehow felt like he belonged to me.

"That sweater's really nice," Julie said to Adam. I shot her a look. It was just a plain white sweatshirt with the school's logo in purple on the chest. Then, I smiled, because I realized that Julie's comment was more timid seduction tactic than genuine compliment.

"Thanks, sweetheart." Adam winked at her and she turned red. I glanced around, trying not to stare too obviously at them.

"Hey, everything okay?" Logan approached, tucking his hands into the pockets of his coat. Autumn had truly arrived by then, and temperatures were falling.

"Yeah, everything's fine. I'm just thinking," I lied reassuringly. In reality, I was destroyed. I couldn't explain how I felt, and the chaos that reigned in my head was eating me alive. I had never been the type to act impulsively. I calculated and planned everything in my life. So now, living on this roller coaster and never knowing what was going to happen tomorrow was really messing with me.

Neil was messing with me.

After a few minutes, Alyssa suggested we go for coffee, so we hit up one of the many restaurants around campus and sat down at a free table. It was a nice place; the mismatched decor gave it a welcoming atmosphere, and it was full of students.

I recognized one of them almost immediately: Bryan Nelson was sitting not too far from us at a table with some other guys from the men's basketball team. I turned my gaze away from him so I wouldn't draw his unwanted attention and ordered a double shot when the waitress came by.

I really needed it.

"Are you sure you're doing okay?" It was Alyssa this time who was worried about me. It was probably my prolonged silence caused by my all-consuming thoughts. They made it basically impossible for me to keep up a conversation, and everyone else was getting suspicious.

"Sure, I'm just a little tired," I said. By now, I was getting pretty good at lying and making excuses, but I had to be because I obviously couldn't tell anyone what was really bothering me.

Plus, my friends knew I had a boyfriend, and I didn't like the idea of them passing judgment on me. I was already well aware that I had screwed up. I was constantly begging Jared to carve out some time for me, but it seemed like all of his other stuff came before me.

"You're seriously telling me you want to fuck Jennifer Madsen? She's off limits," Jake said teasingly to Cory before glancing at a table on the opposite side of the restaurant, next to the window. I heard the name but didn't bother turning around. Something told me that they were referring to the very same Jennifer that I knew.

"Everybody knows she's Neil's faithful little lapdog these days," Adam continued, extending his arm across the back of Julie's chair. She gave a small, embarrassed jolt.

"Like that's ever mattered to Neil. I've never seen the man with an actual girlfriend," Cory answered nonchalantly, looking directly at Logan. "What do you say, Logan? Would your brother give a shit if I hit that?" he continued, sounding innocently curious, as if this were a totally banal question for him to ask. Logan was clearly uncomfortable and annoyed, and it made him uncharacteristically sober.

"I don't like talking about my brother's personal life. I know as much about it as you do," he answered bluntly, obviously trying to tamp down on gossip about Neil.

"Oh come on, Logan. We all know his reputation. I mean, that dude has seen more pussy than a retired gynecologist," Jake insisted, making the rest of the group chuckle. Logan, however, continued to give them a deep look of annoyance.

"I heard he shares the girls with his friends, and that he goes to these parties where—"

Logan pounded his fists on the table, stopping Cory who went mute and stared at him in shock. "Enough!" Logan warned them all, looking like he was thoroughly tired of hearing rumors about Neil. Alyssa and Julie exchanged brief glances, and Jake and Adam quit laughing.

"Here's your coffees, folks." The waitress appeared in her chic black-and-white uniform and politely handed us our orders. Fortunately, this dissipated some of the tension between the boys. Jake changed the subject and everyone started talking again, diverted on to a different topic entirely. I glanced at Logan sitting next to me and dared to give his arm a pat.

"You were in the right, defending your brother. I would have done the same thing, if I had a brother." I grinned at him, and he seemed to appreciate it because I could see his face relax.

"Hey, sweetheart. We've been waiting on our beers for half an hour!" a guy shouted suddenly. From the corner of my eye, I saw him rudely gesturing toward the waitress. He had a wicked grin that gave me the shivers. I turned more fully to get a good look at him and the other people at his table. Immediately, I recognized Jennifer's blond hair. She was wearing a low-cut top and looked amused.

"If Xavier loses his cool, we're in for another one of his typical tantrums," Jake noted. I realized that the guy he was talking about was same slimeball I'd run into on my first day in the city.

To say that the other group of guys was *different* from us was a massive understatement. They belonged to another world entirely. I had felt it the first time I encountered them, but seeing them here now confirmed it. Everything about them—their strange, fanciful appearance and the challenging stares they gave to anyone who dared pass—made it undeniable.

"So who are they exactly?" I played dumb, hoping to get some more information, but everyone just stared at me like I'd grown a second head. Was what I said really that weird?

"You don't know? For real?" Cory tilted his head, and I cleared my throat awkwardly. Logan just sighed and toyed with an empty straw left on the table.

"They call themselves the Krew, but with a K," Jake offered, running a hand through his heavily styled blond hair.

"The Krew?" I echoed with a frown.

"Yeah, apparently it means 'blood' in Polish." This time, it was Adam who spoke. "They get into fights everywhere they go. They've sent more than a few people to the hospital," he explained flatly, looking over at the table of them like they were actual monsters.

"Even the girls are crazy." Alyssa twirled her index finger around her ear to emphasize her point.

I was shocked by this information.

"But why are they allowed here, then? How can they keep attending college?" I asked, and Logan tossed the straw he'd been playing with back on to the table.

"Almost all of them come from very wealthy families," Logan answered with a certain discomfort, training his hazel eyes on the table of them. "The blond girl, whom you've already met at our house, is Jennifer Madsen. There's talk that her stepdad is abusive." I glanced at her and found her grinning, perfectly confident and comfortable. It was the same smile she gave Neil when he wanted her.

I hated it.

"The girl with the blue hair next to her is Alexia Vogel. Her parents died in a car accident, so now she lives with her grandparents. She's a lunatic. Last year at a party, she beat another student so bad she broke the girl's jaw." I turned to Logan in shock. This anecdote of his sounded like something out of a horror movie. I looked around at our other friends who, with their unsurprised looks, confirmed that Logan was telling the truth.

"That... That's...wild," I murmured in shock.

"Yep," Jake muttered.

"And then there's the guys," Logan kept going when he noticed that my gaze had once again drifted over to the Krew. "Luke Parker, the blond dude, his dad's a lawyer and his mom's a journalist. He's probably the most normal-seeming of the group, but he's honestly just as messed up as the rest of them." Logan shook his head in disgust, and I wondered how someone like him had learned such personal details about those people. It seemed like he knew them well.

"Finally…" He dry-swallowed and carefully lowered his voice. "The black-haired one, with the lip and eyebrow piercings, that's Xavier Hudson." He indicated the guy I'd been observing earlier. He was a good-looking guy. I had noticed that about him right away back when I'd first seen him on the side of the road.

"He's a Bronx native. Lives with his alcoholic uncle. Allegedly, he saw his dad murder his mom when he was a kid. He stabbed her twenty-four times." I shuddered at that alarming story and looked mutely at Logan. What could I possibly have said? This was all so surreal that it rendered me speechless.

"He took a gap year before he started school, and it's supposedly so mysterious how he earns all his money, though…" He stopped and heaved a sigh. "It's pretty easy to figure out," he concluded, making a meaningful expression that no doubt alluded to the illicit activities that allowed Xavier to live just like his rich friends.

Right then, Xavier was giving the waitress a sinister stare as she arrived at their table. The poor girl's hand was shaking as she clutched her order pad to her chest.

"So, sweetheart, I asked you for a cold beer. This beer is warm. It's garbage. It feels like a bottle of piss," he snapped. Then he grabbed the neck of the bottle with two fingers and stretched his arm out over the table before dropping it, allowing it to shatter on the floor.

I was genuinely shocked by this atrocious behavior. It was like he was trying to start a brawl.

"This is how he always is…" Cory offered, pushing back a lock of black hair that had fallen over his forehead.

"He picks out a victim and then provokes them until they snap. He especially likes to target women," Jake added.

"Leave! Get the hell out of here!" The waitress pointed at the exit, still scared and visibly trembling. But Xavier just laughed in her face. He stared at her, first at her chest and then at her legs, left exposed by her uniform's skirt. He stood up to his full height. He was slim and tall, though not as tall as Neil.

I glanced around the room, and what I saw was extremely unnerving: everyone was just watching this awful scene play out, totally silent, not doing a thing. This wasn't about staying out of it; it was just pure cowardice.

Things like this couldn't just be allowed to happen—and in a busy public place as well. Someone had to step in. I didn't know what I was going to do, but I instinctively tried to get out of my seat and rescue that girl from this "Krew's" clutches. But Logan grabbed me by the arm and held me down.

"No, wait," he whispered, cautious but confident.

"But—"

"Wait," he repeated more decisively, so I listened to him, but I remained on alert.

A man strode purposefully across the restaurant toward the group as the waitress scurried back to the kitchen.

"Xavier! Off the premises!" shouted the new arrival, whom Logan informed me was the owner of the restaurant and knew those guys very well. Apparently it wasn't the first time they'd tried something like that here.

Xavier smiled insolently, gesturing to his friends with a jerk of his chin. "Let's get out of here, before I bust up this poor asshole's place," he said, shoulder-checking the owner as he moved past him. Alexia and the others followed immediately behind him.

Because we could tell his path was going to take him right past our table, we all sipped our coffees, pretending we were oblivious to what had just gone down. But then my whole body tensed up when I realized that Xavier was slowing down and looking straight at me.

I could feel his eyes on me, but I tried not to react. I kept my head down, swirling the spoon around in my cup until an unfamiliar tobacco smell wafted into my space. It was powerful and pungent.

"Look who it is: Snow White and the Seven Dwarfs." Xavier laughed, and I looked up abruptly only to feel some small relief when I realized he was looking at Logan and not at me. But my relief gave way almost immediately to worry, because I'd come to care about Logan.

"And how are you doing, princess?" The bully rested his hand on the back of Logan's head, and Logan went still beneath him. His jaw clenched and he stared up at Xavier with a bottomless hatred. I was feeling much the same way, though I didn't really even know the guy.

"Please leave," Logan said quietly in his usual refined tone, though his resentment shone through in each word. Xavier shot a sideways glance at our friend group and grinned with delight.

"Fuck, you really are a little bitch, Miller." He patted Logan on the back of the neck before letting go and staring down our entire table.

You could have cut the tension with one of the table knives. Nobody dared to speak, not even Cory, who always had something to say.

Xavier grabbed Logan's coffee cup and raised it to his nose. He sniffed it, gave a groan of mock-appreciation, and took a sip. What happened next left me stunned. He spat right into the mug and placed it back down in front of Logan.

"Drink up," he demanded, pressing his palms against the table. I held my breath. He was blatantly harassing Logan in public. Weren't we supposed to be past this kind of bullying as a society?

"No, thanks. I'd rather gnaw off my own leg than ingest any of your secretions," Logan said steadily, giving him a disdainful look from under his eyelashes. As far as I was concerned, I'd had about enough of the Krew pretending to be all-powerful. We were human beings, not dolls to be pushed around for their amusement. Plus, every moment I spent doing nothing and remaining still was another moment I was complicit with these assholes.

So I jumped up and stared down the idiot in front of me.

"Knock it off!" I blurted out, and only then did Xavier's black eyes turn to me. I was hoping he wouldn't recognize me. For a moment, he examined me minutely like he had no idea who I was. Then, a threatening smile spread across his face.

"And who might you be? Beauty come to save her friends from the beast?" he asked sneeringly. I knew what I needed to do; guys like Xavier put on a front like they were these fearless warriors so they could take their own internal frustrations out on everyone around them. But what they really were was weak.

"You seem to have a weird fixation on fairy tales," I pointed out and my friends laughed.

Xavier glanced around with the aggrieved air of one who was firmly convinced that no one would ever dare to make fun of him.

"Sure I do..." he said in a sinister whisper. "Especially on those little lost princesses whose legs fall open the minute Prince Charming snaps his fingers." He gestured obscenely at me and then winked. For a moment, I thought he was alluding to what had happened with me and Neil, but then I shook myself. He knew nothing about my life and was just talking to me the way he'd talk to anyone else.

"Xavier!" someone thundered in a raspy, angry baritone. Xavier glanced over my shoulder, and his back immediately straightened.

"Neil..." he murmured, his attitude transforming. I didn't bother turning around, because I knew he was behind me. I stood there just observing Xavier. Still, Neil's proximity made me feel those electric sensations in the bottom of my stomach.

"We were just asking your little brother where you were," added Luke, who had remained silent up until now, just enjoying the show.

I felt Neil approach until he was beside me, also facing Xavier. He stared, scowling at the other man for a few seconds.

All around us was this insane silence. Fear and anxiety about what was going to happen next hovered in the air. Neil's golden eyes shifted to the cup of coffee and then to Logan, who had remained motionless all this time, his face twisted in rage. He also gave me a quick look, so brief that I didn't have time to decode it before he looked back at Xavier.

"Drink up," he ordered, grabbing his brother's coffee and handing it to the other man. Jennifer and Alexia exchanged looks of surprise, while Luke wore a disappointed expression that I couldn't parse. Xavier himself looked alternately from the cup to Neil's face and then shook his head with a sly smile on his face.

"We're your friends; we'd never lay a finger on the princess here," he answered, irritation in his voice.

Nice. Were all of Neil's friends like these ones? Xavier gave Logan a smug look. He was bullshitting Neil in the hopes of not provoking him, because Xavier feared Neil and not just a little bit, either. "We know she's protected," Xavier added with a bit more hostility in his tone.

Neil, however, said nothing. He simply continued to hold the cup up in front of Xavier's face, silently demanding that he drink it.

"Drink up," he said again, softly. There was a genuine threat in his voice, as sharp as any blade. Xavier huffed nervously through his nose, considered it for a few moments, and then, with a growl of anger, he snatched the coffee and drank it. He slammed the empty mug back down on the table with a thud that made us all jump and glared disdainfully at Neil.

"Let's get out of here," he ordered his friends, who were standing motionless behind him. Then he slowly squared up with Neil.

"Come find us when you remember who your real family is. I'm gonna make you pay for this, asshole."

After one last tense moment, Xavier shoved his way past Neil and stormed off. Neil sighed, and I suddenly exhaled the breath I'd apparently been holding the whole time. I pressed my hand to my chest, trying in vain to calm my pounding heart. Then, I sat back down and gripped Logan's hand, which was still pulled into an angry fist. Neil turned and gave his brother one of those silent, mysterious looks that were so characteristic of him.

"Don't say it," Logan ordered him bitterly. Neil's actions put a constant spotlight on the family while also unfortunately exposing them to ongoing aggression from the Krew. Neil stared at him, ashamed. The gold of his eyes seemed to soften into a deep well of guilt. In his own way, he did love his brother.

"Don't say anything," Logan continued, as though no further explanation was required. For me, however, there were still a whole bunch of things that I couldn't seem to explain or rationalize.

I knew, though, that I would soon be getting the answers I sought.

12

SELENE

Professor Cooper circulated through the large auditorium. I loved studying and taking notes, but on that day I was pensive and distracted. I drummed my fingers on the table and paged randomly through my textbook, bored.

"I'm starving to death," Alyssa huffed beside me, digging out her phone to respond to some texts. She wasn't being at all helpful in my doomed goal of processing a single word of the lesson, mainly because every five minutes she was making some new complaint. I glanced down at my watch—just a few more minutes and we'd be out of there.

My number one priority that afternoon was calling Jared and asking him to meet me in person and this time, I wasn't going to take no for an answer.

Professor Cooper ended her lecture and reminded us about our next session, and I immediately got out of my seat, examining my copy of the syllabus. I needed to ask some questions, but I wanted to wait until the lecture hall cleared out.

"You're not coming?" Alyssa frowned at me, and I shook my head.

"I'll meet you later; I need some information." I gestured at Professor Cooper, who was intently shuffling some papers on her desk. I waved goodbye to Alyssa and tugged my bag over one shoulder as I descended the stairs.

Unfortunately, my teacher had also left the classroom in a marked hurry, so I had to chase after her. I called her name, but she didn't seem to hear me. I wound up following her for a long time and stopped only when she fled into another classroom that I didn't think I was allowed to enter.

"Damn it," I blurted out huffily. I just needed to ask her a couple of questions; it would really take only a minute or two. I was approaching the cracked door when heard her voice coming from inside. I peered through the crack to make sure I wouldn't be disturbing her when I spotted a man's crossed ankles propped up on a desk and an embarrassed-looking Professor Cooper tucking her hair behind her ears. Clearly this was a bad time. I turned to leave but then a voice, masculine and domineering, froze every muscle in my body.

"You're late, like always," the man informed her in that seductive, almost hypnotic tone, which was now so unfortunately familiar to me.

I held my breath, praying that I was only imagining that it was Neil's voice. Then I turned back, compelled by curiosity and crept closer to the door again. My hand on the doorframe was trembling as I leaned closer to get a better look.

There before her stood Neil in all his glory. The white sweater that hugged his masculine torso and contrasted sharply against his tanned skin. The golden eyes that lasciviously examined Professor Cooper and those lips, curved into a menacing grin. I sucked in a painful breath, afraid I was about to witness something inappropriate.

"I just ended my lecture." Professor Cooper looked at him like she was afraid of him yet wanted him at the same time. I recognized the look because he had the same effect on me.

"Amanda…if you can't do what I tell you to…" He moved closer to her, grabbing a lock of her blond hair and twisting it around and around his index finger. "I'll go public with what happened and destroy your reputation forever," he threatened her with an eerie calm.

Professor Cooper seemed dumbstruck in the face of him. I couldn't see her expression because she was turned away from me, but I could see Neil's—handsome and enigmatic as it ever was.

"Neil, please…" my professor begged, her fingers fluttering around her mouth. She was clearly about to cry and fighting it back. Neil, however, was cool and impassive in the face of the woman's distress.

"Imagine what your colleagues and your students would think. You'd sully the good name of this university and show yourself for what you really are: a slut who fucks her own students." He brought his mouth right up to her ear and stuck his tongue out, licking first her earlobe then the side of her face.

My stomach tightened as though caught in a vice: Neil was really no different from his awful friends. They were all scheming and depraved.

"And I still remember how you loved it," he added in an amused tone. I heard Professor Cooper sob and Neil drank in her vulnerability. He sniffed her neck but didn't kiss it. He restricted himself to fondling her breast instead and grinned, satisfied with the fear he'd manage to generate in the woman.

"You don't want to let me down, Amanda. You don't want that at all," he said, glowering. I stepped back until I hit the opposite wall and decided I had to stop spying on them. I was beginning to think that I had bound myself with invisible chains to someone very dangerous. Someone without a conscience at all.

Had I really imagined that I could trust him? How could I have let someone like Neil touch me without figuring out how dirty his soul really was? And why, despite now knowing for sure what he was, did my body still yearn for his?

I was insane. Just as insane as he was.

I fled to the women's restroom and splashed cold water on my face. I wasn't worried about ruining my makeup because I almost never wore any. I stared at myself in the mirror. My eyelashes, long, black, and wet framed familiar blue eyes; eyes I tried to recognize myself with. The old me. The one who never gave into temptation. The one who didn't lie, who respected other people, who lived her values and believed in her own goodness.

When I was done, I dried my hands with a paper towel and got my phone out of my jeans pocket, hitting the last number in my recent contacts.

"Baby," Jared answered on the second ring. I leaned against the wall and pressed the phone to my chest, sucking in a breath. Then I scrounged up the courage I'd need to tackle yet another of our conversations and put the phone back to my ear.

"Jared," I whispered.

"Selene, are you okay?" He could tell right away that something was wrong, just from the sound of my voice. I felt like crying because all of a sudden it really hit me, what I had really done. It was too late, though.

"Jared, I've been telling you that we need to talk in person," I scolded him too sharply. I was screwing this up—I shouldn't have taken my misery out on him.

"I know..." He gave an exhausted sigh. "But between going to class and my dad needing me at the company, I never have time for other stuff," he lamented.

So I was "other stuff" now? He was the one who was so sure we'd be back together when I went home to Detroit.

"I'm telling you that this is urgent… It can't wait any longer. Please…" I swallowed thickly. My throat was tight and my lips were dry. I wasn't doing well at all. I hadn't been eating; I hadn't slept in days, and I was corpse-pale.

"I'm going to talk to my father. I'll try to get out to you this weekend."

"That's what you said last week." I stared out the open window. The sky was gray and overcast, listless and shadowed, just how I felt that morning. A group of squawking girls entered the bathroom, so I tried to tuck myself further into the corner and go unnoticed.

"You're freaking me out here, Selene. You know that, right?" he said softly, sounding worried. That wasn't my intention. In fact, that was the reason I didn't want to discuss Neil with him over the phone and was waiting for an in-person meeting.

"Let me know if you can come out this weekend, okay?" I tried to soften my tone and turned to observe the girls, who were focused on applying lipstick.

"Yes, I'll try my best," he promised before telling me goodbye and ending the call. I needed to get home, my head was spinning.

I dashed out of the bathroom, completely distracted until my forehead crashed into what felt like a bumpy mountain face. I was saved from falling by two strong hands that caught me just in time. I raised a hand to my aching forehead and the smell of amber and tobacco floated all around me. I glanced up and found Neil's eyes, golden and intense as they always were.

"I'm fine." I gathered myself, pulling away from his touch. I tried to step past him, but Neil grabbed me by the wrist and held me in place.

"You've been avoiding me for days. Why?"

I felt goosebumps raise up at the sound of his severe tone, and I hated myself for responding to him like that.

He was toxic.

Nothing but toxic.

"Please, Neil, not today. I don't feel good and I just want to go home." I tried to free myself, but he tightened his grip until my skin began to feel hot. He could have crushed the bones in my wrist if I kept fighting him. My strength was nothing compared to his.

"I'm headed home, too. I can give you a ride," he offered flatly. But I didn't want to be alone with him. Neil overpowered my critical-thinking abilities. When we were together, I felt lost in slow, aching need. He triggered these insane desires in my body and blurred my very identity. Spending more time with him was extremely inadvisable.

"Don't worry about it; I'll take an Uber." I tugged on my arm, but it seemed he had no intention of letting me go.

I quit trying to leave with a sigh. I knew how stubborn he was and that fighting him was useless.

"I'll remind you that we live in the same house. Avoiding me now won't keep you from seeing me at home later," he observed. He was right: bypassing this particular obstacle was not the solution. I stopped struggling against him, and he released my wrist and we walked down the hall together.

It occurred to me that everyone was watching us. With envy in the case of the girls; curiosity for the boys. What were they thinking about me?

Or rather, what did they think about any of Neil's "companions"?

I avoided answering my own questions so as not to die of shame.

"Everyone's staring at me." I slowed my stride, suddenly self-conscious as I was hit by a wave of inadequacy.

"Ignore them," he said, unfazed by the constant stares from all the students who passed us. Maybe he was just used to it? Well, I definitely wasn't.

"So far I've been pretty anonymous at this school, and I'd like to continue with that," I muttered, clutching my bag against my side. I wasn't at all capable of handling this kind of stress.

"You will—calm down," he answered impatiently.

I came to an abrupt halt in the middle of the hallway. Even I couldn't have explained why, I just suddenly felt like I was suffocating. Neil stopped next to me and heaved a deep sigh, pinching the bridge of his nose as though I was wearing on his last nerve.

"Okay, okay," he muttered to himself before turning to look at the lingering students. "Let's see…" He breathed in sharply through his nose and examined everyone who had the misfortune to be nearby. Finally, he pointed at a dark-haired boy with thick-framed glasses before reaching out and grabbing him by the shirt collar. He dragged the boy over to him, and I flinched when I saw the boy trembling in his grip.

"Ah, an example. What the fuck were you looking at?" Neil asked, pulling the boy right up close to his face and daring the kid to object. Everyone around us had gone into a kind of suspended animation: silent and motionless.

"I… I… nothing! I swear," the poor guy babbled, looking beseechingly at Neil. Neil just gave him a menacing smile before slamming his back against the wall and letting him fall hard to the floor.

I instinctively rushed over to the boy to make sure that he was okay. Had Neil actually lost his mind?

"The young lady here is rather shy. The next guy—or girl—around here who dares to look at her is going to end up like this asshole." Neil gestured to the boy who was now sitting on the floor. *There goes my anonymity.* Everyone was giving me unsettled looks, and the boy who'd been hit jumped up and ran away. As I got back to my feet, I glared murderously at Neil.

"Now walk and quit your bitching," he ordered in a menacing hiss. Everyone went back to talking among one another, pretending to ignore us. Neil proceeded toward the exit, and I just stood there, rocked by that senseless outburst.

I glanced around and spotted Jennifer not far away, staring fixedly at me. A flicker of jealousy lent Jennifer's blue eyes a sinister appearance. Maybe she thought the object of her affections had been marking his territory instead of just trying to mock me? I turned my back on both of them and headed for the exit.

"You are actually insane!" I harangued Neil the moment we got outside. He leaned against the hood of his Maserati and lit up a cigarette. He stared at me, looking irritated but immovable as he took a few drags.

"Get in," he ordered flatly, tossing almost the entire cigarette away. What was with this high-handed attitude? Did he get confused and think he was talking to Jennifer?

"I'm not your little lapdog. I'll walk." I switched directions and headed for the sidewalk that would take me to the nearest bus stop, but Neil took issue with that. Of course.

"Quit being a fucking baby and get in the car!" He grabbed my arm, halting my progress. Clearly Neil would have no problem publicly humiliating me a second time. I, however, still cared about how I appeared in public, especially at school, so I snatched my arm from his grasp and stalked toward his car.

Inside the car, I didn't say a word. I forced myself not to so much as look at him and examined the car's interior instead to distract myself.

The Maserati was sporty but luxurious, quintessentially masculine. A fiery red interior light bathed the rear seats, making them look as if they were swallowed by the flames of hell. It looked like some kind of innovative new spaceship that the devil would pilot.

A chrome trident, symbolic of power and royalty, stood out proudly from the center of the steering wheel. Neil grasped it firmly in his two hands, the backs of them shot-through with veins. Looking at them, I couldn't help but remember how they'd moved against my body: focused, hungry, lusty, and skilled.

I drifted away into indecent fantasies about Neil and hadn't even noticed when we arrived at the house. I unbuckled my seatbelt and shot out of the car, trying immediately to put some distance between us. I felt like I could smell him on me again, even though I knew perfectly well that was just a trick my brain was playing on me.

I tried to climb up to the front door but put my foot wrong on the first step and stumbled, bashing my knee. Luck was just not on my side today. The stab of pain was immediate and froze me for a few seconds. I slumped down on the ground, not caring about dirtying my jeans and tried to touch my new injury, but I winced at the pain.

"I'm absolutely correct when I call you Babygirl, aren't I?" Neil had caught up with me. He knelt down and shook his head in amusement. He gave me such a tender look, and I found him terribly appealing, though a part of me couldn't forget what I had just seen him do.

"You're so aggressive and overbearing. I can't stand you. I fell because I was trying to get as far away from you as possible!" I yelled at him, pointing at my leg, but he ignored the insults and instead just scooped me up into his arms.

I fell silent when my head touched his chest. He emitted such a good, clean smell, and I soaked it in like it was a drug. I couldn't help but wonder then how the cruel person I had seen threatening Professor Cooper earlier could also be so sweet and considerate.

We walked into the house, and he deposited me gently on top of the counter in the kitchen.

"Take your jeans off." Another order, this one more unexpected.

I looked suspiciously at him and inched away, ready to fend him off.

"You don't need to do that; I can take care of it by myself," I babbled in an effort to maintain a modicum of self-possession. There was no way I was going to get undressed in the kitchen right there in front of him.

"Selene," he admonished, resting his hands on either side of my legs. He leaned in closer, staring intently into my eyes and I went still. "I've kissed you, touched you, and fucked you. Do you think a pair of naked legs is going to make much difference?"

Why did those words ignite lust inside me? I pictured us performing lewd acts, and he smiled wickedly, as though he knew exactly what I was thinking. I cleared my throat and tried to look away.

"Wait here," he said before disappearing into the downstairs bathroom. A few minutes later he returned with a first-aid kit. He set it down on the counter to open it up, taking out a can of ice spray. He shook it at me and cocked an eyebrow.

"Take your fucking jeans off," he ordered me again, more severely this time. I huffed but decided to cooperate. I unbuttoned my pants and started to push them down. Neil helped me pull them all the way off before focusing on my red and aching knee. The skin wasn't broken, but I would obviously have a large bruise the next day. When Neil so much as brushed his fingers over the area, I winced in pain.

"We need to get something cool on it; it's already swollen," he noted with a sigh. Then he covered it with a considerable amount of cold spray. I gritted my teeth at the burning sensation caused by the freezing spray. Still, I did feel my pain lessening.

Neil waited a few seconds before taking the opportunity to scope out my bare thighs, which I instinctively pressed together. My panties—white, cotton, and utterly unappealing—were completely exposed for his devouring eyes, and though we had indeed had a history together, I was still embarrassed.

Neither of us spoke, and when I tried to slide down from the counter, Neil wouldn't let me. I looked around and realized that the house was suspiciously silent. Where was Miss Anna?

"Anna must be out shopping. She'll be back soon," he said,

appearing again to read my mind in that unsettling way of his. It felt like a violation of my privacy.

"You scare me sometimes," I grumbled with feeling, and he smiled thinly. He was particularly attractive when he smiled.

"Your eyes can't keep any secrets from me," he answered with an intense stare.

It was in moments like these that his effect was especially potent. I couldn't resist him when he looked at me like that, and he, the giant bastard, knew it. And that was why he felt comfortable getting closer to me and putting his hands on my thighs. I stared down at his long fingers, sinking into my flesh and saw that my legs had started to fall open at his silent command. It was like my body wasn't even my own anymore.

Neil situated himself between my thighs until my sex was pressed against his fly. I didn't say anything, but only because that firm, insistent contact stole my breath.

"So, you wanna tell me why you've been avoiding me these past few days?" he whispered, rubbing my hips with his fingers. My mind was distracted, overloaded with too many uncontrollable sensations. I stared at his full lips and then into his golden eyes, which were waiting on my response. It was difficult to explain my perspective in words.

"Because I know that you're screwing with me," I admitted and his face grew dark. He didn't appreciate the certainty in my voice, but that was what I believed.

"And what else do you know?" He didn't deny my assertion, though. He leaned in until his nose was closer to my neck and seductively breathed in my scent. I didn't fight him off, but I kept my hands tight on the counter's edge. I didn't have the nerve to touch him or be uninhibited like him, despite the fact that I was sitting there in just my shirt and underwear, practically draped all over his body.

"I know that the night we spent together meant nothing to you, that you actively resist love and that—" I said and he put his index finger to my lips and silenced me. I looked into his strange eyes and felt an unfamiliar warmth spread throughout the middle of my chest. It was the kind of warmth that would have been a lot more intense if I could have shared it with him.

"You're a smart girl, Selene, but don't dig too deep into this mystery." He smiled confusingly at me.

"It's a bottomless hole, and your hunger for the truth is only going to hurt you. Each one of us is an enigma. An unanswered question. And that's how it should stay." He moved his thumb over my bottom lip and examined it like he'd never seen one before.

"That's just an oblique way of telling me I'm right, isn't it? I'm not stupid, Neil."

I was, though, because for some strange reason I felt like crying. I had been accumulating all these emotions and states of mind that I'd never experienced before in my life, and it was all because of the fucked-up boy in front of me. I didn't know how to deal with or even understand what I was feeling.

"You can do whatever you want with me: You can talk to me. You can listen to me. You can use me…" He grabbed my hand and pressed it against his crotch. I sucked in a breath when I felt that thick and powerful hardness hidden under the fabric. That had been inside me, moving and bringing me indescribable pleasure. I looked into his eyes, unsettled, as he continued, "But what you can't do is understand me. Or associate me with anything like love." The coldness of his words was even more painful than the resignation in his eyes.

I wondered how a young man could already have so much darkness inside him.

"I don't use people." I pulled my hand back as though I'd been burned, and he tilted his head to one side, frowning. It was second time he'd told me something like that, seeming to take it for granted that it was normal.

"People are not to be used," I reiterated with more conviction, and it was then that he took a step back from me.

He looked bewildered, lost. He glanced around before bringing his gaze back to me and staring like I wasn't even human.

Alarmed, I slipped off the counter, nearly falling, and limped a few steps forward. My knee hurt too badly to put weight on it.

"That's why you can't know me." He gave me a disappointed look and then inexplicably walked away from me. What had I done to make him put that distance between us? A distance that was, more than anything else, psychological?

"Because?"

"Because you can't accept what you can't understand."

I couldn't tell if I was too fuzzy-headed to get what he was saying or if Neil really was just too twisted to be easily comprehended. I stared thoughtfully at him, and just then, the front door opened. A moment later, Anna appeared with a few envelopes in her hands. She dropped them on the floor and observed me, frowning.

She was definitely wondering what I doing in the kitchen wearing just my panties. Then she looked down at my red and slightly flexed knee and figured it out.

"Selene, honey, what happened?" She rushed to me with maternal worry, like I was her actual daughter, while my eyes remained locked on the somber boy just a short distance away from me.

"Take care of her, Anna," he ordered the housekeeper before turning his back on us and going upstairs.

The vibration of a cell phone shook me out of the confusion I was drowning in. I glanced around before realizing that it was my phone. Slowly, I bent down and retrieved it from my jeans, still tangled on the floor.

I swiped my thumb across the screen to unlock it and read the text that had just arrived: I'll be there this weekend.

It was from Jared.

13

....

SELENE

The weekend came too soon.

I only had an hour before Jared arrived, and I was incapable of thinking of anything meaningful to say to him. All I did was think about what to say or how to act, but none of my mental preparations were making me feel at all ready for our meeting.

I was in my bedroom, surrounded by a silence that only increased my agitation. I examined myself in the mirror, and in the blue of my eyes, I saw all the disillusionment I was still feeling about my irrational actions.

My *unforgivable* actions.

I looked down at the black dress I was wearing, very elegant but simple. It was mid-length, exposing my now-healed knee. Naturally, I was reminded of that moment in the kitchen when Neil had tended to me and spoken so mysteriously.

I heaved a broken sigh. Neil had wormed his way into my body and my brain. He had become a full-blown obsession, and the more evasive and elusive he was, the more I yearned to pin him down and uncover exactly why he was so different from all the other guys his age.

He had a man's experience—the sense of disillusionment that came from enduring too much in this life and the inner coldness of someone who was no longer capable of entrusting himself to anyone else. I felt like I had all the pieces of the puzzle spread out before me, but I still just couldn't see how they fit together.

I scraped my hair into a high ponytail, leaving a couple of rebellious strands to frame my face.

I went down to the garden to take some time to myself. After all, solitude was my only consistent friend. I sat down on the wooden bench and admired the garden around me.

A tree nearby cast a shadow that gave me shelter from the sun while a crisp breeze tickled my skin.

"Hey, sis," Logan said, coming over to sit next to me.

"How many times do I have to tell you that I hate it when you call me that?" I mock-grumbled and he grinned. I turned to look at him, and his cheerful face fell when he saw my eyes.

"You're sad. Why?" he asked with concern.

"When you're very sensitive, you get sad a lot." I tucked a strand of hair behind my ear and sighed.

"But aren't you happy to see Jared again?"

It was a legitimate question, but the intense shame I felt over my feelings for Neil made me so generally irrational that it canceled everything else out. "We were only together for three months. I do care about him, but I think I made a mistake attaching myself to him just because we're so much alike. I thought that would be enough for a relationship." I confessed it all with the familiar ease that I always felt with Logan.

"You're young. It's completely normal to make the wrong call in these situations at our age." I looked at him, really examining his facial features. His face was more delicate than Neil's but just as refined and free from imperfections. Beauty was definitely one of the Miller family's strong suits.

"But our mistakes shouldn't hurt other people..." I said, more to myself than to him. Logan smiled at me with understanding.

"Sure, but it's also true that mistakes are how we learn," he said, holding up his index finger in a mocking, smart-ass fashion. Then he gave my shoulder a comforting pat. I immediately felt better, and my lips curved slightly upward. Often, people just need someone to really listen to them, someone to be present, someone they can count on.

"Wait, wait, wait... Is that a smile I see?" He booped me on the nose, and I grinned widely. I was feeling much lighter, despite my imminent encounter with Jared.

"You know what I think?" Logan added. I gave him a curious look and he continued, "I think Jared isn't the right person for you. We get tangled up with people for lots of reasons, and love isn't always one of them. Maybe you made some mistakes, but you can definitely take something away from them. Sometimes the most incredible things are hiding in the chaos."

Just then, a gentle gust of wind moved through my hair, rustling the leaves of the trees. "Incredible things..." I echoed thoughtfully.

"Yeah..." He stood up and extended his hand to help me up.

We walked back into the house and spent the next hour talking about nothing in particular. We were still sitting on the sofa in the living room when we heard the doorbell ring.

"Anna, can you get the door please?" Mia shouted. She appeared a few moments later, leaning over the railing on the upstairs landing with a pen dangling from one hand.

Anna obeyed, and when she opened the door, Jared was standing there with a box of chocolates in his hands.

My heart stuttered, and my nerves increased tenfold.

He paused in the doorway in all his glory. His jade-green eyes seemed brighter than normal, and his blond hair had product in it. Seeing him, Mia came down the stairs, and Logan stood up to greet the new guest. Matt, however, wore a confused expression as he emerged from the kitchen.

I remained motionless on the sofa, fixed in place as though I'd just seen a ghost.

"Please, make yourself comfortable," said Anna as she helped Jared remove his black coat and draped it over her arm.

My former boyfriend bit his lip, looking around sheepishly.

"You must be Jared. I'm so pleased to meet you. I'm Mia Lindhom." Matt's girlfriend approached him and held out her hand. Jared did the same, and in a display of his typical good manners, he presented her with the box of chocolates.

The gesture had Mia melting like snow in the full sun, and my father smiled.

"Please, don't just stand in the doorway, come on in. I'm Matt Anderson," he introduced himself jovially.

"Jared Brown. I'm honored to meet you, sir. I've heard so much about you." He gazed at my father like he was an international superstar, and I realized all over again just how important and famous my father had become in recent years because of his work.

Finally, I was able to shake myself out of my daze. I got off the couch and joined the others with trembling legs, trying to hide my anxiety. Jared, who was saying hello to Logan, seemed to adapt immediately to this new situation. When I got close enough, he turned his eyes on me and my chest felt like it was being crushed in a vise.

"Selene," he said in a whisper full of emotion before looking to my father, as though silently asking for the other man's permission to approach me. Matt stepped aside to let him pass.

"It's been weeks. It's so good to see you again." He hugged the breath out of me and then pulled back to gaze at me admiringly.

"You seem different somehow. You're... You're beautiful." Jared was excited, and I gave him a painful smile that I hoped would look sincere.

"I'm happy to see you, too," I managed, my voice shaking. Jared touched my cheek, and I could tell that he wanted to kiss me but didn't think it was appropriate in the moment.

Once all the hellos were finished, we proceeded to the dining room. During dinner, Jared spoke at length with Mia, my father, and Logan. I was pretty surprised by the warm welcome that Matt gave him. I thought he would take the opportunity to make me uncomfortable, but instead he was so friendly and gracious that Jared completely let down his guard.

I silently observed this tableau. And then, perhaps for the first time, I recognized what a lovely family we could potentially be, and I understood just how many mistakes I'd made in the few weeks I'd been with them.

"Selene, how long have you two been together?" Mia asked, pulling me from my reflections.

"Almost four months," Jared answered for me, giving my thigh a squeeze. I tensed at the intimate contact, but fortunately, he didn't seem to notice anything.

"You're so precious together. I remember being your age, being happy-go-lucky and so in love..." She sighed, lost in the memory.

"With Dad?" Logan asked, raising an eyebrow. I saw Mia's face darken; a cloud of melancholy seemed to pass over her blue eyes. Matt looked at her expectantly, but Logan just smiled, maybe taking it for granted that he'd guessed right. It was the first time I'd heard anyone mention William Miller directly. All I knew about him was that he was the CEO of a major company, that he had been married to Mia, and that he was the father of her three children.

"No..." Mia cleared her throat and fussed nervously with the cutlery next to her plate. "It was with another man, my first love. But that was years ago. It doesn't matter anymore," she added, sounding nostalgic and staring vaguely into the middle distance.

No one dared to ask her any follow-up questions and silence fell over the table, broken only by the click of the latch on the front door. Even though I was pretty sure she was staying over at a friend's that night, I hoped against hope that it was Chloe coming home.

"Oh, Neil's here." Mia patted her lips with her napkin and turned toward the entrance to the dining room. Seconds later, Neil came into the room. He took off his leather jacket and handed it to a waiting Anna with a soft thanks.

"Good evening. What'd I miss?" he began before noticing Jared sitting next to me. He immediately took a seat across from me, next to his brother, and regarded me with a serious scowl.

"Oh darling, I'm so happy you're joining us. Will you stay all evening?" Mia asked him delightedly.

"No, I'm going to a party with Jennifer later," he answered, propping up his elbows on the table. I immediately pictured Neil and Jennifer clinging to one another in some random bedroom and my stomach ached. Was he with her after our night together? I knew I didn't really want to know, but the curiosity remained.

"The rest of the Krew are going too, aren't they?" asked Logan under his breath. Neil gave him a sharp look, but his brother just stared back at him reproachfully.

"Knock it off, Logan," Neil rebuked him, pouring some wine into his glass.

"Bullshit, Neil," Logan whispered, trying not to be overheard by his mother, who had gone back to chatting about work with Matt and Jared again. "I don't like you hanging out with those assholes, and I'll never get tired of telling you that," he continued, sounding tense.

Neil just kept drinking his wine, completely uninterested. Then he looked across the table, first at Jared, then at me. His gaze warmed me, and like always, I was helpless against it. I touched my lower lip with one finger, and it seemed like I could still taste him on my tongue. Neil clocked the movement and watched me, his eyes half-closed in barely concealed lust.

"Oh, how rude!" Mia interrupted suddenly. "Jared, this is my oldest, Neil."

I blinked, realizing that I had gotten so absorbed in Neil's arrival that I'd completely forgotten about Jared. I swallowed thickly and shifted in my seat. Neil and Jared, who had been ignoring each other up until that point, locked eyes menacingly, each taking the measure of the other.

"Pleasure to meet you, Neil," Jared said but Neil didn't move a muscle. He just stared threateningly at him, and Jared was forced to look away first. Logan sighed and scratched his chin with his thumb, observing his brother's demeanor.

"So, Jared, what do you do? We haven't talked about that yet," Matt cut in to dispel the awkwardness. The air had become way too tense, and I was glad my father was trying to salvage the situation.

"I'm studying journalism in Detroit," he answered, squeezing my thigh a bit harder.

I didn't flinch away from that contact, even though I wanted to.

"Interesting," Logan commented with a grin.

"Yep," Jared answered, never taking his eyes from the tantalizing devil across the table. "And what do you do, Neil?" he asked, wiping his lips with the napkin and scrutinizing him closely.

"I survive," was all he said, and an eerie silence fell over us. Mia looked uncomfortable, Matt was frowning, and Logan squeezed his eyes shut for a moment.

Neil's eyes were heavy with sorrow but also with an incredible strength, the kind that comes from fighting something dark and evil. Something powerful and deeply rooted in his soul.

"Dessert, anyone?" Anna broke in, a dissonant voice that relieved the tension and restored the balance of the gathering.

························

Dinner ended shortly after that.

After dessert, Neil vanished into the garden to lay in the hammock and smoke a cigarette. I wanted to chase after him and make sure he was okay after his evasive response to Jared, but I couldn't.

"You're a really great guy, Jared," Matt said, pulling my attention back to him.

"Thank you, Dr. Anderson. Please know that I care deeply about your daughter and that you can trust me," Jared answered.

I tried to cast out the miserable feeling in my chest but to no avail. It felt like many tiny needles were pricking my heart, because I knew that I was going to have to put an end to this farce sooner rather than later.

"I have no doubts about that. Now, if you'll excuse me, I'm going to get ready for bed. I'm quite tired. Don't stay up too late, kids," Matt said, heading upstairs with Mia and Logan, who would be going out shortly. And so Jared and I were left alone in the living room.

"Do you want to watch a movie?" I asked him, somewhat anxiously. If I were being honest, I should have been trying to talk to him about all sorts of things, but my bravery came and went intermittently. It was like it was mocking me.

Jared ignored my suggestion and wrapped an arm around my hips to pull me forcefully against him.

"I think it's time for you to give me a kiss," he whispered, just a short distance from my lips. His breathing sped up, but not from excitement, rather it was from the difficulty of trying to hold that position for too long.

"Hold your horses. First, I need to show you the guest room, then we can watch a nice movie."

I bought myself some time by showing him the room where he'd be staying. While I was at it, I also gave him a quick tour of the house. Jared was stunned at the scope of the place.

I was tense, my body rigid the whole time, but talking about other things helped me build up the courage I needed to deal with what was sure to be the worst part of the evening.

When we got back to the living room, I tried to look relaxed as I sat down on the couch. "So, what genre are you thinking? Horror? Thriller? Crime?" I asked him, still stalling, but Jared didn't want to waste any more time with talk. He sat down next to me and took my wrists, leaning into my lips and seeking contact once again.

"I don't care about the movie; I just want to be with you," he whispered, before stealing a kiss that I know he would have deepened, had I not abruptly pulled away. He gave me a blank look, cocking his head in confusion.

"We need to talk, Jared," I said, trying to gather my thoughts. I rubbed the back of my hand over my lips, uncomfortable with the idea that his saliva might supplant the taste of Neil that remained there.

It was always still there, at least in my mind.

"Selene," Jared sighed wearily. "I'm having a shitty time right now, and you're the only good thing in my life. Everything in Detroit has changed since you left. My father isn't cutting me a single break with work, my classes are intense, and with Mom fighting cancer, I..." A shadow fell over his finely drawn features. His green eyes glistened and his jaw tensed. Immediately, I felt the urge to comfort him, so I took his face in my hands.

"Hey, hey, everything's going to be okay," I whispered gently. I knew all about his troubles; our bond had been cemented by supporting one another through our most difficult moments. Jared really was a guy with a huge heart, loving and completely unselfish. He adored his parents, and the burden of all their troubles often fell on him because he was their only child. His mother was diagnosed with cancer before we even met.

"I just want to be with you," he said again, kissing my neck. He hugged me, seeking the comfort that I had never hesitated to give him in previous months. How was I supposed to confess everything to him when he was in such a delicate and vulnerable mental state?

"I'll make you some hot chocolate," I told him instead and headed for the kitchen, where I rummaged around for a saucepan. When I found one, I got out the hot chocolate mix and grabbed some milk from the fridge. I poured everything into the pot and started heating it. I needed to figure out the most opportune moment to talk to Jared and—

"Did you tell him yet?" asked an unmistakable baritone behind me. I spun around fearfully and found Neil leaning one shoulder on the doorframe, looking beautiful as ever. He was breathtaking.

"That's my business," I snapped shortly.

And why did he care? In the end, what happened between the two of us was meaningless, and I was acutely aware of that fact.

He scrutinized me and I felt myself withering under that golden gaze—sometimes so bright, sometimes so shadowed.

"Don't fall for your boyfriend's whining; it could be a tactic to keep you under his thumb. You really want your freedom? Then go in there and take it." He moved closer, and I gave him a surprised look. Apparently he'd been listening to us. But if he had, how could he be so cynical about it?

"Don't you fucking tell me what to do!" I raised my voice and Neil groaned, closing his eyes. I frowned, confused and dismayed by his reaction. A second later, he opened his eyes back up, and I watched him approach me slowly like a large, deadly cat. I backed away, fully aware that there was nowhere to go.

"Say it again," he whispered, looming over me with his Adonis body. I stared at him and soaked in his pleasant amber aroma. His hair was still a little damp, probably from one of his countless daily showers.

"W... What?" I stammered, my butt bumping into the counter behind me.

"Fuck," he breathed, warm air hitting my face. "I really like the way that word slides off your lips," he added wickedly, locking eyes with me. "Wanna know what I'm thinking about?" He closed the distance between us and put his hands on either side of my body, pressing his chest against my breasts and pushing the air out of my lungs. I could feel the hard outline of every one of his muscles as though fused to my skin.

"No," I murmured in a daze. I didn't know whether it was his voice, his body, or his stare that rendered me so helpless. He nuzzled my cheek with the tip of his nose and breathed in my scent appreciatively.

"I'm thinking about how much I'd like to take you right here in this kitchen with your boyfriend sitting a few feet away from us. About you grinding your hips underneath me while I enjoy a nice, hard..." He stopped next to my ear and smiled. "Fuck," he said again slowly, as though trying to lodge the word firmly in my brain.

I gasped and trembled.

I closed my eyes, imagining my body, delirious with lust under Neil's hands. I quite tried to tamp down those profane thoughts, but Neil grabbed the back of my neck and rubbed my lower lip with his thumb. His hand was big and strong; the pad of his thumb felt cold against my overheated skin. I opened my eyes slowly and saw his own blazing eyes locked on my mouth.

I needed to get back to Jared and quickly.

"Neil," I pleaded softly, trying to create some space between us. I stepped to the side and turned to finish making the hot chocolate. I tried to take slow breaths and calm my furiously pounding heart. I stood up on my tiptoes in an effort to reach the mugs arranged on a high shelf until Neil reached out and effortlessly grabbed them for me, setting them down on the counter. I thanked him softly, staring at my trembling hands.

I had reached such a fever pitch of anxiety that I was completely thrown off-balance.

"Selene, is everything okay?" Jared inquired.

He had joined us in the kitchen. Neil retreated, if only just a bit and remained as austere and unmoved as ever. Jared's face grew guarded, and he watched me with concern.

"Yeah, I was just asking Neil where the mugs were." I pointed up to them and smiled at Jared before pouring the hot chocolate, being very careful not to make a mess with my shaking hands.

"Do you need any help?" he asked, but I quickly shook my head.

"No, I'll be with you in just a minute." I gave him a reassuring smile and Jared nodded, leaving the kitchen. Though not before throwing one last distrustful look in Neil's direction. I couldn't blame him: Neil was not the type to inspire trust in either women or men.

I touched my forehead; I had broken out into a cold sweat. Neil then approached me cautiously and put his hand on my neck, right in the exact spot Jared had been kissing just a few minutes before on the sofa. He rubbed my skin slowly, possibly intending to calm me down, but all he did was cause a blaze of heat in the middle of my chest.

"Wait for me tonight in your room..." he said in a lewd whisper before pressing a gentle kiss to the skin right below my earlobe.

My body's reaction was instantaneous and in sharp contrast to the way I'd reacted to contact with Jared. Goosebumps erupted on my skin and warm flood of liquid soaked my panties, forcing me to clamp my legs together.

After completely devastating me, he left and I was finally alone and could breathe again. I grabbed the two steaming mugs and went back to the living room and to Jared, where I apologized for the long wait.

"Are you sure everything's okay?" he asked as I settled down next to him, cupping the warm mug in my hands. I could still feel that uncomfortable wet sensation between my legs and my body was tense and shaky. Goddammit! Why did Neil have such power over me?

After we finished our hot chocolate, Jared and I watched a movie—I didn't understand a single thing about it. My mind was far away. Still, from time to time, I would nod or pretend I'd been listening to Jared's comments on certain scenes, which flashed before my eyes without actually registering in my brain.

Despite my confused state, when Jared put his arm around my shoulders, I leaned into his chest and allowed myself to be lulled into sleepiness. Jared stroked my hair, which tumbled freely down my back, and I just lay there, enjoying his touch even as I knew, deep down, that my continued silence was wrong. I closed my eyes, trying to hold back the guilty tears that threatened to fall.

Jared kissed my temple, then, unexpectedly, he tilted my chin up with his index finger and brought his lips to mine. Ours was a gentle, sweet kiss, so different from the ones that Neil was making me accustomed to. Our kiss tasted of concealed tears, concealed goodbyes, of unforgivable mistakes, and also of a profound fondness that I now understood would never become love. I kissed him back but only because I didn't want to make him suspicious.

"I love you," he whispered, and I, as though compelled by some dark force, slowly moved my gaze to the stairs where a shadowy figure was observing us from the upper floor.

Neil stood there, his elbows propped up on the railing and his long legs stretched out behind him. His broad shoulders were tensed, as though he had the weight of the entire world on them. I couldn't see the brightness of his eyes but I knew that he was watching us.

"Wait for me tonight in your room..." It seemed that I could hear those words again on the air. Or maybe it was just the echo of my own desire, the need I had to kiss him, touch, and possess him.

Still.

14

....

SELENE

After the movie was over, we talked for about an hour until sleep started to overtake us. After telling my boyfriend goodnight, I walked down the massive upstairs hallway, staring down at the luxurious marble floor as though all my sins were engraved upon it. I couldn't tell Jared the truth. I just couldn't, not with the state of mind he was in.

But this realization brought me no peace. The weight I felt was growing by the minute, and I had discovered that I was actually quite good at lying, which was a skill that I'd never thought I had before.

Lost in my thoughts, I didn't realize that I'd stopped in front of one of the many rooms in the house, one that usually remained locked. That night, however, the door was slightly ajar. I stepped up to, fully intending to close it, but a sudden instinctive urge stopped me. Instead, I peered into the crack and saw that no one was inside. So I put one hand on the cool surface of the wood and pushed it open.

It felt like I was infiltrating a sacred temple, a forbidden place. I had noticed this room during my first few days in the house. It was at the end of the hall across from Matt's office and cloaked in an inexplicable aura of mystery. It had been Anna herself who told me that no one was allowed to go inside. A prohibition that I was currently ignoring.

I groped for a light switch on the wall, and when I found it, a basic room appeared before me, not much different from a home office. There was a leather divan in ivory underneath a large window. A large mahogany desk presided majestically over the center of the room, clean save for an empty pen holder on top.

What was odd, however, were the numerous boxes left haphazardly all over the floor.

I coughed at the thick dust floating in the air and knelt down in front of a random box and rubbed the tip of my nose. I opened the box easily—the flaps weren't even sealed. Then, I pulled what appeared to be a photo album out of it. I ran my hand over the rough surface of the cover before leafing through it, seeing numerous old Miller family photos.

I smiled when I got to one of Logan and Neil as children in a garden. The former was chasing the latter, pretending to be an airplane or maybe an eagle, I couldn't tell. In the background, Mia smiled as she displayed her round belly. She must have been pregnant with Chloe.

I kept browsing and found another photo that featured a tall man with raven-colored hair and deep blue eyes smiling into the camera lens. He was wearing a lightweight shirt that showed off his slim, toned physique, and I assumed this had to be William Miller. His right arm was around young Logan's narrow shoulders and his left hand was buried in the pocket of his slacks.

On his left side, young Neil stood with his head down, staring at the garden. He looked as though he might be feeling left out and wasn't enthusiastic about being photographed. He was wearing a blue tank top with *Oklahoma City* written on it and matching shorts that didn't hide his dirty, scraped-up knees. His golden eyes were fixed on the bright green lawn. His father appeared oblivious to his son's mournful expression.

I touched the photo with my index finger, touched his gleaming eyes. In that child, I recognized the person I had seen rocking in a corner of his room after fighting with Logan. My chest grew tight with hurt. I knew almost nothing about Neil, but I felt so close to him, so connected with him that it seemed that I could feel his heartrending pain inside myself.

Before I could put the album back in the box, though, something else caught my eye. Something much more interesting than family photos. A stack of newspapers covered the bottom of the box. I grabbed one and read the front page headline: "The Children of the Dark Side." I scowled, and with the speed of a thief who is about to be caught red-handed, I rifled through the papers to read the headlines underneath.

"Who Is the Shadow Man?"

"Scandal in New York".

"Children of Darkness."

I pressed my hand over my lips to stifle any noise of shock. I wanted to read through these articles and learn more but a sound from the hallway had me hastily closing up the box and getting to my feet.

I ran to the light switch and flicked it off, holding my breath. I leaned closer to the crack in the door until I could peer out into the hallway. Anna was doing a walkthrough of the house, probably checking that she'd finished all her assigned tasks. She hadn't yet realized that the mystery room was unlocked, but it obviously wasn't safe for me to stay there.

So, after making sure she wasn't looking in my direction, I

scurried down the hallway and took refuge in my own room, shutting the door behind me.

What were those newspaper headlines about? Could it be related to Neil's strange behavior? It was obvious that something had happened to him and his family, but I still didn't know exactly what that was. It was difficult to guess from the few ambiguous pieces I'd seen.

Nevertheless, I was positive that I would solve this mystery. I just needed more time. I was even more determined now, but truthfully, since the moment I met those shining, shadowed eyes I had known perfectly well that Neil was hiding a history that I needed to uncover.

I sighed and toed off my shoes. Then I reached behind my back and tried to unzip my dress as I walked over to the vanity. I was disturbed and pensive in a way I'd never been before in my life. It felt like fate had a design for me and that my meeting with Neil had been meticulously planned by some sort of trickster god.

"I've been waiting for you for a good ten minutes, Babygirl."

I let out a shriek of terror when I spotted Neil in the mirror behind me. He was standing motionless beside my bed.

He smiled at me, and I lost the ability to speak. I swallowed thickly and waited for him to make his move. I knew for certain that I wasn't capable of taking even one step toward that tantalizing body.

Neil, however, had nothing but time. He appraised me lazily before approaching me at a languid, feline pace with all his usual dominance and certainty. Little by little, his smell of amber and tobacco surrounded me. My eyes remained locked on his the entire time, lustful, yes, but above all else dangerous.

"Turn around," he demanded, and I obeyed like a puppet on a string. I feared him. I didn't want to challenge him, but at the same time, I was enthralled by him.

On the one hand, having my back to him helped me maintain a clear head, albeit with some difficulty.

On the other hand, I had no idea what he intended to do back there, and that sense of unknown expectation only intensified the feelings I had until it seemed like I could drown in them.

"Why are you here?" I asked in a small voice, unmoving.

"To fuck you," he answered boldly, right next to my ear. I could feel his chest pressing against my back and his fingers brushing my tensed arm. His breath was warm and controlled, as though nothing in the world could make him lose his self-possession.

"You've already done that." I trembled as I said it. I wasn't trying to provoke him, though I realized that he might have taken it that way. I stiffened when his hand touched the zipper on the back of my dress.

"Not the way I wanted to," he whispered, slowly opening the zipper as though I were some china doll to be handled delicately. I remained motionless, at the mercy of his movements, and I was ashamed of the way I submitted so easily to his every command, but at the same time, I found myself unable to oppose him. I wanted to turn around and look him in the eyes, maybe kick him out and tell him to stop touching me. But I was afraid that he'd see what I really wanted written all over my face, and I wanted to hide it for as long as I could.

"You aren't hurting for women; why do you want me?" I felt his hand stop at the base of my spine. Neil wasn't expecting such a blunt question. I turned my face slightly, resting my chin on my shoulder and waiting for a response that never came. Instead, he inhaled irritably through his nose and continue to undress me.

He let my dress slide down my body until it was just a crumple of fabric around my ankles.

Why was I letting him do all of this? I didn't know. All I knew was that I was clay in his hands, and he was the sculptor. I was the canvas to his painter, the sheet of blank paper to his ink.

"You should watch out for feelings—they can affect the coldest of hearts. Even yours," I continued, trying to needle him even as my body was moved by involuntary tremors. By now it was clear to me that he was no more indifferent to me than I was to him.

"Are you thinking I'm some sentimental guy just because I was considerate with your body the first time, little virgin?" he whispered into my ear, and I didn't like the derisive tone of his voice.

I shouldn't have let him talk to me that way. I wanted to snap back at him, slap him or even kick him in the balls, but when I tried to turn around and do just that, Neil grabbed me violently by the hair.

"What the hell are you doing?" I screamed, beside myself with fear and rage. I tried to struggle free from his grip, the way his fingers clamped down on my hair was painful. I cursed and shouted but none of it made him stop.

Neil swept the books off my desk and forcibly bent me over it. My chest, still covered by my bra, flattened against the cold surface. My ribs and hipbones collided with the wood so hard that I clenched my teeth in pain.

"I'm showing you just how romantic and sentimental I really am," he sneered, and I could hear him fumbling with the fly of his jeans. With one hand still holding me down by my neck, he used the other hand to lower his pants and then his boxers. I couldn't see much from my position but I could make out enough to know what he was about to do.

Stupid.

I had been so stupid but that realization hardly mattered now. This boy was an animal, with serious personal issues and a deep indifference to the feelings of others. Neil was completely different from—

Shit.

Jared.

Was he going to hear me screaming? Was he going to find everything out in the most horrifying way? I imagined him bursting into my room and finding me bent over the desk with Neil behind me.

I tried to push him away, but the truth was: I wanted that. I was too weak. I couldn't suppress the need that I felt flowing through me. I stopped moving, stopped fighting. Pretending to resist him would have been pointless. Neil already knew what I was feeling; he could read my body.

"You want it too; I can tell." He leaned over me, his upper body pressing against my bare back and his pelvis tight against my ass. I could feel him rubbing himself between my ass cheeks, over my panties. He was fully hard and it was just as long and thick as I remembered it.

"This is all wrong," I said, referring to the entire situation. My voice, however, was not as decisive as I wanted it to be, and I had allowed my legs to fall open in a clear invitation. Meanwhile, Neil continued to slowly rub himself against me, panting against the back of my neck, grasping my hair in his fist.

He slapped the palm of his other hand on the wooden surface of the desk, right by my face, and I was hypnotized, staring at those large, strong fingers, the regular nails and raised veins on the back.

I surrendered to our mutual desire with a deep sigh.

"I know how much you liked using me," he whispered into my ear before licking me like an animal might. I could feel his hot tongue gliding down the curve of my neck to my shoulder until it reached my nape. He continued downward, following the line of my backbone and I arched into him, delighting in this utterly masculine display of possession. "Just as much as I liked using you," he finished mischievously.

"I didn't use you." My cheek was pressed against the desk so hard it was difficult to articulate the words clearly. I had to bite my lip to keep from screaming when he slapped my right butt cheek, making the skin burn. My head spun and a sudden wave of cold and heat hit me at the same time from my chest to my toes.

"I did and I intend to do it again," he admitted with the kind of sadistic smile that revealed all his nasty intentions. I watched him from the corner of my eye while he pulled my panties to one side and touched me. I was soaked and ashamed of my treacherous body's reaction to him.

Despite everything, I wanted this—wanted him—and there was no excuse or justification for it. Only this profound sense of shame.

He penetrated me with two fingers and I moaned aloud, tensing every muscle in my body, even the smallest and most imperceptible. He moved his fingers expertly, caressing my tight yet yielding inner walls. Immediately, he found my most sensitive spot, locating it with an ease that spoke to his vast experience.

I pressed my lips together to suppress a moan, not wanting to let him win or give in to him or show him just how much power he had over me. But he felt it anyway.

"You're a bastard," I murmured irritably, grasping the edge of the desk with both hands. I could feel my knees trembling and I had pins and needles on the soles of my feet, a sign that my orgasm was close. But Neil withdrew his fingers and just stood there behind me. I turned my face slightly to look at him. I was enervated but aroused; angry yet eager for him.

He raised the fingers he'd just used to touch me up to his mouth and sucked them with an obscene groan. He licked away the taste of me and pinned me fast with the golden gems of his eyes. He gave me a wicked grin while I turned violently red.

He rubbed my ass cheek with one hand and used the other to masturbate himself from the base to the tip of his enviable length. I was captivated: his body had been created for the express purpose of giving pleasure. He was built to fan the flames of the female libido and to awaken unexplored desires. Though I had played at resistance before, I was now bent over and eager to welcome him in.

Suddenly, the knowledge that Jared was just a short distance away in the guest room brought me back to reality. Hard. A wave of misery washed away the thrill of the moment. I lifted up my torso, intending to put a stop to all of this. Intending to get dressed and flee from this boy who represented for me all that was wicked.

When I tried, however, Neil put his hand on the back of my neck again and forced me down into the same position as before. Except this time he pressed me harder into the desk to keep me from moving at all.

"Jared is right there. We shouldn't..." I was whimpering and I could feel tears forming in the corners of my eyes. My heart was pounding violently and my chest was sore. Neil chuckled. He was enjoying my vulnerable state.

I, on the other hand, was so bewildered: one moment I was aroused; the next moment I was grief-stricken.

"So what? Josh or whatever the fuck that asshole's name is can hear his girl enjoying herself while someone fucks her for once," he said, satisfaction evident in his baritone voice before he penetrated me with one short, decisive thrust. I jolted against the desk and let out a yell that had Neil covering my mouth with the palm of his hand.

"Shh..." His powerful, muscular body was smothering me. He leaned his chest into my back until I was pressed completely flat against the wood. Then he began to move inside me with force, giving me no time to adapt to the large intrusion.

"Neil! Please," I murmured against the warmth of his hand. But even to myself it sounded more like a plea for him to continue.

My hearted battered my ribs, my pants grew faster and faster while my vagina pulsed, accommodating him in all his thickness. I felt an intense pressure against my pelvic muscles. Every time he slowly dragged out of me, I opened my eyes up wide just to squeeze them shut again when he slammed back in with a firm thrust.

He was well aware of his unusually large size. He had taken it into account during our first time, but now he was using it to dominate me, to force me to feel every bit of his strength. He felt like a perpetual motion machine, built only to pound, pound, pound, and pound again. I felt like he was trying to suck out my soul, to corrupt me and then feed off my most intimate desires.

"Softer, please…" I managed as he continued to move against me as though only he and his pleasure even existed. He pressed one hand against my hip while the other was still clutching the base of my neck. He moved his hips implacably against me, slamming against my ass.

"You asked me to show you the real me, your first time," he answered in a shady, sensual tone. He'd waited a few moments to answer me; so long that I assumed he'd forgotten about my request. He sounded thoughtful, lost in some shadow realm. All at once, I realized that my body was only a means to an end for him. In contrast to our last time, he was trying to show me how incapable he was of feeling or connecting sex with anything more significant than an orgasm.

There was nothing of the gentle boy who had undressed me and touched me before left in him now. There were no understanding looks or reassuring smiles or human contact. His burning stare was fixed exclusively on his swollen erection pumping into me, incessant, brutal, and carnal. He saw nothing but my ass cheeks, red from his slaps, and my hips, aching from hitting that awful wooden desk.

"N… Neil," I babbled in a panic, because he seemed too far away and his passion too rough and uncontrollable. I also realized he wasn't wearing a condom, again, which only increased my panic.

"Do you always do it bare?" I managed to ask him in the small space between one thrust and the next. Neil rubbed between my legs with one hand, concentrating on my clit. Then I heard him emit a tiny groan in my ear, one of the few sounds he typically made.

"No, only with you," he admitted, though I couldn't be sure if it was actually true. He kept rubbing me with one hand, fingers slipping between the hot, giving folds of my sex. And despite the minor discomfort, I offered it up freely to him.

"I hope you're not lying," I murmured, closing my eyes. I felt exhausted and sore, despite how aroused I'd become by his shocking show of force. The more he drove into me the slicker I got, in spite of the way my weary muscles screamed at me to make him stop.

He used his tight grip on my hair to force me to bend my back and turn my face in his direction. I opened my eyes again just as Neil breathed against my lips. I met his gaze and noticed a total absence of emotion there. Then, unexpectedly, a flicker of concern moved across his unusual eyes. This was the first bit of human connection we'd shared since he decided to show up in my room. He nuzzled the tip of my nose with his own and then kissed me, urgently and passionately. I moaned into his full, greedy lips, and then Neil showed me just how unrelenting he could be. He began to synchronize the movements of his tongue with the thrusts of his pelvis. He stopped teasing my clit and moved that hand up to my breast, gripping and kneading it forcefully.

I wanted to feel his skin; I wanted to trace his tattoos and learn more of his story. I wanted to soak up his heat the way I did that first time on my bed, but that wasn't possible. Neil kept his clothes on, emotionally far away, consumed solely by his desire to possess me. He broke the kiss and bent me over again, pushing my back down with his chest. Then he continued to move in that firm, rapid way. Always seeking more, like some insatiable beast.

I came abruptly, strangling him and trapping him in that private place where only he had ever been granted access. I ground my lip between my teeth as I felt electrical pulses moving through my body, a rainbow of colors appearing before my eyes. I also slowly became aware of the sound the desk was making as it slammed into the wall. The fear of being discovered mingled with the devastating sensations I was experiencing.

But that was just what Neil was: a lusty man leading me to hell, uncaring about any consequences. I felt buffeted along by a wind that I couldn't outrun, and this little vice of mine was becoming a genuine bad habit.

Pleasure fused with the pain of his thrusts and radiated through every cell in my body. I arched my back and chased his movements, hoping he would come soon as well.

"Fuck," he whispered as he squeezed my still bra-covered breasts and continued to drive into me like a maniac. I silently prayed for him to orgasm because I didn't know how long I could continue to absorb all that power. Now that I'd gone over my own peak, his member was more uncomfortable inside me.

"Look, Selene. Look at that…" He moved my face toward the mirror and only then did I realize that he'd had a full view of us the whole time, lost in our moment of wanton excess. I could see Neil bent over me, his marble-hard glutes contracting with each thrust, his pants lowered to his knees. His flexed forearms were so big they seemed in danger of ripping his shirt. His face was beautiful, with a cruel smile on his red, swollen lips.

Then, I saw myself: legs half-bent, my spine curved and my butt raised up. I saw my reflection's breasts flattened against the wood, cheeks flushed, lips parted. My eyes were shining and my hair was a mess.

I looked like a wild creature, a woman without inhibitions.

It didn't look like *me*.

"Do you like to watch? It makes me crazy," he said, and I felt something wet gliding down my cheeks. I was crying.

It was in that moment that I truly understood the profound differences between the two of us. I had pushed myself so hard, trying to bridge the gap of that difference. But instead I had just lost myself as I followed him.

I continued to stare into the mirror. Neil rested his cheek against mine and ground his stubbly jaw against my smooth, moist skin. Though he clearly saw my tears, there was no apology in his eyes nor understanding. Just a simple awareness that he had put me in this state of distress.

"Look." He withdrew from me slowly and showed me his cock in the mirror. My reaction was instantaneous: I blushed.

"Remember? I told I'd show you how perfectly a man and woman could fit together. Don't you find it romantic?" he whispered sneeringly.

"You're insane," I said harshly, smelling his clean scent mixed with the distinct odor of sex. We were both sweating and breathless.

"You have no idea," he said, pushing into me again and I gasped. I couldn't take more endless minutes of incessant pounding, but his breathing had gotten fast so I knew he was approaching his limit. The last thrust was so powerful and resonating that both of our bodies trembled. He pulled out and marked me right there between my thighs where I was still quivering from his presence. My eyes widened when, moments later, I felt his seed running down my legs until it dripped onto the floor.

Neil grabbed my hips like he needed to hold something to keep from falling over. A soft moan accompanied this tiny moment of weakness; his biceps tensed. After this one instant of vulnerability, he bit his lower lip and not one single grunt, moan, or other animalistic noise left his lovely mouth.

Neil was filthy, vulgar, and perverse but not theatrical. He felt no need to impress a woman with false or excessive chatter during sex. The silence was compelling in its own way.

"Fuck," he said, more to himself than to me, staring down at the evidence on my body of his total loss of control. I stood up from the desk. My elbows were red and my back ached. I got to my feet but staggered when I was hit by a dizzy spell. Neil immediately grabbed me, and I rested my head against his chest. I didn't care if it made me look weak; I was exhausted and it was physically challenging to stand on my own two legs.

He wrapped his arm around my waist and moved my hair off my sweating forehead with his free hand. Neither of us spoke.

Neil helped me to my bed and I lay down on the sheets, curling automatically into a fetal position. His smell was all over me, and I felt like a wreck while he continued to smell and look impeccable.

He backed away from the bed and tucked his still half-hard penis back into his boxers and rearranged his pants, all without taking his eyes off me. It was horrifying, the blank way he could look at me after such an intense, yearning, explosive orgasm. I felt the chill sinking into my bones and my heartbeat throbbed in my temples and wrists. I began to shake again. This act of intimacy hadn't brought us together. If anything, it was the opposite. We looked like two perfect strangers.

Neil continued staring at me in the most detached, almost irritated way, and I felt my self-control slipping more and more. This was the man who had full possession of my soul. I no longer knew who I was.

It was madness.

"Never set foot in that room again. My fucking life is none of your business," he said angrily, and I flinched at his severe tone. Suddenly, I understood his aggression: it was punishment for my intrusion.

"Why?" I sat up on the edge of the bed, trying to ignore the chafing between my legs. I put my feet down on the cold floor. Half-naked in just my white bra, sodden panties, and thigh-highs,

I looked completely worn out. Or maybe Neil was just good at making me feel that way. I sighed and got unsteadily to my feet. I couldn't let him steamroll me anymore; I needed to show him that I was stronger than he believed.

"Because I didn't come in here to be loved or understood by you," he answered, scowling. Then he looked at me with that disarming certainty that set him apart from everyone else. I faced him, fixing my eyes on his. I was going to find all of his weak spots.

"You came in here because you want me more than you want anyone else, and that scares you."

He was expecting just about anything except that. He jerked in surprise and then burst into dismissive laughter. He approached me with confident strides and slowly scanned my body.

"You're so naive, Selene…" He toyed with a lock of my hair, and I tightened my lips into a thin line. His scent was surrounding me entirely and it gave me goosebumps. I hated myself in that moment for the way he made me feel. "Whenever you talk like that, I just want to fuck the innocence right out of you," he whispered in my ear, touching first my cheek and then the curve of my neck. His eyes followed the path his hands made while he breathed me in, absorbing me slowly. He meant to destroy me, I could see it.

"Is that supposed to make me think I got you wrong?" I murmured in a small voice. I had no idea where this unusual bravery was coming from.

"I'm sorry for you, Tinkerbell, but this isn't a fairy tale." He drew close to my mouth and gave me a sarcastic smile. Then he ran his tongue along the contour of my lower lip before walking away and leaving me there, sitting in the wake of his mysterious, shadowy presence.

I still wanted to get some of my own back, though, so I shoved past him and knelt down to pick up the books he'd hurled to the floor when he bent me over the desk. I rubbed my face and closed my eyes.

No. I shouldn't cry, even if I wanted to because he had hurt me. What had really wounded me, however, wasn't his indifferent words, but the way he managed to make me feel.

Filthy, wrong, weak.

Neil was a temptation that I couldn't resist, but every time I gave in, I couldn't live with myself after. I sickened myself; I hated myself. I crouched there with his seed between my thighs, his smell on me, his saliva drying on my skin, and I was ashamed of having allowed him to take ownership of me—of my mind as well as my very being.

"You're bad for me," I said through gritted teeth. It was a truth we both knew, me especially.

Neil swallowed but retained his composure as though my words didn't come as a surprise. "I'm bad for everyone," he agreed. He glanced at my books and then at the desk. He appeared to be considering something for a few moments before he headed for the door.

He left the room, but I could still feel his presence. He was all around me, but most of all, he was inside me.

He was a demon in the shape of a god. He wore his perversion and vice like horns, his confidence like a forked tail, and wielded his damned personality like a weapon—like a pitchfork.

Yet, for all of this, Neil was the person who brought my world to life.

The one who brought *me* to life.

15

....

NEIL

"You're bad for me."

Selene had just figured it out, but I had known it all along.

I'd fucked her, just like I'd done a million times before with every other person in every other erotic encounter.

Sex was my priority—a sick need that often had me forgetting to eat. I used it to remind the world of who I was and what my role here was. I was on the other side now—the winning side. I was in full control of my life, no one else.

I had been locked in the bathroom for more than an hour. I had washed myself again and again. I had scrubbed my skin for so long it had turned red, trying to chase off the nightmares that kept me from sleeping. The dark circles under my eyes were physical proof of the disquiet that had me in its grip. My anxiety was worsening again. I regularly felt disoriented; my chest would hurt, and I struggled to breathe. Basically, my body was clearly showing me that I was becoming more and more unstable.

But I wasn't going to tell anyone. I never did.

Instead, I was going to pretend that everything was fine and that I could handle anything that might be happening to me. The truth was, I needed help. The kind of help that I continually denied myself.

I put my hands around the sides of the sink and squeezed hard. I was completely naked, and as usual, I disgusted myself. I stared at myself in the mirror and tried to mesh that image with the version of me that I couldn't bring myself to accept.

But the truth was, we couldn't both live in the same body.

I would never stop feeling ashamed, just as I would never stop feeling wrong. I would never get free from these feelings of revulsion and the yearning to escape—to die—that constantly knocked around inside my head.

I would never be healed; there was no absolution available for my sins.

I felt like I was trapped—suspended between vice and pleasure, a mockery of redemption. Though I forced myself to live "in the moment," I remained stubbornly anchored to the past. My body had grown, changed, experienced new stimuli, but my mind was still set apart, far away in another world.

All at once, I couldn't help but ask myself what my lovers—Babygirl now included—found attractive about someone like me. After a moment of reflection, the answer became obvious: I stirred the shameful, hidden lusts in women.

I knew that I was desired, and this generated a deep discomfort in me. I hated myself. I hated myself because my looks had only ever been a punishment for me. Now Selene had fallen into my trap, overcome by my enchantments, subjugated by my eyes and my body. In the end, she was no different from the others. She just liked the feeling of my tongue in her mouth, my cock in her cunt, my hands all over her. She wanted from me the exact same thing that they all wanted, and I shouldn't have deluded myself into imagining otherwise.

The truth was, no one would accept a person like me, not if they actually discovered the filth that was inside me. And Selene was no exception.

She was just one of many. What's worse—she was a liar as well.

That morning, before I holed up in my room like a monster in exile, I overheard a conversation between her and Jared. He'd gone urgently to Selene's room, saying something about a call from Detroit, about his mother and her health.

I didn't just listen in, though. I'd also crept up to the half-open door like a stalker to peer inside. Selene had hugged Jared, bursting into tears against his chest, and I couldn't help but smile at the pathetic scene. Babygirl still hadn't told him about us, but in her ocean eyes, I could clearly see the desire to confess it all to him, warring with her inability to do so at that very inopportune moment.

Then, she walked Jared to the front door. Her boyfriend was supposed to stay with us for longer, but apparently he had to leave early.

I felt an insane sense of relief in that moment. I even sighed in satisfaction and stared at my reflection as a perversely pleased expression spread over my face. I truly was a selfish bastard: I wanted Jared's lovely girl for myself. I wanted her in my bed, underneath me, in all the dirtiest, most shameful and profane ways a man could want a woman. To satiate these unhealthy desires, though, dearest Josh needed to disappear. He had to just go back where he came from and quit fucking with me.

For once, it seemed that fate was on my side.

"Neil, what are you doing?" My brother's voice came to me muffled, and I wasn't completely surprised by his presence. I was standing motionless, naked, with my hands clutching the sink as I stared at myself. Who knew how long I'd been there, imprisoned in my own reflection? Logan must have sensed it.

My brother was the one person who knew me better than

anyone. We were linked by a unique, unbreakable bond: we had a shared past that had shaken us. But only I had been destroyed entirely.

I stood up straight and walked past him into my bedroom. I needed to cover myself, though I liked to be naked and soak up the cold in the air. Sometimes, it still had the power to freeze my memories.

"What do you want?" I pulled on my boxers without looking at him, then grabbed a pair of jeans and a dark sweater from the closet. When I'd finished dressing, I turned to Logan and met his concerned eyes. My brother wasn't here casually. I knew him well enough that I could smell the anxiety on him.

"It's about…" he took a deep breath and passed a hand over his face, a sure sign that he feared my reaction to whatever he was about to tell me. "Chloe," he finished in a whisper.

Just hearing her name was enough to make my every sense snap to attention. I walked over to him, a knot of tension in my stomach, and looked at him. We were the same height, but unlike me, Logan had a slim, lean body.

"What happened?" I demanded, alarmed.

Logan was visibly uncomfortable. He hesitated for a few moments, getting up the nerve to tell me. "I think…" he started nervously, "someone hurt Chloe." His words were deliberately vague.

I didn't wait any longer and instead pushed him aside to rush out of my room. I headed for Chloe's room, and Logan followed hot on my heels. The whole time, he kept telling me that I needed to stay calm, that we had to understand the situation and get Chloe to tell us the truth. He said I should control my impulses, because he knew what I was like. I lost my head easily; when I did, no one could manage me.

The short trip to my sister's room seemed to last forever. My head was full of horrifying images, terrifying guesses and assumptions. I burst into Chloe's room and then, I spotted her.

She was curled up on her white bed, her knees pulled up close to her chest and her face tucked down against them. Her blond hair spread over her slim thighs like threads of gold. I approached her cautiously, my heart pounding against my rib cage. I sat down on the side of the bed and gave her head a gentle stroke. She was trembling and a sob escaped her lips.

"Little Koala..." I called her by the nickname I'd given her as a child. Chloe was my Little Koala, and she always would be, no matter how grown up she got.

"Look at me," I insisted in a soft voice, and she slowly lifted her head.

I sucked in a breath when I saw her blue eyes puffy and glassy with tears as well as a purple bruise marring her right cheekbone. I moved her chin with two fingers to get a better look. More marks dotted her neck, ending at an undetermined point underneath her T-shirt.

I had no words. I was shocked. Incredulous.

Chloe's skin was a horrible meeting of innocence and violence. I felt like a cloud of freezing rain was hanging above me; it was too cold to move. Logan, meanwhile, was watching everything with glistening eyes and his jaw clenched miserably.

"What did they do to you? Who did this?" I murmured softly, keeping my voice calm even as I felt a violent, uncontrolled force welling up inside me. I closed one hand into a fist and the other began to tremble. I was the one who always defended my siblings— from everyone and everything. But right now, I felt like nothing but a failure.

How could I have let something like this happen?

I touched her cheek, trying to reassure her, but Chloe just looked down, afraid and deeply wounded. I knew well the feelings she was experiencing: the fear, confusion, and pain. I'd been through them all myself.

"Tell me who did it, kiddo. You need to tell me…" I tried to keep calm, though I was already imagining the reckoning I was going to bring down on the bastard—or bastards—who made the mistake of crushing her like this. *No one* touched my siblings.

"Talk to us, Chloe, please…" Logan urged her, stroking her long blond hair. But our sister seemed to be in shock. Her eyes were vacant. Her legs began to shake, and her lower lip started shaking as well. I was going to make whoever was responsible for this desecration pay.

"Carter," she said finally in an almost inaudible whisper. I stiffened at the sound of the name.

Carter Nelson, Bryan's little brother. I ground my teeth together like an animal and inhaled noisily through my nose.

I was going to kill him.

My twisted mind could neither suggest nor accept any other solution.

All at once I stood up and started running my hands through my hair, tangling it wildly. I could feel my reason slowly slipping away from me until I was completely devoid of any rational thought. A heavy feeling slammed into my upper body, and my heart felt like it was about to be spat out of my chest.

"Neil…" Logan cautioned, realizing what was about to happen.

The madness was creeping over me slowly. I held my face in my hands and tossed my head. I was furious, enraged, completely out of control.

My brother tried to grab my arm, but I was more agile. I fled the room.

I couldn't hear anything; I couldn't see anything.

Anger was riding me. It mocked my weakness and enflamed every fiber of my being.

I went outside, got behind the wheel of my car, and hit the gas, blowing past all the speed limits. I darted around every vehicle in my way, and I wouldn't have been surprised if I'd gotten a ticket.

There was only one thing that mattered to me in that moment: watching that fucker's blood drip down my knuckles.

"Fuck!" I pounded the steering wheel and ran my hand through my hair again. Had that son of a bitch only tried to assault her or had he actually succeeded? Chloe was a virgin, and the idea that he had managed to violate her and take that from her was killing me.

I had no way of knowing how far he'd gone, because I hadn't asked enough questions.

Just hearing his name had been enough to make me completely lose my mind.

I was going to kill him.

I wasn't afraid. I didn't fear the law, prison, or any of that bullshit. What I felt for my family was the only form of love I believed in and I wasn't going to let anyone hurt them.

I came to a halt, braking shortly in front of the illuminated Blanco sign. I knew that I could find Bryan inside, and there was a good chance his brother would be with him.

Blanco was synonymous with cocaine, a very well-known place in this part of town for both using and dealing. That tended to make it more attractive to my peers than the usual clubs or bars.

I didn't bother parking the car correctly and just got out. Immediately, I spotted a black Lamborghini, which I knew to be Nelson's car.

Like every other night, the place was packed; women and men were lounging on sofas and doing lines or touching each other lazily. I moved through the crowds, trying to ignore the sly glances from coked-up girls looking to get railed in one of the bathrooms. I struggled to pick out that Nelson dickhead in the crowd.

"Hey asshole, thanks for finally showing up." Xavier appeared in front of me with a malevolent smile on his face. He looked like he wanted to take a shot at me, probably because of the way I'd bailed on him earlier to get with Selene.

I shoulder-checked him as I passed. I had no time to waste.

"Where the fuck...?" I muttered to myself, viciously shoving any idiot stupid enough to get near me.

"Who are you looking for?" asked Xavier, who I hadn't even realized was behind me. I turned and looked him up and down. He was giving me a cautiously inquisitive look. He had seen how furious I was, and everybody knew when the anger got the better of me, all I did was raise hell.

"Bryan Nelson. Where is he?" I asked, looking past him.

Then, I spotted it: a head of blond hair and a come-on smile aimed at two chicks near the bar.

Bingo.

I walked purposely toward Bryan, who was now heavily flirting with the two girls, even groping one's ass. I took him by the shoulder and landed a right hook square in his face, immediately wiping away that smug dick smile. He toppled to the ground and the girls screamed, scrambling away in fear.

Some of the people around us turned and gave us their full attention but most just continued dancing to the irritating electronica the DJ was spinning.

"What the fuck is your problem, Miller?" Bryan ran the back of his hand over his lip, which had begun to bleed in a trickle from the corner. He glared up at me; I'd only thrown the one punch, but it seemed like he couldn't get up.

But this asshole wasn't my real target.

"Where's your brother?" I demanded as I watched him struggle to his feet.

"What do you want with him?" Bryan staggered and spat blood on the floor next to my shoe in a clear act of defiance.

Did he think I was going to spare him if he demonstrated a little swagger? No. I was going to obliterate him.

"Tell me where he is!" I shouted, grabbing him by the shirt. I clenched the fabric in my fists and locked eyes with him. Bryan stared back at me in shock.

Was he getting a glimpse of the devil inside me? Probably.

"Let him go; I'm the one you want," came a menacing, sardonic voice from behind me. I shoved Bryan away and turned around.

And there he was, Carter Nelson, leather jacket stretched over his shoulders, hair black as night, and a small ring in his left nostril. An arrogant, cynical little fuck.

I stared at him with depthless hatred and clenched my jaw, trying to control the urge to immediately go for his throat.

"I know you, Neil Miller. You don't scare me," he said challengingly. What a brave boy.

I grinned cruelly and slowly advanced on him.

"No, you don't know me at all. Because, if you did, you never would have pulled that kind of shit with my sister." I held my arms loose at my sides and began slowly moving each finger, as though I were warming up before a workout.

Carter's gaze slid over to my hands. Maybe he was finally realizing that he was going to play the role of heavy bag for me tonight.

"Yeah, I tried to fuck her, but don't worry, she's still a virgin," he said mockingly.

And then there was a moment, just one moment, that I imagined must have been much like the explosion that constituted the Big Bang—an explosion that birthed the entire universe. In that one moment, I felt like I was experiencing the very same enormous detonation, except it was entirely contained within my body.

Body temperature spiked, anger expanded, reason disappeared.

My demons seemed to me like galaxies, revolving around me in space. I could see them and hear them, and I followed where they led.

A powerful force coursed through my veins. I could no longer identify any specific voice or face. All I felt was the electric jolt I got as each punch landed.

Everything happened so fast, and I found myself straddling Carter's limp form. His face grew more disfigured with each blow. The smell of blood surrounded me, my knuckles were covered in painful nicks and gashes and my heart pounded wildly.

And then, I came back to myself. I remembered: this *thing* had tried to rape my sister, and when Chloe resisted, he'd beaten her.

"Oh my God… You're going to kill him!" a familiar voice cried out among the chorus of terrified screaming, but I didn't care.

I took Carter's head in both hands and bashed it into the floor as hard as I could. I screamed in rage at what he had done, and then I screamed again at what I was now doing in response.

"Enough! Enough!"

Someone wrapped their arms around my chest and pulled me away from Carter's brutalized body. Both my vision and my thinking were clouded. I couldn't breathe and sweat was pouring off me.

"Neil, calm down! Calm down, please!"

I continued to flail blindly against whoever was trying to restrain me. There was nothing surrounding me anymore. Only blackness, shapes without animation, indistinct faces, emptiness. I elbowed someone, possibly a girl, it was impossible to tell.

I was swallowed up by rage, a destructive force that I couldn't fight.

I blinked several times until a slim figure began to materialize in front of me, its edges still blurry and deformed.

"It's okay, Neil. I'm here with you."

My breathing showed no signs of leveling out; drops of saltwater beaded up on my forehead. I couldn't remember where I was or who I was with. I was confused and lost—the way I always was after one of my uncontrolled outbursts of anger.

Little by little, though, the faces around me grew more precise features and appropriate colors. I could recognize my brother. Logan was there.

"Neil." He held my face in his hands, clearly scared to death. I felt guilty as I shut my eyes and breathed out slowly. My heart was still galloping and my veins were flooded with a sick fury. I had to calm down; I had to do it for Logan.

How many times had he been by my side in a moment like this?

How many times had he seen me in this state?

How many times had I made him afraid?

And yet, he was always there for me. Always.

That was what love meant to me.

"Logan..." I whispered disoriented, and he smiled in relief. I turned my head slightly until I could see who was holding me. I recognized Xavier. I wriggled free, and he let me go. I was tired, drained of all physical strength and energy. It was only then that I was able to look around and realize that we were by ourselves in a dark and gloomy corner of the room.

How did we get here?

They'd probably pulled me away from Carter, or else I would have finished what I'd started.

Oh yeah, Carter.

I didn't even know if the guy had survived my fury. I wanted to make him pay for what he'd done to Chloe, but maybe I had gone a little overboard. I searched myself for any repentant feelings, but I couldn't find one. I wasn't sorry about what I did, only disappointed in my inability to control myself. I might have killed someone, and I wouldn't even have been able to remember it.

"You were out of your mind..." Logan's shoulders slumped, as though admitting this truth was an enormous burden for him. "We need to get out of here. Someone called the police. The ambulance already took Carter. He was on the ground, unconscious." He spoke rapidly, and I was still too dazed to process any of it.

Logan tried to grab my arm, but I flinched away from his touch. I hated being touched without my consent, and I was about to remind him of that when someone else burst in, drawing my attention.

"Logan!"

I turned and saw Selene. Her voice was like the only properly tuned note in an otherwise discordant melody.

Babygirl ran to my brother with tears in her eyes. For a moment, I thought I was having a hallucination and that my imagination was playing tricks on me. But then I got a whiff of that coconut scent that I would have recognized anywhere, and I knew that it was all real.

That *she* was real.

"Everything's okay, Selene." Logan embraced her and reassured her as best he could. Meanwhile, my head had started to spin again, and I felt an instinctive need to lean back against the scraped-up wall behind me. The police could be there any minute, but I lacked the strength to run.

Still reeling, I looked into Selene's terrified face and found the crystalline ocean of her eyes. She was staring at me like I was a lunatic, a serial killer, fucked in the head. And maybe she wasn't entirely wrong about that.

Did she witness some of that horrifying scene from before?

"What are you doing here?" I demanded. I wanted to know why my brother had the bright idea of bringing her along with him and showing her what I really was. Not just a callous man who manipulated women into fucking him, not even just a self-centered, calculating cynic. No, I was something much worse than that, and from the way Selene was looking at me, I could guess that she knew it now, too.

"She insisted on coming. I didn't want her to, but she was worried about you," Logan explained. I smiled at his response.

Babygirl was worried about me?

Only because she didn't know then what I really was.

I kicked off the wall and approached Tinkerbell as though she were an oasis and I was a man dying of thirst. Selene held my gaze steadily while Logan gestured for me to follow him to his car as soon as possible because the police were still on their way.

I, however, was transfixed.

"What did you see?" She jumped when I reached her and spoke softly. She still looked unsettled and afraid.

She gulped, her long auburn hair falling gently around her shoulders. I wanted to touch it, but I forced myself to hold still and wait. I expected her to go off on me, tell me that I was crazy or dangerous or unfit for regular society, but instead she just examined my face discreetly.

"I saw a brother. Trying, in his own way, to punish his sister's abuser because family is everything to him."

Those words, so simple and so true, stupefied me. We hadn't seen or spoken to each other since last night when we were together. I'd fucked her brutally over a desk, and yet, there was no hate in her eyes, no bitterness. Just understanding and maybe even a bit of compassion. She was so little, but she contained such incredible strength.

She was a tigress, that much was for certain.

But how long would she be able to tolerate my insanity before losing her own mind?

"Why are you making excuses for me?" I asked irritably. I wanted her to see me for who I really was. Everyone was afraid of me; everyone kept the appropriate distance from me. They knew that I was rough. They knew that I often slipped outside the bounds of "normal" behavior, and that I was a constant fuckup.

I had *enjoyed* beating the shit out of Carter.

And now this girl was looking at me like I was some kind of hero, keeping the world safe from the monsters. I was no one's hero, though. Maybe she looked at me and saw Batman, but in reality, I was the Joker.

In reality, my life was not a comic book.

"I'm just trying to figure you out," she whispered.

I stared at her lips, red and parted. They formed the shape of a heart. I wanted to kiss them, lick them, and taste them like I'd been doing a few hours before. All at once, I couldn't help but wonder what a creature like her was doing in the middle of my tortured path. I knew that all good things came to an end, and it was almost never a happy one. So I needed to watch my back or Selene would be the end of me.

God had shown me nothing but cruelty since the day I was born, and I firmly believed that she had been sent by a higher power to break me down even further.

But did God think he'd gotten me with this one?

He was wrong.

He wasn't going to fuck me again. Instead, I was going to be the one fucking his ocean-eyed angel as many times as I wanted, even if she wasn't blond or slutty like my usual girls.

"We need to leave right now," Logan urged us, glancing around worriedly. But I didn't stop watching Selene. Her gaze slipped down to my hands. I followed her eye line and saw the blood on my knuckles, the purple-looking stains on my jeans and my rumpled sweater.

I looked pathetic and exhausted.

I shook my head and smiled wryly at myself. I lived my life in that state.

I was addicted to anger.

I used hate like a weapon.

I fed on my awful memories.

I was only deluding myself when I imagined there could be a better future and...I despised love.

Because I had been a victim of it before.

I had seen an unusual, aberrant, *sick* form of love up close. The kind that made an "I love you" into something that could destroy my soul all over again.

That was why I could never love.

That was why the monsters clung to my back.

That was why they whispered to me.

That was why I listened to them.

I was eaten up; I had nothing left to give someone. I couldn't even take when it came to love.

I was incapable of belonging to another person, and Selene was going to realize that sooner or later.

I was just existing in a detached sort of way.

It was how I lived my whole life.

It was who I was and I was *never going to change*.

16

SELENE

I sipped my coffee, trying to get something in my stomach. My mind was still combing over memories of the previous day. I had decided to go to Blanco with Logan. In fact, I'd driven him. I found him in the living room, trembling as he searched for the car keys. All he did was say Neil's name over and over, and that he should have stopped him because he was dangerous in "that state." I had no idea what he was talking about until I finally coaxed the whole story about Chloe and Carter out of him.

I sighed and put my cup back on the counter. Too much about that boy still eluded me. I'd watched him beat Carter bloody; I'd seen how incredibly strong he was, and I'd certainly observed the way he lost control. He had even elbowed me in the midst of his rage and didn't appear to notice. It was like he couldn't recognize anyone in that moment, not even himself.

My silent musing was interrupted by the sound of the doorbell. I watched as Anna straightened her uniform and hurried to the living room.

Chloe was out with Mia, my dad was at the hospital, and Logan and Neil were probably still sleeping. I followed along behind Anna and waited in the kitchen doorway as she opened the door. I held my breath when I saw two policemen standing at the door. They scrutinized the house like a pair of bloodhounds while Anna tried to ask them what they wanted.

"We're looking for Neil Miller. Is he at home?" one of them asked. The officers were middle-aged, tall, and imposing, and they wore their uniforms with obvious confidence.

Anna started and glanced around, perhaps looking for some way to stall or an excuse to offer. A rush of anxious fear ran from my head to my toes. Surely they were here about Carter. I wanted to jump in and rescue Anna from the awkward situation, but the sound of wild footsteps stopped me in my tracks.

I turned my head and watched Neil descending the giant marble staircase. His brown hair was mussed, like always. His golden eyes were lively and gleaming, and his lips were pressed into a severe yet charming expression.

He walked past me without even acknowledging my presence, and a wave of fresh amber smell hit me, giving me goosebumps. He'd undoubtedly just come from one of his many showers. By now, I was very familiar with his habits and his fixation on personal hygiene. He couldn't seem to go without bathing multiple times a day, and weirdly enough, I also found that aspect of him attractive. It made me want to leap on him and drag my tongue over every inch of his skin the way I never had before.

I was a contradiction even to myself. I alternated between moments of sheer exhilaration and moments of deep regret. I still hadn't been able to have a talk with Jared, but I was going to very soon, just as soon as things calmed down for him.

"Officer Scott, what an honor!"

I snapped back to the present moment when I heard Neil's deep baritone greeting one of the men at the door. All I could see was his broad shoulders and the outline of his back's musculature.

"Anna, you go on. I'll take care of things here." He discharged the housekeeper with a polite smile and turned his attention back to the two officers. In the meantime, I hid myself behind the doorframe and spied on the scene.

"May we come in?" Officer Scott asked in a sarcastic tone. He rested his hands on his belt, not far from the holster of his weapon, and eyed Neil warily. Neil didn't react and simply moved aside to allow them inside.

"Are you aware of what happened last night at an establishment called Blanco?" asked Officer Scott, who appeared to be the dourer of the two. Neil just stood there and stared at him, looking for all the world like he couldn't care less.

Not a single emotion crossed his perfect, enigmatic face.

"At Blanco?" he repeated, pretending to think about it.

"Yeah, the club. Your Maserati can usually be found parked right out front."

"And? The fact that I've been there doesn't mean anything," he deflected, maintaining his self-control, even though I saw his shoulders stiffen and his face grow a bit darker.

Officer Scott started walking around the living room while his partner pulled aside the curtains to peer out the window. What were they looking for?

"There was a fight there last night. Carter Nelson was attacked inside the club and beaten to a pulp."

Neil parted his lips slightly. He wore the same bewildered expression he had that night, like he no longer remembered anything.

"He's in the hospital now with major head trauma. He's in a coma," Officer Scott went on, but Neil just continued to stare impassively at him.

"The Nelson family would like to press charges against the

assailant." The officer approached Neil and inspected him with narrowed eyes. "So, Neil, there's only two ways this can go. That poor boy could get better or he could die," he put special emphasis on the last word, just to make sure Neil really got the message. "It's all going to depend on the location, severity, and extent of the brain damage that put him in that coma. You should know all about that, though. You live with a doctor, don't you?" Scott drew back his lips in a sarcastic half-smile, but Neil was stoic and maintained his cold stare.

"And why should that matter to me, Roger?" For the first time, I saw real, barely suppressed hatred in the officer's eyes, when Neil called the man by his first name.

"I get the funny feeling that you had something to do with all of this. Some of the witnesses described the assailant's appearance to me in detail, though no one mentioned you by name. You better pray that boy wakes up and doesn't have irreparable damage. If he dies, Miller, I swear on my life I will see you locked up." He spoke in a half-mutter but with such malice that it raised goosebumps on my arm.

"With what evidence? I had nothing to do with it." Neil gave the man a victorious smile. I couldn't figure out how he was so confident that he wasn't being trapped here. Someone could have recorded what happened, or taken a photo, or simply just said his name, yet Neil seemed completely sure that no such evidence would ever turn up against him.

"You and that gang of thugs you run with..." The officer shook his head, giving him a disdainful look. "Forcing people's silence with threats and cruelty, but don't think I'll forget about you, Neil. You are a thorn in my side that I'm gonna dig out sooner or later. And this time, all the expensive lawyers and rich daddies in the world won't be able to stop me," he promised and I flinched. Obviously, Neil and this man had some unfinished business between them that I knew nothing about.

How could I? The only things I knew about the guy were his

physical strength and his sexual prowess, because those were the only parts of himself he ever showed anyone.

"I think we're done here, officer." Neil smiled menacingly at the man who ran his tongue over his teeth inscrutably. Then he nodded at his partner and together they left.

I kept still, hiding behind the doorframe like a burglar. I just didn't want to stop watching Neil, not for a single moment. He sat down then on the living room sofa, legs spread with his elbows balanced on his knees and his face in his hands. He was worried—clearly tense. All I wanted to do was go reassure him.

"Neil…it's all my fault!" I flinched when I unexpectedly heard Chloe's voice calling into the living room. She rushed to her brother, and he let her curl up on his lap. He held her close and stroked her blond hair.

"It's not your fault; it's Carter's. If he hadn't tried to rape you, I wouldn't have had to hurt him." He rocked her and Chloe wept into the crook of his neck. My chest tightened painfully, and I rubbed it with one hand as though that might ease the pain.

"Don't cry, Little Koala." He kissed her forehead and smiled at her.

So Neil felt things after all. He was human, and he had a heart, just like the rest of us. He simply chose to only gift it to a few people—the ones who were worth it. He was handling Chloe like she was still a girl, a fragile butterfly, and I wanted him to treat me that same way.

In that moment, I realized that I was going to have to earn his trust if I wanted to get to his heart. Neil was a dark knight in a castle of crystal—visible but removed. And he didn't let anyone in, except for the people he loved. And I realized that I wanted a place inside that castle. That I wanted to be counted among Neil's loved ones. I felt stupid for thinking something like that or even hoping that it could happen, but a girl could dream.

I wasn't going to use him the way he thought I would. It wouldn't just be sex between us, but with sexuality—which was the only means he used to communicate—I was going to touch his soul. And I was going to obliterate the barbed wire he'd wrapped around it to protect himself from the world.

....

After the Carter incident and the officers' visit to the house, I got my life back on track again.

I didn't miss another class and tried to socialize more with Logan's friends. I was finding my place in the group and working on fitting in. The group was always welcoming, however, and they were very kind to me. Which is why, despite my introverted nature, it was easy to establish a good rapport with them.

"You should quit ogling everyone's butt," Julie told Adam. This had been an ongoing discussion between the two the entire time we'd been enjoying our break between classes. The sun was lighting up the blue sky, and we were all sitting on benches in one of the many green areas on campus.

"We're men; looking is allowed," Jake cut in, defending his friend. Adam and Julie had only just started dating, but she was already playing the role of jealous girlfriend.

"He's looking at other women? Well, then you get to flirt with other men so he can know what it feels like," Alyssa suggested, giving Adam a cheeky smile. He raised his middle finger in response.

"Fuck. Anyone else see Professor Cooper over there?" Cory turned everyone's attention to the professor who was walking down a main thoroughfare and holding a few books in one arm. She was wearing an elegant cream pantsuit that softly skimmed her prominent curves. Her golden hair gleamed, tied in a high ponytail, and her eyes were the same color as the sky. She truly was a beautiful woman, but I couldn't help but remember when I'd watched Neil threaten her to extract who knew what kind of favor.

It was then that something else occurred to me: the professor, Jennifer, and all the girls he brought home had a lot in common. All of them were blond, seductive, and compelling. All completely unlike me.

"Her ass... My god, what an ass," Jake commented, earning himself an elbow from Logan.

"Is that all you do, cuz? Think about women?" a low voice with an unfamiliar timbre cut in, and I turned to see a pair of magnetic blue eyes. I raised a hand to shield my eyes from the sun so I could get a better look at the new arrival.

It was a guy about our age whom I had never seen before. Maybe he was a fellow student? He was wearing a long, elegant coat, light-weight pants, and a dark sweater. I couldn't tell much about his body, except that he was tall and willowy. His black hair covered his ears and was pulled back into a small ponytail. An earring sparkled from one of his earlobes, and his olive skin contrasted sharply with his dazzling blue eyes.

"Kyle, you son of a bitch! You didn't tell me you were coming here today!" Cory mussed up his hair, but the other boy didn't seem at all bothered. In fact, he gave Cory a hug and slapped him on the back. When he was done, everyone else greeted him with similar enthusiasm. Logan informed me that Kyle was a good friend of theirs whom they'd known for about three years. He didn't live in town, though, so they only saw him twice a year when he came to stay with his aunt and uncle, usually for about a month.

While everyone said their hellos and chatted about people I didn't know, I remained seated on the bench and kept my eyes on the book I'd been reading in my spare time. I tucked a lock of hair behind my ear and kept reading until someone slid a leaf right between the pages I was on. I frowned and looked up to see Kyle—whom I still had not officially met—smiling at me.

229

"They say it's good luck to put a leaf between the pages of a book," he said, and I blushed like an idiot.

"Are you a new addition to the group? You're going to need a lot of patience with these fools. I'm Kyle."

"Nice to meet you, Kyle. I'm Selene." I shook his hand and he lifted mine to his mouth for a chivalrous kiss that made everyone laugh. I knew that I was blushing again, but I tried to hide my shyness with a smile.

"May I?" He gestured to the space next to me on the bench, and I nodded.

"There he is, the wolf on the prowl," Cory teased, but his cousin shooed him off with one hand and turned to give me his full attention.

"So, Selene, you're a reader." He stared down at my book, and I closed it to show him the cover.

"I love the classics. Novels, critical essays…" I typically didn't talk much about my literary tastes or passions, but with Kyle, I immediately knew that I could.

"Favorite author?" he asked.

"Vladimir Nabokov." Kyle grinned enthusiastically at my answer.

"*The Enchanter*," he said immediately, pointing an index finger at me in playful challenge.

"*Bend Sinister*," I fired back.

"*The Gift*," he answered.

We burst into laughter while everyone else stared at us like we were a pair of aliens. I'd rarely found anyone who shared my tastes, and Kyle was a lovely surprise in that regard. He tied his long hair up in a loose bun and raised an eyebrow at me. I shrugged, smiling.

He had a certain allure.

He could have been a rock star or maybe an artist. The guy gave off the vibe that he wasn't afraid to just be himself, and that made him different.

17

PLAYER 2511

There she is, the lovely Selene in the company of Logan and his friends." I smiled, observing the small group in question as they talked and laughed on a bench.

It wasn't difficult for me to trace everything back to her—to the beauty who had somehow drawn the beast's attention. Now I just had to figure out whether she actually mattered in Neil's life or if she was just one more slut he'd fucked.

"Logan's always with her; what are we supposed to do?" asked my right-hand man, sitting next to me in the passenger seat. He was always asking inconvenient questions, but a cool head was the hallmark of a strong person.

Keeping my cool would allow me to plan out everything, just the way I wanted it.

"Logan won't be a problem if we play our cards right." I blew cigarette smoke outside the car. The half-open window gave me a better look at her. Selene Anderson, originally from Detroit.

She was talking with her friends, a book open on her lap and an innocent look on her face. It was a childlike face, the sort that suggested purity and naivete. Who knows, those were probably the exact characteristics that had drawn Neil in.

She was just a girl, after all. She didn't know anything about life yet.

And he didn't realize that enduring pain for too long—the kind inflicted by others—had a way of changing people.

It made them different, cruel, petty, hungry. Yes…hungry.

Revenge had become a vital need for me. The deepest, most intense need I had.

I couldn't smother it; I couldn't repress my true instincts.

Some people say that madness comes from vendettas suppressed for too long.

And I wanted to explode.

It was time to serve up the sweetest morsel that was ever cooked in hell…

18

·····················

SELENE

H ow's your mother?"

"The chemo is really hell on her…" Jared sounded tired,
and I could only imagine how difficult it was for him to endure the
situation. I felt like such a hypocrite in that moment: I wanted to
be there for him, but not the way he wanted. I no longer considered
myself his girlfriend in any sense, but I couldn't tell him that, not
while his mother was struggling for her life.

"I'm so sorry. I'm sure that you being there is essential for her.
You're being strong for her." I couldn't even imagine how I would
have reacted if I were in his position. My mother was everything to
me. Sometimes I wondered why God had set out such cruel desti-
nies for people.

"Being strong is the only thing I can do," he said, sounding heartbroken, and I halted in the middle of the hallway that led to my
room. I'd just finished classes for the day, and I was exhausted. Now,
listening to Jared, I was also agonized and melancholy.

"You'll get through this." All the reassurances I might have made seemed pointless. Every word or sentence was trivial. There was nothing anyone could say in the face of the harrowing reality of cancer. All we could do was wait, endure, and hope to emerge victorious.

Jared changed the subject to ask me if I'd settled in, if I was getting along with Logan's friends, and about other inconsequential information. He was clearly trying to distract himself and avoid thinking about the difficult time he and his family were going through.

After ten more minutes of banal conversation, we said goodbye and I went to my room, tossing my bag down on the bed. I peeled off my coat and stretched my arms up over my head, working muscles that felt tense and sluggish.

Suddenly, a series of strange noises followed by breathless, angry gasping drew me back out into the hallway. I followed the sounds out of my room like I was Hansel and they were breadcrumbs. I stopped at the end of the hallway in front of the half-open door to a private gym and leaned forward to peer inside.

Resting my hand on the doorframe and trying to even breathe silently, I watched Neil, focused on his training.

A bright red punching bag oscillated under violent strikes from his fists. Spellbound, I examined every inch of his tensed body. His track pants clung to his clenched quads. His bare chest was covered in droplets of sweat, outlining his pumped pectorals and an abdomen so sculpted that it would have been the envy of any other man. The thick black lines of his tattoo seemed almost to be dancing around his right bicep. Everything but the top tip of the pikorua on his left hip, however, was covered by the elastic of his low-waisted pants.

His body was a series of natural protrusions and reliefs, a blend of harmonious individual parts that came together to form a living sculpture. He was as beautiful, as worthy of admiration as any piece in an art museum.

I gave myself a shake but continued to watch as Neil landed precise, calculated blows. I didn't know much about boxing, but I knew that the sport required a great deal of speed, strength, and endurance. He wore gloves to protect his own knuckles from possible fractures, such was the power that moved through his masculine form.

His stare, however, was dark and focused. It was all there in his eyes: the weariness of someone who had hoped for something that never happened.

Neil had been let down by life and was now a prisoner of his own hate.

But what exactly had made him this way?

All at once, he stopped and turned his head right toward me. I sucked in a breath, and his golden eyes dominated even that large room, obscuring everything else.

I had two options: I could run away like the worst sort of coward, or I could accept the consequences for being caught spying on him.

"You planning to stay there much longer?" His baritone rocked me just as surely as he'd rocked the punching bag he was now ignoring. Our eyes stayed locked on each other's for what felt like forever, until I decided to enter the room.

The gulf between Neil and me was obvious: I was as jittery as a gazelle standing before a hungry lion. He was arrogant, fully indifferent to what anyone else felt or thought. I moved across the room with uncertain steps, making my way slowly toward his imposing figure as I tried to gather the courage I would need for this moment.

"I can't tell if that unshakable confidence of yours is just a perk of being an asshole or if it's some weird attempt to get girls," I said, and Neil quirked the corner of his lips in an amused expression. I didn't really know what he'd found funny about what I said, but I kept my guard up just the same.

Neil took off his gloves and even that casual movement was appealing. Then, he looked at me again, and I couldn't breathe as he advanced on me, one step at a time, calm and measured. He bent down next to the weight bench, grabbed a bottle of water from the floor and slowly unscrewed the top.

"Why are you here?" He brought the water bottle to his lips and took a long drink, never taking his eyes from me. My gaze dipped to follow the gleaming water droplets that slid down his chest, and I could feel my heartbeat speeding up.

I had to resist, to control the unhealthy attraction that drew me to him, and show him that I wasn't as weak as he thought.

"The right answer would be that I'm not here to try to love or understand you," I murmured. Neil stopped drinking and capped the bottle, setting it back down on the floor.

"And what's the real answer?"

He picked up a folded towel and used it to blot his chest, all the time wearing the smug expression of someone who knew very well that he had an irresistible body.

"I'm here to offer you a compromise…"

What a liar. I'd gotten there purely by chance, and I didn't even know when exactly that idea had come to me. It was just a gut feeling, come to my rescue at an opportune moment.

"What compromise? I'm not the kind of person who folds easily to the will of others," he said in a peremptory tone.

No, he wasn't. Neil was the kind of man who loved to manipulate without being manipulated, who enjoyed using women like sex dolls while never giving more of himself than absolutely necessary.

"I'm not the kind of person who likes to impose my will on others." It was true. I didn't want him to be subject to my will. I didn't want to change him or even judge him, but just to know him. And so I had lied to him, a little bit: I did want to understand him, even if I didn't love him. Love was an emotion that I didn't associate with Neil at all. Even though I was a romantic at heart, I knew that love required more than physical chemistry and sexual satisfaction.

Love was composed of so many more elements that were missing from both my relationship with Jared and whatever strange thing I had going on with Neil.

"I am. I'm the kind of person who likes doing that," he answered bluntly before tossing the towel away and taking a deep breath. Then he began to examine me, analyzing me like I was an unstable chemical compound.

"You can have everything you want...as long as I get something of you." That was my condition. And then, driven by a boldness I didn't think I'd possessed, I made one more attempt to convince him to accept my proposal. I drew one hand along the line of my cleavage, sliding my fingers down slowly. I was wearing a basic blue shirt with a bow at the collar, which was neither sexy nor provocative, but I still tried to appear confident and audacious.

Neil followed my movement with his golden eyes, all the way down to the waistband of my pants, where my hand finally stopped. I could feel the heat in my cheeks, and I hoped I wasn't visibly blushing, or my plan was going to fail miserably.

Neil advanced on me, the smell of him invading the air around me. He was obviously sweaty, yet the clean smell of artificial amber still lingered on his body. I wanted to ask him why he bathed so often that he always smelled like soap, but I was waiting for just the right time.

When he was close enough that I had to tilt my head back to look at him, he grabbed me by the hips like an animal and pulled me violently against him. I let out a surprised sound and a jolt of pure pleasure moved through me.

He smiled at me as he ran his fingers along the front of my pants until he reached the buttons. His intent was clear: he wanted something from me right here, right now, and he wasn't offering anything in return.

"I already gave you my body." He confirmed my thoughts in a

lascivious tone. He clearly felt that should have been enough to satisfy me. I wasn't like the others, though.

"You give that to everyone." I shoved his chest roughly, the only place my hands could reach him. I didn't move him an inch, but he took a few steps back on his own, probably annoyed by my reaction. His gaze had darkened, and suddenly, his expression changed.

"What the fuck do you want then?" he bellowed. I wondered why he seemed to slide so easily into angry bewilderment. One only needed to push a few buttons to make his bad side emerge.

"Tell me!" he shouted at me again, and I flinched, backing away from him. I didn't want to look weak, but I was actually afraid that he might hurt me, even if only by accident.

"I want to talk to you, Neil. There is more than just sex. People have conversations, discussions, they get to know each other and understand each other. Some of them even end up loving each other!" I said in an angry rush, and he stared at me, stupefied. He was breathing heavily, and he looked lost, like he no longer knew where he was. He scrubbed a hand over his face and shook his head, brushing past me to leave the gym.

But I wasn't going to give up that easily, so I followed him to his room. He tried to close the door in my face, but I was faster and blocked it with both hands, managing to squeeze inside. Neil examined me again, this time looking frightened. He was like a wild animal, certain he was about to be captured and crammed into a cage, but that wasn't my intention.

Instead, I wanted to free him from the cage he'd locked himself inside.

"Get out!" He shooed me away, but I paid him no mind and shut the door behind me instead. There was no one else in the house except for Anna, who could probably hear us shouting.

"Calm down." I adjusted my approach, trying to be understanding and placid.

Neil went to the bedside table and retrieved a cigarette from the pack of Winstons lying there. He lit one rapidly, like he'd die if didn't immediately inhale the disgusting thing, and took a deep drag before releasing the smoke into the air. I stayed right where I was, studying his every movement.

A few moments later, he went to the window and threw it open, leaning one shoulder against the wall next to it. Standing there, barely illuminated by the colors of the dying sunset, he looked like a demon for real, ready to feed on me and then spit out my empty husk.

His breathing got more regular as his drags on the cigarette increased, the nicotine having a tranquilizing effect on him. I glanced around the black and cobalt-blue room, trying not stress him out more. With his watchful eyes on me, I took shaky steps forward until I could sit down on the edge of his bed, hands resting on my thighs.

"I know you overheard everything," he said suddenly, regarding me with such intensity that I was immediately cowed.

At first, I didn't understand what he was talking about, but then I realized he was referring to his interaction with the police officers.

"Yeah," I confirmed. "Officer Scott knows you..." I would have given him anything just so long as he kept talking to me, so long as he opened up just a little bit.

Neil sighed and took another drag from his cigarette. He was handsome, despite his drawn appearance. So handsome that it made me feel inadequate, not desirable enough for someone like him. He was so perfect, even if he was a mess on the inside.

"Talk to me," I insisted in a gentle voice. Neil was introverted and wary of others, that much was clear to me by then. He was very reserved, especially when it came to anything about him or his past. It was a paradox: he was so comfortable exposing his body but never his soul. Maybe it was fear that held him back or a desire to hide his weaknesses or maybe he just wanted to hide himself from the world?

I decided that I was going to gently pick my way through the chaos inside him. I would be respectful; I would show him that human beings could also be good and loving.

"When I was fourteen, I got into a bad situation. Fell in with a bad crowd, partying, overindulging in all kinds of shit..." He ground out the cigarette in an ashtray and fixed his honey-colored eyes on me. I gulped when he narrowed his eyes, staring at me through his long lashes. He was concentrating hard, and a small furrow formed in the middle of his forehead, giving him a glowering yet appealing expression. "The fighting was what fucked me up. I've always had problems dealing with my anger, and I've been reported for it plenty of times. I've made a lot of enemies, and I'm not a safe guy to be around. Not even for you..." He said it coldly, maybe with the intention of pushing me away. But what was the point of scaring me off when, in the end, he always came looking for me? He had been the one, every time, to come knocking at my door.

"Why was that specific officer so angry at you?"

"Because I fucked up. I've fucked up a lot. I don't want to talk about this, Selene. Don't ask me any more questions." He walked toward me with a determined stride and grasped my arm. I sucked in a breath when he bent down to look into my eyes.

"You've told me so little," I whispered in disappointment. In that moment, I noticed the tiny amber streaks in the luminous sandy color of his eyes. I could have drowned in those eyes, and it would have been worth losing myself.

"I've told you enough." He tried to kiss me, but I turned my face away.

I could feel his warm breath on my cheek. I wanted to kiss him, but first I needed him to actually accept my conditions, even if I had managed to get something out of him this time. I tried to hold out, but the arm he had in his grasp began to tremble, as did the rest of my body. I didn't know if the trembling was from excitement at being so close to him or fear of his unpredictability. His bare chest made me want to touch him, to run my fingers and then my tongue along the spaces between his muscles. But instead I pulled my arm free and moved away from him. I needed to escape the creature that I was becoming; the one I always became when he touched me.

Perhaps somewhere deep down inside, I was simply afraid of myself and of what I was feeling.

But Neil recaptured me before I even got to the door. He took me by the hips and pulled me forcefully back against him. It was a gesture so possessive that I knew immediately I was trapped, and he wasn't going to release me until he'd taken what he wanted.

"Now it's my turn to get something from you," he whispered into my ear.

"You've already taken the most important thing…" I admitted, thinking of my virginity. Saying it aloud made me surrender to him. I let my shoulders relax and gave myself over to him, letting him do whatever he wanted.

"I want everything." He brushed my hair aside with one hand, speaking slowly and sensually to me. "Everything, Selene." He leaned into me slightly, and I could feel his erection pressing against the cleft of my ass.

I gasped, but his hands moved to my hips, holding me still.

"Everything," I repeated like a robot. My voice cracked and my self-control was evaporating.

"You like feeling me, don't you?" He caressed my stomach with his fingers, and I could feel a trail of fire where his hand had touched me. That hand slowly drifted downward, and I shut my eyes, trying to keep breathing.

"I don't know what you mean," I lied and he made a guttural

sound, like a repressed laugh. His hand slipped down even further until it got to the button of my pants.

"Then I'll show you, Babygirl." He undid the buttons and slipped his hand beneath the fabric, rubbing my sex through the cotton of my panties. I held my breath as I felt the fabric slowly dampening until it clung to my labia, which had been electrified by his touch.

How many others had he pleasured just like this?

"Neil…" I grabbed his wrist, intending to stop him, but when he found the exact rhythm that I needed, I couldn't resist.

I was soaked, and he, giant bastard that he was, just kept gliding his index finger from the top of my slit to the bottom, getting me even more ready to take him.

"Just remember one thing, Selene: women don't fuck me; I fuck women." He continued his teasing game, this time underneath my panties. I sucked in a breath when I felt cold fingertips on my sex, which felt like it was on fire. I stopped breathing entirely when Neil gathered up my juices and used them to wet my clitoris, teasing it slowly and delicately as if his hands had been designed to do just that.

"Let go." He nibbled my earlobe, and I let my head fall back on his shoulder. Oddly enough, I felt protected in that moment; encased in his powerful arms was the only place I wanted to be. I arched my back and let out a moan as my hips began to chase his movements.

Neil, however, quit moving his fingers too soon, making me groan in irritation. Then he grinned and started touching me again, gliding from bottom to top in a cycle of infinite lust and torture. I bit my lip and yearned to have him inside me, but he just kept playing ruthlessly with me, never allowing me true satisfaction.

After a while, his caresses, alternating between vertical and circular motion, caused a tidal wave of overwhelming sensations. I felt my knees buckle, so I leaned against him and reached up behind his neck until I could grab his wild hair.

We stood there, locked together in our lust, unable to resist our impulses. He, however, managed to remain standing behind me, his right hand between my legs and his left cupping my breast. I wanted to have my revenge and torment him like he did me, but unfortunately, we weren't positioned to equal advantage. So I decided to rub my ass against his hard-on, feeling his whole body stiffen as I did so.

"Are you trying to turn me on, Babygirl?" He grinned into the crook of my neck, and I continued to gently grind my pelvis against him.

"Exactly like you did to me," I managed, out of breath. I would have died if he didn't keep stimulating me just as he was. He knew far too well which parts of me to touch; he'd found the rhythm that my body liked the most as easily, as if he'd known it his whole life.

"Actually, I haven't even started yet," he whispered in a deliberately velvet tone.

This thing of ours suddenly seemed more like a war, a genuine battle to the death.

Neil kissed my neck, then sucked and licked it. I squeezed my eyes shut and tried to get a handle on the moans that were vibrating in my chest. I continued to rub my ass on him, trying to make him give in, admit defeat, but Neil was determined to win. He wanted to dominate me, to overpower me.

"You keep that up and I'm going to fuck you against this door," he murmured menacingly, his breath coming in pants. Then he pushed a finger inside me, finding me a yielding, liquid mess.

He rubbed me with a practiced control and a meticulous attention to detail. I lost myself against the marble of his body and soaked up the pleasure that, thus far, only he had ever been able to give me. The knowledge that he had been the first enhanced the feeling that I'd had for some time by then—the feeling that I belonged to him totally.

His breath tickled my neck as I turned my face toward him, meeting his gaze. He was too tall, I never would have reached his lips by myself so I stared intensely at him until he could read my every desire in my face. Then, I lifted myself up on my tiptoes and Neil immediately realized what I was doing. He bent to kiss me, and it was magnificent.

He tilted his head to deepen the kiss, and when his tongue touched mine, an intense heat roared through my middle, all the way up to my nipples. I savored it passionately and he responded with the same intensity. Both of us were starving. Longing for that connection between one another.

I pressed my back harder into him and ground my hips against his hand. The burning strokes of his tongue began to mimic the rhythm of his fingers. I panted against his mouth, our scents mingling. I would let him cross any boundary, take everything from me. I was shaking and my cheeks were flushed. Neil didn't stop kissing me; it was obvious that he couldn't stop himself anymore, just as I couldn't.

In that moment, I decided that I would never let another man touch me like that.

I felt like *his*.

The more I kissed him, the more his fingers took ownership of me, grasping like they wanted to reach my very heart. I moaned and he grinned proudly, devouring my lips until they ached.

And that's when I came.

I came on his hand.

I came in a prolonged climax. I came again, then again, maybe three times. It was slow and devastating each time.

The physical exhaustion that followed was so intense that it had me swaying on my feet for a few seconds. Then, as though I'd just woken from a dream, I twisted in his arms and broke away from him. I needed to clear my head, so I rested my back against the door and tried to catch my breath.

I felt exhausted but sated.

"You know what; I just had a romantic thought," he whispered impishly as I stared into his eyes, enthralled.

"What's that?" I asked, brushing two strands of hair off his forehead. Neil brought his fingers to his mouth and sucked on them, maintaining eye contact with me the whole time. When I caught the smell of my own release, sweet and pungent, I blushed. At the same time, the fact that he seemed to be savoring my taste was flattering.

"I was thinking how nice it would be to taste this straight from the source." He rested his hand next to my head on the doorframe and loomed over me, all six feet, three inches of him. He searched my face, a spark of amusement mingled with his lust, and I blushed even harder.

"You are a rare sort of romantic, it seems," I commented sarcastically. And he was a rare sort of beauty as well. A singular beauty.

"Oh yeah, I'm a *real* romantic," he corrected me with an ironic twist to his mouth, making me smile in return. Then he pressed a chaste kiss to my lips. Finally we had forged a completely new understanding.

Or, at least, that's what I thought...

19

SELENE

I had deluded myself.

In the days that followed our intimate moment, Neil went right back to being distant and brusque, as though nothing had happened.

But it was my refusal to give up on that troubled, fucked-up boy that pushed me back to the room that contained the "memory boxes." But when I tried to enter, it was locked.

"Now, let's see..." The evening after I found the door locked, I sat cross-legged on my bed with my MacBook open to Google.

I cracked my knuckles nervously, then put my fingers to the keyboard, ready to type whatever came into my mind. I started with the word "borderline" and immediately a long list of symptoms of the personality disorder popped up: poor impulse control, frequent outbursts of anger, attempted suicide, substance abuse, self-harm...

"Dissociative episodes, feeling detached from your emotions and your body..." I read aloud. "Intense but unstable relationships, engaging in risky behaviors like unprotected sex..."

I swallowed hard as I remembered our encounter in my room.

"Do you always do it bare?"

"No, only with you."

I kept reading and searched further about causes of the disorder. I didn't even know why I thought of borderline personality disorder, but having considered many of Neil's behaviors at length, I had come to believe that there was something genuinely different—anomalous—about him.

"Research conducted to date on borderline personality disorder has not established a precise cause of the condition," I continued to read carefully. "Prevailing professional opinion, however, is that secondary to genetic factors, anomalies in the early childhood development of the subject may have a particular impact upon emotional pathologies, such as the tendency to react intensely and immediately to even mild stimuli. Early experiences in the family environment could play a key role, particularly physical and psychological mistreatment, violence, abuse—"

Two raps on the door pulled me out of my reading. I huffed and called out a hasty "Yes, what is it?"

Logan entered the room shortly thereafter. I quickly tried to get rid of the shaken expression that I was sure I was wearing and put on a polite smile so as not to make him suspicious.

"Hey, is it cool if I come in?" he asked politely, moving toward me.

"Sure, of course." I cleared my throat and minimized my browser window.

"What are you up to? Studying?"

I glanced at the open MacBook and nodded, trying not to let my nerves show.

"Yeah, just doing some research." It wasn't a total lie. I was looking for an explanation for his brother's bizarre behavior, and though I was hardly a psychiatrist or psychologist, I thought that I might have found one.

"At nine o'clock at night?" He shook his head, disappointed in me. "There's a party I'm going to with everyone, and Kyle asked me if you'd be there." He bit his lip, amused.

I grimaced and gave him a suspicious look. "Well, you can tell *Kyle* that Selene will be staying home and studying." I gave him a mocking smile, and he frowned slightly.

"You're really going to stay home?"

"I'm really going to stay home," I confirmed. I preferred to spend my nights with a good book and a cup of hot chocolate anyway.

"Okay, suit yourself. Mom and Matt went out to dinner with some friends. They took Chloe with them."

Logan shoved his hands into his jeans pockets and rocked back on his heels. He peered at the decorative lights on my bookcase, thinking who knew what kind of thoughts.

"How is your sister?" I was worried about her. I knew that she had been skipping school and that she hadn't even heard from a lot of her friends. It couldn't have been easy, dealing with the fallout from a trauma like the one she'd suffered.

"Not good. She's still scared a lot of the time, but my mom thinks she's just having some trouble at school. She doesn't know what really happened." He bit the inside of his cheek and shot a look at me.

"And you're not going to tell her?"

"Not for the moment." He sighed heavily. I didn't want to argue the merits of that strategy because, ultimately, it was a family issue. A family to which I didn't yet fully belong. Still, I knew that Mia would not have been pleased to learn that Chloe had nearly been raped and that Neil had beaten her attacker to a pulp and no one had mentioned any of it to her.

After Logan left to join his friends at the party, I went down to the kitchen to get some orange juice. I perched on a stool and sipped my drink while mulling over what I'd read about borderline personality disorder. I wasn't certain that it all applied to Neil, but a sixth sense told me I was on the right track.

"Someone's thoughtful," Anna commented as she passed a cloth over the glass doors that led out into the garden. The house always sparkled from top to bottom thanks to her impeccable work. She was diligent and professional, serious yet friendly—the Millers couldn't have asked for a better housekeeper.

As I watched her, I wondered if maybe she could help me gather some more useful information about what was going on in Neil's head. She had known him, after all, since he was a child.

"You've been here for a long time, Miss Anna," I began as Anna continued to buff the already squeaky clean glass of the door. "I was wondering if it was true what they say, that when you work for a family, you can come to love them like they were your own?" I raised my glass to my lips and Anna turned to give me a thoughtful look. Her short honey-blond hair was a perfect match for her hazel eyes, framed by an elegant pair of glasses.

"Absolutely, miss. Mia has become like a sister to me, and I think of her children as my children." She nodded emphatically, and I knew I was on to something with this.

"Tell me about them. You seem to know them so well, and I've only been here for a few weeks." I pretended to be innocently curious about my father's family, the one that had welcomed me and hosted me here in this opulent mansion, concealing my true inquisitorial intentions.

"Mia is completely unlike what those reporters write about her in the tabloids." She flapped the cloth she was holding in the air in annoyance, and I smiled at this funny, unconscious gesture. "She's such a loving woman. She loves her family, and she loves her work, just like Dr. Anderson."

There was a lot I could have said on that topic, but I let it go and just kept listening, smiling and nodding as she brought up positive qualities and things she liked about each member of the family.

"Chloe is a sensitive girl; she's just in her rebellious stage. She adores her brothers, but she's also very possessive of them." She gave me a look that confirmed suspicions that the baby of the family was notably more standoffish with me probably out of discomfort with my friendship with Logan and my... whatever with Neil.

"And Logan? I've spent a lot of time with him since I got here, and I was surprised at the rapport we've developed. I wouldn't have thought it was possible." I got up from my stool and washed the dirty glass in the sink. I was uncomfortable treating Anna like a servant—she wasn't really one for me—so I tried to do my share whenever I could.

"Logan is a true golden boy. There aren't many kids who are as level-headed and intelligent as he is," she said, a deep admiration in her voice. It was the same sort of admiration I had for Logan, who was always kind to everyone, always there with a comforting word in times of need.

But Logan wasn't my goal; my goal was to learn more about...

"And Neil?" I cleared my throat and cautiously drew closer to her. "I don't get to talk to him much." I looked her in the eye. Anna had to have seen the questions that were hovering in the back of my mind. But then, she must have also seen the hard determination that meant I was going to figure that human disaster out no matter what it took.

"Neil is a unique young man." She sighed and looked down, turning the cloth over and over in her hands. A melancholy look stole over her careworn face. "He needs time before he can trust people. He's not a bad person. He loves his family deeply, especially his siblings. He would do anything for them, but..." She tucked a strand of hair behind her ear and hesitated, as if carefully choosing her next words. "You have to respect his emotional distance. Pay attention to his body language; look for the underlying meaning in the things he says… Neil is mostly going to give you nonverbal signals, but if you learn how to read them, then you'll be able to communicate with him," she concluded in a firm yet benevolent tone of voice.

She smiled at me, and then excused herself to finish her household tasks before going home to her own kids. She hadn't told me much that I didn't already know, but she had confirmed that Neil's distrust and difficulty talking about himself were behavioral characteristics, not a result of things I was doing wrong. I just needed to be patient and earn his trust.

I couldn't explain it, but I felt connected to him. I had never believed in that kind of bone-deep understanding that "clicks" between two people. But the totally irrational draw that existed between the two of us had me reevaluating my beliefs.

I shook my head and walked over to the glass doors to look at the now-dark sky, the bright stars, the indistinct colors, the peace and silence of the world. Then, I spotted a dim light shining out from a room in the pool house next to the outdoor pool.

I pushed the doors open and walked out into the garden, wrapping my arms around my chest when the biting air hit my skin. I was only wearing a thin sweater, not enough to really keep out the cold.

I'd thought that there was no one at home except for me and Anna, but I was wrong. My investigative instinct overwhelmed my common sense, so I kept walking toward the small, still mysterious outbuilding. I walked past the swimming pool and approached one of the windows.

Beyond the glass, there was a small but modern and functional kitchen. An open bottle of Jack Daniels and some used glasses sat on the counter. I frowned and moved to the second window, which gave me a view into a bedroom. The curtains inside were pulled open, so I could see the shadows of some figures moving on the wooden floor. I crouched down to one side of the window, trying to hide.

I watched as a girl climbed onto the king-sized bed positioned in the middle of the room, sitting up on her knees. She was completely naked. Her long blond hair fell to the base of her spine, her pale skin and the lush, curving shape of her was completely exposed. She displayed herself proudly with a sly look on her face.

When she turned to address someone behind her, I squinted to see if I could get a better look at her face. And then there, in the silence, I could actually hear the crash of my heart hitting the ground, shattering into a thousand pieces.

It was Jennifer.

I could have walked away at that point. Simply taken a step back and not subjected myself to the pain, but I knew that, if I did, I would spend my life regretting that I didn't know what actually happened in that room. So, with my hand pressed to my heart, I turned my eyes back to the window.

A few moments later, a man approached her and also climbed onto the bed. Neil was wearing just his black boxers, but those would soon join the rest of his clothes, scattered who knows where. And he was so beautiful, with that sinful face and that god-damned smile. I wasn't able to admire his golden eyes because his face was turned away from me, but I did get a good look at his wild hair and his powerful back muscles. It was then that the clicking of anxiety and the low buzz of anger joined the thumping of my heart.

He whispered something into Jennifer's ear and then kissed her neck, making her head fall back in pleasure. They were both on their knees, facing each other. They were gorgeous, like two divinities. Sexuality incarnate.

Apparently, I really wanted to make myself suffer, because I continued watching as, moments later, a second female figure joined them on the bed. She positioned herself behind Neil, who was now sandwiched between the two women. Though I could only see her profile, I recognized the blue hair hanging down over her breasts and knew immediately that it was the other girl from the Krew. Alexia was her name, I recalled.

She was naked as well; her body lean yet soft and offered up to the mercy of this devil who was about to feast on both of them. I couldn't breathe, and I felt a painful pressure in the middle of my chest, like someone was crushing me. Of course, someone *was* crushing me; he was just a few feet away.

Neil started kissing Jennifer and touching her with devastating erotic languor. Meanwhile, Alexia rubbed his shoulders and down to his flexed biceps. She circled him slowly, moving from his powerful back to his marble chest then down to his tense abdominal muscles and slim hips.

She hooked a finger under the elastic of his boxers and started pulling them down. Neil helped her take them off, all without ceasing to make out with the other girl. It looked like this wasn't the first time he'd had to manage two women at the same time.

Alexia grinned, eager to get in on the action. She began kissing his back and licking the skin, hungry to possess him. Neil's muscles contracted with her every touch, and soon his massive erection rose up, nearly touching his belly button. Jennifer stared right at it and bit her lip in satisfaction.

But Neil wasn't wasting any more time. He grabbed Jennifer by the back of the neck and bent her forcibly against his pubic area. Then he turned and murmured something to Alexia, she nodded and got off the bed, walking over to a bedside table and opening the drawer. Instinctively, I stiffened up and tried to conceal myself more effectively from her.

When she went back to him, she had a little silver packet in her hands. I leaned back over to get a better look. Neil tore the packet and removed the condom while Jennifer continued to theatrically suck his dick.

Then, like two devout supplicants worshipping their god, they began licking him in tandem. Jennifer focused on the swollen tip of his penis while Alexia devoted herself to his testicles. Both of them fixed their lustful stares on his honey-colored eyes. I, however, was struggling to recognize him there.

Neil watched them with no emotion on his face. He was cold, remote, calculating, and unmoved. It looked like sex was a disturbance for him—a wild impulse that could not be ignored but involved no virtue or honesty or any genuine feelings of emotional transport. His body was there, but it seemed that the real him was somewhere else, unreachable in the exact same way he had been when he folded me over my desk.

Pretty soon, he was going to give a sublime and intense, yet disturbing, sort of pleasure to both of them. Part of me wanted to stay and examine him to see if even a flicker of genuine enjoyment would pass over that cruel and beautiful face, but I knew that I wasn't going to make it much longer. My stomach was already in knots.

Suddenly, Neil took Alexia by the hips and positioned her in front of him on all fours. He kneaded her ass and slapped one butt cheek, making her jolt forward. As he did so, Jennifer grinned and rubbed him, whispering something into his ear.

Neil lowered the condom to the tip of his erection and unrolled it over his entire majestic length. With his muscles tense, his pectorals tight, and his abdomen rigid, he leaned into Alexia, rubbing himself between her ass cheeks. This produced a moan from her that even I could hear.

Jennifer smiled impishly and stared at the point of contact between Neil and Alexia, and I understood immediately which hole he was about to violate.

I may have been inexperienced, but I wasn't completely ignorant.

That was enough for me.

I wasn't going to stand there and watch them any longer, I had finally reached my limit.

I backed away quickly from that scandalous performance and went back to the kitchen, colliding suddenly with Miss Anna, who grabbed me by the arms before I could fall down.

"Miss Selene." She gave me a look as though she knew exactly what I'd just witnessed. I was in shock and trembling even though I was trying to control myself.

"I'm s… sorry, I don't…" I could hardly get the words out. I felt fuzzy and dazed, like I'd been hit in the head. Maybe this was all just a nasty nightmare?

Anna touched my face tenderly, and I thought about my mother. I thought about going back to Detroit. I thought about begging Jared to forgive me. I thought about dropping everything and running to pack a bag as soon as possible. I thought… I thought…

"Please try to understand," she whispered, sounding mortified. I didn't need to say anything; she already knew.

"What?" I asked her, distressed.

"Don't judge him; understand him." Her shoulders slumped, and she shot a concerned look out the glass door.

"No one can understand him." I couldn't tell her about what had gone on between me and Neil. I couldn't explain to her how let down I felt, I couldn't express my thoughts or tell her why I felt so betrayed. In the end, Neil and I didn't have a relationship. He did not belong to me, and I did not belong to him. And still, seeing him with other people was like a stab to the gut.

"Oh, he can be understood. Just don't fall in love with him; don't make the same mistake as—"

"Scarlett?" I murmured instinctively.

Anna flinched like I'd brought up Satan himself. She stepped back, shaking her head. I could tell from her sudden silence that she was afraid of giving away too much.

"What happened with that girl?" I pressed, taking a step toward her, but Anna lowered her eyes, bringing her hands to her face.

"It's not my place to tell you that kind of thing, young lady." She clasped her hands in front of her and hustled away, not giving me the chance to ask any more questions.

I felt lost, surrounded by clues that needed to be deciphered and questions that had no answers. Neil's odd behavior, that locked room, the girl called Scarlett who was, apparently, part of his past… all of it was a mystery to me.

Nobody was willing to give me any straight answers and that only made my suspicions grow.

....

After classes the next day, I found myself in the usual campus-adjacent restaurant with Logan and the others. But my mind was elsewhere. I spun my straw in my milkshake, searching for an answer to the questions that plagued my mind. I had a terrible headache, and it was hard for me to keep up with what they were talking about.

I hadn't gotten a wink of sleep the previous night, not with images of Neil, Alexia, and Jennifer haunting me for hours on end. All at once, I looked up and stared at the table where the Krew had been sitting days before, when Xavier was harassing Cindy, the waitress. We now knew her well since we were regular customers.

"Here's your coffees, folks," said the girl in question, slipping the last of our orders under Cory's and Jake's noses.

"Thanks, doll." Cory winked, and the girl rolled her eyes, though she gave him a pleased smile.

"Don't be an asshole," Adam scolded him, but Cindy didn't seem to mind. She had probably realized that Cory flirted like that with everyone.

"He's perpetually horny," Jake added, and Cindy blushed, giving him a winsome look. It wasn't the first time something like that had happened, and I suspected she was nurturing a little crush on Jake.

"Selene, you haven't said a word today." Logan gave me a concerned look. It was true, I hadn't been very chatty, and I hadn't been participating in their conversations because my spirits were so low.

"I just have a lot on my mind…" I needed to talk to someone, but Logan was possibly the last person to whom I could confess everything. I was ashamed of what I'd done with his brother. Though, if I could turn back time, I probably would have made the same mistakes all over again.

"Yeah, I think people have noticed…" he answered. He was right. It was all Neil's fault. Neil and my insane life.

But I didn't offer any explanations, and Logan dropped the subject, turning back to talk with his friends.

An hour later, we were headed back home. During the ride, he finally admitted that he was interested in Alyssa. Apparently they were dating and had already slept together several times. But he, like his brother, insisted that there was no room for love in his life and that what he felt for Alyssa was merely a deep fondness.

"You know, there are essays, books, entire encyclopedias that tell us love is an energy, this force that you only experience once in your life, if you're lucky. I don't think I've ever fallen in love. Have you?" he asked as he drove. Being deeply skeptical of human emotions must run in his family.

"No, never…" I looked out the window and thought about Jared. I was positive that I wasn't in love with him. If I was, I wouldn't have such overwhelming feelings for someone else. But at the same time, I wasn't in love with Neil, either. At least, not yet… We had an inescapable connection, marked by an undeniable physical attraction. Still, I was afraid to look too deeply within, because I didn't want to actually confront what I was starting to feel for him. Though I did realize that thinking constantly about a person was one symptom of falling in love.

"Selene, are you listening?" Logan jolted me out of my rumination, and I glanced over at him only to see that we'd arrived home.

"Sorry, I wasn't." I retrieved my bag and opened the door while Logan continued to give me a probing look.

"You're worried about something; that's why you're so distracted." We exited the car and I followed him up the front steps. I wondered how he put up with me, especially these days when I was perpetually lost in my own thoughts. He had an incredible amount of patience.

"You're right, I was just..." I ran into his back when he stopped abruptly on the first step.

"Logan?" I leaned around him to see what was blocking our way and saw a black box at his feet.

"Were you expecting a package from someone?" he asked, frowning down at it. I shook my head and Logan glanced around, but there was no one but us. He bent down to pick up the box and motioned for me to follow him into the house.

"Who's it from? Maybe it's for your mom or Matt," I mused.

We entered the living room and sat down on the sofa, where we examined the box. It was definitely out of the ordinary: all black with no sender or recipient on it.

"We should ask Anna who left it," he said thoughtfully.

"It's her day off," I reminded him.

"Should we open it?" He turned it over in his hands, maybe looking for some sort of marking, a name, anything that might help us figure out what it was. We regarded each other for a few moments, then Logan felt the box all over before placing it on the glass table in front of us and opening it up.

Whatever was inside left Logan completely petrified.

He went white and his mouth fell open.

"What is it, Logan?" I demanded.

"What the fuck is this? A prank?" he snapped.

I began to notice a vile smell in the air, similar to that of a decomposing corpse. I peered inside the box and understood immediately why Logan was so upset.

"Oh my God!" I clapped my hands over my lips and stood up rapidly, thrusting myself away from the package.

"This has to be some sort of sick joke." Logan shut the box again, passing a hand over his face. Just at that moment, the front door swung open. We both turned to see Neil coming over the threshold, handsome as ever and completely in the dark about what was happening.

He observed us with a serious scowl, like he was trying to figure out the reason for our shocked appearance. Then he closed the door and came over to us with slow, decisive strides.

"Why the faces? What happened?" His forehead wrinkled at me over those lovely honey-colored eyes and I gulped.

"Neil…" Logan began. "I think you should look at this." He pointed the box out to his brother, who came closer. His fresh, scrubbed smell washed over me as he bent to open up the package.

"Fuck!" Neil shouted, backing away with a grimace of horror on his face.

"What do you think? It's a shitty prank, right?" Logan asked him, but the dark look on Neil's face made it clear that he thought it was anything but.

A dead raven, putrid and stinking with live worms all over it, feeding on its innards was no run-of-the-mill joke. It couldn't be anything but a threat, macabre and disgusting as it was.

"Who would send something like that?" I hugged myself and rubbed my arms; it was as though I could feel those worms crawling on my skin.

"Someone whose nose I'm about to break." Neil continued

to stare at the contents of the box, his face now controlled and impassive.

"Look, there's something in the corner there." Logan pointed to a section of the box's interior where there appeared to be a loose piece of paper.

"It looks like a note or something," I said skeptically, then I glanced at Logan. Who was going to have courage to put their hand in there and retrieve it? But I shouldn't have wondered, because Neil immediately went over to the box and fished it out, holding it in his thumb and index finger. He shook it to remove the worms that clung to it before reading:

"Let the game begin."

"Let the game begin," Logan repeated. I shuddered, and an eerie silence fell over the living room. The ticking of the clock was the only sound that accompanied us.

Neil stayed there, unmoving, with his eyes glued to that piece of paper for what felt like forever while he wore an ominous scowl.

"The note was typed and printed out." He crumpled it angrily in one hand. I could sense the anger moving through his body, but it was calm that we would need to face this situation. We needed to keep our heads clear and avoid falling into panic.

"No handwriting to identify whoever did this…" I didn't realize I had spoken aloud until his gold eyes landed on me. It felt like it had been years since I'd last looked into them. I had been avoiding him ever since I'd witnessed that perverse scene in the pool house, but despite that, his gaze still burned into me like an uncontrolled flame.

Neil glanced down at the now-wrinkled note. Logan approached him with a frown, but I stayed right where I was.

"Player 2511…" Logan read. "What does that even mean? Who is it?"

"I have no idea," Neil whispered, tossing the note onto the table next to the box. He began to pace restlessly around the living room, obviously anxious. I couldn't blame him, this was an alarming and inexplicable situation. I wanted to offer him consolation. I wanted to go to him and promise him that everything was going to be okay, but my sense of self-respect combined with the lingering shock from seeing that dead raven made me resist. Still, seeing him so torn up hurt me. I felt what he felt, as though we were connected by an invisible thread.

"We need to get rid of this shit." He stopped pacing and pointed at the box before grabbing the note and shoving it into the back pocket of his jeans. The idea of notifying the police briefly popped into my head, but what we would we have said? That we'd gotten an anonymous package containing a raven corpse? They would almost certainly assume it was some sort of prank between kids. Plus, Neil was already on the cops' radar, and this could have made his situation worse.

"I have an idea," Logan said, looking at us. "Come to my room with me."

He went up the stairs, leaving Neil and me temporarily alone in the living room. I turned to look at him: he was so beautiful in that moment, shadowed and vulnerable. I was just as powerfully attracted to him as I'd been on the day we'd met, but the disillusionment I now felt was so intense that I no longer had any desire to speak to him.

After a moment, I shook myself and went up the stairs after Logan. Shortly thereafter, I heard Neil's footsteps coming up behind me. Knowing that he was back there made me anxious. I felt like his eyes were boring into my back like a pair of flaming swords, piercing and burning my flesh.

I couldn't get it out of my head, the image of him with Jennifer and Alexia.

Shit... I had to stop thinking about it. I didn't get to have an opinion on the matter. After all, I meant nothing to him. I wasn't a real part of his life.

I sighed as I walked into Logan's room and cleared my throat, trying to regain some control over myself. Neil propped himself up against his brother's desk and folded his arms over his chest expectantly.

"So, we need to figure out what the raven means and why this person chose it." Logan had put his glasses on and was sitting on his bed with his open MacBook in his lap.

"Does it look like I've got time to waste?" Neil commented in a derisive tone that did nothing to deter his brother.

"We need to figure this out, Neil," Logan chided him, still focused on the screen. I took a seat on the bed next to him and glanced at the search engine results he'd pulled up.

"Ok, knock yourself out, Sherlock." Mr. Disaster dug in the pockets of his black leather jacket for a pack of Winstons, pulling out a single cigarette with his teeth. He lit it and exhaled smoke into the air.

"At least open a window." Logan shook his head and kept typing. Neil obeyed him but muttered incomprehensibly under his breath the whole time.

"Hmm… I'm not finding a lot of positive associations," Logan said after a few moment.

"Seriously? I could have told you that," grumbled Neil. He stood by the window smoking with the typical arrogant ease that set him apart from everyone else. I wanted to snap at him to shut up and stop acting like an ass, but I knew that, if I did, I'd only be venting my anger from the night before. So I resisted the urge.

"Here's something interesting." Logan adjusted his glasses and focused on his reading. "The raven has inspired a number of legends and beliefs. It feeds on the corpses of animals as well as human beings, which is why it has so often been associated with death and evil…" He glanced up at both of us, and Neil gestured for him to continue, so he kept going in a mournful tone. "The raven is often used in black-magic rituals or séances designed to call on evil spirits." I shivered, and Neil must have noticed because he shot me a concerned look.

"This isn't a horror movie, Sherlock. Cut to the chase." He leaned against the windowsill and took a long drag on his cigarette. Then he looked at me again, like he was worried about me. Or maybe I just wanted to believe he was.

"In mythology and esotericism, the raven is often associated with macabre messages or portents of disasters that are to occur in the future...but, listen to what it says here." Logan stopped again, sighed heavily and continued. "Legend has it that a dead raven often heralds revenge," he finished, slowly removing his glasses.

Neil tossed the cigarette out the window and walked over, staring at his brother, who still looked worried.

"We really need to watch out. Trust as few people as possible and watch everyone: friends, relatives, acquaintances, friends of friends. Whoever sent that box knows where we live, knows who we are. They know us and we might know them." Logan glanced between the two of us before standing up and pinching his lower lip between his thumb and forefinger.

I looked from Neil to Logan, rubbing my hands anxiously on my jeans. For the first time, I felt like I was in real danger.

....

Still shaken a few hours later, I decided to make myself a hot cup of chamomile tea. I needed to calm down. I'd even tried calling my mother to improve my mood, but hearing her voice only made me feel worse.

I missed her, like I missed the rest of my life. Yet, I still wasn't sure that I wanted to go back to Detroit.

God, I was so at odds with myself.

I brought the steaming mug to my lips and blew on it slowly. I paused in front of the large glass doors in the kitchen, looking out at a sky robed in total darkness. I'd come to New York with the intention of fixing my relationship with Matt; instead, I'd been thrust into a bunch of problems I had no business dealing with at all. I sighed and gripped the hot cup tighter, basking in the warmth that radiated into my cold palms.

"It had nothing to do with you," Neil said, his voice shattering the silence that had enveloped me. I kept my back to him, though I could feel his presence behind me.

"That's not true. I live here with you. It has *something* to do with me." In reality, I had no enemies in Detroit, and I didn't think I had any New York, either, but I couldn't be certain about anything anymore. I brought the mug to my lips and took a tiny sip as I listened to his footsteps draw nearer to me. It felt like my heart slipped down into my stomach along with the chamomile.

"Have you ever done something truly bad to anyone, Tinkerbell?" I felt Neil's warm breath against my ear, and he began to rub my back with one hand, following the curve of my spine. I tried not to quiver, but I couldn't control the little tremors that moved across my skin.

"No, never. Not before cheating on Jared," I whispered, hanging on to my mug as though it might anchor me in place. Neil made a thoughtful noise and got even closer, until his chest was pressing into my tensed back.

"And has anyone ever done something bad to you?" he continued in that same low, seductive tone. I hesitated before answering. I thought about Matt, about my mother's tears, about the day I caught my father with another woman, about their divorce, and his absence and then...my gaze moved to the pool house. Neil rubbed my arms tenderly, balancing his chin on top of my head and breathing in my scent.

"I know you saw everything," he whispered in my ear, as though it were an unspeakable secret. I stopped breathing altogether. I wanted to break away, to put some safe distance between us, but my legs had turned to concrete and my arms to lead.

"You're just like my father." I continued to stare at the pool house until the reflection of us hovered in the glass in front of me.

The reflection of us…in my room, bent over the desk, Neil behind me. Our fused bodies, our intertwining pants, kisses, tongues, hands…

"You're wrong, Tinkerbell. You're the one who's like him." He stroked my hair and I gasped.

Was I like Matt?

I stared blankly.

He was right.

There was Jared in Detroit, who loved and trusted me and would have welcomed me back with open arms, and I was chasing a man who didn't even want me. It was not very different at all from the way my father had been unfaithful to my mother. My hands started to shake, and two tears rolled down my cheeks until they reached the Cupid's bow of my mouth and then slipped between my lying lips.

"That's not true. I haven't told Jared yet because his mother is sick, maybe dying, and I can't just tell him something like that right now… I don't…." My voice cracked and Neil took me by the shoulders. He turned me slowly around to face him and stared into my eyes. He lifted the mug out of my hands and set it on the counter next to me, then turned his gaze back to me.

"I'm not like my father," I whispered uncertainly. Neil's hands traversed my cheeks; he gathered my tears up on his thumbs and then smiled faintly at me.

"You are, though. You absolutely are, Babygirl. We are all like your father. Flawed sinners, inclined to make mistakes. Mistakes give us the chance to learn things. Like maybe that we can't judge anyone else." He continued touching my face. I couldn't tell if he was trying to break me down or rescue me. He leaned closer and touched his lips to my cheek. Then, he stuck out his tongue and used it to follow the track of my tears, licking them away.

"You smell so pure, and you taste like innocence, but you're a sinner, too," he whispered again.

"Because of you." I grabbed his wrists and tried to pull free from his grip, but Neil didn't budge.

"Another mistake, Babygirl. Never attribute to another a sin you yourself committed." He grinned smugly, like an insolent devil. I tried to move away from him again, but he grabbed my hips and pinned me against the glass of the door, smothering me underneath him.

"You're a bastard." I writhed, trying to get him off me, but he was so much stronger than me. He put one hand around my throat, holding but not squeezing. I was rendered immobile by the feeling of his fingers against my jugular.

"Am I a bastard because you want me all the time? Or because you've conjured up a relationship between us that doesn't actually exist?" He pressed his forehead to mine. "Answer me, Selene. Which of those two reasons were you referring to?" His deep voice was firm and austere.

I didn't know how to answer. I felt all alone, trapped and confused. Maybe he was right and it was all my fault. Mine, and no one else's.

"Not everything has to be explained. We don't have a relationship; we don't have feelings for each other. I'm physically attracted to you just like you are to me, and that's the only truth that brings us together," he finished in the face of my silence, loosening his grip on my throat before gliding his hand from my neck down to my breast. He squeezed it, and I sucked in a breath at the amount of force he used.

He closed his eyes, a deranged desire appearing to get the better of him. "I am what I am and I can't change. I don't expect you to understand, but don't judge me." His eyes opened again and stared at me with the same chill he always showed me whenever he touched me. Whenever he kissed me. Whenever he *owned* me.

"I can't go on like this. I can't do it. I can't keep letting you use me whenever you want. I feel soiled." I stared down at his hand squeezing my left breast then glanced back up at him, silently begging him to release me.

Neil blinked and glared at his own hand as if it had moved by itself—an instinctive, possessive gesture. He relaxed his fingers and stepped back. For a brief instant, he even looked upset, but then he turned inscrutable and apathetic again. Neil seemed to be having these confusing moments more and more often.

But he was in another world, too far away to know.

A person could face almost anything in life—hatred, anger, pain, desperation—but not an absence of love. I could deal with anyone who felt *something*, but I could not deal with someone who didn't feel anything.

20

I stared at the cigarette and vomited a cloud of dense smoke back into the air.

I'd been addicted to nicotine since I was an adolescent. I loved smoking because it relaxed me; it calmed me down, even if calm was not usually one of my strong suits.

The air that day was cold and biting; people were swathed in overcoats and wool sweaters, and I just stood there, looking around indifferently.

"You wanna get a move on? It's fucking freezing out here."

The Krew were waiting impatiently for me to go into one of the restaurants near the university. I didn't get why Xavier always insisted on going to that one shitty place after classes, but I suspected he'd fixated on one of the waitresses there. Wouldn't be the first time.

"Go in. I'll catch up in a minute." This cigarette was sacrosanct, and I was going to finish it.

"Fuck this!" Xavier walked into the restaurant, followed by Luke,

Jennifer, and Alexia, while I stayed outside, deep in thought. I hadn't gotten a wink of sleep the night before. Instead, I mused constantly about the note and its hypothetical sender. The list of my enemies was a long one. I had made a lot of mistakes over the years, and now that was making everything more complicated.

I thought I had left my past behind me, but apparently it was chasing me down like a shadowy demon, impossible to fight. What I was most afraid of, though, was that whoever this maniac was, he might hurt my family, my siblings.

They were my Achilles' heel. I would have killed with my bare hands anyone who dared to touch them.

My nightmares had also come back that night. I had seen Kimberly again, and it felt so real that I vomited up my entire dinner. My only consolation in the morning was the knowledge that she was still in prison, serving her sentence for what she had done, and I would never, ever see her again for the rest of my fucking life.

I chucked the cigarette butt to the ground and stepped on it, sticking my hands into the pockets of my jacket. Then I joined the others inside, sitting at our usual table by the window.

"Finally, asshole. How long does it take you smoke a cigarette?"

Ignoring Xavier, I sat down next to Jennifer. Not because I wanted to be close to her, but because it was the only seat available. She gave me a smile, probably thinking that I was going to accept the suggestion she'd made a half hour before that we lock ourselves in the restaurant's bathroom.

Delusional.

I didn't say anything. I didn't want to talk to anyone, like usual. Instead, I made myself comfortable and stretched my arm out over the back of Jennifer's chair. Then, my eyes caught on a man at the counter who was reprimanding his son. He had him by the arm and he was shaking him all because the boy had spilled fruit punch on his pants.

Suddenly, he slapped the kid across the face so hard that it made my stomach knot up. In that moment, I could feel in my own body exactly what that boy was feeling in his. The burning sensation on my cheek, the throbbing in my head, the hot tears of humiliation… all at the hands of his own father.

My own father.

I hated that piece of shit William Miller with every fiber of my being. I was ashamed to even share blood with him. I dreamed of the day I'd see him dead, because that was what he deserved.

"Hey." Jennifer tried to stroke my face, but I grabbed her roughly by the wrist to stop her. One cutting look from me was enough to make her tremble.

"Don't touch me," I whispered emphatically, though all the others heard me as well. She bobbed her head like a good bitch, and I released her wrist, though not before noticing Xavier's sharp eyes fixed on me.

"Looks like someone's edgy." He quirked up one corner of his mouth and slapped the ass of a passing waitress, making her jump.

"Hey, baby, we asked you for four beers about ten minutes ago." The girl blanched and then walked away without saying anything. We hadn't been there ten minutes, but they never dared to argue with us.

"Can you try, for once, not to be a dick?" I gave him some shit because I hated it when he acted like a fucking bully. I didn't like a lot of ways he acted, though I knew I did similar things.

"Sure thing, boss." He pasted on a phony smile and glanced around, bored. Alexia sat beside him, waiting to be given a scrap of attention. Alexia had some kind of thing with Xavier, even though I fucked her, too. He was fine with me getting down with her. Him-her-me, her-me-him… That was how it had always been. We were used to sharing, especially when it came to women.

"But look who it is. Sweet little doll." Xavier whistled, looking toward the entrance and I followed the direction of his gaze.

The "little doll" he was referring to was Selene.

She had just walked in, followed by Logan. She was wearing a white coat and a scarf the same shade of blue as her ocean eyes. Her auburn hair fell softly around her shoulders, framing her high cheekbones and perfect face. The tip of her nose was red from the cold, and her lush mouth was swollen and pink.

"Whoa, nice stepsister," Luke added with an impish smile. Selene was never vulgar or flashy, but her beauty hardly went unnoticed. She was something rare: fresh and glowing with the kind of angel face that would have attracted anyone's attention. Especially the fucking scumbags next to me.

"I'd know what to do with that ass." Xavier watched as Selene took off her coat and sat down across from Logan. It was just them, but the table had more seats, suggesting their friends would be joining them soon.

"She's nothing special; just a basic ho," Jennifer cut in, glaring hatefully at Selene. I knew that look well; it was filled with the same resentment and sick envy that often had her beating up any woman who caught my eye, even if only for a night.

Unexpectedly, I found myself annoyed by the way she talked about Selene, because Babygirl was definitely not just one of many. I didn't say anything, though, because I knew if the Krew thought I had a soft spot for her, it would make her a target. And I didn't want anything to happen to her. Those assholes shouldn't even have been thinking about defiling her with their poison. So I stayed calm and kept my face blank. I knew that they were testing me, trying to get a rise out of me. But I was a much bigger son of a bitch than any of them were.

"Would she be up for a three-way, do you think?" Luke suggested, just as the waitress came by with our beers. She hastily deposited them on the table and snuck away, taking advantage of Xavier's distraction. He was still laser-focused on Selene.

A three-way? Fuck's sake! These degenerates couldn't even imagine the kind of girl Selene was. They didn't know that she'd only just lost her virginity to me or that she'd never seen or touched a naked man before me. They certainly didn't know how many times I'd fucked her or how intensely attracted I was to her.

Selene was pure in every way. A white rose in a sea of blackened ones, and I was the one who got to defile her. Me and no one else. I needed to be the one—the only one—who devoured her innocence, who sucked her blood, who breathed in her coconut smell and lapped at her delicate curves.

That was an insane line of thought, considering that, just the previous evening, I had made it very clear to her that she meant nothing to me.

And that was true, but I was selfish. A selfish bastard.

I stared at her, watching the way her lips curved into a gentle smile. Her movements were always so elegant. When guys gave her urgent looks, she'd tilt her head down and repeatedly touch her hair in an awkward gesture that poorly disguised her shyness. Even then, I logged her every motion because I didn't just want to know the basics about her, I wanted to know all the little things. Especially those little things that only I had gotten the chance to see, like the tiny mole next to her right areola.

Shortly thereafter, Alyssa, Adam, and the rest of them arrived. Selene greeted everyone politely and moved next to my brother so Julie could sit beside Adam. Then Lucky Kyle or whatever that fucking dude's name was sat down on her other side. All I knew was that he was Cory's out-of-town cousin. He was a tall, skinny idiot with the physique and general vibe of a failed musician.

The dude smiled at Selene and looked at her the way everyone looked at her: adoringly.

Of course he did; she was a fairy. Who could ignore that?

Xavier and Luke tracked my gaze and exchanged knowing looks.

"You fuck her yet?" Luke asked, sipping his beer. I looked at him, pasting on my usual mask of indifference. I would never have thrown my Tinkerbell to the wolves by answering that question honestly.

"No, not my type." I looked at Jennifer. Or rather, I looked quite eloquently at her large breasts, exposed in her low-cut sweater. By that time, I had learned a lot about manipulating people, and the Krew had always been my best practice. Making Jennifer and the rest of them believe that I only wanted her was one way to protect Selene from dangerous repercussions.

"You live together. There's no way a horny fuck like you ain't tapping that ass." Xavier was the smartest of them all but still not smart enough. I smiled at him and took a sip of my beer, looking back at Selene, who was chatting pleasantly with long-haired Kyle.

"You're full of shit. She's Matt's daughter. I don't need that kind of trouble." I shrugged and kept drinking, though the beer tasted worse with every mouthful. Selene continued to smile at that guy, and she seemed comfortable with him. Probably because they'd already hung out several times.

It occurred to me that it would be completely natural for her to be interested in someone other than me. I could stop Luke and Xavier from sniffing around her, but I didn't have the same power over the rest of the student body.

On the other hand, I knew that women tended to fall in love with new guys at about the same rate that I finished cigarettes. She was no different from the rest of them. She was dreaming about fairy tales and looking for Prince Charming. She wanted someone to "make love" to her and whisper sweet nothings while he touched her.

All those things that I would never be able—or willing—to give her.

The room suddenly felt too small and the air too hot. I needed another smoke and to go back home. I got up and made some lame excuse. Xavier shot me a suspicious look, but I didn't care.

I left the Krew and walked directly to my brother's table. Selene hadn't spotted me yet, even though that was the only thing I was waiting for: the moment when her big blue eyes would slam right into me.

"Mmm…great, pineapple juice." I grabbed Logan's glass and took a sip. Logan startled before pouting like a little kid when he saw who it was.

"Give that back, dick." He snatched the drink out of my hands, and his friends all stared wordlessly at me. I wasn't there to intimidate them, all I was looking for was a pair of crystalline eyes. Ones that I noted with satisfaction were already focused on me. Babygirl had finally stopped talking to that jerk and given me her ocean stare, sparkling from behind her long, black eyelashes. I stared fixedly at her until her cheeks turned a soft pink.

"Hey, Tinkerbell," I mouthed and Selene gasped, opening her mouth slightly. Fuck, I wanted to kiss that mouth and then bite it and then soothe it. I wanted to feel it wrapped around me, all over my body.

"See you at home." I clapped Logan on the shoulder and forced my legs to move me promptly away from the table but not before shooting Babygirl one last smile. Good. Now she could continue her *fascinating* conversation with me in her head.

I was going to keep using her just like I did with all the rest of them. I was going to touch her again, kiss her again, fuck her again and again. And then I would tell her again that sex was all that could ever be between the two of us. She would get my body and nothing more.

I went back home to study, because I was in my last year of undergrad, and despite all my issues, I was still hoping to graduate and one day become an architect.

I crossed through the big foyer and stopped when I spotted my mother in an armchair in front of the elegant fireplace. She stared at the flames devouring the wood inside while, outside, hard winds bent the trees and a light rain began to patter on the immense windows of the house.

I got closer for a better look and saw that her blond hair had been messily pulled up into a bun, and her cheeks were streaked with mascara all the way down to her chin. She had been crying; she was completely devastated. I took another step forward and stared at her in shock.

"When were you planning to tell me?"

I stopped. What was she talking about? There were a lot of things I didn't tell my mother. I had stopped trying to be an affectionate son at the age of ten, and I couldn't even remember the last time we'd hugged.

"What are you talking about?" I asked flatly, trying not to display any fear or concern. But when my mother turned her blue eyes on mine, I saw the deep grief in them.

"Lots of things, Neil." She got to her feet, and for one wild moment, I thought she was referring to me and Selene.

But no. There was no way she knew what had happened between me and her partner's daughter. Between me and the girl who I was supposed to treat like a younger sister, who I was never supposed to even remotely consider fucking selfishly to feed my own ego.

My mother stood in front of me, looking up. Her high heels weren't quite enough to let her face reach my height, but her disappointed look surely did. It pinned me where I stood.

"I'm talking about your sister's near-rape and Carter Nelson winding up in a hospital bed, comatose," she said, her voice trembling and her eyes bright with anger. "Why didn't any of you tell me? Why did you go off half-cocked like usual without even informing me?" She scrubbed her face with her hands and started pacing around the living room.

The flickering firelight caught my attention, and then it was me standing there, staring into the fireplace, looking for an answer that I couldn't give her.

"Why? Why do you always have to screw everything up?" she shouted at me, and in the flames, I thought I could see the child version of myself. The Neil who was constantly being scolded by his mother because he didn't want to go to school. The one whose classmates avoided him because he was violent. The one whose teachers hated him because he was rebellious and impossible to discipline. The one who hid in the corner of his room under the window because he needed to get away from the world and that was the only place he felt safe.

I saw the Boy I had been dragging along behind me for all these years.

"No, you're the screwup," I murmured and then turned to look back at her. My mother flinched as though I'd slapped her when she saw my cold stare, full of all the anger that was slowly reemerging from the depths of my damaged soul. I walked purposefully toward her, watching as her eyes widened in fear.

"You are the one who doesn't notice anything that isn't about your life, your work, your partner. You're the one who is completely fucking blind and deaf!" I shouted, just a few inches from her face. I squeezed my hands into fists at my sides and felt the anger flowing immediately into my veins. My heartbeat was throbbing in my temples.

I was never able to deal with the anger; it was my worst enemy. My own mother was standing right there in front of me, but I could have hurt her just then like she were total stranger. I could have destroyed her, torn her to pieces, annihilated her. Fortunately, I still had a modicum of rational thought and was able to control myself.

"Your sister is sick." She burst into tears, and I felt it like a blow to my chest, my heart pounding faster. Not because I cared about my mother, but because I loved my sister. Her pain was my pain.

"Sick how?" I muttered in a small voice. My mother continued to sob, wiping a trembling tear from her chin with the back of one hand.

"She has severe insomnia. She never wants to go to school. She can't focus on homework. She doesn't want to go out with her friends, because she keeps flashing back to the attack." She covered her face with her hands and slumped down on the sofa, weeping like a little girl. She didn't look anything like the famous career woman immortalized by the New York tabloids. Instead, she looked like a woman who had been destroyed by the brutality of life and cruelty of human beings.

I'd known Chloe wasn't doing well, but I hadn't realized it had gotten that bad.

"What?" I was incredulous, incapable of imagining my Little Koala trapped in her room facing such a huge monster all by herself. But I understood... I understood like no one else ever could.

"She's going through so much." My mother got up from the couch and pulled a note from the pocket of her elegant slacks, handing it to me. "I'd like you to place a call to Dr. Lively, Neil. I want Chloe to meet with him."

Did she want my sister to wind up like me? I couldn't let her do that to Chloe. I just couldn't.

"Are you kidding me?" My mother had no idea what it felt like to walk into a psychiatrist's office and be made aware of just how much was wrong with you. Nor how it felt to get loaded up with psychotropic meds.

"I just want to get her some help, and I want you to take her." She drew closer, trying to touch me, but I backed away. I hated being touched without my consent.

"You just want to dump her on a shrink like you did with me!" I snapped angrily.

It was the truth. I was a kid with problems, sure, but my mother hadn't hesitated for a moment before sending me straight to the fucking psychiatrist to get psychoanalyzed and pumped full of drugs. They dulled my senses and kept me docile, like an animal under sedation.

"That is not true, and you know it. You needed help. You still need help." She brought her shaking hand to her mouth, stifling a sob, but I remained motionless, just staring at her.

She was so full of shit.

"Stop it," I warned her sharply. She needed to shut her mouth, to just keep quiet.

"Call Dr. Lively, please. Do it for Chloe and for yourself." She grabbed my wrist. "Do it," she added in a whisper.

I barely heard her; her words from before just kept running through my head like a mantra: *"You still need help."*

A strange, tortured feeling climbed up my throat, making it tighten painfully. I could smell something on me, a smell that didn't belong to me. My skin began tingling, sending signals for help to my brain. It was an uncontrollable feeling. I had the powerful urge to wash myself, to feel the scalding water sluicing over me. I began to breathe heavily, like I'd been running laps. My head was spinning as I dashed up the stairs.

I threw off my leather jacket and barreled through the door to my room. I kicked off my shoes and undid the button on my jeans. My hands were shaking the whole time, like an addict going through withdrawals. I had already taken several showers that day, but I needed another one, right that instant. I pulled off my sweater and threw it on the floor before hurrying into the bathroom.

Horrifying images began flashing before my eyes, sending my soul tumbling back down into the abyss. My stomach lurched, and I hit my knees in front of the toilet.

Why me?

The muscles of my abdomen contracted involuntarily and out poured all the hatred, rage, and frustration that surrounded me like an enormous dark veil whenever I remembered that evil year. The one that was now a part of me and always would be.

I wiped my lips with the back of my hand before curling them in disgust. Then I flushed and got to my feet with difficultly. It was hard to breathe. I could feel my esophagus burning and taste the stomach acid on my tongue. I blinked several times, trying to clear my head.

I bent over the sink and brushed my teeth, scrubbing hard until I saw blood oozing from my gums. I stared at my reflection in the mirror. I was pale; my eyes were glassy and my lips were dry, making it obvious how unsettled I was. My flexed biceps supported my weight as my chest heaved rapidly up and down.

"Fuck this," I whispered. "Fuck this! Fuck this!" My voice got louder and louder. I was so angry, and I hated myself so much. My body, my eyes, every fucking thing about the way I looked. I hated my mood swings, my weak moments, the times when the Boy emerged just to remind me how angry he still was.

I stripped off my jeans and boxers and tossed them furiously away from me. Then I climbed into the shower and turned the water on as hot as it would go. I scalded myself, punishing myself for everything that I had done, for everything that I hadn't avoided, for what I was, for what I had become, and for what I would always be.

Why me?

"Why me? Huh? Why?" I lifted up my face, squinting into the water hitting me, and I addressed a God who probably had as much against me as I now had against him. I could feel the fury crescendoing inside me, quickly outpacing my reason before snuffing it out entirely. So I tried to vent the only way I knew how: I started throwing violent punches against the tile. One after the other. I didn't care about the pain. I didn't care about getting injured. I didn't care about anything. I could have died in there, and honestly, that might have been the best possible outcome.

"Neil! What are you doing?" Logan threw open the glass door of the shower and grabbed me by the shoulders, pulling me out. I collapsed to my knees, staring at my reddened, swollen knuckles and then...then I just started laughing.

Fuck, I was really busting a gut. I must have looked like an actual lunatic.

Or maybe I just *was* a lunatic.

Logan grabbed a bath towel and draped it over my shoulders to cover me. Then he looked at me, terrified and, bit by bit, my laughter died.

"Sorry, it's all his fault..." The Boy's fault, that fucked-up kid. It was always his fault. My body began trembling, rocked by a wave of painful convulsions that I could do nothing to stop. My head was throbbing, and my muscles ached from being held in tension for way too long. My hands felt like they were on fire. I tried to move them, to close them into fists, but it hurt too badly and I grimaced in pain.

I was used to being hurt, though. It was hardly the first time it had happened.

My brother sighed and helped me to my feet. "I'm going to go get you some ice," he said, hurrying out of the bathroom as I trudged slowly across my room. I sat down on the bed and looked down at myself. I was completely naked with nothing but a towel around my shoulders like a cape. The outlines of my muscles and veins showed clearly just how much my body had changed since I was little.

I had grown up but the Boy still lived inside me, more pissed off than ever.

With a heavy sigh, I got up and grabbed a clean pair of boxers from the drawer. I pulled them on and tossed the damp towel on the floor. My skin was still dripping and so was my hair, but I had no intention nor inclination to dry it.

"Logan…is everything okay in there?"

Selene's soft, feminine voice echoed down the hallway from behind the half-open door of my room.

I stared straight ahead at nothing in particular and focused completely on her words. It was ridiculous how my entire body warmed to the sound of her voice, and it was unbelievable how the excitement rushed down between my legs, even in a shitty moment like that.

What would Selene have thought of me if she had known what I really was? A shitshow, a psychopath, everyone's fucking problem. I smiled sardonically at myself and my warped personality.

"Don't worry; everything's fine." Logan's tone was reassuring, but I knew how worried he really was. He was always worried when I lost my head. Moments later, he came into the room with a bag of ice in his hand. He shut the door behind him with a small kick.

"Sit down." He pointed to the bed, but I just kept standing there, staring him down.

"Don't order me around," I told him sharply. I hated it whenever someone tried to tell me what to do. My brother looked at me, and I held his gaze, making sure he knew not to fight with me about it.

"Your hands are already swelling up. I just want to help you." He huffed and approached me. I didn't move. At the same time, I couldn't stop eyeing him warily, and I didn't really know why. My body was acting independently of the rest of me.

"Calm down, okay? It's me, your brother." He said it with such intensity that it actually dissipated the dark clouds fogging up my mind.

It was Logan, my brother.

The same brother who played with me as a child; the only person who had never been afraid of me. The only person who actually knew me and accepted me as I was.

I sat down on the edge of the bed and let my hands rest on my bent knees. I was a big, imposing man, but in that moment, all I felt was vulnerable and tired. I was exhausted from fighting myself once again.

"How come my big, bad brother turns into a baby the moment he needs to get his owies looked at, huh?" he teased, pressing the ice pack down on the back of my right hand. I shuddered at the burning sensation and tightened my jaw, not saying a word. I always felt this way after one of my lost times: confused and unsteady. I never remembered anything I'd said or done. I probably could have committed murder and my mind would have repressed it, so powerful and uncontrolled were my outbursts.

Logan sat down next to me and let me hold the bag of ice in place with my other hand.

"Do you remember when we were little and we used to do pinky swears?" he murmured as I continued to study the backs of my hands, dotted with little red gashes.

Of course I remembered our pinky swears. My mind could easily travel back there, to those distant years that were still alive inside me...

"Logan." I rested my hands on his little shoulders. We were hiding together under the kitchen table. "I'll tell you what you need to do one more time, okay?" I said in a low voice as he watched me with terrified eyes.

"Okay," he whispered, unsure.

"You're going to leave the kitchen and run to the bedroom. You're going to close your eyes while you cross the living room, and you're not going to look." I took a breath and then kept going. "Go in the room and lock the door. Turn on the TV and turn the volume way up."

"Neil." An adult woman's voice echoed off the walls of the house. She had an odd kink: she liked to force me to hide and then come find me.

My heart began pounding in my chest, and I looked back at my brother, waiting for him to repeat the instructions I'd just given him.

"Say it again, now." He was only seven years old and already being tested in ways he couldn't fully understand.

"I leave the kitchen, run to the bedroom, and then . . . " He rubbed the nape his neck and looked upward, trying to remember what came next.

"When you cross the . . . " I prompted him and he continued.

"Yeah, when I cross the living room, I close my eyes and I don't look. Then I go into the room, lock the door, turn on the TV, and turn the volume way up," he concluded in his faint little voice.

"Good pup," I whispered, kissing his forehead. I was his big brother, and I would protect him at all costs.

I started to leave our hiding place. I needed to be found before she could catch us both here and perhaps hurt Logan, too. He held me back, though, tugging on my shirt. "And then you come back to me, right?" he whispered, knowing that we needed to be quiet. He was little, but he was smart.

"Of course, I'll come back. You do everything I told you, okay?" I held his face in my hands and he nodded, though he didn't understand the reason behind my orders. To be honest, I was glad he couldn't understand.

"Should we do our pinky swear?" He stuck his little finger out to me, waiting.

"Pinky swear," I smiled and hooked my pinky with his.

Then he ran away, and I went to meet my fate.

"I could never forget that," I murmured, pressing the ice against my swollen knuckles.

"We've been through everything together," he said softly, thinking of exactly the same things I was.

"You've always been my favorite pup." I reached out and tousled his chestnut hair, cracking a spontaneous grin.

"Come on! Knock it off! You know I hate it when you mess up my hair." He tried to squirm away, muttering like a sulky child.

"I used to do it all the time when you were little," I pointed out.

"When I was little, you tormented me." He threw me a dirty look, and I tried to suppress a laugh.

"That is not true," I argued, pretending not to remember the many disasters I had visited upon him as a child.

"Oh yeah? You once peed *my* bed. On purpose!" he answered, narrowing his eyes.

"Well, you once cut my hair while I was sleeping. Are we going to talk about that?" I said, raising an eyebrow and already scenting victory on the wind. Logan smiled and shook his head at me, then he stared at an uncertain point on the wall, apparently lost in his own thoughts.

"I know you're going to take Chloe to see Dr. Lively. Why don't you…" He swallowed hard and skewered me with his hazel eyes. "Why don't you go back to therapy, too?" he suggested cautiously, and a cold shiver ran down my spine, making me stiffen up. Was he, like my mother, trying to get me to relive that shitty period in my life?

"Fuck." I got up from the bed and glared furiously at him. "I thought you at least would be on my side! For Christ's sake!" I swore and threw the ice bag on the floor. I wanted to smash something up again. The Boy inside me was pushing against my chest, ready to bust out and scream.

Once again, he was feeling misunderstood.

"I am always on your side, but you're not okay, Neil. And you know it, too." He got up as well and walked toward me. I took a step back, because I didn't want him near me—not when I was in that kind of state.

"You're not okay at all. Look at yourself." He jerked his chin toward my hands, but he was surely also referring to the thing in my soul. The thing that was invisible to the human eye that my brother knew perfectly well.

"Leave." I pointed to the door. I wanted to be alone again. I needed to wash myself again. Wash and wash and wash and wash again. The boiling water would ease my discomfort and soothe some of my rage. Actually...I knew of one other way to erase the thoughts that were wrapped around my brain like barbed fucking wire.

"Neil, please...just listen—"

I pointed at the door again, daring him to keep arguing with me. Logan knew my hair-trigger temper, my reactive nature. He knew when he could talk to me and when to just avoid me.

So he sighed and hung his head as he left the room, overwhelmed by me and all the things that came along with me.

I went back to the shower again; this time, I stayed there for a full hour. The amber-scented shower gel was so strong it made me nauseous, but at the same time, it was the only thing I wanted to be able to smell on me. When I was done, I dressed myself in a simple black sweatshirt and a pair of jeans before sitting down at my desk and opening up my laptop.

I should have kept working on my project for Professor Robinson because the due date was rapidly approaching, but instead my eye wandered over the top of my desk, to the folder where I kept clippings of stories that had appeared in the newspapers years before. Back when I had become one of the protagonists of a scandal that had caught the whole city's attention.

It had turned out to be a network.

A complex shadow world.

Something that went well beyond journalistic simplifications about the internet and required an understanding of its hidden depths. The vilest and most dangerous parts.

My hands began to shake, and I refused to open the folder as my false tachycardia started up again. After all, the only reason I kept the thing was to remind me of who I had been: helpless before that woman, when I should have been able to stop her.

I caught her smell again on the air. Her sweat on my skin; her tongue on my neck. My lips twisted in disgust. I found myself, once again, fighting the child version of myself who tried to force me to remember, who muddied my vision with pictures from the past and bewildered my senses with smells and tastes that I didn't want to recognize.

I shut my laptop and sighed in frustration.

Memories were inundating me, ready to pull me under and drown me.

I needed something to distract me; to rescue me.

To calm the Boy down.

I leaped to my feet and left the room with the worst of intentions. I didn't care who else I hurt as long as I got my moment of peace. I looked carefully around, but there was no one there. No obstacles to get in the way of my latest fuckup in progress.

I walked the short stretch of hallway that separated me from Selene's room, and not bothering to knock, I opened the door and went inside. I closed the door behind me and turned the lock. Then, I took a look around.

It looked like a room for a princess.

Everything was in its place. The bright walls and elegant furnishings lent it a sophisticated, refined air. It smelled like Selene, like that coconut scent that had somehow become my favorite smell.

I advanced slowly through the room, in search of my prey. I had been certain I would find her there at that time of night, but there was no sign of her.

Suddenly, a sound drew my attention. It was coming from the en suite bathroom, so I moved toward the open door.

She stood in front of the mirror, intent on putting her hair up in a high ponytail with nothing but a red towel covering her slim, sculpted body. Selene truly had the beauty of a goddess—of a Venus. Her long, defined legs were left exposed by the towel, which only barely covered her ass. I put a hand on my fly because a stab of want had hit me in the lower abdomen and ignited a flame that I wasn't going to be able to control for much longer.

I leaned against the doorframe, arms folded, waiting for her to notice my presence. Selene picked up a jar of scented cream and scooped some into the palm of her hand before slowly spreading it over her still-damp skin. I devoured her with my eyes like a starving animal while she continued to tend to herself. Completely unaware that I was standing there, unmoving, staring at her like a peeping tom.

I decided to end this drawn-out torture and cleared my throat. She should have felt me there.

Babygirl looked up and spotted me in the mirror, finally noting the presence of the wolf, hovering over her like the delicious morsel that she was.

"Oh my God!" She jumped in surprise and whirled around to face me, tightening her hand on the knot of the towel like that was going to protect her from me. I grinned at her.

"Hey, Tinkerbell." I ogled her shamelessly, paying special attention to the thighs that I wanted to feel gripping my waist. I really wanted to fuck, and I had zero qualms about making that clear to her.

"How dare you come into my room without knocking?" she scolded me, her attitude suddenly stern and rigid. That hand tightening again around the towel, however, showed me just how agitated and overwhelmed she was by my presence. What are you doing here?"

She went red when she noticed how my eyes were fixed on her legs. I was just staring at her like a depraved weirdo, and I needed to calm the fuck down. Without bothering to respond, I walked toward her.

I had always preferred action to talking.

"W… what do you want?" she babbled, shaking. Another question that I didn't need to answer. I stepped even closer, until I could smell her clean, innocent scent right in front of me.

Selene had to tilt her head back to look at me; her head barely reached my chest, which only increased my sense of dominance over her. I smiled at her, knowing full well the effect that smile had on women. Then I put my hands on the marble countertop behind her, trapping her. Her slim figure was caged by my larger one like a butterfly in a crystal cloche.

"I want you naked," I whispered in her ear, watching as the goosebumps appeared on her arms. "And wet. For me," I continued, breathing against her tensed neck. I let my lips brush against her earlobe and she swallowed hard.

I was a selfish asshole, and I knew it.

She told me she felt dirty every time I fucked her, but I really needed it.

I needed to put some space between the memories and reality.

I need to make the visions go away, to erase the terrible feelings that I still had inside me, and this felt like the only goddamned way. Sex wasn't a cure, of course. It wasn't even really a treatment. It was just a temporary trick that I used to assure the Boy inside me that I was the dominant one now. I was the one in control.

"No…" Selene whispered, staring vaguely at my chest to avoid looking me in the eye. She knew that if she looked up, I would be able to read in her eyes all the desire she was trying to hide. So I lifted her chin with my index finger and forced her to look at me.

She bit her lower lip and my thumb moved automatically to caress it. I could feel her light, irregular breaths. I was frozen, hypnotized by the sky blue and aquamarine shades in her brilliant eyes.

"Sex is like flying for me. It allows me to spread my wings and get away from everything," I admitted, not even understanding why I was telling her.

Was I making excuses for myself? Or was I trying to win her over, to manipulate her mind the way I did with everyone else?

"You can go fly with Alexia or Jennifer," she snapped bitterly.

"But I want to go flying with you, in your sky," I whispered, pressing close against her ear again. I could hear her tiny gasp of surprise.

"And then you're going to tell me that there's nothing but a strong physical attraction between us, right? That you're just using me and that's all?" she murmured, her lips compressing into a hard line.

It wouldn't be easy to get her to come around. My words had hurt her more than any of my actions. But I couldn't take them back, because I had told her the truth.

So I tried again.

"There's a Neverland for the child that lives inside every man. You're kind of like my Neverland…" She was my utopian ideal, my Tinkerbell, my asymptote, and I had no illusions that I'd ever rise to meet her in reality. Selene gave me a confused look, and I couldn't blame her. I was difficult to understand.

I smiled at her and kept touching her neck, little by little moving down to the outline of her clavicle.

"Use me like I'm *your* Neverland," I whispered again as I continued to traverse her skin, which was like velvet underneath my fingertips. Selene watched my mouth, and her breathing sped up. I could feel her heart beating faster with each passing second.

"Neverland doesn't exist," she said shakily, and her eyes filled up with tears, just like the time I'd bent her over her desk and urged her to watch us in the mirror.

I reached for the knot in her towel then and looked at her.

"I'll show you that it does."

I freed the ends of the towel and let it fall to floor, revealing her naked body. I took a long moment to admire the sinuous shape of her, her firm little breasts, her flat, defined stomach, her long legs pressed together out of sheer embarrassment and her... her pretty pussy, pink and soft. Selene blushed violently under my probing gaze and stared at a random point over my shoulder.

"You don't care about anyone but yourself," she said softly.

I didn't respond. I wanted her, and everything in me was completely fixated on that place between her thighs.

There was no need for her to be embarrassed; she was just perfect. Perhaps the most beautiful woman I had ever seen in my entire life, and I had seen a lot of women before her. I didn't tell her that, though, and I didn't reassure her, either.

I did absolutely nothing to chase away her shyness.

"Where do you want my lips, Tinkerbell?" I whispered, enclosing her hips in my hands. She gasped and went stiff in my arms, her forehead wrinkling up like she couldn't understand any of this. She was awfully adorable when she made certain faces.

"Where do you want my lips?" I asked again, more slowly this time, bringing my mouth closer to hers in an attempt to deepen the trance. Then I abruptly grabbed her high ponytail with one hand and used the other to palm her breast, sliding my knee in between her thighs as I did so. That finally roused her from her confusion, so I also ground my erection into her hip to make her feel how much I wanted her and how hard I'd gotten for her.

Only for her.

"What are you doing?" She stood stock-still and her body trembled, and I realized that I'd exposed the animal that I was too quickly. I'd spooked her.

She was on edge now, and I had to fix it.

I made small movements with my knee between her legs, hoping to help her relax so I could hit that sweet spot that I knew would please her. I hooked one finger under her hair band and undid her ponytail, careful not to hurt her. Selene stared up at me like I was her mortal enemy but also the one man in world she could never resist, and I had every intention of taking full advantage of that conflict.

I was confident that she liked me. I could tell that I had an effect on her, and I knew that the attraction, the goddamned chemistry that drew us together, was mutual.

I kissed her throat and used my left hand to knead her breast. My thumb slowly massaged the nipple, which was already hard as a gemstone, while my leg continued to grind between her thighs.

Completely nude, Babygirl stood motionless, clinging to the clothes that I was just about to peel off my own body. I heard a soft moan and knew that she was about to lose control. I abandoned her breast and snaked my hand down her stomach until I reached her mons. I pulled my knee away and slid my index finger over her slit. I could feel her arousal on my fingertip.

Like the son of a bitch that I was, I grinned into the crook of her neck, because there she was: naked and wet for me, just the way I'd wanted her.

"Is this where you want my lips?" I pressed my index finger against her flesh, still not penetrating her. Selene grabbed my wrist, and I couldn't tell whether she meant to stop me or urge me on.

It was unusual for me to make this kind of offer to a woman. I was bullheaded on the subject of oral sex: I loved getting it, but I did not enjoy giving it. Selene would be one of a lucky few.

I looked at her, and she met my eyes furiously. She hated me in that moment, because I was stoking desires in her that she had tried so hard to disavow. I grinned diabolically at her and used her hips to turn her around until her back was pressed up against my chest. I wanted to taste her—a sick yearning that I'd never experienced before.

I pressed my pelvis against her ass and insinuated myself between her glutes. I wanted to get out of my jeans and feel her skin to skin, but I needed to be patient and give Babygirl the pleasure she needed first.

"What the hell are you trying to do?" She glared at me through the mirror. It was no accident that I had turned her around: I wanted to see the ecstatic expressions I was going to put on her face. And I wanted her to watch herself being pleasured. I wanted her to know just how much she enjoyed being used by me.

Only by me.

Her hands tightened on the edge of the sink, and I pushed her hair over one shoulder, still pushing myself against her.

"I'll show you." I lifted one corner of my mouth, and the starter pistol went off in my head, signaling the beginning of what would be, by my standards, quite a romantic interlude.

I started by using my tongue to gather the water that had beaded up on her bare shoulders, anchoring her in place by her hips while I did so.

The knowledge that she was watching me in the mirror's reflection was unbearably exciting.

I continued licking her, tracing the line of her backbone down the path that would lead me straight to my Neverland. I ran my lips over every inch of her perfumed skin. I pressed my thumbs into the dimples at the base of her spine, and for one perverse moment, I imagined doing what that dumbass Xavier had thought he'd do to her. After kissing my way to the bottom of her spine, I knelt down behind her, putting her incredible ass at eye level. She was completely exposed to my greedy eyes, and I stared at the juicy peach between her legs. It was slightly parted, as though just waiting to welcome me in.

I slapped her ass cheek and bit it immediately after, making her jerk.

Selene gripped the marble sink even harder and I smiled. She was right to hold on, because I was about to destroy her completely.

"Neil," she murmured, like she was going to beg me to stop, but I knew she wanted me to keep going instead.

"Shh, Tinkerbell, get ready to fly with me." I slowly rubbed her ass, which was, in my opinion, perfect. Round, high, porcelain, and completely at my mercy.

I spread her ass open and brought my face to the crease down the center so I could lick her there. Selene started when she felt my hot tongue gliding from her sphincter to her soft, sopping cunt. I sank my tongue into her, and she gasped again at the sudden intrusion.

"Ne...il," she groaned, dragging out the final letters of my name and collapsing onto her elbows. And to think, I had barely even started the torture...

I pulled my tongue away before she fell over the edge. I wanted her out of her mind.

Incidentally, Selene was apparently acutely sensitive in that area, which she demonstrated as I began caressing her from top to bottom with the tip of my tongue. I paused every now and then to kiss her inner thighs, and my stubble created just the right amount of friction—judging by the shivers that shot down her legs.

"Neil!" she called my name again and arched her back. I smiled and said nothing because just wanted to feel her come. I pushed my tongue into her more firmly and Babygirl rocked her hips on my mouth the way I imagined she would if she were to ride my face.

I licked and sucked her relentlessly, and she screamed just like I wanted. My male ego rejoiced and my hard-on leaped, straining against the closure of my jeans. I hastily undid the button and unzipped to give myself some relief.

"I need to learn what you like and how you like it. I want to get to know you my way," I said before plunging back in and stimulating her with my tongue. I helped myself out by inserting my index finger into her heat, and the quivering of her pelvis let me know that I was driving her wild. I paid close attention to all her reactions so

I could memorize what provoked the most enthusiasm from her; because sex was not one size fits all. A woman had her preferences, just like I had mine.

"Keep going," she panted. I was surrounded by her: the sound of her moans, her scent, her divine flavor that hit me like a drug, the trembling in her legs, the arousal that coated my tongue as I drank in her lust. I had never felt so disconnected from the real world as I did in that moment.

I continued battering her with firm, intense strokes of my tongue. Then, I dove inside her again and again, to that secret place that I had been the very first to access.

As I worked, Selene fell deeper and deeper under my profane spell. I could feel her frenetic breaths, her desire barreling forward unstoppably: she was about to come.

I stopped just before she could reach orgasm and gave her a slap on the ass, leaving behind the pink outline of my fingers. I pulled back from her sex and got slowly back to my feet.

I wanted to fuck her and watch as she screamed with pleasure. I wanted to revel in her every excited expression. I wanted to pound her into a stupor and watch the whole thing.

"Did you enjoy that preview?" I turned my eyes to the mirror. The glass had fogged up slightly, and her image was blurry but Selene still looked unrecognizable to me. Her tousled hair, parted lips, reddened cheeks, and eyes hazy with pure lust made her look like something wild. It was sexy as hell. I licked my lower lip, lapping up her juices, and she blushed in embarrassment.

Her taste in my mouth was magnificent

"How did you like it?" she asked, turning on unsteady legs. I gave her a teasing smile and grabbed her hand, pressing it to my erection in answer.

"What do you think?" I held her fingers against me, and she held her breath. I was swollen and so rock hard that it curved up from my jeans. Selene blushed, and her reaction had an entirely abnormal effect on me. I grabbed her by the ass and pinned her between my body and the marble sink. She jumped but didn't try to get away. She had no intention of stopping what I had started. So I decided to let her taste herself and how much she'd wanted me.

I surprised her with a kiss, entangling our tongues, melding our cravings for one another. Her hands moved to touch my abdominal muscles and then up to my pecs. I was still wearing my sweater, but I knew she could definitely feel my burning muscles, throbbing with want.

We kept kissing as I guided her across her room toward her bed. From the first moment that I'd kissed her in the pool, I knew how much I liked kissing her, and I might as well have signed my own death warrant right there. We paused to catch our breath, and she sat down on the bed, completely naked. She was beautiful like an angel: white as snow, majestic as the colors of the sunrise. I looked at her and wanted nothing more than to bury myself inside her.

"Lie down and spread your legs wide," I ordered, pulling my sweater over my head like I was burning up. I threw it randomly behind me then did the same with my jeans and boxers. I went to my knees between her parted thighs with a certain degree of confidence. After all, I knew that I looked good. I had an appealing face and a muscled body that could perform up to female expectations.

Selene was aroused—her cheeks were burning, she was panting, and her eyes were full of lust—but she was also a bit in awe of me. Babygirl swallowed hard and tried to look anywhere but down. I gave her an insolent smile as I grabbed my erection and stroked it slowly while she looked everywhere but at me.

"Look at me," I said. I wanted her to stop being embarrassed, to break down that wall of prudery and let herself go. Selene obeyed me and looked at me, but not where I wanted. Instead, she looked deep into my eyes like she was trying to see into my soul.

"You too," she answered firmly, almost a show of defiance.

I stopped moving my hand and looked at her, just as she'd asked. She lay there on the bed like something precious and delicate. Her body looked small against the mattress beneath her. Her auburn hair was fanned out underneath her on the white bedspread. Her little bare breasts were perfect, her abdomen was stretched out flat, and her legs were splayed with a confidence that she didn't actually possess. I could tell, because they were trembling. And then there, between them, with a need that I deliberately left unsatisfied, was my passport to paradise.

Was this what she wanted me to look at?

Why couldn't she just use me like everyone else did? Why couldn't she just fuck me and be satisfied with my body?

"I looked at you," I muttered hastily, even greedier than before. She looked disappointed, but I didn't know why.

We truly were a disaster together.

"Enough with the bullshit, Selene. Exchanging soulful glances or sweet nothings isn't for me," I added irritably.

How much longer was I going to have to hold myself back? My balls were straining, and my cock felt like it was on the verge of exploding. I could feel the hunger coursing through my veins, and I didn't understand what more she wanted from me.

I shuffled closer to the mattress, still on my knees. I didn't have any more time to waste. I had hit my limit. I stretched myself over her body, supporting my weight on my forearms. Selene gulped and started trembling anew.

"You didn't see the details," she whispered, staring at my lips.

I had, in fact, secretly registered many of them, but she didn't even suspect that, and I certainly wasn't going to tell her. They were at the forefront of my mind whenever I undressed her. I bent my face over her right breast and sucked on it, coaxing a gasp from her. Then I licked her mole right next to the nipple. The shape reminded me of a very small heart and it was one of the *details* I adored most about her body. I looked back up at her and slowly ground myself between her outer lips—so hot and slick against me.

"Then give them all to me here, these invisible details you think only you notice," I mumbled provocatively, sliding my arm between our bodies to take my erection and direct it where I wanted it to go. I grabbed it by the root and rubbed the head against her to lubricate myself.

The eroticism reached its peak when I thrust my hips forward and felt her envelop me in her liquid heat. I enjoyed the raw contact between us too much, which was why I could never wear a condom with Babygirl the way I always did with the others. I slid fully into her, feeling her tight walls reshape to accommodate me. It was hot, slick, and soft. A burning clasp.

She surrounded me, squeezing me and welcoming me as deep as I could get. The feeling was surreal, and I held my breath the whole time as I made space for myself inside her. I buried myself between her thighs at a leisurely pace, and Selene gritted her teeth, breathing in a measured sort of way. I knew that my size was often mildly painful for women. Certainly Selene—who was still as tight as the first time I'd taken her—was feeling some discomfort.

I huffed out a breath as I entered her fully and then stopped. She looked up at me and swallowed hard, waiting for me to move again. She clasped my shoulders with her little hands, rubbing her way down to my lower back. Then she wrapped her legs around my hips and dug her heels into my glutes.

Wrapped around me like that, she seemed somehow even smaller and more fragile. I smiled at her and dropped a chaste kiss on her full lips. It dawned on me, too late, that what was meant as a small, intimate gesture to reassure her might have also made her believe there was more between us than just sex. I couldn't allow myself to keep making that kind of mistake.

I quit looking into her eyes and tried to focus on our breathing, on her little noises and the way our bodies interlocked. I rubbed some of her wetness around on her clit and continued rocking into her, riding the waves of pleasure. I kissed her neck and thought again about how much I loved her coconut scent. I liked women who kept themselves clean, and Selene did that. Very much so.

I lowered my head to her breast and sucked it into my mouth, making her back bend upward. More and more, I was growing to love her delicate curves. I took her small nipple between my lips and nibbled it with my teeth, drawing a moan from her.

"Neil," she said, her murmur broken by a gasp. Then she dug her nails into the flesh of my back and clasped me tightly as I jerked with each thrust. The headboard started hitting the wall and the springs in the mattress began to creak. Selene locked eyes with me again, but this time, I wasn't going to let her manipulate me with her fucking ocean stare. I got too vulnerable when that happened. I became an imbecile that wanted nothing more than to swim out into those waves and drown forever.

I pulled out of her hastily and grabbed her by the hips, turning her face down. This way, I could more easily avoid any compromising eye contact. I pulled her ass up until she was on all fours in front of me. I entered her from behind with one powerful thrust, holding her by the hips.

I didn't want to look at her, but I did anyway.

Selene clutched the bedspread with both fists, her auburn hair was tousled and wild, her arched back slick with sweat, her raised ass the victim of my aggressive thrusting. I couldn't help but stare at the precise spot where our bodies met and the sight of it electrified me. Her pink flower, velvet soft, opened and closed in time with my strokes. It was a rose in full bloom, the delicate petals concealing its depthless center. I took her hair in one hand and tilted her neck back as I leaned over her.

She was beautiful, but I would never tell her that I thought so.

"I love fucking you," I whispered instead into her ear before breathing in her scent from her throat. She didn't say a word; she just gritted her teeth and endured, moaning in satisfaction exactly the way I wanted. Each of her sensual little sounds was followed but a stronger, more agitated thrust.

I slipped a hand under her stomach and clasped her breast, rolling the nipple between my thumb and forefinger. She sucked in a breath. I enjoyed the way Selene responded to me, to the things I did and the ways I touched her. She was so goddamned sensitive, it got me ridiculously hot.

There was nothing in my head then, except for her warm body and my own ferocious, untethered movements. There were no nightmares, no problems. The anonymous package, Dr. Lively, and the poison that always surrounded me all suddenly ceased to exist. Lust was boiling in my veins. Selene's knees buckled abruptly and she collapsed, surrendering to my will.

She groaned into the bedspread and bit her arm to stifle the screams that I would much rather have heard.

"You like being used by me. I can feel it." I tightened my grip on her hair and slapped her flank hard enough to make her shout and moan at the same time. I smiled smugly because I had met my objective, and then I lay down on top of her, putting my weight on my elbows.

My chest rubbed against her back, which was so slender that I was afraid for a moment that I might crush her.

"You asshole," she muttered under her breath, unable to speak any louder. I started moving my hips again, owning her and marking her harder and harder. Suddenly, she pressed a hand to my backside to get me to slow down. Or maybe to speed me up. I didn't investigate either way because I was going to use her to exhaustion no matter what.

I was torturing her at that point. I entered her with sharp thrusts and withdrew slowly, making sure she felt every inch of me. I wanted her to feel like she was being impaled on my cock, and I wanted her to keep feeling that into tomorrow and the days after. We both began to sweat and our breathing was getting ragged. Selene couldn't hold out any longer while I could have kept going all night, if only to avoid coming back to reality.

"You're going to come, Babygirl." I pressed my chest more firmly against her back and felt her tighten all around me, clamping down and sucking me in entirely before finally releasing. And then again, contracting and dilating in a perfectly balanced dance. I sped up the pace of my strokes and her body tensed beneath me. She shifted reflexively back up on all fours and moved her pelvis against me, allowing herself to be transported by the delicious natural spasms of orgasm.

Her forearms strained to support her, and her legs shook. She was beautiful to behold, as much a spectacle as any burst of fireworks. I closed my eyes and allowed myself to be swallowed up by her searing heat and the urgent movements of her hips. A violent shiver ran down my spine, my eyes snapped open, and I quickly pulled out of her. I squeezed her ass with one hand while I used the other to grip myself, quickly moving my fingers up and down my entire length. My abs tensed, a million nerve endings going up like flares, my biceps flexed, a devouring heat burned in my chest, and my veins felt like they were going to burst as my seed spurted across her back.

All rational thought was completely obscured by the sight of Selene underneath me.

"Fuck," I said, out of breath as my orgasm waned, and I slowly came back to reality. I was still on my knees behind Babygirl, trying to catch my breath while Selene collapsed back down, exhausted.

I was covered in sweat, my hair was soaked, my throat was dry, and I had no idea where my heart had gone. Maybe into my stomach, my temples, or even my balls? All of them were pounding.

Worn out, I lay down next to her and felt the strength leaking out of me, little by little. I felt satisfied, the way I always did after a fuck. I stared up at the ceiling, illuminated only by a lamp on the bedside table, and breathed in the air, which was heavy with the smell of sex, coconut, and amber. Heavy with the smell of *us*...strange combination that we were.

Selene turned her head to me. She was still lying on her stomach with her arms flexed under her face and her palms flat on the bedspread. She gave me the same adoring look that every woman gave my body after they enjoyed it thoroughly, and she stretched out a hand toward my left side. She traced the contours of my tattoo there with her index finger, and I shivered at her touch. Her hands were cold, probably because she didn't have so much as a blanket to cover her. Her long, tapered fingers continued running along my skin, and it occurred to me that I'd really like to feel them lower down, maybe encircling my cock and...

Enough.

If I didn't knock that off, I was going to get hard and start the whole thing over again, and I knew that would be asking too much of her. Selene had never experienced real foreplay with a man. I would have to teach her how to pleasure me, tell her what I liked and how to do it, but not right then.

"Do you like my tattoo?" I asked. She startled at the low, hoarse sound of my voice. She pushed some sweaty hair off her forehead and curled into the fetal position, exposing her small breasts, which I couldn't help but linger on.

I couldn't even stand myself anymore. I was acting like a boy struggling with his first teenage crush. How much T and A had I seen in my life? How many women had I used? I couldn't count them. Yet her body felt new to me, an unexplored territory, an unexpected gift, waiting to be unwrapped. Selene was the Neverland I had always dreamed about. The place I fantasized about escaping to for a better life than the one I had.

"I like them both," she murmured and pointed at the one on my right bicep. I'd gotten it when I was sixteen; it extended up to my shoulder and symbolized powerful qualities that I hoped to reflect. I was weirdly pleased by the idea that Selene liked my tattoos.

"Do you think you'll get any more?" she asked.

I loved tattoos and had thought about getting a lot more in various spots on my body, but hold on…

What the hell was I doing? What the hell were we doing?

Small talk?

Since when did I exchange chitchat with a woman after sex? I creased up my forehead, and Selene must have noticed my puzzled expression because she planted her hands on the mattress and pushed up her torso. I immediately copied her.

"What the fuck," I whispered to myself, recognizing just how absurd everything that was happening was—everything that I was doing.

I didn't want a relationship. I wasn't the kind of man from whom anyone could expect sentimentality and that kind of shit, but clearly I had chosen the wrong girl to toy with. I was a deeply troubled man, and Babygirl didn't even have the first idea of the kind of clusterfuck I had in my head. And yet, inexplicably, despite all the women I could have had, I found myself between Selene's legs more and more often.

Selene wasn't even my type. I liked blonds, the bolder and more shameless the better. She, on the other hand, was naive, inexperienced, and—most importantly—auburn-haired.

"What's wrong with you now?" She muttered in confusion. I scrubbed a hand over my face and got off the bed. I retrieved my boxers and pulled them on. I could feel her eyes on me the whole time. Specifically, on my ass, which tensed with every movement. I turned and caught her staring at me, spellbound. She immediately looked away, focusing on her own bare legs.

"I need to leave. That's what's wrong with me," I snapped nervily, making her flinch. This wasn't her fault, not at all. But it wasn't my fault, either.

"Did I say something wrong?" she asked, clearly in the hopes of understanding my mood swings. Good luck to her, because I didn't understand them myself.

I bent down and felt around my jeans pockets for my pack of Winstons; I was in exceptional need of a smoke. Then I remembered that I'd left them in my room.

"Shut up, Selene!" I raised my voice, scaring her. I didn't need her peppering me with questions. I didn't know the answers any better than she did. This situation was getting to be too much for me. It was all getting to be too much.

"Where do you get off?" She jumped off the bed and walked around it, coming right at me. She faced me, her small, slender body completely naked. I smirked down at her from my lofty height.

Did she think she was going to intimidate me?

"What do you think you're doing? Huh, Tinkerbell?" I advanced on her until her smell was right under my nose. She smelled like sex and like *me*.

Selene raised her chin in challenge to me. She was little, but she really did have a tiger's ferocity.

"Talking. You know... That thing you're so afraid to do? Because you only feel like a man when you're screwing something." She skewered me, narrowing her blue eyes. Her hair was messed up, her cheekbones still pink, and her lips were swollen. She had my cum drying on her back and my finger marks on her hips. She looked well-fucked indeed, and it only made her more enticing.

She followed my gaze and saw what I was looking at. I brushed my fingers over the purpling bruises that speckled her pale skin. Then, without warning, I grabbed her by the neck and pulled her to me, taking a handful of her auburn hair.

"And what about you? Don't you feel like a woman when I want you? When I fuck you like an animal? I know you do, just like I know you'll never admit it," I whispered, close to her full lips.

She ground her teeth and said nothing. Her large eyes were full of challenge, telling me the war had only begun. "If you give me something of yourself, I'll do whatever you want," she murmured under her breath. I recalled the dumb compromise she had suggested while I was working out in the gym. Once again, I couldn't understand how she failed to see me for the vile thing that I was.

"What do you want?" I didn't let go of her silky hair, but I was trying not to hurt her.

"Talking," she said again, swallowing hard. I looked at her full lips, and I wanted to kiss her and toss her back on the bed.

"Talking," I echoed thoughtfully, holding her stare. "And I suppose you think you have something to teach me? From all your vast experience, eh?" I asked, amused as I breathed in her pleasing smell.

Selene considered my question for a few moments before replying firmly. "Yes. How to listen to your soul."

21

NEIL

How to listen to your soul."

That's what Babygirl wanted to teach me. I had no idea what that meant, so I let go of her and stepped back, only to see a victorious smile spread across her angel face.

The girl wasn't just a fairy; she was also a dangerous witch.

"You don't know what you're talking about. You can't understand me for who I am," I said, annoyed. Someone like her couldn't deal with a person like me.

I was too fucked up.

I was still trying to find myself, still trying the meld the man I had become with the Boy that I had been. I was searching for a kind of inner peace that I couldn't grasp, and until I actually accepted myself, I couldn't take anyone else along for the ride.

"Why?" Selene asked, hugging her arms. She was clearly freezing, but I did nothing to warm her up. I didn't know how to treat a woman outside of bed.

"Because you'd run." I stepped back from her. This conversation was getting too intimate, more intimate than getting naked with her, more intimate than leaving my imprint in her bedsheets, more intimate than sticking my tongue between her thighs.

"From what?" She advanced on me, but I gave her such a frosty look that she stopped her in her tracks.

"From me!" I raised my voice in frustration. How could she not understand? She needed to stay away from me.

Simple.

"I could understand you and—"

I shook my head, cutting off whatever bullshit was about to come out of her mouth.

"For fuck's sake: no one can understand me, not even you!" I insisted.

She needed to quit thinking of herself as some heroine who was going to save me. There was nothing to save, no one to be redeemed. I was who I was and nothing was going to bring order to my chaos.

She hissed in frustration as she pulled away from me and went to her closet. She pulled out a long sweater, grabbed some clean panties from a drawer, and vanished into the bathroom. I didn't understand why she'd left me there, halfway through a "talk" she herself had started. A few minutes later, however, she emerged wearing her thin sweater and panties that exposed her lovely little ass. She couldn't have taken a shower in such a short time, but I suspected she had done a quick freshening up to calm down while I waited for her, still in just my boxers.

"The sex you have with me isn't like the sex you have with other women, is it? I mean, just look at me." She gestured to herself. "I don't know how to pleasure you; I'd never been with a man before you. I'm inexperienced and probably not even as attractive as all your other lovers. So why do you want me?" She sat back down on her bed and stared at her knees, intimidated.

Was she feeling self-conscious even after what we'd just done?

"You look like a real babe right now," I said, and she lifted her face to look at me. She was blushing, probably because of the roughness of my voice, and she was staring at me like I'd just told her to get on her knees and suck it.

"Neil!" She tossed her head, shaking off who knew what thoughts. "I would like a serious answer for once!" She swore and got to her feet. She was so mad, and I found her extremely adorable. With her looks, she wouldn't have intimidated a squirrel.

I smiled at her and folded my arms over my chest, watching as her gaze moved over my flexed biceps. She liked my body; she liked it a lot.

"Answer me," she said softly, almost like she was already surrendering to the idea that she'd get nothing out of me. I looked at her seriously and decided that, just this once, I could humor her.

"I don't know why." I looked her up and down, scrutinizing her curves. She was beautiful, proportionate yet lush, and her face was flawless. She looked like a doll, handcrafted by an artist. "I just like you…and he likes you, too." I pointed at my crotch, and Selene followed my gaze, reddening immediately. She cleared her throat and looked back at my face, mirroring my position. She crossed her arms under her small breasts and raised her chin confidently.

"That is not a complete answer. You also like Jennifer and Alexia and all the other girls at school," she proclaimed with certainty, but that wasn't really the case. I picked—or rather, cherry-picked—the very best, like I was selecting goods on offer.

I was sleazy, sure, but I wasn't easily satisfied. It wasn't true that I'd fucked all the girls at our university, because I didn't take a woman to bed unless I found her sufficiently attractive. I *had* fucked a lot, though, and I did nasty things with the Krew girls that I would rather Babygirl not learn about. With her, something was different. It was a more intense attraction, a more powerful chemistry, and an uncontrollable wanting.

Usually, physical substance was all I was really looking for in a woman. I could recognize myself in the physical; I could recognize the tragedy of my childhood and understand that it was over now. I knew that this wasn't a normal response, because whenever I finished abusing my own body that way using whatever blond I could find, my soul would once again cry out, looking for some peace. And then the whole cycle would start over again. Again and again. Every time.

With Selene, however, I never felt used up or wrong. With her, I felt removed from everything, far away from the chaos. Far away from myself, even.

"I don't know, okay? I don't know!" I bent down to gather up my jeans and get them back on. I wanted to leave. I was feeling hemmed in, cornered by a girl with eyes as fathomless as the ocean. Selene, meanwhile, tracked my every movement in silence. Surely she had figured out that this "talking" bullshit wasn't going to work and that I was going to leave the same way every time.

"We're not done here." She took my arm and I stopped.

"What more do you want?" I snapped in irritation, noticing my sweater just a short distance away. I wanted to reach for it, pull it on, and get out of the room as soon as possible, but instead I remained there. With her, with Babygirl.

"I want to know why you want—"

Again, I didn't allow her to finish. I wiggled out of her grasp and breathed in deep. I was on the edge of another explosion.

"I do not know. I don't know why I want you," I shouted, making her flinch. "You are the only virgin I have ever been with. You have no experience. You don't know how to please me. I have no idea what attracts me to you. But what were you hoping to hear? That I'm in love with you? That you're 'the one' for me? That I'll only sleep with you from now on? Well, allow me to enlighten you, Selene: I just like you. My cock just likes you." I grabbed it through my jeans.

"It's all just sex. Now, is that enough to bring down your castle in the air? Can you stop plaguing me with all these questions!"

Selene backed up, saying nothing.

I was rude, an insensitive, hot-headed dick, but I had told her the truth.

I needed her to understand that there was no future for us. There was no fairy tale, because I wasn't capable of giving her any more than this. I had so many problems on my plate that thinking about a relationship was not remotely my priority, no matter how hard it was for Selene to understand.

I had been dead inside for too long. There was no salvation, no liberation coming for me. Meeting this chaste and pure girl with her "I can fix him" instinct simply wasn't enough to pull me out of my own personal hell. That was how it happened in books, not in real life.

"You need to live life as it really is." I drew close to her and used my index finger to tilt up her chin. Her eyes, disillusioned now, were still so crystalline that they threatened to enthrall me.

"Illusions destroy the mind, Selene. There is nothing worse than wanting one so much that you start to believe it's real." Selene was far too naive to really understand the dark side of human nature. Her eyes were like permanent rose-tinted glasses through which she filtered the world, seeing only what she wanted to see.

"Don't touch me," she snarled, walking away, and I knew perfectly well how angry and disappointed she was now. Selene had never experienced sex before we met, so she was probably confused and struggling to separate physical attraction from the illusory feeling of "love" that everyone else believed in.

I looked one last time at Selene before brushing past her to finally pick my sweater up off the floor. I could feel the weight of what I had said resting heavily on my chest, but I couldn't apologize for something I genuinely believed, despite the shitty way I might have expressed it.

I sighed and covered my torso, feeling her gaze sharp on my back. Then, I went out the door without giving her another glance.

I didn't deserve a pure white rose like her, and Babygirl didn't deserve my asshole behavior. I knew it, but in spite of all that, I wanted her still. My desire for her was so strong, it couldn't be repressed. I wanted her body without any emotional entanglement that might compromise the delicate understanding between the two of us.

We weren't stepsiblings, and we weren't just roommates or friends, but we weren't a couple, either. Whatever we were, it had arisen purely from a thirst that I wanted to slake. A thirst that would be the source of all her disappointments...

The next day, I decided to relegate Selene to a corner of my mind and deal with the much more serious issue. My sister didn't want to go to school and was locked in her room, drowning in the pain that piece of shit Carter Nelson had inflicted upon her. I knew I should regret leaving him comatose in a hospital bed, but all I could feel was frustration that I hadn't killed him outright.

On top of everything else, I now knew that the Nelson family intended to press charges against the attacker when Carter woke up. There was no way the kid wouldn't mention my name if I didn't find some way to stop him.

"What are you thinking about?" Jennifer kissed my neck, nuzzling the tip of her nose against me to breathe in my smell. We were in my car, but I had no intention of fucking her there, despite her continual advances. She'd asked me for a ride home, and I'd agreed to take her, not thinking about the possibility that she might try to get in my pants the way she usually did.

I didn't mind her forwardness. I was used to it, in fact. Jennifer and I had known each other for four years at that point, and we had established a type of relationship based purely on sex without any sort of commitment. We got along well, especially when we weren't talking. She had an incredible body: huge tits and a tight ass well worth slapping. And she was a real firecracker in bed, which was why I generally preferred to fool around with her in my free time.

"You know I don't like it when you stick your nose into my business."

She was very familiar with who I was and how I thought about things.

Jennifer sat back comfortably in the passenger seat and adjusted the plaid skirt that barely covered her thighs. Today, they were wrapped in a pair of dark tights. Despite the falling temperatures, she never gave up her uniform of knee-high boots and miniskirts, which I used to instantaneously access the only part of her that really interested me.

"Do you know any friends of Nelson's?" I asked as we arrived at the front gate of her house. Jennifer was part of a wealthy family, originally from Ireland. Her father had died in a car accident, and her mother wasted no time at all starting a new life with an entrepreneur out of New York whom she met by chance on a business trip.

"Friends of Bryan, you mean?" she asked, doing up the buttons of the coat that she'd just opened in a desperate attempt to lure me.

"No, the younger brother. Carter," I specified, starting to develop a plan that I could put into action soon to make sure the little bastard didn't press charges.

"Mmm...you should ask Xavier. He always knows everyone." She shrugged and tugged on a black hat, covering the top of her blond head.

"Okay. You can go." With one hand resting on the steering wheel and the other on the gear shift, I glanced out the window again. I kept the engine running, waiting for her to get her ass out of my Maserati. Jennifer, however, just sat there, staring thoughtfully at me.

"You're sleeping with her, aren't you?" she asked suddenly, out of nowhere.

"With who?" I scowled, almost annoyed with her. I hated it when she brought up personal questions, trying to ferret out some kind of secrets about my love life. A love life that I didn't have and, more importantly, would never want to have.

"With the little Virgin Mary who lives with you." She gave me a look of such disturbing rage that it would have sent shivers down anyone else's spine.

"No," I lied. "And even if I were, it shouldn't matter to you." Her bright eyes lingered on my hand gripping the steering wheel, then moved down to take in my entire body and the tension there that I had gotten all too good at hiding.

Apparently satisfied, she brought her eyes back up slowly to mine. Then she leaned into me and put a hand on my knee, stroking up toward my thigh.

"Then why not let Xavier and Luke share her? They'd both like to have her," she whispered, just a short distance from my lips. Her words fluttered slowly around in my brain, conjuring up images of the two of them in bed with Selene while Babygirl shouted and writhed to escape their unwanted touches. A searing heat spread from the pit of my stomach up to my chest. I grabbed Jennifer by the throat and tightened my grip until her nose was touching mine. She held her breath and stared at me, terrified.

"You try to get them to do something like that and you'll regret ever meeting me," I threatened her sharply. Carter's treatment was just a sampling of the many insane things I was capable of doing.

She smiled. Fuck, she smiled! And I knew exactly why: She had won. She'd gotten the reaction she wanted from me.

"You *are* sleeping with her. And I'll tell you what's more: you like the little brat, too." She murmured the last part in a broken whisper that made me abruptly release her. Jennifer rubbed her throat and coughed, staring at me with glistening red eyes.

"You've been warned. Now get out!" I ordered, interrupting our stare-down.

Jennifer had never been jealous of Alexia because she knew that, of the two of them, I preferred her, but she had always been extremely threatened by other women. So much so that she occasionally went to extreme lengths, like beating up girls I had been with. The two of us weren't in a relationship; we weren't together in any real sense, but something had changed between us in the last year.

"She likes you; I like you. Everyone likes you because you're impossible to ignore," she said. I had quit looking at her by then, but I could sense her irritating scent creeping into my space as she leaned close to my ear. I could even feel her warm breath touching my skin.

"Everyone likes you because you are filthy in exactly the way women want."

Women liked me because I was filthy, but none of them knew just how filthy I really was.

I tried not to give her any additional attention, because our conversation was already over, but Jennifer stopped getting out of the car when she saw a man lurching around right in front of the gate. I bent down to see him better. He was wearing a nice suit, but the shirt was buttoned incorrectly and he looked confused. He looked drunk, actually.

"Billy," she murmured, looking alarmed. It was strange to see Jennifer scared of anything, yet in less than a minute, that man had completely changed her demeanor.

"Your stepfather?" I guessed, and she nodded. "Is your mom home?" I had long suspected that Jennifer's home life wasn't the best. Her stepfather was an alcoholic prick, and her mother only got with him for his money and to ensure her life of luxurious excess.

"I doubt it," she said as she continued to stare through the windshield at Billy. He could barely stand upright.

I could have just told her to leave and gotten the fuck out of there, but even though I'd always been callous, I wasn't quite that callous.

"I'll go with you," I suggested, getting the pack of Winstons out of my jeans so I could light up.

"No, you don't need to. Billy's a solid dude; he's just been going a little overboard with the alcohol lately. But it's fine. Go back to your brat," she sneered at me.

She was pissed at me, and she was going to continue being that way until I went back to giving her the kind of attention I did before Selene came here.

"He hits you, doesn't he?" I asked her abruptly, taking my first drag. I'd never cared much about my friends' personal lives, and it wasn't like me to ask that kind of question. But I felt compelled in that moment to learn more about her. I knew what it felt like to be under someone else's thumb.

"I've seen the bruises; you can't lie to me," I added quickly. I knew every curve of her body since I saw her naked on a near daily basis, and I had spotted some suspicious marks on her pale skin. I'd never been overly curious about them before, but now this confirmed my theory. Jennifer shook her head and gave me a sly smile.

"Those are evidence of your passion. When you're fucking me hard, you—"

"Cut the shit! Don't joke about that kind of thing!" I scolded her shortly, and she flinched, dipping her chin in discomfort. I had never seen her yield so quickly. I continued to smoke and sighed. I hated being so aggressive, but it was a part of my nature that I'd been living with my whole life.

"Why do you care what Billy does to me?" she said softly, and for the first time, I saw her suffering. There were tears, clinging to her eyelashes and filling her blue eyes. Blue, but a different shade from Chloe's or Babygirl's. Jennifer's eyes were like two pieces of sky, semi-obscured by smoke. They could be sweet sometimes, like Babygirl's, while other times they radiated all the energy of a furious storm.

"The whole time we've known each other, you've never talked to me about anything personal," she answered shortly. She looked back out the windshield and sank down in her seat.

I mulled over her words, sucking on my Winston again. It was true: Jennifer and I had known each other for years, but I'd never been capable of just having a conversation with her or really getting to know her. I'd often wondered how she felt about being treated that way by me, so coldly detached, indifferent, and insensitive.

Why couldn't I stop myself from taking out what had been done to me on the women around me?

"I know what your skin smells like, how your body feels, and all the things you like in bed, but sometimes I just look at you and wonder if I'll ever really know you at all." Jennifer spoke again, but I just kept smoking and avoiding her gaze. I raked through my hair with one hand while I clamped on to my cigarette with the other. A desperate attempt not to lose control.

"There's nothing else you need to know about me," I said grimly. After all, revealing more of myself meant telling my story, and I was disgusted by what I had lived through. I would rather be a cliché, the typical fuckboy with a revolving door of women who didn't care about anyone or anything with the possible exception of spending my rich daddy's money.

I did love to fuck, but not for the reasons most men liked to pick up women. I was constantly changing women, not because I enjoyed being a manwhore, but because that was my survival mechanism. And I had never used any of William's money. I strove to be independent since I turned sixteen. I'd done all sorts of odd jobs, not because I had to, but because of my pride. That way, I would never have to ask my bastard father for a penny.

"I think I should go..." Jennifer's voice pulled me out of my musings. I watched as she got out of the car, and with a heavy sigh, I put my cigarette back between my lips and got out as well. She wasn't my girl, not my girlfriend, nor even really my friend, but I wasn't going to let her face Billy alone when he was drunk off his ass. I slammed the door behind me, and she turned to stare at me in shock.

"I'll go with you. And I'm not asking for permission," I clarified. I wasn't sure how to describe what I was feeling. Maybe it was protectiveness toward her, or maybe I just wanted to clear my conscience of some of the awful shit I did every day. One good deed wasn't going to make me a better person, but even though I constantly used women for my own purposes, the least I could do was protect them from people like Billy. I finished my cigarette and squashed the butt before walking over to Jennifer, who was giving me a strange look.

"Oh, there you are, sweet pea," her stepfather slurred, staggering toward her. I could smell the Scotch on him and wrinkled my nose in disgust. Jennifer went rigid and took a step back but Billy was so wasted, he hadn't even registered that I was there.

"You back now? Your mother isn't here, and I'm done for the day." He scrutinized her up and down, spending a lot of time on her thighs.

I, on the other hand, was looking at Billy. It looked like he'd walked straight out of his office without a coat, though the day was cold. His suit jacket was wrinkled, and his pants were stained with who knew what concoction. His dark hair was adhered sweatily to his forehead, and his hazel eyes roamed voraciously over Jennifer's body. There was at least a twenty-year age gap between the two of them, but he stared hungrily at her, completely ignoring that minor detail.

"O... Okay," she stammered before turning to me with a doleful smile. "Neil, you can go now."

It was only then that Billy noticed my existence. He stared at me, tilting his neck back to look me in the face, though he didn't seem particularly intimidated by my size.

"And who would this be?" He turned back to Jennifer and took a few steps toward her, trying to keep his balance. "If your mother knew you were out with a boy..." he added with a sinister expression.

He licked his lips and made a grab for her arm, but I shoved him roughly away. Jennifer hid behind me, clinging to my side, obviously afraid. It took Billy a moment to process what was happening in front of him.

"Who the fuck is this? Some friend of yours?" he snapped in annoyance. I looked at him with a cheeky smile and thought about how I wouldn't at all mind breaking this asshole's face.

"Nah, I'm Santa Claus," I answered sardonically and his forehead wrinkled up. "You want your present, Billy?" I added, and Jennifer held on to my jacket in an attempt to keep me from hurting him.

"Pick a hand, Billy. Right or left?" I showed him both palms, ready to throw a punch. He must have finally picked up on my intentions, because he backed away in fear. He was finally getting it. He had registered my size, my cutting stare, the tension in my muscles, and had decided that facing off with me would not have been the wisest choice.

"Jennifer! Get back in the house, or I'll make you spend the night out here," he yelled at his stepdaughter, who was still hiding against me. I turned to stare at her as she came out from behind me to follow him in.

"Billy, let's just chill out, okay?" Jennifer was using the same voice she used on me when she was trying to get into my pants, and she shot him a beguiling smile. I knew every one of these persuasion tactics well, and though they weren't working for me, they were definitely having the desired effect on the middle-aged man in front of us. Billy was hanging on her every word, looking at her like he'd never seen a woman before in his life.

Was she screwing this guy, too?

I wasn't exactly surprised.

I shook my head and stuffed my hands in the pockets of my jeans, turning to leave.

"Neil, wait," Jennifer called after me, but I didn't turn around.

"Could have told me you were fucking him before. I wouldn't have wasted my time." I took out my car keys and unlocked the vehicle. I needed to stop giving other people the help I wished I had gotten. Everywhere I looked, I saw defenseless people at the mercy of monsters who were prepared to destroy them, but I so often got it wrong.

"It's not like that."

"I don't care. It's your life; do with it what you want," I cut her off shortly. I didn't care about her choices. Jennifer knew how it was between us. We weren't together. She could do whatever—whoever—she wanted.

"I only fake like I'm going to fuck him to keep him from hurting me. Most of the time, he's too drunk to know what's happening, and he thinks I'm doing what he asks, but I'm really not," she confessed breathlessly, following me back out to the Maserati.

"You don't need to explain yourself. I really don't care."

I couldn't understand why she was trying so hard. So what if she did? Then what?

It wasn't like I was judging her. I was getting my rocks off with Matt's daughter, despite the risks I ran every time I sought her out, all just to satisfy my own sick needs.

I got into the car, ignoring Jennifer. I had no reason to hang around anymore. Blondie had this one under control.

When you really got down to it, everyone experienced their own form of suffering. And everyone fought against it in their own ways.

And Jennifer was no exception.

22

·····················

NEIL

I didn't want to call Dr. Lively, no matter what my mother said.

I first set foot in his clinic when I was a child. Finally, I had quit taking any psychotropic drugs, quit attending our appointments, and quit even answering his calls.

Every Thursday, Dr. Lively still contacted my mother to ask her about me and about how I was doing, but I avoided talking about my problems with my mother.

Those problems were still there, though. They would always be there.

But I didn't want Chloe to deal with her pain alone. I didn't want her to give up on smiling at the age of sixteen.

I walked out into the garden, trampling the grass. The sun was high overhead, illuminating my sister's blond hair as she slowly moved back and forth on the swing. Its red paint was faded now, and the chain creaked with every slow sway, but Chloe had loved playing on it ever since she was a little kid. She loved swinging, pumping her legs in the air, because she said that it made the sky feel like it was getting closer and closer. Like she might be able to touch a cloud.

"Little Koala." I approached quietly while Chloe stared off into space, lost in her unknowable thoughts. There, sitting on that rusty swing, caught between the two chains, she was still the baby of the family. The same one who always argued with Logan over the swing and would run to claim it before our brother could.

"This was the one place where I was happy. I felt like I could fly..." she muttered, lost in her memories as her hand gripped the chains tighter.

"In dreams, you can touch the sky with a finger..." I added, sticking my hands in the pockets of my jeans and continuing to smile at her, even as she just kept staring into empty air with a blank, lifeless look on her face.

Seeing her like this hurt; it really, really hurt.

"I don't have dreams anymore." She looked up, staring aimlessly into the sky. I knew what she was feeling. I felt it too, every day of my life, so I knew that I had to do something to help her. Help her in the *right* way.

"Think of this swing as a metaphor." I knelt down in front of her and Chloe stopped moving back and forth, looking into my eyes.

"What does that mean?" she whispered.

"You push yourself into the future, and you pull the past behind you." I needed to reassure her, to encourage her, and get her moving forward. "Carter tried to hurt you, but he couldn't. You were brave; you were able to defend yourself." I touched her cheek and smiled slightly. "He didn't take away your chance to share yourself for the first time someday with the person you love. You are going to have sex when you decide, and it will be wonderful; it will be what every girl your age dreams about. You still get to dream, Chloe."

She could do it; she got to make that choice. Life had given her that opportunity, and I was so glad that the worst hadn't happened to her. Still, it wasn't easy to get past that kind of violence. It didn't matter that the son of a bitch didn't do everything he wanted; he had still lured her to a party and pulled her into one of the bedrooms where he tried take advantage of her.

"I can't forget the things he said to me; the feeling of his hands on me..." She looked down, trying to conceal the tears that were already sliding down her wan face. I rubbed them away with my thumbs and turned her face up to me again.

"Do you trust me, kiddo? There's somewhere we need to go." She had to face down her demon and destroy it. It was something I'd been trying to do my whole life, and I hadn't yet succeeded. But she was going to do it. *She* would succeed.

"Where?" she asked, getting hesitantly to her feet.

"There's someone I'd like you to meet..."

Later that afternoon, we pulled up in front of the sleek and modern private clinic.

"Let's go." After we parked, I prompted Chloe to follow me to the entrance. His offices shared a building with a larger in-patient mental health facility. The structure was so large that it was a bit intimidating. I didn't remember it being this grand. We traversed a long avenue of greenery with a fountain in the middle. Then we arrived at the security doors, which we opened by pressing a buzzer that would alert the people inside to our presence. I glanced around, noticing all the typical security cameras everywhere. I couldn't shake the familiar feeling that places like this were nothing but shiny glass prisons.

"Did you seriously take me to a psychiatric clinic?" Chloe grumbled. I could feel her shivering underneath the palm of my hand, which was resting on her shoulder. I smiled at her and cleared my throat, trying not to alarm her.

"No, I took you to one of the best psychiatrists in New York. He does diagnoses and different kinds of therapies, and he only prescribes medication when it's absolutely necessary. In your case, all you're going to do is talk to him," I explained, trying to reassure her.

I noticed a lot had changed since I'd last been here. The vestibule felt more welcoming and modern to me. There were big plasma screens on the walls displaying ads for psychiatric therapy and innovative methods of dealing with mental illness interspersed with picturesque art that gave the otherwise white and antiseptic environment a pop of color. There were ornamental plants hanging from pots in the corners, and it still smelled like fresh paint, which led me to believe the changes were recent.

I led Chloe over to the counter in front of the spacious waiting area where a middle-aged woman sat behind a computer.

"Hi, I'm Neil Miller. I need to see Dr. Lively," I said, drawing her attention to us. She slid her glasses down her nose and looked from me to Chloe.

"Do you have an appointment?"

"No, but I am a long-standing patient of his," I said easily. Dr. Lively used to tell me he would always make time for me, and now it was time to see if he really meant it. She tapped away at her computer, probably checking the patient registry for my profile. I knew exactly what she'd find. In fact, I knew my entire medical history by heart, and it wasn't great.

Dr. Lively also used to tell me that all the time.

The woman squinted at the screen to read the information that had come up about me. Then she cleared her throat awkwardly and looked back at me.

"Yes, there's a...note here," she murmured under her breath sounding a bit daunted. I gave her a cheeky grin and women stiffened up.

"Dr. Lively is with a patient right now. Can you wait? Otherwise, you could see Dr. Keller." I frowned as Chloe clung to me, all tensed up. I had never heard of that person.

"And who is Dr. Keller?" I asked with zero tact. The woman raised an eyebrow, like my question was ridiculous, and took a business card off the countertop and handed it to me. It read:

Dr. John Keller, Psy. D, Lp.

"Dr. Lively's working with another psychiatrist now?" I tossed the card back to her with a frown.

"For quite some time now." She tucked the card back in among the others and looked haughtily back at me.

"Holy shit, so much has changed around here," I blurted out, amused as the woman continued to stare at me like I was a maniac on the loose.

"You're not inspiring a lot of confidence in this lady," Chloe whispered into my ear, drawing the woman's attention to her. No, I didn't inspire any confidence in her at all, but I didn't give a shit.

"Take a seat in the waiting room." She finally excused us with false, calculated kindness. I sat down with Chloe on one of the leather couches while irritating classical Muzak echoed around the white walls. The glass table in front of us was covered in newspapers and magazines. My gaze snagged on the cover of one, which was taken up by a close-up shot of…

"Dad!" Chloe said, eagerly grabbing the magazine.

Yes, it was our father, William Miller, CEO of Miller Enterprise Holdings. The same intrinsically awful bastard who loved to "educate" me via cruel and savage methods of which my sister fortunately knew nothing, thanks only to her youth. Just seeing his icy eyes and soulless smile was enough to get the anger pumping inside me.

Chloe opened up the magazine and leafed through it to find the interview with our father, and all I wanted to do was rip the paper out of her hands and tear it into pieces. I began jiggling my leg and breathing heavily; my throat felt tight and my blood pressure was surely rising.

"Look, doesn't he look younger in this picture?" Chloe held the magazine out to show me. I had broken out into a cold sweat, my heart was pounding in my temples, and my hands were shaking. I was just about to have a complete meltdown when Dr. Lively finally came out of his office.

"All right, Mrs. McChoo, I'll see you for our next session in a month." He guided a woman to the exit and stuck a pen into the pocket of his suit jacket. He hadn't changed a bit; he was still the same gentlemanly guy I remembered. His gray hair fell straight to the nape of his neck, and he had a square face with even features: a nose that drooped slightly and small, bright eyes surrounded by faint crow's-feet, the same sort of wrinkles that bracketed his thin lips.

"Neil." His smile faded, giving way to a look of incredulity when he spotted me. He approached us, and I stood up, sticking out my hand to him.

"Hello, Dr. Lively," I said in a placid voice.

"I haven't seen you in a long time," he reminded me, giving me a pat on the shoulder. I froze for a second with my arm suspended in mid-air before retracting it irritably. I hated to be touched, and he knew that better than anyone.

I took an instinctive step back, and he clearly noticed it because his face darkened.

"And how are you?" he asked tentatively, thrusting his hands into the pockets of his slacks. I didn't want to talk about me or my problems, so I gestured for Chloe to join us. Only then did Dr. Lively register her presence, and he wrinkled his forehead questioningly.

"I'm here for my sister, not for me. You need to talk with her," I explained, putting my arm around her slim shoulders. Chloe was tense and anxious, so I rubbed her arm to calm her down. My former psychiatrist was an excellent doctor, skilled with both the professional and the personal, and I knew he could put Chloe at ease.

"That's no problem. It's a pleasure to meet you, Chloe. I'm Krug Lively. Please don't call me doctor, just Krug." He gave her a benevolent smile, and my sister returned the gesture. I could feel her slowly relaxing, and I was pleased with her positive reaction.

"My pleasure," she murmured.

"Would you care to wait for me in my office?" he suggested, clearly intending to take a moment alone with me. Chloe glanced at me for approval, and I nodded.

"I'll be right here waiting for you. It's all going to be okay. You just need to talk a little," I said softly, planting a kiss on her forehead. She sighed, seeming unconvinced about what she was about to do, but she screwed up her courage and walked toward the doctor's office.

"I thought you were going to come see me every now and then. Instead, you completely vanished. You changed your phone number, and when I tried to meet with you at your home, you never showed. Do you know what a serious thing it is, stopping treatment without your doctor's authorization?" he lectured me, sounding even-tempered yet stern.

"It's fine, Dr. Lively. The meds your psychiatrist gave me made me numb and apathetic," I argued, trying not raise my voice.

"They also allowed you to sleep, manage your impulses, and control your mood swings. You didn't show up for a single one of the follow-up sessions I recommended. I should have been able to evaluate your course of therapy to determine whether you'd achieved your objectives. Instead, you refused care and prevented me from helping you." I could tell that he was angry and disappointed in me. He'd always had my back and had been, in many ways, like the father I never had. And this was how I repaid him?

Dr. Lively was the only man—other than Logan—with whom I had ever discussed my history. His presence had been a huge source of support for me during my adolescence, even when I hated the drugs his team prescribed and the often-rigid course of therapy he forced me to follow.

"Like I said, I'm fine. I've got a handle on it," I lied. I couldn't confess to him how things really were. I didn't have a handle on my trauma. The nightmares were still there, as was the obsession with washing myself, the angry outbursts, and vague thoughts of ending it all.

"Without adequate medical support all this time? Doubtful." He didn't believe me, but he was one of the few people who knew me well enough to tell whether I was lying. I decided to close that conversation and sat back down on the sofa. I balanced one ankle on the opposite knee like a smug asshole and gave him a disinterested look.

"My sister's waiting for you, doctor." I jerked my chin toward the door of his office, and he shook his head in resignation. He was surely thinking that I was lost cause, a total car crash of a person with little desire to reopen the lines of communication.

He didn't push me, though, and fortunately just left me alone in the relaxing environment of the waiting room. My eyes fell back on the magazine that Chloe had left open on the coffee table in front of me. I got up and snatched it away, throwing it as far as I could away from the others.

The last thing I wanted to look at was that prick's face.

"You're making great progress, Megan, keep it up." An unfamiliar male voice roused me from my thoughts. I turned to look at the two people slowly approaching. The first was a doctor, or so I presumed, with an unassuming, professional appearance, and the other was woman about my age.

I scrutinized the latter carefully. She had a mane of dark hair that fell past her shoulders, and she was tall and slightly built but with overflowing curves. Her face was an oval, and she had a pair of full, arresting lips and a dark mole shaped like a coffee bean right above her Cupid's bow. Her emerald-green eyes landed on me, and it only took a few seconds to recognize her. She was Megan Wayne, Alyssa's older sister.

"Thanks, Dr. Keller. I won't let you down." She held out her hand and smiled at him, occasionally darting her eyes my way.

Then, she turned fully in my direction, and I immediately began looking around for an escape hatch. I didn't want to talk to her. I didn't want to look at her or even remember she existed. I jumped up from the sofa, in a hurry to flee.

"Hold on, Miller." She'd reached me before I could even start walking away.

Shit.

I held still and kept my back to her, despite the overpowering scent of orange blossoms that she emitted. "Don't run off like you always do," she said in a low, toe-curling voice. I shuddered and not from pleasure.

We were the same age; we'd often been in the same classes, but it was nothing more than that. I avoided her in school just like I would have avoided her here, if she'd let me.

"I don't want anything to do with you." I turned and locked my iciest gaze on her. The other man, who I understood to be Dr. Keller, looked at us in confusion.

"Logan's dating my sister. If they get married someday, we might become family. Have you thought about that?" She laughed.

I was struck by a wave of dizziness. I'd been aware that Logan was dating Alyssa and had slept with her a couple of times, but I was pretty confident he didn't have any real feelings for her. Logan wasn't in love with her, just attracted to her.

"What the fuck? Was I in some way unclear just now?" I faced her down, talking in a low, menacing tone and inching closer to her.

Any other man would have found her drop-dead gorgeous, with the kind of pneumatic curves that could get a dead man hard. But not me.

For me, Megan was a piece of the past that needed to be forgotten. To be eliminated entirely, if possible.

"Guess you haven't dealt with it yet," she murmured unhappily. She stared intensely into my eyes, and I kept silent. This wasn't the right time to have a conversation about sensitive topics, and she definitely wasn't the right person to tell all about my internal torments.

"I don't think that's any of your concern." It *was* her concern, though, because she was an irrevocable part of the wicked labyrinth that was my mind.

"You should keep going with Dr. Lively. Don't give up." She touched my arm, and it was probably nothing more than a gesture of bland consolation, but I went stiff and jerked away from her. She shouldn't have touched me, and I told her with my eyes just how dismayed I was.

Megan retracted her hand quickly and stepped back. She understood. She turned to Dr. Keller, who had been completely still this whole time, watching us cautiously. She gave him a small smile and then headed for the exit.

As I heard her footsteps get farther and farther away, I finally started breathing again. I felt an immediate, desperate urge to smoke, but I didn't want to go too far away from Chloe. So I rifled in my jacket for my pack of Winstons. I stuck a cigarette between my lips while I searched my pockets for my lighter.

"You can't smoke in here," Keller interjected, standing a few cautious feet away from me. He looked to be about fifty, with fine-boned yet masculine features and the air of someone well-acquainted with life's hardships. His light chestnut eyes dissected me patiently. He was at least as tall as me with the slim, athletic body of someone who maintained a healthy diet and some sort of physical hobby.

I didn't say anything but put the lighter back in my pocket, leaving the unlit cigarette to dangle between my lips. Holding it there made me feel calmer.

"Are you a new patient? I've never seen you here before." He moved closer, but I wasn't there to make friends with my shrink's new coworker. I gave him a severe look in the hopes that he'd stop saying things to me, but he didn't.

"I'm Dr. John Keller. I've been working with Krug for a while now."

Did anyone ask him?

I glanced around for any distraction, but all I saw was the receptionist's saggy ass as she bent over to pick up some fallen papers off the floor. Horrified, I averted my eyes once again and wound up back on the man in front of me.

"I was one of Dr. Lively's patients," I said, and all of a sudden, the room became cramped and suffocating.

"Was?" A frown line appeared in the middle of his forehead; he was puzzling something out.

"Yup, that's right. Right up until one fine day when my psychiatrist told me I was completely cured," I lied, taking the unlit cig between my middle and index fingers and stretching my arm out along the side of the sofa. I couldn't wait to get out of there and smoke in peace.

"That's what he said? That you were 'cured'?" He gave me a small smile that I couldn't quite decipher, and I sat up straighter.

"That's what he said," I confirmed mockingly.

What the fuck did this guy want?

I didn't give a shit about his role at the clinic or how he worked with Dr. Lively. He was Megan's psychiatrist, and that was enough to keep me far away from him.

"Odd. Neither I nor my colleague use the term 'cure.'" He stressed the last word, still smiling. "And do you know why?" he asked. Rhetorically, I presumed, because he didn't wait for me to answer. "Because we do not consider you to be sick, nor do we think of your disorders as diseases. That term 'disease' can be terribly misleading, don't you think? We take a different approach. We analyze your behaviors, all the things you say and do, and then we look for a solution together."

I kept still as I listened to him, focused on his words and the fact that he had lumped me in with the mental patients in his little speech.

"*My* disorder? Don't include me in that; I don't have any kind of disorder," I specified immediately, as though nothing could be more necessary. He gave me that shrink look.

He was analyzing me.

"Denial of a problem is a problem in and of itself." The confidence and little hint of arrogance that came through in his tone irked me. He thought I was like the rest of them. That I was simple to understand or some lab animal he could use to carry out pharmacological experiments.

"You don't know me. You know nothing about me." I took a few steps closer to him, clutching the cigarette between my fingers as I pointed at him.

"*Denial of a problem* is often the only thing that's keeping me alive, but you wouldn't know about that. We're all the same to you shrinks. Just fucking blobs of neurons you can feed the drugs that give your goddamned profession any scientific legitimacy!" I shouted, not far from his face, but the man remained imperturbable, not remotely upset.

Just then, Dr. Lively opened his office door and started leading Chloe out to me. But he stopped short when he saw what was happening in his waiting room.

"Come on, Chloe. Let's get out of here," I ordered her furiously, glancing back and forth between the two psychiatrists who were looking at me like I truly was crazy. I threw my cigarette down and ground it into the freshly waxed floor with the sole of my shoe. Fuck their rules.

Chloe came to me, and I put my arm around her shoulders, guiding her toward the exit. I'd ask her later about how the talk with Dr. Lively went. Just then, I needed to get as far away from that clinic— and those men—as possible.

23

....

SELENE

"S o you're into music?"

I was furthering my acquaintance with Kyle. I had found out that, in addition to being very intelligent, he was also quite nice to be around. I didn't have any romantic interest in him, and I wasn't attracted to him, but I was intrigued by his personality.

"Mostly I like playing guitar, just like Adam and Jake." He gestured to our friends and praised their talent. I grinned and kept walking with them toward a university cafeteria. My stomach was growling because I had been eating less and less. I regularly skipped dinner with the family at night to avoid my father's incessant questions about how my stay was going.

What was I supposed to tell him? That I'd been dumb enough to sleep with his girlfriend's son?

I liked Neil too much, and it was messing with my head. I'd made another dumbass mistake when I let him take me after he'd so presumptuously barged into my room without knocking and found me in the bathroom. He'd done me once right there in front of the sink with his sinful mouth and then again on the bed with his diabolical body.

And it had been just as incredible as it ever was.

Having sex with Neil was like watching a spectacular fireworks display. And then, at the end, there was nothing left behind but a deep, dark sky and few traces of smoke.

I'd tried to talk to him, to keep him from running away, and all I got was a glib, crude response followed by, *"It's just sex. Stop plaguing me with all these questions."*

He couldn't be much clearer than that. The only thing left for me to do was to ignore him, stop giving in to him when he came around, and try to get back to the old me—the girl from Detroit who was full of principles and never would have thrown her virginity away on a stranger. The one who certainly wouldn't have let that same stranger continue to visit humiliation after humiliation on her.

But the truth was, Neil wasn't a stranger anymore. He was an asshole, a selfish prick, and a walking disaster, but not a stranger.

"Hey, there's steam coming out of your ears." Alyssa threw her arm around my shoulders and tried to get me to smile. For too long now, I had needed someone to talk to about the things that were weighing on me. But Alyssa was dating Logan, so telling her my giant secret would be inadvisable.

"I have a lot of homework," I muttered, trying to turn her attention back to classes, subjects we were studying, and upcoming exams.

We walked into the large cafeteria to join the line of students with trays in their hands. The place was packed as usual, but that didn't prevent me from noticing the Krew not far away from us. Xavier was talking to a girl, or rather, he was hitting on a girl while she stared fearfully at him.

Abruptly, he reached out and grabbed a lock of her hair, twining it around his index finger while the girl looked down. It looked like he was trying to talk her into doing something and she couldn't say no; he was Xavier Hudson, and no one said no to him.

"What a dick," Cory noted from behind me. He was; he really was. Xavier was the worst of the Krew: slimy, cruel, and pitiless. I had heard terrible things about him from Logan.

"Yeah," I agreed, pausing to watch him. His black eyes and arrogant smile did nothing for me—except perhaps make me break out in hives.

Once I loaded up my tray with a bowl of soup, some chicken and potatoes, a bottle of water, and a piece of bread in a paper napkin—I turned and headed for the table where my friends were waiting for me. I was careful to keep my meal balanced on its tray as I moved through the crowded space.

Suddenly, however, someone stepped in front of me and blocked my path.

It was Jennifer.

Her blond hair had been wrangled into two elaborate braids that fell over her firm breasts, clearly visible thanks to the tight T-shirt she wore. Her short skirt, on the other hand, barely covered her crotch, though she was wearing dark tights. She looked like an edgy model—beautiful and damned.

"Hey, Saint Selene, wanna come sit with us?" She gestured to a table on my left, and I looked over, almost afraid to see who was sitting there. First I spotted Luke, the seemingly normal blond guy, and then Xavier, who was staring intensely at me in such a twisted way that it made my skin crawl. Finally, I glimpsed Alexia and her blue unicorn hair before looking back at the blond girl before me.

"No, thanks," I answered firmly.

"What's wrong? Are we beneath you, princess? Not worthy to be honored with your presence?" she mocked me, tossing a knowing look back at her friends.

"I hope you all have a nice lunch," I answered with artificial politeness, hoping they'd just leave me alone. My fingers tightened around the edges of my tray, and I tried to move past her, but Jennifer scattered my lunch all over the ground with one slap. I jolted; silence fell over the room as everyone turned to look at us.

My eyes caught on the puddle of soup that was spreading out over the floor before I looked back up at the smug bitch who was grinning at the ridiculous scene.

"What the hell do you want from me?" I demanded, feeling anger making the veins in my neck stand out.

"Show us how you clean up your shitty soup. Lick it all up like a good kitten," Xavier cut in, clearly enjoying the spectacle, while, beside him, Luke glanced around nervously. There was no way I was going to buckle under their harassment.

"Fuck you," I said, clenching my hands into fists at my sides. My heart hammered in my chest, and I could feel my skin getting hotter under the light sweater I was wearing.

"How about *you* fuck me, baby doll," Xavier answered back, winking at me.

I felt trapped. The Krew was known around town, and they scared people. They were unpredictable hotheads who would do anything to feel dominant and in control, and no one was willing to go against them for that reason.

Nobody was going to save me.

So I would have to save myself.

"We hear you've got a boyfriend back in Detroit, even though you're messing with one of ours out here." Jennifer advanced on me, pulling my gaze back to her. "A mutual friend...amazing lay, right?" she whispered into my ear, and I blanched. *How does she know?* Had Neil confessed it all to her? Did he tell her about us or about me and Jared?

I felt almost lightheaded. I was even struggling to stand on my own two feet.

"How… How…" I babbled, and she grinned in satisfaction at my chalk-white face.

"How did I know?" she finished my sentence for me. "Instagram and Facebook are things that exist, and your profile photos are of you and your boyfriend, all happy and smiling in Detroit. You tagged him, sweetie," she said caustically with the pleased expression of someone who has her victim in her clutches.

Well, of course.

That bitch had stalked me on social media like a psychopath.

"He's… He's just a friend."

"Friends don't comment 'I love you' on every single one of your photos," she answered, amused. She really had done her research.

Damn Jared's need to be overly demonstrative on social media.

I didn't care at all what the Krew thought of me, but I didn't want them getting in touch with Jared and telling him what was happening in New York. Undoubtedly, they would frame it all in the worst, cruelest possible way, and while I may not have loved Jared, I did still care about him. I didn't want him to get hurt, especially not during such a tragic time in his life.

"My personal life is none of your concern," I hissed through gritted teeth. Ours was a specifically female challenge, and we were not playing on a level field, as she now knew a lot more about me than I did her. All I wanted to do was take Jennifer by her dumb pigtails and smash her head into a wall, but I couldn't do that. I was like her. I wasn't like *them*.

"Okay, then. If you don't want your man to find out everything, then stay away from mine," she threatened, and I nearly laughed in her face. Stay away from her *what*?

Apparently, Jennifer was having a one-sided relationship with Neil. He wasn't exclusively sleeping with her any more than he was exclusively sleeping with me. But the problem was clear: Jennifer was possessive and jealous all the same.

"Really, now? Can we say that Neil is 'yours'? From what I understand, he's still fucking you through a rubber so he doesn't get an STI!" I'd blurted it out before I even really thought it through. I had grabbed on to Neil's admission that he used condoms with everyone except me, hoping that he hadn't lied to me. Judging by the disbelieving look on the blond's shocked face, he hadn't.

Jennifer's mouth fell open, and then her face turned furious just before she launched herself at me with shocking violence. She pulled my hair until I screamed and then slapped me so hard my eyes shut automatically. I groaned in pain. I fell to my knees and tried to shield my head with my arms as she started raining punches and kicks down on me.

I couldn't see anything; I could only feel my body jerking in the places where she hit me. A blow to my left side, another to the right, another one to my shoulder while the taste of blood spread across my tongue from my lower lip. It already felt swollen and painful.

People saw, people heard, but they did not act. They did nothing at all. It was like everyone was petrified. As I cowered on my knees, taking a beating that I didn't deserve, I realized that no one was ever going to stop people like the Krew from hurting others. Fear, social pressure, and threats always won out over the defense of dignity, which people like them trampled on the daily.

I didn't make a sound, and no tears ran down my face. I was all alone there, my hands raised up to protect my face, unable to get to my feet. In my heart, I had already decided that I was going to hold out; I was going to outlast her. I wasn't going to give her the satisfaction of hearing me beg her to stop.

"Selene!" I thought I heard Alyssa's voice and then Logan's. Finally, it seemed that someone might be coming to help me. It was definitely my friends, but I couldn't see anything except the darkness of my own hands over my eyes.

Someone tried to stop Jennifer; I could tell from her outraged screams, but by that point, she had transformed into a ferocious beast, thirsting for revenge. Her jealousy had completely taken over, and perhaps she really did intend to kill me.

A final strike against my hip made me flinch. Instinctively, I dropped my hands to cover the wounded area, curling forward. My breath caught at the intensity of the pain; for a moment, my lungs were getting no oxygen at all.

"Jennifer!"

That voice… That baritone was the only one in the world that could have given me enough strength to lift up my chin.

Neil grabbed the blond girl by both arms and stopped her blows. He crushed her against his chest and then turned his golden eyes on the victim of Jennifer's ire. When he saw me, he look surprised, like he had been expecting someone else.

I looked at him, and that was the moment when I felt like crying. Tears seemed to well all the way up from the bottom of my heart to the corners of my eyes.

"Oh my God, Selene! Are you okay?" Logan rushed to kneel down next to me, but I couldn't look at him. I remained trapped by Neil's eyes as he just kept staring at me in utter shock and disbelief. Jennifer was breathing heavily, her arms still forced against her sides in his grip. He released her in slow motion, like his body had been drained of energy.

"Selene." Logan touched my face, and I felt his cool hands on my lower lip, examining the wound there. But still my eyes couldn't look away from Neil. He pursed his lips, and in the working of his jaw, I could see how tense he was. Then he tightened his hand into a fist and slowly looked back at Jennifer, who was now surrounded by the rest of the Krew.

"Okay, man, chill out." Xavier tried to neutralize the situation, smiling a nervous smile. "It was just a stupid catfight."

Neil's honey-colored eyes were alight with rage. He ignored

Xavier and continued to stare menacingly at Jennifer, who didn't have the nerve to emit a single syllable. Beautiful and fearsome, he was daring her to say something in her defense, knowing full well that it would be useless. When she kept silent, he advanced on her. She began to shake, taking a step back from him.

Neil put both hands around her throat and slammed her back against the wall. The natural color drained out of Jennifer's face, and it began to go violet. He lifted her cleanly off the floor and the blond girl began kicking frantically against Neil's incontrovertible strength.

"Feeling short of breath, Jen?" he said softly, just a short distance from her lips. He looked like a lunatic. Even his voice sounded deeper and more far away—far from reason. Jennifer shook violently, her body racked with involuntary convulsions, and her eyes rolled back in her head. She was suffocating.

"Breath is the bridge which connects life to consciousness, which unites your body to your thoughts." Neil was quoting Thich Nhat Hanh. "How are you feeling right now?" he said, staring at Jennifer, whose face had begun to turn gray. She made only occasional guttural sounds as she attempted to draw in breath, and even her legs had stopped shaking.

"What does it feel like to suffocate?" He questioned her again as her eyes flicked back to him, begging him silently to release her. But Neil's fingers continued to exert deadly pressure around her neck.

No one stepped up to defuse the insane situation, not even Xavier or Luke. Even Logan just stood there next to me, dumbstruck at what his brother was doing.

This was unreal: Jennifer could very well die, and no one was lifting a finger.

"Touch her again, and I'll kill you. I'll *kill* you, Jennifer," Neil menaced, right up close to her face before opening his hands and letting her collapse to the ground. She coughed uncontrollably. Her face was all red, her eyes were teary, and there were livid marks on her neck.

Neil walked over and knelt down beside me. He didn't speak; he scooped me up gently in his arm. A pained grimace had been etched into my face, but it immediately disappeared when I put my head against his marble chest.

"Show's over, assholes!" he snapped at the people still inertly watching the scene. I didn't have the strength to say anything or to get him to let me go. So I allowed myself to be cradled in his strong arms as I soaked in his amber scent.

He moved through the space like a victorious gladiator traversing the arena after a bout, but there was no enthusiasm in the air around us, no celebratory atmosphere, just a deep, anguished silence.

"Thank you," I murmured, before my eyes fell shut and I allowed myself to lulled into unconsciousness by a sudden drowsiness...

......

I woke up in a colorless but well-lit room. I glanced around, disoriented, and then I tucked my chin to my chest. I wrinkled my nose, smelling some sort of strange disinfectant odor, and that was when I realized I was lying on a bed in the student health center. Nearby, a nurse was writing something down in a folder.

"Welcome back." She smiled at me and tucked the folder under her arm. She was a young woman, probably in her early thirties with blond hair and large chocolate-colored eyes. Her high breasts peeped out from under the light-colored top of her scrubs, and her glasses gave her a distinguished, cultured look. "I gave you some pain relief. Fortunately, you didn't break anything, just some contusions and a small cut on your lip." She gestured to my mouth, and I instinctively lifted a hand to touch it. I could feel the rough surface of a bandage under my fingertips, but I didn't feel any pain.

I guessed the pain meds were still working.

"Thank you." I struggled to sit up and she helped me tenderly.

"You should thank Neil. He's the one who brought you here and demanded I look at you right away. He was worried about you," she informed me in a strangely admiring tone.

"Where is he?" I asked her quickly. She grinned and jerked a thumb at the closed door.

"Out there. Do you want me to let him in?"

I nodded. I was afraid of just about everyone except him in that moment. Neil was only a danger to my heart and mind, certainly not to my body.

The woman went to the door and gestured for him to come inside. When Neil appeared, he looked even more imposing and enigmatic than usual. I shivered and tightened my hands on my jeans-covered thighs.

"All right, she's good to go. Can I get back to my scheduled patients now?" the nurse asked archly. He gave her a knowing look as he moved toward me.

"Well, you did owe me a favor, Claire," he purred, and I realized these two definitely knew each other.

God, even the school nurse was one of his lovers?

"I'll leave you two alone," she answered with a blush before leaving to give us some privacy.

Neil drew even closer to me until I was hit with his amber and tobacco smell. His hair was extra disheveled, and his eyes were luminous like always.

"How are you feeling?" He positioned himself in front of me. I was still sitting on the bed with my legs dangling and he towered over me with his statuesque body. Looking at him always inspired a little bit of awe in me.

"Did you have sex with that nurse, too?" I pointed at the door behind him, and he grinned.

I flushed and tilted my chin down. None of this was my business, but I could never seem to hold my tongue about it.

"Just once, last year," he admitted, searching for my eyes that eventually did look up to meet his.

"So, you're telling me she might take a swing at me someday, too?" I answered bitterly, because the reason Jennifer hated me so deeply was standing right there in front of me, all charm and dark looks.

"That won't happen again. The Krew know what I'm capable of when I lose control," he said with an ominous confidence.

"And what are you capable of?" I said softly.

"I'd rather you didn't know." He moved closer, until his legs were touching my bent knees.

"Why?" I murmured.

"Because then you'd be afraid of me," he answered firmly, not a hint of hesitation in his voice.

But I was already afraid of him. Afraid of what I felt with him, afraid of the person I became with him, afraid of the thoughts I had about him, and afraid for what the future had in store for both of us.

I swallowed and rubbed my index finger on my thigh, considering this whole bizarre situation. Jennifer and the Krew hated me. They were a dangerous group of people, and Neil couldn't be there every time they tried to hurt me.

"Jennifer knows about Jared. She told me to stay away from you or she'll tell him everything." I kept my eyes down, still shocked and upset by what had happened. I wasn't as upset about being on the receiving end of some gratuitous violence as I was at the way women would let themselves be tricked by men, even to the point of harming others rather than accepting reality.

"She's not going to tell him shit." He used his index finger to lift up my chin, and I flinched at the gesture. I was still on edge, and he must have realized it because he touched my cheek indulgently.

"She knows she's going to pay for what she's done," he promised, his eyes locked on the bandage on my lower lip.

I didn't inquire into his method of revenge; Jennifer didn't matter right now, just Jared. I should have been able to break the news to him at the right time without anyone else interfering in that decision.

"Why did she go off like that?" he asked me then, as if I also bore some fault for this. I jerked my face away from his hand and sat up straight. I had to remember that Neil wasn't my hero or my savior. I was just one more trophy in his collection, and I had to keep sight of that.

"Because she said you were hers and I responded in kind," I explained angrily. "Do you think verbal provocation justifies her violence or gives her the right to hit me?" I stood up from the bed and immediately experienced a slight dizziness that made me stagger. Neil grabbed my arm, afraid that I might fall, but I didn't. Instead, I looked around for my shoes, because I was barefoot. Moments later, I spotted my sneakers next to a chair.

"I'm not accusing you of anything, Selene. I'm just trying to figure out how—"

"How it happened? Jennifer is a crazy bitch who is obsessively jealous over you, that's how." I cut him off, reaching for my shoes. I slipped them on and then held onto the back of the chair as another wave of dizziness washed over me.

"You should try telling her that 'you like her and your cock likes her but it's just sex.' Maybe then she'll get that she's not your girl-friend." I rarely expressed myself so crudely, but I repeated his own words to him angrily and then grabbed my coat and bag. I had no idea who had brought my stuff there, and I didn't care. I just wanted to get out.

"Don't be a child. All I did was tell you the truth." Neil came over to me and put a hand on the door to prevent me from leaving, but there was no way I was going to stand there and listen to him. Not anymore.

"There are a lot of ways to tell the truth, Neil. And as if I didn't have enough going on, I'm now the new target of your deranged friends. Did you talk about me behind my back or what?" I gave him a false smile. "Did you maybe brag to Jennifer about your amazing performance? Or maybe you just told her I'm a way to let off steam, a little girl, a pity lay? Did you laugh at me? A naive little virgin who came all the way from Detroit just to get used by you like all the rest?" I seemed to be getting some of my strength back, though I was still dizzy. I was slowly starting to process everything that had happened and really react to it.

"I didn't do any of that. I gave you my word that I wouldn't talk about us to anyone, and I kept it. I'm not a teenager; I don't feel the need to brag about how, when, or who I fuck," he clarified, his voice getting steadily louder.

"And yet they know about it," I pointed out.

"She guessed it on her own, but I never told her anything," he said again, and from the look on his face, I could tell he was being sincere. I sighed then and rubbed my temple. All I wanted to do was go home and forget this disaster of a day.

"I would like to go home," I admitted in a soft voice. Neil slipped his hand over the doorknob and turned it.

"Then let's go home, Tinkerbell," he said decisively, smiling just a little bit when he used my nickname. I looked up at him with every intention of refusing his escort, but I immediately gave in. How could I stay away from the person who shook my heart and ignited my body?

So, instead, I followed him to his car and watched him admiringly as he drove.

Neil even held a steering wheel with his own kind of charm: using one hand while, with the other, he ruffled his thick hair. He also gnawed on his lower lip and stared out the windshield, lost in thought.

As I stared at him, I realized how important his presence had become to me. Just having him next to me was enough to make me forget about everything I'd had to deal with in the last few hours.

"Wanna stop somewhere before we head back?" he suggested, startling me. I composed myself quickly, hoping he didn't catch me looking at him and spacing out.

"Where?" I asked.

"What, don't you trust me?" he asked, with the kind of sneaky smile that gave me goosebumps and a blush.

"No." There was no point trying to lie to him. Even though I had given him parts of myself that I had never given to anyone else, I didn't trust him outside of bed.

"Good. That's the correct response," he answered cheerfully, taking a street I didn't know. I didn't say anything else. Despite what I had just told him, I had placed myself completely in the hands of the walking disaster next to me. From time to time, I caught him sneaking sidelong glances at me, similar to my own.

"Quit looking at me," I teased him.

"You've done nothing but look at me since you got into this car," he shot back, never taking his eyes off the road. Then he turned up the volume on a song by The Neighborhood, and we didn't speak again for a while.

I was still feeling unsettled, though. I was still shaken by what had happened with Jennifer, even if I did know that I was safe with him.

"So, where are we going?" I asked after a while and he snorted at me.

"You're too impatient," he chided me in that grave tone of his that always got under my skin.

"And you're too domineering." I pouted. At the same time, I felt grateful for the painkillers still circulating in my system. I wasn't feeling any pain, but I didn't know how long the effect would last. I preferred not to think about what I'd do then.

"Only in bed," he answered, giving me a meaningful look, and I shook my head at him.

"Disagree. It's not just in bed."

Neil was always domineering, overbearing, arrogant, and overly serious. Apparently he wasn't aware of that—or he pretended he wasn't.

After about ten minutes, he parked the car in front of a chocolate shop. I frowned and leaned forward to get a better look. It was a large space with big windows that allowed me to see the cozy furnishings inside. I also noticed that the tables inside were all full of people, so I turned to Neil with a sigh. I looked bad. I'd just taken a beating, and I had the evidence of it all over me. Neil must have sensed the direction of my thoughts, because he looked between me and the chocolate shop in a considering sort of way.

"Wait here for me," he said, getting out of the car. He didn't even wait for my response; he just walked in the entrance with his usual proud bearing. My eyes dipped down to ogle his firm backside that contracted with every step until he vanished from my field of vision. I made myself comfortable in the passenger seat and waited a few minutes until he reappeared with a small box in hand. He got back into the car and handed it to me.

"Can you hold that for me?" he asked, and I accepted it, noting the blue paper it was wrapped in.

"Aw, did you buy me chocolates? I didn't think you were romantic like that," I said, giving him a little bit of hard time. He started the engine but not before giving me one of his usual severe expressions.

"Do I strike you as cliché?" He rejoined traffic and proceeded along another street that I didn't know; it was taking us farther and farther away from our neighborhood.

"I never thought you were, no," I admitted, holding the box

347

tightly to keep it from sliding around, especially when Neil took hard turns or passed someone recklessly. He drove terribly, or rather, he always drove like he was in the middle of an illegal street race, but I didn't point that out to him because I didn't need another argument. I didn't even ask him any more questions, because I could tell that he wasn't in the mood for talking.

Eventually, we stopped at a park. Neil turned off the car and sat comfortably, looking out at the scene in front of him.

"We can stay in the car, if you'd like. It's a bit cold to sit outside," he said, not even looking at me. I turned to him in amazement. Neil always had the uncanny ability to understand me even when I didn't explain myself. I smiled at him, grateful for the choice, and when our gazes met, I found myself getting lost in his eyes again. They were even more spectacular when they caught the rays of sun filtering in through the car's windshield.

"Open it," he said, jerking his chin at the box still sitting on my lap. I had completely forgotten about it.

But I didn't need to be told twice.

Inside, there were four magnificent rectangular cookies, each one with a smiley face inscribed into it.

"Are you trying to fatten me up?" I grinned, my eyes fixed on the treats. They looked tempting, and I couldn't wait to try them.

"These are the best cookies in New York. The chips are made of artisanal chocolate. Close your eyes and pick one, then read the sentence on the back."

Neil never ceased to astound me. I shut my eyes, perceiving nothing but the sound of our breathing, and grabbed a cookie.

"You can open your eyes now," he ordered, giving me goosebumps.

I did as he instructed and turned my cookie over, reading aloud, "I may be all grown up now, but if I see you without a smile, I'll grab a pencil and draw it in for you like a little kid."

Neil gave me a serious look, almost shocked by what I'd just read. He looked down at the cookie in my hand and then back up at my face in disbelief.

"Are you messing with me?" he asked in confusion, leaning over to make sure that I was being honest.

"Of course not," I said, quickly biting into one cookie and giving him a one-shoulder shrug. They were delightful!

Neil frowned, then let his head fall back against the seat, thoughtful.

"Mmm… These are delicious," I moaned with my mouth full, a few crumbs tumbling out as I did. Neil tracked the path of the falling particles and cocked an eyebrow at me. I stopped chewing and prepared myself for another one of his sharp, insulting comments. But instead he just bit his lip and sighed.

"No one has ever eaten in my car. I don't even fuck in here," he explained, looking me right in the eye. He wanted me to understand that this was a special privilege he was granting me, something he didn't allow any of his other lovers to do.

I took another bite and didn't respond. I was sometimes afraid that I was going to say the wrong thing to him and change his whole mood; he was so terribly erratic. Even now, I wasn't sure whether he was warning me, criticizing me, or just making an observation.

"So…" I decided to change the subject. "Is this some bizarre way of declaring your love for me?" I asked sarcastically. I don't know why I even said something like that. Maybe I was just trying to hide my own real feelings. If I was being honest, I felt shattered, and I was still trying to find the strength to deal with the humiliation I'd suffered at Jennifer's hands.

Neil smiled again in that seductive way he had, and suddenly my stomach clenched.

"These are called 'Good Mood Cookies,'" he explained. "I just wanted you to smile again. Neither Jennifer nor anyone else should have the power to make you miserable. Understand?" He reached a hand up to my face and daubed a few crumbs from my lower lip with his thumb. In that moment, I ceased to think, speak, or even breathe.

"That's not something I can control," I murmured, looking into his eyes.

"We can't control when we get hurt, but we can control who we suffer over, and Jennifer is not worth feeling bad about." As Neil continued to hold my stare, I tried to read his golden eyes like were the most beautiful book I'd ever encountered.

"And what about you? Would you be worth suffering for?" I asked, because everything I had endured from his lover I had endured for him.

Everything I did was for him now.

"No. You should just stay away from me."

He turned his face away and looked back out the windshield. Then, he started the engine and put both his hands on the steering wheel. He was ready to flee that place, our conversation, and most of all, me.

It was always the same story with him: he told me not to believe in love, or silver linings, or fairy tales or the existence of Prince Charmings, and despite all that, I still preferred him and his disenchantment to any happy ending.

24

SELENE

Two weeks had passed since the incident with Jennifer.

Members of the Krew continued to give me shifty looks whenever they spotted me around town, but none of them had approached me again. Jennifer herself seemed to have vanished into thin air. I didn't know if Neil had gone through with his plan for revenge, but I was glad I didn't encounter her again. Neil, on the other hand, proved himself extremely attentive to me in those two weeks. He asked me how I was every day but never touched me. He hadn't once tried to seduce me or sneak into my room.

The last time we'd made love was now a distant memory, and I'd begun to suspect that he'd gotten over whatever weird attraction he had to me. An idea that, if I was being perfectly honest, didn't thrill me.

"Hi," I said as I walked into the kitchen, where my father was sitting at the table sipping a cup of tea behind his laptop. I had explained the bandage on my lip to Mia and Matt with a ridiculous story about falling down the stairs and always kept the bruises on my body covered with my clothes. Fortunately, by then my mouth was completely healed and my bruises didn't hurt anymore, though they had faded from black to a sickly yellow color.

"Hey, Selene." Matt looked and me and halted whatever research he was doing on his computer.

"Is Mia back?" I asked uneasily as I grabbed a carton of orange juice from the fridge.

"She's still at work," he answered, checking the Rolex on his wrist. Actually, it was strange that Matt was already home. He usually didn't get in before ten o'clock at night. I sat down on a stool and drank the juice straight from the carton, not bothering with a glass.

"How are you? How are you finding it here?" And there he went again with his awkward questions. My father still hoped to repair a relationship that I now considered irreparable. A father was supposed to play a central role in daughter's upbringing, protecting her and being responsible for her and providing her with a feeling of security—all things that Matt had never done. Instead, I'd always felt like I was imposing on his life, and that was the worst feeling a little girl could have.

"Suffice it to say I like Detroit better." It was true. Especially after the episode with Jennifer had gone down, I'd been feeling like I was imposing in New York, at school, and especially in Neil's life. He'd basically ignored me lately, and by then, I was sure that whatever had drawn him to me in the first place was completely gone.

Neil had been cured of the Selene virus.

"If there's anything I can do, just ask. Has anyone given you any problems?" Matt's voice cut into my thoughts with a concerned tone that I'd had never before heard from him in all my years of living.

"Don't worry about it. The only thing you could have done is never allow your daughter to catch you having sex with another woman," I said firmly. Matt blanched.

I got back up to replace the juice before I turned to look at him, taking a moment to conceal the unhappiness that those memories still conjured in me.

"I know that I made mistakes, but at the time things with your mother weren't how they once were…" He got up from his chair and approached me, clad in his stylish, impeccable suit.

"Why didn't you just leave her? Why not end your relationship rather than making her suffer while you had affairs with other women? Why?" My voice grew louder as I spoke. I couldn't stand the ridiculous excuses he always tried to give me. A father was supposed to model male behavior for his daughter, to be a Prince Charming in her eyes. But for me, my father was just some rich surgeon, a coldhearted cheater.

"It's not easy, walking away from the woman you've loved your entire life."

"But I was there, too!" I burst out. He should have thought about the consequences his actions would have for me, not just himself. "I was just a child, and you should have thought about the good of the family!" I added, trying not to cry. I had stopped crying in front of him a long time ago.

Matt looked intently at me, troubled by my words. He stretched out a hand, but I backed away. I didn't want any physical contact between the two of us.

"I made a mistake. Who doesn't make mistakes in this life? Let me fix it," he begged me softly.

Again, he was asking me for a second chance, but I couldn't just put it behind me, not when I'd witnessed his infidelity with my own eyes. Not after my father had been gone from my life for so long.

"That's asking too much of me." I shook my head, staring somewhere over his shoulder. I wasn't capable of forgiving something like that. I couldn't do it; I wasn't strong like my mother.

"Selene." Matt took my face in his hands, but I shied away from his touch. Nothing was going to change. I'd known that from the start, from before I ever came to New York. I'd known that trying to reconcile with him would be a total failure.

It was simply too late.

On that realization, I left the kitchen without giving him a second glance.

The next morning, I needed to clear my head and not think about my father. I called Jared and asked him how his mother was doing. He told me that she had lost a lot of weight, that she was vomiting frequently, and she'd lost so much hair that she'd started wearing colorful scarves on her head. The more he told me, the more Jennifer's threats to stay away from Neil echoed in my mind. I needed to prevent Jared from finding out the truth in the worst possible way. I felt so anxious that I went through all my classes with Detroit and Jared lingering in the back of my mind.

The thought did occur to me—of just going back home, ending this absurd situation, and stopping whatever was happening with Neil. But how could I leave him behind? He was becoming increasingly important to me. The questions I constantly asked myself about him and his past, the secret room that housed those mysterious boxes, the ghost of Scarlett, his strange behavior, the disgusting package from an unknown sender… All of it was urging me to stay put and illuminate some of the darkness that now surrounded me.

I was in too deep by then, there was no escape.

....

"Okay, so: William Shakespeare was an English poet and… Why the hell do we need to know this stuff again?" Adam grumbled, drawing our attention to his expression of boredom.

"Maybe because otherwise you wouldn't pass Professor Smith's exam, genius?" Julie cut in.

"Quiet over there!" The librarian was getting tired of constantly chiding us and was about to throw us all out.

After classes, we had decided to stay on campus for a few more hours to study, but we kept getting distracted.

"You're always such an idiot, Adam!" Cory said derisively.

"Everyone, stop it! Let's just go back to studying!" Julie grumbled again. "Moving on. Alyssa, how many sonnets did our Shakespeare pen?" our resident nerd continued, pointing her pencil at Alyssa, who was sitting next to me.

"Umm…fifty? Like iambic *penta*meter?" she answered uncertainly, which made me smile. I appreciated the effort at a mnemonic device, but it apparently hadn't helped her learn these particular facts.

"No, Alyssa. It's actually one hundred and fifty-four. I've told you that several times now," Julie answered in exasperation, brushing her long red hair over one shoulder.

"You know you make a sexy professor, right?" Adam leaned closer to her and touched her cheek, making her blush. I could never understand how those two even communicated with each other. Or how, sometimes, two completely different souls were so deeply compatible with each other that it made for passionate, long-lasting union.

I thought again of Neil, how distant he'd grown and how dissimilar—completely opposite—we were in so many ways. Alas, he and I were nothing close to compatible.

"Cut it out," Julie said in a quiet voice, so as not to get us another scolding from the librarian.

"I'm never going to pass this exam!" Alyssa whimpered in frustration.

"Alyssa, sweetheart, you know there are alternative ways to pass," Jake advised her, giving Cory and Adam a knowing glance. The three boys began to laugh—by "alternative" they surely meant…

"Oh yeah, you give Smith a handy and you'll pass with flying colors, guaranteed." Cory winked, always ready to be explicit about such things.

Everyone burst into laughter, except me and Logan. I didn't like that kind of joke precisely because there were actually people at our school who would sell their dignity to pass a test. Alyssa, though, was definitely not that kind of person.

"Cory, you'd better shut your trap and get to studying," Logan snapped in irritation, gripping his pen tightly.

He and Alyssa had been going out with each other more and more often lately, though they hadn't made anything official.

"Feeling territorial?" I whispered mockingly in his ear, and he cocked an eyebrow at me like I was talking crazy.

"No, I'm just trying to study and keep getting distracted by their bullshit," he explained, before bowing his head back over his book.

"Oh yeah, for sure," I answered sarcastically. If he thought he was fooling me, he was sorely mistaken. I had a woman's intuition about that kind of thing, and I knew that he really liked Alyssa, even if he wouldn't admit it.

"Looks like someone's jealous… So, you two fucking?" Adam asked abruptly, having come to the same conclusion about Logan and Alyssa that I had. Alyssa looked completely embarrassed.

"You should mind your own business. You don't see me asking you and Julie about what you're getting up to," Logan shot back with a harsh look. Julie lowered her eyes and bit the inside of her cheek, clearly uncomfortable.

"Alas! Julie hasn't given it up to Adam yet," Jake said, laughing along with Cory.

"Shut up, you moron!" Adam admonished, throwing a wadded up paper ball at him.

"So this is how you all study, huh?" Kyle came up behind his cousin Cory, resting his hands on his shoulders. He was wearing the same long black coat over his tall, slim body, and his dark hair was gathered into a messy knot at the nape of his neck. A silver ring gleamed in one ear, and his enchanting blue eyes focused immediately on mine. He smiled at me, and I smiled back easily.

"Hey, Nabokov," he teased me.

"Do you really think we get much studying done with these idiots?" Alyssa grumbled as Kyle's gaze continued to burn into me. He watched me with a marked persistence, which made me hugely uncomfortable. Only one person looked at me with that much intensity, and his golden eyes were the only ones I wanted on me.

I looked away, breaking eye contact with him and saw Professor Cooper talking to the librarian not far from our table. There was a swell of dread in my chest when I remembered the way Neil had threatened her in that empty classroom.

I observed her for a long time, focusing on one particular detail that had been right there under my nose this whole time: she had blond hair. She was a blond. Like the nurse at the health center, like Jennifer... like I wasn't. All of Neil's other lovers were blond.

I just kept staring at her as she sat there in her tasteful dark pantsuit, which made her look beautiful and definitely highlighted her rosy glow.

"Blond..." I whispered, as though this was another piece I needed to complete the puzzle that was Neil Miller.

Lost in these considerations, I grew preoccupied, even ignoring Logan right beside me.

"You're quiet today," he told me later when we were heading home in his Audi R8.

"Does your brother have some sort of fixation on blonds?" I murmured, looking out the window at the illuminated signs in all the stores.

Logan was silent for several seconds, and I turned to look at him.

"What makes you think that?" He was watching the road in front of us, but it suddenly seemed like he was on edge. He worried his upper lip and kept drumming his fingers on the steering wheel.

"His lovers are all blonds," I pointed out in a searching tone. I didn't think it was just coincidence.

"Sure, but I wouldn't call it a fixation, more like…" He paused to consider. "A preference," he finished.

So it was true: I wasn't his type of woman, but until two weeks ago, he had seemed to want me anyway. I shook my head in frustration. Logan knew his brother better than me, and maybe I was just seeing connections where there were none. Neil might have preferred blonds to brunettes, but it wasn't like rejected the latter either.

"I think he's also got a fixation on personal hygiene. I mean, how many showers do you take per day?"

We stopped at a traffic light and Logan sighed. He took a long time to respond, and by that point, he seemed actually nervous.

"No, he's just really into cleanliness. He's always been like that," he said placatingly, pretending not to know how many times a day Neil washed himself and how long he spent in the shower.

Whatever Logan knew, he wasn't going to tell me. Neil was still his brother, while I was just…a friend, I supposed.

When we arrived at the house, I got out of the car and slowly made my way up to the front steps. I took them sluggishly, but before I could reach the front door, I spotted a package right in front of it.

Another one.

I glanced around, but there was no sign of anyone, so I knelt down in front of the package, careful not to touch it.

"Selene, what are you doing?" Logan caught up to me and halted when he saw the dark box that had my full attention.

"Shit. Again?" he asked warily.

"Again," I confirmed, looking up at him.

After just a moment's hesitation, we went into the house, carrying the box and all the stress that came with it.

We sat down on the living room sofa, not even bothering to greet Anna, who was occupied with household chores. Both of us were experiencing a wicked case of déjà vu.

Logan sighed, and I gave his shoulder a pat to encourage him to open the package. He did so with such creeping slowness that it shredded my nerves and skyrocketed my anxiety.

When it was finally open, he pulled out an object wrapped in black paper, which he tore roughly away. All we could see was...

"What the hell?" he blurted out.

"It's a music box..."

It was white and blue, decorated with clouds and angels, presumably to represent heaven.

"This should make it play." I turned a small crank on the back of the box, and a strange piece of music began to waft through the living room. The music box slowly rotated on its base and then opened like a shell to reveal an angel with clipped wings, its face painted red and its eyes gone.

"God!" Logan flinched back, as if to protect himself from the shocking figure, but I watched the angel as it spun, accompanied by the delicate yet macabre melody. Eventually, I spotted a small note carefully folded up and tucked between its wings.

"Logan." I swallowed hard and tapped his shoulder, pointing out the paper.

He set the music box down on the coffee table in front of us and grabbed the note to read it:

AN ANGEL WHOSE WINGS HAVE BEEN CLIPPED, DEPRIVED OF ITS OWN GLOW,

   THROWN INTO THE DARKEST SHADOWS, UNABLE FOR SO LONG TO SEE THE SUN'S LIGHT...

AN ANGEL WHO DID NOT KNOW THE WORD HATE, AN ANGEL WHO DID NOT

CONDEMN THE WOUNDED ROSE, AN ANGEL WHO LEARNED TO DANCE

IN THE DARKNESS, TRANSFORMING ITSELF INTO THE WORST OF DEVILS,

TRANSFORMING ITS WORLD INTO THE WORST OF HELLS.

THE DEVIL IS IN THE DETAILS.

THE DEVIL IS ALSO WITH YOU.

THE MYSTERY OF THE MUSIC BOX.

PLAYER 2511

Logan and I remained silent for an unknowable amount of time. The sender was Player 2511 again, and this note had also been typed and printed. My heart was pounding like a jackhammer against my rib cage. I looked over at Logan and saw that he was as shocked as I was. Neither of us knew what to do or say in that moment.

The sound of footsteps drew our attention to the marble staircase in the center of the room. Neil. His black sweatshirt clung to his chest, displaying its breadth and strength. His easy, masculine presence sidetracked my train of thought, making me forget for a second the situation we were in.

We didn't need to explain anything to him. Neil stopped right before the table and stared at that damned music box. The he looked at the open package and the note in his brother's hand. "Him again?" I could hear concern in his voice.

Logan nodded and handed him the piece of paper. Neil's golden eyes flickered over the ominous words, and his face twisted into a focused, thoughtful expression.

"Does it mean anything to you, Neil?" Logan asked. Neil threw the note back onto the coffee table and glared at the music box.

"No, I have no idea what it means," he answered. He ran a hand over his face while the other went to his hip. For the first time, he seemed agitated as well.

"I think we should go to the police," I said, and his honey-colored eyes snapped to me. I sucked in a breath at the force of his stare, which had pinned me to the sofa as surely as if he'd done it with his large, strong hands.

"And tell them what? All we could do is file a worthless complaint against an unknown person and nothing would come of it," he bit out, making me flinch.

"I'm just suggesting solutions. You don't need to snap at me like that." I scolded him, regarding him with narrowed eyes.

"Calm down, everyone." Logan cut in to defuse the tension. "Try to think, Neil. Could it be someone you know? Maybe one of the Krew?" he asked thoughtfully, but Neil tossed his head and gave him a mocking smile.

"I know you hate them, little brother, but my friends would never do something like this to me. Not to *me*, for fuck's sake!" he answered firmly, pointing at himself as though it were impossible to even imagine such a thing happening.

To be fair, Neil wasn't just a member of the Krew, he was clearly their leader. Someone whom both Luke and Xavier seemed to fear quite a bit, which I'd seen for myself on several occasions.

"I'm just trying to figure this out," Logan argued, getting to his feet.

"Planting doubts about the Krew? Nice move, bro." Neil winked at Logan and ran a hand through his chestnut hair, ruffling it.

"Would you really be surprised if it was them?" Logan insisted. "They're insane, and that blond you're screwing beat the crap out of Selene not even two weeks ago!" he shouted, then turned to point at me. Neil turned to me as well and examined me thoughtfully. A shadow passed over his face, further darkening his grim expression before he turned back to his brother.

"That blond I'm screwing," he repeated pointedly, "has learned her lesson, and she, like the others, knows not to touch Selene again."

They were talking about me like I wasn't even in the room and had no say in this matter. Yet, I felt strangely...protected.

"You should distance yourself from them. It's your fault we're even in this situation. You and the people you hang around with and all the shit you pull!" Logan accused him, and Neil recoiled as though he'd been slapped. I didn't understand what specifically they were talking about, as I knew little about Neil's past and somehow even less about his present.

The human disaster in front of me, however, must have known exactly what Logan meant. He huffed an annoyed breath and then quirked a corner of his mouth as his gaze shifted to the music box. He picked it up and held it in his hand, turning it this way and that for a few moments as it rested in his palm and then... he hurled it against the wall, reducing it to a thousand tiny pieces.

The deafening, unexpected noise bounced off the walls of the living room, and I shut my eyes against it. When I opened them again, I saw Logan standing frozen, observing the entire scene.

"Feel better now?" he asked coldly while Neil panted. The skin on his cheekbones was red, and the tendons in his neck stood out. One raised vein protruded from his temple, and his full lips were parted and dry.

"Fuck you," Neil hissed menacingly, leveling a glare at his brother.

Just then, someone opened the front door and walked in. Chatter filled up the room. It was Mia and Matt, along with Chloe.

"I'm so happy you're going back to school tomorrow and..." Mia's smile fell as she noticed the shards of ceramic scattered all over the floor. Matt, on the other hand, shut the door and immediately put an arm around the baby of the family.

"What's going on here?" Mia looked from the destroyed music box to her children before turning back to Chloe and shooing her away. "Go on to your room, darling," she said in a soothing voice, though I was sure that she herself was feeling shaken and concerned.

With just a fleeting glance to her brothers, Chloe went across the living room and up the stairs without offering a reply. Matt stepped up to join his girlfriend, and apparently not at all surprised by the situation, looked closely at Neil.

"Are we back to this, Neil?" Mia addressed her eldest child directly with a stern, investigatory tone. Neil said nothing but held his mother's gaze without any sort of fear. "If you can't stop having these sorts of reactions, I'll be forced to—"

"Kick me out? Or send me to the nuthouse?" he said with a goading smile as he turned to face his mother. Mia swallowed hard and shook her head, shifting her eyes to the music box that had been demolished by her son's rage.

"Where did I go wrong with you?" Sadness shadowed her pale face, and Matt rested a hand on her shoulder to bolster her.

"Everywhere," Neil answered, staring intently at her.

"It was my fault, Mom. I provoked him," Logan added, but his mother didn't even look at him. She stared stubbornly at Neil.

"You got every part of it wrong," Neil continued. "You never listened to what I was trying to tell you with my silences. You never looked into the things I drew or my teachers' suspicions." His gave her a mirthless smile as he moved closer to her. "You were too focused on yourself, too busy with your career and the dinners you were going to with William while the world pulled me down and the monsters devoured my soul." He wasn't merely looking her in the eyes, he was incinerating her from the inside out; the tears that had started pouring down her cheeks were evidence of that.

Matt remained silent, saying nothing in Mia's defense.

Presumably, he knew something that I didn't and maybe it was somehow justified, this hatred that Neil had for his mother.

"I *drew* it for you. The black was for fear, yellow was for her hair, and red...red was for hell. Was it really that hard to decode? I was a kid; I didn't know any other way to tell you what was happening to me..." he continued in a whisper. Mia bowed her head, audibly sobbing.

For my part, I couldn't understand any of this, but I could feel Neil's pain. Surprisingly, I felt like crying myself. A chill crept under my skin, despite the warmth of the room. The chill of his words and his faraway eyes, sucked into the darkness.

"I'm sorry..." Mia's thin voice shattered the intense silence. Matt allowed his hand to slide from his girlfriend's shoulder and lowered his arm, surrendering her to her cruel fate. There was nothing to be done to fill the void in Neil's golden eyes and in his beautiful, miserable face.

"Doesn't matter. That doesn't matter anymore."

Peter Pan had ceased to fly.

He didn't *want* to.

The stars were winking out; the curtain was descending.

The show was over.

25

SELENE

I stood motionless, staring down the door of the room that contained the memory boxes.

It was still locked, so I could only stare at its wooden surface as though hoping that at any moment the answers I sought might be inscribed upon it.

I understood that something terrible had happened to Neil, and the newspaper articles about a scandal only increased my suspicions. Perhaps I should have been understanding and patient with him, waiting until I had completely earned his trust. He was a unique man, after all. Every day, he grappled with his problems and never allowed anyone to stay by his side.

But I didn't want to give up. At least, not that easily.

"Selene, are we going?" Logan drew my attention, and I turned to find him right next to me. I hadn't even heard his footsteps echoing down the hall. We'd agreed to meet up that afternoon because we were going to spend some time in Matt's private library. We intended to do some research and try to solve the riddle that Player 2511 had sent us.

"Yeah." I followed him to the library, and as soon as I walked through the door, I was amazed. The smell of paper and books overwhelmed me, drawing me deeper into an environment I preferred above all others. The dark wood of the floor gave the room a magical ambiance. A ladder leaned against the high shelves to allow readers to retrieve the volumes placed up near the ceiling. Daylight filtered in through an enormous window, lighting up the sleek mahogany desk where my father usually sat to read his medical periodicals. Not far away from it were some Gothic-style armchairs with sage-colored cushions and a wooden table with a vase of fresh flowers on it. Undoubtedly, it was replaced every day by Anna.

"How many books are in here?" I asked, visibly shocked as I gawked around the room, tilting my head back.

"More than six thousand. There are also a number of first editions," Logan told me, giving me an amused look.

"Damn! It reminds me a little bit of the library at Hearst Castle," I noted with a smile.

"Whose castle?" He asked.

"William Randolph Hearst's. A newspaper magnate who lived in California." I continued to gaze admiringly at the incredibly high shelves all around me, slowly rotating to see them all. This had officially become my favorite room in the house.

"So, what are we doing here?"

I jerked when I heard Neil's voice, and all at once, the books were no longer the center of my attention.

"Thanks for being on time," Logan chided, but Neil remained unmoved. He leaned against the edge of the desk and crossed his arms over his chest, waiting for a real answer.

He didn't pay me any attention, so I decided that I could be indifferent as well and made myself comfortable in one of the armchairs.

"Okay," Logan began, putting on his black eyeglasses. It gave him a scholarly look. "We've got a library full of books here, and I've already identified some that might help us." He grabbed a volume and handed it to me before doing the same thing to Neil. "Look at these carefully and try to find anything you can about the music box: its origin, its function, possible stories or legends connected to it... Basically anything that helps us learn more about it. It's the same sender as the first one, so just as the choice of the raven wasn't random, the music box probably wasn't, either," he finished gravely, sitting down in the armchair opposite me.

"Agreed." I opened the book he'd given me and began leafing through it. The pages were marked by time, with tiny characters so faded in places that deciphering the writing was difficult. Neil was turning the pages of his own book, an unlit cigarette clamped between his full lips. His pack of Winstons sat on the desk next to him. The pack was never far away from him, and I wondered just how much he smoked per day and how old he'd been when he started.

His eyes were lowered to his book, his powerful shoulders pushing him slightly forward. A messy forelock hung over his forehead, and his stubble punctuated the contours of his perfect face. His long eyelashes dipped downward.

He took the cigarette between his index and middle fingers, and with that same hand, paged through the book. He never took his eyes off it, the way I should have been doing, if I wasn't sitting just a few feet away from him. Even the way he held his cigarette was beguiling.

Logan cleared his throat, and I looked up immediately. Logan was staring at me with his brows furrowed. I blushed violently and ducked my head back into the book.

After Logan's nonverbal scolding, I didn't have the courage to lift my nose out of the books or to divert my attention to the gorgeous human disaster to my left.

About thirty minutes of intense silence passed, during which I genuinely committed myself to searching for anything that might help us.

"Find anything?" Logan asked, taking off his glasses to rub his eyes.

"No," I sighed and he nodded, as though willing himself not to lose heart.

"What about you, Neil?" He turned toward his brother, who had opened another book, abandoning the first.

"Fuck all," he answered, blunt and impatient, and kept on ignoring me. He didn't even so much as glance in my direction. It was like I wasn't even in the room.

"Okay, let's keep looking then. Onward!" Logan encouraged us as he pushed his glasses back on and resumed his desperate search.

Another twenty minutes of silent concentration passed. The only sound was the occasional faint rustling of paper whenever one of us turned a page, hoping to find something of interest. Suddenly, I huffed out a breath and took a break to stretch my arms, which were starting to feel sluggish. As I did so, I turned my face to Neil and caught him watching me.

He was looking at me—just me. I could hardly believe it. I lowered my arms awkwardly and returned his stare intensely.

Then Neil did something unexpected: he inserted his right index finger between the abandoned pages of his book and made an opening there. Then, he slowly glided his finger back and forth, as if he were petting the smooth paper.

I watched him from under my eyelashes and saw how his chest rose and fell. Seconds later, I realized that he was making an obscene gesture and concealing it with the book. I gulped and turned red.

He quirked a corner of his mouth, delighted by his filthy simulation, and I tilted my face down in embarrassment. But not before checking to make sure that Logan hadn't noticed anything.

I cleared my throat and gave Neil another sideways look, keeping my face tilted down. I could feel his golden gaze hot on me, and I struggled not to fall into its trap once again. Had he lost his mind? Right there in front of his brother he was…trying to provoke me? Seduce me? Mess with me? He had been ignoring me for two weeks, and just then, I was wishing that he'd kept that up.

"Hey! I think I found something!" Fortunately, Logan interrupted the intimate moment, drawing our attention to something far more important.

"Fantastic, good job, Sherlock," Neil teased, closing his book.

I was never going to be able to look at a book again without thinking obscene thoughts.

"Let's see." Logan got up from his chair, holding the book in both hands. "The music box emerged in the late seventeen hundreds. They are sentimental items, cloaked in mystery and a powerful fascination. Many legends swirl around music boxes, but one of the most significant is that of the famous…" He looked up at me and Neil and then continued to read. "Angel of the Music Box." Logan appeared to have hit upon exactly what we were looking for, but I wasn't sure I wanted to know exactly what was hidden inside the puzzle.

"Keep going," I said, sounding uncertain.

"The Angel of the Music Box is one of the earliest folktales about music boxes. It tells the story of a young girl who lived with her father and brother. On her twelfth birthday, her father gifted the girl a music box with an angel inside, promising that the angel would protect her for the rest of her life. The angel was God's messenger, bringer of justice, peace, and love."

"So far it doesn't sound like anything to worry about," I commented.

"Keep going," Neil prompted, staring intently at his brother, who immediately resumed his recitation.

"However, the father forbade the little girl to touch the music box, as it was a very fragile and valuable object, and he stored it in his own room. One day, the little girl disobeyed her father and crept into his bedroom to take the object of her desires. But the music box fell to the floor, and the angel shattered into countless pieces." Logan sighed and glanced up nervously at us before continuing.

"Upon returning to the house, her father found the destroyed music box and shouted at her. He upbraided her for her disobedience but did say that he would attempt to repair the music box. A few days later, the girl entered her home and found the music box sitting on a table as though it were brand new. She turned the crank, the music box opened, and she saw that her angel was no longer inside it; instead there was a monstrous demon. Frightened, the girl backed away and encountered her father. 'This is your punishment for disobeying me,' he told her, and the little girl burst into tears," Logan finished, looking thoughtfully at us.

"So what's it supposed to mean?" I asked skeptically.

"The devil in the music box basically means punishment," Logan stated.

"So, we have a raven that symbolizes revenge and an angel painted to look like a demon, which suggests punishment…and…" I rubbed the back of my neck, still confused. I didn't get the relevance of the music box to the raven and vice versa.

"Maybe the punishment already happened," Neil said, staring off into space. He'd been silent this whole time, just listening to us. I regarded him carefully. The smile, the charming expression, and the sly look had disappeared completely, giving way to a grave awareness.

"What are you talking about?" Logan asked with a frown.

"That some disobedient person has always paid the price for their actions." Neil explained in a low voice, causing a frosty silence to descend in his wake.

"And do you know who that might be?" Logan stepped

cautiously toward Neil, who slowly fixed his golden stare on his brother's face.

"No." Neil swallowed hard, moving closer to Logan. "But whoever it is, I give you my word that nothing is going to happen to our family." He said it with such simple confidence. There was no fear in those luminous eyes, just a deep sense of responsibility that lay heavily on his shoulders.

"Why would anything happen to the family?" I got up from my chair as agitation began to stir in my blood. He might not have been afraid, but I sure was.

"Because every game has winners and losers, Selene," he answered inscrutably, and I straightened my spine. I hadn't heard my name on his lips in a long time; it seemed somehow even more melodious to me.

"So, let's be winners," I answered so decisively that Logan's hazel eyes also darted to me. Neil stared at me in that deep, dark way of his and then smiled pityingly at me, as though convinced that only an idiot could believe we might win at this game.

26

NEIL

I was in the living room watching cartoons like usual when I heard my mother's voice, talking with some girl at the front door.

"Really? That would be amazing, Kimberly! Unfortunately, my schedule at the company means I'm never home, and our previous babysitter is expecting her second child!"

I turned to regard the young woman without any particular interest. The first thing I noticed about her was her long blond hair, falling over her light shirt.

"No problem, Mrs. Miller. We are neighbors, after all. I'd be delighted to look after your kids. Is there another on the way?" The girl smiled, pointing at my mother's prominent belly where Chloe was waiting.

"Oh, yes. It's going to be a girl this time."

"I wish you all the best, Mrs. Miller." The girl said, her voice delicate and innocent.

"I could come over in the afternoons after school, if that works for you?" the girl offered.

"And you're in your senior year of high school?"

I quit watching them and took out my notebook where I loved to draw. Just then, I had decided to finish my draft of the grandfather clock in our house, which showed two o'clock in the afternoon.

"Yes, I lost a couple of years but I am trying to make them up. I want to graduate, and I need to work so I can pay for college."

"You're a girl with a good head on her shoulders, Kimberly. Come with me. Logan is asleep, but Neil is here in the living room." I heard their footsteps drawing closer and closer, but my hand didn't want to stop tracing lines across the paper.

"Neil, darling." My mother knelt down beside me and pulled the pencil from my hand until I looked at her. Then, I was able to get a better look at the girl with her: the long blond hair, the tight shirt, the short black skirt, the slim body, and fresh, innocent face.

"Darling, this is Kimberly. She's going to be your new babysitter." I sat there, just staring at her. I had once read somewhere that children had the power to see beyond superficial appearances, and I discovered in that moment that I, in fact, had that capacity. There was something odd in this stranger's gray eyes, something sinister.

"I don't understand why he's so quiet; he isn't usually," my mother said, touching my cheek. My eyes couldn't pull away from the new babysitter's hypnotic face.

The girl knelt like my mother, while I lay on the floor, my legs crossed behind me and my hands motionless in front of me.

"You really are a beautiful boy, Neil," she said softly, examining every feature of my face. It wasn't a compliment to my mother for having given birth to a child who looked like me. Instead, it was flattery directed at a child, one that she was already thinking of in a very abnormal way.

"I love kids, Mrs. Miller. You'll see—your children and I are going to get along great," she added, still staring fixedly at me.

"That would make me so happy," Mom said hopefully.

"We're going to spend a lot of time together, Neil," Kimberly whispered with a devious smile that sent shivers down my spine...

Light from a small lamp on the dresser dimly illuminated the dark of the pool house. I was soaked in sweat; it was beading on my forehead, plastering my hair to my neck.

"Yes…" the blond beneath me groaned as I fucked her from behind. All at once, my stomach burned at the reminder of her presence and the sound of her gasps nauseated me. I covered her mouth with my hand, and she tightened around me, probably because she saw it as a possessive gesture. In reality, I hadn't gone out that night with the intention of bringing anyone home, not after the second puzzle had riddled my mind with suspicions and uncertainties. Then, I starting thinking about Kimberly, and it made me so angry and confused.

So, I took refuge in sex to avoid reality. Though I'd tried several times over the years to break the unhealthy habit, this destructive escapism, I always fell back into temptation.

I'd also spent the past two weeks wanting Selene, but she still had the marks of Jennifer's violence all over her body. I forced myself to keep my distance and didn't bother her with my advances. At least, not until the library, when I'd once again found myself in close quarters with her and her damned coconut smell.

The oval of her face, her ocean eyes rimmed in long, black lashes, her auburn hair in loose waves, her tiny, upturned nose and those lips… Those fucking lips that I had imagined on my own.

"Yes, keep going…" the blond beneath me whined again as I slammed my hips against her ass. I didn't even remember her name. All that mattered was that she had blond hair and a willowy body; that was enough to silence the Boy in me.

He talked all the time and often cried. He begged me to remind him that it was all over. That he was no longer a victim. That he was now the one in charge.

"You like being fucked this way?" I whispered to the girl, grabbing her sweaty hair in a tight fist. She bent back her neck and babbled something unintelligible, her eyes glazed. I rammed into her ass, creating the unmistakable sounds of rough sex to which I had grown accustomed.

Beads of sweat ran into the creases of my flexed abdominals and my tanned skin flushed with effort. My bare chest was pressed against her sweaty back. I could feel her slippery skin meeting my own, just as I could feel her juices soaking me in the area where the condom didn't completely cover me.

I looked down at us and the troublesome feeling only increased: I was disgusted by this.

"Y.. You're...incredible," she fawned over me, pushing herself up to meet me. She couldn't get enough; she really was just like the blond from my nightmares. She was lewd, experienced, and...

Perfect for me.

I insulted her roundly, whispering the filthiest things a man could say in an intimate moment, and she made noises of appreciation because she thought I was doing it to get her hot and not because I truly meant it. But how was she supposed to know that I needed to use women like her to carve out a moment of peace and remind myself that I was now the one dominating others?

Yet, I never really felt any better.

I was marked and stigmatized now, destined to only experience sexuality and eroticism the way I'd been taught: perversely.

I closed my eyes, and the Boy appeared again inside my head. He was wearing what he always wore: his Oklahoma City tank top and a pair of blue shorts. His knees were scraped up, and he had a basketball tucked underneath his arm. He smiled at me and bored his bright eyes directly into mine as he said:

"Finally, I'm no longer the one being subjected to this vast and

intolerable threat. Finally, I don't have to endure an unendurable situation. Finally, I am the one with all the power, and that bitch is the victim."

He winked at me, and I just kept moving. My conscience listened to him and everything I did was to satisfy him.

"G… Gently… I can't breathe." The blond beneath me complained about the way I was squeezing the back of her neck and how I had her other hand pinned against her hip. I was using my weight to flatten her, fucking her crudely and pounding all my frustration into her. I was sure that if the Tigress could see me right now, she would run like hell in the other direction.

"Shut up and the enjoy the moment because this going to be your first and last time with me." I rarely fucked anyone more than once. Jennifer, Alexia, and Babygirl were only exceptions.

With Selene, though, everything was different. I tried to think about Kimberly with her, but I couldn't manage it.

"You're hurting me…"

I silenced the girl underneath me by using my hands to tilt her neck back, driving my hips into her with even more force. If she had kept talking, I might have broken her back. Fortunately, that wasn't necessary.

The more I moved, the more she moaned, grasping the sheets in her fingers. Her spread thighs writhed in an attempt to get some relief and her toes curled. Her pale skin had turned red and glistened with sweat, as did her forehead and the hair at the nape of her neck. I hoped she would come soon because the smell of her arousal was starting to bother me.

At that point, the blond came for a second time in ten minutes, and after three more strokes, I came as well, filling the condom with my hot seed. Sex for me was like playing a game of cards with nothing at stake.

I clambered off the girl's now-inert body and tossed the condom into the trash. She stayed prone on the bed, and if I hadn't seen her back rising and falling, I would have thought she'd collapsed. Her eyes were hooded, her mouth hanging half-open, and her hair was disheveled, but I could only imagine the kind of state I was in. I stank of sex, and both our noses wrinkled in irritation.

"The stories are true. You do fuck like an animal," she whispered, giving me a satisfied look in the dim half-light of the room. I was still nude, my head spinning from the orgasm, but I felt nothing inside.

"Get out," I answered shortly, and she turned to look at me incredulously.

Her body was completely exposed now, and I could get a good look at her. She didn't have anything the others' didn't: she was blond and hot. And when she looked at me, she saw a normal, good-looking guy who was great in bed, and she never suspected the deviant monster-victim that I concealed within.

The girl left without bothering me any further, and I took a long shower to scrub her tongue, her smell, and her sweat from my skin. I didn't get out of the shower stall until the smell of bath gel was so strong that it had imprinted itself upon my nostrils.

I wrapped a towel around my waist and brushed my teeth, scrubbing until my gums were bleeding again. Then I rinsed the toothpaste and spit into the sink, making note of how the white foam mingled with the smears of blood.

I wiped my lips with the towel and turned off the faucet, staring at my reflection in the mirror. I frowned when I noticed a purple mark on my neck and a few more on my chest. My lips were red and swollen. I ran my tongue over my upper teeth and tasted the fresh mint that permeated my palate. Then I put my hands on the marble countertop and stared at my eyes with their strange yellow-gold color, streaks of bronze visible only in the reflected light.

Was it my unusual eyes that had attracted the attention of that evil woman? I scoffed at myself with a fixed smile and thought about how truly different sex with Selene had been.

I had been captivated by her.

I kept on taking my blonds to bed, but the only person I really wanted was the redhead with the ocean eyes.

My Neverland.

My fairy.

My tigress.

My Goody-Two-shoes…

"Tink…" I whispered, giving voice to my thoughts. I just wanted to use her again, because when I did, I wasn't thinking about Kimberly for the first time in a long time. I could feel something closer to human, less different from everyone around me.

The next moment, something appeared in my reflection that snapped my single thread of reason. It was him again, the child. I sighed and prepared myself for what he had to say.

"You like her…" murmured the Peter Pan who lived inside me, holding tight to my memories.

The attraction I felt toward my beautiful tigress was palpable, a visceral want that had me imagining her naked underneath, though I was well aware that I'd never be able to give her anything other than sex.

"We can't have her, and you know it too," I told the Boy in the mirror, who fixed me with an insolent stare and an unpredictable smirk. "There's no Neverland for us. There's nothing but reality," I added impatiently. Both of us longed to escape, but we were trapped together in my soul.

"There's nothing but blond women who remind us that we're not victims anymore, you got me?" I told him, tired of fighting with myself.

For a second—a fraction of a second—I thought about how much I missed talking to Dr. Lively. He was the only person capable of listening to both me and what lived inside me. I ducked my head, ending my internal monologue, and spotted my iPhone lying right next to my hand. I saw the tiny circle of the front camera and immediately snatched it up and turned it face down. I sighed in relief but too soon: now the back camera was pointing up at me. I was motionless as I stared at it, getting lost in the darkness of that tiny lens that wanted to draw me in, confound my subconscious and take me far away from this reality.

And thus the memories began...

"Smile, Neil." Kim aimed the lens at me. She had rummaged through my father's stuff and found an old Argus C3 camera that she'd been turning over in her hands for several minutes.

"I said smile," she ordered, irritated because I never listened to her. I hated it when she gave me orders, and she never tolerated my attempts at disobedience.

I was sitting on the Persian carpet in the living room drawing, and I gave her a serious look. With an angry motion, she launched the camera at me and I flinched. She regularly had angry outbursts that she couldn't seem to control, and I always tried to hide how much she scared me then.

"You are such a spoiled, stubborn kid." She sat down huffily on the couch, spreading her legs wide. She was wearing a tight shirt and an extremely short skirt. Short enough that I could see her white panties underneath it.

She caught me looking between her thighs and grinned. I'd never been a particularly brazen kid, but Kim was teaching me to become one.

"What're you looking at?" she asked, as I hastily went back to my drawing.

"Nothing," I answered, refusing to turn back in her direction.

"Little perv," she chuckled, blowing a big bubble with her chewing gum.

I began to experience all the usual awful sensations: anxiety, trembling hands, heart racing in my chest. I shifted uncomfortably in my shorts. At the time, I couldn't tolerate wearing my underwear. Kim's attentions had irritated my groin and caused redness on my genitals, but I'd never told my mother about it.

I was too ashamed.

"Do you want to play?" she asked then, amused. That was what she always proposed. Kim loved to play; I didn't.

I didn't like the games she played. I didn't like the things she did to me. I didn't like the way she looked at me or touched me.

I shook my head slowly and continued drawing. I was trying to draw a vase, but I couldn't concentrate.

"Cat got your tongue? Come on—answer me," she urged impatiently. She got up from the sofa and came toward me. The floor seemed to vibrate with every step she took, and my heart sank as the familiar fear twisted through my body. I wasn't brave enough to look up at her. Instead, I stared at her white ankle socks and the flat black shoes that matched the rest of her outfit.

"What do you want to do instead? Watch that stupid cartoon again? The Peter Pan one?"

Suddenly, I no longer saw anything at all. I just heard her voice, mocking me the way she always did.

"It's my favorite," I answered in a shaky voice.

"For real?" she said in mock surprise. "I don't give a shit."

She knelt down to look me in the face, and only then did I look into her eyes.

They were gray. Cold. Cruel. Dangerous.

"I don't want to play with you." I continued to be stubborn even though I always knew how it would end.

Kim was going to win. She always won.

"I've got a lot of things in mind. I need to get you ready." She reached out and pushed a curl off my forehead. Then she smiled as she stared fixedly at my lips.

"Get ready for what?" I managed to ask, trying to ignore how my soul splintered every time she touched me.

"When you're ready, I'm going to introduce you to some people. They'll be your new friends," she continued, petting my hair, and I smacked her hand away from me. Kim frowned and gave me a severe look.

"I don't want any new friends, and I don't want you, either!" I yelled. Then I scrambled to my feet, wiping away a tear. I hadn't even realized I was crying, and I knew that I wasn't supposed to. My father would have been mad at me. He said crying was for sissies.

"Pick up the camera. I'm going to teach you something new today," she said, gesturing at the old Argus lying on carpet. But, once again, I disobeyed. I kicked the camera away from me, cracking the lens. I didn't care; I was used to challenging Kim.

She tried to bend me to her will, and I fought with everything I had not to give in to her.

"You little shit." She took me by the wrist and bent down to look into my eyes. I got a whiff of her vanilla perfume and turned up my nose at it because I couldn't stand it. I couldn't stand having it on me, on my skin, inside me. That smell had invaded me; it had insinuated itself into every part of me without my permission, and I was disgusted by it.

"Should I go play with Logan instead?" She grinned smugly, because she knew she had me in her clutches.

She always used the same tactic in the end: blackmail. She knew that I would never allow her to touch my brother, that I would give in to her instead.

I did what I had to do to protect Logan.

"So pick up that camera and go wait for me in your parents' bedroom. We're going to play a new game." She released my wrist and looked at me expectantly, waiting for me to follow her orders.

"In Mom and Dad's room?" I repeated incredulously.

"In Mom and Dad's room," she confirmed.

When I was little, I never worried about monsters under the bed or in the closet. I never believed stories about aliens coming through a kid's *window in the middle of the night to abduct them. One thing that had scared me, though, were tales of child-eating witches. And Kim was a real life child-eater.*

She fed on their innocence, ended their childhoods, annihilated their lives, and destroyed their dreams.

And, every time, I tried to fly away. Far away from Kim.

But she always reached out and caught me.

She ate the child in me; she devoured his purity, and there was nothing I could do to stop her.

I picked up my phone and walked out of the bathroom to toss it on the bed. I wrinkled my nose at the smell of sex that hung around the room. I'd forgotten to open the window and gather up the sheets for Anna to wash. I did both hurriedly with just my towel on.

Then I got dressed, putting back on the same clothes I'd stripped off a couple hours earlier. I rolled up the sleeves of my white sweater. It smelled clean, like the rest of my body, and it made me feel a bit calmer.

It was about eleven p.m. by then. After spending the afternoon in the library with Logan and Selene, I'd gone out with the Krew to distract myself and have a drink. About an hour later, I'd ended up in bed with a blond I'd picked up at Blanco. Or rather, she offered herself to me on a silver platter, and I took her up on it.

Exhausted, I sat down on the edge of the bed and put on my shoes. The air outside was cold, so I also put on my brown leather jacket before I left the pool house. I felt in my pockets for my phone and keys before I shut the door.

As I turned to cross the lawn and go back inside the house, I spotted a figure huddled on a chaise longue next to the pool. A blue blanket was draped over her slim shoulders, and her auburn hair was scraped back into a high ponytail. I recognized her perfect profile and generous mouth immediately. Selene.

How long had she been out there?

I walked toward her, the shape of her gradually solidifying as I approached. She was reading a book by the light of a tiny reading lamp, though I didn't see why she'd be doing that outside in the garden in the bitter autumn air rather than in her warm bed, clad in those awful pajamas with the tigers on them.

"You've chosen a rather strange place to dedicate yourself to your reading." I took out my pack of Winstons and extracted one cigarette with my teeth before fishing my lighter out of my jacket's inside pocket. A mild breeze scuttled my first attempt at lighting the cigarette, so I cupped my hand more tightly around it and turned to protect myself from the wind before trying again. I succeeded in my goal and put everything back in my pocket before taking a seat on the chaise longue in front of Babygirl. The dark sky, devoid of clouds, stretched over us like a starry blanket. A view I would have happily enjoyed, had I not something more beautiful right there in front of me.

Selene's long eyelashes stayed lowered, protecting those crystalline eyes as they scrolled line by line through her stupid book. She was ignoring me, and I was absolutely not used to it. I inhaled deeply and then pursed my lips to exhale directly into Tinkerbell's beautiful little face. She lifted her ocean eyes to me and coughed, wafting a hand in front of her nose.

"What the hell was that?" she snapped. Finally, I'd caught her attention. Though I didn't understand why she was so surly and irritated.

"I asked you a question," I insisted.

"And I didn't feel like answering. Where I choose to read is none of your business." She turned back to her book, but I immediately knew that something wasn't right. We didn't know each other very well, but I had learned a thing or two about her. I knew how to read the things she wasn't saying in her eyes.

"What did you see?" I asked her bluntly, and I heard Selene's sharp inhalation. Who knew how long she'd been out there; she'd probably caught me fucking that blond. Not that I cared about her reaction—I didn't have to justify myself to her or anyone else. It was just that I knew she wasn't capable of separating sex from emotions, and she couldn't differentiate a physical encounter from a relationship; she perceived the whole situation very differently than I did.

"I don't know what you're talking about."

She was lying. I could tell by the way her hands were trembling.

"How long have you been out here?" I tried again. I didn't even know why I was sitting out there in the cold, chasing the whims of this girl instead of just going into the house and falling blissfully asleep. She sighed and looked at me with those ocean eyes that infected my thoughts every time. And in that moment, I could perfectly recall every time I had touched her, every time I'd kissed her and dominated her body.

The occasions had been few, yes, but each one was so intense, giving me the kind of all-encompassing orgasms that I'd never experienced with anyone else.

"Long enough to realize what an asshole you really are." She finally admitted what had been eating her up this whole time. She'd seen the blond, though I didn't know exactly how much she had witnessed.

"You enjoy spying on me, huh? This is the second time you've done it." I teased, delighting in the blush that painted her high cheekbones. Selene stood up immediately, and she was in such a hurry to escape that she left her closed book on the chaise longue. I knew by now how reactive and even childish she could be, and on one hand, this aspect of her personality irritated me, but on the other hand, it also got me hot.

"Sorry to disappoint, but it actually only happened once, and it was repulsive," she snapped back. All of sudden it was confusing to me, how we'd gone from ignoring each other for weeks to collaborating on solving a puzzle to arguing now about…what?

About nothing.

I grabbed her wrist and dragged her down onto my lap. Selene clutched the thin blanket that had fallen off one shoulder and wrapped it close around her, like she was trying to protect herself from me. I stubbed out my cigarette in the ashtray and put my hand on her hip. The other one traversed her thigh, concealed by black leggings. Soon, my fingers were not far away from her crotch, my palm so large that I almost covered her completely.

"What, exactly, was so repulsive?" I whispered sensually a short distance from her lips. She watched me with wide, wary eyes. She was afraid of me, and I didn't like that at all.

"Seeing you do those things…" she answered vaguely, looking into the crystalline pool water illuminated by underwater lights rather than facing me.

"What things?" I wanted to hear her say something filthy, but I knew Selene would never do that. I rubbed her side in an attempt to get her to relax, because, perched there on my legs, she felt as stiff and taut as a violin string.

I examined her face, that little upturned nose, the dark pink lips pressed together, and long eyelashes that stood out clearly around the crystals she called eyes. It was a beautiful face, and I couldn't stop analyzing it like it was some architectural masterpiece that I wanted to re-create in my notebook.

Suddenly, my mind suggested that I do something very dumb. I lifted my index finger and delicately traced the outline of her profile. Selene gently turned her face toward me, watching and letting me touch her. My index finger continued down her nose, over her lips, along her slim jaw. A little gasp told me she was nervous, and I couldn't tell whether it was from fear or anticipation, but I had known for a long time by then the effect I had on her.

I inched closer and sniffed her. She smelled like coconuts and a clean and that made me want to do other, equally dumb things.

Dumber, even.

I cocked my head and put my lips on her neck. I traced them up and down and up again, letting my tongue make a wet trail across her skin. Her hands clamped down on the blanket and my hands clamped down even harder on her hip and thigh.

"There's no point in covering yourself up when the shivers are under your skin," I whispered into her ear, grasping the lobe between my lips and sucking it, strong and slow. She dropped her hand to my stomach and clutched my sweater between her fingers.

"I can't give you what you want. But you can use me and take what I have to offer..." I grabbed her hand and pulled it lower, right where I wanted it. "And it's not my heart, Selene." I underscored the point by pressing her hand into my crotch. I wanted her to understand and stop spinning up these nonexistent fantasies. Love was for the delusional; this right here was for the disillusioned. Like me.

"I'm not blond," she murmured. I expected her to snatch her hand away at that point and run screaming. Maybe even slap me. But none of that happened.

Instead, she stroked me and my breath caught as I considered her words.

"I'm the only darker-haired girl you want..." she said thoughtfully.

She was the only one I wanted because she was Neverland, a fairy from a story, the door between reality and illusion. She was all of that, and at the same time, nothing at all because she didn't even exist in my world. I wanted to say all of this to her, but I didn't. Instead, I just soaked in the heat of her hand, touching me just the way I'd been wanting for the last two weeks.

To be perfectly honest, I'd only been giving her time to recover after Jennifer's attack. Fortunately, I'd been able to come to her rescue then, but I since wondered many times further Jennifer, in her frenzy, would have gone if I hadn't been there.

"May... May I touch you?" She had stopped rubbing me between my thighs, and I had to shut my eyes as I nestled into the crook of her neck, only then registering how ridiculously close we were to one another.

She was me asking for permission to touch me? Where? And more importantly, *why*?

She had probably realized a long time ago how weird I was in that way. She had noticed that I hated to be touched without my consent and that was why she was now asking my permission.

I didn't say anything but nodded. Selene lifted her index finger and touched my forehead, which wrinkled as I frowned, realizing what she had in mind. Her finger stroked down my straight nose and she smiled.

She was echoing my gesture from before.

The tip of her finger was cold on my skin, but I didn't object to her touch, which was soft and delicate.

"You have a perfect face," she whispered, staring at my lips before moving her finger over them as well. She traced the shape of my mouth and swallowed. She wanted to kiss me; I could tell by the way her pupils dilated, shrinking the circle of ocean blue around them. She drew her finger farther down to my chin and stroked the scruff on my jaw, continuing along to my throat.

The fabric of my sweater kept her touch from reaching my collarbone, yet it still felt as though I could sense her presence on my skin. Then, her palm flattened on the left side of my chest, right over my heart.

"Pounding. I can feel you, you know? Pounding so hard," she murmured, as though she were actually speaking directly to the muscle inside my chest. And in that brief moment, I felt like I actually understood what it meant to be human, but it was such a fleeting feeling that I immediately snapped back to who I really was.

"It's called *arousal*." I moved into the crook of her neck again and pressed a small kiss there, breathing in her good smell. "Tachycardia is just a symptom of physical arousal. You look at things from the wrong angles, Tinkerbell, and it's no good." Destroying her illusion, I felt her legs shift as she moved to stand up, but I held her down on top of me. She was going to stay there until I decided she could go. "It pounds for a lot of women, you know? And not because I love them," I added in a soft voice, and Selene tried again to wriggle away, but I still didn't let her.

"Stop it," she pleaded, squeezing her eyes shut. She shouldn't have done that. She needed to look at me and listen to me and understand me.

"It was pounding for the blond from before, the one you saw coming out of the pool house," I continued, not because I wanted to hurt her, but because I wanted her to see things the way I saw them.

"I said stop it!" she said, raising her voice and glaring at me. She tried with one hand to push me away, but I knew it was in vain. She was too small and delicate to fight someone like me.

"You should tell your boyfriend everything and start over fresh with a person you can actually fall in love with. And not because he knows how to fuck you or because you find his problems fascinating, but because he's a serious man with whom you can build a future," I said, making it all clear to her. All the things I couldn't give her and all the hopes she should never, ever project onto me.

I was older than her; maybe I could give her some good advice and help her figure out how to separate attraction from that illusory feeling called love, but nothing more than that. "Or…" I whispered, offering an insane alternative. "You could stay right here and explore this attraction we share, purely as a physical desire that needs to be satisfied, until one or both of us gets tired of this shit." We looked at each other. Both of us knew that was the stupidest possible thing to do, and I fully expected her to reject me, to agree that she should turn her attention to someone else, someone less troubled, someone who could get closer to her ideal man.

Not to mention that we could be found out at any time. I, in particular, ran the risk of losing Matt's trust forever, all to indulge my sexual fantasies with his daughter.

"Or you could talk to me more often, like you're doing right now, without me needing to ask you," Selene retorted, surprising me. She knew how to shut me up, and she didn't even need to get my pants down to do it. I shook my head in shock. I was talking to her, and what's more, I was the one who'd started it.

I was reminded of her stupid compromise. Selene wanted to learn something about me every time I demanded something from her. I realized that I needed to be cunning and anticipate her next moves. So I leaned forward to kiss her and keep her from starting in with the fucking questions again. But she spotted what I was doing right away.

"Nope." She pulled back to prevent me from reaching her lips, which then curved into an insolent smile. "If you want a kiss, you have tell me something about yourself." She recited her damned condition, and I sighed in defeat.

"My favorite color is blue," I said, which was the first bullshit that came to mind as I stared into her beautiful eyes. Then, I tried again to steal a kiss from her, but she pressed one hand to my chest, clasping her blanket around her with the other.

"I want more," she insisted.

What could she possibly want to know about me? I didn't talk about myself with anyone. I didn't talk like that to women.

Ever.

And I couldn't understand why she wanted to do it or what she hoped to achieve. I'd already fulfilled a few of her fantasies about being with a man, what else did she want from me? I glanced around and noticed the cigarette butt stubbed out in the plastic ashtray beside me.

"I started smoking when I was twelve," I said. It was banal but just as true as my previous fact, and her forehead creased thoughtfully.

"Do you smoke... Are cigarettes all you smoke?" she asked hesitantly, as though afraid of how I might react. She was trying to figure out if I used drugs, that much was clear, but she was far too polite to ask me outright.

"Cigarettes are my only addiction, so no, I don't do drugs."

Because I can't. But I didn't tell her that, because then I would have had to explain how both drugs and alcohol altered my psychological state and made me dangerous. Or maybe I would have even blurted out a confession about the heavy medications I used to take and how combining them with illegal drugs could have killed me.

"You're wrong. You have at least one other addiction," she said. "The blonds," she clarified, smiling at me in amusement. I sighed and gave her a serious look until her smile faded. She had no idea what kind of shit hid behind that seemingly simple statement, nor the pain I carried with me.

"My real addiction is sex...with the blonds," I corrected her, and her expression darkened before she shook her head to banish whatever she was thinking about.

"I'm not blond and yet—"

I cut her off before she could finish. "It's been so long since I fucked you; you were clearly just an outlier," I told her with a certainty that I knew would prick her feminine pride. Truthfully, we had only spent a little time together, but I felt like I'd known her for years. And that was strange.

"After that last time, you..." Selene cleared her throat and turned red, clearly thinking about what had happened in her room. And in her bathroom. "You didn't seek me out again. Why?"

If she had been any other woman, I would have thought it was a come-on, but Selene seemed genuinely curious and even a little afraid of the answer I would give her.

"Maybe I stopped wanting you?" I offered, smiling my sleaziest smile. Babygirl sucked in a breath and pursed her lips. I hoped she wasn't about to start crying; instead she just took a deep breath and leaned closer to my ear, hitting me with her hot exhalation.

"Or maybe you want me so much that you have to stay away from me? I think you didn't want to jump my bones because you didn't want to see the bruises your whore left on me," she said, sounding unlike herself. The word "whore" took on a lewd new appeal when it rolled off her innocent lips.

I grasped her side more tightly as my other hand crept closer to her crotch. I didn't want to think about what Jennifer had done to her, or I would end up showing her the side of myself that I hated. Instead, I preferred to focus on what we'd gotten up to in her room.

"Would you like to be my whore?" I taunted her, just a short distance from her lush mouth, which I needed to taste. We were doing way too much talking and not enough acting for my tastes.

"At least with me you wouldn't have to worry about catching a disease," she answered shortly.

"But you'd be too much of an innocent to go along with all my twisted requests," I replied and it was true. I would never have shared Babygirl with the Krew. I would never have let her do any of the things I usually did with women—Jennifer and Alexia in particular—and the other assholes I hung out with.

"Like?" She was blushing even as she showed me all the typical inquisitiveness of an inexperienced girl trying to hide her embarrassment by pretending to be more worldly.

"Like, would you want to share me with another woman? At the same time? In the same bed?" My whisper was like a caress and her eyes went wide before darting away from me. She was uncomfortable, stiff as a block of wood.

She didn't answer me and just glanced at the pool house behind her, obviously considering something.

"And would you want to share me with another man? At the same time? In the same bed?" she said finally, sounding embarrassed, but there was a determination in her eyes that rendered me speechless for a few moments. Sure, I would have enjoyed that, but only with another woman. Not her. A strange feeling in my stomach made me close my lips into a thin line. If Xavier or Luke had heard Selene say something like that, they definitely would have tried to share her.

With or without her consent.

I took her chin roughly and pulled her face closer to mine. Selene gasped and stared fearfully at me while I glared at her.

"Never say that kind of shit in front of the Krew," I ordered her sternly. She stared back at me as though in a trance, and I jostled her chin to bring her back to earth. "Did you hear me? Don't you dare say anything like that in front of Xavier or Luke. Never." I turned red from the rage that filled me at the mere idea of her in bed with either of those two. "If something like that happened, I would end up going straight to jail," I finished shortly, not mincing my words.

The Krew took the things they wanted, ignoring any rules or morals. They didn't care about anyone or anything. Women were just objects to be played with, and Selene had already been on their radar for a while.

She couldn't show herself to be vulnerable or available to them or they would pounce.

I shook my head.

Well, now that I had talked to her, I was going to demand my compensation.

I drew closer to her lips and seized them with my own, and

it wasn't because I was trying to lure her into bed like the girl I'd picked up outside Blanco. It was simply because I wanted to kiss her. That kiss tasted of rich chocolate because she might have had a hot chocolate or enjoyed a sweet while reading. I didn't know and I didn't care; I just wanted her tongue entangled with mine even if, for me, it meant nothing.

Nothing was going to change between us.

Then I looked into her eyes and realized how much I hated doing this. It was the same thing every time: I saw my own end there, yet I couldn't stay away. I always felt so vulnerable and incapable of controlling myself when I got too close to her.

In that moment, the stars scattered across the dark sky seemed to lose their brilliance, overshadowed by the pale, lustrous glow of her face. Selene closed her eyes and lifted herself up a bit to straddle me. The blanket started to slip from her shoulders, but I caught it just in time and restored it. She whispered a fleeting "thanks," and then my lips were sealed to hers again. I ran my hands down her back and groped her ass, pulling her into me.

She was sitting too far away, and I wanted her right on top of me, as close as we could get. I ground myself between her thighs as my knees squeezed her sides. I knew she could feel my hard-on, just like I was feeling the arousal that had inflamed all her senses.

"Kiss me and don't stop," I demanded when she pulled away from me to catch her breath. She wasn't used to kissing the way I did: I devoured her lips and fed off her desires. I wondered how she kissed that idiot Jared, since she seemed to be having so much trouble keeping up with me.

I slipped a hand behind her neck and pressed her against me while using the other hand to forcefully grope her ass cheek. She whined something unintelligible, or maybe it was just a moan before closing her eyes, and she slowly gyrated her pelvis against me.

If she was trying to kill me, she was going to succeed.

I grinned against her lips and moved my hand along her flank, imposing a more insistent rhythm on her shy and awkward movements.

Oh, yeah, that was just how I wanted it, right there...

"Get a little closer," I ordered because I wanted to feel her properly. I pressed her against me again until her breasts were plastered to my chest. Her thighs trembled and opened wider to accommodate her new position. The thin fabric of her leggings allowed her to become aroused as she bucked against my hard cock.

The more I kissed her, the more I wanted her. Her taste had merged with my own, to the point of creating an entirely new flavor. My lips pulsed from the nonstop friction, and my muscles tenses with every movement of her tongue because...I wanted to screw her right there.

I didn't care that we were in the garden, in the cold, in an extremely vulnerable location. All Matt had to do was lean out on one of the numerous balconies on the back of the house and he would see us, but I wanted her so intensely that I could no longer see reason.

"Let me in..." I pressed a finger to the cleft of her ass, following it down to her labia below and what was beneath them, which I was sure I'd find wet and gripping, just for me. I moved my other hand to the button on my jeans, but Selene grabbed my wrist and stopped me.

Just then, I felt her quiver and turn stiff before burying her forehead in the crook of my neck. Her breathing had gone shallow and she kept emitting small sobbing moans that she couldn't seem to control. And then I understood: she was about to come.

Shit, just from that?

The idea thrilled me, so I traced the contours of her mouth with my tongue until her lips fell open. Then I moved beneath her so she could feel even more of me. She was so sensitive precisely because she was inexperienced. She wasn't used to all these sensations to which my own body seemed to have become numb. I never could have come from so little stimulation. I was too depraved, too hungry, and my soul was too damaged.

Selene trembled again and hid her face in the space between my neck and shoulder as she began to move her pelvis faster and more uncontrollably, overtaken by the intense pleasure that preceded a climax. She stopped only when her hips ceased shaking from the involuntary shuddering tremors. The idea that a mere passionate kiss had caused her to orgasm brought an easy smile to my face, and I stroked her hair with one hand. I couldn't see her face but I knew her cheeks would be blazing.

"Did you enjoy that frenzied humping?" I asked archly, and she made a noise of frustration and embarrassment. She truly was a delightful Babygirl. She nuzzled the tip of her nose against the curve of my neck, still straddling me.

"Just shut up. Don't say anything else," she pleaded, still keeping me from looking her in the eye.

I burst out laughing at the ridiculousness of the situation. I took pride in the power that I wielded over her, but at the same time, it frightened me. I didn't want her to grow dependent on me, to forget what I told her and to disregard all my warnings.

"We have to get back..." was all I said when I could finally see her luminous eyes, brighter than the stars that peppered the sky as she gazed at me like she were getting drunk on me.

On *me*, for fuck's sake.

We got to our feet, and I adjusted my jeans on my hips. Out of the corner of my eye, I spotted a figure just a short distance from the chaise longue. Anna was staring at us with violently reddened cheeks and the look of someone who had just been caught red-handed in the midst of a crime.

My eyes widened, but I wasn't overly agitated: Anna was far from the worst person who could have surprised us in that moment.

I turned to Selene to let her know that we weren't alone, but from her pallid face, I could tell that she had already noticed.

"Oh, God!" She shielded her eyes and mumbled a series of curses, completely mortified.

As I was the unmoved one between the two of us, I decided to manage the situation and reassure Babygirl. After all, Anna had seen a lot worse from me.

"Don't worry, I'll talk to her. Go on into the house." I pulled her hand away from her face and Selene stared at me like it was weird of me to remain so calm. But I just knew it was pointless to angst about a mistake that had already been made.

"Wh-what?" she stammered, clutching the blue blanket, which, paired with her tennis shoes, made her look so young.

"Go inside," I ordered her again and gave her a gentle slap on the ass. She jumped and gave me a reproachful look, but I didn't care. Either way, she walked awkwardly away toward the French doors that led inside and wished Miss Anna a feeble goodnight.

I sighed and stuck my hands in the pockets of my jeans as Anna cautiously approached me.

She was wearing a long coat and a black purse dangled from one of her hands.

"I've finished up a bit late, and now I'm leaving," she mumbled, looking down at the lawn instead of at me. She was possibly even more embarrassed than Selene, while I just stood there, casually waiting for her to have her say.

"Miss Anna——" I started, but she lifted her chin and gave an indulgent shake of her head.

"I've known you since you were a little boy, Neil. And I've never judged your choices, but Miss Anderson…" Her gaze shifted to the chaise, and she took a deep breath before continuing. "She's not like the others," she finished, telling me something I'd already figured out on my own.

Anna had seen countless girls coming out of my room or the pool house and had surely seen how far removed Selene was from my world and the reality I lived with every day.

"This thing," I spun my index finger in the air, not sure how to even define the situation with Selene, "needs to stay just between us," I ordered, and Anna nodded, though she still seemed concerned.

"Remember Scarlett, Neil."

When I heard that name, I stiffened, suddenly cold.

"Don't make the same mistakes with Selene. Don't toy with her. You have so many women around who would do anything to spend the night with you, but she…" She stopped and clutched her bag more tightly to herself. "She is still very young and believes in love so much."

"I know that. I know it very well," I sighed and ran a hand over my face, licking my lower lip, which was still swollen from my tigress's intense kisses.

Despite Miss Anna's good advice, I still wanted Selene in my bed. Mostly to attend to the enormous erection that she had provoked.

"Then you have two paths before you: either let her go or start off on a new journey with her. I'm sure you'll do the right thing." She stood up on her tiptoes to press a kiss to my cheek, like a mother might do with her child. Then she smiled at me and left, wrapping her coat around herself to protect herself from the cold.

Start off on a new journey with her?

What the fuck…

"How do I know what the right thing is?" I called after her, not caring if anyone else heard me. Anna turned back with another indulgent look.

"If you do what makes you happy, then that will be the right thing to do." She lifted her hand in farewell before turning away and starting to walk again.

I watched her as she moved away, her bright hair rustling in the mild breeze, her stride slow but determined, and I thought about what she had said.

What if the right thing to do for me was the wrong thing for Selene?

27

NEIL

I came to my senses.

As compelling as Miss Anna's words had been, I had realized once again that I was never going to be able to undertake any sort of *journey* with Selene. My issues were far beyond the ordinary emotional problems experienced by regular people who lived their lives while clinging to pointless illusions.

Just then, the dawn of another goddamned day was filtering through my bedroom window where, for more than an hour already, I had been hitting my punching bag with just my black wraps wound around my hands. Working out every morning was a good way to vent some of my anger, especially when the nightmares seized my brain. Boxing kept me from succumbing to the wrong temptations and gave me an outlet for my anxieties—other than sex.

I threw punch after punch, alternating hooks with uppercuts and uppercuts with jabs. I controlled my breathing, bounced in place and then struck again.

Hook, hook, uppercut, jab.

Now, however, another even more dangerous problem had been added to my long list of them: the girl from Detroit. I smiled as I thought about her.

I was a bundle of contradictions: I wanted Selene all to myself, but at the same time, I didn't want her to get attached to me, because I knew I could never give her the things she really deserved. Knowing that made me feel increasingly uncomfortable, so I rolled my shoulders and hit the bag again with a powerful strike, making it swing wildly from side to side.

I shouldn't have let myself get distracted.

Overthinking could have ruined the last ten minutes of my training, but that happened anyway because of my phone. I searched for it, following the sound, and found it on the dresser next to the bed. A bead of sweat rolled down my temple, and I stopped it with the back of my hand before I answered.

"What the fuck do you want?" I spit out breathlessly, hearing a sardonic laugh on the other end of the line. I was tired and sweaty, my black tank top was sticking to me along with my sweatpants. I wanted to take a shower; until I could, my anxiety wasn't going to lessen.

"Good morning to you too, dickhead. Don't tell me you're fucking right now?" Xavier ribbed me, and I sighed.

"What do you want?" I asked again. He snorted, and I heard a female voice near him, a sign that he was probably with Alexia or possibly someone else.

"Hold on, kitten, give me a break. I'm on the phone," he chided the girl, and I rolled my eyes. It wasn't Alexia, then, because she hated being called kitten.

"Spit it out," I ordered impatiently, earning myself a curse from him.

"I heard that Carter Nelson woke up from his coma and that he's planning to turn you in." He dropped the bomb all in one breath, and I went still.

Shit.

By then, I had completely forgotten about the kid's existence. I had been hoping I could simply wash my hands of him, but now he was back just to fuck up my day.

"How do you know this?" I scrubbed a hand over my sweaty face and repositioned the phone in my hand.

"Reliable sources have informed me," he answered, vague but confident.

"Fuck," I swore. Now this was a real shitshow. I needed to find some way to stop Carter from bringing up my name, or I would be immediately arrested.

"You got something in mind?" Xavier knew me well.

"I'll see you tonight at Blanco," I answered, telling him nothing.

Then I hung up and got in the shower. I had a short amount of time to come up with a plan I could execute immediately that would resolve the whole sticky situation.

⸻

I didn't go home after my classes to avoid running into Babygirl or making my brother suspicious. Instead, I went straight to Blanco.

The LED sign illuminated the packed parking lot adjacent to the club. As usual, the place was full, packed with men and women of all ages, intent on entertaining themselves in the worst possible ways.

I stepped out of my Maserati and leaned on the hood, lighting a cigarette. My leather jacket pulled against my biceps with every movement, and my imposing presence attracted a number of stares, especially from women.

One girl in particular, wearing a short, slutty dress, stared at me insistently, making it very clear to me that she wouldn't mind at all if I were to plow her in any corner of the lot. A glance at her hair— the color of wheat—made me momentarily consider wasting half an hour with her. My body, however, seemed numb to the concept and didn't give me any arousal signals. My heart did not pound the way it had the night before.

I inhaled the smoke and looked away from the blond to the entrance where two women were walking right toward me.

Alexia swung her hips, propped up on a pair of tall leather boots that enhanced her soft curves. She had small breasts but her ass was first-rate. Jennifer, in her braids, had a more hard-edged and provocative style. She had a shapely body, and her plump lips could work magic when they were wrapped around my cock. Though, after what had gone down with Selene, I had stopped paying any attention to her.

"Where are the others?" I asked immediately, without saying hello and addressing myself only to Alexia.

"Inside," she answered with a shrug. She reached out to me with her fingers in a V shape, wordlessly requesting that I pass her the cigarette. After one final drag, I obliged her.

"Thanks, boss." She grinned, bringing it to her lips. Jennifer, by contrast, watched our interaction with rage because she hated being ignored.

"You're the one who talked to Paul and told him not to let me set foot in his place again, aren't you?" she started in, already furious, her voice low and menacing.

Paul was the owner of Blanco as well as the only person who really mattered in the local cocaine trade. I was, in fact, the person who asked him to cut Jennifer off, because she needed to pay for what she'd done to Selene.

"I haven't been able to score in two weeks because of you." She thrust a finger at me, but I just continued to lean against the car, my arms folded and my posture unruffled.

"Chill out, Jen." Alexia tossed the cigarette butt to the ground and drew close to Jennifer before she could go off on a psychotic rant.

"Chill out? He's been acting like a total asshole ever since I laid a finger on his little brat." She moved toward me, and I darted forward like I was spring-loaded.

"You don't talk about her," I threatened. And then Luke arrived, grabbing my arm as he did so.

"What the fuck is your problem?" he asked in confusion as Xavier walked toward us without a care in the world, a sinister grin on his face.

He zipped up his pants as he glanced between me and Jennifer. "You two wanna knock it off? I can't even take a piss without finding you out here fighting," he grumbled with a dismissive wave of his hand. But Jennifer ignored him and went right back on the attack.

"You fucked her raw! She must be really good at spreading those legs because she's literally fucked your brains out!" The bitch kept shouting as Alexia got between us, trying to push her away from me.

"Better than you, that's for sure," I lied, giving her a wink. Selene wasn't more skilled than Jennifer—she couldn't have been, considering her inexperience. But the sex I had with her was indeed better than what I had with Alexia or Jennifer.

"Did you fuck her bare? Seriously?" Xavier cut in, but I had no intention of telling that story or of confessing that Selene was as pure as any princess from a fairy tale.

"Enough! Let it go!" Luke came to my defense. I backed away as he continued to hold me with one arm.

I scrubbed a hand over my face and walked away to try to regain some control over myself. I could hear Jennifer cursing me, yelling and shouting all kinds of nastiness, but I didn't care.

I didn't give a damn about her.

I went back to my car and signaled Xavier and Luke. "Get over here, guys. Stop wasting time with that bitch," I said bluntly. It was sufficient enough to shut Jennifer up and make her realize that I was no longer in the mood to fuck around. Alexia whispered something into her ear and she sighed, saying nothing.

Good. If she hadn't shut up, I would have shut her mouth for her in the least pleasant way possible. Once the blond was dealt with, I looked to Xavier and Luke, who were both frowning at me.

"I need you. There's somewhere we have to go," I informed them decisively. They exchanged blank looks with one another before turning back to me.

"Where?" Luke asked, skeptical.

"Is this about fucking shit up?" Xavier interjected with considerably more enthusiasm.

"It's about one of our fuckups, yeah," I answered, and we understood one another without exchanging another word.

"Fuck yeah! I'm in!" Xavier exclaimed, pulling out his car keys. Luke, by contrast, took a deep breath before murmuring "okay." But he didn't sound convinced.

"Do you have a problem with that?" I asked him bluntly, making him flinch. He narrowed his eyes at me and jerked a thumb back toward the entrance to the club.

"I was on track to fuck a crazy-hot redhead in the bathroom in there, but now I need to postpone it because of you," he answered, irritated.

Was that really why he wasn't thrilled to be coming with us? I cocked an eyebrow and leaned in to within an inch of his nose.

"There will be other fucks. Now focus, because I won't tolerate any kind of distraction." I gave him two light slaps on the cheek to emphasize my point, and he just clenched his jaw without saying anything.

"Let's go," I said. I looked to Alexia and informed her that she was coming with me. Xavier and Luke would have to follow us in Xavier's car.

"I'm coming, too," Jennifer interrupted in a defiant tone before I could turn away.

"No, you're not. You're staying here," I ordered without the slightest hesitation.

"Do I need to remind you that I'm a member of the Krew also?" she argued, moving toward me until my fierce expression made her halt.

"Whether you like it or not, I make the decisions here, and you are *not* coming. End of story. Don't fuck with me," I reiterated in a grave tone.

When she fell silent, I turned and walked toward my car with Alexia.

"Where exactly are we going?" she asked, briefly glancing at me once she'd settled into the passenger seat.

"To The Royal," I answered without looking back at her. I quickly checked my text messages before starting the engine.

"Are you shitting me?" She looked at me with her little doll face and fluttered her fake eyelashes a few times in disbelief.

"Do I look like I'm shitting you?" I cracked a cheeky grin, and with no further conversation, drove her to the club I'd indicated.

The Royal was Nelson and his friends' hangout. Earlier in the afternoon, I heard from some other people about a party that was to take place there that evening and that Nelson's whole group planned to show up.

When we pulled up in front of the club, I immediately took note of the line at the entrance. I had been informed, however, that the real party would take place in the parking lot behind the venue and not inside.

"I can already feel the blood on my hands," Xavier commented as we gathered in front of the cordoned-off entrance that prevented access to the enormous parking lot. The open space was filled with people, tall outdoor heaters were placed around at intervals, and the bass of the music was amplified by a pair of subwoofers connected to the DJ's mixing table. People were getting wild to the sound of it, swinging around plastic cups full of booze as well as other stuff. There were half-naked girls all over and parked race cars, lovingly displayed by their owners in advance of the race that was to take place after midnight.

"Don't do anything until the time is right," I ordered the three people flanking me.

Notes of Malaa's "Notorious" accompanied our determined strides, hunting for the prey that had brought us here. Luke, Alexia, and I were focused on the objective, while Xavier stared at the girls asses as they waggled in front of us and winked at a few of them who seemed to be returning his interest.

"Knock it off. You're not here to pick up girls," I snapped irritably at him. He rolled his eyes but immediately took on a more cautious attitude like the rest of us.

We moved through the crowd, the loud music booming from the speakers keeping us from communicating with one another, except in meaningful glances as we searched for Nelson's clique. I looked around just then, and from the alarmed looks on the faces around us, I realized that our presence had been noted.

One guy in particular seemed fixated on the red X that stood out starkly in the middle of my sweater, matching the leather jacket stretching over my shoulders. The guy whispered something to his friend, who turned to stare at us. Both of them looked at first surprised and then afraid.

I smiled slightly and kept moving. It was written on our faces what we were: we were an offense to public decency; devils who would happily roast anyone who dared to provoke us.

"There they are." Xavier put a hand on my shoulder to turn my attention toward three guys. They were leaned up against one of the race cars. One of them was about to fuck a girl over the hood while the other two drank beers and chatted. When they spotted us stopped short just a little ways away from them, they quit laughing and looked at us suspiciously, suddenly at attention.

I could smell it immediately, their fear and my victory: Carter wasn't going to turn me in, because I knew exactly how to stop him.

"Who the fuck are you?" one of the punks demanded. He had

gauges in both earlobes, and there were tattoos clearly visible on both sides of his neck. I didn't respond and resumed my approach, followed by the others.

I leaned casually against the car next to theirs, having no idea whose it was. Then I took out my pack of Winstons and pulled out a cigarette, bringing it to my lips before I lit it.

The guy jerked the girl off the hood of the car before wiping his glistening lips with the back of his hand and glaring at me. My eyes roamed over the piercings that jutted out from both of his eyebrows as well as his left nostril. I showed not the slightest interest in his infuriated expression.

"Hey, dickhead! That's my car," he snarled at me as my gaze moved on to the DJ's speakers, which were pumping out another Malaa song, "Prophecy." I often listened to that one in the car or when I was working out at home.

"I'm talking to you!" The guy tried to draw my attention back to him, but I continued to smoke with calculated indifference.

"Which one of you is in charge?" was my opener, but only after I'd made them wait for a while. I blew smoke out into the air and awaited their response, staring into the guy's black eyes.

"Until Carter comes back, I am," the tattooed one answered proudly.

"And your name is?" I asked, pretending like I cared.

"You're the one who needs to tell me your name, asshole! You're in my territory, and you're smoking on my car!" he informed me, grinding his teeth.

Calm down, kiddo.

"Neil," I said in a placid tone, and he tilted his head to one side. His friends all frowned and exchanged worried looks with one another.

"Miller?" the leader finished.

"Exactly. How perceptive of you." I taunted him while Xavier and Luke stood ready beside me, like two attack dogs waiting for my signal.

"You're the one who put Carter in the hospital," he hissed under his breath.

"Bravo, so you're a smart guy as well," I said derisively, taking another drag off my cigarette.

"Wh-what do you want?" he stammered, his attitude shifting. He was wary now.

"To talk." And suddenly, I thought about Babygirl and our compromise. In that moment, I might have agreed with her on the importance of conversation, but I still preferred to do it on my terms. All I was really good for was fucking things up.

"About what? And get off my car!" he shouted, probably to disguise how afraid he was, but I didn't listen either way. I finished my cigarette and ground it out right on the hood of his beloved car. I folded my arms over my chest and just kept staring at him, focusing on the hardware that he had definitely got because he thought it made him look badass.

"Why are you staring at my piercings?" he continued. "I got another one right here, if you're so interested. Wanna see?" he sneered, grabbing his crotch.

The shameless gesture made the two idiots he was with laugh. Meanwhile, I was approaching the end of my patience. Xavier and Luke both gave me worried looks—they knew exactly what happened whenever someone stepped to me.

I stretched my arms out to the sides and got up off the car, moving determinedly toward the group of guys who all backed away, confused by my sudden movements. It was in moments like this that my reason fled, abandoning me to the madness, and I made the choice to let my demons take the lead.

I snatched a beer bottle from one of the leader's friends and chucked it against a nearby wall, making all three of them flinch.

"Hey! What the hell is wrong with you?" the leader shouted again, hurling himself at me. But I never let him touch me, dodging out of his way with a small twist of my torso. I pulled back my arm and punched him full in the face. The boy stumbled and then hit the ground; his hands jumped to the injured area, which had started to bleed.

"Do you know what that was?" I moved closer to him, circling him as I soaked in his fear, which I could feel now, strong and clear. "A *jab*," I continued. "In boxing, that's a straight punch that can KO your opponent in half a second," I explained with a devilish smile.

I leaned down and grabbed him by the arm, then yanked him to his feet, pinning his wrists behind his back.

"What the fuck are you doing? You some kind of psycho—" He didn't get to finish because I jerked him closer to me, getting right up next to his ear.

"Just sit tight, Wes," I whispered menacingly.

The kid went white, realizing that I had known who he was from the beginning and that I had only ever been toying with him.

"Alexia." I motioned for her to approach, and she did so, swinging her hips in that tight miniskirt that I would consider pushing up later on.

"Undo his jeans and pull down his boxers. Our friend here has a piercing he'd like to show us." I grinned as she reached out for the guy's jeans. He kicked like a pussy while I easily held him in place.

"What are you doing? Let me go! You really are as crazy as people say!" he sneered at me again, and I tightened my grip on his wrists, actually hurting him.

"Really? And who says that, Wes?" I jerked my chin toward Alexia who immediately tugged down his jeans and then his boxers.

"Huh... Kinda small," she said with an exaggerated grimace of disappointment. Xavier and Luke burst out laughing in unison, while Wes's friends just watched the scene, gobsmacked. They didn't try anything, because they realized that none of us was playing around.

"Yank out his piercing," I ordered and a ghastly silence fell all around us. All I could hear was the music and the distant shouts from the throng of dancers. Alexia gave me a concerned look from under her false eyelashes but my mind was made up.

"Get on with it!" I demanded again, and Wes started crying like a baby. He shook in my arms and immediately stopped even trying to resist what Alexia was about to do with him. His friends tried to rush me then, but Xavier and Luke shoved them violently to their knees.

"Try to move and we'll bash your face in." Xavier whispered to one of them, who immediately paled and didn't move another muscle. We were stronger, more dangerous, and much bigger bastards than them, and finally, they understood that, too.

"You sure about this?" Alexia asked, looking into my eyes. She didn't want to obey me, that much was clear. I was going overboard, and even the Krew knew it, but I didn't care if I hurt people, just like no one had cared about me when I was the victim in the situation. Still, I tried for a moment to consider the possible consequences of my actions. As I did so, my right hand began to shake and my heartbeat throbbed in my temples.

"I can feel you, you know? Pounding so hard."

I could hear Selene's voice echoing around in my head. I could see her ocean eyes, scrutinizing my chest in search of the heart I didn't have because it had long ago sunk into the abyss.

What would she think if she could see me now? Would she have been disgusted? Afraid? Would she pity me?

Suddenly, I wasn't sure about what I'd told Alexia to do. I wasn't sure about anything, actually. I remained motionless for a few seconds, frozen in thought, until my arms decided, seemingly by themselves, to release the guy. He fell to the ground, naked from the waist down.

Alexia instinctively took a step back and gave me a relieved look, as if to let me know that I had done the right thing. But even though I had spared Wes, I wasn't sure whether or not to feel good about it.

"Hand over your phones. Now," I demanded. I knew that Carter got up to all sorts of shit and his friends loved to record it. I knew I'd find something worth blackmailing him over in there.

Terrified, the two other guys gave their phones to Xavier and Luke. I crouched down and felt the pockets of Wes's jeans while he was still on the ground, staring off into space.

I avoiding glancing at his naked body and took the thing I was interested in, rising back up to my feet.

"Get dressed. Your little cock hanging out in plain sight is making me nauseous." I slipped his phone into the inside pocket of my jacket and looked down at him from on high, noting as he eyes dropped in shame.

Wes didn't have anything to say now. He'd quit acting like the leader. Now, he was just a guy who had encountered a bigger monster than himself.

Once I had what I needed, I turned my back on all of them and headed for home, alone.

....

The day after our assault on The Royal, I headed over to Xavier's tattoo parlor. For two years he'd managed to own and operate it by himself. Xavier was the oldest of all of us, despite his frequent immaturity and tendency to act without thinking things through.

"Easy, man," Luke huffed. He lay stomach-down on the table, his jeans pulled up over his calf, which was at Xavier's mercy as he concentrated on giving him a tattoo.

"Stop whining like a bitch!" Xavier scolded him, irritated.

I'd snuck into the shop without announcing myself, like I always did, and neither of them had noticed my presence. Then, I pulled back the black curtain that divided me from them and made my entrance.

"You know I saw you come in, right?" Xavier grumbled, continuing to jab Luke's skin. Luke had surrendered by that point, resting his forehead on his flexed forearms.

"And I smelled your body wash," Luke added before lifting his face and wrinkling his nose. "How much of that shit do you use?"

"It's true, you do smell like a high-priced prostitute," Xavier sneered, pausing for a moment to look at me. He was wearing black gloves and held the tattoo gun in one hand.

I gave them both a hard look, not particularly entertained by their musings. No one knew why I was such a freak about hygiene or why I had an obsessive compulsion to shower, least of all these two, who immediately realized I wasn't in the mood to deal with their bullshit. Appropriately, Xavier went back to his work, and Luke went back to enduring the pain.

I moved closer to them and sat down on a stool, bending one knee. I looked around, bored, as Luke continued to mumble complaints at Xavier. I examined the dark walls, splattered with red paint; the sterilization tools; and needles of various types and sizes—shaders, round, flat, and otherwise. I concentrated on the sound of the gun as the needle repeatedly pierced Luke's reddened skin.

It was his second tattoo, and he'd chosen a thorny skull.

"It barely hurts on the calf; I don't know what you're crying about," Xavier said, continuing to follow along the lines of the design he'd stenciled on.

When I got the toki on my bicep at sixteen, I didn't feel much pain. Probably because I was so excited about getting my first tattoo that I didn't even notice. The pain I experienced when I got the pikorua on my left flank, however, I remembered vividly. It had felt like the needle was sticking all the way into my bones.

"You need to send me all the material you get off Carter's friends," I told them.

"You know that everyone is going to know what we did, right? They all recognized us at that party," Luke cut in, gritting his teeth while Xavier continued to labor over his calf.

"So what? They also know we're the Krew," a female voice responded. A second later, Alexia shoved aside the black curtain and advanced on us. She was wearing another short leather skirt and teetering atop a pair of knee-high boots. Xavier shot her a quick look then immediately returned to concentrating.

"Hey, Neil," she greeted me with a wicked smile. I looked her up and down, admiring her body and paying special attention to her ass, which was the part of her I liked best.

"What are you doing here?" I asked, meeting her eyes again.

"Lynn has a fever. I'm filling in to help out with client appointments."

Lynn was a friend of Xavier's, one of the rare girls he didn't sleep with because she was anything but the easy type. And also because she was a bit butch and would punch anyone who dared to touch her without her consent.

Alexia approached her pseudo-boyfriend and folded her arms over her chest, watching him admiringly as he continued Luke's tattoo. Xavier hated to talk while he worked, and he could get really focused when he wasn't high. Honestly, when he was sober, he was a pretty calm person.

"Why are you over here? You should be waiting for calls," he scolded her. He treated Alexia like a friend and like a sex partner, but never like a woman he actually wanted.

I had no room to judge since I regularly did much worse, but Alexia had obviously been in love with him for years. We all knew it. We all could see it, except for him, apparently.

"I like to watch you work," she admitted, sounding sickeningly sweet. I was surprised by her tone; she wasn't usually like that.

"And I don't like you hovering around," he snapped back.

They had a strange relationship.

They'd been sleeping together for years, but ever since Alexia had started fucking me as well, something had changed with Xavier. She'd chosen to be with me. Usually neither he nor I cared about sharing a woman, but ever since then, Xavier seemed to be nursing a strange grudge against me.

I was still hoping I was wrong about that.

"You're a dick. As usual. I have no idea why I'm here helping you." Alexia stalked off angrily, but Xavier just kept working without batting an eye.

"What's your problem? You need to stop treating her that way." Luke was always trying to restore harmony to our group's sick dynamics. I rarely argued with him, but lately women had become a problem between us.

"It's how she deserves to be treated." Xavier gave me an ambiguous but not remotely friendly look before sighing and continuing with the tattoo. Immediately, I felt a distinct tension in the air, a feeling that Luke only confirmed when he cleared his throat to very obviously draw our attention elsewhere.

He started talking about Carter and his friends and what we'd done, but I knew he was just trying to avoid the impending fight between me and Xavier. I could already feel my nerves lighting up. Something wasn't right, and I was likely the problem. I tried to keep my mouth shut—I needed to keep my mouth shut—but...

"What the fuck is going on?" I snapped defensively, because that was how I was feeling. I couldn't pretend that everything was fine. I'd always had the balls to face a situation head-on before, and I wasn't going to turn aside now.

Luke stopped chattering, and Xavier stopped tattooing. They both knew not to lie to me, I hated it when they schemed behind my back.

"Nothing," Luke answered immediately.

"Nothing?" I smiled mockingly, getting up off the stool. "I've known you two long for that. You can't bullshit me." I underscored the message by staring them both in the eyes.

This was how it always happened.

As soon as I got their backs against the wall, they turned into punk kids incapable of fighting back.

"Nothing, man, seriously. Don't stress about it." Xavier gave me a fake smile and returned to his work. Luke, by contrast, sighed and looked worried about my reaction.

I would have liked to probe their elusive behavior more fully, but I decided to let it go for the moment. If I'd really wanted to, I could have made them spill their guts with my fists, but I would rather avoid that if I could.

"Do you get what I'm saying? I don't give a shit what's going on with you, just send me the stuff that I need. After all, that's what I came here for," I told them shortly. I headed toward the curtain to leave but a calendar hanging on the wall caught my attention.

The twenty-fifth of the month was circled thickly in red. I frowned and looked at it. I couldn't say why, but I suddenly felt an uncharacteristic curiosity about that number. Acting on instinct, I lifted up the calendar page and saw the twenty-fifth was also circled on the previous month. In fact, all the months were like that.

"It's the day my mother died," Xavier said, though I hadn't asked him anything. I didn't like sticking my nose in other people's business the same way I didn't allow other people to snoop around in my shit.

"She died on November twenty-fifth, twenty years ago now." He set down his gun and stood, peeling off his gloves. He wasn't finished talking, but I had no interest in hearing his story, despite having heard various rumors about it. Allegedly, he saw his father stab his mother to death. But I was firmly convinced that admitting certain things aloud meant crossing a boundary that couldn't be uncrossed. If Xavier or Luke told me about their lives, then sooner or later they were going to expect me to talk about mine as well.

"Okay, I'm going," I said shortly. "We'll see each other later."

And that was how I left, as insensitive and uninterested as I could possibly be. I had good reasons for behaving like that, though.

Each member of the Krew came from a disastrous background. Each one of us had suffered somehow. Each of us carried a deep hurt inside. Each of us was fighting an unending battle with ourselves. I shared a lot of things with the Krew: my perverted thoughts, my sexual desires, my questionable habits, even my women. But there was something that I would never share with any of them, a part of myself that I guarded jealously: my soul.

28

SELENE

M iss Anna knew.
  Shit.

She had seen us on the chaise longue, lost in our moment of sin. I didn't know how it could have happened.

I could feel my cheeks heating up; I was sure that I was blushing just from recalling Neil's lips on mine, his demanding tongue, his golden eyes staring at me so full of lust and that enigmatic smile that made me lose my mind. I'd felt like I was dying last night when I watched that blond girl come out of the pool house. Fortunately, I hadn't seen what happened inside, though it had been easy enough to intuit.

I was so furious and eaten up with jealousy that I fixated on my book and sat out in the cold to punish myself and prove to myself that Neil was all wrong for me. That I shouldn't hold out hope that he would change and become the perfect man I'd dreamed of having by my side since I was a little girl.

I was there in the garden because I needed to accept reality. But all I needed was to see him again, handsome and brazen as ever with a cigarette pressed between his lips and his mind caught up in his own problems, and I fell right back into his trap.

Neil had been clear with me.

I could not hope for a future with us. In fact, there was no *us*. He was never going to be mine, and yet something inside me still told me that there was hope, even if it was small and fragile.

It might have been because Neil looked at me like he'd never seen a woman before, or maybe because he kissed me like I was the only person in the entire world that he wanted. Either way, I was convinced that there was something holding him back from really feeling human emotions toward me.

He was afraid to show his true self. He was afraid to talk to me and make himself known.

But why? What did he really fear?

I wanted him to bare his soul to me, not just his body. I wanted to know what his hopes were, his dreams and his fears. I wanted to know the kind of music he listened to and what he did in his free time and everything that had happened in his past. I yearned to know who Scarlett was and what those papers in the locked room meant, but he was too locked inside himself.

Plus, we still needed to figure out the identity of this lunatic who was forcing us into a macabre game full of riddles to decipher. Logan had held on to the threatening note but declined my suggestion that we go to the police, which continued to be the only option that made sense to me.

In any event, I could no longer trust anyone. There wasn't a single day that I left the house without first peering around cautiously. I felt like I was being watched and frequently glanced over my shoulder only to see no one behind me. Sometimes, I figured it was just a manifestation of my fear that my brain was projecting into reality. Other times, I was certain that there really was someone trying to follow or keep tabs on me.

"Selene." I jerked when Alyssa put her arm around my shoulders. "Your coffee has been here for ten minutes." We were at our usual spot where all the students went after classes, and she was gesturing at my mug of coffee.

"Yeah, I was just…thinking." I paused and thought about a plausible excuse to give her. "I was thinking about my mom. I need to call her later." I gave her a smile and took hold of my coffee to drink it.

"Did you hear what went down at The Royal last night?" Adam leaned in toward us as if imparting a dire secret. He even glanced around first to make sure no one was listening in.

"No. What happened?" Logan asked, sounding bored.

"Apparently a dude got sexually assaulted, and they found him on the ground with his pants around his ankles," Adam answered in a lowered voice while Logan looked thoughtfully at him.

"Seriously?" Jake interjected, horrified.

"Yeah. There was a party going on, and it seems that the Krew crashed it just to stir shit up. The guy in question was a friend of Carter Nelson," he added, and Logan sat back in his chair, his eyes fixed on a vague point somewhere on the table.

"Are you sure the dude was sexually assaulted?" Cory asked.

"He was beaten up, too. His nose was broken." Adam touched his own nose, ignoring Cory's question.

"The Krew are monsters," Kyle noted, turning his blue eyes on me. He was well aware of Jennifer's assault on me. Ever since then, he had vocally despised the Krew.

"We need to just ignore them. We're different from they are," I murmured, stirring my coffee with a spoon and recalling how passive I had been while Jennifer was hitting me.

"Someone's going to have to stop them sooner or later. It's ridiculous that they can just act like that without anyone doing anything," Alyssa put in, shaking her head.

"There's never any proof of what they do. And the people who witness their freak-outs are too afraid to do anything," Adam explained, thoughtfully biting the inside of his cheek. Then, he shifted his gaze to Logan, who had remained silent the whole time.

"You don't know anything about what happened last night at The Royal, do you?" he asked Logan suspiciously. Logan frowned and gave him a serious look.

"Why would I? Of course not," he answered immediately, clearly bothered by Adam's question. Truthfully, I didn't get where Adam was going with this either.

"Well, Neil is part of the Krew and..."

"And I'm supposed to know all the stupid shit he does with them?" he snapped furiously. "Well, I don't. My brother doesn't tell me anything," he said defensively, and I instinctively rested my hand on his shoulder to calm him down.

I understood where he was coming from. It couldn't have been easy always having people's eyes on you, always feeling singled out just because of the choices your brother made.

"You should help him get out of that gang," Kyle put in, pulling his long hair into a messy bun at the base of his neck.

"I've tried. It's not easy," Logan answered, his shoulder slumping in resignation.

Just then, my eyes were pulled to the entrance of the bar as though compelled by some dark, magnetic force. There, five intimidating personages had appeared. Neil loomed over the others with his great height and caught everyone's eye.

"Speak of the devil," Kyle commentated, looking directly at the newcomers. The gossip session ended, and Adam settled back in his chair, sipping his coffee. Logan stared hard at his brother, who was leading his friends to their usual table next to the restaurant's big window, apparently not noticing us.

I watched him the entire time until he'd settled in at the table, because I couldn't seem to tear my eyes away. Alexia sat next to him while Jennifer positioned herself between Luke and Xavier. Neil didn't pay her the slightest bit of attention; he stretched his arm across the back of the chair belonging to the girl with blue unicorn hair, smiling at something she whispered in his ear. My chest tightened as I recalled how he'd touched her, in the pool house, smacking her ass before undoubtedly giving him a savage orgasm that I had absolutely refused to witness. Should I have been more worried about Alexia than Jennifer all this time? I didn't know which of the two was actually his favorite.

It occurred to me that I was being stupid and screwing everything up, but I couldn't fight the sick feeling that gnawed on the inside of my stomach. I only had one name for it: jealousy.

"Lolita, light of my life, fire of my loins. My sin, my soul," Kyle whispered in my ear, making me flinch. He had moved next to me, giving his seat to Alyssa who was now clinging to Logan's arm, and I hadn't noticed any of it because I was too absorbed in my own thoughts.

"How many times have you read it?" I grinned at him, trying to shift my attention to anything other than golden eyes and messy hair that I longed to run my fingers through.

"Quite a few. And I sense that you are maybe fascinated by passionate delusion, impossible love, insidious emotions, and the thorniest parts of the human psyche," he teased, and I was impressed with his thoughtful analysis. Kyle was a clever and intuitive guy, characteristics I often saw—and adored—in other readers like me who appreciated the great classics.

"Me, on the other hand, I'm fascinated by intelligent girls." Kyle smiled at me, and I blushed. Not because I liked him, but because I was always embarrassed by compliments. "There aren't a lot of people who would rather read or expand their knowledge than go out and get wild," he added in tones of genuine surprise. After one of the few evenings out on the town I had ever hand, I'd come home drunk and promptly lost my virginity to a boy who had infected my mind ever since. So that was the end of the "exploring partying" chapter of my life.

Just then, I turned my face in Neil's direction and caught him looking at me.

Yeah, he'd seen me.

His eyes were on me even as his arm still rested on Alexia's chair. In that brief moment when our eyes met, the walls of the bar, my friends, the customers around us, the background voices, sounds of glasses clinking, and the Krew themselves seemed to disappear. We were communicating with a silent language we might never fully understand.

"Do you want to go with me? I can take you home." Kyle broke the visual connection, seizing my attention.

I thought about it for a second, but I couldn't find any reason to turn down his invitation.

After all, Kyle was just a friend and nothing more.

I stood up and told Logan I was getting a ride with the literature-loving musician. He nodded, and Alyssa winked at me, but I shook my head and made a face to let her know we weren't going to do anything weird.

I gathered up my bag and put on my dove-gray coat before following Kyle to the exit. I forced myself not to glance at Neil or his friends when we had to walk past their table. Still, I held my breath until we got out the door. Fortunately, none of them paid any attention to us.

I spent about two hours with Kyle as we drove around town, listening to one of his favorite albums in the car. I also got a call from Jared while I was with him, and I inquired, as always, about Jared's mother and asked him to tell me when he had the time to talk for longer.

Regardless of how things went with Neil, Jared deserved to know my true stance on our relationship.

When Kyle brought me home—or rather, to Matt's home—he complimented me on the impressive facade. I didn't invite him in and got out of the car immediately after thanking him. I didn't even allow him to walk me to the front steps.

I slowly approached the front door, and even from the paved driveway, I could see the light on the pool house, spilling out the windows. It had to be Neil. He was the only one who used the pool house, and exclusively to be with women.

It had been a while, actually, since I'd heard moans and groans coming from his bedroom, and I wondered why he'd made that change to his routine. I wondered even more if it had anything to do with my presence.

I shook my head and kept walking, shivering from the cold. I stopped short again, however, when I spotted Neil's silhouette on a chaise longue. He rested his elbows on his knees, his head first lowered as he focused on the crystalline water of the pool, illuminated by colorful lights, before he raised it to look at me. In the semi-darkness, alone and partially obscured, he inspired a kind of fear that I had only experienced a few times in my life. An intense shudder run down my spine when his eyes, which I could barely see from such a distance, scrutinized me from top to bottom.

For a moment, I imagined that he'd been there the whole time, waiting for me to come back. But I quickly dismissed that ridiculous idea. Neil didn't care about anyone except himself and his physical needs.

I hesitated for a few seconds, unsure of how to proceed.

Part of me wanted to just go into the house, eat dinner, and go to bed. But before I could really even consider what the best decision would be, my legs were taking me toward the pool, walking around it to reach him.

His lips wrapped around the cigarette, sucking in the smoke before falling open to release it out into the air.

"You're going to have so many things to tell your boyfriend." His baritone broke the silence as I stood there, still staring at him. "First you'll have to tell him that you lost your virginity to me, and now you're going to have to explain that you're into some musician who just came to town." There was no mockery in his voice, nor any irritation. He sounded serious and reflective. He smiled without looking at me, as though savoring the taste of the nicotine while he looked into the pool. The smell of chlorine came over us in waves because of the light, brisk breeze that made me occasionally shudder from cold.

"Not every human relationship has a sexual element. Kyle is my friend," I answered him. "And he's not my boyfriend," I added, though I felt a stab of pain in my chest. I wasn't at all sure that Jared would agree with that assessment, but how was I supposed to conclusively dash his hopes when he was already suffering so much?

"Not your boyfriend," Neil repeated, sounding amused.

"Don't be tedious. It's my business." I was irritated because I already knew that I'd done wrong by Jared.

"You should be honest, especially with yourself. I saw how you blushed when Lucky Kyle or whatever the hell his name is looked at you earlier. You're no different from the rest of them after all," he accused, bringing the cigarette back to his lips so he could inhale even more toxic chemicals.

I tilted my head to one side and looked at him before taking a few confrontational steps forward. "What do you mean by that?"

"Just that all a man needs to do is give you a wink, pretend to be a gentleman, pour on the compliments, and off you go with him," he said, finally looking me in the eyes.

He sounded calm, but it felt like he was in the mood to hurt me, like I was no longer the Selene of the other night, the one he had kissed and touched right there where he was now sitting.

"And what's wrong with that? It's not like I slept with him."
I raised my voice in vexation. I didn't even know why we were
talking about Kyle or what purpose this ridiculous conversation
served.

"Don't get upset about it, Tinkerbell. You're a woman, and as
such, you're weak when it comes to men." He ground out the butt
in the ashtray and spit the last plume of smoke into the air with an
arrogant certainty that got right under my skin.

"To men in general?" I repeated in surprise. "The only man I've
allowed to violate my boundaries thus far is the asshole I'm arguing
with right now. I'm sorry, Neil, but I happen to find Kyle interesting
because I can talk to him, because he's cultured, and because I like
cultured men who can carry on a conversation." I was praising Kyle
just to further provoke Neil. His reaction to all of this was completely incomprehensible to me, but I had no intention of letting
him walk all over me.

"Cultured..." He got to his feet, looming so far above me that
I had to tilt my head back to look into his face. The certainty I had
felt up until that point was starting to wane. I felt a sudden wash
of helplessness, and I could only attribute it to his imposing size,
which, unfortunately, was having exactly the effect he was hoping
for: I was intimidated.

Neil moved closer, and I breathed in slowly, smelling his body
wash. He leaned down to my ear and parted his lips.

"Some people—and I am one of them—hate happy ends. We
feel cheated. Harm is the norm," he whispered, leaving me speechless. "That's what your beloved Nabokov said," he added in a sensual tone, the heat of his breath traversing the collar of my coat and
moving down my body, all the way to center of me.

Then, he pulled away just far enough to look me in the eye, and
he smiled because he had demonstrated something about himself
that I hadn't known before.

"You've read Nabokov?" I murmured softly, like a child afraid to speak. I was definitely surprised.

"If you want to know something more about me, you have to give me something of yourself in return," he answered, walking off toward the pool house.

Two minutes later, I found myself inside the pool house, taking in its homey furnishings. The walls were bright; a large glass door led out onto the outdoor patio and the pool. There was a kitchen in one corner with a large fridge, a stove, and a breakfast bar complete with stools. The dining table was small, though, and tucked between the kitchen and the larger room, right where I was standing, gaping like a fish. There was a modern pellet fireplace, an enormous plasma screen, a wall storage unit, and a white leather sofa in the corner.

Finally, a door led into the infamous bedroom, which had an attached bathroom. In short, the pool house was a real luxury, small but extremely comfortable. Matt's money was well spent.

"You seem tense." Neil opened the fridge and grabbed a can of beer, which he opened and lifted to his mouth. I wasn't just tense; I was extremely anxious.

"Make yourself at home," he added, glancing at the coat I was still wearing and the bag that still hung from my shoulder. I followed his advice and put both my coat and bag on the coat rack by the door. I glanced around before tugging down the hem of the sweater I was wearing over my basic, light-wash jeans. I rubbed my hands together, and after spotting the gesture, Neil pointed at the fireplace.

"That'll warm you up, though…" He advanced on me slowly, leaving his beer on the bar. "I do know some other ways to fix that problem," he said, shamelessly looking my body up and down with a disappointed expression on his face.

"Wh-what is it?" I stammered, suddenly feeling awkward.

"Don't you ever wear skirts?" His golden eyes came back to my face as he waited for my response.

"Should I? I don't really like them." And I didn't understand this absurd question. Was he trying to dictate how I dressed?

I backed away from him and examined the living room to buy myself some time.

"I don't dress the way your lovers do. Is that what's bothering you? Do you not like my look? Is it too…babyish?" I teased him, while I looked at the colorful painting mounted right above the fireplace. Then, I turned to face him, displaying an uncharacteristic confidence that I was mostly just pretending to possess.

He seemed far away, yet he was slowly undressing me with his eyes. I caught him staring at my ass, outlined clearly in my tight jeans as well as the curves of my body, highlighted by my thin sweater. I thought about how many times his hands had traced over those same curves.

"Do you want to play a game?" he suggested, and his low voice didn't bode well at all.

"What kind of game?" I asked in a feeble voice.

Neil walked over to me and touched my cheek, making me go rigid.

"You're too tense." He kissed my neck and fit our bodies together. He brushed his lips along my jaw and then exhaled against my mouth, locking eyes with me.

"I don't want to go into that bedroom. I don't want to go to the same place you take everyone else." I made myself very clear, my voice low, although I quivered when his hand continued touching my cheek. He smiled and slid his fingers along my arm, pulling a gasp from me.

"You're already in the same place I take everyone," he whispered in my ear. "But we can stay on the couch, if you prefer," he added.

Whatever game we were about to play, I already knew it was going to involve both of us getting naked.

He backed away, and I felt cold where his hand had been. He

vanished into the bedroom and returned a few moments later, toying with something in his cupped hand.

"What do you have there?" I asked, sitting down on the edge of the sofa.

Neil crooked one corner of his mouth and moved toward me slowly, holding himself in that decisive way that always sapped me of any strength. He sat down beside me and opened his hand, revealing two...

"Dice?" I said as I looked at them. "What are you going to do with two dice?" I turned my gaze to him and saw that he had taken on a cheerful expression. Was he screwing with me or something?

"Details, Selene. Go on, take a closer look at them." I liked it when he said my name; it generated a painful but gratifying tension within me.

I leaned over to get a better look at the dice: they were blue with black writing carved into each side.

"These dice are for real romantics, like me," he said, under his breath. It was then that I looked more closely at the writing: *breast, penis, butt*. On the other one: *suck, kiss, lick*, and other words that I stopped reading because I was too scandalized. How had I ever believed that Mr. Disaster would ask me to play a normal game?

"Ar-are you insane?" I stammered.

I tried to stand up, but before I could, Neil grabbed my wrist to stop me.

"It's just a game; don't be a baby," he smiled. "You're lucky I didn't ask you to share me with another girl at the same time, in the same bed," he whispered, echoing a phrase I had heard from him on another occasion. I swallowed hard and forced myself to get a handle on my impulses and not simply run away.

"I never would have agreed to that," I said firmly, and a quiet, guttural laugh—deeply masculine—escaped him. I found it

428

fascinating, despite everything. It suddenly occurred to me how completely crazy I was. I was a total idiot, humoring him like this.

"Choose a die without looking," he instructed, holding his open hand out to me. I kept my eyes locked on his, those irises so unique that I couldn't stop admiring them, and he stared back at me in return.

I grabbed a die and only then did I lower my eyes, breaking our connection.

"You chose the body parts," he pointed out, glancing at the die still in his hand. "And left me with the actions," he added with a triumphant smile, pleased that luck was on his side.

"And which…" I cleared my throat. "Which actions would those be, exactly?" I was having trouble even formulating a question, because I was so nervous that I couldn't process anything anymore. I glanced at the front door, and for a moment, I thought about hurling that damned die into the air and running away. Another part of me, however, was dying to know what he was thinking.

"Kissing, biting, touching, sucking, licking, and stroking," he explained. "Nothing painful; nothing sadistic. Bondage and all that other shit isn't what turns me on. You know that. My vices are something else," he murmured and settled himself more fully on the large sectional sofa, lit up by the glow of the fireplace.

"What does that mean?" I asked, hoping I wouldn't regret the question. Neil grinned like the worst kind of sinner and leaned into my ear again.

"I like to play games with bodies. Ever since I was a kid."

For a moment, I just stared at a point on his right shoulder. I wasn't sure how to understand that confession. There were a thousand theories and assumptions in my head, but I didn't want to think through any of them right at that moment.

"I'll play games with you, if you can just answer my questions. If we can just talk." I offered my condition again, and he stared into my eyes. He sighed before reluctantly nodding, giving me just a hint of a defeated smile.

"Okay. Roll your die, then I'll roll mine," he instructed. I closed my hand over the die and shook it before throwing it down again on the low table in front of us. He did the same.

"Area: neck, action: suck." He read the first combination, and I breathed a sigh of relief. That wasn't too bad for a first turn.

"You got lucky, baby." He moved closer and brushed my hair behind my shoulders to expose the curve of my neck. He blew on it, giving me goosebumps. Yet I remained seated with my knees locked together and my hands dug into the material of my jeans.

"Relax," he said, putting his lips on my skin. I smiled at the friction of his stubble, which tickled me. He lingered over one spot for a few moments before suddenly beginning to suck, which made me exhale in surprise. I could feel it all: his soft, inviting mouth exerting an unmistakable pressure on me, the heat of his breath, the capillaries in my neck fracturing, though not painfully.

"Let's go again." He pulled back way too soon and reached for his die again. I followed his lead; together, we rattled them in our hands before tossing them both down on the table. We leaned forward to read the next combination.

"Area: breast; action: suck." *Sucking again, dammit.* He looked at me like he'd just read the recipe for a sweet treat rather than some obscene writing on erotic dice. I stiffened. Why had I agreed to stay here?

I pushed my palms down on the giving surface of the sofa and looked expectantly at him. I wasn't even capable of undressing; I was so worked up.

"It's nothing we haven't done before," he reassured me, and he was right. He'd already seen me naked on multiple other occasions. He had undressed me and touched me, but things were different somehow that evening. He felt so far away, emotionally speaking. We hadn't even kissed.

In a flash, he fixed his eyes on me and grabbed the hem of my sweater, slowly raising it up. I lifted my arms to assist him, and he threw the sweater to a far corner of the sofa before fixing his ravenous stare on my bra. He traced the edges of it with just his fingertips until he reached the hooks to open it. I was terribly embarrassed, but Neil didn't notice as he peeled yet another article of clothing off me, leaving me naked from the waist up.

I instinctively tried to shield myself with my right forearm and turned red. It was not the action of a bold, self-confident woman.

Neil gave me a solemn look. I couldn't tell if he was irritated or moved to pity by my gesture, but I didn't have too much time to think about it because he grabbed my wrists and pulled them away from me so he could look at my now-exposed breasts. They were small, but high and firm, and my nipples were stiff, pointed right at him as though waiting for him to lavish attention upon them.

The flash of desire in his golden eyes accompanied the movement of his hands as he placed them underneath my breasts, like he was testing their weight. I flinched at the sudden contact, but he didn't stop, and I didn't resist. He felt them with a kneading motion before bending his head down and flicking his tongue over my left nipple. I trembled.

"I like the way your skin smells," he commented before capturing my nipple with his lips and sucking, drawing a shy but perfectly audible moan out of me. I touched his hair, digging my fingers in and tightening them. His scruff rubbed against my sternum and his mop of hair tickled the base of my throat.

"Who is Scarlett?" I asked abruptly, forcing him to honor my condition. Neil stopped suckling my left breast and moved to the right, still in a calculated, expert fashion. Once my nipple was in his mouth, he battered it with his tongue, causing alternating hot and cold sensations that practically made me vibrate.

He looked up at me, letting me see just how much he was enjoying everything he was doing, while making it clear that he knew I was enjoying it, too.

Oh, yes, I was enjoying it a lot. But only because he was one doing it to me.

"Answer me," I murmured, but Neil just licked all around my areola in response. The slide of his saliva, his hot tongue, the slow, rhythmic movements had me clenching my lower lip between my teeth. I flexed my thighs to relieve some of the throbbing caused by my reawakened libido. My heart was pounding in my temples, and my head began to spin.

"My ex," he said finally, and my eyes went wide because I thought for sure he'd never answer me. He pulled away from my breast and licked his lips as though he were sorry to no longer be tasting my skin.

"How long were you two together?" I pressed, regaining some control over my breath, which had previously gone fast and irregular. Neil ran a hand through his hair and picked the dice back up, not looking at me.

"We didn't have a real relationship. It's a long story, but about a year, I guess." He closed his fist around his die and shook to reroll it. This was obviously a painful topic, but knowing that the infamous Scarlett was indeed an ex of his and not just another lover like Jennifer and the rest of them stirred up a prickly, tormented feeling in my stomach.

I touched my right breast with one hand. It was still glistening wet with his saliva and the nipple stiffened again when I thought about his lips playing over it. I picked up my die and tried with all my might to hide how uncomfortable I was being half-naked right beside him, though he wasn't even looking at me.

"Area: penis, action: stroke," he read with a slightly ironic tone that made me blanch. I straightened my spine and breathed in slowly. I had no idea how to touch a man that way; I had no idea where I should even start. It was a little absurd to be twenty-one years old and to have so little sexual experience with anyone—certainly not Jared—and I felt the burden of my inexperience every time I needed to do something for or with Neil.

"I'll show you how." He turned to me and lifted my chin with his index finger because I had been staring into the fireplace, looking for a pretext to escape or perhaps to just a place to hide my blazing face.

"I don't know... I mean, I don't think I'm..."

"Capable?" He said, his voice overlapping mine. "Trust me," he whispered and made me stretch out on the couch. A moment later, he positioned himself alongside me, propped up on his elbow. He stared at my breasts as he took my hand and guided it to the zipper of his jeans.

My god! I needed to... I just needed to...

"Touch me," he ordered under his breath, pressing his nose into the crook of my neck as I lay there inertly. I opened my hand and sucked in a breath when I felt him under my fingers, swollen and hard even through the fabric of his pants.

"O-okay," I murmured in mortification, as I moved my hand from top to bottom. I followed the contours of his member, pressing against his jeans, and was amazed all over again at how long and thick it was.

"Good. Now, unzip me," he said softly. I moved my hand to the button of his jeans and tried to free it but with no success.

I was incapable of performing even the simplest of actions: pulling down his fly.

"A true babe." He gave me a sensual smile. "Let me help." He undid the button and lowered his fly before pausing expectantly, ready for me to do the rest.

At the same time, he began to rub my breasts and kiss my neck until, little by little, my anxiety evaporated.

I pulled his jeans down over the curve of his butt and he lifted his hips to assist me. Then, I glanced down and spotted his erect penis beneath the white Calvin Klein boxers he wore. I moved my gaze to the V shape leading to his pelvic area and touched the lateral lines with my fingertip. The movement made him flinch.

Then, I traced the outline of his tattoo on his left flank, and he sighed.

"You're really into my tattoos, huh?" he said, sounding pleased with himself, and I nodded. I loved the pikorua just as much as I loved the toki on his right bicep, currently covered by his fleece. They were marvelous embellishments on his marble statue of a body.

"God, so much," I whispered against his lips, using my fingers to stroke the tip of his erection where it was peeking out of his underwear elastic.

"Pull them down," he demanded. I swallowed and grabbed the waistband with both hands, scrupulously not looking down.

"Look at me. I like being looked at by you." He smiled a predator's smile at me, and I shifted my gaze to the hard-on that now curved over his navel. Veins along the sides of his member made it appear even more starkly masculine; his testicles were contracted. His glans dark and not yet fully emerged. I felt embarrassed, but despite that, I couldn't stop staring at him.

"I'll teach you how to make me feel good." He grasped my hand in his and guided it to his bare flesh.

"Squeeze." He helped me wrap my fingers around the base of him, though my fingertips and thumb could not connect.

"And move you hand like this." He manipulated my hand in a slow but precise up and down rhythm. His skin was sleek and hot, sliding perfectly against my hand.

434

"I like it best right here." He glided my hand to bottom of his glans and encouraged me to move my fingers over that sensitive area.

Despite all of this, Neil was breathing in a slow and controlled fashion, so I had no idea whether he liked what I was doing. I decided not to worry about that and simply mimic his movements, delighting in the incredible sensation of trying to stroke him off.

I really liked touching him.

"Never make the mistake of forgetting about these." He guided my hand lower, specifically to his swollen testicles and I gasped. "Focus on this area." He used my index finger and made me rub the crease that ran down the center, sliding up and back down slowly.

Neil breathed in deep and then exhaled, bathing my face in his hot breath. Then, he slipped his hand away from mine and urged me to keep going by myself

"Every man has his own preferences. You're learning what I like and how I like it," he informed me. "The way to a man's heart is through his cock. You want to get at my soul? Touch *me* the way I like," he concluded with a brash grin that made me blush. I supposed that this constituted a romantic statement for him.

Either way, I concentrated on trying to move my hand the way he'd taught me as we lay facing each other. My breasts were pressed against his chest and our bodies stuck fast to each other. Neil began to touch me, fondling my breast, rubbing a thumb over my nipple. I moaned timidly, not sure if he was trying to arouse me or himself. He smiled and clasped his hand over mine again, pushing me to speed up my strokes.

"I'll never come like this. You need to work harder, Tinkerbell." He moved his hand back to my face and stroked my cheek this time before leaning in to kiss me.

He didn't ask for my permission; he demanded contact between our lips as he bucked his hips against my fist.

Despite that, Neil didn't pant; he didn't moan. He was completely silent. It made it difficult to know whether he was really engaged with what was happening, and more importantly, how much he was enjoying it. I applied myself—truly applied myself—even if performing this kind of foreplay on Neil wasn't easy, considering how long it took him to reach orgasm and how unused I was to doing this kind of thing for a man.

Occasionally, I would pause and rub him with my open hand just to get a break. I hoped, in those moments, to see him more fully engaged. I stretched my hand down to his testicles and fondled them. They felt slippery under my hand but also tightly contracted. I glided my hand up his erection again, hard as a steel blade, then I alternated those movements several more times.

Neil, however, seemed to remain unmoved, and for a moment, I thought I wasn't doing it right. Plus, my wrist had begun to hurt as well as the muscles in my arm. I quit kissing his mouth and refocused my attentions on his neck, licking and nibbling it. At the same time, my hand moved back to his testicles, tugging them absently downward.

"Yes. Good job," he murmured, closing his eyes, and for the first time, I heard his hoarse, aroused voice. Apparently this movement was good for him?

So I repeated it, and Neil pushed his pelvis against my hand, wordlessly commending my initiative.

"Fuck," he mumbled. "Faster, now," he suggested, letting his head fall back against the couch and squeezing his eyes shut. I gripped his erection firmly and gave it fast, rhythmic strokes right against his favorite spot. I had now memorized the things that gave him pleasure, and the rush of power that gave me was incredible.

I slid my thumb over the long slit at the head of his glans. I collected a pearlescent bead of liquid from the tip and thrilled at the idea of him getting wet like that.

"Precum. It means I'm almost there, Babygirl." The rumble of his baritone made me flush. The idea of him seemingly being able to read my mind and confirm my ideas was currently very appealing to me. Neil parted his lips and bit the bottom one. His body went rigid and his testicles seemed to harden and it looked to me like he was being entirely undone by pleasure. It was a marvelous spectacle, and I was the sole spectator.

It didn't matter how many there had been before me or how many there might be after; in that moment, Neil was experiencing this pleasure exclusively thanks to *me*.

He was still contained, he didn't make a sound, but the increase in his breathing told me he was likely close to orgasm.

"You're beautiful when you're aroused," I blurted out and his eyes snapped open, focusing on my hand. His golden gaze lit up with desire, even brighter than usual.

"Yeah?" he asked, turning his attention, and I nodded before approaching his lips with my own.

"Yeah," I confirmed and kissed him. He slipped his hand into my hair and welcomed my tongue as it passionately pursued his own until I was breathless.

On instinct, I bit down on his full lips for no reason but that they were fantastic. They felt hot and swollen between my teeth. It was one of those moments that could never be measured with a clock but only in the beats of our hearts as our mouths and limbs were intertwined.

Neil broke the kiss, exhaling on my lips and resting his forehead against mine. Then he swiftly yanked his fleece over his torso so as not to get it dirty just as he exploded in hot spurts against my hand and his own lower abdomen. He tightened his abs as the spasms hit him, squeezing his eyes shut.

Then, that muscled chest heaved breathlessly while his forehead broke out into a slight sweat. His cheeks and neck had reddened, and his mouth was swollen and moist.

"That was... I mean... It was—" He didn't let me finish. Instead, he opened his eyes and kissed me again.

His kiss was crude, all domination and control. His kiss left no room to breathe and he moved his tongue in my mouth so fast and so deeply that it was impossible for me to match him.

"You did good, but you have no idea how much I want your lips wrapped around me," he murmured, and a nanosecond later, I found myself straddling him. I didn't care that his cum would get on my jeans. I didn't care about anything other than the need to feel him more fully.

His hands on my hips coaxed me to rock my pelvis against him while our lips continued to communicate in a new language, all their own.

Kissing him was like finally quenching my thirst in a vast, burning desert, and I wanted to suck every last drop him from. His bare erection chafing between my thighs encouraged me to rock more violently. Suddenly, I pulled away from his lips and lifted myself up, putting my hands on his pectoral muscles. His fingers glided over the fabric of my sweater, and I wanted to touch every part of him, but then something shifted in his gaze.

His golden eyes narrowed, and Neil began to look at me as though he no longer knew who I was. His fingers clamped down on my hips until I felt a wave of pain sweep through my body. I rocked on him again, but almost immediately, I had to stop because Neil was resisting me. I held still, astride his hips, and Neil touched my sides softly, moving up along my rib cage to my breasts. Then, he squeezed them so hard it made me whine and flinch in pain.

"You're hurting me," I told him, confused.

The game was over, the lust was ebbing and the pleasure had evaporated. His eyes had been emptied of all human emotion so completely; in that moment, Neil scared me. He let his hands fall down to our thighs. His gaze wandered to the junction of our bodies, and he frowned. He began to breathe irregularly, like he was struggling for air.

"Neil," I said, taking his face in my hands. He rubbed his throat and then his chest, opening his lips in a desperate attempt at speech.

He looked like he was suffocating.

"Neil!" I spoke louder as I raised myself off him. His eyes were pinned to the ceiling and his eyelids didn't move—it was like he'd taken a strong dose of some paralytic toxin.

"Neil! You're scaring me!" I shook him but he still didn't move.

"Neil, please! I'm going to call for help!" I scrambled off the couch and searched for one of our phones, but before I could find one, he clamped down on my wrist and shoved me face-first against the wall. He was strong; it didn't take much for him to throw my body around. He pinned my hands behind my back and pressed against me, crushing me.

"You're done hurting me," he whispered menacingly in my ear.

I had no idea what he was talking about. I began shaking and burst into the tears from the confused feelings that lanced through my chest like a lightning storm.

"Get out of here. Get the hell out of here, Selene." His tone of voice changed suddenly again. This time he sounded like he was pleading with me. He released me abruptly, and I turned around, covering my bare breasts with my forearm.

I looked at him fearfully, and Neil put his head in his hands, confused and disoriented.

"I said get out of here! Now!" he shouted, grabbing a nearby vase and hurling it at the wall. I gasped, snatching my sweater off the couch and hurriedly pulling it on, not even bothering to look for my bra.

There was no time. I needed to get out of there. As fast as I could.

Suddenly, Neil began smashing everything within his reach. While he vented his rage, I gathered up my coat and bag, and with both my hands and legs still shaking, I somehow managed to get to the door.

I turned back once to look at him and the room he was systematically destroying. The vase, the painting, the television, the chairs… Everything was reduced to broken pieces. My eyes stretched wide, and with my heart in my mouth and fear slithering snakelike through my body, I threw open the door and ran panting into the yard.

Something had summoned the secret beast inside him. I had watched the metamorphosis in his eyes. His golden gaze had been absorbed by his dilated pupils and a shadowy veil had passed over his face, a dark, ominous expression had replaced the look of desire, and I'd known right then that Neil was no longer with me.

I knew then that there was a monster living within him.

And I…

I had seen it.

29

....

SELENE

I'm coming to see you tomorrow.

That was the text Jared had sent me the night before while as I was in the pool house with Neil.

He hadn't added a salutation or any cute nicknames of his own. He'd just warned me that he was going to come find me, and I wasn't sure if I was actually ready to face him.

I was still shaken up by what had happened with Neil. Not just by our intimate moment when I'd felt the voluptuous satisfaction of his kisses, his hands on me, my own desire coursing through my veins. But also by the moment when all of that had been rapidly replaced with a blind fury for which I still had no explanation.

What had made him react that way?

I had no idea. Just like I had no idea how I was supposed to act if I ran into him the hallway, or the kitchen, or the garden.

It was for this reason that I'd gone to classes that day and returned home in the afternoon while trying every way I could think of to avoid Neil. It was seven p.m., and at eight thirty, Jared would be there. Then, we were supposed to go out. I had no idea where he was planning to take me, as he'd been rather vague and mysterious when he called a couple of hours ago.

After taking a shower, I wandered around my room in futile anxiety. The time had come to have the talk with my erstwhile boyfriend. I would no longer be able to keep this secret inside me—a secret that was rapidly growing too big to hide.

The situation with Neil had taken a new turn, possibly an even worse one than before, but I couldn't keep Jared hanging on when I didn't have feelings for him anymore. He had a right to know the truth, and he was going to learn it tonight.

I wanted to wear something comfortable but stylish, so I opted for a white button-down, a blue pullover, and a pair of jeans in the same color. I wore my hair down past my shoulders and put on a little mascara to highlight my eyelashes. Then, I slid on my shoes and packed my purse with all the typical essentials.

"Are you going out?" Two knocks on my half-open door drew my attention. Logan was standing there, looking curiously at me.

"Jared's going to be here soon." I gave him a smile and grabbed a puffy jacket from the closet.

"Oh, you two are finally meeting up," he said, demonstrating an enthusiasm that I did not share. Logan, after all, could have no idea that my evening was sure to be a complete disaster. "You don't seem very happy, though…" he added thoughtfully, and for a moment, I stopped pretending everything was okay. At least with him.

"I need to tell him something serious." I sat down on the edge of the bed, and Logan frowned as he regarded me with those lovely catlike eyes of his.

"What could you have possibly done that was so serious?" he asked dismissively, taking a seat next to me.

"I'm not getting back together with him. Our pause is really a stop, and I've already moved on. I've already…done things with someone else." I said it all in one breath, staring down at my legs instead of at him. A deafening silence fell over us. I didn't have the courage to look up at the disgusted expression he probably had on his face. Who knows what he must have been thinking about me.

"You can say it: I'm a slut. I'm a terrible person; it's all true…" But he just rested his hand on my shoulder and shook his head no.

"I'm not in any position to judge your choices," he told me kindly. "Jared? Sure. And maybe the other guy. Speaking of…do you love him?" he added, sounding slightly awkward. I looked into his eyes, but I couldn't give him an immediate response. Did I love Neil? Even I didn't know. Mr. Disaster wasn't like other men, and his outburst the day before had provided ample demonstration of that.

"I… I don't know," I murmured in a very quiet voice, fixing my eyes on a vague point out in the middle of the room.

"Well, whatever happens with the other man, one thing is for certain: you didn't love Jared," he pointed out. I thought the same thing, but it hardly excused my behavior.

"I screwed up," I admitted.

"Selene, everybody makes mistakes," he said, trying to console me, and I appreciated his approach to this. Logan always had a kind and soothing word for everyone; he was never insulting or reactive. He thought carefully before he spoke or acted.

"Everything's going to be okay. You'll have a heart-to-heart with him, and Jared will understand." It was clear that he was trying to soothe away some of my worries. "And if anything happens, if you need me for any reason, don't hesitate to call me." And now he sounded a little worried. Probably because he knew that coming clean about something like this wasn't a simple process. People tended to take this kind of news poorly.

I gave Logan a hug goodbye and promised him that I would call if I needed him. Then, I headed out and met Jared in his car. He'd told me when he'd be arriving in his text, so I walked down the main driveway trying to take deep breaths. My legs felt like jelly, and my heart wouldn't stop pounding in my chest at an uncontrollable tempo.

"Hey." I gave Jared a nervous smile as I slid into the passenger seat. He was put-together as always, wearing a light winter coat over his black shirt and pants. His blond hair was slicked back against the nape his neck with gel, and his jade-green eyes were fixed on me, examining me all over.

"Hey." He moved closer and planted a kiss on the corner of my lips, still unsmiling.

"I'm glad to see you," I babbled inanely as he started the car's engine. "How... How's your mother?" I decided to open with that familiar question, trying not to seem too nervous, though it was difficult to hide.

"Bad," he answered simply, driving off on a route I did not know.

His hand was tense as he gripped the steering wheel, and he often clenched his jaw as though it were a new nervous tic.

"Is the chemo not working the way you'd hoped?" I asked. I actually did want to know how his mother was doing, but he gave me an unreadable smile. He ran his hand through his hair as we came to a stop in front of a park. I glanced around. It was dark outside, and only a few scattered lamps illuminated the road we'd stopped on for who knew what reason. I'd thought we were going to go out for dinner or a drink together, but apparently Jared didn't want to do either of those things.

"Why are we stopped here?" I asked him, confused, but he just cut the engine and let his head fall back against the seat rest, staring vacantly through the windshield.

"I've been thinking about you a lot recently. More than usual..." he began, sounding more like he was talking to himself than to me. "I've been thinking about that first time I saw you there in the library, so focused on picking out one of your novels. I still remember exactly what you were wearing, did you know that?" He paused for a moment, and I considered all the possible reasons for this monologue, then I clutched my purse against my thighs.

"You had on this blue dress that matched the color of your eyes and you were...fuck, you were incredible. Just the most beautiful girl I had ever seen, and you were in some random library in Detroit." He smiled and shook his head as if to mock himself.

"Why are you telling me this?"

"Before you, I only got with girls for the sex, but you know that already. I didn't think I would ever have those kinds of devastating feelings for anyone in particular, until you came into my life, looking so innocent with your pure little face," he continued, not answering my question. He seemed completely lost in his own memories, and all I could do was listen, psyching myself up to tell him everything. Right now.

"Jared..." I murmured but he hushed me.

"I felt so lucky to have met you. I thought you were the one. Maybe the love of my life." I had not failed to notice that he was speaking in the past tense. He turned to face me, his bright eyes now gleaming with a pain that I had not expected. I felt as though I'd been skewered to my seat, unable to move. "I've always treated you with respect. I gave up dating and regular sex all to wait for you. For you to be ready." He leaned in and touched my cheek. His touch was gentle, even delicate, and he looked at me like I was something precious that required careful handling. But his eyes...they were strange, different from before.

"I don't understand," I whispered, intimidated, and he bent his head to kiss me. The way he did it was completely unexpected: he seized my lips with his own and violently stabbed his tongue into my mouth, forcing me to accept him. I put my hands on his chest to push him away, but Jared fought me, using his body to exert terrible pressure on me.

"Show me what he taught you," he muttered against my lips, renewing his attack. He began groping my breast with one hand while the other felt up my thigh. I felt trapped, helpless, and bewildered.

"Jared," I panted in terror, trying to get him off me but to no avail. "Jared!" I said again, my back slamming into the window behind me. His mouth moved down my throat, and his hands tried to wriggle under my sweater. That's when I started kicking.

"Stop it! Stop it right now!" I shrieked, but Jared, with a strength that surprised me, grabbed me by the hair and bent my head back until he was looking me right in the eyes. He had swollen lips and wild hair, a face that I now struggled to recognize, and eyes filled with hatred. And those eyes were boring into me as though he wanted to kill me.

"Did you really believe I didn't know?" he whispered hatefully, right next to my mouth. "I got a message from someone who thought it was in my best interest to know what my girlfriend was getting up to here in my absence." He smiled and tightened his fist around my hair.

I went white, my stomach closing as though trapped in a vise, because this wasn't at all how I expected this to go.

"I wasn't... We weren't—" I barely got to speak before he cut me off again.

"I received some photos. Photos of you in his car, of you and him in the pool house at your father's place. How many times did you screw him? You weren't ready for me, but suddenly it was okay with him. Was it *just* him, or did you give it up for his little brother, too? Huh?"

He knew everything.

Jared knew *everything,* and I was so shocked that my heart felt like it was pounding out of my chest. My throat went dry. I couldn't decide what was worse: the fact that someone had secretly taken photos of us and sent them to Jared, or that he had found out the truth in such a horrible way.

"Jared, I . . ." I burst into tears, but no look of pity or understanding crossed his face. His face, which now had none of the sweetness that I'd known him for in the past.

"Shut up! You've been acting like a whore." He nuzzled my cheek with the tip of his nose and breathed in my smell, pressing his temple to mine. "I never would have expected this from you . . . Never," he murmured in a jagged voice, a sign that he was about to break. I held myself as still as I could, quivering in his arms.

"This is the way it always goes, isn't it? Men who respect women and treat them like princesses aren't enough for you, are they? They're just total idiots as far as you're concerned. Isn't that right?" He sighed heavily, and I could feel his heart beating at a gallop. His grip on my hair just got tighter and tighter. "You want these messed-up assholes who'll just fuck you like an animal and don't have the first clue how to treat you," he added, his voice pure malice, and his breath still hot on my skin. "But if I can't have you, he doesn't get to either," he threatened under his breath, running his hand from my breasts to my thighs.

"Please, let me explain . . . I'm sorry, I know I made a mistake and—" I grimaced as his fingers clamped down violently on my thigh until I let out a groan of pain.

"You're going to tell me where he is right now, and we are going to go see him." He jerked my neck back again and glared into my eyes, baring his teeth. "You are going to cooperate with me, Selene, or I swear on my life, I'm going to hurt you. Badly." His breath hit my lips, and I closed my eyes, feeling tears leak down the sides of my cheeks.

"Aw, don't cry, baby." He caught one tear with his thumb and gave me a mocking smile. "You enjoyed messing around behind my back, didn't you?"

I kept my eyes tightly shut, feeling humiliated, hurt, and imperiled. Jared wasn't acting like himself, and he seemed capable of anything.

"Answer me!" He grabbed my jaw, and my eyes went wide with fear.

"Yes!" I screamed. "Yes, I enjoyed it, and I would do it again!"

My confession was met by a deadly, treacherous expression on his face. Automatically, he raised his arm and stuck me with a loud slap that left me disoriented. I touched the affected cheek and felt my flesh throbbing under my fingertips while Jared just glared in my direction as though he were about to leap on me like some deranged beast.

Immediately, I opened the car's door and jumped out, trying to run away, but he was faster than me. He grabbed me by the arm and slammed me down against the hood, pinning both my wrists behind my back. I could feel the cold paint under my cheek and my hips struck the bumper.

"Let me go! Let me go now!" I screamed, looking around for anyone who might help, but there wasn't a soul in sight. I started crying again as he forced me back into the car.

I tumbled into the passenger seat, and after slamming my door, Jared got hastily back behind the wheel, where he immediately started the engine.

"I already know where he is; you don't even need to say a word."

He really did know everything.

He knew where to find Neil, and there was nothing I could do to stop Jared from going to him.

I glanced down at the cell phone sticking out of my coat pocket and inched it out, trying to make sure the lunatic next to me didn't notice.

"Selene!" He snapped, his eyes still fixed on the road. "Neil goes to Blanco on Friday nights, doesn't he?" he demanded furiously, even though he didn't require any confirmation from me. He just wanted me to collaborate with him because he had me trapped.

"I don't know," I mumbled, trying to control the fear that was blooming throughout my body. My legs were trembling along with my hands.

"But you're his whore; you know that much at least," he sneered as he shifted gears. As he spoke, I swiped another tear from the cheek he'd hit and winced again at the pain. I shuddered to think of the state I must be in because of him, but I was determined to warn Neil. So I slid my phone out of my pocket and hid it alongside me, between my leg and door. I quickly tapped out a text to Logan and sent it, staring straight ahead so as not to arouse suspicion.

"You never loved me. I should have known," Jared said. I immediately put the phone back in my pocket. Love was no longer a feeling I associated with him at all.

"You just hit me," I answered hatefully, and he laughed, like I'd just said something hilarious, like I was out here telling jokes. My face hurt so much it was hard to breathe. I stared down at my hands, which wouldn't stop trembling and tried to calm myself down.

"Here we are." Jared pulled over right in front of the Blanco sign and immediately dashed out of the car, slamming the door behind him. I got out as well and followed him, hoping that Logan had gotten there already.

"Has anyone here seen Neil Miller?" he shouted outside the club's entrance, drawing every eye to us. I couldn't even blush or feel embarrassed because the only emotion inside me was fear, and I was completely filled with it.

"Oh, there he is." Jared spotted Neil a second later in the parking lot, leaning against the hood of his Maserati with a cigarette in his hand. He strode briskly toward him.

"No! Jared, wait!"

I screamed and my voice drew Neil's honey-colored eyes to me.

He turned confusedly in my direction, not understanding what was happening.

"You! You son of a bitch!" Jared rushed Neil and punched him in the abdomen, making him double over.

"Jared!" I screamed, my hands clasped against my stomach as though I'd felt the blow myself. Neil's shoulders slumped forward, and he rubbed the injured area. For a fleeting moment, a pained expression crossed his beautiful face, but it immediately gave way to fury. His gaze grew ominous, and the lines of his face drew tight. He had turned his stare on me, and he was looking very intensely at one specific point: my cheek.

"What the fuck are you doing?" Xavier and Luke approached Jared, ready to defend their friend, but Neil immediately raised a hand to halt them.

"Selene!" called an alarmed Logan, who had just arrived. "What the hell is going on… What happened to your cheek?" He stared at me in shock, and I was trying so hard to hold back tears that I could barely speak.

"Jared… He already knew everything… He knew that—" But I didn't get to finish because the furious voice of the man in question shouted over me.

"You fucked my girlfriend!" he screamed at Neil.

And now Logan knew everything, too.

His eyes went wide and he stood motionless, staring at the scene in front of him. He was in completely shock about everything that was happening.

Just like I was.

"You… I mean, you and Neil… You two…" he stammered, totally bewildered, but there was no time for me to explain, not then. I turned to Neil, his shadowy, imposing frame towering over Jared.

He tossed his cigarette and ground it out with his shoe, all the while continuing to stare at his adversary.

"You hit her," he stated in a voice I didn't recognize. It was like another version of himself had been imported from an alternate reality.

Jared quirked up the corner of his mouth and gave me a disgusted look. "She won't be able to blow you for a little while, so sorry. Do you mind?" he sneered at Neil, and I flinched at yet another insult. Logan put a reassuring arm around my shoulders and Neil grimaced.

"Xavier, hand me that bottle." He extended his hand for his friend's bottle of beer, which Xavier gave to him without complaint.

"Why does he want that?" I murmured fearfully as a small crowd began to gather to watch our little drama.

"Not for anything good," Logan answered, worried.

Neil stared Jared down for a moment, the bottle in his hand before casually cracking it against a nearby wall, making all of us jump. The bottom broke off and Neil was left holding a long, sharp splinter of glass.

What the hell...

Everyone's attention was entirely on Neil now, all of them just waiting to witness whatever happened next.

Nobody even tried to step in because people loved to see a fight, but I feared the worst.

"Logan, stop him!" I lifted my hands to my face as Logan went immediately to his brother, who stood there fearlessly challenging Jared.

"Neil, don't lose your shit. Put that down. You're not yourself right now." He approached him cautiously, holding out both hands. "I know you hate being touched without your consent, but you can't react like this. You're not going to solve anything with that piece of glass," he added in a persuasive tone, but Neil just kept staring at Jared as though trying to murder him with his eyes.

He squeezed the shattered bottle in his hand until drops of

blood fell to the ground, but no expression of pain appeared on his face. It was like he was carved out of ice. It was disquieting, like he'd become detached from the world and was floating away into the darkness.

"Jared, leave!" Logan shouted, getting in between the two of them.

"Let him go, Logan! This piece of shit doesn't scare me!" Jared taunted as Neil's eyes grew narrower and narrower.

"Jared, you don't know what you're talking about!" Logan insisted. Neil's pupils were dilated, and his stare was completely devoid of emotion, just like it had been the night before. It looked like he was dissociating, like he was observing himself from outside his body.

"Jared, let's go." I took his arm and tried to pull him back with me but he resisted, glaring at me in disgust.

"Don't you dare touch me!" he shouted at me, and Neil's hand tightened on the bottle, causing even more blood to drip onto the pavement.

"For fuck's sake, Neil! Give me the bottle, you're cutting yourself!" Logan cried, trying to snatch it away from him, but Neil's fingers held firm. He was clenching his jaw, and his breathing was deep but controlled.

"Neil, please. Just listen to me. Don't do something stupid here! I know you're angry right now, but please put the bottle down." Logan was using a reassuring tone, as if trying to communicate with his brother on a different level. But Neil continued to glare at Jared like he was the only other person in the world.

"Do it for me, please. You trust me, right?" Logan was clearly using his own well-developed method to get through to Neil. It was obvious when I watched his measured steps, the slow way he stretched out his open hands, his balanced tone of voice, and his compassionate gaze.

"I'm the one person you do trust. So listen to me and drop the glass," he added softly and Neil finally looked away from Jared and at his brother. He seemed to recognize something in Logan's eyes. Neil allowed his hand to relax and the splinter of glass fell to the ground. His blood started flowing in earnest, but that didn't seem to bother him a bit.

"Christ's sake!" Logan sighed, kicking the bottle away as Jared observed the scene in confusion.

"No one is going to touch me or her, Jared," Neil told him in an authoritative tone. "No one," he repeated and his voice seemed to echo in the silence that had fallen over the gathered crowd. In my mind, it was as though the hands of an imaginary clock were ticking, counting down the seconds remaining before Neil's *real* reaction.

Brushing by Logan with one arm, Neil advanced on Jared and I broke into a sprint, insinuating myself between the two of them before Neil could completely lose control of himself.

"No! Don't hurt him!" I mustered up all of my courage, and Neil just looked at me, cold and vacant. I could smell him, though, that satisfying mixture of amber and tobacco that belonged to no one but him. That scent confirmed that it was Neil who was standing in front of me, even if his stare was so dark and menacing.

"Please don't hurt him. For me," I whispered, and his golden eyes moved to my cheek. He touched it, and I winced in pain. His touch was warm and tender, though. It felt like he was trying to tell me something but couldn't figure out how.

His eyes suddenly turned inward, lost in his unknowable thoughts, and he compressed his lips into a bitter line and took his hand away from me. Then, he brushed past me as well.

"Let's make a bet, shall we? I bet I can hurt you without ever touching you." He approached Jared and regarded him disdainfully, curling up one corner of his lips. I had no idea what he was planning, and I clung to Logan's arm when he came up beside me to offer support.

"Did you think hitting me would bring back your girl's virginity?" A sneering smile was painted across Neil's handsome, fiendish face as Jared's eyes went wide with surprise.

"Oh, God," Logan whispered.

"You know, Jared, there is such a thing as psychological violence, which has nothing to do with the physical kind," Neil murmured, still moving closer to him. "And, believe me, I am speaking from personal experience when I tell you it's a whole lot more painful than a punch," he went on maliciously.

"Oh fuck, this is finally getting interesting!" Xavier cut in before he and Luke burst into laughter. I ignored them and kept my eyes on Neil, who had started speaking again.

"So, Jared," he put extra stress on his name, circling him slowly. "I suspect that I am capable of destroying you without ever laying a finger on you, but let's find out," he said decisively. "Did you think you could come here and somehow erase what has already happened? Yes, I absolutely fucked your *girlfriend*." He grinned impudently at him.

"Do you want me to tell you all about it? From the very beginning?" Neil proposed, continuing to circle Jared who appeared to be in a trancelike state.

"Where do I even start? Oh yeah, there was the first week, when we kissed. Her lips are so soft and inviting," he said, pretending to be aroused by the memory. "And when I say 'lips,'" he put extra emphasis on the word and then paused for effect, "Well… You know what I mean…" He gave Jared a suggestive wink, and I blushed violently. I was going to be sick.

"Then there was her first time, and you have no idea how hot the sound of her moans are," he continued in that low, provocative voice. He made another circuit around Jared, who stood there with his fists relaxed in shock.

Logan put a hand on my shoulder and tugged me closer to him.

454

"He doesn't have any limits or inhibitions, Selene," he said resignedly while I could do nothing but stare at the scene in front of me, wishing it was just a terrible nightmare.

"And then there were her incredible orgasms, which only I have ever given her and those…" he circled Jared again. "Fuck, feeling her come will just fuck up every single part of you. Brain, body, soul… Everything…" he murmured, his gaze briefly sliding to me with a taunting, arrogant smile.

I leaned into Logan as if I might faint. My legs were wobbling, and my heart was pounding in my ears, and the whole world went blurry and started to spin around me.

"Selene, are you okay?" Logan asked me, alarmed, but I didn't answer him. I didn't have the strength.

I glanced around and saw that the people who'd witnessed the scene were starting to send curious looks my way while Alexia and Jennifer were watching me proudly from their place next to Xavier and Luke. The blond girl, in particular, was smiling like a plan had just come together, and in a flash, I knew…

Her threats that day in the cafeteria; she'd talked about my Instagram, Jared, Detroit…

"Should I keep going, Jared?" Neil's baritone drew my eyes back to him, reveling in the humiliation of the boy in front of him.

"And, in case you were wondering about it… Yes, we did also fuck while you were staying over at our house. In the room next door, in fact, and I can't tell you how much I enjoyed that one. Oh yeah, it was satisfying on an animal level. It was the most incredible orgasm of my life." He taunted him again, coming to a stop right in front of his face.

Jared's gaze was lost somewhere out in space, and his arms hung limp at his sides. His breathing was shallow, his lips slightly parted. It looked like he soul had left his body.

"You lost the best thing that's ever happened to you, and it doesn't matter how or why it happened. I found it, and that's all that matters to me. Life's a game, you know. And there are people who win and people who lose," he said seriously, and Jared took a step back, leaning against the wall behind him.

Jennifer quit smiling and looked at Neil in disbelief, as did several other members of the Krew. I, on the other hand, was sure that I'd heard him wrong…

"I fucked up, Logan." Neil turned suddenly to his brother, who was regarding him seriously with no reaction. "But if I could go back in time, I'd do everything exactly the same."

Then, he approached me, towering over me with his great height. I bent my head back to look at him. He raised a hand and touched my cheek and moved his thumb along my lower lip. I winced, because I could still feel Jared's slap throbbing against my face.

"You're not going to touch her again, Jared. And I won't be so forgiving if you try it again." He took one last look at my ex-boyfriend, who was still motionless with his back against the wall.

"Let's get out of here." Neil gestured at me with his chin, inviting me to follow him. I hesitated, because I was still so shaken up and confused that I no longer had any idea who I should trust or what was the right thing to do. Next to me, Logan was watching the entire disastrous scene gravely but he didn't intervene.

"Neil! Where the fuck are you going?" blurted out Jennifer as she advanced on us furiously, jealousy written all over her face. Mr. Disaster stopped and turned to her with an indifferent look.

"I'm taking a trip to my Neverland," he answered, sounding amused and turning his eyes on me.

Everyone looked befuddled, including Logan, because no one else knew what he was talking about. I was the only one who could have understood his words—ours was a secret language that we could use to conceal our real thoughts.

I appreciated, then, that Neil had been defending me in his own way, even if he had aggressively kicked me out of the pool house the night before.

I didn't know if trusting him was the right thing to do, just as I didn't know if following him into his darkness was going to lead to inevitable suffering. What I did know, however, was that my entire soul wanted to take the risk and give Neil a chance instead of spending the rest of my life wondering what might have happened, had I listened to my reason instead of my instinct.

This man, beautiful and troubled, had dug a hand into my chest and clasped his fingers around my heart, marking me as his.

I was now subject to all of his disasters. And he himself was my disaster. My beautiful disaster.

It would be him and no other.

30

What story are you going to make up to explain this gnarly bruise?" I asked Selene as she perched on the marble counter of my bathroom. I had no idea why I'd decided to take her away from Blanco with me. I just knew that I categorically refused to leave her there with that prick Jared. I had no idea he'd come in from Detroit at all, much less that Selene had decided to confess everything to him without telling me first. I could have helped her manage the situation, but once again, she'd done the childish thing.

She didn't answer me, though. Her ocean eyes were still beautiful but listless; they had lost their usual light.

"Why didn't you say anything about Jared coming here?" I pushed again, putting the first-aid kit away underneath the sink. I'd already dressed the cut on my palm and put some bruise cream on her cheek. Over the course of one evening, I'd become a fucking nurse.

"He texted me yesterday when I was with you," she said finally, slipping down from the marble counter and turning to look at herself in the mirror. She was always beautiful to me, even with that large violet stain that stood out against her pale skin. "And I still don't know whether to be pissed at you for the way you ran me off last night or for announcing everything we did in public or whether..." She turned and looked at me. "Or whether I should thank you for standing up for me, in your own way," she finished in an uncertain whisper, looking at the jacket I was still wearing.

I thought back for a moment on the evening's events. I'd gone out to distract myself, to spend one night with the Krew without dwelling on my nightmares, my mood swings, and all the other fucking problems that swarmed my brain.

It had been incredible the night before, feeling Babygirl's hands on me as she followed all my instructions, learning how to touch me. For all the experienced women I'd been with, I had never come to easily as when I felt those timid, questing, and uncertain fingers on me. It was impossibly arousing.

I couldn't tell her the real reason I'd made her leave: that some mechanism in my brain had been triggered in a way that would have seemed convoluted and illogical to anyone who didn't have my precise traumatic experiences. Unfortunately, my memories had been resurfacing more and more often, and sometimes even the smallest, barely perceptible detail was enough to set me off. Sometimes, it was blond hair, or something someone said, a look, a situation—it could be anything, and I would be back there in the worst part of my life. My demons would rear up to remind me they were still there and I would never heal.

That was why I couldn't have a relationship with anyone and why Selene needed to stay away from me.

I couldn't believe in love, because the kind of love I'd known had destroyed me completely. The damaged remains of my psyche had no capacity for love.

"Jared called me a..." Selene spoke, and my thoughts turned

back to her. She was wearing a simple outfit that was nonetheless attractive on her. I wanted to touch her, and strangely, to be touched *by* her. I wanted to feel those fingers clasped around me again, the way they had been before the moment evaporated because of my broken brain. "A..." She couldn't finish her sentence, and I stroked her cheek softly.

I didn't need to hear her say it; I already knew the kind of insults she'd heard from him. She was still afraid and upset. I could hear it in her trailing speech and see it in her trembling legs.

"And did you believe him?" I asked her, trying not to focus too much on those full lips whose taste was still impressed upon my tongue. Selene looked thoughtfully at me, and I stared at the upward curve of her eyelashes, ringing her ocean gaze that currently looked so tempestuous.

"I don't know if a woman who has only ever been with one man can really be described that way," she said, sounding both reflective and saddened.

Did she actually have to think about it?

That one man was me, and she wasn't a whore; she would never be.

"He doesn't know shit," I spat, in reference to her boyfriend. Or rather, her ex-boyfriend now. Selene was everything that was pure and unsullied; she was magnificent, and she was light-years away from a whore.

Sure, she'd made mistakes, but that was probably mostly my fault. She had a good soul, and that didn't change.

"Don't let other people tell you who you really are. Quit giving a shit about other people's opinions." I pulled off my leather jacket and headed for my room, gesturing for her to follow me. I tossed the jacket onto the desk chair and rolled the sleeves of my sweater up to my elbows. Selene stood at a distance, inspecting her surroundings as though it were a torture chamber where she was about to receive her umpteenth punishment.

"You can sit down, if you want." I didn't know how to interact with a woman outside of bed. I was experiencing so many firsts with Selene; she couldn't possibly realize. I rubbed the back of my neck and sighed.

I was feeling unsettled. I hadn't really given that dickhead Jared the lesson he'd deserved, and just the night before, I'd kicked her out of the pool house like nothing had happened between us. I should have at least tried to apologize about that. I was also discomforted by the two riddles I hadn't been able to solve and the idea of some unknown person stalking me. Finally, I felt weird about Logan having learned the whole truth.

In short, I had a lot of reasons to be antsy in that moment, yet my mind was fixed on Babygirl as she sat down on my bed and everything else seemed to fall away.

"Why did you kick me out like that last night, and why did you smash everything?" Selene asked softly as she stared at the crumpled papers I'd tossed to the floor the previous night. They were covered in my attempts at solving those goddamned puzzles. I flexed my left hand, the one with the bandage over the cut I'd given myself with that bottle, and sighed.

"Because my brain doesn't work right sometimes, especially when it gets stuck in the past." She didn't really want to start up this "talking" bullshit again, did she? We'd had sex several times now; I liked her body, and I liked her, but the possibility of Selene becoming a real part of my fucked-up life was still extremely remote.

Babygirl pulled down the sleeves of her own sweater and clamped her thighs together nervously. She was still troubled, and it made me feel helpless because there wasn't anything I could do to erase the shitty evening she'd had.

"Did he put his hands on you in any other way?" I asked suddenly. I crossed my arms over my chest and planted my ass on the desk, mentally preparing myself for whatever answer I was about to hear. Selene kept her head lowered and didn't say a single word.

God, she was ridiculously sweet: she seemed somehow smaller and more innocent like that. I moved slowly to her and crouched until I could meet her big blue eyes.

"What did he do to you?" I pushed a strand of auburn hair behind her ear, and she went rigid.

Was she afraid of me, too?

Of course, she had watched me smash up an entire room less than twenty-four hours before, so could I really expect her to feel safe in my company?

"He kissed me and..."

She paused and my mind ferreted away that information. He had kissed her, and the realization that he had done so against her will revived my poisonous anger. "And he did touch me." Shit, I didn't want to know any more.

I got up and stalked around the room like the lunatic that I was. I wanted to break that fucker's nose, crack his head open, and chop off his balls for what he'd tried to do to her.

"Fuck," I swore, understanding exactly what it was like to have to live with that kind of trauma. "Why did you tell him you'd slept with someone else? Specifically with me? You shouldn't have done it, not by yourself. You were being stupid!" I yelled, making her flinch.

"He knew everything already. He knew about me. He knew about you. He knew that you go to Blanco regularly. Someone had already told him everything; that's why he came here tonight," she explained, getting to her feet and facing me.

What did she think she was going to do against someone like me? I smiled and regretted going off on her but not calling her stupid.

"You should have done some investigation before you went out alone with him. This could have been a lot worse," I blurted out.

But how bad had it actually been? I looked her up and down, from her auburn hair to the toes of her shoes, that entire soft, pure little body that had only ever been touched by me. *Would* only be touched by me, until I got tired of her.

I realized that she was scared, but at that moment, all I wanted to do was feel her again. I wanted to do it my way, in my room. The same place everything began that fateful evening when she'd come to me hammered, thinking I had company and instead found me drunk-training.

"How far did he go?" I asked her because I needed the pain—I needed to know. She glanced up at me and swallowed before biting her lower lip, where my eyes lingered, greedy for her.

"As far as the blond in the pool house went with you."

Fuck, no!

That blond had done just about everything with me; did that mean her shitty ex had managed to force his way into her pants?

"Don't screw with me!" I grabbed her elbow and felt her shivering. I needed a real—and precise—answer.

"Why, are you jealous?" she taunted me. She had no idea the dark things this conversation had really awakened in me. No, I wasn't jealous, but I certainly would have castrated any man who tried to assault my women, whether it was my sister or my…*her*.

"Don't joke about that kind of thing, Selene. Jealously has nothing to do with it! You and I are not together, and I would never try to forbid you from fucking whoever else you like, but if someone tried to assault you… Well, I wouldn't be responsible for my actions," I confessed, willing her to understand that it was the sexual-abuse element that had the alarms going off in my brain and all of my instincts leaping to action. It was true, after all, that I would never have kept her from sleeping with someone else. I had no right to do that, even if…

"Really? So, if I got down with Xavier or Luke or someone else from the university, you'd be just fine with that?" she teased me, the smirk on her face so impertinent that I could have bitten it off.

No! Of course I wouldn't allow Xavier or Luke to touch her, because they were twisted perverts like me. They were worse, even—they were genuine sleaze bags. Plus, I was very familiar with their sexual fantasies—I'd even participated in a few of them—and none of it was right for an innocent woman like her.

I would never have done anything like that with her.

"Some other guy at school, sure." I pasted on a cocky grin, because I could accept that, but only once I'd gotten tired of her.

She could have other men but only *after* me.

"But for the moment, Tinkerbell…" I leaned into her and breathed in her coconut smell. She smelled freshly scrubbed, something that drove me crazy in a woman. "You'll just have to settle for my cock," I whispered, making her jolt.

Oh, yes…. She rubbed it and stimulated it at length the previous night. She had examined its length and diameter, and I was confident she wouldn't easily forget it.

"What the hell was going through your head!"

My lustful reminiscences were interrupted by a furious Logan, who burst into the room without even bothering to knock. I turned away from Selene and braced myself for another tedious lecture from my brother.

"It was an accident," I said mockingly, and Selene turned red, sitting back down on the bed. Logan was so enraged that he had thus far ignored her presence.

"An accident?" he repeated, looking first at me and then, finally, at Selene. "Neil! Losing your phone is an accident; a fender bender is an accident; knocking over a vase is an accident. Sleeping with Matt's daughter is not an accident, for God's sake! What were you thinking?" he snapped, and I glanced at Selene, who was looking extremely troubled.

Logan followed my eyes and allowed his shoulders to slump, scrubbing a hand over his face. "Selene, I know you've have a rough day, but I really need to talk to this dickhead." He gestured at me, and I looked back at him, threateningly this time.

"Be careful," I warned him, because he was approaching a line.

"Do you have any idea what is going to happen when Matt finds out about this?"

"Keep your voice down," I hissed through gritted teeth. I hated verbal aggression; I hated it when people raised their voices at me. I knew that I'd fucked up and that sleeping with Babygirl was a huge mistake, but Logan knew how I was.

"How long has this been going on?" My brother looked exclusively at me, possibly because he blamed all this shit on me or possibly to avoid embarrassing Selene. If that was his goal, though, he was failing miserably at it.

"Since two weeks after she got here," I admitted evenly. After all, it wasn't like I killed someone. I had sex with a girl I liked. What was so wrong about that?

"So, for nearly a month, you mean?" he exploded, running both hands through his hair.

What a drama queen.

"I told you to lower your voice," I repeated sternly, moving closer to him with my usual despotic authority.

"You didn't even give her time to unpack," he commented. "I'm used to your bullshit, but even I didn't think you'd do something like this," he continued, sounding anxious.

"I already told you; it was an accident." I answered him with a false air of calm that I hoped wouldn't completely evaporate.

"Yeah, tell it to someone else," he snapped back.

"Neil's telling the truth. We were both drunk." After a prolonged silence, Selene's delicate voice pushed in between us, drawing both of our attentions to her pallid face. She was visibly exhausted by her nightmare day. "It happened the night I got drunk, and…"

"And I took you back to your room," Logan guessed with a heavy sigh before giving me a speculative look. "And you were drunk, too? Why?"

I didn't know if that was a serious question, but I gave a nonchalant shrug either way.

"That's none of your business," I answered bluntly, mincing no words. I couldn't tell him the real reason I was getting trashed with Selene right there. I would have, if we were alone and I hoped he could see that.

"Neil, don't push me," he threatened in a low tone. I grinned because no one could stop a person like me or instill any sort of fear in a soul that had already been through hell.

"Little bro—don't push *me*." He knew perfectly well, after all, what would happen if he did that. And appropriately, my cutting look seemed to be enough to make him step back behind the line. Where he belonged.

"How many times has this happened? I mean, what I'm saying is…is this thing still going on between the two of you?" He gestured between us with his index finger, and Selene blushed violently, looking adorable the way she always did when she wore her perpetually prim expression. Even when she came, even in the midst of her orgasm, she maintained that aura of innocence.

"Yes," I confirmed, drawing my brother's hazel eyes back to me. Judging by the look on his face, he was preparing to cut my balls off any second.

"And were you drunk all the other times, too?" he asked mockingly, shaking his head as he resigned himself to the reality of what we had done.

"No. But while we're here, would you also like to know how long it took me to get hard?" I answered with false gravity, and his head shot up. He looked at me like I was an alien, but if Selene wasn't used to my vulgarity by now, that was her problem.

"This is going to end badly, and you have to know that. You have never had a stable relationship because you are an unstable person," he accused me, right there in front of the Tigress. If he'd brought up my mental issues, I would have immediately tossed him out.

"I don't even have to ask if you have feelings for her or if you're actually together, because I already know what you're going to say. I know you, Neil. I know you better than anyone." The fact that he was talking like Selene wasn't even in the room with us was upsetting me. I hated how he just said and implied things that I would never have explained to her.

"And don't give me that look, Neil!" he continued in the face of my forbidding expression. "It's only fair that she hears this and understands the kind of trouble she's gotten herself into." He turned to Selene now. She raised up her chin, her hands tightening on her thighs. Fuck, I didn't want him to scare her. Couldn't he see she was already terrified?

"Stop it," I ordered him, trying to hold on to some fucking self-control, even as I felt it slipping away from me like water.

"He's going to use you, Selene. He'll use you until he's had enough of you, and when that happens, you won't want to let him go because while he was using you, you will have fallen in love with him the way everyone else does."

Selene's mouth fell open, but she seemed unable to respond. I lunged at Logan and gave him a shove.

I loved my siblings. In fact, the feelings I had for them were the only form of love that I actually believed in, but that wouldn't stop me from tearing a strip off them when they deserved it.

"What the fuck are you saying to her?" I yelled, close to Logan's face. He was just as tall as me, but his face, like his frame, was less imposing and slimmer. He didn't fear me, though, because he knew that I would never lay a hand on him, that I would never really hurt him. He knew I would lay down my life for him or Chloe, and it was this knowledge that allowed him to challenge me.

He gave me a disappointed look and shook his head.

"Only the truth. And you should be telling her, too. You could have had any girl you wanted; why pick Selene? She needed to stay out of your collection, because we both know how this is going to end."

And…how *was* my twisted fairy tale with Babygirl supposed to end?

Certainly not happily ever after, and Logan could see it already. Even if I didn't appreciate him saying all of this in front of Selene, my brother was telling her the truth. A truth that I had only given her in a partially obscured way, because I was selfish. Because I knew I needed to warn her, but I didn't want to destroy any possibility of getting to use her again.

And again and again.

I wanted her because, when I was with her, the memories were less resurgent. Which wasn't what happened with the blonds.

"Logan," she said, getting up to approach my brother. "Neil's told me many times that we aren't in a relationship and that I shouldn't project any imaginary delusions on him. Don't worry about me; he was straightforward."

Incredible: Babygirl was defending me, but she didn't realize that I had never been as completely honest as she'd thought.

Yes, I had made it clear that I was fucked up in every way and that my brain worked only intermittently. But I hadn't been explicit, and that was out of pure self-absorption. I was even happy when she finally ended things with her shithead ex, even if I did hate the way he'd done it.

"And now, if you'll both excuse me, my head feels like it's exploding and I need to rest," Selene murmured. Then she walked, shoulders hunched, to the door.

"Clean up the mess you made of the pool house before Mom gets home," Logan ordered, following her.

Fortunately, Matt and my mother were away on a business trip, and they'd taken Chloe with them. Otherwise, there was no way I'd be able to explain everything that had happened in the last two days.

I glanced back at my brother, who still stood in the doorway of my bedroom. He gave me a saddened look and sighed again.

"Your angry outbursts are getting more and more frequent. You realize that, don't you? Maybe it would do you some good to talk with Dr. Lively…" He ducked his chin and concluded, "Just think about it." Then he walked out and left me alone to consider his words.

....

The next day, I cleaned up the pool house with Miss Anna's help. My mother and Matt would be coming back that afternoon, but since I'd thrown out and replaced everything I'd broken, they shouldn't have noticed anything. My credit cards had come in handy, and I'd never had a problem using money to fix the damage I'd done.

"I'd say we're finished," Anna commented after we wiped down the bathroom. It was the one I'd been using most often lately.

"You're an angel, Anna." I smiled at her and put the new vase on the living room table before glancing around. The pool house gleamed and smelled clean, like it was brand new. It had taken us a good five hours to put everything right, but we'd gotten great results.

"Why have you been using this as an apartment and not your room anymore?" asked Anna, who was fussing with the pointless fake flowers my mother loved to use to brighten up the decor.

"Because this is more private." And it was the truth. The women I took to bed were too loud, and bringing them up to my room was no longer sensible. Chloe had suffered from insomnia after what Carter had done to her and could have easily heard what was going on in my bedroom. Plus, now Selene slept next door, and it made me feel oddly uncomfortable to know that I was causing her sleepless nights. I couldn't help but imagine her listening in on me when I was with someone else, which only made me think of her at inopportune moments.

"Oh, I understand... Your habits haven't changed then?" Anna glanced at me, and I detected a hint of reproach in her tone.

"Why would they change?"

I needed to do what I did. It might have been psychologically questionable and morally unacceptable, but my survival mechanism was the only thing that gave me moments of slight relief from the memories that constantly tormented me.

Miss Anna didn't answer but only heaved a great sigh and left me by myself.

I spent most of the rest of the day in the pool house, and not because I'd summoned a blond to fuck, although the thought did cross my mind a few times. No, instead it was because I needed to be on my own.

After a few hours of solitude, I'd taken another one of my long showers and stretched out on the sofa to stare up at the ceiling, still wearing just my boxers. My hair was still damp and my skin still red from the heat of the shower.

Abruptly, I tucked my chin and gazed down at my body. With my index finger, I tracked the edges of my tattoo on my left flank, just as Selene had done. I thought about how delicate her touch had felt on me. Even when she was trying to pleasure me, she did it so gently that it made me smile.

God...how could she be so gentle with me?

I thought back on her luminous eyes, her full lips, her pale skin, her hands that shook at my slightest caress, her shocked expression at my teasing, her shyness, her innocence, and for the first time, I thought about how things might have gone differently for us. If only I'd been a less complicated person.

But I wasn't. And I knew that if she ever found out everything there was to know about me, she would have run like hell in the other direction.

Thus, I decided in that moment that the best course of action was to get completely out of her life. I needed to stop wanting her, stop touching her, stop trying to protect her, because the only person she really needed to be protected from was me.

She was a moment of perfection, and as such, had always had an expiration date. Yes, I needed to move on from her and do it so gently that she didn't even notice.

This thing between us would remain just a brief but intense period in my life that I would remember forever. One of the few positive memories in the swamp that was my mind. Still absorbed in these thoughts, I let my head fall to look toward the enormous window that overlooked the patio, because I had felt eyes on me.

And I wasn't wrong.

I caught a glimpse of a figure in the twilight of the evening, a figure in a hood, but I saw them for such a fleeting instant that I wasn't completely sure. I leaped off the couch, still half-naked, and ran for the door, throwing it open.

"Who the fuck is out there?" I demanded, seeing no one. The freezing air combined with the heat from indoors had hit my exposed flesh, making me shiver.

Maybe I was starting to see things?

Dammit. I didn't use drugs, but I really felt like I'd just had a hallucination.

Worried, I took a step back inside, but before I could retreat completely, something caught my attention.

A sealed black envelope lay on the doormat at my feet. I frowned and retrieved it. I flipped it over to read the sender's information, but there was nothing written on the front except a name that was, oddly enough, not unexpected: Player 2511

I looked around the darkness that surrounded me, examined the swimming pool, the long walkway that led to the entrance gate and to the front stoop of the house.

Nothing.

There was no one there.

"Are you enjoying yourself?" I whispered to my imaginary conversational partner. Someone I couldn't assign a name or a face.

With one last cautious look, I retreated into the pool house and closed the door behind me, staring at the envelope in my hands. I headed for the kitchen bar and tore it open angrily, eager to see what was inside.

I pulled out a sheet a paper with a padlock drawn on it and an almost poetic composition written on it:

> LOOK NOT TO ANY GOD, ONLY ONE SAVIOR EXISTS. GIVEN
> TO US EACH A DEVIL AND I AM YOURS. NO MAN ESCAPES ME
> FOR LONG.
>
> SOLVE THE PUZZLE.
>
> PLAYER 2511

I scrubbed a hand over my face and threw the piece of paper down on the bar. What was he talking about? What did he mean? This was the third warning I'd received in the space of a few days, and the fact that I'd found this envelope when I was alone in the pool house suggested that the son of a bitch was specifically angry at me.

"So now you want to play with me," I mused, taking the note between my fingers, but unfortunately that wasn't the only thing inside.

The corner of what appeared to be a photograph, which I hadn't noticed before, peeped out from the open envelope. I pulled it out carefully and saw that it was a picture of Logan studying in his room.

"What the...?" I muttered in shock as I realized that there were several more photos. There was one of my mother leaving her workplace, another of Matt getting out of his Range Rover to enter the hospital, one of Chloe walking across a courtyard at her school, and one with Selene in the foreground, smiling at Alyssa on the university campus.

A mixture of rage and disbelief filled my chest until I had to take a seat on a stool. I realized that whoever was behind all of this had been stalking us. He'd been analyzing our lives, watching our every movement. He knew what we did, where we did it, and at what times.

I tried to muster up my courage, which had crumpled like ash when I saw those pictures and examined the back of them, starting with the one of Logan.

"Who will be the first?" was written on it.

It wasn't just an idle question—it was a warning and a threat. I frowned as I flipped through the other photos of my family members furiously. Each one had a word written on the back, presumably intended to link up with the others.

I lined up the photos, moving them around until I could read the sentence that bastard Player 2511 wanted me to see:

"You are all targets."

I sat there, dumbfounded with my mouth open and my eyes wide. I couldn't even feel my heart beating because I was completely petrified. I swallowed hard and stood up off the stool, running a hand through my hair.

I wanted to break something, preferably the skull of whoever thought it was so much fun to do this to me.

I looked over the photos again before sweeping them away across the bar. Everyone was there, everyone except...

"Me," I whispered, my voice so low it was almost unrecognizable. I wasn't in any of the photos. Why?

"You're loving this, aren't you? Fucking with my head with all these riddles." I blurted out, glaring down at the photos and that goddamned note. I had no idea who Player was. After all, I had few friends and a lot of enemies, which made it extremely difficult to identify the architect of this scheme from among them.

One thing, however, was now clear to me: the son of a bitch had started his game because of me.

He wanted me for his opponent, so everyone around me had become a potential target for him. But in what way? What would he do to them?

Shit, I needed a smoke and to get some air.

I dressed in a hurry, pulling on black track pants and a hoodie, and went outside, flicking the hood over my head. I sat down on the chaise longue and stretched my legs out in front of me, crossing my ankles.

I wasn't just in shock; I was also pissed off. I now had this enormous weight hanging over me.

I had an entire family to protect.

I would have died if anything happened to any one of them, especially because of some unresolved issue that bastard had with me. Whatever this was about, it was clearly my fault, and if he wanted to play, he should have come to me instead of dragging them into it, too.

Fuck, even Selene.

There had been a photo of her as well. She was also a potential target, and all because I'd allowed her to get close to me. I didn't mean to, but I had dragged her into my shit.

That, after all, was what being around me meant: certain doom.

"I knew I'd find you out here." Logan approached me at a leisurely pace. He was wrapped in a gray sweatshirt due to the cold.

Lost in my thoughts, I hadn't realized how late it was. When I isolated myself like that, time seemed to lose all meaning.

"Just like I knew you'd spend the day locked up in the pool house. Selene asked about you earlier, and I told her you needed to be alone for a while."

Logan did know me better than anyone else, and I'd often wondered what I would have done without him; what would have happened to me if I hadn't had a brother like him?

"You do know me." I stuck a cigarette between my lips and lit it. If people really did have soulmates, then Logan was mine: he was definitely the better half of me.

"You're my fucked-up big brother; of course I know you." He smiled and sat down on the chaise next to me, hands stuffed into the pocket of his sweatshirt. I gave him a thin smile and kept smoking, watching the dense smoke cloud rise up into the air.

"The cold freezes the memories, right? How long have you been sitting out here?"

Logan really did know everything there was to know about me. He could interpret all the details, every tiny quirk of my bizarre behaviors. I was vulnerable to him, stripped of all my barriers. I became nothing but myself, with all my endless flaws and issues.

"About five minutes," I answered, pinching the beige filter of my Winston between my lips. They were my favorite brand because they relaxed me without leaving too much of a nicotine aftertaste on my tongue. Every one of my quirks had a reason—they were waiting to be discovered.

"Can I bum one?" Logan pointed at my pack of cigarettes, and I shot him a skeptical look. I didn't like him smoking, though I knew he wasn't addicted like me.

"No, just finish mine." I took one last drag before passing it over to him. He took it in his fingers and lifted it to his lips to try it.

He almost never smoked, except when he was nervous.

475

"So, tell me about it. Do you like her?" he asked, looking at the glowing cherry on his cigarette rather than at me.

I could have pretended I didn't know what he was asking about, but I knew that would have been pointless. But, hold on... Wasn't he still pissed off at me?

"You know that I get confused about stuff like that," I answered, vaguely but truthfully. I was confused by human relationships in general and with women in particular. For one thing, since I was child, a woman had never provoked anything more than a physical interest in me. For another, there were my sexual inclinations, which the monster inside forced me to impose on everyone.

Especially on blonds.

"Do you think the world might be less scary for you if you had someone by your side?"

I turned to examine my brother, trying to figure out why the fuck he was talking like this now.

"Need I remind you that you were the one who said I was unstable?" I threw his own words in his face and he sighed.

"Nah, I still think that and the reasons why I do are clear, even for you. But that doesn't mean you can't at least try to open your heart to someone."

What the hell was he doing? First he was warning Selene away from me and now he wanted me to...date her? Try to start a relationship with her?

"Did you come here to play Jiminy Cricket for me? Why?" It would have been insane to open myself up like that to anyone, let alone someone like Selene. It would have been like a death sentence for her, and I didn't want Babygirl to die—I wanted her to live.

To live by the side of someone much better than me.

"They aren't all like Kimberly or Scarlett. Have you ever tried just talking to a woman? Have you tried really getting to know someone and figuring out if you want her in your life and not just your bed?"

The answer was obvious: I never showed an interest in anything about a woman beyond her body. But I didn't answer and Logan kept talking:

"You should give yourself a chance. You can't keep forcing yourself to relive that torture all the time. I know that sex is nothing but pain for you."

Something cracked open in my chest at the sound of these words because...Logan *saw* me. Or maybe he had always known the truth about my behavior, deep down.

"I do it for the Boy..." I whispered, rubbing a hand over my chest where the patter of my heart was suddenly loud, so loud and then something abruptly caught my attention.

It was the Boy himself, the one who couldn't rest, the one who forced me to soothe him in the most illogical way.

I saw him.

I saw him right there in front of me, standing on the other side of the pool with his blue shorts covered in dirt. His knees were scraped up, golden eyes filled with tears, long brown curls hanging over his forehead, his Oklahoma City basketball jersey and a ball tucked under his forearm. It was the same one he used to play with out in the yard. By himself.

We stared each other down and then he shifted his gaze to the clean, clear water in front of him for just a second before looking back at me. I frowned, unsure if he was trying to tell me something but I didn't know. He smiled at me and then dropped like a dead weight into the water.

"No!" I screamed, leaping up to run for the edge of the pool.

But the Boy was gone. He had vanished. I searched the bottom of the pool and the paved area all around it but h-he...wasn't there. Instead, the memories came to take his place.

Those fucking memories...

It was raining.

It was the middle of the night, and my parents were asleep.

I got out of my bed and left my room.

I padded barefoot down the hallway, glancing briefly at my brother's closed bedroom door.

Silently and on tiptoes, I descended the stairs. I was only wearing my underwear because I had taken off my pajamas and neatly folded them before putting them away in my drawer.

It was pitch-black outside, but the orange glow of a garden lamp filtered through the large window, cutting the floor into neat segments. It was this light that guided me outside.

I opened the glass doors and walked out onto the lawn, under the pouring sky and the slashes of lightning. I brushed my wet hair out of my face with one hand and proceeded toward the pool.

I didn't yet know how to swim, and that was exactly why I was there.

I glanced up at the dark sky, and it seemed as though the storm had waited for me.

Like it didn't want me to cry alone.

I had learned to endure the pain, but I could no longer keep it inside. In that moment, I felt like a wild bird beating its wings against the storm, knowing it would never survive the tumult, would never watch the sun come out from behind those black clouds.

I opened my hands and held them out, letting drops of rain patter against my skin.

I saw them; I heard them. I was alive, but I was still filthy. Too filthy. All the water in the world wasn't going to make me clean again.

Every drop of rain in my hands felt like another piece of me that I could no longer hold together.

I balled my hands into fists and stared into the pool in front of me. It looked like the deep, dark pelt of a sleeping animal.

It had never been so scary as it was in that moment.

In that moment, I felt a fear more ancient than any other emotion: courage, excitement, insanity, desperation.

I didn't look back once as I opened my arms up wide. I looked just like an angel then. Or maybe not.

I would probably become an angel, though, after I went through with it.

Mom wouldn't have been happy with my choice, but I didn't care. I couldn't go on the way I was.

Just then, the garden's flowers bent against the rain, wind shook through the leaves on the trees, and the world looked like a painting.

Fate had spoken, and it had told a story about a boy who was ready to stop fighting.

He'd already stopped hoping, and he couldn't keep living with the sadness, with the dulled colors and the knot that constantly tightened around his heart.

I thought about the note I'd left on my desk for my family:

"When the rain is over, I will be on my way to Neverland."

And so, after one deep, final breath, I shut my eyes and let myself fall forward, held fast in the silent arms of the storm.

....

"N-Neil," Logan stammered, but I didn't look at him. Instead, I just kept staring at the water, which now reflected my adult self, my powerful body and mature features.

"He, the Boy… He was just here… He was here just a second ago." I pointed vaguely in front of me, but I felt completely disconnected from reality, shaken and confused.

Where did he go?

"There was no one there, Neil." My brother sighed and put a hand on my shoulder to get my attention. I turned and the pity in his eyes made me crouch down at the edge of pool, in total surrender

"There's no one," he repeated miserably.

31

SELENE

People said makeup could work miracles, and in my case, it certainly did: concealer perfectly covered the bruise on my cheek.

It didn't hurt anymore, but without the makeup, it was still highly visible on my light skin.

Jared was definitely out of my life after that terrible night, and I found myself having conflicting feelings about that: On one hand, I was relieved that I wouldn't still feel the stress of knowing I needed to reject him. On the other hand, it was shocking to discover that Jared had a violent side. I never would have thought him capable of that.

It did make me feel freer, though, and less guilty. I felt less in the wrong, and now I was free to pursue this connection I had with Neil with no obstacles. Well, no obstacles except the single insurmountable one that was Neil himself and his complicated personality.

I didn't think I would ever fully understand his mood swings or what caused him to have such sudden and frequently unreasonable reactions. One moment, he could be so passionate and sensual, like he'd been during our dice game in the pool house, and the next he turned angry and dangerous.

Sometimes, he could talk to me and be communicative, while other times he turned in on himself and got lost in his own thoughts, like he was living in a world of his own.

I sighed and shut the book I was reading, stretching out my numbed muscles. I was sitting cross-legged on my bed, bored and obsessing over Neil. I'd studied all afternoon before taking a shower and putting on my tiger-print pajamas. I smiled as I remembered the first time Neil had seen me in them, when he made it clear that he hated them and they would never be able to "get a man hard."

It felt like such a long time since that night.

Two knocks on my door pulled me out of the memory.

"Come in," I said, watching Logan's lean figure enter my room.

"I hope I'm not disturbing you," he said, looking as embarrassed as I was.

He knew. He knew everything, just like Miss Anna.

"Logan, I..."

"I'm not here to pass judgment on you; I just want to talk to you." He walked over to my desk chair and sat down it, resting his elbows on his knees.

I had no idea what he was going to say, and despite his reassurances, I was still afraid he was thinking horrible things about me.

"Neil is not like other guys," he began, staring down at the floor as if searching it for the right words. "He went through certain things. Things that led him to develop these ways of acting and thinking that are...out of the ordinary." He sighed, and I hoped he was about to get more specific. I had long ago realized that Neil was not like other people, but his being different didn't scare me.

"What are you trying to tell me?" I asked, encouraging him to be more explicit.

"I'm trying to tell you that, if you're looking for a fairy tale or a Prince Charming or even a love story, my brother is the wrong person for you." He met my eyes, looking utterly heartbroken. "He's not an evil person. In fact, I owe everything to him. He sacrificed himself to protect me, but...in doing that, he damaged himself." His words were like a direct strike to the heart. His eyes were shining and full of the kind of fraternal feeling that I hadn't experienced and could only imagine. Logan loved his brother deeply.

"His experiences made him who he is today, and I don't think any one person—or their love—is going to cure him. That's how it happens in books, Selene, but this is real life. Have you noticed that Neil..." He paused and took a deep breath before continuing. "He easily loses control, he takes countless showers every day, chain smokes, is emotionally isolated and addicted to sex, often acts irrationally, and has confused thinking patterns?"

These were, in fact, things that I had already noticed. The same things that had led me to search the internet for information about his possible psychological conditions.

"Does he..." I wanted to ask, but at the same time, I didn't want to say something that he might interpret as insulting to Neil. I needed to know, however, so I cleared my throat and took the plunge. "Does he have borderline personality disorder?" I said, my voice little more than an uncomfortable whisper. I hoped Logan wasn't going to get angry at me or see me as an enemy that he needed to defend his brother from.

"No," he answered immediately, and I got the feeling that there was a part of him that wished he could have said yes. "I know he's a good-looking guy, and I know he does well with women, and I know that he likes you more than the others, but I care about both of you. And I'm afraid that one—or both—of you are going to wind up getting hurt in this crazy situation." He ran an anxious hand through his hair before getting up and walking over to sit by on the edge of the bed.

"Don't get me wrong, I would be thrilled if he opened his heart to you, but he still has so many problems to resolve. Enormous problems, Selene. He's not going to be capable of loving another person if he doesn't learn to love himself. Just like he'll never be able to move forward if he doesn't get closure with his past."

I stared down at my legs. What could I do to help him? Nothing.

Being with him wasn't enough; having feelings for him wasn't enough. In fact, it might have made things worse. But I couldn't just give up. I couldn't let myself be scared off by his personal issues. Maybe I couldn't fix everything, but I could at least support him as he tried to make choices that might improve his current reality.

I looked up at Logan and smiled, giving his hand a squeeze. I saw where he was coming from; I understood his concern for his brother and for me, but I had entered into Neil's labyrinth now, and the only way I was leaving was with him.

Maybe that made me crazier than the person I was trying to help, but my heart told me it was the right thing to do.

After Logan had left, a very stupid and possibly even dangerous idea popped into my head. I left my room and walked the short length of hallway between my room and Neil's. I hadn't encountered him in two days, and despite Logan warnings, I still wanted to see him.

Maybe he wasn't even in the house. Maybe he was out with the Krew or was with whichever blond was on deck tonight, but none of these possibilities made me abandon my search. I knocked three times on his door and immediately felt my heart rate speed up. Footsteps, sure and measured, on the other side of the door told me he was about to appear. When he finally opened the door to reveal himself, I had the immediate urge to run away.

Neil stood there in just a pair of gray sweatpants. My eyes roved over his broad shoulders, the half-moon shape of his pectoral muscles, his sculpted abdominal muscles and divots of his lower abdomen, below which his manhood was concealed. I examined what I could see of the pikorua on his left side and thought about how I'd touched it those few times when Neil had been naked beside me.

"What do you want, Tinkerbell?" he began in his low baritone. "Or is it Tigress tonight?" He added, sounding amused as he looked at the decidedly unsexy, even childish print of my pajamas.

I swallowed hard and forced myself to look him in the eyes. God, but those were magnificent as well, that uncertain gold-yellow color that shifted hues depending on the light.

"Well?" he prompted me.

My throat was so dry, and I probably had the same look on my face as the girls who gawked at him every day. "So, I was bored and…"

What the hell kind of answer was that?

"And so you thought it was fine to come bother me at this hour because you're unattached now and want to fuck more often?" he taunted me, giving me a smug smile, one of the few kinds of smiles I ever saw his perfect face. My eyes went wide when I processed what he'd said.

"No!" I said immediately, trying to recover. "Oh my God, no, that wasn't… I don't…" But he'd already stepped back and made it obvious he wasn't going to stand there listening to my rambling explanation.

"Come in," he offered, and I obeyed, feeling like my body was responding more to his will than my own. I also had no idea why I'd come looking for him or why I wasn't more wary of him, especially after what he'd done in the pool house.

I glanced around, taking in the sophisticated yet typically masculine decor. It was a space that I had memorized by that point. His amber scent lingered in the air, and the half-open door of the bathroom emitted steam, as though it had just been used.

"You covered it up..." he murmured in reference to my bruise, moving closer to examine my face in more detail.

"It doesn't hurt much anymore," I answered, trying not to get distracted by all those exposed muscles.

Why the hell am I in this room?

Neil was unpredictable. At any moment, he could fly into a rage and kick me out or he could suggest playing an erotic dice game or...

The train of thought was derailed when he grabbed my wrist and pulled me against him.

"You're not wearing a bra," he said in a sensual whisper. My hands came to rest on his bare skin; I could feel his warmth beneath my fingers. I didn't have the guts to move or even utter a word. I barely came up his sternum, and my eyes got caught on a random portion of his abdomen.

"I...don't think it was a good idea to come here... I..." I started to back away to leave, but he grabbed a handful of my shirt and tightened his fist around it. Again, he pulled me to him. This time, he pressed my back against his chest and breathed against my neck, plastering me to his body.

"Where do you think you're flying off to, Tinkerbell?"

That tone... That was the tone always presaged his desires, and right now he wanted me. I could feel it.

"Tell me something about yourself before you take something from me," I whispered, shutting my eyes as I felt his erection nudging the base of my spine. I had to admit that his overwhelming physicality excited me, and I liked the feeling of him exerting his will on me.

"Player 2511 sent me another envelope with a puzzle," he confessed to my surprise. I turned, prepared to ask him more questions, but Neil just bent down to kiss and lick my neck. I let out a stupefied moan at the voluptuous feeling of his tongue on my skin. My head was spinning; I felt like I'd pounded a bottle of vodka.

"W-what was in it?" I managed, though I could feel his hands touching me all over, even the places where we were separated by my horrendous pajamas.

"Photos of every family member and a riddle that I don't want to think about right now," he whispered in my ear, using his body to coax me backward, toward the edge of the bed.

This was a ridiculous way for us to "talk."

I really hadn't been expecting such a serious response when I asked him to tell me something.

I fell onto the mattress, a dead weight, and Neil loomed over me, crawling between my legs. He kissed my neck and caressed my body with one hand, supporting his weight on the other elbow.

"What photos?" I gasped timidly as he slipped a hand under my shirt to feel my bare breast. He covered it with his warm palm and gave it a hard squeeze, making me arch up into him.

"Help me forget it all, Selene." He pleaded with his eyes, and then, growing impatient, he pulled my shirt off. I had no higher thoughts; I just followed his instructions like a puppet. He tossed the shirt aside and moved immediately to my nipples, sucking them. He squeezed my breasts between both hands and then slipped his tongue between them. He lapped at them like he was losing his mind.

As he did so, his wild hair tickled the base of my throat, and his stubble prickled against my tender skin, which only made each devastating sensation more acute. I emitted a tiny cry when he took one nipple between his teeth and nibbled it, exciting nerve endings I didn't even realize I had.

"Neil," I slurred in the throes of passion. Just like always, he knew the exact places to touch, how to coax forth my desires and make my sex pulse as I rubbed it against his hard-on, still covered by his sweatpants.

"Spread your wings *wide*, Tink," I thought I heard him say over the furious pounding of my heart in my ears. Then, Neil licked his way down my sternum, across my stomach and finally to my belly button. He circled it with his tongue and grabbed the waistband of my pants, pulling them down.

Abruptly, he bent to sniff my cotton panties, and I reddened at the bizarre gesture. He grinned at me and took my panties off and slid them down my outstretched legs.

"You're perfect," he whispered, staring right into the center of me, where I trembled in anticipation of welcoming him. He spread my legs wider then and continued to stare at my vulva, heedless of the blush that was now turning my cheeks purple.

"You know, baby, I've never been attracted to a girl like you before." He gently stroked the tops of my thighs, make me quiver with excitement. "But I like you," he declared, opening my legs even wider. My breathing sped up as Neil bent to kiss my knee. He tickled me with his beard scruff as he moved up to my inner thigh, making me flinch and gasp sensually.

"You're still too sensitive." He continued to drag his lips across my skin with a wicked smile while I just stared at him, hypnotized by his luminous gaze.

I was naked, entirely exposed before his eyes, and all I wanted was for him to touch me and own me the way only he could.

As though sensing my indecent thoughts, Neil drew close to the spot where I needed him and blew gently on my sex, making me acutely aware that his mouth was just a millimeter away from me. He wasn't touching me yet, but I could feel his warm breath as he continued to exhale against me, and I observed the reactions of my body: I trembled. I shuddered. I grew slick for him.

"Mmm, you like it, too," he commented, almost talking more to himself than to me. He pressed a wet kiss on my mons, and I sighed with pleasure. While my eyes were locked on his, he gave my skin another kiss, slow and sucking, close to my cleft but still not close enough. My arousal, however, went from zero to a hundred in a nanosecond.

God, it was torture.

"Neil," I begged, instinctively moving myself closer to his mouth with a groan of desperation.

"Shh…" he shushed me, and I felt his breath caress me again, right where I wanted his warm, wet lips to go.

"I'm begging you." I could barely recognize my own voice. I was completely out of my mind. I put my hand over his where they were squeezing my hips and rolled my pelvis slightly in a circular motion. By now, Neil knew he had me where he wanted me. I tried to arch up again but his hands kept me immobilized.

"Easy, Tigress," he whispered sardonically, but I couldn't listen to him, because I was just waiting to feel him between my legs. His mouth traveled down my thigh, farther from where I needed it, and I let out a frustrated noise.

"You are such an asshole," I muttered, my voice dipping into a lower register. *A beautiful asshole, though*, I thought.

Neil moved back up again and breathed hotly on my sex. He still didn't talk to me, but I automatically let my legs fall open to fully experience his bewitching breath.

"I could make you come like this, couldn't I? Without ever even touching you." He grinned confidently, and I had no doubts that he was correct.

"I want to feel you," I answered, chewing on my lower lip.

"Where?" he asked slyly in that low, rough voice of his.

"Everywhere." I splayed my legs, completely insensible, drunk on him and this entire insane, thrilling situation.

Neil grinned and finally approached me. He gave me look laden with eroticism, and then, with just the tip of his tongue, he began to lick and suck delicately at me. He teased me with a feather-light touch, moving from the top to the bottom of me.

He knew exactly what he was doing, and I almost couldn't believe that he'd only done this for a few women.

"N-Neil, slow…" I stammered because I couldn't speak clearly, but he was unstoppable. He continued to deliver the most sublime pleasure with each attentive stroke of his tongue while he moved devotedly over my clitoris. I gasped and shook, my feelings so intense that it was making me lose all control.

I jolted again when he swept his tongue around my clitoris until it stiffened. Then he pressed two fingers inside me, intoxicating me beyond anything I might have imagined. I gripped his hair as I tumbled over the edge into an abyss of lust and perversion, driven by his implacable touch.

"God." The arousal was so intense that it made me bow my back.

"I like tasting you, too," he whispered, and I bent my knees, lifting my pelvis to meet his face. Even just the sound of his voice rendered me helpless and aroused.

I wanted him to talk forever.

His hands rose from my legs to my stomach to my breasts, he fondled them roughly then slowly reached back down. All the while, his tongue swirled languid and expert over me as I panted and fluttered against him.

Neil locked eyes with me, looking up from under his brown lashes. With his disheveled hair and his lips on my sex, he presented a magnificent picture. In an unconscious—or perhaps a little wicked—reflex, my thighs squeezed together, and I admired the image of his face framed between them. In answer, he moved his tongue so quick and obscene, as though to penetrate me with it.

"How do… How… Oh yeah, right there," I babbled, sweating. My chest rose and fell in time with my ragged breaths as Neil devoured me in a frenzy, unceasing. I lost all track of time: my clit throbbed, my labia swelled, a consuming heat began to burn in a line from my toes to my chest, through the middle of me.

A violent tremor made all my muscles go rigid as I reached an intense, acute, immediate, and, above all else, passionate orgasm.

I tossed my head back into the pillow, gripping his hair, and a rainbow of colors blurred my vision as I came apart on his tongue.

Every part of me relaxed, and I swallowed hard as I watched his face slowly approach mine, staring down at me with those beautiful eyes.

"How was your flight, Tinkerbell?" He licked his lips, savoring the taste of me. Seeing his mouth all wet and swollen made me flush.

"Turns out I really like being a member of the mile-high club," I said ironically, and he first frowned and then burst into laughter, making my chest vibrate with the sound. I'd never heard him laugh so heartily before. It was almost a tender moment.

Almost.

"You are adorable. An adorable virgin." He smiled as he propped himself up on his elbows. His hair tickled my forehead, his chest pressed against my chest, and his erection twitched between my thighs. I could feel it hard there, and my desire for him was reignited.

Mine.

In that moment, he would be only mine.

I stared at his lips, gleaming with my fluids, and then lifted my face until I could pass my tongue over his mouth, rendering him speechless.

"You're becoming bolder," he answered in a guttural voice that sent a wave of pleasure through me.

"I'm learning from the best, apparently," I answered, and he frowned, staring inexplicably at my cheek. I couldn't always tell what he was thinking, and in that moment I definitely couldn't.

Suddenly, his pupils shrank to pinpricks and the gold dominated his eyes, exposing all his confusion.

"You don't think you can project all your fantasies about love onto me now that you don't have a boyfriend, do you?" He lifted himself off me and grabbed my sides, flipping me over on my stomach. In less than a second, I found myself with my breasts pressed against the bedspread as his index finger tracing down my spine.

"And what if you're the one fantasizing about a fairy-tale love with me?" I needled him.

I jolted as a loud slap landed hard on my butt cheek. I glanced at him over my shoulder, trying to make out his face, but all I could see was the toki on his right bicep.

"The only fairy tale I would imagine you in, Tinkerbell..." He lifted my hips, posing me on all fours in front of him. He stroked my butt cheeks with both hands, squeezing my flesh with zero delicacy. "Is the one where the prince gets to fuck the princess's ass." Then he bit me, and I could feel his teeth sinking into my flesh in the very same place where he'd slapped. Then he pulled his hands away from me, only to yank down his pants and boxers.

"Pervert," I said, as I remained there, bent over and naked with my hair fluttering loose around me, just waiting for him to do what he wanted to me.

"You don't find me romantic?" He rubbed between my thighs, and I could hear him laughing in a self-satisfied way.

Anything but. I wanted to answer but I couldn't speak. I was embarrassed, even though Neil was so good at readying me that I wanted nothing more than to feel him moving inside me.

"Fuck, you want me, don't you, baby?"

I just twisted to stare back at him. He ran a finger through my arousal, and then brought it to his lips, sucking it off like it was a rare delicacy.

I did want him; I wanted him so much I felt like I'd die from it. And I, too, could feel how wet and ready I was to take him.

I arched my back as his erection moved between my thighs again. "Condom," I reminded him because we'd always skipped it previously.

"I've never worn one with you," he answered, sounding annoyed at my interruption as he continued to grind himself against me.

"But you should," I pointed out, watching him out of the corner of his eye. I felt awkward, and I didn't really get why he loved this position so much. It kept me from seeing or even touching him. It felt impersonal, distancing, and it occurred to me that he probably liked it for that very reason. He wanted to make a woman feel helpless and subordinate.

"You're on the pill, so it doesn't matter," he shut me down firmly. "And I'm tired of talking now, Tinkerbell. Just shut up and use me." Before I had a chance to argue, he pressed his hips flush against mine. His cock slid hard inside me, stealing my breath and I shouted.

I molded myself to accommodate him with considerable difficulty, just like every other time. I could feel every inch of him, as though he were deep in my abdomen. Neil paused for just a moment and allowed me to adjust to him.

I made a slow exhalation just as he withdrew and breathed in again when he surged back with a firm, forceful thrust.

"Gentle…" I murmured, and all at once his hands seized tightly on my hips and his thrusts became increasingly ferocious until I had trouble keeping myself up on my knees. His pace was too fast and insistent, but I tried to relax into it and concentrate on what we were doing. Out and in Neil went—out and in—and with every drive into me, I let out a sound of mingled pleasure and pain because I still wasn't used to his size.

"Fuck, your body makes me crazy." He bent over me, taking my hair in his hand and licking my neck. His torso pressed against my back, and feeling him sweaty and panting behind me made that carnal contact—the contact he had tried so hard to turn into something purely mechanical—feel intimate.

"You're so tight. You're crushing my cock, baby," he whispered to me in that rough tone that made my head spin.

I took a deep breath. I needed to relax; I needed to concentrate on the parts of our embrace that felt good, not the hands holding me so hard they left marks or the thrusts that were sometimes incredible, sometimes painful.

My knees, however, could only take the pressure for so long, and so I collapsed, my chest flattening against the warm bedspread. My nipples chafed against the soft fabric and my ass rose and fell to match the movements of his hips.

Neil was so sure of himself, so dominant and forceful that I had to bite my lower lip to keep from moaning as I rested my temple against his outstretched arm. I clung to his wrought iron headboard as it rebounded off the wall, providing an obscene soundtrack to our scene.

After a few moments, Neil rested his chin on my shoulder and breathed heavily next to my ear. I could smell him, I could feel his slick chest, his burning skin. All of it only heightened the moment and highlighted the fusion of our bodies.

When he touched me, it was like an out-of-body experience because suddenly, every part of me belonged to him, not me.

"Neil," I murmured while he continued to penetrate me and my arousal rose along with his.

"Let me kiss you," I said, almost without realizing I was speaking. I wanted to create more intimacy between us and not simply be pushed around by him like I was just another body.

Neil didn't catch my request right away; he kept fisting my hair while, with the other hand, he supported his weight over me, hovering so as not to crush me.

He looked down at the place where we were connected and put all his focus there, on the way he was dominating me, ignoring all emotional involvement.

"Why won't you kiss me?" I asked again. That time on the chaise longue out by the pool, he himself had said "kiss me and don't stop."

But now it seemed like the idea of putting our lips together disgusted him.

"I want to touch you and look into your eyes," I tried to lever my torso up but ran out of strength. Instead, I lay motionless beneath him and allowed him to take full mastery over me.

Neil planted his hands on either side of my head and shifted his weight onto his forearms, plunging himself even deeper inside me.

On one hand, the crescendoing desire made me groan with pleasure, but on the other hand, it also exhausted me. It was a surreal sensation. I felt like I was aflame, like an actual fire had broken out around us.

"Shh…I need more," he said, probably referring to more interminable minutes of humping because he clearly had no intention of stopping. He kept thrusting and thrusting for what felt like forever while a strange ringing began to sound in my ears, and I stared vaguely at the middle of the room, my cheek pressed to the bedspread.

My breathing grew labored and my skin was soaked in sweat. Through all of this, Neil still had not kissed me, and by that point, I had resigned myself to the idea that he never would. Instead, he slapped my butt cheek and I flinched. After that, he started talking again, whispering obscenities into my ear. Just hearing the sound of his voice was enough to have me gripping the sheets, ready to come.

Neil covered my mouth when I screamed through my orgasm and pushed my legs wider. My ass was pressed against his lower belly, and I trembled, at the mercy of a storm I was never going to control.

"You really are a fairy creature." He chuckled, continuing to rock against me, this time in a slow, sensual way designed to intensify my orgasm. As soon as I became lucid again, however, he started pounding his hips frantically against me, biting first my shoulder and then my neck where salty dribbles of sweat had collected. He swept them up eagerly with his tongue.

On the edge of a third orgasm, I was babbling random words while he slipped a hand under my tensed stomach and slid it all the way down. He pinched my clit between his thumb and index finger and applied pressure before massaging it oh so gently. His touch, so skilled and decisive, sent me over the edge and he gave a self-satisfied chuckle at my body's involuntary reactions. Seconds later, my sex pulled his in ravenously and I exploded again.

"S-stop," I managed, my eyes squeezed shut because I was humiliated by the way he made me lose control. He grinned into the crook of my neck and pushed his chest against my back, moving again.

"What, don't you like flying with me?" he said mockingly. Instinctively, I rose up to slip my hand into his soaked hair.

I began to writhe under his body again as I felt another orgasm building. I bowed my back, and Neil grasped me by the hair, pulling my head to the side so he could kiss me. My lips opened, ceding to his tongue, and our tastes commingled. Moments later, he gave one more intense thrust, and his cock grazed that magical place inside that I'd heard so much about but hadn't really believed existed—I was struck dumb by a wave of pleasure.

By that point, I could no longer feel my arms or my legs or my torso. Nothing but the involuntary reactions coaxed forth from my nerve endings. Neil really knew how to stupefy a woman. I guessed that was why Jennifer was so hooked on him and so possessive over him. I hoped, though, that I wouldn't become the same way.

It seemed that our lips wanted nothing more than to chase one another to the ends of the earth, and I rose to follow him. I pulled away from his kiss and my head fell back against the bedspread as Neil pulled rapidly out of me.

I gave him a sideways glance: he was terribly close.

He grasped himself and rapidly moved his hand, hot seed spraying over my ass and lower back. His was a trembling orgasm but not an ostentatious one, and it was nearly devoid of emotion.

Then, satiated, he collapsed by my side, sweating and panting. He stared up at the ceiling while running his fingers through his tousled hair.

I gazed at him worshipfully, as one might regard a god.

My eyes traced the lines of the Māori-style tattoo on his muscular bicep before slipping down to examine his abdominal muscles, covered in a sheen of sweat, and his hairless pubic area from which his swollen member still sprung upward.

"Did I hurt you?" He sat up slightly to lean against the headboard and reached over to the bedside table to pick up his pack of Winstons.

He didn't look at me, though I could tell he was waiting for my response.

"A little," I admitted under my breath, making a fist against my lips. Though I could still feel the aftershocks of pleasure between my thighs, I was sore from basically my pelvis down. Neil pulled out a cigarette with his teeth and lit it before sliding the lighter back into the pack and putting it back on the bedside table.

"You need to learn how to fuck without kissing," he said, staring into the cloud of smoke he'd produced to pollute the air.

I frowned at the caustic words. Suddenly, I felt humiliated and discomforted: I was cold and sweaty. His cum was dripping down my back, and I could still feel him between my legs. I sat up, covering my breasts with a forearm and looked around for my clothes.

"What did you expect? Look at the kind of asshole you're sleeping with," I muttered to myself, cursing myself for being so stupid. But said asshole grabbed my wrist and pulled me to him until my breasts were crushed against his chest and my eyes were level with his.

"Do you know why you need to learn?" He plucked the cigarette from his mouth, and with the same hand, placed a lock of sodden hair behind my ears. He exhaled the smoke through his nose as he did so. I couldn't stand that smell.

"Because I should be more like the blonds you fool around with, I suppose?" I answered, now truly infuriated. I was genuinely prepared to slap him if he said one more offensive thing to me.

"No." He smiled as he stared fixedly at every line of my face, as though I were a portrait to be analyzed. "Because if you keep on acting like a child, all I'm going to want to do is fuck the inexperience out of you," he added in frustration, as though this were some insurmountable desire inside him to which he felt enslaved.

"Are you trying to give me a compliment?" I arched one eyebrow, deeply confused, but he just busied himself with his cigarette, leaning his head back to stare at the ceiling.

"I don't give compliments, Selene." He continued to smoke pointedly as though to transfer all the buzzing thoughts from his mind to his cigarette. He was so fascinating when he was reflecting on something.

"Look at you, all serious," I teased him, feigning a pout. Neil looked at me and wrinkled his brow.

"And dangerous, right?" he asked, lifting one corner of his mouth slightly. I was trying to keep myself from ogling his body, so I got closer to him, brushing my nose against his jaw. I breathed in his scent: he smelled like sex, like aftershave on his neck, and body soap on his chest.

"Could be more so." I stared at the cigarette clamped between his lips, and he gave me a provoking smile. "Why do you poison yourself with those?" I wrinkled my nose and made a grimace of disappointment.

"What, have you never smoked a cigarette?" he asked archly, not touching me and not giving any sign that he intended to so in the near future.

"No, never." I'd never picked up one of those self-destructive habits, never even tried indulging in the things I thought were bad for me. Though, to be fair, I had become very good at making mistakes recently.

"You wanna try?" he asked in that baritone voice that could make a woman do the worst kind of things for him. I alternated looks between him and the cigarette, which he now held between his fingers, as I considered the proposition.

"I'm not sure," I answered, as unsettled as I might be if he'd asked me to jump off one of the city's tallest skyscrapers without a parachute.

"There's a first time for everything." He brought his hand up close to my lips, and I opened them automatically to accept the filter of the cigarette, the same one that had so recently been between his lips. I inhaled the smoke with awkward, exaggerated movements.

Within seconds, I was hacking loudly and Neil immediately took the cigarette from me, sticking it back between his own lips.

"At least now I know for sure that smoking sucks," I managed, through another cough. I felt like my throat and chest were both on fire.

"And that you're a baby." The asshole grinned as my eyes grew watery from coughing. "Don't start. This shit is habit-forming, and it's too hard to stop," he added, blowing smoke out his mouth only to inhale it again through his nose, like a seasoned smoker.

"Trust me, I have no intention of starting," I answered, making a disgusted face. I sat up to face him and pulled up the covers to conceal myself, at least from the waist down.

Neil moved his cigarette to the other side of his mouth and narrowed his eyes, peering at my bare chest. His lascivious stare made my nipples stiffen and goosebumps break out across my skin.

I looked away to hide my blush and noticed the desk. A few crumpled pieces of white paper caught my eye, and I thought about riddles again, about Player 2511, about...

"What did the third riddle say?" I turned to look at him; he was focused on grinding out the cigarette butt in a black ashtray shaped like a skull on his bedside table. The guy was really committed to weirdness, even when it came to home decor.

Then, Neil sighed and ran one hand through his hair, the other stroking his…

Goddammit!

I'd been trying not to look down, and he must have noticed because he smiled, delighting in my discomfort.

"Do you know what I want from you right now?" he asked in a seductive tone as he continued to rub himself. Abruptly, he bent one knee and left his other leg stretched out in front of him. I continued to do everything I could to avoid turning my gaze in the direction he clearly wanted it to go and instead stared seriously into his face, waiting to hear this new perversion of romance.

"It's one of those things you'd never do because it goes against your morals," he said mockingly, so I knew that it was something depraved. I tossed my hair over one shoulder, allowing the ends to tickle my right breast and his ravenous eyes immediately relocated to that spot.

"You have a very low opinion of me," I answered back challengingly because I was proud of who I was. I'd rather be me than any of the many iterations of Jennifer he'd been with before.

"I do, because you like to talk and I like to act. It's a clear mismatch." He balanced his elbow on his bent knee and finally stopped stroking himself. I breathed a sigh of relief because, if he had continued, he might have succeeded in distracting me.

"So, considering that you'd rather be *acting* right now, try *acting* like less of an asshole and start doing something important, like answering my question?" I gave him a confident, one-shoulder shrug to emphasize my words.

He pulled his back away from the headboard and leaned his face closer to mine, ready for an argument.

"Every time you act naughty, I just want to shut your mouth with my cock," he whispered impishly, breathing against my lips. I held my own breath because imagining him doing that to me both frightened and thrilled me. I couldn't even tell which was the predominant emotion.

"And I'd let you, if you'd only start trusting me," I answered softly, staring into his eyes and trying to wordlessly tell him that he could let his guard down with me. I was an ally, not an enemy. I wanted to feel his soul, not just his body.

Neil, however, got serious again and stared at me as though I'd just said something astounding. He slid away from me and sat on the edge of the bed with his back to me.

And then he retreated.

He retreated the way he always did whenever I got too close to the bright red line that marked a boundary I could never cross.

"There was a picture of you along with the rest of them in Player's envelope," he said, not looking at me. I couldn't see anything except the sharp muscles of his back and those broad shoulders that spoke to all his potent strength.

"The riddle had a padlock symbol on it and a weird, blasphemous poem thing. There was also a threat on the back of the pictures." He got to his feet, displaying the perfect musculature of his tight backside and stooped to put on his boxers.

"Everyone around me becomes a target for him. All of you are targets, even though I'm the one he's really after. He wants to play with me, and he'll use you to do it." He turned to look at me, and I was stunned by these revelations.

"I had my suspicions before, but now I know for sure." He ran a hand over his face and sighed.

"I don't know what to say." I lowered my gaze to the comforter I still had clenched in one hand. Honestly, there were a lot of things I wanted to say, but they only would have added to his stress and

I didn't want to do that. I would rather be useful to him and stay close.

"I don't know your history, Neil, and I don't know what that lunatic wants from you, but whatever happens you won't face it alone," I promised, pulling his golden stare to me. He stared at me like he wasn't sure if I was real or if he'd heard me correctly.

But I was very real and he understood perfectly. I wasn't scared, and I wasn't going to abandon him either.

"You've got nothing to do with the situation." He tossed his head, growing agitated. I could tell from the way his muscles bunched up in tension and his voice, which got deeper and more forceful.

"You said there was a photo of me in there too, right?" I said, trying to conceal some of the terror I felt at finding myself in the crosshairs of some anonymous psychopath. "So, whether you like it or not, we're in this together." Voicing this conclusion out loud only increased my fear because my mind was finally able to accept the danger. "And quit looking at me like that," I scolded him when I noticed that the was staring at me like a man who couldn't accept the reality of the situation.

"I'm going to make sure that nothing happens to any of you," he whispered, a stormy, frightening light in his eyes. My shoulders slumped, and I had a feeling of foreboding.

"How?" I needed him to explain more to me because Neil acted on instinct and tended to do the wrong thing, driven by impulses he could not control.

"I'd sacrifice my life to save any of you, just like I did before..."

32

NEIL

The horrible Muzak in the clinic's waiting room did nothing but get on my nerves.

The plump receptionist with the saggy ass was observing me over the top of her black-framed glasses, looking like a watch dog just waiting to attack the moment I stepped out of line.

"I'm nervous." Next to me, Chloe swung her ankles to relieve some of the tension coursing through her. She was just about to go in for her second session with my old shrink, and I was with her because I'd decided I was always going to go to the clinic with her.

I was the only one of us who understood what it meant to go through something like this.

At least the Carter issue was resolved. I'd gone to visit him in the hospital and blackmailed him with some pictures immortalizing his drug-dealing career. If he mentioned my name to any cops, I'd immediately go to the station with my overwhelming evidence against him. He'd accepted my deal; the matter was closed as far as I was concerned, though my sister was still suffering the aftereffects of trauma.

"Everything's going to be okay. Dr. Lively is a good person. You said it yourself," I told her reassuringly. In truth, I was feeling anxious and short of breath myself. I needed a smoke and to clean myself. It had been fifty-eight minutes since I'd last been in contact with water.

"Who were you with last night?" My sister kept her face tilted down, and for a second, I thought I'd imagined her question, so I gave her a confused look.

"What?" I muttered in a weak voice I barely recognized as my own.

Shit!

"Last night, I heard strange noises coming from your room. You were with a girl." Chloe blushed.

"Are you sure it was coming from my room?" The house was huge, and our bedrooms were pretty widely spaced, but that didn't exclude the possibility of other people overhearing what went on in my bed. It had happened before, but knowing that it was Selene this time made me worry.

"I'm sure, Neil. I may be inexperienced and a virgin, but I'm not an idiot," she grumbled, giving me the stink eye. Chloe was possessive of me and Logan the same way we were with her. I smiled at her and wrapped an arm around her shoulders.

"Kiddo, that was just me training on the heavy bag, like usual," I told her, trying to sound casual and lighten the mood. Discussing sex with my sister was hardly my idea of a good time.

"Sure. Of course." She rolled her eyes, and I pressed a kiss to her temple. Just then, Dr. Lively's office door opened, and he approached us with a beaming smile. He greeted me first, then Chloe.

"Ready?" he asked kindly, and she nodded as she got to her feet. She took a deep breath and then looked back at me.

"I'll wait right here," I said softly, reassuring her.

Chloe followed the doctor into his office, and I was left by myself, huffing at the vaguely classical music that continued to bug the shit out of me.

"What's going on with you?" carped the receptionist, who continued to watch me from a distance.

"The Muzak. Instead of relaxing a patient, it just boils his piss," I snapped, scandalizing her with my vulgar language. I got off the couch, which suddenly felt uncomfortable, and poked around the room, ignoring the bulldog in a wig seated a few feet away from me.

White walls, potted plants, abstract paintings, windows made of safety glass up to the ceiling, cameras everywhere, reinforced doors to prevent access from one part of the building into another, a top-of-the-line alarm system… All of it made me feel like I was in prison. In fact, the suffocating feeling I got whenever I was there was one of the reasons I'd stopped therapy. My "therapy" was dredging up old memories, talking about myself, analyzing my personality on an introspective journey that Dr. Lively assured me would help me but had done nothing but damage me even further.

I paced the waiting room in agitation, and when the bulldog wandered away with some paperwork in hand, I began to feel freer. I glanced around cautiously before approaching the office adjacent to Dr. Lively's. On the door (entirely white, of course) was a gold nameplate inscribed with "Dr. John Keller."

I saw that the door was slightly open, and I moved closer, sure I would see the clinic's other shrink inside, but the office was empty. I frowned and looked quickly back at the reception desk. She wasn't back yet, so I pushed the door the rest of the way open and went inside.

I was very clearly trespassing in a space I was not permitted to enter, but I didn't give a damn about the rules. I examined the room's furnishings first. There was a huge desk in the middle of the room with two stylish armchairs positioned in front of it. The walls were white with a blue undertone that was illuminated by the large windows. Apparently, Keller was an art lover. I was particularly struck by one painting, which appeared to be a photorealistic rendering of a shell on a beach at sunset. I leaned in to get a better look at it until someone behind me cleared their throat, making me jump.

"Hey, my office got more interesting in my absence." Dr. Keller walked into the room, wearing a tasteful blue suit without a tie. His bright hazel eyes examined me carefully as he stood there, holding a steaming cup of something in one hand and using the other to swirl a teaspoon around in it.

"I got bored out there," I admitted, poker-faced. Then I went back to looking at the picture with the shell in the foreground.

"You know, kid, Blaise Pascal once said that all humanity's problems stem from man's inability to sit quietly in a room alone," he murmured, sounding amused before taking a determined step forward. He came over to stand next to me and joined me in staring at the painting. I moved back slightly to put some distance between us.

"What did you say your name was? I've only met you once, and my memory isn't what it used to be," he said, sipping on what I presumed was some kind of herbal tea.

I kept quiet and looked at the steaming mug in his left hand. I noticed that he wasn't wearing a wedding ring on that hand, so he presumably wasn't married. Probably didn't have kids.

"This is one of the best tea blends they make at the café here in the clinic; you should try it. It's passionflower," he continued, making me cock an eyebrow.

"So do you just habitually have conversations with yourself or what?" I asked, somewhat coldly. He brought the mug to his lips, which pulled up in a tiny smile.

"I have conversations with all sorts of people. And you are a person, correct?" he answered cheerfully.

Of course I was, but Dr. Keller had apparently failed to notice my inability to speak or engage with someone for more than five minutes.

Either way, he knew nothing about me.

I glanced around again and saw another painting, this one behind thick glass. The frame around it was silver with little gold streaks. The painting depicted a shell with a white pearl in the middle of it; I found it singular, to say the least. This office seemed more like a shrine to the sea rather than a place to cure troubled minds.

"Do you know the legend of the pearl and the shell?" the doctor inquired, probably eager to tell me some more of his useless bullshit. I looked back at him and gave an irritable shake of my head.

"Look, I don't know what you take me for, but I'm not crazy, and you can't do your psych shit on me." I made a motion for the door, intending to leave, but Dr. Keller spoke again.

"The pearl is a precious object, which the shell cares for, protecting it inside itself." He stared at the painting and smiled. "The hardness of the shell symbolizes strength; the gleam of the pearl symbolizes life, purity, something precious and concealed." He stuck one hand into the pocket of his stylish pants and used the other to bring the tea to his mouth again.

What the hell was he talking about?

"The early Christians associated the pearl—white and intact—with virginal maidens and the shell with the man first charged with safeguarding them," he explained, as if I gave a shit about any of these nonsensical stories.

"Sure, yeah, interesting." I started for the door again, but he kept talking.

"Together, the pearl and its shell symbolize life, love, and eroticism. A man who finds his pearl is a lucky man indeed." He stared down at the liquid in his cup and swirled his wrist in a circular motion, as though hoping to spot something inside the mug. All at once, he turned thoughtful.

"Why should I care about a story like that?" I blurted out impatiently, regretting having ever gone into his office.

"Legend. It's a legend," he corrected me.

"Yeah, same thing," I huffed.

God, which one of us was the crazy person again?

I ran a hand over my face and gave him a flat look. Dr. Keller still stood there, just staring into his steaming mug, his hand in his pocket and his brow furrowed.

"Have you found your precious pearl?" I asked him mockingly, and he looked up at me. He ignored my question and moved quickly over to his desk, circling around it to sit down in the armchair and crossing one leg over the other.

"I asked you a question." Suddenly, the door was no longer my focus but rather this man who was ignoring me.

"Why should I tell you anything about it? It's just a story, after all." He smiled at me and put the mug down on the desk, knitting his hands over his abdomen.

"You're wasting my time." I shook my head and ran a hand through my tousled hair.

The man was mocking me; it was obvious.

"Neil, what do you see in front of you?" he asked, an unreadable expression on his face. I was surprised: How did he know my name? I never had actually introduced myself.

"A shrink who's trying to fuck with me, but the game's over, Dr. Keller." I was starting to bristle. My hands trembled, and he glanced down at them. That was happening more and more often: hand tremors exposed my anxiousness. The doctor put his elbows on the desk and interwove his fingers beneath his chin, giving him a reflective posture.

"What do you see?" he asked again, and I realized that he was actually asking me. I looked over his shoulder at the white wall and then back at him, waiting for a response behind that imposing desk. There was a neat stack of papers on his right and a lamp to his left.

"A desk?" I answered finally with an insolent smirk, because *fuck him*. Whatever his actual intentions were, I was going to play this my way.

"Hmm...so you see a basic rectangular desk, made of high-quality wood with assorted documents and a useless lamp on it, right?" He touched his index finger to his chin, rubbing his neatly groomed beard, and I frowned at him.

"That's right. I also see a guy who's trying everything he can think of to piss me off," I shot back. He nodded, looking thoughtfully at me.

"The problem, kid, is that you see but you don't observe," he pointed out, as though he'd just made some significant discovery. "You see a desk, but you aren't really observing the object in question." He shook his head as though disappointed in me, and I couldn't tell if he was being serious or not.

"This desk," he pressed his flattened palms on the wooden surface, "may seem like just a basic, clearly defined, static object, but you need to look at it from multiple points of view. On one hand, you do need to take notice, as you have done so well, of the object and its most obvious characteristics: shape, structure, function and so forth..." He waved a hand. "On the other hand, we also have to consider the symbolic and social aspects of the object. This desk in particular is a tool for gatherings, relating to one another, sharing a space. Do you see?" he asked as I stood there, now observing him.

"Just like how the story of the pearl is a lot more than just a story." He pointed an index finger at the painting I'd disparaged.

"Oh, I see." I smiled and put my hand on the back of one of his armchairs, my posture typically arrogant. "You're offended because I wasn't impressed by your stupid legend." I spotted a tic in his left cheek. Maybe the good doctor was about to lose his patience.

"I have something for you." He pulled open a drawer and took out something that I couldn't identify because it was enclosed in his fist. "You can give this to your pearl, someday. I'm positive that you will one day understand just how real the legend I've told you is."

Dr. Keller opened his hand and showed me the object he wanted me to have. It was a cube of transparent glass about the side of a walnut. Enclosed within it was a white, perfectly smooth, and luminous pearl. I reached out and took it, staring thoughtfully at his gift.

"Interesting," I said derisively. "And how am I supposed to know who my pearl is?" I pretended to play along with his game, and he smiled in satisfaction.

"You'll feel it inside. The cube will help you protect your pearl until its shell finds it. When you're ready, you'll have to give it to the woman you believe is worthy of receiving it," he explained, perfectly serious.

"Aren't I the shell?" This was all ridiculous. Perhaps his herbal tea was dosed with some high-end drug favored by headshrinkers.

"Exactly," he confirmed.

I shook my head and walked away, heading for the office door again.

"Have a good day, Dr. Keller." I dismissed myself with mock-courtesy.

I walked out into the hallway and followed it back to the waiting room. There, on the sofa, I discovered—

"Nice to see you, Miller." Megan winked at me. Immediately, I looked around in hopes of seeing Chloe, but my sister wasn't there. Probably hadn't finished her session yet.

"Can't say the same." Hell, not only did I not like seeing her, I didn't like having her anywhere near me. Megan made me feel agitated and exposed. We'd known each other for too many years, and she knew too much about me.

"What are you doing here? Have you started therapy again?"

Her green eyes scanned me up and down, pausing on the hand that held Dr. Keller's glass cube. "My doctor has this weird thing about the legend of the pearl and the shell. Apparently he told you about it," she snickered, and I immediately shoved the pearl into my jacket pocket. I didn't like the idea of her making fun of me over that bullshit.

"Listen: you need to stay away from me. How many times do I have to tell you that?" I snapped, needing her to understand that I wasn't screwing around. She frowned, crossing one leg over the other. My eyes traced the provocative shape of her body: a thin T-shirt beneath her studded black jacket covered high, large breasts; skintight leather pants stretched over a pair of firm thighs I wouldn't have minded feeling up, had Megan not been Megan.

She was athletic, her muscles defined and feminine and suggestive of an aggression that was usually very attractive in a woman.

But I did not find her attractive in any sense. I wouldn't have taken her to bed even if I'd been about to explode with want.

"I'm here for the same reason you are. You need to stop dwelling on the past." She stood up, and anxiety made my chest grow tight. I didn't want her to get any closer to me, because with every step she took, my mind retreated further into a time I didn't want to recall.

"Don't come closer," I murmured as the waiting room suddenly shrank and narrowed. She was dangerously close already, and her smell was getting more and more intense.

"We were children without history, and now we are adults with history. Our memories will always be part of us, but spending your life clinging to them is absolutely going to hold you back." The more she talked, the faster my breathing went. I didn't know how to regulate these moods; I was feeling unstable, and her words did nothing but bring out the worst in me. I'd broken into a cold sweat, and I wanted to tear off every layer of clothing I wore and throw myself underneath a shower, staying there for as long as I needed.

"Shut your fucking mouth!" It wasn't me, it was the Boy with his heart full of pain who didn't want to hear more.

"You didn't hurt me, Neil. Ryan is the one who forced me, not you."

Ryan...

I staggered backward and rubbed my forehead. My heartbeat pulsed in my temples, and a sudden dizzy feeling forced me to bend my knees into a squat.

"Shut up," I whispered, trying to catch my breath. But I didn't even get to breathe because she refused to stop.

She sat down next to me and put a hand on my knee. "I know Kimberly's in a psychiatric facility in Orangeburg," she said carefully. I knew it, too. After she was sent to prison, she'd made a suicide attempt and the judge deemed it appropriate to declare her mentally ill. They transferred her to a mental health facility because she was a danger to herself and others.

"She only exists in your head now, Neil," Megan added, rubbing my knee. I could feel my skin burning in the place where she touched me.

"Why are you doing this to me?" I clenched my hands into fists and pressed them against my head, which felt like it was going to explode. I was being overloaded with memories, and it made me sick, made me tremble, made me suffocate. I felt shaken, teeming with hurts I couldn't heal. I clenched my teeth as a familiar rage coursed through my veins like a bolt of energy, demanding to be violently expelled.

"Because we have the same history. No one can understand you better than me," she whispered as she rubbed my back. Why did she keep touching me without my consent?

"You don't need to touch me, goddammit!" I shouted and my voice, loud and furious, pulled Dr. Keller out of his office. He approached at a speedy clip.

"What is going on here?" he was alarmed as he looked between the two of us.

"Don't you ever touch me again without my permission, or I swear I will make you regret it!" I pointed a finger at Megan. I was shaking uncontrollably by that point, my fury having grown to unmanageable levels. A couple of men, probably clinic employees, approached me cautiously, like I was an enraged lion that needed to be locked back in his cage as soon as possible.

"Neil." Dr. Lively had also showed up, raising a palm to the stop the men who were trying to get a hold of me.

"Leave him be; don't get any closer," he ordered pointedly, and they stopped in their tracks. I would have hit them if they'd come any closer, and my old psychiatrist knew it.

"Neil," Chloe called out to me. She was staring at me, terrified, as she walked up next to Dr. Lively. Her big blue eyes were huge with fear, and all my attention focused on her. I didn't want to scare her.

I tried to focus on breathing, despite feeling the eyes of two psychiatrists on me as they tried to anticipate my next move. I rubbed my forehead again. I was lightheaded and waves of nausea made me stagger back.

"Chloe…" I muttered, feeling the lack of air in my lungs. "Let's go." I reached out and took her by the hand, yanking her toward me. My sister looked bewildered and confused and that just made me more anxious.

"W-what's going on?" she managed, and I tried to reassure her by stroking her hair.

"Nothing. We just need to leave." I shot Megan a warning look. She had sat down on the couch by then and was staring at me like I was a lunatic. Then, I turned to the two doctors who were still watching the scene play out, positive that there was something broken inside me.

Something I had always denied both to them and to myself.

It was impulsive and violent, and when I did vent my anger, I felt an electricity, a sick thrill that I couldn't control.

Hitting other people, hurting them, gave me a kind of relief. A fact that demonstrated that I did, in fact, suffer from a mental illness, but I nevertheless refused any medical or therapeutic treatment.

I slid into the car and steered with one hand while I rubbed my head with the other. Chloe sat in silence next to me. She knew better than to try to talk to me when I was in that state.

Because of Megan my mind was trapped back in a place to which I never wanted to return.

I was back with Kimberly, who always wore plaid skirts, the short, high-waisted kind. I was back in those moments when she demanded we play hide-and-seek because it excited her to hunt for me and find me hiding, terrified, in some corner of the house. And if I tried to say no, Kim would make the choice for me.

She'd insult me, tell me what a spoiled little bastard I was all because I defied her.

I defied her when she told me to touch her. Defied her when she told me to lick her.

I defied her when she told me to "make love" with her, trying to justify the filthy things she did with an emotion that didn't exist.

"There's nothing wrong with loving someone, Neil, and we love each other," she whispered into my ear as she moved over me or when she stripped me of my Oklahoma City basketball jersey and my shorts, which had concealed a body, still small and undeveloped.

"I'll hurt Logan if you don't do as I tell you," she'd threatened and manipulated. So I never had the guts to tell my parents everything, because then she might have started hurting Logan, too. Kimberly had broken down my emotional resistance, assisted by my tender age at the time she started abusing me. She was able to isolate me, making our relationship impenetrable from the outside, and she guaranteed my silence with blackmail.

The only way I could communicate with the world was through my drawings, where I tried to express some of my secrets. Yellow for her hair, black for my fear, and red for hell. Additionally, I used explicit language and demonstrated sexual behaviors and knowledge that no child that age should have. I evinced a broad understanding of sex, even using toys in a sexualized way. I suffered from an acute rash around my genitals as well, and these were just a few of the red flags my mother should have picked up on.

....

When Chloe and I got home, the first thing my body required to survive the memories was a shower.

I went into my bathroom and stayed there for an hour and a half. I scrubbed and washed away the horrible feelings that felt like they were carved into me, like still-bleeding cuts. If I could have, I would have torn off my skin and sewed on a new one. But that wasn't possible. Though I was emotionally monstrous, physically I was still very much a human being.

I rubbed my skin and felt my muscles, slippery under my fingertips from the excess of bath gel I used. In the past, it had given me contact dermatitis. I glanced down and was disgusted by myself: I was aroused.

I was aroused by the memory of what that whore had done to me. Not because the memory was pleasurable, but because it flipped the monster-victim switch inside me that made me want to get her underneath me. To drag her down into hell along with me.

I clutched my erection in my fist and stroked along its full length. I didn't understand why women thought it was visually appealing, but I did understand why they loved it so much.

They loved it because it satisfied them.

They loved it because I'd been learning how to use it since I was a child, a fact that revolted me.

I began to masturbate, but that was never a solution to these moments of total abandon. It wasn't pleasure that I sought from sex but *revenge*.

It was a revenge that gave only the smallest feeling of relief as I used whatever blond I could find, pretending she was Kimberly. I'd been fucking her in my head because that was the only way I could feel sated. But it was a satisfaction with a short expiration date, because the whole mechanism would just start up all over again, like my brain was a record player with only one song, over and over again.

I abruptly stopped stroking myself because it would have been pointless to continue. I was just going to have to live with a persistent hard-on for a few interminable minutes because I knew I couldn't come on my own.

Sure, I could have gone to the next room and asked Babygirl to remedy it for me, but for fuck's sake, I hadn't even spoken to her since before I went to the clinic. After our last time in bed, I'd barely looked at her, purposely ignoring her so she would realize how insignificant this thing between us was for me.

Our postcoital "talk" had generated a new turmoil inside me. I was only used to my familiar sort of inner chaos, the kind I'd been living with my whole life.

I got out of the shower and wrapped a towel around my waist, trying to distract myself enough to release some of the physical as well as the mental tension. I walked back into my room, and just then, my cell phone rang insistently. I didn't even have a chance to get my sweatpants on.

Instead, I reached over and grabbed my phone to answer the call.

"Matt?" I asked as soon as I picked up. It was strange for Matt to be calling at that hour. In fact, it was strange for him to be calling me at all.

"Neil," he said brokenly. He sounded profoundly upset.

"You… You need to come here to the hospital," he added, his voice anxious.

"The hospital?" I frowned and immediately headed for my closet to find something clean to wear.

"Yes, Saint Vincent Medical Center. It's Logan," he said.

After that, I no longer felt anything at all.

After I dressed and asked Anna to keep an eye on Chloe, I got into my car and sped down the street to get to my brother.

33

SELENE

It all happened so fast.

Logan took Alyssa out for her birthday. He'd gotten her a gift and planned a romantic dinner, but after he took her home, something had gone awry.

We still didn't know exactly what happened, because Logan couldn't talk to us. Logan couldn't hear us. Logan wasn't conscious.

At that particular moment, Mia was sobbing in my father's arms as he tried to support her. Her blond hair tumbled gently around her shoulders, and mascara streaked down her cheeks. I, meanwhile, was still so shocked by the news of his accident that I wasn't even completely sure where I was.

"What happened?"

For a second, I thought I'd imagined that baritone. But then I realized he was actually there, in the hospital, because I could see him running toward us, his beautiful face a portrait of fear. Mia turned to her son and kept sobbing, trying in vain to speak.

"Logan lost control of his car," Matt explained, moving closer to Neil as though preparing to handle him if he had another huge reaction.

"He lost control of the car?" he repeated, his golden eyes intent. "How is he? Where is he? He's okay, right?" he demanded, panting. He was out of breath and clearly shaken up, so Matt rested his hands on Neil's shoulders, trying to calm him down.

"Neil," he said, giving him a gentle squeeze. "They had to rush him into the operating room. He had internal bleeding and—"

"I need to see him!" he shouted, shooting agitated glances all around.

"Neil, calm down, you need to understand that—" Matt tried again, but his words were useless in the face of Neil's anger.

"I need to see him! Christ's sake!" he continued shouting, attracting the attention of a few nurses who turned to watch him. His voice was so loud, so full of rage that it made me flinch.

"Neil, calm down." Matt reached out for him again, but he dodged out of the way. Neil hated being touched; my father should have known that. Mia, meanwhile, looked like she was going to faint, so I rushed over and took her arm.

"Mia!" I exclaimed fearfully, my hands trembling as I helped her into a chair.

"Neil, don't be this way," she whispered to her son, and I could see how anxious she was. I realized that, in that moment, Neil's reaction was what Mia feared the most.

"No, goddammit! Let me see him!" He began stalking around in an agitated fashion and a couple of nurses approached him, which only made the situation worse.

My father attempted again to calm him down, but Neil wasn't listening to anyone.

"Neil, please!" Mia burst into tears again, but he just raged harder. It was a disturbing scene.

"What is going on here?" a doctor with an arrogant air asked disdainfully as he approached, regarding Neil warily.

"Let me see my brother!" he shouted again. His golden eyes, shiny with pain, darted to the doctor who maintained his cold-blooded expression.

"Son, try to calm down," he told Neil. "Do you know how many people I see in this place every single day, crying their eyes out while their loved ones fight for their lives?"

"Calm down?! It's not your brother lying in a hospital bed! Let me fucking see him! Now!" Neil screamed, grabbing the doctor by the lapels of his white coat.

My father and the nurses stopped him, wrapping their arms around him, but Neil was more than six feet of beast, powerful and impossible to control. He threw off their grasps roughly, and still holding on to the doctor's coat, he shouted again, "Don't touch me!"

He was completely out of his mind. His forehead was covered in sweat, the veins in his neck were standing out sharply. His black sweatshirt pulled tight over his tensed biceps, and his sweatpants similarly strained against his quads and calves.

"Call security!" the doctor instructed the nurses.

"I'm not some maniac! I just want to see him!" Neil screamed again. "And don't get any closer, or I'll tear you a new asshole, moth-erfucker!" he shouted at a security guard who had rushed over to stop him.

"Neil, listen to me." My father took him by the shoulder and dragged him over to a distant corner.

"No, Matt! Let me go!" His screams were heartrending; they were so full of fear and pain, and I felt so helpless. There was nothing I could do to make him feel better.

Seeing him this way hurt me: His chest heaved frenetically, his disheveled hair was plastered to his forehead, and his eyes were full of anger but also fear.

"Neil, listen carefully to me." My father grabbed his face in both hands and stared deep into his eyes. "Logan's in surgery right now. They cannot let you in. You'll see him as soon as they are done. I give you my word," he said kindly, trying to comfort him.

Neil swallowed and stared at him, breath still coming in pants.

"He has a head injury and internal bleeding," Matt went on. "He has a compound fracture to the femur and one of his lungs was at risk of collapsing. That's why they have to operate on him," he finished wretchedly while Neil seemed to be in total shock.

Just then, a different doctor approached us, peeling off his mask and gloves as he did so. Mia leaped to her feet while the man just looked at us in silence.

Neil bypassed everyone else and approached him.

"How is he?" he demanded, alarmed, as the doctor continued to look at the group of us, probably searching for the right words to explain everything to us.

"The boy is in critical condition," the doctor said gravely. We all rushed over to him, and I instinctively positioned myself next to Neil, squeezing his arm. I didn't even know why I did it, I just knew that, in that moment, I needed him.

"What does that mean? Explain in detail," my father said. The doctor scrubbed a hand over his face and sighed.

"He's in a coma for the moment. We've stopped the internal bleeding, but unfortunately, he is experiencing pulmonary collapse," he answered with a polite, albeit saddened look on his face.

"Pulmonary collapse?" my father echoed.

"What does that mean?" Mia sobbed, lifting her hands to her face.

"Pneumothorax or lung collapse occurs when air escapes from the lung—in this case due to major trauma—and gets trapped between the chest wall and the lung itself. The increased pressure causes part or all of the lung to collapse and the patient cannot breathe properly," the doctor explained in a professional tone.

"Did you perform a needle aspiration to get the air out of his chest?" Matt interjected, demonstrating his expertise in this field. The doctor's face clearly showed his surprise.

"Yes, of course. We've also surgically inserted a fiber-optic camera and searched for the air leak so we could seal it...but... Are you a doctor?" the man asked, frowning slightly.

"Yes, I'm a surgeon. Could I take a look at his chart?" Matt proposed, hastily shedding his jacket.

"Of course. If you scrub up, I'll take you into the OR," Logan's doctor answered before turning back to the rest of us. "Wait here; we'll have more information for you later," he said, turning to leave.

"Matt!" Neil reached out and caught my father's arm, pulling away from me. "I have never begged anyone for anything, and I never thought I'd need to, but please save him," Neil pleaded, looking into Matt's eyes. Matt touched the side of Neil's face and smiled at him, like a father would do with his actual son.

"I'm going to go," he murmured and said nothing further.

He departed in a hurry while Mia remained in the waiting room, head in her hands. She was devastated, and there was nothing I could do except try to give her some moral support.

Overcome, I turned to look at Neil and found him staring off into space, lost in his inner torment.

"Neil," I moved toward him, intending to be with him, but he just fixed me with a cold stare and brushed past me with a shoulder check that made me stumble.

He headed for the exit, and though it was my instinct to follow him, I didn't. Sighing, I glanced back at Mia. I walked over to her and took a seat beside her.

"Everything's going to be okay," I said softly, swallowing hard. She lifted her blue eyes to me, so full of suffering. Then, suddenly, she embraced me. I stiffened at the unexpected show of affection but returned the gesture.

"My baby, my son…he could die, Selene," she sobbed into my shoulder, as though transmitting all her misery to me.

"He's strong, Mia. He's going to recover." I was surprised, as I wept with her in that moment, at how close I'd gotten to my father's family in such a short amount of time.

"Selene, please go after Neil." My father's girlfriend put her hands on my shoulders and looked me in the eye. "He cares so deeply about Logan, and I'm afraid he's going to do something foolish. Please, don't let him out of your sight," she begged me.

I reassured her that I would and left to figure out whether Neil had calmed down.

Cold air stung my face as I exited the hospital, making me pull my coat more tightly around me. I looked around, searching for Neil's golden eyes and then I spotted them, staring off into space. He was sitting on a wall by the primary parking structure, smoking a cigarette.

He looked as good as ever and just as imposing. He sat in the only pool of soft light provided by a streetlamp, surrounded on all sides by gloomy semi-darkness. He'd pulled up the black hood on his sweatshirt to protect himself from the cold, as all he was wearing was basic sweatpants and a T-shirt with a black hoodie over it. He'd probably rushed here without bothering to find something more appropriate for the weather.

"Did you come out here to check up on me?" He shot me a fleeting glance before returning his gaze to the cigarette he was smoking.

"I just wanted to keep you company," I answered, debating whether or not to sit down next to him. With Neil, I had to strategize my every move because his mood fluctuated like a seesaw.

"I don't need company," he answered seriously and took a drag from his cigarette.

"Neil, whether you like it or not, I'm not going to leave you here to face this on your own," I said firmly. He had to stop running away from me. There was no reason for it.

"I've always faced everything on my own, with help from no one." He smiled bitterly, staring at nothing in particular. Then, he frowned thoughtfully and parted his lips to let loose a cloud of smoke into the air.

"Well, not anymore. I'm here now." I sat down next to him. I was probably risking one of his fits of rage but I didn't care.

Then, Neil turned to me and blew more smoke directly into my face. I coughed but didn't complain. I knew he was doing it to irritate me, knowing how much I hated the smell of cigarettes.

"He's going to be okay." I refused to give up, and I was going to keep supporting him, even when he tried to thwart me at every turn.

"And why do you think that?" he sneered and turned those magnificent eyes on me, staring intensely.

"Because Logan is stronger than he seems," I said softly, swinging my legs against the wall. Neil's gaze dropped from my eyes to my lips and my heart flipped.

"You really believe that?" he asked in the barest whisper.

"I'm certain of it."

We kept staring at each other, and it occurred to me—not for the first time—that in addition to being the most beautiful in the world, his eyes were the only ones capable of peering right into my soul.

I wanted to kiss him, and I got the feeling he wanted the same thing. But we couldn't, not out here where we ran the risk of being caught by Matt or Mia.

"Maybe it'd be best if we went back inside." It was Neil who broke eye contact first, and I was grateful because I could finally breathe again.

We hopped off the wall and returned to the hospital. I followed him, confused and increasingly convinced that I was never going to understand what he and I were.

We weren't kissing.

We weren't having sex.

We weren't in love.

We were blank sheet of paper onto which something still had yet to be inscribed.

....

That night was devastating for everyone.

Alyssa, Cory, and the rest of Logan's friends all rushed to the hospital as soon as they heard about the accident. Alyssa, in particular, was distraught, and she told me that night that she was in love with Logan. I thought about how happy he would have been if he'd been able to hear her declaration of love. But I was positive that he would hear Alyssa's voice again, that he was going to wake up and come back to us.

Anna and Chloe joined us later, the latter of whom supported her mother through the hours of agony. I knew having her children close by would help keep Mia's hopes alive.

What no one saw coming, however, was the sudden appearance of the man Neil hated most in all the world.

"Where is my son? What happened?" The voice was strong and deep but nevertheless revealed the agitated state of mind of its owner, Mr. William Miller. He was a good-looking man, impeccably turned out with an icy stare. The kind of person who aroused suspicion with the very perfection he showed off so ostentatiously. I'd heard about him and seen the occasional picture of him in the tabloids, but I'd never seen him in person.

"Are you kidding me? Get this piece of shit out of here!" Neil barked, stabbing a finger at his father while never taking his eyes off Mia. Unexpectedly, I found myself standing between the two men, unsure of what I should do.

I didn't know much about his history with his father, because Mr. Disaster had never really told me anything about him. He refused to confide in me or allow me to get to know him in even the smallest ways.

It wasn't that I wanted to invade his personal life or force him to change or pass judgment on him. I just wanted to be a touchstone for him, a person he could trust.

"Neil…" I instinctively put my hand on his shoulder, perhaps trying to get a handle on this ridiculous situation. Mia was looking between her ex-husband and her son in such a bewildered fashion that I felt pity for her.

"Don't touch me, Selene!" Neil barked out the order, making me take a step back. It was as though his body was being lit up by the fires of his hatred, a hatred that was driving him further into oblivion.

"Neil, William is your father; he has a right to know your brother's condition," Mia said finally, though her voice was a barely audible whisper.

"This is your fault, isn't it?" William gestured at his son, ignoring my presence completely.

"I wasn't with him. I have no idea what happened," Neil snapped defensively, and his mother got to her feet, clinging on to his arm. Was she afraid an actual fight might break out between father and son? Could they really be that far gone?

"I have a funny feeling that you had something to do with whatever happened. It's always been this way with you, ever since you were a child. You make a mess and everyone else has to suffer the consequences," William answered threateningly through gritted teeth. So this outwardly handsome, put-together man had something to hide after all. There was something deeply ugly way down in his soul that made me shrink back from him.

"Shut your mouth if you don't want me to boot your ass out of here," Neil barked.

"You solve all your problems with violence," William answered with a dark, shameless smile.

"Just how you taught me, you son of a bitch," Neil whispered grimly, his golden eyes glaring daggers at the man. Mia's fingers tightened around her son's bicep.

I got the sense that William Miller had not been an exemplary father to Neil. Maybe he'd even hit him. The idea made me shudder. I didn't want to picture Neil as a defenseless child, suffering violence at the hands of that icy man. That was probably why Neil never wanted to tell me about himself, why he was so introspective and mistrustful, walled up in his own world.

"I want to see my son." William turned to his ex-wife, apparently deciding to end this ill-advised conversation with Neil. Just then, Matt approached us, wearing a white coat and looking exhausted.

Everyone's attention shifted to Matt. In that moment, any pre-existing resentments were set aside for one reason and one reason only: Logan.

"How is he?" Neil asked.

"They've intubated him for now. He's sustained severe trauma, and now all we can do is wait. He won't be out of the woods until we can get him to breathe on his own," Matt explained, leaving room for negative outcomes that he didn't elaborate upon. Neil staggered back from him, running his hands through his hair, and Mia burst into tears with a wail so anguished that it pierced my heart.

"Thank you for everything you've done, Matt." William smiled woefully at him before taking a seat next to his ex-wife and balancing his elbows on his knees. Neil, on the other hand, remained on the fringes of the group, and seeing how isolated he was, I decided to get closer to him. I didn't want him to endure all of this alone.

He stood perfectly still—his stare vacant and his plush lips compressed into a line of bitterness. I sat down next to him, not asking for permission.

The clean scent of his clothing washed over me. It smelled freshly scrubbed, exactly like his skin.

"You know what my mother always says?" I said, out of nowhere.

I worried he would shoo me away, but surprisingly, he didn't. He just kept leaning forward and staring intently at the floor as he listened to me.

"That life is a violin, and hope is its bow." I gave him a small smile. I wanted to touch him but held myself back, knowing Neil wouldn't like it. "And do you know why?" I went on, leaning slightly to get closer to him. "Think about it: Can you play a violin without its bow? Maybe, but it certainly wouldn't sound the same," I mused aloud. "In the same way, you can't really live without hope."

Neil turned in my direction and stared at me with those gleaming, honey-colored eyes. He studied my face for several moments before sighing and turning his gaze back in front of him.

"And do you think hope is enough to save him?"

"Yes and you should do everything you can to find it inside you." I put an instinctive hand on his knee, an unconscious gesture that I regretted the moment I did it. I was prepared to apologize and put the appropriate distance between us, but then, Neil did something that left me speechless.

He squeezed my hand with his own and pulled me closer to him. He didn't look at me, and his other elbow was still propped up on his leg, but he kept my forearm pressed to his thigh as his fingers toyed with mine.

I held my breath because even just the touch of his hand was all-consuming for me.

"You really are a strange girl, Tinkerbell," he murmured as he looked at my hand, which seemed so small compared to his.

I smiled. "And you're a little bit of a disaster," I answered with a hint of irony.

"A lot, I'd say," he corrected, chewing on his lip.

Perhaps Neil was finally letting me touch his soul...

We spent the whole night in the hospital, waiting for news about Logan.

Several times, Mia told me to go home and get some rest, but there was no way I was going to leave my family there alone, especially not Neil. I fell asleep in an awkward position on one of the chairs in the waiting room and woke up a few hours later with a powerful headache that made me grumble with pain.

"Selene." A hand rested on my shoulder, and I blinked to focus on the figure looming above me. I could see dark stubble below a pair of hazel eyes.

"Matt," I whispered, my voice still thick with sleep.

"I thought I'd bring you something hot. You haven't eaten." He handed me a cup of hot chocolate, and I reached up to take it.

It was a weird feeling: this was probably the most intimate moment the two of us had shared in years. I occurred to me then that Matt sometimes seemed different from the man I remembered and that thought led me to wonder if it might actually be possible for things to improve between the two of us.

"Thanks," I said awkwardly, my hands tightening around the warm cup. I blew on it before taking a sip of the chocolate.

"I wanted to thank you." He sat down next to me and smiled.

"For what?" I asked, feeling the hot chocolate trickle down into my empty stomach.

"Being there for Mia and the kids."

"No need to thank me. We have to support each other at times like this." I was convinced of this: we were a family, albeit in our own weird way.

"You remind me so much of your mother," he said softly, and a melancholy look passed over his weary face. All it took was one mention of my mother, and I was suddenly reminded of my adolescence in a kind of flashback that conjured up all the pain I'd felt in those years. I lowered my gaze to the steaming cup avoiding my father's eyes.

"Selene." He paused. "I know very well that I've made a lot of mistakes. That I've always put my career first and that I was..." His voice broke because it was never easy to expose oneself in that way. "Unfaithful to your mother. I know you saw me with another woman. Everyone makes mistakes. The most important thing is that we understand our mistakes and try to fix them." He rubbed his palms against his stylish pants, the same ones he'd worn the day before. None of us had gone back home—none of us would until we knew more about Logan's condition.

"I wanted you from the moment your mother told me she was pregnant. Please, try to forgive me. You can't know how much it hurts that you won't call me 'Dad.'"

It hurt me too, and maybe I should have been less extreme and more willing to bend. Matt's behavior had hurt me in a soul-destroying way that irreparably poisoned my perception of him. The struggle to forgive him was basically synonymous with the intense pain that I still felt inside.

"I don't know." My frosty tone extinguished his hopes as well as my own. "I don't know, Matt," I repeated thoughtfully, staring at the cup as though I might find all of life's answers at the bottom of it. Forgiveness meant forgetting about our painful past, and I wasn't ready to do that. I was a slave to my anger and resentment and maybe that pain was always going to be inside me, even if I did try to stuff it down into a corner of my soul.

"Think about it. That's all I ask of you." I had never heard my father plead like that. He had always been a man who never asked for anything, the invincible and untouchable Matt Anderson.

He swiped a hand over his face, and only then did I notice the dark circles under his eyes. He was really having a rough time, and surprisingly, I was worried about him.

"You should go home and rest," I suggested.

"No, not until we have more definitive news about Logan," he answered, sounding exhausted as he gazed at Mia, sleeping next to Chloe. Suddenly, it occurred to me that Neil was nowhere to be seen, and I immediately started looking around for him.

"Where's Neil?" I asked, maybe sounding slightly too concerned. I heard it as I said it and hoped Matt wouldn't get suspicious.

"With Logan," he answered. "The doctor let him go in and he hasn't moved all night."

"So he hasn't eaten or rested or...?" Matt started shaking his head before I could even finish. Neil's love for his brother ran deep; they had an unbreakable bond like I'd never seen before.

"Nothing. Neil's sitting at his brother's bedside, and he doesn't want anyone to disturb him," Matt said, and my chest got tight at the thought of how much he was suffering over Logan. "I'm going to check in with the doctor and see if there's any news. I'll be right back." Matt got up and walked off, and I stood up as well, stretching my stiff muscles.

I smiled ruefully at the sleeping Chloe and Mia while a few nurses walked through the silent lobby, the smell of disinfectant filling the air around us. I headed quietly for the vending machine. I got two coffees and took them back over to Mia.

She opened her eyes, blinking in the fluorescent light.

"I thought you might want some coffee." I handed a cup to her and she smiled slightly as she accepted it.

"Thank you so much." She stroked Chloe's hair as she took a sip. The girl was now spread out over her mother's lap. I set the other coffee down on the chair next to the baby of the family so she could have it when she woke up. Then I sat down and rubbed my palms against my jeans, feeling slightly discomforted.

"I'm grateful for everything you're doing, Selene," Mia said abruptly. "I can't imagine how difficult it's been for you to accept your parents' situation and the relationship between your father and me."

I looked uneasily at her because we'd never discussed that before. When I moved to New York, I had a completely different idea of who Mia was, mainly due to my own dumb preconceptions and the things I read in the tabloids.

"I consider you a member of our family. I'm glad you came to live with us, and I would never want you see me as a threat."

I ducked my head because that had happened so often when I was a teenager. My insecurities and jealousy led me to take a hostile position toward my father's new romantic situation. I felt he had abandoned me and my mother for her, making me see Mia as a danger to us.

"Your father and I met by chance," she said and I stared at her, waiting for her to keep going. "I had breast asymmetry. Ever since I was a girl, my condition was...traumatic for me. But I dreaded the idea of an operation and didn't want to undergo surgery. I thought the situation might improve with pregnancy, but it never did." She licked her lower lip and took a deep breath before continuing.

"So I decided to turn to one of the most renowned surgeons in the country—your father. He helped me not just through my physical journey but my psychological one as well. After the end of my marriage, I thought I'd never commit to someone again. I thought I'd never meet a man capable of changing my life and...I was wrong," she said in a low murmur.

"At first, I hid our relationship from my kids. When I finally brought him home, Chloe took it pretty well. Logan was a bit shocked. And Neil..." She gripped the coffee cup in her hands and her voice trembled. "He didn't speak to me for months," she confessed, and I felt a strange tension in my chest. Mr. Disaster was so strong, but at the same time so fragile.

"Months?" I whispered.

"Yes. Neil is very rigid: he gives his trust only to a few people, and he hates anyone he believes has betrayed him." She gave me a resigned look and continued. "He never forgives. Our relationship was already troubled because of my ex-husband and the problems Neil had in his childhood, but after Matt came on the scene, I lost him completely. The only people who truly have a place in his heart now are his siblings." Her eyes moved down to Chloe, and she stroked the girl's blond hair as she continued to doze on her mother's lap.

"And that's how I know that, if I ever lost Logan or Chloe, I would lose Neil as well. He lives symbiotically with them; he won't survive without them." The gravity of her words kept me from speaking. I'd known already that the bond between Neil and his siblings was deep, almost uncanny, but now Mia had added another piece to the puzzle. She had made it clear that something had happened, something specific that made Neil cling so tightly to them.

"Let's not think about worst-case scenarios. Everything's going to be okay; you'll see," I tried to reassure her.

"As for your relationship with my father, I didn't know about your operation and I'm glad that you told me. I appreciate the trust you've placed in me," I admitted, a little embarrassed. "You're not a substitute for my mother, Mia, but..." I cleared my throat before continuing. "But maybe we could be friends."

I didn't know if "friends" was the most precise term to define our relationship, but I considered it a reasonable proposal, if unexpected. It occurred to me that even in the worst situations there were opportunities to be seized and maybe this turning point in my relationship with my father's girlfriend could be one of them.

Mia and I talked for a bit longer, and then I got up and went back over to the vending machine and got another coffee. Not for me, but for Mia's son, the walking disaster I hadn't seen in several hours and with whom I very much wanted to "talk," though I already knew how he'd feel about that.

I headed for Logan's room. I wouldn't be allowed to go in, but I needed to at least make sure Neil was okay. But before I reached the door, his imposing form appeared right in front of me.

His handsome face was etched with suffering, his hair as wild as ever, and his golden eyes lusterless. With every step that brought me closer to him, my heart beat a little faster, throbbing in every corner of my body.

"Hey," I said as soon as I'd caught his eye. "I brought you some coffee," I babbled. Neil got me agitated, and I hated how I lost the ability to form meaningful sentences whenever he stared at me in that dark, mysterious way of his. I could never tell if he was admiring me or disgusted by me.

He didn't say anything and instead just fiddled with a piece of paper in his hands. I frowned, intending to ask him what it was, but before I could say anything, Neil took me by the wrist and pulled me into an isolated corner. He glanced around to make sure no one was watching us and then opened up the crumpled paper to show it to me.

"Do you remember what I told you about the puzzle with the padlock and the photos with writing on them?" His baritone startled me, like this was the first time I was hearing it in years, but I focused on what he was actually saying and nodded.

"Okay. So, I solved it, spent the whole night thinking about it." Dark circles shadowed his incredible eyes, now alight with a dangerous anger.

"What?" I managed, bewildered.

"Logan's accident wasn't an accident—all of it was planned. He was the first. Logan's car went off the road because someone messed with the brakes. Player intended for Logan to die." He handed me the paper, and I saw that it was scribbled all over with calculations and connections. I tried to decipher it, but I couldn't pick out any conclusions from the scrawl, so Neil had to explain it to me.

"The note had a padlock drawn on it. The lock means a

pattern-matching or puzzle game. In this case, the asshole made an encoded tanka." He rubbed his face and sucked in an anxious breath.

"And what's that?" I looked again at the paper where he'd written out his reasoning using a series of diagrams, but it was hard to find a thread in such a complex labyrinth.

On the note right beneath the padlock, there was this sort of poem thing:

"Look not to any god, only one savior exists. Given to us each a devil and I am yours. No man escapes me for long." He recited what sounded like some sort of macabre religious-themed poem, and I shivered, frowning in confusion.

"Fuck, Selene," he said, getting impatient with me. "It's a tanka; it's a type of five-line poem with a five-seven-five-seven-seven syllable structure. In Japanese, they're written in one line, but in English, they're broken up. And if you break this one up…"

Look

Only

Given

And

No

Logan.

"Oh, God," I whispered, swallowing thickly because my throat had gone dry. I looked at Neil and noticed the tension behind his bright eyes.

"Logan was just that sick fucker's first hit. Player's going to keep making moves; he's going to strike again and again until he destroys whatever scrap of sanity I have left!" He clenched his fists at his sides, as though longing to smash up something and vent his anger. Wordlessly, I begged him not to do it, to get control over himself because I understood now how hard he had to work to manage his impulses.

"We're going to get out of this." I drew closer to him and locked my eyes on his. Neil wasn't good with words, but he could hold entire conversations with his eyes. In fact, they frequently screamed out his feelings for anyone who was looking.

"We'll get out of this? When? When Logan dies?" His tone grew sharper. "Or when someone else does?" he continued, his jaw tight.

"I don't know, but I do know we are going to fix this, all of this." Actually, I was mortally afraid, but I didn't want to torture him or make him even more anxious.

I watched his expression grow stiff and allowed myself to reach out one hand as if to rub his arm. He glanced down at my silent request and then back up at my face. I expected him to brush me off roughly, but oddly enough, he didn't. I rested my hand on his arm comfortingly.

"There's no point in getting riled up now; we need to stay calm and clearheaded. I'll be with you, whatever happens," I promised him again. I would have done it a thousand more times, too. Whoever this psychopath intent on hurting us was, we would face him together.

Neil gave me an unreadable stare. I had no idea what sort of thoughts were buzzing around inside his head. He was good at masking what he was thinking, just like he was good at being unpredictable.

Suddenly, he lifted a hand and cupped the back of my neck. His fingers tangled in my long hair, which he then used to pull me to him. His touch sent my heart racing at exhilarating speeds. It reached a peak when, with his own brand of possessiveness, he kissed me.

The kiss was firm but almost chaste, without indulgence. It wasn't one of his rough or violent kisses, far from it. It was innocent yet still dominating. My hands were pressed against his chest and my fingers splayed over his powerful musculature. I could feel his soft, plush lips against mine. Our breath hung suspended in the air, fused together in an inexplicable yet perfect fit.

After what felt like an infinite moment, he broke the kiss and rested his forehead against mine, breathing in deep. I should have been afraid that someone would spot us. If I were thinking rationally, I would have pushed him away and told him not do impulsive things like that when we were with our family, but at that moment, all I really wanted to do was stay in his arms and soak in the scent of him.

"It's impolite to kiss someone without their permission," I whispered, staring at the perfect lips that had so recently been pressed against my own. Neil quirked one corner of his mouth in a teasing smile.

"Then I must be very rude because I don't ask for kisses, Tinkerbell. I take them."

34

NEIL

I thought that life had already given me enough storms, enough rainy days, enough sunless ones. Enough losses and injuries. But I was wrong. I was wrong because now I could see that there had been something worse coming all along: my brother in a hospital bed. I had gone with Matt to Logan's room, which I would not normally be allowed to enter, and it was there that I truly realized exactly what had happened to him.

"Here we are. Logan's in a coma at the moment, so I don't..." Matt was trying to say something, but I couldn't listen to him. My head was spinning and my temples were still pulsing from all the screaming I'd just done.

"I want to stay with him, Matt. I need to." The Boy and I both needed it—we had survived thanks to him. Logan was a part of us. Of me.

I stared at the door to his room for a few moments, hesitating before I went in.

I knew I wasn't ready to see him in that state, but I had to do it anyway. I had to be with him. Sighing heavily, I walked inside slowly, and it seemed like I could almost feel a gust of cold air against my face. Finally, I could see him there, lying on the hospital bed, intubated. One of his monitors showed a heart rate that was far too slow, almost imperceptible. I leaned toward him and gulped, swallowing down the sharp thing that was suddenly in my throat.

Then, I screwed up every ounce of courage I had and sat down next to the bed, staring at my brother's white face, marred by the trauma he'd sustained. His bright eyes were closed, but as Babygirl had told me, it was time to look within myself for that flame of hope.

The bow.

"You're in a fight with death now, Logan." I took his hand and held it in my own, and for the first time in my life, I was genuinely afraid of losing the person I cared about most in the world.

"Logan," I said in a simple murmur. "I don't know if you can hear me…" My voice broke; I barely recognized it. The room was silent except for the beeping of the monitors, which echoed hauntingly, reminding me that his life was hanging by a fragile thread.

I looked up at the line that recorded his heartbeat: the waves were small and showed no sign of growing. I looked back down at my brother and took his hand again.

"Logan, you still have a lot of life ahead of you; don't leave us." I stared at him, overwhelmed by this huge feeling of despair, like I was on a dead-end road with no escape route.

"Don't leave me," I added softly, and I felt my heart break in two at the thought of never seeing him again. Of never hearing his voice or seeing his smile.

"Do you remember our pinky promises?" I smiled weakly as I remembered his big eyes staring up at me nervously every time I had to go away from him. "Remember how you made me promise to come back to you?" I rubbed the back of his hand with my thumb.

"Now you've got to make that promise to me." I took a deep

breath because I suddenly felt short on air. "You have to promise me that you'll come back to me. That you'll keep lecturing me and we'll have our talks in the garden and that I'm going to be able to watch you eat your cereal every morning." I continued, watching him closely, even though his body showed no signs of life. It was inert, devoid of any spark.

"Promise me you'll come back to me. We'll get through this, Logan." I gripped his fingers. "We'll get through it. But if you're not there, then I won't stay, either. If you leave, I'm going to go with you…" The pain I felt was indescribable. If someone had shards of glass stabbed into their body all over, the feeling might have gotten close.

"I wish I had been there, Logan. Actually, I wish I could have taken your place. I should have protected you the way I always have." My chest ached, and I massaged it with one hand.

"I'm so sorry, Logan." I squeezed his cold hand in mine and kept talking, "You're the air I breathe, the best part of me. I never said it but…I love you. I care more about you than I do my own life. The only kind of love I've ever understood is the kind I have with you and Chloe. So, you see, you have to stay with me. I promise you that I'm going to find whoever did this to you." My voice was flat but filled with hatred. "I'm going to find him and kill him. I promise, Logan." I licked my now-dry lips and hung my head, closing my eyes. Was this really all life was? It was like Roberto Gervaso said: a crystal pendant, dangling from the ceiling by a silken thread.

It was a fucking lie that each of us could be the architect of our own destiny, because destiny was the one who chooses for us. He was a piece of shit teacher who inflicted only punishments on his pupils.

Suddenly, my cell phone rang. I leaped up from the chair and walked over to the window before pulling it out of my pants pocket. Glancing at the screen, I saw that it was an unknown number. My hand was trembling with rage as I accepted the call and brought the phone to my ear.

"Did you like my surprise, Neil? It was so simple, tampering with the brakes on your brother's car." The person on the other end was using a voice modifier, making him unrecognizable. But actually being able to hear whoever was doing this to us felt like a nightmare slowly materializing in front of me. Automatically, I thought of the puzzle, the lock, the poem...

"You've made a serious mistake," I hissed, cold and menacing.

The son of a bitch never should have touched Logan, just like he shouldn't touch any other member of my family. I wasn't afraid of him. I just needed to find out who he was so I could go beat him to death.

"Oh, for sure. Little bro's in a bad way, huh? He's going to die, you know." The motherfucker laughed aloud. I clenched my fists as I stared at Logan, limp and motionless on the bed.

"Listen to me, you sick son of a bitch," I began softly, feeling the anger surging through every part of my body. My jaw had begun to ache from grinding my teeth. "And remember these words," I continued in a grim, deliberate tone. "I am going to find out who you are, and I am going to kill you. From this day forward, that will be my only goal." I gripped the phone tightly. I wanted to destroy the anonymous person on the other end of the line, but I needed to keep my cool. I had to think and act strategically.

"Who will be next?" He burst into laughter and hung up before I could respond.

I remained frozen, staring at the white wall in front of me before slowly lowering my eyes to my phone, where my usual lock screen had appeared: flames on a black background. The same kind of flame seemed to rage inside of me at the idea of getting my revenge.

I turned to Logan and examined him closely. This was no fucking accident. It had been completely premeditated. Player had tried to murder my brother—Logan was the first pawn to be sacrificed in his sick game.

This was my fault. I'd had the solution to the riddle right there in front of me, but I hadn't been able to figure it out.

The anger inside me burned like acid, eating me from the inside out. My hands shook again, heat spread like oozing lava into every fiber of my being.

I looked at Logan again and sat down beside him, taking his hand in mine.

"I'm going to stay here with you tonight. I won't leave you," I promised him, watching his chalk-white face. "But you've got to wake up, Logan. I'll be with you, however fucking long it takes." I leaned over him, pressing a kiss to his forehead. "And I'm going to find the person who did this to you," I repeated, still locked in the grips of an anger that I fought to control. She was a ferocious beast, however, and she demanded to be let out of her cage.

Player, that bastard, wanted his revenge, but now it was time for me to get mine.

....

I had a sleepless night.

I was feeling agitated because I was still wearing the same clothes I'd worn the day before and my skin hadn't been in contact with water for several hours.

I felt like a drug addict going through withdrawals.

All I did was wander the edges of Logan's room, like a caged lion, rubbing my temples because my headache was wearing me down.

My mind was now completely fixed on solving Player's puzzles. I needed to figure out how to read his messages and analyze his language. That was the only way I'd be able to spot more hidden threats.

I asked the on-duty nurse for a pen and paper and began writing down my thoughts. Then, I tried my hand at cryptography to see if I could figure out how this fucking guy thought. Whoever he was, he had a sharp mind; his secret message was unintelligible to me.

But he also clearly wanted me to read these riddles and understand what he was trying to say to me.

I sat by Logan and used the dim nightlight to write everything on my mind down on that piece of paper.

I concentrated my efforts on the most recent puzzle, the vaguely satanic verse. I was certain there was something I had missed, something I should have been able to see before he'd caused Logan's accident.

"Fuck," I whispered. I had no idea what time it was, but my headache was getting more intense and all that thinking only made it worse. I was counting the syllables in the little verse and the number—thirty-one—felt vaguely familiar.

I grabbed my phone and searched "31 syllables," which brought up a number of results, most prominently a type of Japanese poem that included thirty-one syllables broken into chunks of five and seven. Hastily rewriting the verse to fit into that format, I realized what I was looking at.

It was an acrostic.

A fucking acrostic—which I hadn't even remotely considered—was the mechanism my enemy had used to reveal his plans to me before ever attacking Logan.

It was then that I truly understood the game he wanted to play with me. He was hoping that I would attempt to stop him and that I would fail and feel guilty as I watched his targets die because of me. Player had given me the answer; it was only slightly hidden, and I was supposed to decipher it. If I had, I might have prevented him from doing what he'd done. In this case, however, my inaction had made me his accomplice.

"What a fucking nutjob."

I was finally starting to get the rules of this game, and now I knew that I needed to guess who would be next so I could stop his attack. However, I had no new clues and the photos of my family members seemed too vague to give me any leads.

He could have gone for any one of them.

I swiped a hand over my face and decided to get out of the room because I needed some fresh air or I was going to lose it.

Then, there in the hallway, my eyes were inundated by an ocean that I had learned to recognize intimately. I stared down Selene, who was walking timidly toward me. Her steps seemed unsure, and her cheeks were colored with a blush that revealed her discomfort. She held a cup of coffee in one hand, and she was still wearing her outfit from yesterday. So she hadn't gone home, either.

Her long auburn hair was different, though. Loose around her shoulders in messy waves that made her look disheveled yet irresistible.

I needed to tell someone what I had discovered—keeping everything inside was only going to make me feel worse. And Selene, after all, already knew about the last riddle I'd gotten at the pool house. So I pulled her over to a secluded corner and spilled my guts.

I told her everything, even showing her the paper covered in my handwriting where my underlying theory was laid out—the way out of this labyrinth we'd suddenly been dropped into. Her crystalline eyes widened in shock, and I got a glimpse of the fear that Babygirl was usually so good at hiding from the world.

And then I kissed her, without really knowing why.

Maybe there wasn't even a reason, and it was just in my nature to do dumb shit sometimes. Or maybe it was my way of showing her that I appreciated her attempts to stay by my side, to help me through this shitty situation, even if I didn't really believe all that crap she told me, like the thing about the violin and the bow.

I tried to humor her so she wouldn't feel hurt, and I didn't tell her that I was a realist, unlike her, and I didn't live my life based on illusions. I'd been sincere when I admitted that I liked her smell and her taste and when I told her about how aroused her body made me. I was sincere when I kissed her, lashing her tongue with my own like I was trying to punish her for being so naive and inexperienced. I was especially sincere when I took her hand and put it between my legs to make sure she understood that, even in those hideous pajamas, she made me absurdly hard…

All of that, though, was light-years away from an actual emotion.

For women, the smallest gesture could take on countless meanings. Everything was simpler for us men: a kiss was just a kiss and fuck was just a fuck.

I looked from her inviting lips to her glowing eyes and stepped back, putting a halt to the fucked-up thing I'd just done before I did it again.

"Go home and get cleaned up. I'll stay here," I said.

Selene gasped like I'd just told her she stank and looked like shit without her makeup on. But I really was just trying to tell her get some rest because those dark circles under her eyes were irrefutable signs of her exhaustion. Otherwise, she was completely beautiful, even all messy like that.

She didn't say anything, so I just stared down at the paper cup she was still holding in one hand. Fuck, she'd brought me coffee, and I hadn't even bothered to thank her.

I took it with a sigh, startling her. I gulped down the hot coffee in one shot and tossed the cup into a nearby trashcan. I licked my lips to savor the bitter taste—just the way I liked it. My stomach rumbled in protest because I'd gone too long without eating.

"I'm going back to Logan." I gestured at my brother's door and she nodded, still not saying anything. She walked away, but before she could get back to the waiting room, I snatched her wrist and drew close to her.

"Thanks for the coffee." In reality, I was thanking her not just for that but for everything that she was doing for us. She must have realized that, because she smiled at me and her ocean eyes lit up. It took so little to make her happy, and she never wanted anything in return for all that she gave. She just did it out of the kindness of her heart—her good and pure heart.

"No problem." She stood up on her tiptoes and planted an unexpected kiss on my jaw. I was so much taller than her that I would have needed to bend down for her to reach my cheek or my lips. I hadn't moved for her, however, because I had not anticipated the gesture.

"I didn't give you permission to kiss me," I said, stern and cynical. I even narrowed my eyes at her in a threatening sort of way to reinforce the concept.

"Well, then I must be very rude." She gave me an indifferent, one-shoulder shrug and grinned cheekily at me.

Did she really think herself rude for stealing a kiss from me?

So what did that make me, who had stolen her virginity, her innocence, and everything else that belonged to her out of pure male ego? What right did I have to demand everything from her, leaving nothing behind for anyone else?

"Go on, get out of here." I shook my head. Now was not the time to think about how tight and hot she was around me or how she moaned timidly beneath me or how many times I'd been able to make her come as I fucked her because she was still so inexperienced and couldn't handle the physical sensations.

I was going to keep on using her until her last day in New York.

Fortunately for me, she did walk away and I watched her body, slim yet shapely, proceeding toward the waiting room. In that moment, I remembered that she too was a potential target, and I decided that I was going to make sure she returned to Detroit as soon as possible. I didn't want anything bad to happen to her because of me. I knew, though, that Selene was stubborn and just telling her to leave wouldn't be enough to make her do it. I'd have to figure something else out. I needed to show her what I really was or I had to act like such a bastard that she'd actually hate me.

It wasn't important how I did it, but I was going to have to hurt her.

It wouldn't be too hard—the Boy would help me, after all. All I needed to do was think of Kimberly, and I would become the monster, the worst of beasts, and Babygirl would understand exactly why I was incapable of love, why I was so disturbed and deviant.

I quit thinking about Selene and returned to Logan's room. Every time I saw him lying there in that bed, I felt a hollowness in my chest. I sat down next to him again and took his hand.

"Logan, I'm back." I wasn't going anywhere; I was going to stay by his side for as long as it took. I didn't care if I ate or drank or slept; I just needed to hear his voice again.

I started talking to him again, like I'd been doing all night because I had once heard that talking to someone in a coma helps keep their spirit alive.

"What do you say I play some music for you?" I asked as his chest slowly rose and fell. I took out my phone and opened the music player, scrolling for his favorite song among my files.

"Here we go." I played "See You Again" by Wiz Khalifa and Charlie Puth and adjusted the volume so it wasn't too loud. Slowly, I brought the phone closer to him.

"Do you remember when you used to listen to this every day? You had just watched that Fast and Furious movie for the third time and every time this song started, you'd tell me about how choked up you got during the scene where Dom met Brian at the crossroads and they thought back on all the good times they had together," I murmured, my voice weak as I rubbed the back of his hand with my thumb.

"You were obsessed with those fucking movies. You still have all the DVDs in your room," I said archly. "Remember when you said you wanted to be as yoked as Dwayne Johnson?" I smiled at the memory of him pumping his biceps, pretending to be his favorite actor.

"And you had a thing for Michelle Rodriguez. You said you wanted to marry her someday," I added, thinking back fondly on his hormonal teenage discourses on the subject. "You were so funny. Who's going to watch our favorite movies with me if you don't come back?"

It was hard to say it.

Meanwhile, the song echoed off the bare walls, my melancholy clashing with it—like dissonance, like arrhythmia, like a discordant note.

"This is it, this is your favorite part. You hummed it ad nauseam." I truly wanted to cry. Maybe if I did, I could have gotten some feeling of release instead of just more suffocating pain.

When the song ended, I closed the app and locked my screen again. Everything was silent once more and the beep of the monitors bounced incessantly between the walls. I glanced at the clock and saw that Logan had now been in a coma for twelve hours, and he still hadn't woken up.

I sighed and squeezed his hand again. I wasn't going to give up. Life had always been cruel to me. I never got the opportunity to choose or even escape my destiny, but Logan still could. For him, there had to be another possibility.

"Come on, Logan. Wake up."

I stared at his closed eyelids. He was immersed in a world of shadow, and I wanted to pull him out, but nothing happened. I sighed and lay my forehead on our linked hands.

"If you leave me, I won't be able to do it anymore," I admitted, struggling to breathe. "Losing you would destroy me for good. I'd have to go with you," I told him, staring at his expressionless face.

I blinked, trying to banish the sudden irritation I felt at the corners of my eyes. I hummed his song under my breath, struggling to control the emotions that were making my chest feel tight. I closed my eyes and pressed my forehead to his hand again, where it was enclosed within mine. I felt like my head was caving in, or rather that I was going out of my head entirely. All I wanted to do was wake up from this nightmare, talk to Logan, mess up his hair, and bust his chops like nothing had happened.

Suddenly, I felt something moving against my forehead. I lifted my face and frowned down at his still-relaxed fingers. Shit, now I was starting to hallucinate as well.

I ran a hand over my face in exasperation. I already hadn't been doing well, and this situation was fraying the last threads of sanity I still had. I stared at his inert hand and shook my head, scoffing at myself because my mind had clearly started playing tricks on me.

Just then, however, my brother's index finger began to tap on the mattress, and I blinked to make sure I wasn't dreaming.

"Logan." I turned my gaze to his face and saw his eyelids tremble.

"I can't believe it." My heart began to pound so hard that I thought I would have a heart attack. I grinned uncontrollably and my eyes filled with tears. I felt like I was living in a dream and I was afraid that, at any moment, I might wake up.

"Logan," I said, getting closer to him. "Can you hear me? Open your eyes," I urged him as his eyelids continued to twitch. "Come on. You've got this. You can do it!" I continued to hold his hand as I got to my feet.

With aching slowness, he opened his eyes and immediately looked at me.

In that moment, it was as though my soul itself finally let out a long-held breath.

"Hey, little brother," I whispered in relief and he squeezed my hand. I knew it. I knew he'd never give up. I stared down at our linked hands, connected like always, like they were each part of the same whole, like a cardinal point aimed toward infinity. I looked at his face, and he tried to wink at me.

"Welcome back." My heart felt like it would actually burst. "You're awake, Logan! I have to tell Matt!" I said enthusiastically. "Just d-don't go to sleep," I babbled. I didn't even know what the fuck I was saying. "I mean, stay awake. Don't close your eyes," I added, still in shock and never letting go of his hand.

"I'll be right back." I didn't want to leave him, but it would only be a few seconds, just a few seconds and then I could return to his room.

I ran out into the hallway and collided almost immediately with Matt.

"God, Neil! What's going on?" he asked, sounding alarmed, but I didn't know where to start. I couldn't even catch my breath long enough to talk. I put my hands on his shoulders and tried to force the air into my lungs.

"Matt, h-he…" I sputtered in agitation.

Meanwhile, my mother and sister had approached, trailed by Selene and Alyssa, and all of them were waiting to hear what I had to say.

"Neil, speak," Matt said, sounding concerned. He probably thought it was bad news, but instead…

"He woke up, Matt! He's awake! Logan's awake!" I practically shouted the words with an excess of joy and the expression on his face shifted first from worried to shocked to delighted.

"What?" My mother burst into tears and ran to me, throwing her arms around me.

"He's awake, Mom! He woke up!" I said, stroking her hair. I was so happy that everything else just fell away. I didn't even care that she'd hugged me without my consent. Chloe hurled herself at Matt while Alyssa clasped Selene tightly as they both wept.

"I can't believe it!" Matt grinned, passing both hands over his face in disbelief. I let out a sigh of relief and returned to Logan. I was almost afraid to go back into his room, afraid I might find that I'd only imagined the nightmare was over. Instead, I found his hazel eyes focused clearly on me.

My brother was waiting for me, just like he waited for me when we were children.

"Here I am." I approached the bed and saw his hand resting palm up, toward me. He spread his fingers, and I understood the gesture immediately. I took his hand and smiled at him. He'd come back to me, and he was never going anywhere ever again.

"I love you," I said and one solitary tear slid down his cheek.

If just then someone had asked me what happiness was, I would have to told them that happiness is a house with all the people you love inside. It's the knowing looks we share with our partners in crime, the smiles of our loved ones, the warmth that comes from being near those who are dear to us. Even the strength to defend those people at the cost of one's own life, if necessary. But, above all else: happiness is the luminous gaze of someone who fought through a nightmare to come back to you because…

He made it.

35

SELENE

Logan spent two more weeks in the hospital. The doctors said they needed to monitor him and check in daily to avoid complications. Since his femur was fractured, he'd also have to wear a cast for at least a month.

Overall, though, things had gone well. It was a genuine miracle that he'd survived such a major accident, and despite the worries and fears that still shadowed us about this invisible, menacing stranger, the air in the house felt different. The tragic accident had brought the Anderson–Miller family together like never before. Something had changed inside me as well. I had realized that family was a precious resource, meant to be cherished. Family meant lending strength and support to one another. It meant facing challenges together and overcoming them. It meant being united in the face of everything and everyone.

We were all in the living room after finishing dinner. Matt and Chloe were playing a game of chess (the loser had to do dishes). I was perched on one of the armchairs, while Logan sat on the sofa wearing a blue tracksuit. He had his broken leg stretched out in front of him and two crutches lay to the left of his body.

"So, are you two a couple?" Mia asked, glancing between Logan and Alyssa.

Alyssa had been by Logan's side every day during his hospital stay, and their bond had only gotten stronger.

"Checkmate!" Chloe exclaimed, sitting on the rug in front of the glass coffee table in the center of the room. Matt, on the other side of the table, snorted and rubbed his meticulously groomed beard.

"Sheesh, you really are good," he grumbled to himself, but the little exchange between the two of them didn't pull Mia's attention from her son and Alyssa.

"Yes, Mrs. Lindhom," Alyssa answered finally, picking back up her conversation with Mia.

I glanced at Logan: he was smiling, pleased with his girlfriend's presence. His face still showed evidence of the accident—he wore a couple of bandages over some injuries on his brow ridge—but none of that seemed to temper his happiness. Alyssa cuddled next to him, resting her head against his chest, breathing in his smell. I thought about how lovely they were together and then felt sad.

It was then that I realized there was something else that was different after our return to the house, and that was Neil's attitude. Mr. Disaster had gone back to being cold and unfriendly. He barely paid me any attention, only greeting me brusquely whenever went ran into each other around the house and he felt he had to. He hadn't kissed me or touched me or attempted to get close to me.

I often thought about how it might have been between us if he had been willing to let me into his life. If he had trusted me enough to let me know him and stripped himself of more than just his clothes. I also often thought about whether or not he'd started sleeping with Jennifer again or if he'd started seeing new blonds I didn't even know existed.

In any case, I would always bear with me that storm he'd made inside me when his lips touched mine in those carnal kisses that froze all words and thoughts. Automatically, I pinched my lower lip between my thumb and index finger, as though I could still taste tobacco on my tongue, the essence of him on my palate.

"I heard Neil's voice..." Logan's words disrupted the flow of my memories, bringing my attention back to him. Someone must have asked him about the coma. "It was the only lifeline I had to hold on to in all that darkness," he said in a voice barely above a whisper, staring at an indistinct point in front of him. Even Matt and Chloe had stopped their game to turn and listen to him.

"I could feel his hand warm on mine. He talked to me and I remember everything he said to me. Every word was like an electric shock to my chest." He smiled and looked at Mia, who swiftly wiped a tear from her cheek.

"I really thought I wasn't going to make it; I was so scared. But his determination helped me keep from losing hope." The thoughtful silence that fell over us was impressive: no one uttered so much as a sound as we all concentrated on what Logan was saying.

"So I kept my promise and—"

An intense baritone overlapped with his voice. "You came back to me."

Neil was leaning one shoulder against the doorframe in a way looking like he'd just returned from parts unknown, the keys to his Maserati dangling from the pocket of his dark jeans. His lips were curved into a smile that was entirely for Logan.

"Just like you always came back to me," Logan answered, though none of the rest of us quite understood what he meant.

That's when Neil shifted his gaze to me, and I gasped as though I'd been burned. It was extremely difficult to conceal the effect his eyes had on me, and he surely noticed it because he let his stare dip down from my thin sweater to my dark pants, before slowly crawling back up to my face. He'd stopped smiling and was instead biting the inside of his cheek pensively. Yet again, I couldn't tell if he liked what he saw or found something about me lacking, probably the way I looked. Maybe my hair didn't look good loose and wavy or maybe he thought I should be wearing makeup.

Then, he met my eyes, and with a nearly imperceptible jerk of his chin, he gestured toward the door. I frowned and examined his face. Neil turned then and walked toward the kitchen. Clearly, he meant for me to follow him.

I glanced around to make sure we weren't making anyone suspicious but everyone else had gone back to chatting with each other again. Everyone except for Logan, who was looking at me with something like concern in his face.

He was, after all, the only member of the family who knew about us, besides Anna.

I ignored him, crossed the living room, and slipped into the kitchen, all the while feeling his hazel eyes boring into my back. When I got into the kitchen, I realized that Neil wasn't there, so I went out the French doors into the garden. Immediately, I wrapped my arms around my torso as a blast of cold air hit me, making me shiver.

I strolled at a slow pace under a sky filled with stars as I searched for the damaged boy who couldn't stop stealing pieces of my soul. I spotted him not too far away, swaying in a hammock.

I took a deep breath and felt my knees wobbling as I approached him. Like always, I was completely taken in by his charm.

"Come here," he said, even as he continued to stare up into the darkened sky like the only things he cared about were the stars above him and the cloud of smoke dissipating in front of him.

I took a few steps toward him and paused to consider: Where was I supposed to sit? There wasn't enough room for me in the hammock and asking him to sit up would be embarrassing.

"There's room for both of us," he added, turning to look my way. That ability he had to know what I was thinking was always disarming. Slowly and carefully, I climbed into the hammock alongside him.

Neil lifted up his arm, and I stared at him in shock because I wasn't expecting that kind of gesture from him. Did he want me to lie down next to him? Or...*hug* him?

I decided not to irritate him with either question and situated myself next to him. I stretched out my legs and rested my cheek against his chest. I felt one of his arms reach up to wrap around my shoulders. I breathed in his good, familiar scent and reveled in his warmth against the cold of the night.

"'Selene' means 'moon,' right?" He brushed my arms with just the fingertips of his right hand while holding his cigarette in his left and stared up at the sky. It was the first time he'd asked me a personal question like that, and a spontaneous smile perked up the corners of my mouth.

"Mom teaches classical literature, and she's passionate about Greek mythology. Around the time she discovered she was pregnant, she'd been reading a myth about the goddess Selene, so she decided to name me after her," I explained with a shy smile as I looked up at the moon, glowing all alone up in the sky. There was a deep feeling of peace in the air, a pleasant solitude and a brisk chill that slapped against the bulwark of human heat our bodies had created.

"She's usually depicted as a beautiful woman with a pale, delicate face. And in Greek mythology, she was said to have many lovers due to her indisputable allure." I blushed as I related this detail, even though it was only the truth. I certainly didn't consider myself a goddess or even a very beautiful woman, but I was still honored to share her name.

"Many lovers," he repeated thoughtfully and not a single emotion showed itself on his inscrutable face.

"Yeah," I confirmed and he turned to face me, resting his hand on his stomach with the cigarette still giving off smoke between his index and middle fingers.

"You should go back to Detroit," he murmured, gazing into my eyes like they were some mysterious place to be lingered upon. I didn't know why he'd say something like that to me, and I certainly wasn't pleased to hear him talking that way.

"Why should I leave?" I asked, clenching my hand into a fist and pressing it into my lips. I was curling up against myself like a hedgehog, perhaps out of fear about how he was going to answer.

"Because you're not safe here," he answered. He turned his stare back up at the sky and continued smoking.

"Because of the person sending those riddles?" I demanded, clinging to him. I couldn't imagine being far away from there, from his family and from him. It was irrational, that thought, and it was stupid to hope that there was a real connection between the two of us, but I also didn't want to exclude the possibility that he might feel something—anything—for me.

"Yes, but it's not just that. I don't want you to..." He stopped, rubbing his jaw where the hint of an incoming beard gave him a particular masculine appeal.

"Want me to what?" I prompted him, and he took another drag on his cigarette, holding the smoke in for longer than usual before he released it through his nose.

"The heart can create illusions that destroy the soul. Often, we see only what we want to see. Even when it's not there," he answered cynically. He spoke with a removed sort of certainty that was difficult to gainsay.

"I'm not under any illusions," I answered firmly. Neil took one last drag and put it out before turning to give me his full attention.

"You don't understand. You shouldn't—" And he didn't finish because I leaned closer until I could capture his mouth with my own. Neil's eyes widened in surprise, and he clenched his teeth to prevent me from deepening the kiss. I slowly rubbed myself against him, and after a few moments of resistance he caved with a frustrated groan. He opened his lips, warm and full, and allowed me to soar beyond desire, to lose myself in the thrill of his taste. I put a hand on his chest and my fingers slid against the warm fabric of his sweater. I could feel his heart beating, but it was his soul that I wanted to touch.

Neil slipped his fingers into the hair at the nape of my neck and guided my head back to intensify the kiss. His tongue began hunting mine in that crude, passionate way that made it so hard to keep up with him. My heart flipped wildly with each languid touch. The more he kissed me, the more of me ignited. Jolts of electricity moved from the middle of my chest straight down between my thighs. Neil moved his lips against mine so confidently and expertly that it instantly aroused me, made me hunger for him. I was forced to interrupt our lustful collision, however, to take a breath of air. I paused, resting my forehead against his.

"You should get far away from me," Neil insisted, licking his already-wet lips.

"I don't see why," I said miserably, and he looked into my eyes, irritated. I could read his moods perfectly now.

"If you continue to stay near me..." His hand stroked my neck before moving down my body, touching every part of me: breasts, stomach, torso, hip. He stopped at the button on my jeans and undid it, slowly pulling down the zipper.

"I would make you feel wanted every day." He slipped a hand into my jeans and brushed his fingers against the fabric of my panties. My eyes went wide because I realized what he was going to do, but we were out in the open, in a hammock, extremely vulnerable to being discovered.

And yet...I couldn't bring myself to stop him.

I felt paralyzed, overwhelmed by lust.

"You'd become addicted to my touch." He began to rub me through the cotton, which was already feeling damp.

"N-Neil," I stammered.

We were in the garden…in the garden…and…

"I'd give you intense pleasure…" He brushed aside the fabric that was in his way and grazed my outer labia with his cool fingertips. I was already hot and swollen with arousal. I blushed violently, embarrassed by how much my body wanted him and how little I could hide it.

"Urgent." He pushed his index finger into me and my walls accepted him, yielding and wet. Although I was getting lost in his touch, I tried to grab his wrist and catch my breath.

"Deep." Neil continued to knock me flat with his hoarse, mature voice. He pressed his finger in all the way and I gasped, squeezing my hand around his wrist but unable to put up any real resistance.

"Stop," I begged, though my breathless tone undermined me.

"Uncontrollable." He began moving his finger in and out of me with a perfectly calculated rhythm. "Powerful." He sped up and I bit my lower lip to keep from moaning or screaming. I squeezed my eyes shut and pressed my forehead to his chest.

"I'd make you enjoy it, Selene, and I'd give you this exhausting, sublime pleasure every single day."

I arched my back as his thumb began to tease my clit, making my hips buck against his wicked hand. A moan escaped me and he grinned with pride.

"Shh, Babygirl," he chided me, continuing his slow, seductive torture. All at once, I trembled and he bit my lower lip, pulling hard on it as my sex contracted around his finger. I sucked in a breath and buried my face in his chest, trying not to cry aloud.

"I'd let you use my body, my hands, my mouth, my tongue, but…" His baritone pushed me over the edge.

I collapsed back into reality and opened my eyes, struggling to control myself again, and more importantly, to get some oxygen into my lungs. My lower lip was sore and swelling, my chest rose and fell wearily, and my slick center was still being rocked by the thrilling, unstoppable tremors of orgasm.

I only caught a few words of his intermittent speech, but that last sentence was clear to me: this would be all I ever got from him.

He pulled his hand out from between my thighs and brought it up to his mouth. He sniffed at my arousal like an animal and I went red, though I should have been used to his bold, obscene gestures by them. Then he stuck his index finger between his lips and sucked, locking eyes with me. He didn't speak, but it felt like he was telling me *"I love the taste of you,"* and I gasped at how powerfully his masculine voice echoed in my imagination.

"Did you get any of what I just said to you?" he asked, sounding amused. He looked at me like the inexperienced girl that I was; I hated that part of myself, so shy and insecure. Sometimes, I wished I was more like other people: audacious, uninhibited, shameless. But those weren't qualities that I had. So instead, I ducked my head and quickly zipped up my jeans, pressing my thighs together and staring at a random point on his chest.

"I'm not suited for relationships. I wasn't meant to be with a woman like that. And it's not because I don't want to. Believe me, I would like to be that way..." He lifted my chin with his index finger, forcing me to look him in the eyes. There, I caught a glimpse of words unspoken, hidden thoughts, secret fears, and the terrible memories that had made him into such a troubled, disillusioned man. "But the Boy and I still have so many problems to deal with..." He raised his torso away from me and sat up in the hammock, which only pulled me along with him.

Then we both sat, our bodies swaying back and forth as the moon watched over us. Who knew what she thought of us. Of a girl with her heart full of hopes and dreams and a disaster of a boy with a brilliant mind that was nonetheless caught up in the web of the past.

"Who is the Boy?" I asked hesitantly, resting my hands on my kneecaps. My shoes grazed the green lawn with every tiny swing of the hammock.

"Neil," he said simply, not looking at me.

I didn't understand his introspective reasoning. Sometimes, the things he said were too abstruse and mysterious for me to decipher them, but this part of him fascinated me more than anything else.

"There is a star in the sky for each of us, far enough away that our mistakes cannot tarnish it." I murmured under my breath. "Christian Bobin said that. You should recommend him to the Boy, for when he's feeling sad," I whispered. Neil turned to look at me and furrowed his brow. I knew he wasn't going to elaborate on that idea, because he'd already said too much by his standards, but I needed to be patient.

"Think about what I said. I've fucked other people these last two weeks, just like I've been doing since the beginning. Do you know what that means?" he asked, but he didn't wait for me to answer before continuing. "It means that I like you, Selene, but you are not indispensable. You get me out of my head for a minute and nothing more. I want to be honest with you. If you don't have any illusions, like you say, then I won't be disappointing you."

It suddenly occurred to me that I was looking at a frozen person, trapped inside himself, surrounded by walls so high and thick that they would be impossible to break down.

I looked away when he confirmed what I'd feared: that he'd been with other women. The thought of other women touching him or him touching them the way he touched me made me feel nervy and vulnerable. A quiet ache in my chest kept me from replying. I opened my lips and then closed them several times, unable to say a word.

His capacity for destruction was enviable. He truly was a magnificent bastard.

"I hope that behind your mask of ice there is a heart that can one day beat for someone." It was difficult to get the words out. A strange sensation crawled over my skin; there was a stabbing pain in my chest and nausea rose from the pit of my stomach at the memory of what I'd just allowed him to do to me.

I was afraid that I had fallen hopelessly in love with him, and that knowledge scared me. But love happened at random and could not be planned for or controlled. Love was an unpredictable and irrational little monster, sometimes good, sometimes evil. It was frequently insane and inexplicable, controversial and illogical.

For the first time in my life, I had been a victim of love, and I still couldn't say exactly what love was, only that I knew it when I started to see the perfection in Neil's imperfections. And that I wouldn't have found it in anyone else.

"Oh, one last thing: from now on, feel free to touch the other girls, kiss them, really show them a good time," I taunted him, echoing his own words. "But don't come near me again."

I climbed out of the hammock, and putting on a tranquil facade, I showed him just how serious I was about that demand. Neil stood up as well, preparing to loom over me with his great height, but I refused to be intimidated.

"We both know that you'll let me touch you whenever I want," he answered, all arrogant certainty. But I just gave him an insolent smile and moved closer to him, narrowing my eyes.

"Or maybe I'll let one your friends touch me and get rid of this inexperience. After all, you said it yourself...." I paused for effect and gave him a slow, sensual blink, pursing my lips. "I need to learn how to fuck without kissing," I whispered, sounding amused. I spoke slowly to really imprint the message in his mind.

Maybe I was being immature and reacting out of unhealthy

jealousy, but if he was going to live freely, sleeping with all of kinds of women, I should be able to go my own way as well.

Neil stared darkly at me. His bright eyes had ceased shining and had given way to a stormy, menacing expression. I might have found it thrilling if I didn't know how hard he struggled to control his impulses.

"You'd better leave, Tinkerbell." Something ominous now lurked behind the nickname he always called me.

Neil stared intensely at me and some feminine instinct urged me not to continue arguing with him. Then, suddenly, his right arm, which had been hanging at his side, began to shake, drawing my eye. The fingers of that hand moved as though he were playing an invisible piano, and I realized that he was probably trying to express some sort of tense energy he felt moving inside him.

I took a step back because standing there, immersed in the darkness and lit only by the faint glow of the moon, that man looked like a fallen angel, a tortured soul trapped in a divinity's body and…

Dangerous. He looked dangerous.

36

SELENE

I miss you so much. Campus isn't the same without you."

I couldn't help but roll my eyes. Alyssa kept calling Logan to tell him again how much she missed having him at school. Ever since they'd made their relationship official, she'd done nothing but tell me all about how perfect, sweet, considerate, kind, smart, erudite, romantic, sensitive, and intuitive Logan was. Not to mention how well-endowed and good in bed he was, which was apparently characteristic of the Miller men.

"Okay, puppy, see you later," she said in a baby voice, flirting with her new boyfriend.

"You're really laying it on thick." I gave her a sideways glance as we walked down the hallway of our university, books clutched to our chests and our heads in the clouds.

"I'm a lucky woman," she answered dreamily. I was a little afraid she was about to do a little twirl right there among the other students.

"And an extremely mushy one," I muttered.

"You're so sour. When was the last time you got fucked? You seem frustrated." She arched an eyebrow and examined me carefully as my cheeks turned red at her observation.

That wasn't the point, though. I hadn't yet established a good sex life for myself, so it wasn't like I was going into withdrawals. I was just feeling unsettled by the things Neil had said to me the previous night. In that moment of abandon, I hadn't been able to give his speech the appropriate consideration, but I'd thought and thought about it all night until I came to a conclusion: he and I were traveling on two completely separate tracks, perhaps even parallel to each other, thus destined to never meet.

For him, it was just a physical attraction between us; while for me, it was something more, and it had been ever since I agreed to reenact my first time with him so that I could recall every feeling, every detail.

"It's not that, the problem is…him. Him and his twisted personality," I admitted. I felt an enormous need to just talk to someone about it. I was tired of keeping everything bottled up inside and never being able to hear an opinion other than my own. I was tired of only having my own conscience to bounce things off, and I needed advice and perspectives from other people.

"Him who? Jared?" Alyssa obviously wasn't aware how ridiculous my love life had gotten or of the fact that I'd broken up with Jared.

For a moment, I rethought the idea of telling her everything, but I needed to free myself from the enormous burden that was weighing me down. I had to confide in someone.

"No, it's not Jared."

We went into the lecture hall, but I already knew that we wouldn't be paying attention to the lesson. In fact, Alyssa immediately started in with her questions, and I told her everything. Absolutely everything.

"So, you're sleeping with Neil? *The* Neil?" she practically shouted.

"Shut up or we are going to get kicked out. And yes," I whispered, bowing my head and pretending to scrutinize my notes.

"Oh my god. There are girls in this room who would sell a kidney for one night with him. You know that, right? But everyone says he's only into super-hot blonds and doesn't have sex with just anyone," she whispered with her hand over her mouth, preventing others from reading her lips clearly.

I sighed because that wasn't just a rumor; it was the plain truth.

"Do your parents know?" she asked, getting more and more curious.

"Are you kidding? Obviously not." And I had no idea how they would react to that kind of news. I'd often wondered, but ultimately, I tried to avoid thinking about it because I didn't want to worry about my father's reaction. I'd never really talked to him about my personal life, and he'd been gone before I had the chance to tell him about any first crushes. Indeed, the topic of "men" had always been a bit taboo between us.

"Is he aggressive in bed like he is everywhere else?"

Ugh.

What kind of question was that?

I blushed and dropped the pen I was holding onto the floor. Alyssa giggled delightedly as I bent down to pick it up.

"What are these questions you're asking me?" I answered, trying to keep my tone low but appropriately threatening. *Of course he was*, was what I wanted to tell her. He was aggressive, rough, and passionate. But I wasn't going to say any of that to Alyssa, because it was private. The things I shared with my fucked-up not-a-boyfriend belonged to him and me alone.

"And what about *it*? What's he working with?" She stretched out her hands to indicate an average penis length and my eyes went wide.

Has she lost her mind?

I gave her a perplexed look, and she stifled a laugh as she drew her fingers even farther apart and…

"He's well-endowed, yes. Now knock it off." I slapped her wrist to put an end to the lewd gestures. Then she touched the end of her pen to her lips and shot me a mischievous look.

"Try not to fall in love with him. He's a peculiar guy with a complex personality." Alyssa had suddenly grown serious again, and she looked at me with concern. I couldn't blame her. Neil was incapable of forging connections with most people. Logan and Chloe were the only real people who existed for him, and he kept his heart locked up in a tower too high to climb, almost insurmountable.

"What's worse is that he's always getting into trouble. I mean, he hangs out with the Krew and you see how everyone here is afraid of them. They're a pack of animals, and he's their leader," she murmured, horrified, and I found myself agreeing with her entirely.

Of all of Neil's friends, though, Jennifer was still the one I hated the most. I hadn't forgotten what she'd done to me. And yet she was Neil's preferred choice among all his lovers because she was shameless, wicked, and most of all blond.

I shook my head and kept answering Alyssa's questions, trying not to think about Krew Barbie, because even picturing her awful braids or sexy-yet-vulgar body made me feel anxious and ill at ease. Instead, I tried to focus on the unsolicited but still helpful advice that Alyssa tried to give me at the end of class.

According to her, I was much too good and naive a girl, and my personality wasn't suited to someone like Neil. He was a person with a forceful, intractable character; he was clever and calculating.

Experienced and shrewd.

And I knew that better than anyone.

Later, at home, Alyssa's words continued to echo through my mind as I sat in the living room with Logan. He was munching on his favorite cereal despite the fact that it was well into the afternoon.

"Neil isn't a boy, Selene. He eats innocent girls like you for breakfast. You need to be a woman to be with him, someone capable of standing up to him."

And then, *"Learn how to deal with him, or he'll end up grinding you down like one of his cigarette butts."*

"I can see the gears in your brain whirring at an impressive speed," Logan observed. He was sitting on the sofa with his leg stretched out in front of him, per doctor's orders. He was supposed to rest and take painkillers for at least three weeks before resuming his normal activities.

I didn't answer and just lifted my glass of juice to my lips. I wasn't sure if I could tell Logan the true reason for my torment. I opted instead to change the subject slightly.

"Alyssa knows about the situation with Neil," I said. Logan abruptly stopped chewing and watching the rerun of a basketball game, turning to stare at me with an indecipherable expression on his face.

"And she gave me some advice," I added awkwardly, hoping he wouldn't ask about it in detail because Alyssa had also given me some sex tips that I'd rather not recount.

"You already know how I feel about that." Logan sighed. "Neil's a unique sort of person." And he was, he truly was. He was a riddle that was nearly impossible to solve. "You can keep it casual with him, Selene, but there's no future with him. I'm only saying this because you don't seem like..." He looked at me, a small, sweet smile flitting over his lips. "You don't seem like the kind of girl he usually surrounds himself with. You put so much feeling into everything you do, so you need to be careful and never forget that he's different from other people."

I knew perfectly well that Neil wasn't a boy who needed a little coaxing and a fix-him-up mindset to get him to bond with someone. He wasn't just hostile to love; he refused, from the outset, to admit that love even existed.

My train of thought was interrupted by a glance from Anna, who was busily polishing the silverware. Her attention had been drawn by Logan's sincere speech. Here was a woman who had known Neil since he was a child. She was the one who advised me not to judge him but to try to understand him. To learn how to interpret his silent language and figure out what he was saying even when he had no intention of exposing himself to me.

However, that was considerably easier to say than do.

I shook myself and changed the subject again, spending a couple of easy hours hanging out with Logan. We were both trying to distract ourselves: him from his accident and me from my worries. Later, Chloe joined us, but instead of getting in on our conversation, she just fell asleep next to her brother, lulled by what she called "this boring game" on the TV. When it finally ended, Logan made a grimace of pain, which I noticed immediately.

"Logan," I said, putting a hand on his shoulder, and he shook his head reassuringly at me.

"There's some pain every now and then, but it's fine." He smiled at me in that sweet way of his, and I sighed in relief. It couldn't have been easy, living with trauma caused by a maniac who was bent on harming us for some inexplicable reason.

"I saw him, you know." He leaned back against the upholstered sofa and allowed his head to fall back, staring upward. His eyes, fixed on the ceiling, were shadowed with memories of his horrific accident. "He was wearing a white mask," he added before I had a chance to ask him any questions.

If he'd gotten a good look at him, we might have been able to take a description of his appearance to the police. It wouldn't have been much, but it might have helped a little. Instead, fate was conspiring against us. Whoever Player was, he knew what he was doing, because he never left a trace of himself, other than the puzzles.

"He was behind me in a black Jeep. I don't remember the license plate. He just kept screwing with me, blinding me with his high beams." His voice dipped to a pained whisper as he hung his head, staring at his outstretched leg. "Other than the mask, the only thing I saw in the rearview mirror was him waving at me right before I..." He stopped and his voice shook. I didn't want to push him to talk to me, so I just waited and rubbed the back of his hand as I did so.

"I tried to brake before a curve that was too sharp, too deadly. But the brakes wouldn't respond, and I lost control of the car and..." He couldn't finish and swallowed thickly instead, squeezing his hands into angry fists. I regarded him intently, surprised by this revelation. This added an additional clue to the puzzle that Neil was attempting to decipher. How many more riddles would there be? How many of us would Player attack? And above all else: Who would be next?

"Does Neil know about this?" I whispered, squeezing his hand in mine, a muted pain weighing down my chest. Logan nodded and chewed his lower lip nervously.

"Yeah, I told him everything, and he's pretty on edge these days." He looked at me like he was trying to give me some sort of warning. I had no intention of trying to change his brother's mood, but Logan still seemed worried for me.

Player 2511 had now shown himself to us, albeit while wearing a white mask, and according to the photos he sent, he'd been watching us like a true stalker. He was hunting us. He might have been there, right outside the house, or maybe he was lurking underneath the windows of our rooms or on campus or around the cafés we frequented. He was always watching us, like an invisible devil whose presence we could only sense but never confirm.

It felt like we were walking a labyrinth filled with insidious dangers and we were all wearing blindfolds. No one was above suspicion; anyone could be an enemy, even the nicest neighbor or most unassuming friend.

I thought about it for the rest of the night, even as I took a long, hot bath to ease some of the tension from my rigid body. But none of it reassured me, so I got dressed and decided that I needed to talk to Neil. The only people who knew the truth of the situation were the three of us: me, Logan and…him.

I went to his room at nine o'clock after putting on a big, loose hoodie that fell to below my butt. Underneath I wore a simple fitted T-shirt and a pair of leggings. My hair was down and wavy because I had just let it dry without doing anything to it. My face, as usual, was pale and bare.

I knocked twice on his door, feeling the usual stormy sensation in my stomach. It felt like a full-on tropical hurricane in there. Images of what had happened the last time I was in his room rose up in my mind like a dirty movie, creating a certain yearning sensation between my thighs. It was a physical reaction that I was finding increasingly difficult to control.

This boy had taken my prudish soul and molded it into a creature of lust.

I took a deep breath to calm myself down and toyed with the string on my sweatshirt as I waited for him to open the door. But I didn't hear footsteps or any other sound that might suggest his presence on the other side of the door. So, eventually, I pushed it open. I glanced inside: the room was empty. Neil wasn't there. I had no idea how long he'd been gone, and I had even less of a clue where he was.

I walked inside slowly and turned on the light. Cobalt blue contrasted with the black that dominated the entire atmosphere, from the walls to the masculine furnishings that made the room feel oppressive. I advanced further and looked around. I could smell his fresh scent in the air of this perfectly tidied and sanitized room.

The king-sized bed in the center was covered with a dark comforter. The same one I'd clutched in my fingers while his body dominated mine, turning me into a slave of pleasure. It seemed that I could still feel the powerful thrusts of his hips, the shocking strength of his hands, his irregular yet controlled breathing that never managed to outstrip the limits he'd imposed upon himself. I could feel his brutish lips and his electric tongue—I relived all of it, and all of a sudden, an exhausted feeling came over me, forcing me to sit down on the bed.

My breathing sped up as I reviewed the indecent memories, and my eyes darted over to the sleek bedside table with its skull-shaped ashtray. Next to it, however, was something new. It appeared to be a small notebook or journal. I picked it up and examined the matte brown cover that featured no design or words to indicate anything about it. I opened it, though I realized that I had already violated Neil's privacy the moment I let myself walk into his room.

He would have screamed at me if he ever found out. I shuddered at the idea, but it did nothing to lessen my curiosity, so I began to page through the notebook. I was astonished.

"Damn…" I whispered, seeing precise and perfect architectural drawings. The first was of a series of ancient Greek columns, the second a temple, the third was our house, rendered exactly true to life. There were also measurements, geographical features, numbers and notations that I understood nothing about. Nevertheless, the precision and organization of it was impressive.

I leafed through the rest of the notebook, occasionally brushing the incredible drawings with my fingers and thought about good he was at this. Neil enjoying drawing, and he appeared to have a real talent for it.

"Keeping your skills a secret from the world, huh?" I said to myself, smiling I turned a few more pages until I stopped on a drawing of the pool house. He had rendered it perfectly, just like all the other buildings. *Does he want to be an architect?* It seemed so. I didn't know much about the discipline, but I was convinced that he had a true gift and that his hands were capable of creating incredible things.

I put the notebook back where it had been and stood up from the bed, looking over at his bookshelf. It wasn't like the rest in the house but was instead composed of a series of L-shaped ledges mounted together to form an irregular and original shape on the wall. Each piece scattered across the wall was painted to match the other shades of the room.

I had noticed it before, of course, but never paid much attention to it—I hadn't imagined Neil as someone who owned many books or had much interest in reading. But if he knew Nabokov and the other authors he'd quoted during our conversations, he was probably concealing a deeper well of knowledge that he chose not to flaunt.

My suspicions were confirmed as I browsed through his books—his collection spanned everything from Octavio Paz to Salinger, with a stop at Ian Fleming. I spotted Nabokov's *Lolita* and whole lot of Bukowski. Neil had several of his books: *Women; Tales of Ordinary Madness; Absence of the Hero; Erections, Ejaculations, Exhibitions, and General Tales of Ordinary Madness; Notes of a Dirty Old Man...* I raised an eyebrow at the last one and gave a tiny smile.

Then, I spotted another one: *"Love Is a Dog From Hell,"* I read aloud and grew serious again. Maybe this was why Neil loved this author so much: he was a transgressive man who entangled love with sexuality and had a great capacity for describing erotic male fantasies but in a deeper, more poetic way.

"Bukowski's his favorite." I started at the sound of Chloe's voice and the book I'd been holding fell to the floor.

"Oh my God. I'm sorry, I was just…just…" I crouched down to pick up the book and put it back where it belonged while the baby of the house approached me with an amused smile on her face. Who could say what my face looked like; I was such an idiot.

"You don't have to explain yourself, Selene. My brother doesn't talk about himself, and it makes people curious." She folded her arms over her chest and studied Neil's odd bookcase, rearranging a few of the books I'd touched. "Better not to leave a trace, though. He doesn't like other people going through his stuff," she murmured, making sure to keep her voice low.

"I came here to talk to him but then…well…" I didn't even know what to say. There was no excuse for my disrespectful behavior. I should never have gone through the door of his room without his permission.

"I won't say anything." Chloe gave me a knowing wink, and I sighed in relief.

"We've been studying since we were very young. Our grandparents were particularly strict and demanding about it. They forced our parents to enroll us in the city's most prestigious schools as soon as we were old enough. They wanted us to be educated, knowledgeable model students," she explained, staring at nothing in particular on the bookcase. "Neil loves literature, philosophy, and astronomy, but he doesn't share those passions with anyone else. He reads every night, especially when he can't sleep. Or sometimes he draws. Buildings, objects; he can basically reproduce anything he sees." She smiled, turning her intense blue eyes to mine.

"I always thought there was more to him than just a pretty face," I said lightly, trying not to expose my deeper interest in Neil, because Chloe didn't know about us.

"Anyway, if you're looking for him, he's probably in the pool house, but—" I didn't let her finish.

"Okay, I'll go there then," I said quickly. "Thanks, Chloe. And if you didn't mention anything about this huge screwup of mine, I would really appreciate it." I clasped my hands in gratitude and hurried for the door.

But learning more details about Neil's life had only increased the already dire levels of attraction I felt toward him, urging me to chase him into the darkness that surrounded him. After this, I regretted having praised Kyle for being well-read that night in the garden. I'd underestimated Neil and his intelligence. I'd been condescending, and he'd immediately turned around and proved me wrong.

Breathlessly, I headed downstairs, down that enormous marble staircase and then through the kitchen and out the French doors to the garden. I shivered in the cold and walked a bit faster. I walked past the swimming pool and sped toward the glowing pool house, the lights on inside filtering through the large curtains despite the fact that the curtains were drawn this time.

Is he alone in there?

Just to be on the safe side, I knocked and waited, my teeth chattering as I rubbed my hands together. I should have put on something warmer, but my eagerness to see him had me forgetting just about everything, including my own name.

"Hello, baby doll."

I stared in shock when I found myself faced with Xavier. His slashing dark eyes were glittering and his pupils were dilated. I glanced at the metal piercing in his lower lip and then at the black sweater that covered his chest and tight, dark-wash jeans he wore. Then, a slow, malevolent smile spread across his face, and my confidence wavered.

"I'm looking for Neil." I cleared my throat, mentally cursing my stupidity. I should have just backed off and walked away instead of asking to see him. My biggest mistake, though, was going into the pool house when Xavier stepped aside and invited me to make myself comfortable.

"That hoodie you're wearing is too big, baby doll," he said as he closed the door behind me. He turned to stare shamelessly at my ass, and I zipped the hoodie up to my throat, completely concealing the tight T-shirt underneath. I moved into the living room, which I had last seen in a state of total destruction, but now it was perfectly tidy.

The pellet fireplace was lit, and the heat emanating from it was so powerful that it warmed me immediately. I saw Luke sitting on the sectional sofa, bent forward with his elbows on his knees. His blue eyes watched me warily, and his brow was furrowed in a pensive expression.

"What's she doing here?" he asked Xavier, like I wasn't standing right there.

"How the fuck should I know?" Xavier answered, coming up alongside me. He looked at my chest and then down at my legs, giving me a mocking smile. "Someone should give you lessons in femininity. What are you wearing? I can't even tell you have tits." He taunted me before sitting down next to the blond boy, who at least didn't make any nasty comments.

Then, I noticed a strange smell in the air that I couldn't quite recognize. It was mingled with the odor of sex, which I learned to distinguish thanks to one particular person's efforts.

"What's up, bitch?"

I started when Jennifer appeared behind me, half-naked as usual. She was wearing just a black bra and a pair of barely-there panties that were essentially see-through. She walked past me to Xavier and sat down on his lap, tossing a disgusted look my way.

God, I hated her, and she could see in my eyes just how much.

"Getting angry, princess?" she taunted, wrapping her arm around Xavier's neck. In response, he kissed her breast, which was packed into the tight, vulgar lingerie.

"Apparently you keep finding new ways to lower yourself,

hopping from one man to the next," I snapped with zero restraint. I couldn't help it, that fake porcelain doll face of hers triggered a rage that I just couldn't control.

"The girl's got balls," Luke muttered, getting up off the sofa. I shrank back when he approached me, but fortunately, he didn't bother me and just passed by on his way to the kitchenette. Maybe he was the only sane man among these lunatics, but I couldn't trust any of them so I stationed myself in a corner of the room where I could keep an eye on all three of them.

"Don't lecture me. You're no saint yourself, considering you're fucking the worst of us." She winked at me, and I had to squeeze my lips together to force myself not to answer. If I did, there was going to be another fight. This time, though, I would have fought back.

"I'd be curious to see how you are in the sack." Xavier dropped another kiss on Jennifer's neck and then looked at me, raising one corner of his mouth in a wicked half-smile.

"She's shitty. Seems pretty obvious to me." The blond girl leaned forward and picked a white paper cylinder from the table. It looked noticeably different from a regular cigarette. She brought it to her lips and lit it, inhaling deeply and exhaling a thick cloud of smoke. Only then did I pause to examine the glass surface of the table, which was strewn with bags of snacks, some empty glasses, two open bottles of alcohol, and two clear baggies with some pills inside. Beside them, the ashtray was overflowing with cigarette butts and chewing gum.

"Do I need to get more?" Luke asked from behind me. He approached with a can of beer in one hand, watching the bizarre couple on the sofa.

"No, there's plenty," Xavier answered, rubbing Jennifer's thigh while she enjoyed what was, I presumed, a joint. She locked her blue eyes on me as she blew smoke into the air.

"Ever had sex on ecstasy, princess?" Jennifer challenged me

again, but I wasn't going to listen to her. I didn't have any more time to waste on someone like her.

"Where's Neil?" I asked resolutely, which earned me a sinister, mocking laugh. I hated her just a little bit more.

"He's playing hide-and-seek. He's waiting for you, you know? Go find him." She winked contemptuously at me. I gave a furtive glance at the closed bedroom door and my chest tightened in agony.

If Jennifer was out here then who was in there with him?

"I think you should leave." Luke stepped in front of me, blocking my view of his two friends. I raised my chin to look him in the eye and frowned. Was this a member of the Krew trying to...spare my feelings? Or give me advice?

"These two won't stop otherwise. But bear in mind that they're going to be done soon, and the situation can get worse." This was the first time Luke had spoken to me with anything like kindness. But he was still Krew, so I still didn't trust him.

Just then, the bedroom door swung open and revealed exactly the person I had been searching for. His gleaming golden eyes landed on me, slowly traversing the outline of my body before returning to dive into my blue gaze.

He gave me an indecipherable look for a long time, blinking repeatedly as if to ensure that I wasn't a hallucination. Then he heaved an irritated sigh and walked toward me, his muscles contracting and expanding with every step.

Behind him, unicorn-haired Alexia emerged from the room along with another girl. She was blond and petite with a perky body. Both of them wore surprised expressions on faces still flushed from arousal.

Alexia—who was, fortunately, clothed—sat down next to Jennifer with a smug look on her overly made-up face. The other blond was wrapped only in a bedsheet, and she had the unmistakable look of someone who'd just been well fucked. She paused behind Neil, who completely blocked her smaller figure and then craned her neck to one side for a look at me.

I was the one in the wrong here, not her.

I was the one who was imposing, not her.

Luke cleared his throat while Neil just stared at me, coming to a halt right in front of me.

If he had wanted to ignore me, he would have done so. Instead, he chose for me to see him. He wanted me to smell the shower gel he emitted because he'd just scrubbed away the evidence of sex with those other women, though other evidence was still clearly visible. His lips were swollen, his cheekbones pink, his muscles were still tense, and his arousal showed on his face in a way that felt like a slap.

And it burned. It burned so much.

"What's wrong? Cat got her tongue?" Alexia asked, but I didn't so much as glance at her. After all, the blue unicorn meant nothing to me. Instead, I stepped back and took a deep breath. I felt something pressing down on my chest, something so heavy that it made it impossible to breathe properly.

Meanwhile, Neil just looked at me, motionless and inscrutable. He reminded me of a wild animal behind a wall of glass. An animal who filled his life with empty sensations, shared with equally empty women.

"The trouble with a mask is it never changes," I murmured after a long silence that had drawn everyone's eyes to us. "Bukowski said that," I added challengingly, staring him down.

His forehead creased as he absorbed the blow. "'A pro does as well as he can within what he has set out to do, and a madman does exceptionally well at what he can't help doing.' He also said that." He glanced at my eyes and then at my lips. I stared up at him, still enthralled but so disappointed.

"What the fuck are they talking about?" Xavier grumbled, breaking the hush that had fallen all around us. Neil broke eye contact and took a seat on one of the stools in the little kitchen. He crooked his index finger at the nameless blond, and she obediently approached him.

"He's not satisfied yet, baby doll. He won't be until he breaks you in half," Xavier jeered crudely with Jennifer still perched on his knee.

"Selene, I really think you should go" said Luke who had since returned to the kitchen. But I couldn't tear my eyes away from Neil, who had begun to unwind the sheet from around the girl, revealing her delicate yet proportionate curves. He skimmed the edges of her with both hands and I noticed a red palm print on one buttock as well as scratches along her flanks.

Signs of passion.

Neil started rubbing her breasts then, baring them only to his golden, emotionless eyes. Her back arched as he cupped them in his large hands. Then, he bent to put his lips against her nipples and swirled his tongue around them, staring lewdly into her eyes.

He was trying to hypnotize her, to put her in his thrall the way he did with all the rest of them. A knife between the ribs would have hurt less.

I staggered back in shock, but he continued to lavish attention on her with his mouth and hands, weaving his fingers through her long hair and encouraging her to get on her knees.

The girl obeyed this wordless command. Holding her tightly by the hair, Neil pulled down the elastic of his boxers and freed his stiff, imposing erection.

That shameless move was too much for me. I immediately shifted my gaze down to the toes of my sneakers. I avoided looking at them, though I could still hear.

Everything.

I heard the guttural noises the girl made. I heard her gag when Neil had presumably thrust too hard. I heard a feminine complaint, perhaps because his member was too thick and she couldn't accommodate it all. Then I heard sensual moaning as the girl undoubtedly found her rhythm and began to enjoy herself.

I couldn't say for sure; I didn't have enough information. I just extrapolated as I continued to look away. I didn't want this profane scene lingering in my head forever.

"You aren't gonna watch, baby doll? You're fine to fuck him, but now you're gonna be shy?" Xavier asked, and only the two bitches sitting next to him laughed at his sarcastic questions. I glanced up at Luke who was just sipping his beer like whatever was happening in the kitchen was perfectly normal.

Finally, I looked at Neil. Not a single gasp or moan came from his lips. He never lost control, not even after he orgasmed into the girl's mouth, slackening his hold on her hair.

"Clean it off," Neil said in a flat tone of voice that sounded bizarre on a man who just came, and she obeyed. My eyes roved over his tense body, and I watched him adjust his boxers before staring into his eyes.

I screwed up all my contempt and all my courage to spit at him, "You're depraved." I shook my head in disgust. "You all are." I looked at the blond girl who was now standing and facing me. Her tongue flicked out rapidly to catch a pearlescent drop from the corner of her mouth. Her naked breasts, heavy with arousal, were clearly visible, as were her hairless mons and flat stomach. She had a belly-button ring shaped like a rose.

Neil remained seated on the stool and folded his arms over his chest, looking more like he'd just finished sipping a coffee than getting head from a girl he didn't know in front of five other people.

I watched as Luke set his can of beer down on the kitchen island right next to the asshole and continued watching as Luke approached me again.

I didn't think before I did it.

I let myself be guided by pure instinct, because nothing I could have said would have fully expressed all that I was feeling. I felt like I had countless knives sticking in me: my chest, my stomach, my back, and explaining it in words felt impossible.

I grabbed Luke by the collar of his leather jacket and got up on tiptoes so I could reach his lips.

Then I closed my eyes and kissed him. Maybe I'd regret it or maybe I'd have to soothe my conscience with some lame excuse, but all that was something I would think about later.

After a moment of surprise, Luke parted his lips and returned the dumb, insolent gesture. His hands moved down to my hips and clasped me close to him. I could feel the bulge in his jeans poking me in the abdomen.

My fingers clung tighter to his collar, and I tasted beer on his tongue. I felt his hand slide down my hip and over my ass. When Luke squeezed me there, I shut my eyes and willed myself to remain immobile. Truthfully, I wanted to cry because the lips I really wanted belonged to someone else. *I* belonged to someone else.

Was it really so wrong to feel something pure and want to be near the person who brought out those overwhelming emotions? Was it so wrong to not know much about sex? To believe in love and in the possibility that anything might be overcome? Perhaps even overcome together?

Apparently it was.

I forced myself to refocus on Luke and the expertise he was demonstrating with his kisses. Luke was a really good kisser. He was passionate and carnal, though not as much as Neil. Not as much as that disastrous, insane, and profane boy. It seemed that my body only recognized him. My senses only perked up for him. My skin only warmed for him. I realized that, unfortunately, nothing and no one could match the intensity I'd felt in those moments with Neil.

Luke rubbed my check with one hand, wiping a tear from my

cheekbone with his thumb. I realized that I hadn't merely kissed him: it had been an instinctive protest born from suffering and rage.

"You've really fucked up now," he whispered, yielding to me. He rested his forehead on mine, giving us both a moment to catch our breaths.

I couldn't tell if he was referring to any regret I might feel or how Neil was going to react.

"I'll deal with it later," I answered with a sad smile.

"What did I just witness?" Xavier pushed himself up off the sofa, dislodging Jennifer from his lap. I turned away from Luke and looked at Neil, who was now standing up and glaring at his friend with a thunderous expression on his rigid face.

Suddenly, he came at me like a ferocious beast, grabbing me by the elbow and shoving me against the door. He smothered me with his body, and I could feel the heat of his naked skin even through my clothes. Every seductive edge of him, fitting perfectly against mine. He was much taller than me, and my nose was level with his pecs until he bent his neck to align our faces.

Eye to eye, we faced each other down as though preparing for a duel.

"Babygirl," he said, his voice the barest whisper. "You had your fucking fun, and I'm gonna pretend like I didn't see anything. But you need to get out of here in the next few seconds, or I'm gonna fuck you against this door and show my friend here how much you like it when I pound it into you, all that love you want so badly," he threatened me, staring at my lips, which glistened with someone else's saliva. I ran my tongue over them as if to taste Luke's essence again, hoping for a reaction from Neil.

"Maybe I like him better than you. And maybe you'll have to see us, the way you wanted me to see that girl—" but I didn't get to finish because Neil grabbed me by the elbow, threw open the door to a blast of icy air, and shoved me roughly out of the pool house.

He was infuriated. I could see it in his panting breaths and the tension of each protruding vein. He looked like he was about to burst.

"Fuck you!" he erupted before slamming the door in my face.

"Fuck you, too! Prick!" I turned and screamed it at the wooden surface, behind which I knew he could hear me. A strange heat erupted in my chest. I took a few steps away before walking back again, allowing my anger to take control. "You twisted asshole!" I yelled again, blind fury leading me to rain kicks down on the door while delighted laughter and mocking shouts floated out from inside that goddamned pool house.

Neil was a monster crafted by the gods. Beautiful but, ultimately, a lure into destruction.

37

....

NEIL

She'd kissed Luke.
Not just "a guy," but Luke Parker, one of the Krew, and that meant only one thing: she was in danger.

I had specifically told her she could do whatever she wanted with whoever she wanted except for one of them, for fuck's sake.

I was so anxious that I smoked an entire pack of Winstons in a matter of hours.

A few days before, I had already decided that I needed to push her away from me, and the blond girl that night was just another means to achieve that end.

But Babygirl hadn't looked up once while I'd stared at her the whole time.

I was angry because seeing her standing there in shock among the Krew, her innocent face looking so disappointed, had only brought back the urgent need to send her away as fast as I could. Immediately, if possible.

I heard the Krew cracking their obscene, needling jokes about her, but Babygirl had ignored them with her typical fierce elegance, because she was so much stronger than she looked.

When I saw her kiss with Luke, I knew perfectly well that it was merely an attempt to provoke me, because Selene wasn't truly into it. She kissed him with passion but without emotion. No blush colored her cheeks and no shivers had moved over her slim yet devastatingly appealing body. Fuck, all I wanted to do was slam her up against that door and remind her just how much she liked taking me. And *only* me.

I wanted to bite her swollen lips, which so often stuck out in an automatic pout, or see that ocean stare up close, framed by long, thick eyelashes. I wanted to feel her hips moving in sync with mine, to fit her rounded breasts so perfectly into my mouth, and not because the Boy needed to dominate her sexually like he did with all the others, but because he simply…liked flying with her. To his Neverland.

It was true: I was depraved, just like she said, but I would never have actually done any of that in front of the Krew, no matter how pissed off I was. I would never allow my friends to hear the sensual little sounds she made or see the mole dotting her right breast, right next to the nipple. I would certainly never let them know how tightly she gripped me and how much she screamed when I was pounding into her. Those were little secrets that only I knew, and I liked the idea of keeping it that way.

Despite all of that, I still had so many issues to resolve. Issues that prevented me from leading a normal life like any other guy my age. And it only increased my certainty that I could never tie Selene—or any woman who dreamed of a loving relationship—to me.

I sighed and reluctantly returned to the present moment.

Chloe had another appointment with Dr. Lively that afternoon, and like always, I was going to take her. First, however, I needed to solve a puzzle: Who was Player 2511?

The bastard had called me while I was in the hospital and masked his number so I couldn't find out his identity that way. But I knew that there were ways to trace even anonymized numbers, and Luke happened to know a lot about that. So I went to him, and without telling him any details about the situation, I asked him just to try to figure out where Player's call had really come from.

"You have to give me your phone." Luke held his hands out to me, and I gave him a flat stare. We were sitting in his car, parked outside the house. I'd asked him to meet me without Xavier because we needed to take care of this by ourselves.

I handed over the phone and leaned over to peer at the laptop he'd brought with him.

"What are you doing?" The vibe between us was different, the tension in the air was as palpable as the awkward silence that filled the car.

"I'm jailbreaking your cell for this program. It's pirated software that can be used to catch mobile and landline numbers," he explained, plugging the phone into a cable and typing in a series of numerical combinations.

"Hmm…" I murmured thoughtfully as he continued to avoid looking at me and cleared his throat in obvious discomfort.

"Now we just need to wait a few minutes for it to download," he added, staring at the black screen where a loading symbol had appeared.

While we waited, I dug out my pack of Winstons and pulled one out with my teeth, feeling around in the pockets of my jacket for a lighter. I was outwardly calm while Luke kept silent, clearly unsettled.

I lifted one side of my mouth and said nothing because I knew he'd start talking soon. I'd known the Krew for years, and I fully understood the character of each one of them, Luke included.

The blond guy beside me was someone who couldn't bullshit.

The foundation of our friendship was honesty, which is why I often preferred him to Xavier, who was underhanded and calculating.

"Listen, Neil..." he began, right on time. "I don't know what the fuck I'm supposed to do now. I mean, nothing like this has ever happened to us before. The girl's hot and everything, but if you're interested in her, I'll never let what happened yesterday happen again," he said, all in one breath. Then, he continued, "She's not even a very good kisser, not like the girls we're used to, but she is fucking stunning and she smells nice and she has a picture-perfect ass and who knows what else she's hiding under those baggy clothes, but hey, if me talking to her is a problem for you, just let me know. She caught me off-guard yesterday, I wasn't prepared to..." He stopped when I casually propped open the car door and blew out a plume of smoke before taking another drag off my cigarette. I didn't look at him, though I heard every single word of his little speech.

"It can't happen again. You're not to touch her. I want her far away from our group and all our bullshit," I ordered pointedly. Then I turned to fix him with the stare of someone who would not be contradicted.

Luke considered my answer for a few moments. Maybe he'd been expecting me to say the kind of thing I usually did: "Do whatever you want. Fuck her. Hell, let's have a threesome." Or maybe he thought I'd ask "heads or tails?" the way I so often did when we were about to share a woman.

"Okay, I won't touch her, but..."

I didn't want Selene to become like the blond from the night before, like Alexia or Jennifer. I didn't want her to piss away her innocence and be contaminated by a world that ran on appearances and degradation. Selene was different, and she needed to stay herself, no matter what.

Of course, I knew that she enjoyed the sex, though she never would have admitted it aloud, but she liked it with me, because

587

I'd been the only one, and for whatever reason, she felt a powerful connection to me. What would have happened if she decided to give herself to Luke? Or what if she started sleeping with other random guys?

She wouldn't be the Tinkerbell I'd gotten to know.

That innocent stare would have given way to a feline look of seduction, her willowy body would become soiled and experienced, her natural smile grown sly, her mind poisoned with profane desires. She wouldn't want to make love the way she dreamed about. Instead, she would have taken men to bed not out of any emotion but out of perversion and need, just the way I did. Just the way I'd been taught.

And wasn't that exactly how I was now wrongly teaching her?

If Selene changed, got mixed up with the scum that surrounded me, it would have been no one's fault but mine. All the more reason to push her away from me as fast as I could.

"Neil?" Luke prompted me because I gotten completely lost in my thoughts about Selene. I was thinking about her and Luke or her and some other assholes, and I wasn't understanding shit at the moment. I looked over at him and put out my cigarette, brushing some ash off my jeans.

"I've got bad news for you," he said when I looked him in the eye.

"What is it?" I sighed.

"The dude called from a coffee shop, Brooklyn Bagel. He probably didn't want to be traced, so what better way to do that than to call from a landline in a public business?" He shot me a cursory glance, his words smooth as butter now.

"Shit," I swore.

"Hey, don't punch the car," he broke in, trying to prevent me from venting my anger on the dashboard of his Bugatti Veyron, a particularly beloved gift from his father.

"How did he alter his voice?" I asked him, watching as his

eyebrows lifted in surprise. He clearly wasn't expecting me to give him that kind of detail.

"Well, the voice modifier doesn't have to be incorporated into the phone. All kinds of tech exists to do it," he explained, sounding detached. That was another thing I appreciated about Luke: his lack of curiosity and good sense of discretion. He just did what I said without poking around, unlike Xavier, who always wanted to know every little detail before he did anything.

My two friends were total opposites, for all that they were cut from the same cloth.

I scrubbed a hand over my face in resignation and pushed open the car's door, but before I could climb out, Luke grasped my arm. I forced myself not to react to his uninvited touch.

"Are you sure everything's cool with us?" he murmured uncertainly, as though already afraid how I might react.

What was he so worried about?

"You'd fuck her the minute she gave you an opening. Why wouldn't we be cool?" I answered sourly and gave him a brazen grin. Then I got out of the car to avoid reopening a discussion that I was finding too uncomfortable just then.

Unfortunately for me, Selene had ignited a flame I had no real power to snuff out, because Luke and Xavier were just like me. They would have done anything to have her, even just to slither between her thighs one time. Plus, I suspected that a strange curiosity about Babygirl had been kindled in Luke. She'd given him a thin slice of her inexperience, but he wanted the whole pie.

He wanted to take my place at the table and feast—that's what he wanted.

Without sparing Luke another glance, I went back into the house and headed for my room. I needed to get my car keys and take Chloe to the clinic. As soon as I walked into my room, however, my eyes landed on my bookcase. I noticed immediately that someone had moved my books. Miss Anna always respected my rules, one of which was that no one was ever to touch my stuff. I quickly deduced that there was only one person in the house who would have invaded my privacy like that: Selene.

I didn't yell at her only because I didn't have time. I would have to bawl her out later.

"I'm ready to go." Chloe walked into the room, wearing a coat that let me know it was time to head out.

Once we were in the car, I did nothing but dwell on everything that had happened in the last few days: that fucking puzzle, Player 2511 and his anonymous call, the kiss between Selene and Luke, Logan and his accident.

On top of everything else, my brother had recently told me that he'd seen Player in a black Jeep before the accident. He'd followed him and even waved right before Logan went off the road and nearly died. I felt anger flare up with a passion at the idea of that bastard delighting in causing my brother's near-fatal accident.

"I need to know your every move from now on," I said abruptly to Chloe as I parked in front of the psychiatric clinic.

"What?" she asked confusedly.

"You heard me. You have to tell me where you're going, who you're going there with, everything you do," I repeated firmly as we got out of the car.

"Are you feeling okay?" She followed along behind me with her eyebrows raised. I locked the car with the fob, and we headed for the entrance.

"You do as I say, end of discussion," I ordered in my typical rough fashion, and fortunately, she chose not to reply.

We walked into Dr. Lively's high-end clinic, and I glanced around. There was the usual classical Muzak, the usual saggy-assed woman behind the latest generation of computer, the usual orderlies wandering the halls, and the usual waiting room where we would sit on chic sofas and wait for Dr. Lively to receive us.

"I'm feeling antsy," Chloe groused, snatching up a magazine to flip through in the hopes of soothing some of the nerves she got every time she had another session with the psychiatrist.

"It'll be fine, just like the other times," I reassured her, taking a seat next to her. I balanced one ankle on the opposite knee and tried to tamp down the thoughts that were filling up my brain. I already had a giant headache, and there was still a lot of day left.

"Oh, Chloe, it's nice to see you. I was just waiting for you to arrive." Dr. Lively approached us, and as soon as she stood to join him, he put an arm around her shoulders. "Ready for a nice little talk?" He smiled at her and Chloe nodded uncertainly as they walked toward his office.

I tried to avoid my former psychiatrist's gaze, but when I felt his eyes boring into me, I had to lift my chin.

"I hope that one day you'll come to my clinic to do more than just accompany Chloe," said the doctor pointedly. I had to give him credit: Krug wasn't a man who gave up easily. But I was a stubborn patient who had no intention of letting him shrink my head again.

"People say hope springs eternal, but that seems hard on the knees, doctor." I gave him an irritating smile, and he didn't answer but only scowled at me and stuck his hands into the pockets of his jacket.

"I'm confident you'll change your mind one day." He turned and vanished into his office, closing the door behind him.

Once I was alone again, I stared at the white clinic walls, which did nothing but bring back memories and trigger the urge to flee, to escape. I couldn't, though, because I needed to wait until Chloe was done.

I stood up from the couch and started pacing the waiting room.

Distantly, I heard melancholy piano music that was supposed to soothe patients but only managed to irritate and aggravate me.

"This music is shit," I said, aware that the receptionist could hear me, but I didn't care.

I always said what I was thinking.

Bored, I stopped abruptly to stare at one of the paintings on the wall. The caption read: "Titian, *Sacred and Profane Love*, oil on canvas, 46 in × 110 in, circa 1515."

"I'm sorry you're not enjoying the shitty music," said an immediately recognizable voice. The tall, impressive man was watching me with a delighted smile—it was Dr. Keller. He nodded at me and considered the painting I'd been looking at. I'd only been looking out of boredom, not because I was especially interested in art, though I supposed I knew enough about it.

"So what do you think? What does it mean?"

Did he think that I was stupid? Uncultured or ignorant?

"You're asking me?" I sneered, stepping back to put some distance between us again. I hated it when people tried to invade my space.

He made a skeptical face and then just looked at me in amusement. "I would like to hear your opinion about this reproduction of a painting we have on display here in the clinic," he answered, shrugging one shoulder.

I glanced from the man to the painting and sighed. This shrink was even stranger than I'd thought.

"Considering that the woman on the left is wearing clothes and the other one isn't, I'm guessing she's the chaste lady and the other one's the whore," I answered nonchalantly. Dr. Keller scratched his chin with one hand, his forehead creasing thoughtfully.

Why was he looking at me like that? Weirdo.

"You were close. The clothed woman does represent a sacred, pure sort of godly love and the semi-nude woman represents profane, carnal, passionate love," he added, looking me in the eye. "But Titian suggests that we all contain both types of love within ourselves." Then he pointed out the infant Eros situated between the two women and splashing intently in the water that filled the stone sarcophagus upon which the women sat.

What was he trying to tell me with this?

"You know, Neil, we can look beyond appearances with just about anything. Last time, I offered you the example of my desk, remember?" he asked, still examining the painting. "This painting, for example, might be interpreted in such a way that it could become relevant to your life." He gave me a small smile, and I looked at him in bemusement. Understanding the man was genuinely difficult for me.

"Think about it…"

I turned to stare at the naked woman in the painting, and my mind immediately leaped to Kimberly.

There were also two types of women in my world: ones like Kimberly, who represented profane love, and then there were the others, those peerless women who represented universal strengths. They were intelligent, capable of both giving and receiving love. They were passionate, but they also had pure and precious hearts. They were sacred love.

I had learned about profane love too early in my life and thus had grown up with the belief that it was the only kind that could exist. But in reality, pure love was also out there somewhere, offered by those people who were capable of giving not only their body but also their soul. Perhaps I was the one who had been depriving myself of that kind of pure love—of pure women—because I was a man without limits. Emotionally unavailable, incapable of feeling things, and only willing to give anything of myself in bed.

"I don't believe in love," I pronounced after a long, meditative silence. I looked up and finally met Keller's eyes.

"What about sex? What do you think of that?" he asked, scrutinizing me. That was an even more complicated question, and I wasn't about to explain to him the psychological mechanics that required me to perpetuate my abuse over and over again. I took a step back and put my hand to my throat where it felt like my sweater was getting tighter. Maybe it was some kind of conditioned response in my head. I always felt like I was suffocating when I thought back on my history.

"Sex is a form of pleasure that one human shares with another for various reasons. I do it to survive," I whispered, feeling my voice break the way it always did when I talked about personal things.

"Is there a difference for you between sex and love?" he asked again, clearly intending to get at the heart of the matter.

"No. 'Making love' isn't something that exists as far as I'm concerned. It's just a more romantic way to say what people really mean which is: 'I want to fuck you.' Women in particular want men to be romantic and not treat them like sex objects, so they need to hear all the typical clichés about love." I shrugged, giving voice to more of my thoughts than I'd planned.

"I see. So, you argue that two souls can never connect via their bodies? In your opinion, intercourse is solely physical. Is that right?" He lifted an eyebrow and waited.

I couldn't figure out whether he was intrigued by the way my mind worked or if he was trying to pry into my personal life.

"Well, if souls really could connect through their bodies, a couple would never get bored in the bedroom, would they? But that happens even to people who stood up before God and promised to love each other forever. Why do you think that is? If there's a genuine bond between two souls, why does that happen?" I asked bitterly. "Why do women who have been married for years fantasize about a man giving them a good hard fuck rather than about making love with their husbands?" I quirked a corner of my mouth with arrogant disregard.

"Why do men fantasize about nailing random sluts instead of desiring the women they claim to have such feelings for?" I continued. "Why do people cheat? Rape? Divorce? Abandon their children? Why are there people who, despite having been married or partnered for years, still keep looking for some illusory, imaginary love? Perhaps because they are dissatisfied? Perhaps because the high expectations they'd placed on their much-vaunted 'love' left them disappointed?" I gave him a bitter smile, and his gaze turned reflective.

"You don't have an answer for me, do you, Dr. Keller?" I asked him, victorious. "So don't try to tell me that love really exists, because I don't have illusions about anything. I'm just a realist," I finished bluntly, holding his bright hazel stare, which never stopped assessing me.

"There's some truth in what you say. Love is rare and difficult to find but not impossible. It doesn't really have a fixed definition; it's an abstract force. Invisible but powerful and none of us can escape it. But love isn't just a feeling—it takes many forms. You know, Neil, you might be surrounded by it already. For someone like you, love often comes wearing sexy clothes, maybe with a pair of eyes or lips that draw you like a magnet. Sometimes it hides in the movements of a body, in the tone of a voice, in one particular smell that you can't seem to get away from. It's in a smile, a look, strengths and weaknesses, or even in a body to which you are powerfully attracted. And then, one day, you'll realize that all of it put together means more than just sex. It means love," he explained, his tone calm and his expression thoughtful.

So, in addition to being a weirdo, this guy was also a fucking romantic who believed in fairy tales like my little Tinkerbell.

"And have you experienced it?" I asked.

"Of course I did. A long time ago, with my pearl," he answered immediately. A melancholy expression moved across his face, shadowing his otherwise indulgent look.

"You seem quite leery of me," he muttered, nevertheless sounding like he was enjoying himself. "You need to get out of this glass prison you've trapped yourself in. I know your heart feels like it's been anesthetized, but you can fight and bring it back to life, you know?" He glanced down at his watch and took a few steps away. "Don't let fear eat away your soul, kid." He smiled and headed down the hallway opposite us. "It's time for my tea break. It was a pleasure talking with you." He immediately raised his stiffened right hand to his forehead in a military-style salute, which he paired with a friendly wink.

I furrowed my brow as I watched his figure walking purposefully away. I wasn't someone who talked easily, especially not to complete strangers. Yet, that doctor seemed to coax thoughts and words from me that I'd expressed to others only rarely and with difficulty. Still, I hadn't gone so far as to confess everything to him. That, if love was pain, then sex just made more of it.

How was a person supposed to experience love after one's tormentor had hidden a threat in every "I love you"?

How was a person supposed to feel something they couldn't even define?

It was all too abstract to me. I needed realistic, concrete things. I left the illusions to people who were afraid of ending up alone. People who needed to cling to someone else so they could project their fantasy of love upon them.

Yeah, a fantasy.

Because love was nothing but an idea. The invention of some human who couldn't accept a solitary existence and insisted on finding someone with whom they could share their life.

But loneliness didn't scare me.

I had grown up without love, and I'd survived up until this point, so I didn't feel the need for it now.

It was just me and the Boy for now.

"How'd it go?" Chloe and I walked out to the car after her session with Dr. Lively. My sister seemed peaceful, and that made me feel relieved.

"Good. Carter is slowly fading from in here." She tapped her index finger against her temple, and I put my arm around her shoulders, pulling her close to me.

"He's going to disappear completely. We'll lock him in a drawer and throw away the key." I kissed her forehead, breathing in the pleasant scent of her, and we got into the car. I thought then about how my psychiatrist had once explained memory to me. It was the brain's information storage system. The mind processed information gleaned from experiences or sensations in the form of memories. If those memories were particularly traumatic, one could learn how to lock them up in drawers or "cerebral containers" where they couldn't impair one's cognition. If that was what she was doing, Chloe was on the right track, and she was going to pull out of it. She would overcome the trauma Carter inflicted upon her and learn to smile again like any other girl her age.

"I'm hungry as a bear," my sister said as soon as we got home before hurrying into the kitchen. I heard her calling Anna's name, asking if she had prepared anything Chloe could eat. I, on the other hand, walked across the living room, intending to go upstairs and take another shower, but something blocked my way.

Logan was sitting on the bottom step of the staircase, one crutch next to him, the other lying on the floor. I rushed over to him, alarmed, as he struggled in vain to get up on his own.

"Logan." His cheeks were damp and his head hung down as he stared blankly at the broken leg stretched out before him. How long had he been sitting there? What had happened to him?

I knelt in front of him on the marble floor and looked into his face, trying to figure out how he was doing.

"I…I can't deal with this anymore." Logan put his head in his hands and sighed miserably.

"With the crutches? Is your leg hurting? Tell me." I sat down next to him. It was then that I noticed the childish expression on his face. It was the same one he wore when he was little and he couldn't figure out how to properly brush his teeth on his own. Or tie his shoes. Or find two socks of the same color to wear. Logan had been a determined kid who always wanted to do everything himself, and he had always been a perfectionist. No matter what he did, he wanted to do it better.

"With everything. I can't go to class. I can't get out of the house. The meds the doctors have me on keep me so doped up that I just lie around all day like a stoner. And I can't even go up the stairs because, every time I do, I could fall. I can't do fucking anything, and I feel so useless," he admitted in a burst of frustration. I hugged him automatically, just like when we were kids and I found him hiding under his bed, waiting for me to return after "playing" with Kimberly.

Logan rested his head against my chest, just like he used to do back then, and I patted his shoulder because he wasn't going to face all of this by himself. I was going to be right there with him. We were going to do it together.

"I know it's really difficult, and I can see how demoralizing the immobility is for you, but you're strong, Logan. You've already gotten through the worst part, now you just have to be patient." I smiled at him, but he turned away from me, staring at nothing in particular as his shoulders continued to shake with sobs. "Don't call yourself useless. You have no idea how important you are to me. I was so afraid of losing you; I think I died during those twelve hours you spent in a coma, and now that you've come back to life…that brings me to life, too." I told him sincerely, and his hazel eyes finally lifted to look into mine.

It was right there, in my brother's eyes and in Chloe's: the truest form of love that existed in this world.

"Come on, let's order a pizza and watch an action movie with a lot of gunfights and hot, half-naked chicks giving lap dances." I put my arm around his waist and helped him to his feet. He was tall and heavy, but I managed to support him the whole way to the sofa in the living room.

"The ones where they wear the star-shaped nipple pasties?" he asked slyly, and I shook my head, glad to see that the pup was getting over this crisis. Surely it was only one of many he'd face during his long convalescence.

And I'd be right there next to him.

Always.

"The ones with the star-shaped nipple pasties," I confirmed, grinning at him.

A few hours later, Logan had finally calmed down and seemed to have completely moved past his momentary breakdown.

In the end, I knew where he was coming from.

Dealing with the trauma of an accident like his wasn't remotely easy, but he was a capable guy. He would come out of this stronger than before. We were lounging on the sofa together watching *Miami Vice* when our tranquil moment was interrupted by a call from Xavier.

"Ignore it," Logan groused, glaring at the phone's screen where my friend's name was displayed. I gave him a look, knowing that I was going to answer. I couldn't ignore a call from one of the Krew. Too often, they'd fucked something up and needed my help. Help that I never denied any of them.

But my brother hated them, especially Xavier, whom he thought was the worst of them. He couldn't imagine how we could be friends, nor could he accept it.

"You know I can't." I stood up and lifted my index finger, asking him to give me a minute. Then, I answered the phone.

"What do you want?" I asked.

"Hey asshole. Wanna go get a drink?" he offered. I glanced at Logan, watching the movie intently with a serious expression on his face, and I sighed. My brother would be upset with me if I accepted Xavier's invitation, but at the same time, I could really use a distraction. I needed to let off some steam after everything that had happened. My talk with Dr. Keller, Logan's breakdown... I needed to clear my head.

"Okay," I said simply, accepting a dirty look from my brother who shook his head as if to say, *"I knew it."*

"I'll be back shortly," I lied, ending the call with Xavier. Typically when I went out with the Krew, I never got back early. I glanced at the time. It was already past eleven, and I was probably going to end the night in the pool house with some random blond, giving her the only thing I was capable of giving anyone.

Heedless of my brother's protests, I took a shower and changed into clean clothes. Then I headed out for the address Xavier had texted to me. I sped down the streets with The Neighborhood blasting from my speakers as I ran a hand through my hair, trying to tame it. My hair was still wet, and like always, it smelled too strongly, but I didn't care. The scent of shampoo overpowered Kim's vanilla perfume in my mind.

It was a smell that I would have recognized anywhere, even after so many years.

Thinking of my tormentor, I sped up even faster and cranked the volume. I wanted the music to push down all those irritating thoughts, but I knew that nothing and no one was going to erase what I had experienced. It was embedded in me, like a giant scar across my heart.

The bright red LED sign was the first thing I noticed as I went inside. The interior was full of people, many of them beautiful women. There was a bar along one wall and lots of low tables with leather sofas. I headed for Xavier, who I'd found sitting at one of the stools in front of the piano bar, intent on his beer.

"Finally," Xavier said, chuckling. It seemed he was already pumped. I took a seat on the stool next to him and rested my elbows on the bar. I didn't even know why I'd agreed to come out with him. I would have rather stayed on the sofa with my brother, watching movies and commenting on them. But that was something I only realized in that moment. What a dumbass I was.

"Are you already drunk?" I looked my friend up and down. He didn't seem completely wasted, but from his vacant look and pink cheeks, I figured another beer would probably be enough to finish him off for good.

"Has the baby doll recovered from that perverted show you put on for her? Bet she's never fucking seen anything like that before." He chuckled, chewing on his lower lip piercing. He wasn't wrong. Maybe that's why I felt so twitchy. I wasn't proud of what I'd done, but it was necessary. Selene had to realize who I was. She had to know every part of me so she could run away and seek refuge in the arms of some much better person.

"I don't want to talk about it." Not only did I not want to talk about it, I didn't even want to think about what had happened after that with Luke. I hadn't fully dealt with that kiss yet and it was ridiculous of me.

I never cared about anyone. Never.

"Scotch," I demanded of the bartender, turning entirely to face the bar. Fortunately, the soft music created just the right atmosphere to distract me from my thoughts. I might have called it meditative if Xavier hadn't been there talking shit the whole time. Now he'd started in on Alexia and their undefinable relationship, the jealousy and the constant fighting. He couldn't figure out why she was acting like an overbearing girlfriend.

"The hot blond over there had been eyeing you since you walked in," he informed me abruptly, giving me a small nudge. The bartender gave me my Scotch and I took a drink, glancing briefly at the blond in question. She was with a friend and had to be at least thirty. She was attractive, sexy, and confident. She was sipping a cocktail and smiling at her friend while never taking her eyes off me.

I could read every one of her desires.

Body language held no secrets for me. I could thank Kim for my education there.

The blond smiled strategically, and I observed that even her basic posture was sexually inviting. She traced the curve of her own neck with one hand, intending to draw my attention to that erogenous zone. Typically, that kind of overt trick strongly appealed to me—I liked it when a woman tried to seduce me. But in that moment, I found myself inexplicably bored. I turned my attention back to my Scotch and took another drink, savoring it slowly.

"Well?" Xavier asked, gesturing instead to the girl's friend.

"Well nothing. I'm not in the mood for fucking," I admitted bluntly.

"Are you shitting me? Did you see them?" He finished his beer and got off his stool. "I'm sorry for you, bro, but I'm not gonna miss an opening." He gave me a friendly shoulder pat and walked over to the two women, clearly attempting to pick up one or possibly both of them. I shook my head, smiling. I had forgotten that going out with him when I didn't plan to pick someone up meant spending the night alone for sure. I decided I'd stay for another ten minutes and then I'd head back home.

"Is that you, kid? What a coincidence."

I turned immediately to see a man was now occupying Xavier's recently vacated stool. Dr. Keller gave me a sidelong glance and ordered a gin and tonic. I'd already sat through his introspective bullshit about love and whatever once today and that had been plenty.

"Fuck," I grumbled, visibly annoyed. "You go to places like this?" He didn't strike me as a late-night barfly, yet there he was, sitting next to me, dressed impeccably as always. His unique charm was not going unnoticed by the women around us and I wondered why someone like him didn't have a wife.

"Did I fail to notice some sign forbidding entry to men who are pushing fifty?" he asked sardonically, adjusting his stylish jacket. The more I looked at him, the more he struck me as a rare bird here among these horny degenerates. His air of refinement clashed with the atmosphere around us, full of men looking to pick up girls half their age.

"No, but the people who come here are usually looking to drink or fuck. Choice is yours, doctor." I took another sip of my Scotch and traced the rim of the glass with my index finger, bored.

"Is that how it works, then? You have to come in with a pre-defined objective?" He glanced around, frowning at a group of men standing nearby. "I just came here for a gin and tonic. That's it," he explained easily.

When the bartender handed him his drink, Keller thanked him before swirling the straw around inside the glass.

"Don't you have someone waiting at home for you, Dr. Keller?" I couldn't seem to hold my tongue, even though I didn't really give a shit about his life.

"Nope. Just the occasional friend." He smiled, making it clear what he meant by "friend."

"So you're an inveterate bachelor who enjoys sleeping with different women when the mood strikes him?"

"I didn't say that," he answered.

"But that's what you meant."

I considered it pointless to dig into the life of a man I barely knew, but I also hated being taken for a ride, and that's what he had tried to do. "Your pearl and all that bullshit…" I shook my head, unable to finish the sentence. I didn't need to.

"She definitely existed, but we didn't get the chance to marry." He drank his gin and tonic and sighed. "We didn't even get the chance to really be together."

I had finished my Scotch by that point, and I should have just gotten up and left. I watched the doctor's face as he became absorbed in his musings, and when he lifted his wrist to grab his glass, I took notice of a small patch of skin exposed by the movement of his shirt. There appeared to be some kind of symbol tattooed there.

"Haven't you ever seen a doctor with a tattoo?" he asked when he caught me looking, but I remained impassive.

"Nothing surprises me anymore," I answered cooly. "It's faded, though. You should get someone to go over it again. I have a friend who does tattoos," I added, referring to Xavier, who had vanished to God knew where with the blond or the brunette, whichever one he'd managed to hook.

"No, for me it's mostly got sentimental value. I don't really care how it looks. I got it done more than twenty years ago." He lifted his shirt sleeve a bit and showed me. It was some Japanese characters that I couldn't read. I could have asked him what it meant, but I decided not to because I didn't want to seem nosy. I hated nosy people.

Still, I stared hard at those intersecting lines and wondered all the while how the fuck I'd ended up in this situation. I was sitting here talking to this guy when I could have been propositioning the flirty blond from before and getting blown in one of the club's bathrooms.

I really was in a bad way.

I looked around, no longer paying any attention to Dr. Keller. I needed to find Xavier and let him know that I was leaving. That was no easy feat, however. Who knew where he might have gone to feed his urges?

"Did you come here with someone?" Keller asked, trying to figure out who I was looking for.

"Yes, with a friend who's currently busy nailing some random." I sighed impatiently and got off my stool. I took my wallet out of my pants and offered to pay but Dr. Keller beat me to it.

"Leave it, it's on me."

Usually, I never allowed anyone to pay for me, but I wasn't in the mood to argue just then.

"Thanks." I put my wallet back in my pocket and turned to go. I didn't want to be there any longer. Logan would be pleased to see me come home. Maybe I still might have found him on the sofa watching *Miami Vice*, and I could have sat down next to him, cursing myself for having left him alone.

"Kid." Dr. Keller called after me, and I turned my eyes on him, waiting to hear what he had to say.

"Maybe I could come see your friend sometime?" he smiled and I frowned, not understanding what he was talking about. "For the faded tattoo." He lifted his wrist, and I understood. Of course, the tattoo.

"Whenever you want." I pulled out my pack of Winstons and jerked my chin in a farewell gesture. I stuck a cigarette between my lips and made for the exit, still musing on just how weird that guy was.

38

SELENE

Leaving was the best choice.

I'd thought a lot about going back to Detroit, especially after the furious argument I'd had with Neil.

Even worse, because of him, I'd done something extremely stupid. I'd kissed Luke to show him that I could be like him; to show him that I, too, could kiss someone without feeling anything. That I could be just like Jennifer and Alexia who...

No.

I wasn't like them, and I wasn't like Neil. To my great misfortune, I cared about him a lot even if he didn't reciprocate my feelings. After our fight, I had begun to see him in a different light. Though I still felt a sick attraction toward him, I had to admit the reality of the situation: Neil was a person with a lot of problems; he was extremely hostile to sentiment, and I couldn't be the only one fighting for something that would probably never exist between us. Because, unfortunately, he was and always would be unattainable.

I didn't want to get drawn into his darkness. I didn't want to change myself or the things I believed in to make him happy. Maybe we just weren't meant to be, and I needed to accept that.

"So you're going back to Detroit?" Alyssa sat on my bed wearing a cute yellow dress and tall boots, looking mournful.

I nodded and propped myself up against the desk to watch her.

"But you'll come back to visit me every now and then, won't you?" she asked, and I nodded again, though I wasn't really sure that I would.

A few minutes before, I had called my mother to let her know that after Halloween, in about one week, I would be coming back home. I'd made the decision to tell Matt and Mia later and then I'd sort things out at the university before leaving.

"I need to get back to my old life."

And that was the truth: I needed to remind myself of who I was, my values, and my principles. I needed to get some perspective and space to clear my head—all things I'd been losing steadily ever since I first met...

"Who said you could come into my room and rifle through my things?" Neil burst angrily into the room, startling both of us. Alyssa jumped to her feet, and I adopted a ready stance. His baritone bounced thunderously off the walls, and his golden eyes cut into me like daggers.

We hadn't seen or spoken to each other since that night in the pool house. Where did he get off bursting in here and acting like this?

"What are you talking about?" I looked him up and down—he loomed so large in that small space—and my heart beat faster.

"Um... I'll give you some privacy and go see Logan." Alyssa shot me a furtive look and slipped away, embarrassed. She quailed as she moved past Neil because the walking disaster was in full fury.

"You know exactly what I'm talking about," he answered after my friend had left, shutting the door behind her. I swallowed hard and considered my options. I could tell him that I had indeed gone into his room or I could deny it tooth and nail since he hardly deserved my honesty after what he'd done. But in the end, I opted for the truth.

"You know what? Yes, I went into your room. But just for your information, I don't care about you anymore!" I exploded, throwing my arms out in exasperation. "Run through every blond in the city if you want, but I'll no longer be an audience for any more nasty performances with those wretched friends you think so highly of!" I didn't care that I was screaming or that I sounded like a crazy person; I was tired of being treated badly. I was tired of his behavior, tired of the Krew, of Jennifer; I was so tired of the blonds that I'd started having bad dreams about them.

"Oh, really? But you do care about sticking your tongue down Luke's throat. You know he'd love to come back for more, don't you?" He winked at me before leaning back against the door and crossing his arms over his chest, a posture that made his fit biceps pop.

"I'm going back to Detroit in a week," I said, watching the arrogant smile slowly slide off his face. He stood frozen in that smug stance, but his eyes grew thoughtful. Doubts and silent questions swirled in the gold of his eyes.

"Because of what you saw with the blond?" he asked me in a tone I could not decipher.

"Because of what you are," I admitted with a horrified expression.

Neil was imposing, and he was too powerful for a girl to handle. And that's what I was to him, just a girl.

"In addition to not knowing how to kiss or fuck, you apparently also don't know shit about shit, Babygirl." He moved toward me, and in a nanosecond, my hand flew up to slap him, but Neil immediately grabbed my wrist, squeezing it hard.

My arm remained locked in mid-air while his eyes lit up with too many emotions to catalog, though I definitely spotted rage and excitement in there.

"Since when are you so violent?" He mocked me with a smirk that only increased my agitation.

"Fuck you," I muttered under my breath, and he stared at my lips as though bewitched. If he had tried to kiss me, I would have hit him for real.

"I still have three more limbs; try to kiss me and I'll castrate you," I threatened and his grin only got wider, like he found me amusing or had caught me in some lie. To be perfectly honest, I wanted his sinful mouth on me. I wanted to taste it and feel his savage tongue that halted my breath. I wanted to stop clinging to the mere memory of our kisses.

"I'd rather you do something else with my balls..." He leaned closer to my ear and inhaled slowly, making my whole body go rigid. "They're full again..." he said in a low whisper. I made a face and he pulled away, regarding me warily before shaking his head and finally letting go of my wrist.

"You really are a baby, Tinkerbell." He looked me from head to toe before going to the door, putting some space between the two of us.

I staggered back until I hit the side of the bed and sat down, staring at my wrist. The delicate white skin there was starting to display red marks from his fingers.

"One week. Just one more week and I'm out of here," I whispered, though I didn't know if I was talking to myself or to him. Neil rested his hand on the doorknob and turned to give me a cautious glance. "We never talked seriously; you never really honored my compromise..." I kept going, feeling my heart slowly decelerate because now he too knew that this was the end of us.

"You ought to give me something of yourself, something that I can take back to Detroit with me." Only then did I lift my face to look at him. I felt a familiar warmth spreading throughout my chest and goosebumps sprouted along my arms and legs.

And then Neil left without saying anything, taking his impenetrable silence with him. He hadn't reacted at all, as though he were completely unmoved by my impending departure.

....

I made my way down to the living room after a while to avoid wallowing in my thoughts. I sat down in one of the armchairs while Alyssa and Logan talked to each other.

"I said you should go."

As I watched, Alyssa started to gesticulate in a way that made it clear she was trying to convince Logan of something while he just shook his head and told her to stop.

"No, because you won't be there," she grumbled, touching his face, but her boyfriend responded with a disappointed look and a huff.

"Halloween's a big celebration. You should go and take Selene with you." Logan looked at me, and I gave him an understanding smile, but honestly, I still wasn't tracking the conversation.

"What are you talking about?" I asked, arching a curious eyebrow.

"About the huge Halloween party Bill O'Brien's having. He's rented out this actual mansion for a spooky costume party," Alyssa answered excitedly.

"And who's Bill O'Brien?" I asked.

"You don't know? He's one of the hottest basketball players on campus," she answered, like we all had a moral duty to keep tabs on the university's hot dudes. I shrugged and draped my legs over the arm of the chair.

"Okay. So?"

"So every year, he and the rest of the team throw a big rager that

everyone goes to and now Alyssa wants to skip it because of me."
Logan gestured to his leg and his girlfriend sighed, rubbing his arm.

I understood Alyssa perfectly. If my boyfriend had been injured
in an accident, I wouldn't have gone to a party, either. I would much
rather have spent Halloween with him.

"I don't know; it just doesn't seem right," she murmured, looking
down.

"Bring Selene along with you. It's her first Halloween here in
New York," Logan suggested, as if I'd never seen a pumpkin before
in my life.

"Shall I remind you, Logan, that Halloween is celebrated across
the United States of America, including in Detroit?" I muttered
archly, and he rolled his eyes. Too late, I realized that he was probably just using me to get Alyssa to agree to go.

"It would be better if you came, Selene," Alyssa agreed with him,
clapping her hands in excitement.

How would I improve the circumstances?

"Not a chance. I don't like parties." I gave my head a decisive
shake.

"But it's not just any party—it's Halloween. And if you don't
go, I'm not going, either," Alyssa insisted like a mischievous child,
while Logan smiled and gave me his puppy-dog look, which was
impossible to ignore. I glanced back and forth between the pair of
them several times before rolling my eyes and giving in.

"Fine," I huffed.

"It can be your last party before you leave," Alyssa noted, her
expression growing sad. Logan, unaware of my plans, also slowly
stopped smiling.

"What?" he asked, and I ducked my head guiltily because I
hadn't yet told the rest of the family about my decision.

"Yeah," I confirmed, uneasy. "I'm going home. I miss my mom,"
I said, though that wasn't the real reason.

"Are you sure? But you will come back, right?" Logan asked, sounding concerned as he searched my eyes. I nodded at the first question and didn't answer the second. I worried my upper lip and smiled, trying to defuse some of the tension. I didn't want to talk about it, so I changed the subject.

"Okay, then, so how about we watch a movie?" I suggested and the other two agreed.

We watched an extremely sad two-hour film. At one point, Logan fell asleep. Alyssa cried her eyes out at the ending, while I inhaled an entire bag of high-calorie chips that would probably go straight to my hips.

When Logan opened his eyes and Alyssa leaned into him, looking for cuddles and attention, I wished them both goodnight. Matt and Mia wouldn't be home until later, so I decided to creep up to my room to give the pair a little privacy.

I took a hot bath to a soundtrack of "The Scientist" by Coldplay, my favorite band. Then I got into my oversized tiger-print pajamas. I slid my feet into fluffy slippers and flopped down on the bed, opening my MacBook. I reflected on how much I truly enjoyed my solitude. Unlike many other people, I'd never experienced it as a negative—far from it. Being on my own gave me time to get back in touch with myself and think about my choices, weighing what was right or wrong for me. The silence became meditative—a total peace that calmed my nerves and allowed me to relax.

Just then, my phone vibrated with an incoming text message alert. I jolted at the sudden buzzing sound and grabbed the phone with an annoyed exhalation.

You look bored...

I sat up and crossed my legs underneath me as I read the message, sent to me by an unknown number. I glanced around fearfully. Was someone spying on me?

Another message came in, drawing my attention.

Those awful pajamas again...

Now that message… That could not have been from anyone other than…

I lifted my head and instinctively looked at the glass doors that accessed the balcony, the only place someone could possibly be looking in on me and I saw…Neil. I saw him in all his cursed beauty, leaning on the balcony's railing with a lit cigarette hanging from his lips.

What was he doing out there?

How was he not freezing cold?

Neil was now wearing another sweater and a pair of jeans that emphasized his tall, muscular form. It couldn't be enough to keep him warm. He bent his head over his phone and tapped out something.

We have adjoining balconies.

It was strange to be texting when we were within just a few feet of each other, but then Neil and I had never been exactly "normal" together.

Wait a second…

How did you get my number?

The answer came shortly: **I might have taken it from Logan**

"Taken," of course, not asked for.

I lifted my face and looked in his direction, beyond the large glass barrier, but he had vanished. Where the hell was he now?

I frowned and slid over the edge of the bed, leaving behind my laptop, because all of my attention was now fixed on the messy scene playing out on the balcony.

My phone vibrated again in my hands and my heart leaped.

Do you want to...talk?

I reread the question three times, and I still wasn't sure whether he was sincere or just messing with me.

Either way, I needed to answer him. I could give in and say yes right away, or I could say no and forever deprive myself of the potential opportunity to communicate with him. Finally, I just typed:
Why?

I looked out at the balcony again, hoping he might reappear. But he wasn't there, and he probably wasn't coming back, either.

My phone buzzed again.

Because today I told the Boy that there is a star in the sky for each of us, far enough away that our mistakes cannot tarnish it, and he seemed to agree. He would like to find it with you.

My heart throbbed as I read his response, so odd and profound.

I looked up at the glass doors and suddenly, Neil was there. He gave me a small smile, and just then, it felt like I had an entire colony of butterflies flying around inside my chest. I understood it then...

We weren't nothing. We were something that could be seen, sensed, felt, something that did exist but knew no meanings or definitions.

There was no explanation for the likes of us.

I accept.

After typing out my answer, I lifted my chin to look at him and noticed an odd detail. Neil had a marker in his hand. He hesitated for a few moments and then rested the tip of the marker against the glass and drew a medium-sized star there. The lines were so perfectly symmetrical, I was enchanted by them. Neil really did have gifted hands and not just when it came to pleasuring a woman.

I approached the door slowly, meeting his eyes through the glass and then opened it. The cold air mingled with the heat of the room.

"You really are a disaster," I noted, looking at his sinfully appealing body. He smiled and walked into my room without asking for permission. A wave of his pleasing scent washed over me. I immediately shut the door behind him and just watched as he wandered around my room, scrutinizing everything curiously.

He dragged his fingers along one edge of my desk, and I could guess what he was thinking about. He'd once taken me violently on that desk, showing me all his uncontrollable carnal desire.

"You're here to talk." My weak voice cut through the uncomfortable silence that hung over the room, and he turned to look at me, paying special attention to my pajamas. I didn't care if he thought they were childish; I wasn't going to change for him or anyone else.

"You'll have to take your clothes off," he murmured, sounding intrigued but quite serious, and I shook my head.

It was no use trying to get anything out of him. All he did was tease me until he'd gotten what he wanted. Again, I felt dumb and deluded.

"Goodnight, Neil." I sat down on the edge of my bed and grabbed my computer, settling it on my lap.

"You'll have to take your clothes off...." he repeated and a muscle in my cheek twitched angrily. "Because I'll be waiting for you at the indoor pool, and you'll need to wear a swimsuit," he continued with a dictatorial scowl, so I would understand just how silly I'd been to mistrust him before I'd even let him finish. I lifted my face to meet his eyes, but he had already turned and headed for the door. I saw the marker tucked into the back pocket of his dark jeans.

I didn't move for a few moments, staring at the hallway his frame had vanished into. I blinked as if to make sure I hadn't imagined all of it, and then got quickly off the bed, shaking myself out of my trance.

Before I left my room, I put on a black one-piece with a bit of a revealing neckline. It was sexy but not vulgar, because I wanted him to want me but I didn't want to be as flashy as the women who typically surrounded him. I also brushed my teeth, let my hair down to fall past my shoulders, and even did a quick check to make sure I was shaved and presentable.

Then, I took the elevator up to the third floor to meet him.

My legs trembled with every inch closer I got to him, and when the elevator doors opened and signaled my arrival, I had to be careful I didn't fall down. Strong emotions swirled in my gut like planets orbiting a sun.

I went to the pool and immediately spotted Neil floating in the water. His upturned face was wet, his eyes closed as water dripped from their long lashes. His pectorals were especially prominent as his arms stretched out wide on either side of him. His full lips were curled into an insolent smirk, and his skin gleamed.

"Took you long enough, Tinkerbell," he commented, opening his eyes to fix his golden gaze on me. I glanced around and noticed the soft, white deck chairs scattered around the pool. I peeled off my bathrobe and put it on one of them next to his things: the pack of Winstons, his phone, and the marker from before. Neil was eclectic to say the least.

I cleared my throat as I watched his gaze travel along my curves. I approached him in my bare feet, and choosing not to dive in, I sat down on the marble edge of the pool and dunked my legs just up to my knees. The water was pleasantly warm.

"What, don't trust me?" he teased, swimming to meet me with elegant, feline motions. His lips broke the crystalline water line while his eyes remained above the surface. His chestnut hair hung down damply over the back of his neck. The toki stood out on his powerful bicep, begging me to touch it.

"Not enough. Remember: we're here to talk," I answered honestly, because I really couldn't share too small a space with Neil without giving in to the temptation of his kisses.

I needed to shift my attention to something other than his body. I could feel my cheeks getting hot, and I was pretty sure it wasn't because of the water.

"Bukowski's your favorite writer," I began with what felt like a good jumping-off topic.

Neil paused just a short distance from me and ran his hands through his wet hair. He licked his lips and they almost certainly tasted like chlorine and *him*—a combination I longed to experience.

"And you went through my stuff without permission," he answered, irritated. But he remained a safe distance away from me, for which I was eternally grateful.

"So...you like to read?" I pushed onwards because, goddammit, I needed a win.

Neil snorted and moved closer to me, which set off my invisible alarm. I imagined a tiny red light blinking inside me.

"There's a bluebird in my heart that wants to get out, but I'm too tough for him, I say, stay in there, I'm not going to let anybody see," he answered with a Bukowski quote, staring at my legs and floating over in front of me. Too close. I shifted uncertainly on the marble and tried to refocus on why I'd followed him here.

"And you've read Nabokov. *Lolita*?" I couldn't help a small, pleased smile because it made me happy that Neil was familiar with my favorite author.

"It's about a pedophile," he noted colorlessly, brushing my left ankle with one hand. I flinched and automatically clapped my knees together in a protective gesture, which only made him laugh his guttural laugh at me.

"Exactly." I cleared my throat and felt another caress, this time on my right ankle.

Neil watched me through his long eyelashes and gave me a sly smile, floating closer to me once again.

"Get in the water with me, Tinkerbell. I won't bite," he murmured huskily, and I blushed at the sound.

"It was a gift from my maternal grandmother," I told him,

referring to the sweater which had since become one of his favorite objects of ridicule.

Neil frowned in confusion, so I explained.

"The sweater with Tinkerbell on it, it was from my grandma Marie. People might think it's hideous or childish, but it has a great deal of sentimental value for me," I informed him, feeling my heart beat a little faster at the memory of my beloved grandmother, who'd been gone for two years at that point. Neil grew serious again and stroked my calves with both hands, drawing lines and circles with his fingers and igniting a white-hot flame within me. Then, he moved up to the hollow behind my knee and rubbed me there slowly, so slowly that a shiver moved across my shoulder. A spark of irrepressible cunning flickered in his golden eyes.

"All the more reason to keep calling you…" He paused for effect. "Tinkerbell," he finished, his tone light and pointedly angelic as he ceased the minor contact between us. "So are you coming after me or not?" he demanded before diving back into the water and swimming away from me along the bottom.

My eyes widened in sync with the elegant movements of his strong arms, pushing through the water. Neil seemed to me like both a marvelous dolphin and a dangerous shark at the same time. I took advantage of his submersion to pull the hair tie off my wrist and put my hair up into a high ponytail, a few strands falling loose around my face. Then I lowered myself slowly into the pool, though I continued to hug the edge. With my back to the crystalline expanse, I looked over my shoulder to see where Neil had gone. Suddenly, I sucked in a breath as two hands positioned themselves on my hips and a flawless body pressed itself into my back.

"Finally…" he whispered, brushing the nape of my neck with the tip of his nose, and the sheer wickedness I heard in his voice had me standing at attention.

My body tensed immediately, and I gulped as I felt his erection poking between my butt cheeks. Neil had no problem letting me feel it. In fact, it seemed he was trying to provoke me because he slowly ground himself against me, triggering the familiar yearning between my thighs.

Damn it.

"You... You..." I babbled softly, unable to articulate the questions that hung on the tip of my tongue. I licked my bottom lip and exhaled in a desperate attempt to get the words out.

"I... I... What?" he asked in a singsong voice. His voice was low and teasing, and this time my lower abdomen quivered as well.

Goddamn it.

"Weren't you... I mean.... What happened to...stargazing?"

"They can gaze at us," he whispered, and I raised my face to look at the glass ceiling over us, offering a panoramic view of a spectacular starry sky. I turned to him and met his eyes, which could have given the stars a run for their money, so golden and luminous.

I lowered my gaze and slipped away from his humid breath on the back of my neck and the curve of my collarbone because I didn't want him to seduce me, though he could have done it without much effort.

"What else do you like to do? Besides reading?" I swam a distance away before stopping and looking at him.

He heaved a defeated sigh, and after a few moments, answered:

"Draw, play sports." He moved toward the steps, giving me a sidelong glance.

"Wanna get out?" he suggested with a severe expression, as though something were suddenly irritating him.

I watched his masculine hands grasping the ladder and then Mr. Disaster used his biceps to lever himself up and out of the pool. He stood there, pausing to allow me to appreciate his sculpted form. I saw what appeared to be a white bathing suit wrapped around his rock-hard backside. The fabric, extremely thin and practically transparent, made me suspicious.

I climbed out as well, following him over to one of the chairs, and sincerely hoped that he wasn't just wearing his boxers.

Neil stretched out on the lounger, crossing one ankle over the other. I swallowed hard when my eyes caught on the massive, crude bulge visible through what I now realized were, indeed, waterlogged white boxers.

"Well? Are you going to join me?" He looked at me, pretending not to see how obviously embarrassed I was. His gleaming golden eyes, however, rimmed with wet eyelashes, lit up with mischief, and a slow smile curved those beautiful lips.

Feeling uncomfortable, I grabbed my bathrobe and patted my chest and thighs dry. Then I tossed it back down and walked right toward the mysterious devil who was brazenly staring at my breasts. My nipples were hard, and the wet fabric did nothing to hide them. I was feeling especially appealing in that moment, and I sincerely hoped he was suffering as much as I was.

"You can sit next to me or on top of me. Your choice." The evil glitter in his eyes was terrifying yet inexplicably seductive.

"The last time I sat on top of you, you destroyed the pool house," I reminded him and twisted my mouth into a thoughtful expression. I had never really understood what had happened in that moment, right after we…

"Because I hate that position. It makes me feel suffocated," he answered vaguely, his gaze sinking down hungrily to my legs. I let him trace their lines with his eyes, like I was a blank canvas and he was a paintbrush.

"Then why did you just suggest that I—" But he answered before I could finish the question.

"Because I know you like feeling me between your legs." His voice was a sweet whisper, a stark contrast to his burning gaze that laved me slowly as though Neil longed to envelop my body in his hands.

"What makes you think that?" I asked but Neil leaned forward, and in one firm movement, took me by the wrist.

"Shut up and get over here." It was a subdued order but an authoritative one. In no time at all, I found myself lying motionless on the chair, like a mouse in the clutches of a venomous snake. Neil moved on top of me, supporting himself on his forearms on either side of my head. Then, his hips slipped between my thighs and pressed down right there, where I had been throbbing for so long.

Silvery drops of water streamed down his tanned skin, while his eyes grew dark with deranged desire. I tried to resist, but I began quivering all over: my shoulders, my hands, my legs, everything.

"Don't tense up," he said, his whisper like a caress. He pressed his lips to my neck and pulled them slowly up to the space beneath my ear. He touched the lobe with his tongue, making me gasp.

"I'm right here…" he added when he noticed that I was staring up at the sky through the glass ceiling rather than looking at him. In all honesty, I was focusing on the sensations he coaxed from me. I could feel my heartbeat throbbing in every square inch of my body, to the point where it made it hard to breathe.

"You know, Tinkerbell…" He went back to teasing my throat with his mouth before slipping down to my clavicle. It felt like he was etching the way into my skin with his hot breath. "I showed you what I like and how I like it…" He began moving his hips against me, swaying in a slow, lovely way until my knees locked around him. "Now I just need to show you when I like it and how much I like it…"

And thus he declared his true intentions, which I should have known right away. I also realized that it was now up to me whether I chose to go "flying" with him or not.

I closed my eyes and arched my back as he tugged down the neck of my swimsuit, freeing one breast. He cradled it in his hand before bringing it to his lips to suck. My first reaction was surprise but then my craving body recognized his touch and a look of pleasure and approval spread over my face.

"You told me we would talk and…" My words died as he began to worry my nipple with his teeth. Like a delicate new bud, it stiffened in his mouth as his tongue flickered over my areola. I couldn't focus on anything just then other than what he was doing to me.

"I'm about to tell you lots of things, Tinkerbell." He helped me get my bathing suit off with rapid, impatient movements and tossed it aside, turning immediately back to me. My now uncovered sex rubbed against his hard-on, and my nipples dragged against the muscles of his chest.

We provided a spectacle unparalleled for the stars which, shining down from above, illuminated our bodies as they trembled with need and want.

He stared at me, and in that moment, I caught a glimpse of the beautiful yet terrible creature inside him. All at once, his lips cracked in a lewd grin, showing off the white gleam of his teeth. Then Mr. Disaster tilted his head slightly and licked the curve of my mouth, deliberating leaving a trail of his saliva on me like a brand of possession. He gave me another look, this one more ambiguous, as though he were waiting for me to understand something. Then he leaned in and kissed me the way he liked.

He pressed his tongue into my mouth, and I returned the intense, voluptuous gesture, tangling my tongue with his. My hands slid along his arms, tracing the muscles that stood out in sharp relief and the many visible veins. His hand went the other way, moving down my stomach until he reached my mound. He touched my clit, rubbing it slowly with two fingers.

We were supposed to talk…talk and…instead I began to move my own pelvis in rhythm with his movements, a slow, shy swaying back and forth.

My hands climbed up again until they reached his broad

shoulders while his fingers stroked my labia, soft and wet, before finally invading that quivering place that was so ready to welcome him in.

I made an indecipherable noise, and he smiled, adopting with his fingers the same exhausting rhythm as his tongue.

My legs began to tremble unmistakably and Neil stroked my thighs, urging me to calm down. We didn't speak, but suddenly, all his gestures became perfectly clear and easily readable for me.

I was still waiting, though, for the moment when he would finally shed his fears and offer me his soul as well as his body. The moment when he would willingly expose his weaknesses to me, trusting that I would take care of him. But seeing him there, hovering over me with his gleaming eyes and his hungry mouth, his energetic tongue and his fine, strong fingers, it was still such a shocking, incomparable experience that it drew such intense emotions out of me. My eyes filled with strange tears. I wanted to cry because it felt so good and because I couldn't control it and because it made such a victim of me.

My back bowed again when his fingers sank into me until his knuckles were flush with my labia. Then, he began moving them so rapidly that my vision went fuzzy. I saw sprays of color, waves of it like paint splashes. I heard a jumble of sounds, and my body became a shapeless puddle as involuntary convulsions rocked me through the wave of my orgasm.

"Mmm..." was the only comment I could offer as my eyes slowly opened to catch his. We stared at each other from a negligible distance. Both of us were visibly panting and an innocent smile turned up the corners of my mouth. I stroked the curves of his perfect body and Neil allowed me to touch him, his eyes predatory and voracious as he watched me.

I kissed along his jaw to his throat when I inhaled the good smell of his skin. As I did so, my hands sank down to rub his firm glutes, and with my index finger, I traced the central furrow between them. His lips parted to let out a low, guttural gasp, and I smiled in surprise because it was so rare to hear his pleasure. I worshipped him with my touch and thought that perhaps he was right after all: there was a silent language through which much could be communicated without ever using words.

"You have a perfect body," I praised him, but he pretended he couldn't hear me and rested his forehead against mine, breathing me in. I hooked my fingertips under the sodden elastic of his boxers and pulled them down slowly, immediately assisted by Neil, who tossed them aside. He was now completely naked.

I couldn't see him, but I could feel it. I felt it with every part of me, and soon, I would feel him inside me.

Neil shut his eyes, rocking slowly in a regular yet sensual rhythm. His stiff member slid back and forth over my cleft, readying my body, though I was already quivering at the prospect of fully abandoning myself to lust.

Then, his cheeks became tinged with red as though he were embarrassed and his fingers dug into the base of my spine. Mr. Disaster opened his eyes, turning that penetrating golden stare on me, and I felt unsettled in a way I hadn't before.

He adjusted his pelvis and used one hand to guide his erection where he wanted—where we both wanted—it to go.

"You said you wanted something from me…" he said in a faint whisper as he pushed gently inside me, invading me. I gritted my teeth against his size, which he was very cognizant of, so he stopped and looked into my eyes.

I read an implicit concern in those eyes; never had he looked at me so seriously or so courteously. I realized that there was an entire universe in his eyes, a universe I could only admire, where I had not yet been able to find the answers to my questions.

We stared at each other as though time had stopped, our breath suspended in the air, our lips drawn close together in anticipation. With decisive, sultry movements, he applied the lightest pressure from his hips, and I let out deep moan as he bottomed out inside of me.

I thought it magnificent, how my body united with his. I could feel everything about him: his mind, his emotions, his heartbeat racing faster and faster. I hoped he wouldn't notice how I was blushing, but Neil looked at me again with those big, intense, serious eyes and I knew that he'd seen it.

He pressed his cheek against my temple and began to move, rocking back and forth with deep, decisive strokes. He pulled back without ever coming completely out of me and pushed powerfully back inside, his chest colliding with my breasts.

After a few moments, his thrusting sped up and all of my muscles tensed. My hand ended up clinging to his glutes, which contracted with each thrust. His breathing got uneven as he kissed me, swallowing my every sound as his tongue tangled with mine. Abruptly, he looked down at me, and I could see an atypical confusion on his face.

Then, he instinctively lifted up his torso and got to his knees, taking me by the hips. He began to move more forcefully and lifted my pelvis so he could drive himself deeper. His rough, savage side took over, and I arched back into him, startled by the shocking carnality of it.

My lips parted to emit a visceral scream but Neil hovered over me and kissed me again, stealing my breath.

It was a liberating, powerful…passionate kiss.

His hands on my hips had turned into a possessive clutch, and I looked at him in bewilderment.

"Neil…" I murmured, unable to speak properly while he continued to plunge into me, emitting small, low masculine sighs that gave me goosebumps.

"Be quiet, Babygirl." He growled it, like a big, ravenous cat, and the rough sound of his voice was enough to make me peak. My muscles locked up too quickly, I lost control of myself. I squeezed my eyes shut and yanked on his hair, letting my euphoria explode around him like a volcano's eruption.

My channel sucked him in deeper, energetically, convulsively. My pelvic muscles contracted and dilated at the mercy of sublime sensations that moved freely across my body. It was an intense, heart-wrenching, indelible moment.

I shook beneath him and his hips gave me the briefest reprieve. Neil glanced at me, maybe expecting he'd have to immediately address complaints because this coupling had been quick, brutal, and not at all gentle.

In that moment of hesitation, his gaze fell to the place where our bodies were joined. Then he leaned on his elbows and looked back up at my face.

"Yes, you are truly a Babygirl..." he whispered, delighted by how I hadn't yet learned to control my emotional and physical reactions to these sensations.

But even though I'd come almost immediately, Neil had every intention of starting again and continuing relentlessly. For eternity, it felt like. I blushed and my shoulders shook as I breathed in deep in my chest. Then he pressed his hips flush against me again, signaling the end of our little pause. I dug my nails into his back flesh and absorbed the fierce, powerful strokes that marked me again as belonging to him. My brow furrowed and I caught my lower lip between my teeth as I began to feel a slight ache in my lower abdomen that I couldn't seem to ease.

Neil was forceful, huge, and overpowering while I was small, slim, and delicate. Sex with him was always a mixture of pleasure and pain because of his stamina and ability. He overwhelmed me, he took possession of me, he penetrated me deeply until I had submitted fully to the power of his body.

There were many women who would have envied me and wanted his body mounting them instead. They would have wanted to kiss his full, pink lips and lick his wet, glistening tanned skin. They would have wanted his lewd touch and his filthy tongue. And there I was, feeling like something made of glass in the hands of this godlike creature, imbued with superhuman strength and energy.

As he kept moving, his eyes were stuck on mine, like he was afraid of losing me. His elbows still supported his considerable frame and his hands stroked my hair. Neither of us uttered so much as a word, only our moans floated out around us while I became lost in his stare.

"N-Neil..." I stammered because my ragged breathing wouldn't let me get words out correctly. He grinned into the bend of my neck and licked the skin there, tasting my sweat. I was sweating all over. In fact, I felt like I was aflame.

"I like it when you can't talk," he noted mischievously as my legs tightened around him.

Our faces and chests were so close together that I could feel his heartbeat chasing mine. All the sensations were amplified; I could smell his skin and his breath, it was so intense that it made me sad. Because this sex would change nothing for Neil. I would still mean nothing to him, and I would still be leaving.

In a week.

Then, Neil redoubled his efforts, raising himself up on his forearms and penetrating me more forcefully. I stared at the inverted triangle of his hips slamming into me, the tattoo on his left hip, his abs contracting, his chest flushed with effort.

The sight of us locked together was so thrilling that I chased his movements, participating in his race to orgasm. His eyes raked over my nude body, rocked by more waves of pleasure, and with a growl deep in his throat, his body stiffened. His thrusts got sharper and deeper. I jolted forward and slipped back in time with his hips, but what was he going for?

I could feel him in my stomach and between my breasts. That sensation of feeling him was so all-encompassing. Neil filled me completely, and it wasn't merely a physical fullness but an emotional one as well. He enveloped my soul in his chaos. His sultry sighs were full of erotic appeal as they harmonized with mine into a single melody. Together, we allowed the magic of the moment to sweep over us as though we'd been caught up in a sandstorm, in an unstoppable wave.

With his forehead pressed against mine, guttural male sounds emerged from his parted lips, and I knew that, perhaps for the first time, he was losing control. He gripped my breast with one hand while the other clutched my hip as though he were afraid of falling into some void.

His breathing grew rapid, his cheeks blazed. His skin was sweaty and when he froze inside of me, at the mercy of his muscles' powerful contractions, I could feel him pulsing in my low abdomen. A bizarre heat spread deep inside me and I realized that he…he had reached his peak by giving himself completely to me.

He continued to thrust slightly, and I felt his member slide more easily, seed slicking the way between my thighs and it was…it was fantastic.

Just magnificent.

Neil had come inside me and something had broken; a barrier had collapsed. He lay breathless on top of me and panted against my ear, the sound giving me goosebumps.

"You made me do something really fucking stupid," he muttered, sounding disappointed.

I stroked his spine, and his breathing grew gradually more regular and measured.

"What do you mean?" I asked him with a serious expression.

Neil rolled off me to the side, and I curled up against his chest, both because space on the lounge chair was limited and because I loved his warmth and his smell anytime, even times like this.

"You gave your first time to me, now I've given you mine. We're even, Tinkerbell." He looked up at the starry sky as if to hide his eyes from me. I felt tired, satiated, and a little lightheaded, but I turned an embarrassing shade of maroon when I realized what he'd just said to me.

He doesn't... He didn't...

"Have you never done that with a woman before?" I whispered gently, pushing my sweaty hair off my forehead so I could more closely observe the graceful lines of his face.

"I showed you how it is when a man likes it." His expression displayed a certain troubled look that I couldn't quite interpret because his presence was so overwhelming. Every time I tried to take in oxygen, my breasts grazed his chest, and I became pathetically aroused, even as I still shook with the aftermath of pleasure.

"And how much..." I added smugly, and he turned to give me a scrutinizing look, which made me feel terribly embarrassed. He was somehow even more beautiful after sex, his eyes lazy and glittering, his lips swollen and red, the relaxed expanse of his glistening skin... I, meanwhile, was in who knew what sort of condition.

"Now you'll have something of me to take back to Detroit with you." He slipped his forearm under the back of my neck and let me rest next to him. Or rather...on him. I flattened my palm over his chest, and naked and in disarray, we gazed up at the sky together. We grew drunk on the stars in that echoing, deafening silence.

"Tell me about yourself," he said suddenly, staring at me in that serious, penetrating way that made him look so breathtakingly beautiful, and I didn't even try to hide my astonishment at hearing such a request from him. It was unexpected to say the least.

"What would you like to know?" I answered softly, blinking a few times in disbelief.

"Whatever you want to tell me," he said, looking upward.

"I'd just finished my freshman year of college in Detroit before I transferred here. I was fairly well known. I had my group of friends and…" I stopped, licking my lips. "Jared," I said, clearing my throat awkwardly because I didn't know how Neil would react to hearing that name. But his golden eyes stayed fixed on the starry sky, so I went on.

"I had a normal life. I've always appreciated the simple things: a good book and a cup of hot cocoa…" I said, lightly stroking his chest as our bodies lay intertwined on the lounger. "I hated frat parties and the obnoxious basketball players who hit on everyone…kind of like you," I said teasingly, though I knew it wasn't at all accurate. It was women who hit on Neil because he was appealing, gorgeous, and reserved. So much so that it was nearly impossible to get close to him.

"I'm more discerning than you might think," he said defensively, turning to look at me. I examined his features and wondered once more how he could be so perfect. That forehead, eyes, nose, lips, and chin—they looked like they'd been situated with the utmost precision by an especially perfectionistic god.

"Tell me more about yourself." He shook me from my musings, looking actually curious about my life. I smiled at him and picked up where I'd left off.

"There's not much to tell. I was mostly raised by my mother. The year my father left us, I stopped calling him 'Dad.'" I glanced down at my index finger, stroking the skin between his pecs almost absent-mindedly and continued. "I knew he was living here in New York, but for four years, I always tried to avoid talking to him or meeting his family. That is to say, all of you…" I looked up to see him watching me with his usual dark, imperturbable expression.

"I was lucky to always have my mom at my side. I have a really great relationship with her."

"What's her name?" He continued to watch me, and I felt his warm breath on my face.

"Judith Martin. She's a literature professor," I said with pride. I was proud of the woman she was, not only in the professional sphere but also within our family.

"She was a very present mother who always gave me lots of attention. I miss her so much..." My voice broke because my mother's absence was something that constantly hung over my life in New York. "I don't get to talk to her that often because of her job, so I have this deep feeling of homesickness and loneliness," I confessed, admitting this to myself for the first time as well as to him.

I'd always tried not to dwell on those feelings, but I couldn't deny that I'd often felt alone, like I couldn't count on anyone except for myself. True, solitude was sometimes meditative for me, but at other times, it could be painful.

"I feel lost," I said in a small whisper. "Like I'm setting out on this journey through life on my own," I continued and his golden eyes never left my face for even a second.

"Sometimes, I think I'm better off alone and that all I want is to live in a little place that's just mine, untainted by the badness of other people. But there are other times when I also want someone else there to share it with me." I swallowed, surprised by my own words. "It's a contradiction, I know, but I have my...weirdnesses as well." I tried to brush the admission aside, smiling shyly at him, but Neil just continued to stare at me in that grave way. He frowned a little bit—thoughtfully—and slipped his arm out from behind my head. He sat up, splendidly nude.

He ran a hand through his wet hair and glanced around as though looking for something. Then, apparently spotting what he sought, he stood up and gave me a full view of his chiseled physique and hard, firm ass.

I still didn't know what he was doing, though, so I followed him with my eyes as he walked purposefully over to another deck chair and grabbed something. He returned to me and I saw he had the marker clutched in one hand. Then, he sat down next to me and pulled the cap off the marker with his teeth, leaning over my pelvic area.

I was… I was…nude with my privates exposed and rosy, still branded with his cum. I pressed my legs together out of embarrassed reflex but Neil didn't even glance between my thighs. He was focused on something else.

He pressed the tip of the marker against my hip and began making lines that gradually resolved into a larger design. I lifted up my torso and craned my neck to see what it was and recognized a… shell. A solid black shell with a white pearl inside.

"Every time you feel alone, draw a pearl inside a shell," he said softly, blowing on the drawing. Then he kissed my lower stomach, tracing a path up my stomach and over my breasts. He licked a nipple, making me go rigid with arousal and then, finally, he moved his face up level with mine. He stared at me, his golden eyes sly and laughing.

"What's the story with the pearl and the shell?" I murmured with an honest smile that I couldn't hide. Neil was just incredible on the whole with his crazy, creative ideas.

"It's not a story," he corrected. "It's a legend." He hovered over me, putting his hands on either side of my hips, covering me. Then, he touched his lips to mine, not quite kissing me. I stared deeply at him, examining the lines of amber that radiated from his pupil and dispersed into the gold of his iris.

How was it that this boy steeped in shadows had the sun in his eyes?

I bit my upper lip, embarrassed, and an automatic question slid off my tongue before I could stop it. It was probably a mistake but I had to try. At least try to know him.

"And us? What are we?"

It was a legitimate question, though I knew that there were plenty of things in the world that couldn't be so defined. But we had shared something important. He had given me his first, confessing that he'd never done that with anyone else.

Was I deluding myself, or was it possible that I mattered just a little bit to Neil?

He looked me up and down and then smiled his enigmatic smile, leaning down until he was only a hairsbreadth away from my ear.

"Everyone knows Prince Charming and the princess live happily ever after," he said softly in his deep, mature voice. His chest grazed my nipples and I held my breath, helpless against the feelings his body triggered.

"But have you ever wondered what happens to the princess and the dark knight?"

39

NEIL

I came inside her.

Goddamn it.

I—*me*—had done something so stupid after years of experience, after having done everything a man could do to a woman without ever screwing up like that.

But it hadn't been just a meaningless gesture, or a careless mistake made in the throes of orgasm. I made a choice; it was premeditated. I wanted to make sure that Selene truly understood what it was like when a man was enjoying sex. More importantly, when *I* was enjoying sex.

And the truth was, I'd only really understood that when I entered her without any barrier between me and her velvet-soft skin. Until I exploded inside her body without worrying about controlling myself or stifling my urges. And I wanted to show her just how much I needed to have her, to have her body, her soul, everything that was hers. As I sank into her and put that exquisite pressure on the junction of our bodies, I felt safe with my Babygirl.

I felt like I was where I was supposed to be in a way I never had with anyone else.

After the fucking and talking, Selene asked me to stay a little longer with her, but after I'd gotten what I wanted, I decided I absolutely needed to get dressed and go back to my room. I knew that I'd already done more than enough for one night, and the image of her face as she came was destined to haunt me, consuming my thoughts relentlessly.

"Selene is just a woman, just one woman, like so many others," I repeated to myself as I thought about how much I'd enjoyed smelling myself on her skin and how much I'd like to be back inside her, in that place I most adored, the place that absolutely fucked my head though I'd thought myself immune to its power.

But I knew I couldn't stay there. Selene could not be allowed to bond with me because there would be no happy ending for us.

The things that brought me pleasure were all immoral or filthy because I needed to soothe my spirit and feed my desires. My life, at the end of the day, was a pendulum that swung between cruelty and sorrow, boredom and disappointment, nightmares and reality.

It swung between me and Babygirl.

And so I took the path of least resistance, where a pack of Winstons and some hot blond were enough to keep me satisfied and relieve some of the suffering that weighed me down.

Selene was a fairy creature, a being that fell from heaven with the single goal of bringing me to the brink of madness, and it was my job to keep that from happening.

Even if I had shared things with her that I hadn't shared with anyone else. Usually, I didn't like to linger over details, on the smell and the touch of it all, but with Babygirl, it was the opposite. I loved to immerse myself in the curves of her body, kiss each line and angle, take refuge inside her and show her a world of sin. A world she didn't even know existed, a world in which we smashed into each other, two contrasting forces of nature, constantly in conflict, but at the same time, so interconnected that one could not exist without the other.

I told myself that I wasn't going to let her chain me down to her. Because Selene was forbidden fruit. A surreal illusion. A creature of mystery. A crystalline body that contained within it a soul so pure that someone like me shouldn't have been allowed remotely near it. And yet, I continued to kiss her, I continued to fuck her and do whatever else I wanted to her because I was selfish and twisted. And because her willowy little body kindled a burning desire in me that I could not contain.

The idea of her leaving for Detroit didn't thrill me, even though I agreed it was the right decision. After all, we had a faceless psychopath on our backs, fully capable of hurting my family and already plotting something diabolical for his next target. Selene could be in just as much danger as my mother, Chloe, or Matt.

And I would never have forgiven myself.

....

The morning after our lustful interlude by the pool, I ignored Selene as she ate breakfast in the kitchen. She watched me the whole time with those crystalline eyes, waiting for me to look at her.

I managed to resist the urge to go to her and kiss her.

Fuck, honestly, it took all the strength I had not to walk over to her, lift her up on the table, and throw her legs open so I could lose myself in the heat of her. In her purity, in her sweet taste, or the depth of her eyes…

Her body, the way she moved, the way she looked at me, the vastness of her heart, the integrity of her soul…everything about her stunned me. Even when she was wearing all her clothes or yelling at me or giving me her disappointed look.

She was the most beautiful of angels, and I was always going to be a monster. And that was why we were impossible together.

I took a closer look at her: she looked tired but satisfied, the familiar expression of a woman who had thoroughly enjoyed herself and would love to get another taste of my body. It was the effect that I had on everyone.

And, of course, that satisfaction was immediately followed by the dissatisfaction of realizing that body was still attached to me. And I, better than anyone else, knew how she was feeling.

Hours later, I lounged restlessly on the waiting room sofa at the psychiatrist's office where I had once again brought Chloe. There was a woman, approximately my mother's age, who wouldn't stop staring at me. She was wearing a form-fitting pencil skirt that emphasized her body and a fur-collared coat was draped open over her delicate shoulders, leaving her large breasts exposed. She leafed through a magazine, legs elegantly crossed, and every now and then, she'd toss a quick glance in my direction.

She had short, bright hair—a shade of blond that particularly appealed to the Boy in me.

The familiar sick machine had been triggered.

The woman before me continued to give me heated looks, fluttering her eyelashes. I saw a shrewd gleam in her chocolate-brown eyes, so I adopted a predatory posture of my own.

I made myself comfortable on the sofa, spreading my legs, leaning my left elbow on the sofa's arm and letting my right hand fall to my crotch. I touched myself. Or, more accurately, I palmed myself crudely before rubbing my cock through the material of my jeans, showing her just how big it was. I enjoyed the expression of shock that instantly flashed across her face as she glanced around in alarm, making sure no one else was there.

My clear and unequivocal signal had made her uncomfortable. I was, after all, extremely good at creating sexually provocative situations.

Kimberly had taught me how to be perverse, filthy, and libidinous. She had likened our relationship to the love affairs among the Olympian deities. There were plenty of myths, she said, where various Greek gods fell in love with humans due to their great beauty and then simply abducted the mortals to do with them as they pleased.

Thus, I learned from her that beauty was a powerful tool for predicting and influencing human behavior. It was at the root of so many choices people made or actions they performed. Kim herself had always told me, "I use you because you're beautiful."

Like the child-eating witch she was, the quest for beauty was the universal driving force behind her frequently disgusting and immoral behavior. She didn't care how old I was; she didn't care that what she was doing was a crime, she didn't care that she was damaging my mind, body, and spirit. She had reduced me to an object. An object that she claimed to love.

So, from a yen for beauty, we moved on to violation, justified with an "I love you." All that it really meant was: *I love that you are beautiful, and I'll fuck you for the same reason. But remember: this is our little secret.*

In fact, a declaration of love invariably followed each abusive act. An attempt to soothe the victim's soul. Kim felt entitled to seize and possess me, because she felt a desire for me that she wasn't willing to control. And so the child-eater tried to make me feel guilty for my beauty and her violence because, in her depraved mind, I was the one who had offended first, not her. I was the one who exerted an irresistible power over her, and Kim could not accept being at the mercy of anything, least of all the way I looked.

It was exactly the kind of insane justification sexual predators—men and women—typically offer their victims and the people around them. I had experienced it firsthand, years before...

I was naked, sitting on the edge of the bed.

I didn't move except to rub my forehead and wipe away the sweat.

Kim stood in front of me, getting dressed again. I stared at her with contempt, the way I always looked at her.

I hated her.

I hated the things she made me do. I hated her abuse. I hated the way she reached inside me and ripped out my soul without ever even bothering to ask permission.

I was a happy kid before she arrived. I laughed a lot. I loved playing basketball in the backyard with Logan. I loved racing him to see who could get to the swing first.

I loved life.

But ever since Kim arrived, everything had changed.

"You need to take a shower and get dressed right now," she said, taking a long look at my body. I lowered my head, overcome by a sudden feeling of shame that I had been experiencing more and more frequently. I could still feel her hands on me. The agony, the rage, the inability to fight back and stop all the disgusting stuff.

I was too little, and she was too big.

"It isn't normal, what we do. Mommy will be mad," I whispered, rubbing my knees nervously. I still didn't really understand sex. Perhaps because I had never done it voluntarily. But I knew enough to realize our relationship was wrong. Still, I had to go along with her and keep my mouth shut.

"And whose fault is that? You're the one who's wrong, don't you see? You want a woman so much older than you," she accused, like she always did. Kim said that if I told anyone about what was happening, people would think that I was sick in the head. Naively, I believed her and had started avoiding people's eyes so I could hide my sickness and keep from getting locked up in some mental hospital.

"That's not true! It's disgusting when you touch me!" I screamed and Kim slapped me, enraged. Then her face softened, and she kneeled before me to touch my injured cheek. She always alternated moments

639

of kindness with those moments in which she became the worst sort of monster.

"I don't want to hurt you. Stop making me angry," she murmured so softly. She pushed a strand of hair away from my left eye and smiled at me.

"You always hurt me," I answered miserably.

"You enjoy it. Your body reacts when I touch you." Her hands brushed against my chest, and I leaped up, getting away from her as fast as I could. I looked down at her and shook my head. I felt weak and muddled. I looked around, memorizing every detail of the room. There was a weird smell in the air. The sheets were crumpled up. My clothes were scattered all over the floor.

My desk lamp was on and next to it sat my little red model car, my sketchbook, a pen holder, and a piggy bank shaped like a basketball. Then I looked at my babysitter in her usual uniform, her long blond hair, grayish eyes, a small mole dotting her right cheek…

I realized that everyone had a breaking point. My suffering was ready to explode. I wanted to scream out what I had been enduring now for months so everyone could hear, but I was too afraid of not being understood or, even worse, not being accepted.

The misery and trauma had grown so huge that I had started to dissociate while I was being abused. I abandoned my body and sought refuge deep in my mind because it was the only way I'd survive the experience.

"Someday, women are going to love you just like I love you," she continued as I rushed to a corner of the room, curling up with my knees drawn tightly to my chest. I didn't even know what love was supposed to be, but thanks to Kim, I understood that it felt awful.

My life was unavoidably changing now: I had begun to die at the exact moment Kim first "loved" me.

Returning to the present moment, I watched the woman who had just been sitting across from me leaving with a boy who had probably just finished a session with Dr. Keller. Meanwhile, Chloe was still shut up in my former psychiatrist's office. I realized I'd gotten lost in my internal reverie again, losing sight of the prey I'd identified. She had surely noticed my distraction.

I sighed and looked down at the glass table in front of me, littered with numerous magazines as well as a notebook and pencil.

That was weird.

I picked up the notebook and paged through it, seeing that every page was fresh and blank. I frowned and looked around to see if there was anyone who might have lost it, but there was no one except me and the bulldog at the reception desk. So I decided to pick up the pencil as well and do what I always did to relax: draw.

"I'm pleased with your progress." Dr. Lively's voice cut through the quiet of the waiting room, overpowering the ever-present classical Muzak that I tried not to listen to.

The doctor was walking toward me with his hand on Chloe's shoulder, and I quickly shut the notebook before tossing it back on the table. His eyes focused on me warily before shifting to the notebook. He gave me a small smile as he leaned over to pick it up.

What the fuck was he smiling about?

I considered his demeanor for a few moments and then I understood.

Dr. Lively had known me since I was a kid. He knew my likes and dislikes, and he knew that my drawings had always revealed my secrets. They were the medium I used to communicate. He had left that notebook in the waiting room on purpose, hoping that I wouldn't be able to resist drawing in it and giving him something of me to analyze.

"Chloe, could you wait here for a minute?" I stood up and touched my sister's cheek and she nodded, albeit looking somewhat confused. Then I shot a look at my former shrink, and without waiting for him to follow, walked swiftly into his office.

"What's the fucking meaning of this?" I blurted out as soon as I heard the office door close behind me. Dr. Lively stood there, the notebook open in his hands, and stared down at my drawing.

"I needed to get you into my office somehow. And I understand the human psyche, yours in particular," he said wryly as he headed for his desk.

"That's playing dirty," I said accusingly because I hated being fucked with like that.

"What is this?" He opened the notebook to the page with my sketch and then looked up at me. His eyes searched my face for answers, but I had none to give him.

"Look, I don't have time to waste on this. I was done with all that therapy shit, and I'm not about to start again now," I said baldly as Dr. Lively leaned on the desk in front of me, his arms folded.

"I have other problems to deal with," I added, thinking of Player 2511, though the doctor knew nothing about that issue.

"For example?" He furrowed his brow, giving me an inquisitive frown.

I wasn't sure whether or not I should tell him everything. After all, that whole thing had nothing to do with my mental issues or my prior trauma, even if I did feel the weight of it inside me, crushing me a little bit more each day.

"There's a psychopath after me," I confessed bluntly. "He sends these riddles to our house, and he's launched my family into this game where anyone who gets close to me is a target," I explained as the psychiatrist remained calm, focusing on my words. "I don't know why I'm telling you all this." I scrubbed a hand over my face and started pacing before him, suddenly anxious.

The smell of lilies emanating from the flowers on his desk was nauseating, and it took me back to a time when I had to go to this office three times a week.

"Who solves these riddles?"

His question made me halt in my tracks, and I turned to look at him.

What the fuck was he asking me that for? I frowned and took a deep breath before answering. "Me and my brother, and Selene helps."

Upon hearing that last name, Dr. Lively made a questioning face, so I preempted his curiosity. "Matt Anderson's daughter, but that's another story..." I waved a dismissive hand and he pushed himself off the desk and went around it to take a seat in his chair.

"Who solves them?" he asked again, opening his notebook in which he wrote down everything and grabbing a pen from the glass container on his right.

"My brother and I," I answered quickly, not mentioning Selene's name again so as not to draw his attention to her. "I solved the last one, and it was the most complex, I think." I looked cautiously at him, trying to figure out what he was thinking, but Dr. Lively was busy writing down everything I'd just said in his notebook. For a moment, it was like a flashback in a movie and I was seeing the same scene, only years before.

He sighed and adjusted his glasses on the bridge of his nose, darting a glance at me.

"When you were in high school, you claimed that there were men lurking outside in a pickup truck," he said, bringing up an admission I'd made as a teenager. I took a step back just as he calmly interlaced his fingers and rested his wrists on the wooden surface of the desk, still looking at me all the while.

"You said that those men were kidnapping children, locking them in their truck, and raping them." He sighed and lowered his gaze to the notebook still open in front of me. He reached out and dragged it under his own nose to get a better look at my drawing.

"But there was no pickup truck and no dangerous men," he concluded, fixing me with a skeptical stare.

"What are you trying to say?" I asked in an incredulous whisper. He couldn't possibly think I was lying. He couldn't possibly think that I . . .

"My brother's life was in danger, Dr. Lively. He nearly died!" I raised my voice and felt the uncontrollable tremors start in my muscles. I advanced on him in a blind rage. But he did not give up.

"Where were you when these riddles were delivered to your home?" He took his pen, turning it over in his fingers as he leaned back in his chair. I couldn't believe he would actually ask me that question. I looked at him in shock and waves of disappointment and anger hit me right in the chest.

"Stop it! Stop insinuating this bullshit!" I grabbed the glass pen holder and hurled it violently against the wall.

I needed to vent some of this feeling. I was no longer in control of my impulses and my reason, as usual, had fled, abandoning me to my demons.

My tachycardia intensified, and I began to sweat. My temples pulsed painfully, my clothes were suffocating, my hands shook. Anger was an involuntary energy that surged through my body and pushed inside my head, searching for an escape route.

"Neil, part of my job is outlining the challenges that may arise following the kind of trauma you experienced at a very delicate age." He resumed speaking like I hadn't just obliterated one of the decorative objects on his fancy desk. Then, he leaned toward me, resting his elbows on the wooden surface of said desk. "In your case, I diagnosed you with OCD at age eleven and IED at the age of fourteen," he said as though he were a medical robot designed to talk and talk and talk some more . . .

I recalled the day I had been diagnosed with intermittent explosive disorder, or IED. It happened after I had a violent episode at school. I'd punched a boy after a minor argument, and I'd completely lost control. During my adolescence, that kind of episode got more and more frequent as well as more extreme. Dr. Lively instructed me to partake in cognitive behavior therapy and to take various medications.

As time passed, I learned to recognize the warning signs of an episode: the tremor in my hands, the sudden-onset heart palpitations, the feeling of pressure inside my head. But although I was aware of these problems, I continued to deny them and eventually refused to go back to therapy.

"Where were you when you received these puzzles?" He looked up at me, and I pushed the memories away to refocus on our conversation.

"You've known me for years." I was so tired…my legs crumpled involuntarily, forcing me to take a seat in one of the chairs next to the desk. My brain felt like it had been overloaded with information, my psyche nothing more than a blocked and damaged electrical network capable of nothing but confusion.

"Yes, Neil, I've known you for years," he said, taking a deep breath before he turned back to my drawing and frowned reflectively.

I had drawn a pentagram.

A perfect pentagram, a symbol of magic and occultism.

Spirit: top point.

Air: upper left.

Water: upper right.

Earth: lower left.

Fire: lower right.

The circle that enclosed it all represented the gods, the divine embrace of everything that existed inside the pentagram. It also represented the continuity of those forces, flowing forever, never stopping, involving all energies. Benign, for some people. Evil for others.

Fortunately, Dr. Lively didn't ask me any questions about it.

"When you were a teenager, I diagnosed you with Dissociative

Identity Disorder." He closed the notebook and took off his glasses, setting them down on the book's dark cover.

"You told me about yourself, about the Boy, and about the conversations that took place between you…" He turned his gaze on me again and a sudden, powerful headache had me clutching my forehead as his words fluttered around aimlessly in my brain.

"As you well know, the primary characteristic of that disorder is the presence of two or more personalities which manifest not just explicitly but via a discontinuity with one's sense of self." I had heard this speech over and over again, but I had excised it from my brain in order to live the version of normal life that I created for myself.

Dr. Lively paused, his expression probing. Maybe he was trying to make sure that I was listening to him? Then, he went on, "People with this disorder—people like you—can feel depersonalized. They observe themselves as if from outside, doing atypical things and relating to their loved ones as if they were strangers or not real people at all. Sometimes, they may be convinced that their body is different, like that of a child or they may hear internal conversations between different states of personality. Sometimes, when a patient is not aware of this kind of condition or does not accept that they are affected by it, the voices of the other identities can address them or comment on their behavior."

A cold shiver ran down my spine because that was exactly what had been happening to me on a regular basis. And when it happened, it was so intense that it made me…afraid.

"The disorder can also involve insomnia, panic attacks, impulsive behavior, and psycho-sexual dysfunction." He looked at me and I clenched my hands into fists, trying to breathe.

"Delayed ejaculation, in your case, which is primarily situational. In one of our last sessions, you told me how that manifests in some of your sexual relationships, especially when you seek out women who remind you of Kim and therefore allow your mind to be convinced to relive your trauma. Is that still the case?" He interwove his fingers, looking sympathetically at me as he waited for my response.

Yes, goddamnit, yes, that was still the fucking case.

It was no coincidence that intercourse lasted so long for me and that my thrusts became increasingly energetic as I embarked on a violent, anxious race to orgasm. For most men, climax was all about losing control and letting go. For me, however, it meant going to war with myself because my mind had been conditioned to avoid fully enjoying a woman.

"What does all this have to do with the riddles?" I said, trying to cut to the chase because this conversation had become a Rubik's cube I couldn't solve.

"DID can also include dissociative amnesia. Subjects find themselves in places with no memory of how they got there, they find unfamiliar objects or…" he paused, which only increased my agitation. I was jiggling my leg, clenching my hand into a fist over and over like I could prevent my life from bouncing away from me like an unruly tennis ball. "They may find notes or other writing that they don't recognize as their own and cannot explain. They might do things and not remember…"

A chilling silence descended inside those four white walls and not because I was buying his theory but because I had begun to seriously wonder if he wasn't the one showing signs of a mental imbalance instead of me.

"I have never had amnesia. What the fuck are you talking about?" I said vehemently, leaping up as the chair I'd been sitting in suddenly felt like nothing so much as an expanse of sharpened blades.

Dr. Lively gave me an almost pitying look before getting gracefully to his feet and putting his hands in his pants pockets.

"The son of a bitch called me using an anonymized number. I heard his voice through a modifier. He threatened me and caused the accident that almost killed my brother. Do you have any idea the gravity of what you are suggesting right now?" My voice kept rising. It seemed inconceivable that this man who I once thought knew me better than anyone else in the world, this man who had watched my mind develop since childhood, could insinuate that I was that kind of psychopath.

"When you were a child, you used a burner phone to fake calls from Kim. You claimed that she was the one who called you and that you had spoken with her. But Kim was in a psychiatric facility at the time, isolated from the outside world and sedated practically into a vegetative state for her own protection. Yet you continued to insist that she was calling you, and when I found out you were lying, you explained yourself by telling me that it was the Boy. That he wanted to play and it was all his idea. Do you remember that, Neil?"

He came around to my side of the desk and I stepped back, disturbed by what he had just told me.

No, I didn't remember that at all.

Dr. Lively regarded me sadly, his shoulders slumped, lips folded into a bitter line.

Perhaps he was lying to me. Maybe he just wanted me to see him again so he was trying to convince me of the seriousness of my issues so I'd agree to restart therapy. He was a psychiatrist, after all, so he knew how my mind worked.

I stepped back further, increasing the distance between us until my back collided with the door handle.

"I am sorry, Neil. The human mind is a vast cosmos and the most fragile among us get lost inside it very easily," he said, giving me an anguished look as I opened the door and left his office with all speed.

I met Chloe in the waiting room and signaled that it was time to leave. She jumped up to walk alongside me, hurrying to keep up with my longer strides.

"What's going on?" she said softly, sounding both worried and out of breath. Instinctively, I put my arm around her shoulders so I wouldn't scare her. I gave her my most certain, most arrogant smile as I led her to the car.

"Nothing. Dr. Lively says I'm in tip-top shape," I said tonelessly, opening the car door for her. "Do you want to get some of the good ice cream before we go home?" I suggested, full of false joviality.

My mind was a complex, even confusing cosmos, but I was going to force myself to find my way through it. To prove to Dr. Lively that he was wrong.

40

SELENE

Halloween.

The long-awaited day had arrived. Children went from house to house, reciting the fateful incantation, "Trick or treat!" The pumpkins had carved faces—sometimes smiling, sometimes scary. The interiors were lit with candles or artificial lights.

I didn't want to go to Bill O'Brien's party, but Alyssa insisted that I had to come or else she wouldn't go either, so I gave in. The iconography of Halloween was all death, monsters, dark magic, the occult, and evil things, but I wasn't quite sure that the dress Alyssa had selected for me to wear was evoking any of those things. She, on the other hand, had settled on a look decidedly more suited to the occasion.

"You look great," I said, looking her over head to toe.

Alyssa and I were in my room as I appraised her simple yet sexy witch costume. The black polyester bodice hugged her breasts tightly and her tulle skirt, cut shorter in the front and longer in the back, was overlaid with a layer of satin-y fabric and another one of seductive lace. A pair of black fishnets and a pointy hat completed the whimsical look, while her bold makeup in shades of black and purple made her look more aggressive and sultry.

"You don't look half bad yourself," she said, examining my body, and a twinge of embarrassment made me wobble in my high heels. I didn't look scary at all, far from it.

I wore a golden Venetian mask made of lace over my eyes. It was mysterious and seductive and left the bottom half of my face clearly visible. Alyssa herself had applied my cherry-red lipstick, highlighting the shape of my mouth.

My hair fell in a long auburn sheet down my back; it had taken Alyssa more than two hours with a straightener to do it. My hair had gotten so long—I'd need to cut it sooner rather than later. I wore a stiff corset with straps. It was a tight fit, designed to shape the body into a womanly silhouette. It was black with gold embroidery, and it was embellished with little gems in the same colors. The skirt, which was rather short, was made of black satin and also featured sumptuous lace and gold embroidery, perfectly matching the top half of the costume.

I also wore a pair of high heels designed to streamline my figure and expose my legs, which were covered only by a pair of sheer black tights.

"But I'm not a witch or a monster or anything Halloween-y," I pointed out, examining my reflection in the mirror.

Alyssa came over to me, resting her hands on my shoulders and giving me the kind of sly smile that told me this costume had been selected precisely to avoid looking like any of those Halloween creatures.

"You're gorgeous, and you know your *lover* is also going to be at this party. It'll be good for him to see what he's missing out on while he's being a dick and ignoring you," she answered, pulling on her black coat to protect against the cold

Since she already knew all about me and Neil, I'd told her about that night in the pool and about the complete indifference Neil had shown me afterward. I had omitted a few details, though, like him drawing the shell and pearl on my hip.

It had been such a strange feeling, knowing that he was engaging with me without any physical or emotional barriers. It was made all the more unique because I knew that he didn't feel those same things with the blonds in the pool house.

After hours hidden away in my room, we finished getting ready and went downstairs where we found Logan on the sofa waiting for us. He had been watching something on TV but his eyes immediately snapped to his girlfriend, roving over her with desire, and perhaps a little hint of jealousy.

"I'm begging you: steer clear of horny assholes." He pulled a worried face, and Alyssa bent down to press a chaste, reassuring kiss on his lips. Then, Logan looked at me and his eyebrows flew up in surprise.

"Wow, Selene, you're…" he hesitated. "I mean…you don't even look like yourself," he finished, sounding astonished. I went red and managed a shy "thanks," which earned me a satisfied look from Alyssa, the architect of everything.

"We're heading out, don't wait up." Alyssa went to the front door, and I followed her with my coat thrown over one arm. We were taking her car to the spooky house party. We met our friends outside the enormous gate in front of the stately residence, which from the outside looked like one of those abandoned estates where someone would go ghost hunting in a movie. A row of illuminated pumpkins along the walkway leading to the door completed the scene.

I wasn't exactly calm. I had a strange feeling inside, something that kept me from relaxing the way I would have liked—something that kept me on my toes. Though I had no idea why I should be. It was just a Halloween house party, nothing to fear, even if the house itself was a little macabre and eerie-feeling.

I looked out over the sea of people around me. The party had been highly anticipated in the last week, and there had been a lot of publicity surrounding it. That was how it always worked: the rich basketball star rented a mansion big enough to hold an enormous crowd and then invited his buddies, who invited their buddies, who invited other buddies, and so on and so forth. It kept spreading through DMs, posts on Instagram, and group chats until it was the most talked-about event on campus.

"What's your costume, Selene? You shine like a star, doll." Cory turned his attention to me as we walked into the party, focusing particularly on my exposed legs beneath my excessively short skirt. I felt uncomfortable, and I could already feel the looks from everyone in their masks.

"I don't actually know, either." I shrugged and cracked a small smile, examining my friends' costumes instead. Julie had come as a vampire, wearing an ankle-length dress in black and red. Jake was a pirate, exposing some of the tattoos on his arms, while Adam was wearing a sophisticated velvet cloak and a white *V for Vendetta* mask. Cory, on the other hand…well, Cory was…

"Are you a magnet?" I cocked my head to get a better look at his outfit: a black pair of pants and a shirt with an enormous red and silver horseshoe-shaped…thing around his neck. Yeah, it had to be a magnet.

"You got it. Though tonight I'm hoping to be more of a pussy magnet." Only the guys laughed at his joke, while Alyssa, Julie, and I exchanged looks. It seemed our male friends had only one thing on their minds tonight: sex, sex, and more sex.

"Oh God, don't start with that. Let's go!" Julie grumbled, leading us toward the entrance. I walked down the paved pathway, trying not to trip while Alyssa held on to me because her heels were even more dizzyingly high than my own.

Once we got inside the luxurious manor, we found it all decked out for Halloween. I was a little bit in awe. The walls were illuminated by the suggestive play of light, turning them a fiery red. It gave life to the frescos on the high ceiling. They were so high that I had to bend my neck back to admire them. In the background, the DJ's mixer hummed softly.

We were greeted at the door by a girl in what appeared to be a sexy bunny costume and she took our coats and personal items.

"Damn, there's so many people here." Cory strolled delightedly into the crowd while Julie took Adam's hand and Jake glanced around, evaluating his prospects for the evening.

Alyssa took me by the hand and led me along with her to check out the cavernous main room where a tall staircase led to the upper floors.

"Wow, this place is incredible," she whispered into my ear over the music that echoed off the imposing walls. We stopped at a table laden with food and took note of the meticulous attention that had been paid to every last detail. Everything was appropriately monstrous: Halloween-themed deviled eggs, little toasts cut into the shape of tombstones, breadstick witch's brooms, tartlets shaped like skulls, puff-pastry mummies, fried pumpkin pieces. There were even a number of fake spiders and other bugs hidden among the desserts and frozen in the ices cubes for drinks.

Over in the bar area, cocktail glasses were filled with liquids that varied in color from fiery red to blue and black. It made the idea of drinking them considerably less appealing.

"Blech," I said in answer to Alyssa's suggestion that I try one. She pinched a glass between her fingers and threw it back all in one gulp, leaving just an ice cube at the bottom with a…cockroach encased in it.

"Yum." She licked her lips and I shook my head, amused. She was definitely braver than I was. Shortly thereafter, Adam, Julie, and the rest of the group joined us, and everyone managed to drink the stuff, except for me who was imagining those fake spiders crawling along my bare arms.

"Welcome to the big Halloween bash!" The DJ, situated on a mezzanine festooned with cobwebs and stick-on bloody footprints, called out, drawing our attention. He was dressed as a skeleton, holding the microphone in one hand while he used the other to rapidly adjust the mixer. Guests started approaching him, whooping and complimenting his choice of music, which was doing a lot to create an all-around creepy atmosphere that was genuinely unsettling. After a few more ominous notes floated out into the large space, everyone began to dance—it was a creepy mix of monsters, ghosts, assorted scary creatures, animals from some shadowy forest, alarmingly realistic vinyl masks, and costumes straight out of the worst horror movies of the last century.

"Come on! Let's get dancing!" Cory leaped into the fray, followed by Jake and Adam, who wasn't willing to leave Julie alone for even a second. Suddenly, Alyssa started elbowing me hard in the side until I spotted a small group dressed as ghouls in blood-soaked hospital gowns. They looked like they'd come out of some haunted insane asylum. Looking at them, I realized just how out of place my costume was for this kind of party, and I shuffled awkwardly.

"Stop freaking out. You look great, and he's going to notice that any time now." Alyssa's voice made me cast out a glance for the "him" in question. I spotted him right away, clear among the crush of indistinct bodies.

The Krew took up space, as usual, with their beauty and their presence. None of them wore a costume that was like anyone else's. Xavier and Luke were stationed on either side of Neil, each wearing tracksuits and white plastic masks. The masks were lit up with LEDs, red for Xavier, yellow for Luke.

It was a frightening look, and not because they were pretending to be some monstrous creatures, but because they themselves were entirely capable of being monstrous and not just on Halloween.

Next to Xavier, Jennifer was dressed as Harley Quinn in *Suicide Squad*. Her blond hair was in two pigtails: one dip-dyed blue and the other pink. Her lean body was on display in a short T-shirt with "Daddy's Lil' Monster" written on it, red and blue shorts, and fishnets. She wore a matching leather jacket, high-tops, and studded bracelets and held an actual baseball bat in one hand. I was horrified at the idea that she might just swing that at anyone who came close to the object of her obsession.

Alexia had gone with an intense evil clown theme. She wore a black and blue polka-dotted skirt and a corset in the same colors, thigh-highs and multicolored high heels. Her face was covered in greasepaint, and her eyes had been emphasized with a bold, dark smokey look. Blue lines of face paint ran up her cheeks on either side of her mouth, and she'd stuck sparkling rhinestones to the outside of her eyes, like tears.

She was beautiful and frightening in just the right way, just like the other members of the Krew. But the person who stood out most in that room full of people attempting to terrify was Neil. He wasn't wearing anything weird or overdone, just a nice black suit that was fitted to his athletic body. His chestnut hair was neatly arranged for once, and he wore a black mask with intricate silver designs over half his face. The left half, specifically, and a little bit of the right eyebrow, leaving everything else on display, including his mouth.

It was the mask from *The Phantom of the Opera*—an appropriately seductive and enigmatic vibe.

The group cleared a path in front of themselves as they moved through the crowd because everyone knew who they were and that it would be better to get out of their way. Neil crossed the room with determined strides, his bearing particularly masculine, and people (mostly girls) admired him. Like he was some dark angel or an enchanting demon that had come to drag them off into a secret spot somewhere in this immense mansion.

"Okay, so, yes: he is very sexy. I get it, my friend. It can't be easy to resist that." Alyssa's comment was not at all helpful. A strange, intense burning sensation had spread from my chest to my cheeks. I was sure that, despite the mask, my blush would be visible to anyone looking. I suddenly felt unsettled, hardly able to even stand on my own two feet.

Neil hadn't seen me yet, but I knew that the moment he did, I was going to die right there on the spot.

I silently prayed to whatever God was listening that Mr. Disaster wouldn't come any closer than the bar. Because, just a few feet beyond that, was us. Or, rather, me, bemusedly ogling his chiseled musculature in that tight black suit. His sculpted body and more than six feet of masculine energy had not gone unnoticed at all, and I bristled at the knowledge that Jennifer or some other little monster would soon be offering him their pumpkin on a silver platter.

"You've gotta be seen, come on!" Alyssa grabbed me by the wrist, and I dug my heels in like a recalcitrant dog, willing myself not to give in to her.

Damn it! I didn't want Neil to see me. I was feeling good there in my anonymous corner where no one would bother me.

"Don't be a baby! Get a move on!" She grabbed me with her other hand and my heels skidded a little on the floor, but I continued to resist her.

"I said no!" I snapped irritably.

"Selene, if I didn't want him to look at you, you'd be dressed as a zombie bride right now. But I did want him to look at you and die mad over your incredible legs," she continued, pulling me to her with more and more force until I finally gave in.

I surrendered and followed her into the crowd of dancers. I felt suffocated by all the bodies accidentally rubbing against mine.

Someone even touched my hair, but I couldn't tell who it was because there were so many people all around that it made me dizzy.

I stuck as close as possible to Alyssa, hoping to keep any of the guys around us from groping my ass. I looked around trying to find Neil but there was no sign of him. Suddenly, I felt Alyssa's hands tighten on my hips. I looked at her and found her rubbing herself against me.

"What are you doing?" I tried to wriggle away from her, but she got up close to my ear and explained her plan.

"Try to look like you're really into it. Men love this stuff." She stroked the back of my neck while I continued staring at her through my mask. Then, I uncertainly attempted to mimic her movements.

"You have to move your hips seductively," she explained, and I tried to give them a kind of natural sway, hoping to look fluid and confident. I could feel the ends of my hair hitting my low back and the bottom of my skirt rising slightly as my corset strained against me. It was so tight it had actually slimmed my waist until Alyssa could encircle it with one arm.

We put on a sexy show together, our bodies chasing one another as if we were lovers.

"Good job, keep going," she whispered, close to my lips and I grinned conspiratorially back. Evidently there was a lot that I could learn from my friend. Alyssa was more experienced than me. She'd dated a few guys before Logan, and she definitely knew some tricks to make them fall at her feet. Neil, though, wasn't like other guys and—

"He's a man, Selene. Just a man, and he's got the same weak points as any other man," she said, like she was reading my mind as she continued to grind against me even more audaciously. I raised my arms over my head and bent my elbows, moving my hips with more force. This wasn't so difficult after all—all you had to do was let yourself be transported by the music, by the joyful laughter of your friend and then the whole world took on a different flavor.

Dancing was like a puzzle: a series of tiny movements that joined together to create something beautiful.

Alyssa gave me a sly grin as she backed slowly away from me, stretching out her arms to put distance between us. I frowned, not understanding why she was retreating but then, just as her smile widened victoriously, two hands grasped my hips possessively, halting my movements.

Oh shit.

"Let me see you work that little ass…" The hoarse baritone of my personal disaster filtered into my ear like a whispered melody, somehow drowning out the music and the yelling of the people around us. I held still, rigid and more embarrassed than ever. Now that the shark had actually taken the bait, I found myself no longer capable of the sexy swaying I'd been doing before. I quivered when his chest pressed against my back and something poked into me.

I held my breath. Yep, that was a mighty erection shamelessly on display for me.

He moved his fingers upward, tracing the embroidery on my corset before sinking back down to my hips and using them to pull me into him with more force.

"Have you forgotten how to move, Tinkerbell?" he asked in a sultry whisper, and I could feel his hot breath hit my neck, followed almost immediately by his lips.

Barely twenty-four hours had passed since we'd last touched each other, but to me it felt like an eternity. I shut my eyes and let my head fall back against his chest as his tongue drew a wet trail up to the shell of my ear where a golden gem winked, matching my outfit. He nibbled on my earlobe and unexpected flood of warmth spread out of me, soaking the regular cotton panties I'd worn even under this sexy costume. I was still me, after all.

"What are you supposed to be? A princess or a fairy?" he spoke again, his low, deep voice leaving me stunned.

"It's a pleasure to meet you, Erik." I was astonished at my ability to speak, let alone remember the Phantom of the Opera's name while his big hands roved over my hips, holding me even closer to him.

In that moment, I felt exactly like Christine, the young woman in the novel who'd been Erik's obsession. Here he was, right in front of me, my own captivating phantom.

"The pleasure is mine, little fairy," he answered in tones of velvet, having apparently decided that I was not a princess. Then, he leaned in close to my ear. "I'm on to your little game, you know," he said, sounding faintly amused. He was surely referring to Alyssa's scheme to make me irresistible to him.

I swallowed hard and moved closer to him, crushing my breasts against his chest.

"And did you like it? Our little game?" I put my hands on his hips before sliding them around to the base of his spine. His black shirt was so tight that I feel the ridges of his muscles under my fingertips. My eyes were drawn to his unbuttoned collar suddenly. I found myself staring at his throat where, I pressed a sweet kiss. Neil squeezed my hips reflexively and parted those full lips that I longed to taste.

"Oops," I whispered facetiously, as though I had overstepped. Something lit up within his golden eyes, something that made him lean down over me until he could touch my nose with the tip of his own. His clean scent was even more powerful than usual, which only increased my longing to get him undressed and take him entirely.

Take everything he had: body, mind, and soul.

"You're playing with fire, Babygirl," he said in a seductive warning just before his lips crashed into mine. He grabbed my glutes with his hands, groping them possessively, and in the same moment, he plunged his tongue into my mouth. The kiss was urgent, passionate, and dominating and I returned it eagerly.

My hands crept around to his front, worshipping his tensed abdominals. A tiny moan slipped out of my lips as he devoured me like it was all he could do to keep himself from fucking me right there on the dance floor. He cradled my face in his hands and continued moving his tongue hungrily inside my mouth. He confounded my thoughts, my desires, my fears, everything.

His body, stiff with arousal, began to grind against me in a firm, unmistakably male sort of way, and in that moment he became the center of my world.

"Come with me," he whispered impatiently. He grabbed my hand before I could really understand what was happening and led me through the crowd of people.

I followed him without argument.

He could have been leading me straight to hell and I would have cheerfully gone with him.

I squeezed his arm when someone shoved me and Neil turned to shoot a warning look at a skeleton who apologized immediately with his hands raised defensively.

"You okay?" he asked, eyeing the other guy in irritation as he walked away and I nodded. The last thing I wanted was to incite a fight or watch Neil struggle to control his anger.

Fortunately, he just started walking again, and I sighed as I followed him up the stairs to the second floor. I didn't know exactly where we were going. All I could see were his broad, powerful shoulders, a sight that made me feel protected. Safe.

I was not so naive, though, that I didn't realize that Neil wanted me and we could really only have one destination: some free bedroom.

My conscience prickled me then. *What am I doing?*

After our night at the pool, Neil had ignored me completely. He'd gone so far as to pretend I didn't exist. He made me feel used and tossed aside.

I needed to resign myself to the truth: Neil liked my body, but he didn't like *me*. He didn't feel the way I felt. Because I liked him even with all his problems, and that was why I had to go back to Detroit. I would have stayed if he'd asked me to. If he'd wanted to try to really get to know each other and build something together. That was the only way I could have stayed.

"You want to use me again," I said to him, using his term for what we shared.

Neil stopped, fingers still interlaced with mine, and turned to face me.

I thought once again about how beautiful he was. The mystery and the darkness of him worked to create a man of uncommon, inexplicable allure.

"I just want you to understand," he answered ambiguously. An almost imperceptible look of sadness moved over his face, half-concealed behind his mask. He opened a door and waved me inside. I looked from his long fingers to the open door, uncertain whether I should cross the threshold.

After a moment's hesitation, my legs seemed to move under their own power, taking me into the room. I looked around, admiring the decor. This ceiling was also quite high and decorated with a fresco that my eyes lingered on.

It looked like a bedroom fit for a queen. Velvety ivory hangings around the canopy bed and two armchairs positioned in front of the enormous window gave the room an intimate yet welcoming vibe. Mini pumpkins with lit candles inside were here as well on the bedside tables and the antique desk with a few more scattered around the room.

There was no need to look for a light switch; the room was softly yet amply lit. Our shadows moved across the walls, the same ones that reflected the candle flames.

"Finally. I've been waiting for you."

I flinched when I heard a female voice, then I turned and found Harley Quinn before me, leaning against another door that probably let to the attached bathroom.

"Aw, did you think you were gonna be alone with him, princess?" Jennifer sneered, walking toward me. I looked at Neil, who had yet to utter a single word. He stood a short distance away from us with his usual arrogant posture—his body rigid and imposing, his expression serious and austere.

"What's going on?" I managed in a low whisper, so shaken that not only did I not know what to say, I didn't even know what to think. Neil didn't answer me, except to grab his leather belt and open the metal buckle before sliding it out of his belt loops.

Jennifer looked at him and bit her lower lip. To me, however, his movements seemed cold, distant, domineering. The actions of a man who was going to do what he was going to do, no matter who objected.

"You thought he was going to fuck you, didn't you?" Jennifer brushed past me, wafting her irritatingly sweet scent my way and closed in on Neil, taking the belt from his hand. She set it down on a nearby piece of furniture and then turned her attention back to his body.

She was devouring him with her eyes, and soon she was going to do it with her viper's mouth and her siren's hands.

"It's a game," Neil said in a faraway tone and the blond girl grinned enthusiastically. She turned to me and swayed her hips on her way to the bed.

"The game is simple: whoever can seduce him gets to have him. Alexia and I are the ones who usually play. I don't understand why he's chosen you," Jennifer explained, sitting down on the bed and patting the space next to her with one palm. I kept staring at her like I was watching a scene from a horror film.

Why had Neil set up a...a trap for me?

"Join me, princess, if you have the guts to play." Jennifer needled me with the wicked grin that I'd done nothing but hate for too long.

"He's not an object. He's not a trophy up for grabs for anyone who plays a stupid, pointless game," I snapped, turning to Neil because he was the one I really wanted to talk to. Though I was shaking all over, I went to him immediately and stared into those eyes. Eyes that, at the moment, communicated exactly nothing.

"Why are you acting like this?" I asked. It felt like I was trapped in a nightmare. He couldn't be treating me like that, like something else to play with along with Jennifer.

"If you don't play, that means you forfeit and he'll spend the night with me." Jennifer's voice behind me struck like a whip. The idea that someone else would get to touch him, take pleasure from him, kiss him, and use him as though he were a sex doll made me feel unbearably sick to my stomach.

Normally, I would never participate in a game like that, and as I looked at Neil, I realized that he knew that. After all, he knew me. I could practically see in his eyes that he was sure I'd refuse. It almost seemed like that's what he wanted me to do. But if that was so, I couldn't figure out why he'd engineered this whole insane situation to begin with.

"I'll play," I declared, continuing to stare at Neil, and I didn't miss the flicker of surprise in his eyes, which now looked unsettled.

What was Neil's real purpose here? That I watch him with someone else? That I understand I meant nothing to him? That I get another reason to leave and go back to Detroit?

I stared at him, full of disdain and anger, and then I headed for the bed where the Queen Bitch waited for me with a sly smile on her face. She was the person I hated most in the world at that moment and the one upon whom I was about to take my revenge.

"May the best woman win," she offered, a mocking challenge as she lay back on her elbows and made herself comfortable.

I waited patiently to find out how this stupid game was played, sitting on the edge of the bed with my legs pressed together. I tugged down my skirt. The positions Jennifer and I had adopted illustrated the vast gulf between us: I sat there, nearly motionless and trembling like a helpless baby chick while she half-reclined and waited with feverish impatience to spread her legs, like a cat in heat.

My thoughts were interrupted by Neil, who approached us at a slow, measured pace. His gleaming eyes met mine as I lifted my chin, silently begging him to either send Jennifer away or leave with me because whatever was about to happen was only going to hurt me.

But he pretended not to recognize my wordless request and instead grabbed me by the back of the neck, leaning down over me. There was something deeply unsettling in his kiss, and it occurred to me just how hard it would be to really escape his allure.

As if to illustrate that thought, my lips parted in spite of me and chased the aggressive movements of his tongue. Then, Neil forced me down with his powerful body. He crawled over me, slow and elegant, never breaking our kiss, which became increasingly greedy.

I squeezed his hips between my knees and he arched his back, making me feel every inch of his massive hard-on against my groin.

I allowed my fingers to roam over the smooth fabric of his shirt and I felt his breathing deepen when I drifted down to his glutes. But just as I had managed to forget about Jennifer's presence right next to us, Neil's lips pulled away from mine. Jennifer had grabbed his arm and she lunged for him, drawing his attention away from me and onto her.

Neil kissed her exactly the way he had just kissed me moments before. He migrated slowly into the center of the bed, positioning himself between us. He propped himself up on his knees and forearms, never lying down next to anyone because he wanted to remain distant. Impersonal, dominant, the one who decided how the evening would end.

Though I was aroused, the sight of him and Jennifer kissing passionately made my stomach clench so hard that I felt nauseous from the jealousy that was slowly poisoning my body, like the venom from a snake.

Suddenly, I no longer knew what I was doing. Instinct told me to get up and get away from that room, but reason along with my desire to strike back at Jennifer in some way told me to stay right there. I wanted to show Neil that I was the one he wanted, the one he made love to without a barrier, the one he'd lost himself inside.

Jennifer began to moan loudly, likely in an attempt to further excite Neil. She reached between his legs with one hand and used the other to bare her breasts.

He took note of the bold gesture and kissed down her neck, across her collarbone and then, finally, to her nipple. He pressed it between his lips and sucked, coaxing more moans from her. Meanwhile, I just watched it all as though I'd lost the ability to move.

I should have played the game, tried to lure him over to me, used him like an object and got one over on that blond bitch. But whatever there was between me and Neil, it wasn't a game. He wasn't a thing, and what's more: I suddenly realized that I didn't care about "winning" against anyone.

My conscience poked its head out, seconding my instinct's proposal that we make a quick escape. I raised my torso up but Neil didn't pay me any mind because he had decided from the beginning that he was going to go with her. Even if I'd done everything I could to seduce him.

If there was one thing I was sure of, it was that my walking disaster wasn't going to let a woman choose. He was the one who chose, always. And in this case, he had deliberately chosen Jennifer so that I could bear witness to another one of his obscene performances.

When Jennifer opened his fly and unzipped him, rubbing him through his black boxers, I immediately got up from the bed. I needed to leave before he got inside her, before she started scream-ing, and before I got sick for real. The two of them must surely have heard my high heels clattering across the room, but he didn't stop me. He didn't even give it a token try. So I went out the door and slammed it shut behind me.

I hated him. I hated him with my whole being.

I ran down the hallway, allowing tears of rage to stream from my eyes. I wasn't crying for him but for what I had let him do to me. I would never be able to join his world, to share him with other people, to accept the inexplicable perversions that drove him.

I could no longer tolerate the power he had over me, the vulner-ability he exposed in me. I could no longer tolerate the jealousy I felt toward womankind in general because of the fear that anyone could at any time take him away from me. Because he wasn't mine; he didn't belong to me. He didn't *want* to belong to me.

"Selene."

I halted, bumping into a firm body that was suddenly in my way. I looked up into the blue eyes of an unmasked Luke. His finely drawn features were creased in a perplexed expression. A black track suit covered his slim, athletic body. It was nice but less impressive than Neil's. And then I cursed myself because, once again, I was comparing someone else to him.

It was the same story every single time: I couldn't think of anyone the way I thought of him; I didn't believe there was anyone out there capable of measuring up.

"What happened?" he asked with a serious expression as he grasped my bare arms.

"Does this have to do with Neil?" he asked incisively. "Come on, let's get some air," he suggested. After retrieving my coat to protect myself from the brisk night air, I followed him out the exit. I still wasn't sure how much I trusted him, considering that he was part of the Krew, and if he hung out with those people he was likely similar to them in some ways. His vibe, however, felt anything but dangerous.

We sat down outside on a wooden bench, also decorated with fake cobwebs, while nearby a group of people talked and smoked. The fact that we weren't in a particularly isolated or secluded place calmed me down a bit.

"Do you want to tell me about it?" Luke brought a cigarette to his lips and felt around in the pocket of his jacket for the lighter. I took the opportunity to really evaluate him and realized that he wasn't a bad looking guy at all. I'd even go so far as to say he was hot, just like that sleaze bag Xavier, with the main difference being that the latter was, in fact, a sleaze bag...

Luke had a masculine yet angelic-looking face. His blue eyes shone bright even in the dark, gloomy night. His blond hair was all ruffled and fell over his forehead. His nose was straight and proportionate and he had the lean body of a male model.

"Your friend is depraved with no empathy or respect for other people," I snapped automatically, and he burst into laughter.

Well, I was glad to see someone was having fun, at least.

"What did he do this time?" He exhaled smoke into the air. I still wasn't sure if I was confiding in the right person, but at least I knew his friend's dirty deeds would come as no surprise to him.

"He took me into a bedroom where he knew Jennifer was waiting." I wrapped my coat around myself more tightly and squeezed my thighs together against the cold. I saw Luke's eyes flicker briefly down to my legs before returning to my face.

"And he suggested a sex game, right?" he asked, smiling. He might have found the situation amusing, but I was just disgusted and disappointed.

"He wanted Jennifer and me to play. Whoever was better at seducing him got to..."

"Fuck him," he finished for me, taking another drag from his cigarette. I looked at him again, and the longer I analyzed him, the less I saw him as a friend of Neil's or a member of the Krew and the more I saw just another nice, normal dude.

"I think he probably wanted to show you how different you are from the rest of them," he explained.

"Luke, he kissed me and a few days ago we…" I paused because I wasn't entirely comfortable telling him that kind of thing about myself. I bit my lip and fell silent, hoping he'd figure it out on his own.

"He definitely likes you, that's for sure. But I think he sees you more as someone to be protected than someone who could actually be a part of his life." He took one last drag and put out his cigarette, looking back at me. My brow furrowed as I tried to follow his reasoning, and it occurred to me that he might be on to something.

Neil did like me, but he also thought I was a girl—too naive and inexperienced to be with him. I sighed, and as I watched the cloud of frozen breath slip from my lips, I thought about what Neil was doing at that moment up in that room. I wondered if he was done already or if he was just starting. Did he enjoy it the way he'd enjoyed it with me? Was that bitch Jennifer happy that she'd finally got what she wanted?

"You need to stop thinking that someone like him might change. People like us, we don't change," he declared firmly, looking first at my eyes and then down to my lips. I felt a jolt of electricity at his powerful, plain, and, above all, truthful words.

Luke was probably waiting for me to argue his claim, but instead I just dipped my head and accepted that uncomfortable truth within myself.

"But you, Selene…"

He tilted up my chin with his index finger, and his voice turned gentle and understanding. "You're so beautiful and so smart. Do you realize how much better you can do than him?"

I appreciated the attempt to make me feel better, but I needed to close this Neil chapter of my life. The chapter about the screwed-up boy who, with just the sound of his voice, could reach places inside me that I hadn't even realized existed.

Nevertheless, I smiled at Luke and he got to his feet, rubbing the back of his head and looking around anxiously. I didn't understand the sudden change in his demeanor, but I didn't question him.

"You don't seem to be like them," I pointed out, looking up at him. Luke eyes locked on mine and he frowned.

"You mean like the Krew?" he asked.

"Exactly." I nodded and wrapped my coat more tightly around myself again. Luke smiled when he noticed. I was shivering from the cold.

"And what makes you think that?" he continued, apparently intrigued by this avenue of discussion.

"I don't know; it's just a feeling." A feeling that fluctuated because, sometimes, Luke took on a persona that made me think differently of him, while at other times he seemed harmless, nice to talk with.

"Wrong feeling," he answered, a teasing look on his face. He continued to stand a little bit away from me. He seemed uneasy. He kept glancing around like he wanted to make sure no one saw him there with me.

Was he ashamed to be seen with me?

"Afraid Xavier's going to laugh at your for hanging out with me?"

"Do I look stupid to you? I don't give a shit what Xavier says." He ran a hand through his blond hair and propped his foot up on the bench, a short distance away from me. "But I don't want any problems with Neil…"

I nearly laughed in his face.

Was he serious?

"I think he's a little busy with something else at the moment.

Believe me, Neil doesn't care about me." A hysterical bubble of laughter rose up from the back of my throat. There was no need to worry about Neil. He couldn't care less if someone approached me, even—

"Remember how, after you kissed me in the pool house, he threw you out?" Luke said, crossing his arms over his chest. He'd adopted a brazen posture that contrasted with his oh-so-angelic face. I hoped I didn't blush at the mention of our kiss, that childish, almost involuntary gesture I'd made.

"So? Do you think he'll get mad at you if he sees us here just talking?" It was insane to think about. I would have slapped Mr. Disaster myself if he pulled something like that after what had just happened with Jennifer. He had absolutely no right.

Luke shook his head and smiled like the answer was obvious to him.

"He's shared every other girl with us, except for you," he pointed out, scrutinizing me like he might figure out why.

"He just tried to share me with Jennifer tonight." Nausea clenched my stomach at the very idea. The more I thought about it, the more I wanted a long detox from Neil and the feelings he generated in me.

"He wanted you to share him with Jennifer, which is very different." He looked me up and down, pausing on my legs. I cleared my throat and looked over his shoulder at small group passing by. The girls called out flirtatious greetings to Luke while the boys avoided his eyes, intimidated. I realized then that he produced that same sense of awe I felt from people when I was in a public place with Neil. It seemed that everyone knew who Luke was and they feared him.

"Apparently you're just as infamous as your friends," I said, nodding at the passing group. Luke smiled mysteriously and looked back at my face.

"I never said I was any different," he answered, shrugging.

I got up from the bench, wandering around a little and trying to ignore the cold air against my skin. I felt horribly vulnerable, a broken heart close to another boy who could probably cause me to make similar mistakes.

But what I really wanted was to prove that I wasn't like Neil, that I couldn't just use other people for personal gain.

"I don't want to have beef with Neil, but..." Luke spoke again, and I turned my full attention on him. He took a few steps toward me, towering over me, and looked down into my face like he was tracing every line. "I was clear with him that, if you ever wanted anything from me, I wouldn't hold off," he finished with a provocative smile.

Did he really mean that?

I blushed violently, and I was sure that this time my cheeks were actually blazing. I wasn't completely unmoved by someone like Luke, and perhaps if I had been a different sort of person, I could have just taken the opportunity that had been presented to me. I'd liked our kiss. It wasn't as devastating as Neil's, but it wasn't bad either, far from it.

"I'm not... I'm not that kind of person. I couldn't—"

"I understand the kind of person you are; you don't have to explain yourself. I think the person who doesn't understand is Neil." He looked deeply into my eyes for a moment before continuing. "Now, I think I really should go back into the house. Are you here with anyone?" he asked considerately and I nodded.

I needed to find Alyssa and get out of there right away.

After telling Luke goodbye, I hunted Alyssa down, determined to get back home. I told her everything, sparing no details, and she didn't hesitate to call Neil an asshole, a pervert, and a dickhead. I was glad she could because, unfortunately, there seemed to be something inside me that prevented me from hating him the way I would have liked.

I got back home at two in the morning and thanked Alyssa for the ride. I tried not to make any noise as I entered the house, even taking my shoes off outside so I didn't wake anyone. But when I walked into the living room, I found Logan still on the sofa, with a thousand-yard stare pointed at a package that sat in front of the lit fireplace.

"Logan..." I murmured in concern, dropping my shoes near the front door and running barefoot to him. I didn't even need to hear him speak to understand how upset he was.

"I found it out the porch, in front of the door..."

A delivery from Player 2511.

The fourth riddle.

41

SELENE

I watched as Logan stared, petrified, at the letter in his hand.

Another puzzle. Another warning. Another nightmare.

That evening had already turned into a complete catastrophe— the only thing missing was this anonymous lunatic. My hands wouldn't stop trembling; my fingers gripped and regripped the mask I'd taken off, but they could do nothing to grasp on to this disorienting new reality. I mentally reviewed the contents of the riddle that I'd just read with Logan:

> WHITE HORSE
> TWO
> THREE
> "INSANITY" IS REPEATING THE SAME THING OVER AND OVER AGAIN AND EXPECTING A DIFFERENT SOLUTION.
> FIND THE SOLUTION.
>
> PLAYER 2511

Suddenly the door swung open, and Neil, maskless, walked slowly inside. As he tossed his keys onto the usual spot on the entryway shelf, the familiar feeling of dread in the pit of my stomach came back stronger than before, as if to mock me.

I took a closer look at him: he was still wearing his stylish suit from before, but his hair was messed up, his shirt was wrinkled, and he wasn't wearing a belt. Presumably, he'd left it in that room at the mansion. He looked entirely like someone who had spent the night with Jennifer, doing what they usually did.

For a second, Neil stared blankly at us as though he hadn't expected to find us sitting there on the couch in the middle of the night. Then he walked forward and spotted the note his brother was still clutching between his fingers and he understood.

He stopped a little ways away from me, and my traitorous heart sped up. Tension rose between us, and when I smelled her scent on him, I shuddered like I'd been hit with a blast of cold air.

"Him again?" He snatched the note from Logan's hand and read it. It wasn't going to be easy to decipher. Like the others, it would probably take some research and more complex reasoning. Neil seemed to feel differently, however.

As soon as he finished reading the note, he folded it back up and stuck it into his pocket. The muscles in his arms made short little movements as he did so. Logan furrowed his brow and I kept silent.

"I have a terrible headache right now. Let's meet tomorrow morning in the library and figure it out," he said. Logan glanced at me as though I might have some explanation for Neil's behavior. But I didn't understand him and probably never would.

"Are you... Are you feeling okay?" Logan asked hesitantly, clearly trying to understand.

"I just need a long shower..." Neil said, like we hadn't just been issued a puzzle by a dangerous maniac. Like nothing had happened at all.

He turned, dragging a hand through his hair and slowly climbed the stairs, looking exhausted and disillusioned. Surrendered to a fate that had been his prison for who knew how long.

....

I didn't get a wink of sleep that night. Thoughts invaded my brain and wouldn't give me a moment's peace.

Fresh morning air caressed my face as the new day found me out on the balcony with my elbows resting on the railing and the facial expression of someone who had been defeated. Defeated by Neil and the evil that surrounded him.

Soon, I would have to go to the library to figure out what the damn puzzle meant, and the thought of seeing Mr. Disaster, of spending time with him, stirred nothing but anxiety and anguish inside of me. I knew it from my stomach that throbbed, my tongue that felt thick and heavy, and the emptiness inside me. Still, a part of me didn't want to leave New York.

My flight was only twenty-four hours away, but so many things had happened that I still could have changed my mind. Could I really just walk away and leave Neil alone to fight both himself and some psychopath bent on revenge?

Sighing, I made my way to the library. I immediately spotted Logan sitting in one of the sleek armchairs. Neil arrived shortly after me in a pair of sweatpants that perfectly highlighted the powerful shape of his muscular body. I tried not to look at him too much. He didn't deserve any more of my attention.

"Good morning," Logan said, turning his hazel eyes on me. I greeted him with a faint smile and sat down in the chair next to him, hoping to avoid Neil's stare. It seemed that I could feel his honey-colored eyes on me, but that could simply have been my brain playing tricks on me, trying to convince me he cared even a little about me.

He'd been with another woman last night, after kissing me, after sharing something unique with me on the chaise by the pool, and I could not conceive of forgiving that kind of slight. Luke had been right: people like them didn't change.

"So..." Logan looked from me to his brother, who stood at a distance from us, leaning against the windowsill with his arms folded. Rays from the sun filtered through the large window, lighting him up and making him look like a fallen angel. I tried not to let myself be distracted and focused on Logan as he went through all the clues Player 2511 had sent.

"To recap: we've received four packages. The first had the dead crow and suggested revenge. The second was the angel of the music box, which was connected with the story about the little girl and the theme of punishment. The third package was different, containing photos of each of us with 'who will be first?' written on the back as well as the acrostic with my name." He looked at his broken leg and sighed. "Now we need to figure out this latest note as well," he said, speaking more vigorously and trying to chase the negative thoughts from our minds. It was important that we remained focused and clearheaded and didn't allow ourselves to be overcome with emotion.

"What do you suggest we do?" Neil moved away from the window, eating up the space with his firm, masculine strides. I didn't want to, but damn it, I had to give in to temptation and look at him, and I regretted it immediately.

"We need to look for anything that could be related to a white horse," Logan said, calling my attention back to him and what he was saying. "We should find plenty of research material here. Anything might be useful to us." He pointed at some books stacked on the coffee table in front of him and reached out to grab one.

I started researching as well, and as soon as I opened my book, I sneezed at all the dust. Then, as if my eyes were magnetized and had been drawn elsewhere, I looked up and met Neil's golden gaze.

Why was he staring at me like that?

Still, every time, his gaze had the power to commingle our souls. It went beyond words, pulling me into his madness. It took all the courage I had to finally break eye contact with him and go back to looking at the open pages.

"Find anything yet?" Logan asked, and just when I thought my answer would have to be no, I spotted something that could be interesting.

"There is something in here, but I don't think I'm on the right track," I said, looking doubtful.

"Come on, read it," Neil said, speaking directly to me for the first time since the previous night. I cleared my throat and dipped my chin to read the page.

"The white horse is symbolic of beauty and purity. Over the centuries, its meaning has broadened and it is often considered a divine animal with the power to free itself from the earthly, material world…" I looked up at the both of them; they'd been watching me the whole time with serious looks on their faces.

I might have found it funny, if we weren't in such an insane situation.

"I don't think that's what he's trying to tell us." Logan shook his head and scrubbed a hand over his face. "Let's keep looking. But, Selene…" He caught my eye and gave me a smile. "Great job, sis." Then he winked at me before going back to his research, abandoning the book he'd been using and dedicating himself to the next one.

His willpower and determination were admirable. He was working so hard for Neil, to help him and support him as he fought a battle of wits against a worthy opponent, a true strategist.

It was incredible how, though none of us knew who Player 2511 was, we each felt his presence like some hard-to-exorcise demon.

"Um…I think I found something interesting," Logan said, his eyes locked on an illustration in his book.

"What?" asked Neil, tossing his book onto the wooden table and taking a seat on the arm of Logan's chair. He stretched his arm across the backrest and peered down at his brother, involuntarily adopting the stance of a curious kid.

"Look at this." Logan pointed to the page he had been so fixated upon so, of course, I had to get closer to them until my legs brushed against Neil's knee. I jumped at even that minimal contact, while he remained impassive, staring at an image that was included in the book.

"It's an illustration by Gustave Doré. Listen…" Logan pointed at the caption underneath the picture and we waited in silence for him to continue. "Gustave Doré's work, entitled *Death on a Pale Horse,* is a depiction of the personification of death: a skeleton brandishing a scythe, often pictured in a black robe or cloak with a hood." He looked up, first at Neil and then at me and swallowed audibly.

"Fuck, this is it. Keep reading," Neil urged him and Logan continued.

"The personification of death is tasked with accompanying souls from the land of the living, symbolized by the white horse, to the land of the dead as represented by the skeleton. It is a juxtaposition of life and death when we discuss the passage of the soul from one world into the next," he concluded in a chilly tone as a meditative silence fell all around us.

"So this letter means—" I murmured in a tiny voice.

"Death," Neil finished for me, jumping up from Logan's armrest.

"Player already tried to kill me once. Maybe he's telling us that he's going to try again?" Logan asked, worrying his lip anxiously.

"Don't forget about the numbers; we still need to figure those out," I added, pulling their attention back to the note, which held an even more complex puzzle to solve.

"You're right; we shouldn't jump to conclusions." Logan gestured to a notebook and pen on the desk, encouraging him to start making notes on possible connections between the words and the numbers. Neil followed his brother's suggestion and leaned against the edge of the desk, trying to make some sense of the note.

While his brother looked for a solution, Logan's shoulders slumped in resignation. The sparkle of determination that had lit up his eyes so recently had gone out, giving way to wary suspicion that perhaps that bastard Player was just messing with our heads. Maybe he already knew that he'd win either way.

I pushed those disheartening thoughts out of my mind and looked at Neil, who was writing something down with the pen cap between his teeth.

"Three, two…" Logan muttered quietly, pondering something.

"Insanity is doing the same thing over and over again and expecting different results. It's a quote that people think is from Einstein," he said abruptly, looking over at his brother, who simply nodded.

"What does an Einstein quote have to do with the numbers in the riddle?" I asked doubtfully, but just then, Neil made a catlike leap off the desk and came over to us, staring all the while at the notebook in his hand.

"I might have the solution." He laid it down on the coffee table in front of us, and Logan and I craned our necks to get a better look.

"It's multiplication." He looked at Logan, who had tilted his head confusedly to examine his brother's scribbles.

"Multiplication?" he asked blankly.

"Yes. Two times three is six." He glanced back and forth between me and Logan and then sighed deeply. "'Insanity is *doing* the same thing over and over again and expecting a different *result* is the quote, but our note said *repeating* and *solution*.'" He looked down at the paper and pointed to the six with his index finger. "What happens if we repeat the solution?" He grabbed the pen and wrote out a series of them, "Six...six...six..." He looked back up at us and threw the pen onto the coffee table. "Madness is just a metaphor. The word 'solution' implies a mathematical problem, and then 'repeating' it is an instruction to verbally say the answer several times," he concluded decisively, rubbing his face while Logan and I exchanged troubled looks.

"666 is the devil's number, right?" Logan breathed.

"Yeah," Neil confirmed. "We need to learn more," he added, going back to the desk for two more books before returning to us. He handed one to Logan and kept the other for himself, flipping quickly through it.

It took another thirty minutes of tireless searching before Logan made another shocking discovery. "Listen to this verse from the book of Revelation, referring to a prediction about the coming of the Antichrist: 'Here is wisdom. He that hath understanding, let him count the number of the beast; for it is the number of a man: and his number is Six hundred and sixty and six,'" Logan read. He turned to look at me, and I shuddered at the idea that this goddamned Player 2511 was also some sort of devil worshipper.

"Keep going," Neil ordered, pacing as he watched us. His agitation was palpable; I could feel it in the timbre of his voice and see it in the rigid way he held his body.

"Contrary to common belief, the number 666 does not identify the king of the demons—namely, Lucifer—but a being very near him," Logan continued, reading along further. "The significance of the number involves very complex numerological and kabbalistic concepts, but to make a long story short: in the Bible, the number seven often indicates wholeness or completion. Because six approaches but does not reach seven, it is symbolic of imperfection. Repeated three times—another sacred number—it takes on the meaning of arrogance, human evil, and death." He swallowed hard and shut the book, staring off into space with a troubled expression.

"For God's sake," I whispered, trembling with involuntary shivers. There were no words to explain how unsettling the situation had become.

"What is Player trying to tell us with that? That he's a devil worshipper? We got that," Neil said with a laugh that was not remotely amused, instead sounding full of contempt. Then he began to pace more frantically.

"No," Logan argued. "Pay attention. I think he considers himself perfect—a seven, as it were. So the six suggests there's a person who is very close to him." He swallowed again and clenched his jaw—a nervous tic.

"You're telling me this asshole has one or more accomplices?" Neil retorted, pausing to give Logan a look like he was talking crazy.

"That's exactly what I'm telling you. I don't think he's acting alone," Logan answered, his voice heavy with worry.

"Shit, you might be right." Neil raked a hand through his hair and emitted a low noise of frustration that made me flinch.

"So what do we do now?" Logan asked uncertainly. My heart was pounding so loudly, I was afraid one of them was going to hear it.

"Now we should expect an attack," Neil answered. He was right: Player 2511 wouldn't wait long.

He was going to hit us again. In some new way.

And who would be his next target?

....

The rest of the day didn't go any better. I guess I wouldn't have happy memories to cherish of my last hours in my father's luxurious mansion.

When I told Matt that I was going back to Detroit the next day, his face was at first dismayed, then disbelieving, and then heartbroken because we never had actually resolved anything between us. Work had continued to take up the majority of his time, and I hadn't stopped being silent and mistrustful every time he tried to communicate with me. If anything, I felt like the emotions that had tied me to him for so many years were becoming increasingly far away.

After seeing my father, I sorted out a few final things at the university and then spent the rest of the afternoon packing my suitcase. It felt like I had just arrived the day before, and now it was already time to leave.

But while my decision may have been drastic, it was quite comprehensible: I couldn't continue to live under the same roof as Neil, screwing up every other day, stumbling over my own mistakes only to make them again and again. I was trampling my own dignity.

I could understand that Neil wanted to be free from any constraint or responsibility and that love, the idea of a stable relationship, terrified him so completely that he did extreme things, like at the Halloween party. But I could not accept a man who treated me the way he had, forcing me to constantly compete with other women for his attention.

Once my bags were packed, I went to bed, but I didn't sleep. Eventually, I glanced at the alarm clock: it was the middle of the night, and there were six hours and forty-seven minutes until my flight. Yeah, I was counting down the minutes until I left.

Wearing my familiar childish tiger-print pajamas and leaving my hair disheveled, I went down to the kitchen. I sat on a stool and ate some of Logan's cereal and drank a glass of warm milk. The room was lit by the soft glow of the moon that streamed in through the large French doors, and the entire house was bathed in silence. Only my small noises echoed faintly off the walls as I jiggled my feet, covered in colorful socks.

I thought and thought about my decision to leave, only confirming to myself even more that it was the right one.

I needed to stop reading books where all a woman had to do was try to save the beautiful-yet-damned hero to get her love story. Fairy tales didn't exist and neither did men who allowed women to rescue them so easily. Instead, there were deep fissures, bleeding wounds that could not be erased by love. Which was, after all, only one of the ingredients required to redeem a profoundly damaged soul.

"I thought I heard noises in here." I jumped at the sound of Neil's voice puncturing the silence and the opalescent gloom in which I had been pleasantly conversing with myself.

I swallowed my bite of cereal with some difficulty before turning to look at him. He was leaning up against the door frame, and I struggled not to show him just how much his lethal appeal still affected me. To distract myself, I imagined that he'd just come from the pool house or some other "date" with one of his lovers.

"What are you doing here?" I sipped my warm milk, gripping the glass too tightly with shaking fingers, intimidated and excited at the same time. Neil gave me an enigmatic smile before slowly approaching and resting both elbows on the kitchen island. He stretched his torso out perilously close to me.

Once again, I willed myself not to be bewitched by him. Not even when a fresh wave of scent hit me right in the face, rekindling my longing to touch him.

"Do you know why I like the night, Tinkerbell?" he whispered in a velvety tone, like he'd never disrespected me on Halloween. I didn't answer and avoided looking at him, pretending to be unmoved by his charms. "Because every night is followed by a new day, and I need to get up before destiny so I can anticipate its evil plans," he continued, though I hadn't encouraged him at all.

I couldn't pretend I wasn't affected by his words, though, because Neil really was such a strange, intriguing guy and so different from anyone else I knew.

"Were you out in the garden?" I set my glass down on the kitchen island, concentrating on its rim so I didn't have to meet his golden eyes.

"Yes," he confirmed, not moving from his position. I looked up at him through my eyelashes and caught him paying meticulous attention to me. I knew I couldn't look like much at the moment, with my messy hair and my exhausted face, but he was looking at me like I was...something beautiful.

"In this cold?" I finally got up the nerve to look into his eyes, but he seemed focused on scrutinizing my lips as though memorizing the shape of them.

Instinctively, I swiped out my tongue to catch the last of the cereal residue, sure that was the reason he was staring at my mouth. Neil swallowed thickly and slowly bit down on his lower lip, looking somehow even more attractive than usual.

"I'd rather the freezing cold than the heat of old memories," he answered flatly, turning his eyes to mine.

"You really are strange," I whispered, thinking how little sense our conversations made.

"Would you say the darkness going hand in hand with the moon was strange?" he asked before strolling around the island to get closer to me. I stiffened as, step by step, he further invaded my space, turning my stool toward himself.

Thus I found myself facing his abdomen, my field of vision obscured by his broad chest and my bent knees touching his legs.

"I... I don't understand you," I admitted, raising my chin to look at his face, contorted into a serious, impenetrable look. He touched my cheek, and I winced at his cold knuckles, radiating winter against my warm skin.

He was frozen.

"You don't need to understand me."

I could sense his suffering.

"And Jennifer? Does she understand you?" I murmured in a curious, deliberately wounding tone, causing him to stop touching me. He took a deep breath and exhaled it slowly, ready for a fight.

"No, and she doesn't even try, which is why I prefer her to you," he admitted bluntly, not caring in the least if it hurt me. My heart seemed to hit the floor, shattering into thousands of pieces. I tried to get up off the stool, but Neil grabbed my hips and forced me back down.

He didn't want me to cut our conversation short; he wanted me to stay right there and suffer. And all at once, I understood the motive behind his strange behavior.

"Oh, now I get it! You're trying to get me out of New York! That's why you wanted me to see you fuck her. That's why you suggested a threesome with a girl who beat me up. That's why you sought out her and the others even after you got in my bed, that's why—" But his annoyed voice overpowered mine, cutting me off.

"Because of all that and lots more, I'm not fucking right for you!" he insisted forcefully, digging his fingers into my hips. His touch was all flame and pain, passion and peril.

I held my breath and touched my own chest, like he'd just stabbed me.

I felt like a butterfly alighting on a blade of grass, and Neil just kept stomping over me, keeping me from flying away. Killing me slowly.

"Thank you so much. Everything's very clear to me, and in just a few hours, you'll be free of me." I pushed him away with a strength I didn't realize I possessed and then I brushed past him, trying to leave. But his hand seized my wrist, halting my steps.

"Let me go," I commanded under my breath. And then I turned to look at him with the kind of anger that, for my entire life up until that I point, I had reserved exclusively for my father.

Neil's expression softened, and he glanced down at my pajamas and then back up to my face with the faintest smile tilting up the corners of his full lips.

"Don't think that I didn't enjoy what we had together," he murmured in a pitiable sort of way.

Why in the hell was he looking at me that way? I didn't want to feel pity for anyone right now, least of all him. It didn't matter that my eyes were blurry with tears and my heart was shattered. Traitorous emotions, why did they have to work against me when I most needed to control them?

"Of course you did. You got to use me like all the rest," I snapped at him.

The instant I said it, my legs went weak and my wrist burned from being trapped in his relentless iron grip. It felt like there would be a brand there, something I would carry with me forever.

"That's not what I mean…" he answered, annoyed. Perhaps he was feeling somewhat degraded by my accusation? But what about me? How was I supposed to feel?

"And what did you mean, Neil?" I prompted him. "After all, you have always been extremely clear on this point. 'I like using you, Selene; use me too,'" I taunted, reminding him of his own words.

Because I certainly hadn't forgotten them. I never could.

"Stop it," he said in a menacing hiss, his hold on my wrist tightening. But I didn't care. I didn't care so much that it wrought a change in me. I began to spew out words, barely even registering what I was saying.

"'Selene, it's just sex. Selene, it's no love story. Selene, you don't know how to kiss, how to fuck, Selene, you—"

With one powerful tug he brought me suddenly closer to him and I fell silent. His face was just a couple of inches from mine, and from the cruel expression on his face, I knew that his patience was gone.

"Are those the memories you'll be taking back to Detroit with you?" he whispered, a hairsbreadth from my lips, clearly trying to intimidate me. There was neither lust nor desire in his eyes but something darker and more dangerous that he was struggling to keep at bay.

"Yes," I lied. I would never have admitted to him how I was going to remember so much more about him, about me and what we had shared with each other.

"Then you really don't know shit." He released me roughly and took a few steps back with a diabolical smirk that made me waver on the spot. He stepped away and leaned on the kitchen island, palms down, shoulders slumping forward as though something heavy weighed upon him.

"If I don't, it's because you've never given me anything of yourself other than your dick," I blurted out, hoping to provoke him, and he turned to look at me like he couldn't believe I'd spoken. He perused my entire body attentively, from my colorful socks to my baggy pajamas. Then he smiled the kind of intriguing smile that could have made anyone do something stupid.

"Since when is a girl like you so brash?" Something about his low baritone told me that he'd enjoyed my pathetic imitation of his usual lines, though it was obvious to the both of us that I belonged to a different world entirely.

"Since I met a deviant like you," I answered in kind.

"Trust me—I kept it as sweet and romantic as I could with you, Tinkerbell," he said with a mocking look.

"And what would you have done differently? If you were with one of the others?"

Neil considered my question for a few moments, wrinkling his forehead in an expression of concentration that was almost fatally appealing.

Then he laughed sardonically and walked toward me as I trembled. I knew that I should have left, I should have gotten away from him as fast as I could. But something kept me stuck there, at his mercy.

"I would have grabbed you..." He took me by the hair and tilted my head so we could look into each other's eyes. His tight grip along with the rough tone he used to address me generated only one feeling in me: fear.

"And I would have ordered you to get on your knees," he whispered slowly, still weighing and evaluating me with those golden eyes. Inside them, an explosion of emotions showed just how unstable and dangerous his soul really was. "I would have forced my way into here..." His eyes darted to my mouth, and I saw desire painted all over his face. "And I would have made you swallow it all down. I would have emptied myself into your mouth until you begged me to stop." He clenched his jaw and released me abruptly.

I had to grab on to the kitchen counter to keep from falling to the floor while my heart pulsed so rapidly that I was afraid it would burn a hole in my chest.

"You're shaking like a leaf." Neil regarded me from head to toe, studying the reactions of my body. "This is why I've always tried to suppress the real me when I'm with you," he concluded, taking another step.

In that moment, it seemed certain to me that Neil was a demon, wrapped up in gold and black to camouflage what he really was and bewilder my senses.

They say that, in life, we have to make the right choices, but we don't always have the ability to recognize them. Who establishes right and wrong? Does the right thing really make us happy? Was going back to Detroit really the right decision? The one that would make me happy?

The first rays of sunlight began to peak through the window of my room where I had dragged myself after my fight with Neil. They turned everything they touched into gold, but the peaceful silence of the moment wasn't enough to soothe my melancholy.

I looked at my reflection in the mirror, and all I saw was a girl in pain—alone, disillusioned with everything, but most of all, with herself. I knew from the beginning what I was getting into with a person like Neil. I knew from the beginning that, sooner or later, I was going to pay the price for what I'd done, but still, I chose to follow my heart.

"Always follow your heart," my mother often said, but her maxim now seemed like a huge pile of bullshit to me. A heart could cause irreversible damage, the kind that all the reason in the world couldn't fix.

It occurred to me how strange this feeling really was: I had made a mistake and kept on making it, and yet, I didn't regret it. In fact, if I had access to a time machine, I would have done the exact same things over again.

With him.

I opened my closet and gathered up the last of my clothing to put in my suitcase. I was still concerned and disturbed over what had happened on Halloween, about the puzzle we'd received. And what was I doing? I was running away like a coward.

I still couldn't believe myself.

"Selene," Alyssa called to me, but I didn't answer. She was sitting on the edge of the bed and had been watching me with increasing concern for approximately the last hour. I didn't want to explain what was wrong with me, however, because she just would have scolded me and told me I should just stay away from a guy like Neil. That he was too complicated, too troubled, and too lots of other things as well.

"I have to hurry, Alyssa," I said shortly, glancing around so I could avoid meeting her eyes or revealing how hurt I was about my impending departure.

I looked around my room and saw it as clearly as if it had been written on the walls: the hopes, the expectations, and good intentions…they were all faded now.

I had failed in my attempt to save Neil, but he had failed as well. He lacked the courage to let himself be saved.

"Selene, your silence is really worrying me," Alyssa announced, getting to her feet. I shut my suitcase and took it off the bed, setting it down on the floor.

"I've just got a lot on my mind." I smiled weakly at her and put on my light-colored trench coat, leaving my hair loose around my shoulders.

"I still can't believe you're leaving." Her voice broke a little, and it made me sad to hear her feeling so down.

"Alyssa, you can come visit me whenever you want." I moved closer to her and put my hands on her shoulders. "We'll stay in touch. What's a two-hour flight, anyway?" I smiled, but that only seemed to make things worse, and soon Alyssa was on the verge of tears. I hugged her tightly and held her for a very long time. Then, I pulled away from her and grabbed my suitcase because it was time for me to go.

"Ready?" When I got down to the living room, Logan was standing there with the aid of his crutches. He gave me a glum smile and Alyssa quickly went to him to allow him to lean on her.

"As I'll ever be." I pulled my suitcase along behind me as I said goodbye to Anna.

"We will always be here for you if you need us, Miss Selene. It was a pleasure meeting you." She pressed a kiss to my cheek with a maternal warmth that made me blush, and I walked past her to see the melancholy faces of Matt and Mia.

"You are a wonderful girl. Come back soon; I'll be waiting for you." Mia pulled me into a heartrending embrace that I hadn't been expecting. I felt almost suffocated in her arms, but at the same time, I knew how sincere her kindness was and had always been. I wrapped my arms around her waist and gave her all the time she needed to come to terms with my abrupt decision to leave.

"Selene, I can't tell you how sorry I am that you're leaving." Chloe also showed unexpected warmth. She embraced me and I smiled at her, advising her to stay safe and keep her grades up.

"Are you sure you want to take a taxi? We can take you to the airport," my father suggested for the umpteenth time, but I shook my head.

"No, don't worry about it," I answered firmly. Then, just as he took one step forward to hug me, I took one back to avoid any physical contact with him. His eyes couldn't hide the devastating sorrow that he felt in that moment, while mine remained cold and detached even in the face of heartbreaking emotions.

I went to the front door and opened it out onto the front stoop, followed by Logan and Alyssa. I hadn't been expecting Neil to come and say goodbye to me, so I felt my heart lurch when a black Maserati drove through the enormous main gates and down the driveway toward the house.

Everything inside me suddenly switched on, as though my soul had been abruptly awakened. My knees trembled and an overwhelming feeling of turmoil had me swaying on my feet. Alyssa and Logan exchanged knowing looks before turning their attention to me.

"Maybe it would be best if..." Logan began.

"We gave you some privacy," Alyssa finished.

"Call us when you get there," she added, giving me one last hug.

Logan hugged me as well, saying with certainty, "We'll come to visit you."

"I'm counting on it." I broke our embrace and gave him an honest smile, trying to hide how ill at ease I truly was.

Occasionally, one encounters special people with the power to reach deep inside with only a smile, a hug, or a gesture of kindness. Logan and Alyssa were those kind of people, and I would carry them in my heart forever.

"Selene." Neil's baritone startled me, making every cell in my body vibrate. I looked him from head to toe: the sun made his wild hair and golden eyes even more brilliant.

But I immediately wrapped my fingers around the handle of my suitcase and kept walking, brushing right past him.

"You told me everything you needed to tell me last night. I have to go now, Neil," I said as I hurried away from him, knowing that this would be the hardest part.

I would never see him again. I would never get to drink him in the moment I woke up with his eyes still all sleepy and his lips swollen, ready for kissing.

I'd no longer be able to watch him bite into a protein bar or smell his shower gel or feel his constant presence.

I would never argue with him about his lovers and then allow him to make me forget it all with his kisses.

I would no longer get the chance to share spaces with him or share anything at all. Not friends or family…certainly not a life.

"Wait." Neil reached out and took me by the wrist.

I turned to face him and his mouth dropped open slightly, as though he were about to tell me something. Instead, he closed his lips and chewed anxiously on the inside of his cheek. We stared fixedly at one another for a few seconds, which felt somehow infinite. If I could have stopped time right then, I would have. I would have stayed there just like that, rooted to the ground in front of him, getting lost in his golden eyes.

I felt like a fairy sitting paralyzed in the palm of Neil's hand, unable to take flight, and I realized then that he had been my Neverland, too.

"I just wanted to say goodbye…" He moved closer to me until he was surrounding me with his scent, and I closed my eyes to soak it in. Deep in my heart, I was hoping he'd say something to convince me to stay. But that wasn't what happened.

Instead, Neil just pressed his warm lips to my forehead and gave me a sweet, chaste kiss before he pulled away with the faintest smile. He shot a glance at the Tinkerbell sweater I wore, just like the night we first met, and his eyes gleamed with an intense but indecipherable light.

"Safe travels, Tinkerbell." His voice reached down to touch the recesses of my soul for the last time. Then, as my taxi pulled up, he stepped back away from me.

The driver got out, opened the trunk, and stowed my bag inside. I moved around to the passenger door and took a quick look back at Mr. Disaster while he continued to stare at me in total silence.

"Take care of yourself, Neil," was all I said as I got into the car. I watched him through the window one last time and met his eyes, which continued to bore into mine as he said nothing. As he didn't ask me to stay.

"We good to go?" the driver asked, tossing a glance at me in the rearview mirror. I looked at Neil again and felt my heart pounding against my chest. A warm feeling spread across every inch of my skin. My eyes were stinging, but I refused to give in and cry.

Not again.

"Yes," I confirmed in a small voice.

The driver started the car and we pulled away slowly. I turned back to Mr. Disaster and watched him until he had faded from view.

My lips began to tremble powerfully, and as I rested my head against the window, I couldn't hold back my tears any longer.

What would become of us?

Maybe there wasn't an *us* anymore. Or maybe there never had been in the first place.

It felt to me as though I could feel his fingers stroking me, his lips kissing me, his hands traversing my entire body.

I still vividly sensed his presence, like an enchanted dream that was, at the same time, the sharpest torture.

Unfortunately, there was no cure for memories. There was no cure for the past.

There was no freedom from it, either.

I needed to stop thinking about him.

I sighed as I reached into my pocket for my phone so I could text my mother that I'd be home in a few hours. But then my fingers encountered something that was, from the size and shape of it, definitely not my cell phone. I wrinkled my forehead in confusion as I pulled out the object that had somehow ended up in my pocket and studied it closely. It was a transparent glass cube with a pearl suspended inside it.

"What is this?" I murmured, watching the way it glittered as it reflected the sunlight.

This thing didn't belong to me, and I couldn't figure out how it had gotten into my coat pocket, unless...

"I just wanted to say goodbye..."

Neil had gotten close to me to kiss my forehead, and perhaps, at the same time, he'd...he'd...

I grinned like a little girl and clutched the small iridescent cube tight to my chest. I would take this gift with me to Detroit along with so many other things about him.

But what no one—including me—knew was that I wouldn't get back to my city. I would never arrive at the airport, never take that flight. My journey was about to end right there.

"Miss!" the driver called out to me, and there was palpable concern in his voice. I leaned forward to speak with him.

"What happened?" I asked, still a bit shaken up by Neil's surprise. The driver kept looking behind us in the rearview mirror.

"There's a car, a black Jeep that's been following us for about twenty minutes now, but it's getting dangerously close!" he exclaimed, his hands tightening on the steering wheel.

I turned around to see the vehicle in question, and my eyes went wide when I spotted a figure behind the wheel, his face concealed beneath a white mask. He raised one black-gloved hand and waved sarcastically at me.

"Go faster!" I shouted at the driver, who stomped on the accelerator, causing the odometer to spike. But the Jeep continued to follow us.

It was him.

Player 2511.

How had he known I was leaving?

I gripped the seat and stared out the back window. The Jeep caught up with us quickly and began flashing its brights.

"Please! Can you go faster?" My eyes bounced between my driver and the Jeep, which, in a sudden maneuver, rammed the back of the taxi, sending us into a skid.

And that was it.

It happened in the space of a second.

The whole world stopped.

I heard the driver scream. I saw the too-tight curve.

I didn't have time for any realizations as the car veered off the road and crashed into the guardrail.

My head was thrown violently against the window and a dull pain began to spread throughout my entire body.

I tightened my fist around the glass cube as my eyes drooped closed.

All at once, it seemed like I could feel Neil's fingers gliding through my hair, his golden eyes warming like rays of sunlight and his lips curving into a loving smile.

"Would you say the darkness going hand in hand with the moon was strange?"

That's what he'd asked me and it occurred to me that, if I had a second chance, I would have answered him, "Yes. I would call it strange. As strange as calling a woman Tinkerbell and likening her to Neverland. As strange as slipping a pearl trapped in a cube of glass into her pocket. Everything about you is strange, my disaster, but please keep on making the darkness walk hand in hand with the moon because...because the stars seem to have aligned over you."

42

....

PLAYER 2511

I took my phone out of my pocket and dialed his number again, hoping this time would be the right time.

He answered after two rings.

"Finally! I called you six fucking times!" I burst out furiously.

"Yeah, sorry about that," he sighed. "Everything went as planned," he told me.

"Is she alive?" I asked, bringing a cigarette to my lips.

"I don't think so," he answered uncertainly, which only intensified my anger.

"What the fuck do you mean you don't *think* so? I hope for your sake she isn't. Don't forget: you've already fucked up once with his brother!" I ground my teeth and crushed the cell phone in my hand as though I longed to break it into pieces.

I didn't have a great relationship to my more impulsive side.

"I know. You remind me all the time," he lectured me, though he was in absolutely no position to do so.

"Do what you're supposed to do, or I swear I'll get rid of you, too!" I hung up the phone without waiting for him to reply and crushed the spent cigarette butt in the ashtray. I stared at a picture on the wall of the only god I could believe in.

The same one that led every man to his natural state.

The same one that set his sights on evolving man into his own state of divinity.

Yes, because we humans would become the true divine.

One did not live in opposition to Satan but for Satan.

Without reservations.

He was the only judge capable of accusing the perpetrator of his crimes. He was not an adversary. He was not a prosecutor.

He was a spirit guide.

Man was free to act.

Free to choose.

While God, the famous Yahweh, attempted to take over men's minds.

He tried to prevent their spiritual progress. Prevent inner growth. Prevent them from accessing cosmic wisdom. Prevent them from surpassing their limits.

He favored ignorance, a lack of knowledge. And ignorance was the true sin.

Not perversion. Not the world of the forbidden. Not the illegal. Not the shadow realm. Not...us.

I regarded the inverted five-pointed star—two points extending upward and considered the details.

Dark energy descended from above and empowered the soul of man.

It was that energy that I believed in.

That energy that would allow me to carry out my revenge.

I stared at the pentagram and I smiled.

THANKS

We have reached the end of the first volume in this series, and I want to thank everyone who has undertaken this journey along with sweet Selene and troubled Neil.

As you may have noticed, many questions remain unanswered. Mystery still looms over the lives of our protagonists, and a dangerous antagonist will do anything to have his revenge.

It wasn't easy to work with such delicate subject matter, and I hope I was up to the challenge. It is also my hope that Selene has touched each of your hearts and that Neil has made you fly momentarily into his version of Neverland, a little madder and more mixed up than the original.

I thank my readers, who have always believed in me since the debut of this story three years ago, and I thank my family for supporting me in every choice I've made.

I hope you can continue to come along with me and that you are curious to discover everything our two disasters have in store for us...

Each of you is important to me. You are my strength.

Thank you from the bottom of my heart.

Yours Always,
Kira Shell

READ ON FOR A SNEAK PEEK
AT THE NEXT THRILLING
INSTALLMENT OF NEIL AND
SELENE'S ANGSTY DARK ROMANCE
IN *A DANGEROUS GAME*.

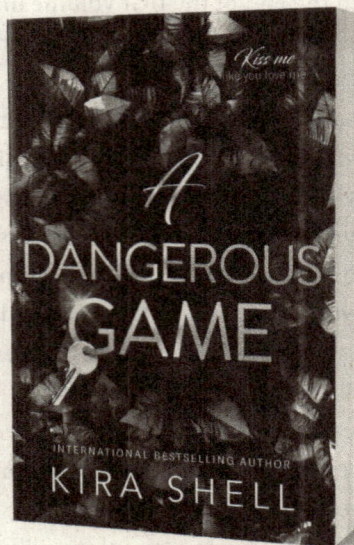

PROLOGUE

NEIL

I sat on the living room sofa and stared at a painting of Jesus.

My mom had told me I needed to thank the Lord every day, say a prayer to him every night and go to church with her every week. She said there was something wrong with me, that the child-eating witch I talked about so often was a monster who only existed in my head and that only the church could offer me salvation.

She didn't understand what I was saying.

"I swear she exists," I'd told her over and over again, especially whenever I got home from school to find that the teacher had already called her about my bad behavior.

Like the teacher had that day.

"Stop telling stories!" My mother scolded me. "What you did was unacceptable!" She shouted at me because my teacher had told her I'd groped a classmate but that wasn't really what happened. All I did was put my hand on her thigh while she was crying about getting a bad grade. The teacher found us and assumed I was touching her in a way that wasn't appropriate for a child. So I tried to explain to Mom that *she* did those bad things to me—the child-eater—but that I would never do them to anyone else. But it felt like she didn't hear me.

"You have to believe me, Mom," I said, soft and defeated.

"This is the second time they've called to tell me about your unmanageable behavior. What the hell is driving you to do these things? Are you trying to get my attention? Huh?" She rubbed her belly with one hand. We were only a few months away from Chloe's birth and my mother was far from calm.

I didn't want to make her mad the way I did last time. When that happened, she got sick and Dad punished me.

"Mommy, I—" I didn't get to finish because she stalked over to me and slapped me across the face. It hurt so bad my lip started to tremble. I looked up at her, my eyes full of tears, my cheek aching but my mother just coldly pointed up the stairs with her index finger.

"Go to your room!" She ordered and I hung my head and obeyed her. I ran to my bedroom upstairs and shut the door behind me. I didn't want to see anyone. I knelt down at the foot of the bed and put my hands together in prayer just the way Mom always told me to and then I bent my head as I spoke:

Please God, make this torture stop.

Why did Kim pick me?

Did I do something bad?

Please tell me, because I can't figure it out.

I'm sorry.

I'm sorry for asking for too much for Christmas last year.

I'm sorry for talking back to my Mom sometimes, even on accident.

I'm sorry for hiding Logan's after school snack just to spite him.

I'm sorry for being jealous of my little sister Chloe who isn't here yet but I'm just afraid my mom will forget about me.

I'm sorry for making Dad angry by getting a juice stain on his new shirt.

I'm sorry for everything but please...just help me.

Children were afraid of monsters that hid under the bed, behind the curtains or inside the closet but that wasn't how monsters really were.

They walked carelessly through our world, their appearances misleading, their smiles enigmatic. They stretched out a hand to you and offered you something sweet before kindly asking you to follow them.

There, in the shadows, in some murky, hidden place, they peeled back your skin and your screams died a slow death.

One day, one of those monsters descended on me and without ever even asking, battered down the door to my soul, invaded my heart and contaminated every inch of my body with poison.

I fought for a long time to protect myself but the monster had confused—and fused with—me so rapidly, making a mess of everything.

That was when the enemy had been born inside me. Two souls began to co-exist—different, opposed, removed. Thus I learned to control and accept them, becoming, with time...

My own worst enemy.

1

....

NEIL

H aving sex, making love, fucking; for me, all of those acts
belonged to one broad category: pleasure.

My pleasure, though, wasn't like other people's. I didn't have sex
for the orgasm, which often didn't even happen for me.

No, for me sex was a way to get a sick thrill, imagining that I had
beneath me the person who had so gravely wounded my psyche and
my soul: Kimberly. People who experienced that kind of abuse in
their childhood often developed strange ways of relating to other
people in adulthood. They could become manipulative, antagonis-
tic, perverse and easily agitated.

Like me, basically.

My personality had been seriously warped and I knew that the
earlier the abuse occurred the greater the long-term damage would
be. Eventually, it resulted in a psychopathological change to my
innate tendencies. Dr. Lively had once explained the concept to me
in detail during a session. And, he added, the suffering and humiliation that I continued to feel inside would manifest themselves in

the sexual and platonic relationships that I had with women, spilling over irreparably onto them. In fact, all I was really doing was forcing myself to reenact my abuse but this time I played the role of the perpetrator. This was a condition that my doctor referred to as "compulsive ego-dystonic behavior"

All at once, my brain, which had been wandering in its own chaos, pulled me back to the present.

I was in bed and I was not alone.

"Neil." Jennifer continued to rock back and forth on me, groping my sweaty pecs. She bit her lip as she undulated, which only intensified my goddamned nausea.

I used my fingers to direct her, tightening them on her hips as I stared at the steel ring I wore on the middle finger of my right hand. Anything to avoid looking at the place where her body sucked me in greedily and released. Jennifer didn't want anyone but me and I didn't want anyone but...Babygirl.

To keep from thinking about Selene, however, I mused on how much I hated the position in which I was currently fucking Jennifer. As usual, I couldn't stand being underneath a woman for more than five minutes so, when that fifth minute ticked over in my brain, I flipped our positions until I could straddle her. My erection, still wet from her fluids, rested on her abdomen.

I pulled off the used condom and her eyes followed the motion ravenously.

She enjoyed my size, like women always did and I knew it. Jennifer, though, didn't even try hide her longing to savor it like a delicious lollipop.

She wanted me...of course she wanted me...

She looked up at me pantingly, her cheeks rosy and eyes filled with an expectation that I was about to satisfy. I got up on my knees and aimed my swollen tip right into her beautiful mouth. I put my hands on the headboard and set the same rhythm once again.

In-out, in-out, but this time I watched as I possessed her sinful lips. I watched and I enjoyed what I saw but, even more, I enjoyed the way she had to work to pleasure me. It was hardly easy, taking all of me but Jennifer knew how far to go, she knew how to meet my needs.

Suddenly, she sputtered and I paused for a few moments in the heat of her mouth. I waited for her nod before I started moving again. Her hands squeezed my ass as it contracted with each thrust. I could feel her nails sinking into my flesh as I continued to take what I wanted from her.

When Jen started to gasp and the bobbing of her head slowed down, I realized that Xavier had rejoined us on the bed. This time, he'd stuck his head between her thighs. This whole scene, obscene yet quotidian, had started about an hour earlier the same way it always did, with him and me sharing a woman.

"You really missed my tongue, didn't you, babydoll?" Xavier's rough, aroused voice significantly slowed my rush towards an orgasm that was feeling increasingly far away. My brain didn't want to cooperate at all that day. I felt tense and so nervous that I couldn't let go in the way I wanted.

"Fuck," I grumbled under my breath, pulling out of Jennifer's mouth so I could move away and get up off the bed. I glanced back at the two of them, continuing to seek their own pleasure and I took note of how Xavier focused on pushing her over the edge with his mouth.

My friend was certainly more generous than I was. Lately, I'd only been granting that kind of privilege to the girl with the ocean eyes who had just gone away: Selene.

Jennifer gave me a pleading look, begging me to come back to where I was before, buried between her lips. But I shook my head and went to the bathroom instead, shutting the door behind me. I could still hear their moans from behind me as they continued to go at it in earnest.

I rested my hands on the edge of the sink and stared at my reflection: my hair was a riot, my lips were red, the tendons in my neck were too tense and my muscles were still rigid. I really did have the look of an unsatisfied man. Sexual desire circulated through my body like a poisonous drug. I was still stubbornly erect, my body refusing to give me that moment of abandon, those five seconds of total explosion, the chills that went from the base of my spine straight up to my brain. The same ones I'd felt with only one woman.

With my Babygirl.

I could still remember the way I'd climaxed in that soft, oh-so tight little body; the way she pulled me inside herself and allowed me through the gates of a cursed paradise. I remembered the delicate way her fingers dug into my back, so afraid of hurting me. I remembered the rough kisses she couldn't completely match because no one had ever kissed her while they fucked her before.

I remembered the way she looked at me as I showed her just how much sex with her pleased me. I couldn't hide it because every orgasm we experienced together was so all-encompassing that it stole my breath. But even when I didn't pant, even when I tried not to lose control, she stole a little piece of me. She took it in tiny doses, creeping in on her tiptoes just like a fairy and leaving a little bit of pixie dust sprinkled on my soul each time.

I had thought about calling her and asking her if she'd gotten to Detroit, if she was doing okay and if she'd found the little present I'd left in her coat pocket.

I had slipped a glass cube with a pearl inside it into her pocket, using the lame excuse of a forehead kiss to get close enough to her that I could do it undetected.

She'd just left that morning and it was only ten in the evening at that point yet it felt like an infinite amount of time had passed since I'd last immersed myself in her ocean. I wanted to wrap my arms around her and kiss her and drag her into my bedroom with me but I told myself not to fuck it up and to let her go because it was the right thing to do.

The right thing.

I kept repeating it to myself like a crazy person just to keep myself from pulling out my phone and sending a text saying: *Come back to me right now, Tinkerbell.* Because, even if she did, nothing would have changed. I wouldn't have changed. I would still have been the same disturbed Boy who used his blondes, who took countless showers every day, who refused to return to therapy, who couldn't control his impulses, who talked to himself, who was incapable of love. A person like me would never, ever have been able to accept love because even the most innocent "I love you," would have brought out the beast within.

It was right to let her go, to let her live her own life, maybe with some normal man who didn't have DID, IED or OCD the way I did. A man who treated her with kindness and touched her gently and didn't sleep with anyone except his woman. A serious, respectful man with whom she could build a family, have children and get her happy ending.

Selene deserved all of that but it was something I could never have given her. If I hadn't had the problems I did, I would have tried, I really would have tried to hold on to her. But, unfortunately, that wasn't my reality and I, being the way that I was, would never have considered trying to initiate a stable relationship with a woman.

Not so long as Kimberly was still in my head.

ABOUT THE AUTHOR

Kira Shell is a bestselling Italian author with over 600,000 copies of her dark romances sold. She began writing the Kiss Me Like You Love Me series in 2017. The series has over six million Wattpad reads. Kira is a law graduate and lives in Italy.

Instagram: @kira_shell_autrice_
TikTok: @kirashell